EXILES' REFRAIN

MEL TODD

BAD ASH PUBLISHING

Paperback ISBN: 978-1-950287-49-9

Harback ISBN: 978-1-950287-50-5

Page edge design by Painted Wings Publishing

Cover Art by Galen Dara 2016

Cover design by Ampersand Covers

❀ Formatted with Vellum

To everyone who's ever been cast out, cut loose, or told they didn't belong:
This story is for the stubborn hearts who refuse to fade quietly,
for the fierce souls who build family out of wreckage,
and for anyone willing to burn the world down before they break.
May you always find your own place—and the courage to claim it.

CHAPTER ONE

JADAYA

"What do you see when you look at the ocean?" Kol asked, his eyes locked on the horizon.

Jadaya looked at the man sitting on her right, his slim, pale body, webbed hands and toes, silvery hair, and a sense of peace, all in direct contrast to her. She let her gaze move from him to the worn dock they sat on, supported by coral reefs and constructed from the hulls of wrecked ships. They gleaned the beach daily to collect the ocean's bounty, while divers scoured the ocean floor for the remnants of shipwrecks. The seas around Aois were not normally dangerous, but Pel, the god of the sea, was both temperamental and easily distracted.

The waves lashed against the piers' coral supports, swirling around as pieces of jetsam floated to the top only to be dragged back down, leaving bits of white foam in its wake. She looked out further to where the deeps were, where monsters and gods held sway. The dark blue a hungry maw ready for its next victim, the sharp swells, teeth yearning to sink into another ship; the grey underbelly of the water mimicking the dead that floated in its depths.

"Hunger, rage, a need to destroy all that might try to claim it," she said, memories of salt in wounds and clinging to a splintered piece of hull too fresh to have faded. "Mockery of our attempts to sail and contempt for our ships." Her words in Aoisan were thicker and broken compared to Kol's smooth, almost lyrical speech. She learned fast in the six tendays since she washed up on the shore, but she would never sound like these people who sang as naturally as they breathed.

"Ah," he said with a soft musical exhale. "That explains much."

Jadaya frowned and pushed her dreads out of the way, the salt encasing them left crystals on her hands. "Why, what do you see?" The ocean would never be anything to her other than a threat and a reminder of all that she lost.

He kept his gaze on the distant horizon, though she knew he wore a slight smile as he stared out at the endless appetite that was the ocean. "I see the depths that provides us food, the palace that houses Pel, the water that holds us as we bring life into the world, the ever-changing face of the sea that protects us and nourishes us, and the secrets to life yet to be discovered." The lyrical sway to his words made the sea out as a place of wonder, not the ravenous beast she knew it was. Pel, the god of the ocean, was one of their gods, not one worshipped by Zuyika, not that she worshiped her own divines anymore. They had cast her out, exiled her here, and now she had no idea where to go or what to be.

Or what to live for.

She cast her eyes back to the waves and shook her head. "I envy you what you see. For me, there is too much pain and fear wrapped up in those waters."

"Yes. And that is why you are still here, neither Aoisan nor Zuyikan. You are not Ged. You are adrift." He glanced at her now, the soft smile making the words an observation, not the attack they could have been.

Jadaya avoided his eyes, locking her gaze on the view. "Do you think I should become Aoisan?"

"I think very little. I know you are welcome here, especially after your actions. But Ijo would never turn you away if you requested it." There was nothing in his voice, but a simple statement. Ijo was the Priestess of Rian. Between Rian and Pel, the Aoisan gods were both kind and standoffish. If a stranger had washed ashore in Zuyika, her divines would have come almost immediately to interrogate and decide their fate.

But they are no longer your divines.

Jadaya shook off the thought, though it still burned that the ones she had spent her lifetime in service to would throw her away because... She drove the thought away. Unwilling to face her flagrant breaking of the rules and her rightful punishment. Instead, Jadaya rose and stretched to her full height. At six and a half hands, she was almost two hands taller than Kol, and wider across the shoulders. Her skin, once darker than a locked room, had lightened to the color of charcoal on a seashell. The idea of losing more of herself, of her skin and hair color changing even more filled her with an atavistic dread. Her hair, long thin twists that stopped at the middle of her back, had acquired hints of red and blue in it that still startled her. The gods had taken that too when they exiled her here. While she retained her clearly delineated muscles and lanky build, she saw a stranger every morning in the still water of the washbasin.

Kol possessed smooth silvery blue skin that flushed in pale rainbow colors, silver white silky hair that barely touched his shoulders, and pale eyes that saw too much. To become an Aois would mean to not be her, at least the *her* in her mind, any longer.

"I will keep that in mind. Or maybe join the Ged. Though it would be the land Ged. I am too uncomfortable with the sea, to be able to live the life of a sea Ged. But I have little desire to lose even more of who I am. To become another people." She stared at the sails in the distance and shuddered at the idea of getting back on a boat.

"True. Though it might be interesting to see what Pel and Rian would make of you." Kol leaned down and picked up the repaired net.

"I believe white hair and skin with silver tones would not fare well with me," Jadaya said, keeping her voice amused, as she grabbed the basket of fish. When you joined another family, via wedlock or choice, the gods changed you to match their people. Every race reflected what their gods thought best fit them. For Aoisans, it was the webbed hands and feet, ability to dive far under water, sharp claw-like nails, and hair so silver and fine it was used to make jewelry. While the people had taken her in, Jadaya was unsure about becoming Aoisan.

"Maybe not, but they did an excellent job with Jukochka." Kols' voice was mild as they walked up the pier. The woman in question was from Agrina. She fell in love with an Aoisan and had moved here, switching her allegiance to Pel and Rian. Already her skin had lightened three shades, and formerly tree needle green eyes had paled to the color of new-growth leaves. Her hair had lightened from its original dark brown to a rich blonde, and she had lost at least twenty tellaweight in her bosom.

Jadaya let her mind drift for a moment, imagining her own bosom twenty tellaweights heavier. Tellanuts were popular everywhere, and more than a few were provided to her the first few nights on the ship. Her back ripped to shreds, grateful for the narcotic effect. Every nut weighed roughly the same, and they were the size of the first knuckle of her thumb. The tree grew like a weed, and most families kept a tella tree in their dwelling, a gift of the old gods. The image of twenty tella nuts filling her chest bindings was amusing.

"Yes, she seems happy," Jadaya said. The rest of what he said registered. She could not imagine her skin the color of sand with silver hints or her hair becoming fine silver ringlets. Just the idea made her hands twitch for her ajo oil, to start twisting in her grow out. But her hands were full with the basket of fish, so she resisted.

"You will never be happy here if you are unable to see where you fit," Kol said as they approached his house.

As always, her eyes drifted to the gleaming oyster shell that was the city of Pelisic, with the pearl the temple to Pel and Rian. It sat at the base of the mountain, staring out at the sea like a mournful lover. The walls and the streets of

Pelisic were created with crushed shells, the thick clay that lay under the sand of the beaches, and the bones of the sea monsters that washed up on shore. Together, it created a gleaming whiteness that seemed almost divine coming from her world of browns and yellows. The iridescence of the shells made the entire city glitter, and she thought she could spend days watching the shifting light.

Then there was the singing that never stopped. It was part of the foundation of the city. All Aoisans had the innate ability to stay in tune, and they sang while working, while playing, while driving their carts into the city, and while praising the gods. They sang a song for every need and every emotion. It was captivating, and Jadaya could lose days just listening to them sing.

I was blessed or lucky to wash up here and not be food for the Deep.

Kol and his wife Ola had found her lying on a shard of a hull, the tides beating her against the shore, her re-opened wounds oozing blood and crusted with salt, barely able to speak. They spent three tendays nurturing her back to health. Since then, she had been something between a guest and a daughter, their only child having died while still young.

Together they entered Kol's house, Jadaya having to duck through the door. It consisted of one large room that held a clay oven for both cooking and heating the home, a sink with water running from the spring, simple woven swing chairs attached to the ceiling, and a table with three chairs. Three arches led out of the room, one to a needs room, the others to bedrooms made up of soft seaweed mats on the floor and hooks and shelves for belongings. The needs room held a waste bucket that was emptied daily, a sea shower that just added more salt to her hair, and soaps and oils to keep your body clean and supple. Their cat, a small version of the terrifying sabers, a white and brown one with a curved tail called Hunter, wound around Jadaya's legs as she carried the fish to the kitchen. Ola would clean the fish and create some of the best food Jadaya had tasted since she found herself on this shore. The rest Ola would cure and sell at the market in a few days. Few had Ola's touch with dried fish and it was a favorite among many.

"I have no idea where I want to be. I still struggle with the knowledge that I am exiled, much less that all my thoughts for the future are no longer valid." She stopped speaking, unable to say what she felt as she had no idea what her own feelings were yet. There existed a gaping hole in her mind and heart where her land, her lover, her gods once occupied. A hole that nothing she found so far would fill.

"Study the ocean. It lets others beat against it and it goes where it will. There is solace in its eternalness," Kol advised, but Jadaya shuddered at the idea of becoming one with the bottomless hunger she felt from the sea. If she could figure out how to never get on a ship again, she would. Kol laughed, seeing her expression. "But you will find your own way, just like the sea birds do."

Jadaya nodded. "I thought I would go hunt. Some red meat would be nice." She ached for something to do and while she had never hunted for food in Zuyika, she had been trained thoroughly in sword, bow, staff, and spear. Those skills had not left her with her exile. It was as easy to put an arrow in an animal as a target. The cleaning of her prey had taken some practice, but Kol bartered with Pak, a butcher he knew, to teach her. She had learned quickly, both out of gratitude and a need for more protein. While the fish delighted her tastebuds, she was accustomed to heartier fare, hence her desire to hunt.

Kol looked at her with pale eyes that saw too much, but he only nodded. "If you chance to see any fowl, Ola could use some feathers."

Grateful at the release, Jadaya grabbed her kit, bow, and quiver and headed out. Everyone said that Kol and Ola treated her like a daughter, but she barely remembered having parents. Growing up in the temple as a Chosen, among all the others offered as their family's tithe, meant she rarely had authority figures, just rules. It unsettled her to not have rigid lists of rules and duties. The freedom felt unnatural.

Jadaya stepped out of their house to stare at the wall of the city. The majority of the residential area was outside the wall but built against it on the ocean side. They often had either doors, ladders, or stairs that lead up and over the walls. It was a huge defensive weakness.

With a sigh, she lifted her hand parallel to the horizon. Two of her fingers filled the space between the rising sun and the ocean horizon. If her bow worked as well as she expected it, she should have food and be back at least four fingers before sunset.

She set the gleaming sun to her back and headed toward the mountains. The Aoisan's preferred the ocean to the mountains. Lack of access to the sea made them uncomfortable. Many of the rich had personal pools to swim in, and the temple to Pel had large heated pools that were open to all Aoisans as well as the temple auditorium where nightly they gathered to sing. It was a way of life to let music guide them, encouraging the creation of new songs, new harmonies, and it all made Jadaya feel even more out of place. Her height, the color of her skin, her coarse curly hair, plus the fact that she sounded like a croaking frog that was confused about what sound it wanted to make, made her stand out more than anything else.

With the song of the city, a thousand voices lifting up in multiple tunes, as her companion, she headed to the back gate. It required her to go through the city proper, but that also saved her four fingers of hiking around the city. Besides, she always found something new wandering through Pelisic, even if everyone stared at her. There were still Aoisans that had never seen her and she drew looks standing a full two hands above most of them, dark against their lightness. But she embraced their curiosity. It was better than hate. They were never rude and often smiled at her. To her intense amusement, at least three had approached Kol and Ola, asking if she cut her hair could they buy it. If she decided she needed money that badly, she would. But for now her hair, and the scars on her back, were all that she had left of her home. Her former home.

Jadaya shook her head and continued moving through town, intent on getting to the mountain gate. Pelisic had three gates: the so-called ship gate that led into the sheltered harbor, the trade gate that opened to the road that traveled over all the islands, linking them with rope and wooden planks, then the mountain gate.

From a defensive standpoint, there were so many weaknesses her hands twitched with the need to repair them. But this would never be her place, her home. The trade gate was an actual gate, but from her observations in her time here, it was shut more to block the winds that came swirling through the islands and encourage livestock to not go wandering at night.

The city was almost pure Aoisan, as they had little desire to travel and fewer reasons for others to come here. Of all the races, the Ged were the ones with wanderlust. The question was, should she join them?

Pushing away the thoughts for another day. She moved further into the city, where the temple to Pel and Rian lay at the center. The temple gleamed with pearls brought up from the oyster beds, each one shimmering with colors. The wide entry let into a courtyard that honored Raine, while a clever channel had water from the ocean surging up and splashing. It contained rooms for both Pel and Rian when they chose to visit. She had yet to figure out how entwined they were in their people's lives, but no matter, they seemed distant and aloof compared to Zula and Yika.

A familiar bittersweet pang lashed through her, and she sped up her steps, running as much from her own memories as anxiety to get out of the city. The dogs that roamed during the day raced alongside her, barking, tongues lolling, and tails wagging as she moved through the city. To her ears, even they seemed to bark in harmony with the songs.

The mountain gate was an arch in the wall with no door that opened to a trail leading up to the shrine for Rian on the tallest peak, and often her priestesses were the only ones to use it besides the occasional hunter. Jadaya's stress lightened as she stepped through, and just the difference of having a wall between her and the people of Pelisic made the music less of an overpowering force and more like a gentle harmony between her and nature.

Jadaya moved up the mountain, headed for the shrine to Rian. The sparse trees with needle-like leaves mixed with the thick underbrush absorbed the signing from below. By the time she reached the shrine, the music of Pelisic was but an inaudible murmur she felt more than heard. She walked into the shrine, intending to leave a token for the goddess. While she was unwilling to forgo her gods, even though they exiled her, she appreciated that Rian had not forbidden her from living here.

The small shrine was five pillars of white coral and clay, inset on all sides with pearls and etched in notes of music. She had been told if you could read the notes; it was a constant song of gratitude and love for all the gifts Rian gave her people: rain, love, friendship, rivers, and music. The roof was a series of metal sections that provided no protection from the rain, but instead created chimes for the rain to produce its own music. Standing inside while the rain came down created a sound that filled her with joy and peace.

She set down a shell discovered on her last walk along the beach, small but perfect with a pearly surface and refracted colors. She put it on the shrine, where a few others had laid their gifts.

"Aryix bless," Jadaya murmured, head bowed for a moment as she expressed her gratitude to the goddess, letting the barely audible hum of music, the rustle of the wind through the needles, and her own breathing fill the silence. Letting it go, she turned and stared out at the Pool of the Gods, where Pel resided, to her right and the open sea toward Vykland to her left. Sails spotted the sea with black.

Jadaya took the breathtaking view in, frowning at the sails. In the time since her arrival, she occasionally observed white or yellow sales, never black. She struggled to focus on them, but Yika stripped the gift to see far away along with her other gifts when she banished Jadaya. Pushing down the pain, Jadaya forced a shrug at the reminder of all she lost, and turned her mind to red meat and hide from the wily dryn that lived up here. They had long, thick fur, cloven hooves, and sturdy legs. Tt would take skill and patience to bring one down. With a smile, she hoisted her bow, one she made not four tendays ago. No Aoisan could pull it, but with her long arms and strength, it conformed to her will, and her accuracy was almost what she could do with the master bows of her home. *Former* home.

She shook her head, leaving the past where it belonged, no matter how much it hurt, and slipped out of the shrine, intent on meat for her rescuers.

CHAPTER TWO

JADAYA

The needles of the trees scratched at her, but Jadaya ignored it, happy with the dryn on her back. After about four fingers of hunting, a dryn had crossed her path and her bow proved its value. A quick field dressing and she headed back toward Pelisic, but mostly Kol and Ola. The sticky blood dripping down her back attracted flies that darted in and out, much to her annoyance. Her hair sat in a bun on the top of her head, out of the way, enabling her to drape the deer across her shoulders. It was a good-sized buck, and maybe an Aoisan would have struggled to carry it, but she moved down the mountain with ease.

The surrounding trees created their own type of music as the breeze rustled the needles and creaked the branches. Those sounds mixed with her breathing and the crunch of her sandal shod feet in the underbrush almost created a harmony around her. Lost in her own thoughts and the sounds of nature around her as she traveled down the mountain the only sounds being the forest, when she rounded a curve in the trail and the walls of Pelisic loomed in front of her, she froze, off balance the sounds wrong for where she was. She stood there blinking; the trees blocking the sky, and the skin on her neck rose as she stared at the mountain gate.

Where is the music?

Jadaya stood there seeking the sound that had been ever present since she awoke in this land. The songs that amused, confused, and even annoyed her. It was gone. She stood there for far too long, trying to remember when she had heard no music from these people and she failed. Even at night, there were priestesses that sang songs to their goddess and god.

Her nose crinkled at the scent of smoke, and her brain finally woke up. She dropped the dryn, pulled the bow to her, set the quiver on her back and sprinted toward the gate, instincts taking over. She slipped into the city, taking a second to orient and see what information she could parse out. There were pillars of smoke coming from the harbor, while the music from the temple was silent. She raced down streets, toward the school, and stepped into a battle. Men of an unfamiliar land were grabbing children, carrying them away, and attacking anyone that tried to stop them.

Aoisans lay on the ground, blood seeping from their cooling bodies, and screams of children filled the air as more people ran to stop them. In the harbor, she could see one ship already pulling out, even as someone tossed another struggling child up on the deck.

The men were shorter than her, but with hard muscles softened by a layer of fat, with wavy brown hair pulled back in a thick tail, and skin the color of fish belly gone bad, ash from the fires adding more gray to their skin. Most of the Aoisans just threw themselves at the men, flailing against them, and died for their efforts. They had no standing guard or even warriors. The closest thing to guards was the fire brigade, but the coral and shell walls were hard to burn and fires were easily put out by rain or seawater.

Jadaya took all this in with a few glances. Training of the Chosen for Zula and Yika was thorough, and part of it had included assessment. Her first assessment was that she possessed reach and probably strength on the attackers. Her second was she needed an up close weapon as she only had seven arrows.

She pulled her bow up, aimed at a man who shoved his sword through a woman flailing at him. Even with the sword in her, the Aoisan woman still fought with him, trying to stop him from grabbing a child. Jadaya slipped into her a hunting mental state, where all that existed was the target. She sighted down the pale wood, the head of the arrow locked on his heart and released. Even as the arrow flew toward her target, she drew and nocked the next. Her bow was short and strong. Kol, even with his suncycles of fishing and pulling up nets, was unable to fully draw it. The arrow punched through the invader's leather armor and through his heart, assuming his gods had left it in the normal place.

Jadaya paid no attention to how others reacted. She had already sighted another invader and loosed the arrow. Again the short bow propelled it forward at impressive speed and it punched through the ribs of this one. She kept moving, another arrow nocked and aimed. This time at someone who realized what she was doing and raced toward her. The arrow released without conscious thought and slammed into his throat.

Four arrows left.

She spun, looking for a clear shot. There, to her left, a man coming out of the school area with a terrified child tucked under one beefy arm. The silvery skin of the Aoisan child stood out starkly against his dark brown armor. She let loose a breath, then the arrow, the speed of it faster than she could follow before it took this one in the neck.

A bit high, but better than low. Need to keep the children safe.

There were no other obvious enemies, so she moved further down, the school mostly empty except for a few screaming little ones. All the adults were dead. She scanned the remaining children quickly. While terrified and possibly hurt, none of them looked like they had life-threatening injuries. The street toward the harbor was littered with too many dead bodies, though she saw some that were moving though wounded. Another invader rushed out of a house, his hands full of cloth and other valuables. He never saw her before the arrow was quivering in his chest.

She kept moving, headed toward the chaos at the harbor. More and more people were fighting, some with more skill than witnessed in the other sailors, but desperation had a power all of its own. A group of three men, all with swords and leers that made it all seem even more obscene given the blood splattering their exposed skin, trotted up the street toward her. Jadaya sank into herself: draw, aim, fire, nock, draw, aim, fire, nock, draw, aim, fire.

The last of her precious arrows sank all the way to the fletching in the man's chest not five feet in front of her. He toppled backward, a look of surprise in his eyes as his life flew away almost as fast as her attention. She reached down and grabbed the sword that fell from his hands. It was a straight sword, shorter than she was used to, but given his height, the length made sense. She glanced at the other two men, but their swords looked similar, though not identical. They were still too short. Dismissing other options and taking the sword as the best in a bad situation, she sprinted the rest of the way to the harbor, where one of ships with bold black sails was still at the dock, the other two headed out the sea gates.

Jadaya wasted a bitter second to wish they were actual gates, then dove into battle. The first man she intercepted sneered at her in contempt, then coughed in surprise as her parry translated into a smooth thrust that gutted him. The next man must have seen that, as he avoided leaving himself as open. The rapid *clang, clack,* of steel hitting steel created music she was familiar with, but the screams and cries of children and wounded added a frenetic pace to the beat.

He was skilled, but it was obvious the last fifteen suncycles practicing almost daily had set her skills much higher. Though her back protested as her movements pulled against scar tissue. Proof she had been avoiding her routines. That would not be happening again. Anger at her weakness lent her extra energy, and she kicked out with her leg while their swords locked, making him stumble. She slid her sword across his neck, spraying her with his blood before he had a chance to recover.

"They are leaving!" The panicked shout grabbed her attention as another man lunged at her. The moment of distraction cost her. Along with the protesting skin that had healed tight over the whip marks on her back, a new pain blossomed as his sword cut her, laying open a gash across her upper left arm. Jadaya snarled and doubled down on him, her skill overwhelming him quickly. He fell at her feet and she turned, looking for more. But what invaders remained were rushing toward the last ship. They were followed by a slim Aoisan, black hair shocking against silvery white skin, who fought with two knives the length of his forearm.

The ship gate was really just two tall pillars with flames on the top build on either side of the harbor opening, acting more as guides at night than security. The local fishing boats went in and out, as did the occasional trade vessel, and usually there was a Ged vessel docked. But it had no way to prevent the ships from leaving.

Jadaya took no time to think, just raced after them. Her long legs caught up easily with the Aoisan, who glanced at her with a quick nod. Then she was on the last of the three men running for the ship that was pulling away from the dock. There was no hesitation or break in stride as she shoved the sword in the back of the man in front of her. With a grunt of effort, she lifted and pushed him to the right, letting his falling weight pull free from the sword. She caught up with the next man as they raced up the gangplank. She lunged forward and slashed the sword across his knees, hamstringing him. He fell into the water with a cry and she jumped onto the deck without hesitation.

There was a cry of rage from the men crewing the ship, some wearing armor and bearing swords, others obviously sailors, though not sea Ged. That knowledge flashed through her as unusual, as sea Ged crewed all trade ships, but these invaders had crewed their own ships. It also removed any hesitation.

The memories swamped her for a second, but the roar of men attacking snapped her back to reality. She swung the sword hard at a sailor charging her with a belaying pin. The sword sliced across his body and he stumbled back, grabbing his stomach as she snatched the pin from off his hand.

Her world dissolved into blocking with the pin and swinging the sword. The lurching of the ship made the fight more difficult. Especially as the fighters on the ship were much steadier than she was. Every swing, every stab, and every block helped bring back her training. The movements ground into her, since she was coordinated enough to pick up a training sword. No matter what happened, she was and always would be a warrior.

The last attacker went down, and she spun, looking for the next threat, but the only living person she saw was the other Aoisan. His chest heaved, and she realized he was covered in blood, both from others and himself. She looked around as the ship rocked, her confidence vanishing as she fell out of combat.

"Turn the wheel until the bow is pointed toward the dock. Drop the ladders into the water, then lower the sails." The order came from the young man, but she just nodded and headed to the helm. It took them a while to turn the ship back to the dock, but as they got closer, multiple Aoisans jumped off the dock and started swimming to them. Their speed in the water was a direct counterpoint to their lack of fighting ability. Anyone that could move that fluidly should be able to defend themselves.

She pushed the thoughts away and turned over the helm to the first Aoisan that came up offering to take it. The black-haired young man had been pacing back and forth, and as soon as others got on board, it had only increased.

"You have any issues with cramped spaces?" he demanded the second she got down to the main deck.

Jadaya frowned, then followed his gaze to the hatch, and everything snapped into focus. There would still be people down there. And that is where the children must be kept, as there were none on the main deck.

She looked at him, lips pressed into a tight line. "Yes. Jadaya."

"I know. Hard to miss you. Note. Ready?"

It took a second to realize Note was his name, but by then he was already at the hatch, waiting for her. She grabbed the sword, replacing the belaying pin with a knife from one of the sailors. She nodded, and he pulled the hatch open.

CHAPTER THREE

NOTE

The lack of music woke him. The music he hated and loved with equal passion. Hated because they had tainted it past his ability to enjoy singing ever again. Loved it because it meant he was home, for all that he felt like an exile in his own land.

Note lay in bed, his little corner of safety, listening, trying to figure out what was wrong. He constructed his sleeping space in such a way that he had weapons and two exits always available. He heard nothing in the room immediately outside his bed. This silence let him slide open the panel and look out. His white living area, a never-used sleeping sling, and a board, salvaged from a wreck, covered with intricate carvings, inset pearls, and other shells, hung on the wall. His bed had a separate airflow channel, and another tight escape tunnel.

He slipped on his sandals and walked to the door, pushing it open, still trying to place what might have stopped the music. He lived outside the too-confining walls, on the north side of the harbor. It made him smile to watch the sun rise over the harbor filled with boats of people he knew.

His door opened on the harbor, and the second it swung open, black sails obscured everything. His heart slammed into his chest so hard he could barely breathe, and he stood there frozen in the doorway as the past played in his mind. A scream pulled him out of his paralyzed shock. A quick glance to the right and he saw a child being carried, screaming in terror, to the waiting ships.

Ships, three ships. Rian, why have you forsaken us now?

He refused to waste time asking the goddess questions, if she even was paying attention. He reached back in and grabbed his blades. Most Aoisans regarded his need to have his knives as a remnant of his suffering. And maybe they were, but they were also the reason he made it back alive, and he spent time daily to ensure his skills remained sharp.

The knives were the length of his forearm. He wore them strapped to his legs, uncaring of anyone's reactions. He kept them even upon entering the temple, only Rian refusing to force him had allowed Ijo to drop the matter. If Rian had forced it, he would have never spoken to her again. Maybe she knew, maybe not. The gods rarely reacted like people and after praying for rescue for suncycles and not receiving an answer, it meant he depended on them not at all.

The sheathes were on his legs, the knives in his hands, as he went racing out of his house to the dock.

If I can kill them before they get to the ships, I can prevent them from taking the children.

He let the ones that had already gotten to the ships go, though he cursed himself for his insulated sleeping area. Instead, he attacked the first sailor he could reach, a large man, with a squirming, crying child, of about ten cycles under his arm.

The man just laughed at him, and from the trail of bodies along this path, Note knew he assumed all Aoisans were unable to fight. It was more accurate than Note would like, but it meant he had an advantage going into this fight, and he grabbed it.

Note allowed the knives to waver in his hands, as if he had no idea know how to use them. The man grinned, revealing tella-stained teeth. Tella nuts made you feel as if the powers of the gods coursed through your body. It made you feel immortal, invincible, and stupid. The invader fell for Note's faked ineptitude and raised his sword high to bring it slashing down. Note ducked under it, the knives severing the veins running up to the torso from the legs. The man stumbled and dropped the child.

Note nimbly stepped aside and grabbed the boy. "Run. Hide above the walls. Call any other children you see. Stay hidden until the songs are sung again." His words were harsh as he shoved the boy toward the walls. The youngster just nodded, little legs pumping as fast as possible toward the walls and innumerable hiding spots children that age always found. Note had no time to watch as another raider bore down on him.

The feigned incompetence only worked once, so this time Note went straight into fighting. The thing with knife fighting was it excelled in cramped spaces and unexpected attacks. It put him at a disadvantage in a straight fight, one on one with a sword. If the sword hit him, death would take him. Especially considering at this point he wore loose pants and a sleeveless shirt that already had sprays of red slicing across it. He darted in, avoiding the sword swing, Note practiced staying limber and quick, and traced one knife across the underside of the raised arm, while slamming the other into the lower left flank of the man's back to provide leverage.

He pushed past the raider with the knife in his back as leverage, then ripped it out, letting the man fall behind him. Note went after anyone carrying a child, ignoring the others unless they came right at him. He knew who the raiders were, and he tried to replay their methods in his head. He had hoped, dared to hope, they would never return. Stupid to think men like that, gods like that, would ever deny themselves.

They would have come in after dawn, after they had seen all the sailboats go out, the ones filled with strong men who, while not warriors, would be tougher. Sailed in quietly, probably acted like traders until they had enough men on the dock. Three ships. They would have been able to move quickly. Pelisic was peaceful, and no one expected trouble.

They should. After all, it happened before. Why not again?

The thoughts left trails of acid in their wake and he fought harder, biting back howls of anger. These men were not the ones responsible for his own abduction years ago, but they would serve well as stand-ins.

Note dashed and slashed, but they avoided him, running to the other ships. And even one attacker, now that they knew he was a capable fighter, could keep him from moving in far enough to get the others. Two ships pulled up their gangplanks as he struggled to stop them, watching his fellow Aoisans get cut down around him. A scream of pure rage burst out of him, but the gods, as usual, were silent, and the invaders were happy with the wanton destruction.

The shift of their attention to the main road into the city, the one that led to the school and other businesses, grabbed his. He followed their eyes toward a figure walking down the street, her black skin making her look like an avenging shadow against the white of the walls. He watched for the space of two heartbeats as three men rushed her, and she put arrows in their chest before he could have even aimed.

Jadaya. The storm refugee that Kol had succored. He had seen her around the city but not thought much about her either way. Her people had not been part of his past. It had not occurred to him she might be part of his future. Before he could drag his eyes away from the avenging woman, she grabbed a fallen sword and was cutting through the raiders like a fillet knife through a fish's belly.

He took out the next two and looked around, only to see in the chaos the two ships had reached the gates, far enough out that he could never catch them. But the last one still had mooring lines and a gangplank. Note raced toward it. Thudding feet caught up to him, heavy long strides. He glanced to his ready to attack, only to see the woman racing ahead, taking out another invader as she ran. Blood covered her and the clothes she wore, even to dripping down her back.

How did she manage that?

He brushed the question from his mind as he raced up the plank after her, the splash of wood hitting water telling him how close the timing was. Knives at the ready, he dove in, this time fighting invaders and sailors. They could all die. Just for starting on these voyages, they earned their deaths. To his left, Jadaya more than held her own. She made most of them look like trainees who were still learning what weapons they should use. Even the lurching of the ship was unable to stop her until the top deck held only them and dead bodies.

Note stood a second, scanning. But the dead and the refugee were the only figures still on the deck. He glanced at her. "Turn the wheel until the bow is pointed toward the dock. Then drop the ladders into the water and lower the sails."

He was glad she just nodded at him and headed to the helm. Note went and dropped the ladders and nets as people were already swimming toward the ship. Fighting they might be useless at, but handling a ship was a different matter. As soon as the first person grabbed the ladder, he checked everything again and while she had pointed the ship back toward Pelisic, there was no sign of the children he knew had been dragged aboard.

Eyes locked on the hatch, Note pulled his daggers out. "You have any issues with cramped spaces?" he asked the dark woman next to him, her twisty black hair half falling down half in a silly bump on the top of her head.

"No. Jadaya," she said, her Aoisan still stilted but completely understandable.

Does she really think anyone in Pelisic is unaware of who she is? She has two hands of height more than most of us and pulls in the light with her skin. How could anyone miss her?

He kept most of his thoughts out of his response. Most. "I know. Hard to miss you. Note. Ready?"

The stranger to his shored blinked, then nodded. At least he had company as he went down there. A slow smile crept up his face as he set his hand on the hatch and pulled up. Down there, knives were an advantage and being small and limber might keep him alive. Hopefully, the slavers below would never know what killed them.

CHAPTER FOUR

JADAYA

She blinked as he said his name. Every other Aoisan she met so far had a one or two syllable name, one that could become music at any time. Jadaya put her curiosity about this young man into the back of her mind and nodded. She clenched the sword in her hand, a knife in the other, and waited. Her height caused issues down there, but she had no idea how cramped this ship was - yet. The young man, Note, slipped in first, his skin almost glowing in the low light. She followed cautiously, stopping three steps in to let her eyes adjust. Zula and Yika had not given their people better sight in the dark, though they could see further than a hawk when they wanted to.

The sounds below were muffled, but she could hear the notes of panic and the higher pitch that indicated children. The steps led down at an angle, and she crouched to look behind them, but all she could see was shadows toward the front of the ship.

Note had made it to the bottom of the stairs, and he spun in a slow circle looking for those waiting to kill them. Jadaya watched him, trying to make sure they worked together. He looked up at her, skin almost shining in the faint lantern light. Rather than talk, he jerked his head toward the back of the ship.

She nodded and finished her descent, head just brushing the ceiling. He moved to the left, and she went right. As they crept through the constantly changing shadows from the lanterns on the wall, he was the only constant with his almost glowing skin.

Night work is not what he should do.

The random thought resulted in curved lips, but she let it go as a muffled sound caught her attention. She looked at the barrels and saw a sliver of that same silvery hair. Knowing she was hard to see in the shadows, she darted forward, her sword braced diagonally in front of her. Worst case, a child might be terrified but alive. Though she somehow doubted that the child was hiding from her, if the child had seen her at all. The sudden side rush elicited a curse, and then the man hiding down there lunged out at her. She blocked the attack with her sword, while with her left, she slid the knife in and gutted him in one move. He fell with a muffled cry, and she turned to check on the child, slamming her head into a support beam.

"Uhhh," she groaned through clenched teeth.

"Night warrior is hurt?" The question came from the child behind the barrels, and Jadaya forced herself to shake off the dizziness.

"No," she said, though the pounding when she shook her head belied her words. "Run up the stairs. We already cleared off the top." She pointed to the light that highlighted the stairs as a hope of salvation. "Run," she ordered.

The child darted out and up the stairs with a speed only the young ever seemed to have. Jadaya could hear muffled sounds of a fight on the other side, but she let him be and worked her way toward the stern. There was a room directly ahead of her. She tried to check every area, but the shadows and the fact that only the center of the hold was high enough to let her walk without hitting supports slowed her down.

She made it to the room at the same time Note did. He spoke without preamble. "Still prow to check out, and one more hold below us. Too small for both. Can you handle this?" He waved his arm to take in the level they were on.

"Yes," she said simply. He was right, and she already felt cramped.

So be it, instead I can use the sword as a shield and the knife as my weapon.

Matching action to her strategy, she swapped the sword to her left hand, grasping the pommel so her thumb rested against the end of the hilt, while the blade lay back against her arm. Not perfect, but it would give her minimal protection from an overhead blow. Note had already disappeared back into the shadows. She reached for the door, a smile settling on her face. It was foolhardy in the extreme, but this fighting, the rescuing, it was what had been missing the last six mooncycles. This was what called to her: battle and the proving you were better than those you fought.

Not that these had been much of a challenge.

Banishing that thought, for arrogance could only get her killed. She turned the door handle and pushed in, left arm in front of her. Whimpering and crying met her ears, but the flickering light revealed a man with a child in his arm, knife against her throat.

He snarled something, and she shook her head, her eyes not leaving him as she took in the scene. There were multiple tiers of beds that were crammed with children, all looking at her with wide eyes reflecting the light. The man stood in the doorway, so any child would have to scramble around him to get to her and safety. The way he held the child implied a willingness to slice open the child's throat to defend against an attack.

He spoke again, but this time in Ged. All the lands had their own tongue, sometimes similar to others, sometimes not. But everyone spoke Ged. It was the trade tongue and everyone learned it along with their mother tongue.

"Let me go or I kill child," the man threatened, the child crying silently in his arms.

"There is nowhere to go. We have the ship," Jadaya replied calmly, though she kept her stance. Her arms and legs were long enough that one large step and a lunge would allow her to gut him. If there was no child in the way.

His mouth dropped open, arms trembling, though she had no idea why. "Did other ships get out?"

Jadaya tilted her head to the side slightly. "Why?"

"Did get out?" he demanded again.

Even his Ged was basic, and it added to her confusion. After a moment, not seeing what difference it would make, Jadaya nodded. "Yes, we will chase." She was unsure if they would or not, but letting this go seemed horrible.

"Percit bless," he breathed. In one motion he released the child, who dropped to the floor in with an awkward thump, and slit his own throat. Blood splashed across her face and arm. Blinking her eyes to clear them, she looked around. There was no one else there except the children.

Licking her lips, spitting as she tasted blood, she took a moment to assess. "Stay here. I want to check the rest of the area first, but we have the ship. You are safe."

The crying slowed and solemn eyes looked at her from under silver locks. As a group, they nodded, and Jadaya stepped back out to search the hold. It took three more impacts with supports and tripping over thick rope twice, but the area was empty. Note met her on her sweep.

"Two dead below, no children." He looked at her, obviously waiting for something.

"Room full of children. I told them to stay until it was verified safe. Two dead here, plus the two you killed opposite me. So six?" She tried to remember the Ged ship she had been dumped onto, and the numbers seemed roughly right.

He nodded once and headed up the stairs. She went back to get the kids. They all scurried up the stairs to the deck. They were coming back to the dock by the time she emerged, and Jadaya stood and looked at the city. Pelisic had always radiated joy, shining light, and a jumble of whiteness that somehow came across as friendly.

Now smoke drifted up in the street, splashes of dark red spread under pale bodies, the brightly colored clothes seeming garish. But worst of all, there was no song. Even the grim-faced Aoisans getting the ship back to dock had no music. The sky clouded, and in moments a light rain began falling. Note stood in the middle of the deck and sneered up at the sky. He shook his head, walked to the edge of the ship, and jumped off. A moment later, Jadaya could see his form gliding toward the dock.

Aoisans swam like fish, they introduced their babies to the ocean at birth in the birthing pools. They had gills on the sides of their chest, letting them dive to incredible depths. Jadaya would wait for the gangplank. She could swim, Kol made sure of that. But in his words, she looked like a dryn trying to dance and failing horribly. Personally, she was sure a dryn could dance better than she could swim.

She walked off the ship and down the dock. The high priestess, Ijo, was coming out of the city proper. Instead of her normal white pants and white shirt, she was garbed in a brown apron over a simple women's wrap that bound the breasts and went between your legs, then tied around your waist. It was standard in many lands, but Jadaya had always worn her loincloth and binders separately. It made it easier to get to wounds earned during training.

As Jadaya headed toward the priestess, Note moved faster than her and intercepted the woman as she got to the deck. His voice was loud enough that Jadaya figured everyone on the dock heard him.

"Where were your precious gods, Ijo? Why were there no guards set? Why was this allowed to happen?" His words hit with the impact of sword strikes and Jadaya slowed her gait, not wanting to be in the middle of this. Others had paused and looked at him and, to her surprise, she saw shame on multiple faces.

"You know I do not control the gods, Miy," Ijo said, her voice calm, but with a tightness in her face that was at odds with the normally serene woman.

"Miy died twenty suncycles ago. And that was not my question. Where are they?" He waved his hands around them, taking in the dead, the wounded, and the children, some crying over a fallen figure.

Ijo took in a deep breath and let it out slowly. Jadaya was close enough to see the tears on her face. But the priestess kept her eyes on Note. "I have no knowledge of that. I will ask."

Slow, fat drops of rain fell, each one soft in a way that made them feel like tears.

Note sneered and glanced up at the sky. "Nice to see you finally decided to pay attention." Jadaya was unsure who he was talking to. Surely he never talked to his gods in that manner.

Ijo reached out a hand to touch him, but he pulled away from her touch.

"That still leaves the question of why there was no watch here. In all the years, there have never been guards placed. Why? You knew this could happen, *has* happened, over and over. Explain that failing to me." Note stood staring at her, arms across his chest, his face a carved statute, unforgiving, unmoving.

The priestess let her head drop and stared at her hands. They were covered with blood, cuts, and they looked old and trembled under her gaze. "We were lacking the knowledge of how to guard, how to protect. None of us are trained, and it had been so long. We thought maybe they might not come again or had found another way to solve the issue."

Note turned and spat on the ground, and half the Aoisans hissed, pulling back in surprise. "Then you are fools, and I should have died rather than come back to a people and gods that care so little for their children."

The shame that covered everyone left Jadaya confused. The sky darkened and a bolt of lightning came down, striking the entrance to the city. But rather than an explosion of sparks and boom of sound, two people stood there, a woman and a man. The woman wore robes the color of a ripening sky, with bits of jewelry of pearls and silver made to look like leaves or branches. Her hair, the same color as most Aoisans, was twisted and wound around her head. Her face was streaked with tear tracks and she held herself tight, with arms wrapped around her waist. She paced forward to where Note glared at them and Ijo was falling to her knees.

A man walked beside her. He had a clean face, with skin that looked like most Aoisans, but his had tiny scales that reflected the light, making a constant shift of rainbows across the skin. Well built, clad only in a swimming cloth. Jadaya could see the webs between his toes as he walked and the slight ripples of gills along his torso. His silvery hair was pulled into a large, thick braid that went down his back.

Neither of them carried anything, but they moved as if weighed down by something. Their eyes, both shifting rainbows of color, took in the damage and deaths, and they moved slower and slower as they approached Ijo and Note.

Their gods.

Jadaya was unable to decide if she should kneel, bow, or flee. Frozen, she just watched the drama unfold in front of her.

CHAPTER FIVE

NOTE

"Amazing how you show up after the damage is done. And here I thought the gods prohibited slavery of their people," Note said, facing the two gods without a shred of humility or deference. Why should he? They had done little enough for him.

They ignored him as usual, though Rian darted a look his way and a few more tears fell from her eyes.

"What happened, Ijo?" Rian asked the priestess.

Note snorted derisively. "Why ask questions you already know the answer to?"

This time, the gods did look at him. He could see the guilt on their faces and had no sympathy.

"Will you never let us live down the mistakes we made?" Rian asked, her voice the sound of breeze on the trees and a brook running over stones. He fought the need, the urge to let his anger fade. They were his gods. They should have protected him, all of them.

Note swallowed and looked at the body of Doi, the local bartender, though there was little worth drinking in Pelisic. Doi's silver hair was now red from his cut throat, as lay not five feet in front of him. Knowing that others had fought and died, pushed back Note'ss desire to waver.

"I might have, someday. But this?" Another wave of his hand. "This means your protestations of loving us are false." He was aware everyone around him was kneeling, except Jadaya. That was interesting. But at the moment, immaterial. This fight had been a long time coming. Though the hope maybe something had changed had remained in his heart. So much for that hope.

"No!" Rian burst out, but subsided as Pel put his arm around her. She turned to put her head on his shoulder.

"We… We were tricked and distracted. Lied to almost," Pel said, looking out at the sea instead of them. "The ways of the gods are complicated, and time passes so fast here. We will have words with Cassix. But you, of any, should know the consequences of this not happening."

Cassix is involved? Why? I thought he avoided his siblings.

Note jerked back as if slapped at her comment, and snarled, "Then maybe you should deal with your brother. Or are your people dying not a valid reason to quit catering to him?"

The two gods exchanged glances that held a wealth of information that meant nothing to him, and bile rose in his throat. They were toys to the gods, and a few broken toys were the price you paid to keep harmony in the family.

"Ijo, do you have the jar?" Rian asked as more tears ran down her face.

Ijo fumbled at her waist, trying to untie a belt that held two jars. They were smallish jars, large enough to hold a two cupped hands of liquid. She pulled the one with a raindrop on the lid and gave it to Rian. The goddess took the jar and held it up to her face. Tears ran down from her eyes into the jar, each one glowing slightly. It seemed like no time at all and the jar was full. As if in response, the light rain slowed as her tears dried up.

"The other one, if you please, Ijo. Though where is Lir?" Pel asked, looking around.

Ijo handed the other jar to Pel, and her hands shook. "He was killed defending the children." Her voice broke on the last word and Note dropped his head, hiding his face. There had been issues with Lir over the suncycles, he never wanted him dead. He never wanted to deprive Ijo of her husband. Note forced the thoughts away. Many people had lost spouses or children this day.

Pel's head dropped for a moment and Note wanted to scream, but he kept silent as Pel brought his braid of hair over his shoulder and squeezed moisture out of it into the jar. The drops of water glowed as they filled the glass jar until it was full. Pel sealed the jar and handed it back to Ijo. "I am sorry. It was never supposed to be like this. Build the funeral pyres. I will wait for all of them and escort them myself to Percit's domain."

"Three of my tears will heal all but death. Pel's water should be mixed with seawater, one drop per container. It will lessen the grief and help with the aftermath." Rian slid him a glance, and he nodded. She turned back to Ijo. "Mix one drop of my tears with one drop and Pel's and give it to anyone seeking to conceive. If it is possible, it will happen. But first heal, then look to the future."

"What? You want to make sure there are more children to steal? After all,

Percit is the reason behind all of this." Note's voice was acid, and the gods stiffened, focusing on him again.

"You are unaware of the complication of this situation," Pel said, his voice heavy and anger touching the words. "It is more than you think."

"More? You never listened when I called you, did you?" Note's rage flowed into the words, driving him and his need to know why. "Every tear we cried. When we begged for release. Some of us even prayed to Percit, asking her to take us. But of course she didn't respond. Because she couldn't." Each word snapped out like a blow and Ijo cowered from his words, her eyes watching the gods, waiting for them to snap.

Maybe I desire their wrath? For them to smite me so I no longer exist like this anymore?

"No," Pel said, the anger in his voice matching Note's. "When you are there, Xyl blocks all to any other gods. But they would not abuse you, nor treat you like slaves. At worst, you are servants to the temple. Most regard that as an honor." Pel waved his hand with a dismissive gesture, as if to erase the past.

Note's jaw dropped and rage melted into incredulity, then his control slipped and he started to laugh. He could hear the insanity in his laugh, but was unable to stop it. All the anger, all the fear, all the crying, and they had never heard, never realized what had happened to him. To the others. It was that knowledge, the memory of what those children were headed toward, that stopped the laughter. At some point, his eyes had closed and when he opened them, he was the center of attention. Even the gods watched him with wide, worried eyes.

Jadaya stood, her arms crossed over her chest, lighter scars shown at the edges of her shirt. Her concerned look, complete with furrowed brow, meant more than those from his fellow countryman. Note had heard the stories of her back, how Kol and Ola had to hand feed and bathe her for three tendays before she could walk to the needs room herself without ripping open the wounds again. They were able to make her comfortable in a simple tub of spring water from the temple. Ijo had even let them take a single tear to help. She understood what suffering was, even if he would never know who had given her the wounds.

"So be it. You want the story. I shall give it to you, but not here. Not now. You need to understand, but for now, I need to help. I will be there tonight. If you wish to hear the story of what they will use our children for, I will share it." He had no need to add that if they skipped this story, the proof they were uncaring would be clear.

The two divine beings glanced at each other, then back at Note. "We will be there," Rian said, her voice the sound of wind through the trees.

Note nodded and then turned to look at Jadaya, dismissing the gods from his attention. "Will you help me with the bodies? We need to start the rites for those that died." He had no idea what to do about the abducted children, but maybe after the talk with the gods, their attitude would change.

I will keep my gills open, rather than try to breathe with that hope.

"Yes. What would you like?" Her rough, hesitant voice was so different from the melodic ones of his people. Right now, he preferred it. Her voice brought with it no memories of songs.

Oh. Right. Song.

Note heaved a sigh, wanting nothing more than to go crawl into his space and hide from all of this. From what had been allowed to happen. "Ijo."

The woman in question looked up at him. The two gods had vanished, not that he ever expected them to stay around.

"I told the children to hide until they heard the songs. They need to be restarted so they will come out. I am sure there are many more that might still be hiding."

Her face pale Ijo nodded. "I will. Tell all injured to come to me. I will prepare the tears for healing."

Note nodded, wondering when this had become his job, but all of them, even the foreign woman, looked at him. He wanted to scream, rage against their lackadaisical attitude, but he tamped it down and began giving orders. First was a wagon to place the bodies. There were too many for easy caring.

Those who were only injured made their way to the temple as the song started. Rather than the normal paeans to the gods, this was a song of mourning, of loss, and it filled the city with a level of sadness the threatened to make him cry. As if Rian heard them too, soft rain began to fall. Tears from the sky, though these had no ability to heal like the ones from her eyes.

Jadaya pulled the wagon easily, her strength and height a benefit as together they collected the dead and sent the wounded to the temple. To his relief, she stayed silent, not pestering him with questions, though he caught curious glances at him. In the end, the toll was both better and worse than he had feared. Many that he had thought were dead were instead wounded or unconscious. Those were soon put right by the temple. Those neither injured nor mourning set about cleaning and putting things to right. The count of the dead lay at thirteen, much fewer than he had feared.

The worse was the number of children that were gone, even after the songs had restarted and they had filtered out of their hiding places. As always, the raiders had focused on those between the ages of six and twelve. They had killed no children, which was a relief, yet thirty were gone. They had knocked the older ones down with harsh blows, giving them little chance of fighting their attackers. But with so many gone, you could feel the emptiness in the city and the low musical wails of those who were now childless.

By dark, the worst had been cleaned up, though it would take days to put the city back to its normal pristine condition. He kept his thoughts to himself, but he preferred the darker look. The soot was more honest, where the white gave the impression everything here was perfect. With an aching heart and sore body, he approached the temple. Ijo awaited him at the door, dressed once again in white with her hair smoothly held back. If not for the lines of grief on her face, you would have thought she had been untouched by this day.

"You are here to speak with them?" She stood, almost blocking the door, trying to deflect his anger.

He shrugged. "I came here to tell them what happened if they actually care. They never seemed to before."

Ijo's eyes darkened, but she spoke no defense of their gods, simply nodded and let him into the inner chambers. He followed her to the chamber of worship, through it to a small door at the end that led into a sitting room with another door out. He knew from his lessons as a child that beyond that door were the living quarters for the gods when they were here. It was kept always clean and ready for them, though they used it but rarely. Pel had a home in the sea and preferred the water over land. Rian stayed with her husband.

Each set of gods dealt with their people differently, and while Pel and Rian were active, they maintained a life distant from their people.

And ignorant of our suffering.

He tried to let the bitterness flush away, but it was hard. A sound had him turning, and he saw Rian and Pel entering the sitting room where he and Ijo stood.

Pel crossed arms over his muscular chest, looking at Note with tight lips and narrowed eyes. Rian stood beside him, her hands clasped in front of her, a pensive look on her face.

"You wanted to tell us the truth of what was done. This is your chance," Pel said, his voice flat.

"I shall go," Ijo said, her voice almost a whisper. Her face provided the only evidence of tears. Note flinched, remembering Lir had lost his life trying to protect the children. For all that the man had refused to take Note's comments seriously, when Note had first returned to Pelisic, he grieved for Ijo's loss.

"No. Stay. You should hear this too. Maybe then you can spearhead some changes." Without asking permission, Note dropped into a chair, suddenly too tired to remain standing. He looked at his feet, eyes lingering on the blood and dirt still coating his legs and feet. "Listen, as I tell you what I experienced and the fate that awaits the children stolen from Aois."

CHAPTER SIX

JADAYA

The amount of disrespect Note had for his gods shocked Jadaya into silence. Even now, even after her exile, she was unable to imagine talking to Zula or Yika like that. They were her gods. How could she not treat them with honor? The memory of her punishment and the words Elike had whispered to her before they took her to the ship drifted through her mind, but she shied away from it, unable to see her gods as fallible. She had broken the laws knowingly. Her punishment was just.

"Will you help me with the bodies? We need to start the rites for those that died."

Note's words pulled her out of her thoughts and Jadaya glanced down at the man looking at her, ignoring the divines staring at him.

"Yes. What would you like?" She fumbled the words, but nodded as he talked. What he asked was relatively easier for her. Relieved to be out from under the eyes of the divines, not wanting them to ask why she was Exile, she went and grabbed the two-wheeled cart normally used for moving trade goods from the ships to further into Pelisic.

She grabbed it and brought it to the first body. She placed the body on the cart, her height making it relatively easy to pick up the smaller Aoisan. Even with the added load, the cart moved easily, and she followed Note as they went through the town. Others were moving ahead of them, seeing who might still be alive. More lived than expected, but the bodies placed carefully on the cart still carried a weight that was more than purely physical.

The attackers were gathered along with the locals. No one wanted to leave bodies just lying there, and it was better to treat the bodies with some level of honor. You never knew which god might get upset because of the treatment of the dead. Especially one whose wife was the goddess of death.

When the last body had been claimed and laid in the cart, Ijo met them at the entrance to the temple courtyard. "Jadaya, Aryix bless for your assistance. My priestesses will take them from here. We will prepare them for their final rites."

Jadaya nodded and watched as they took the bodies from the cart, and Note and Ijo headed into the temple. Part of her wanted to know what had happened to Note and what fate was in store for the children, but the lure of getting clean and resting won.

She climbed back up the path to the mountain gate, grabbing her discarded bow and quiver as she did so, and reclaimed the dryn. The meat sitting there for a few fingers had not hurt it. She threw it back over her shoulders and then made her way back down through the city toward Kol and Ola.

The songs had restarted, but the sadness that lay under every note pulled at her heart. She had almost made it back to Kol's when the soft rain that had been more cleansing than anything began to intensify. Lightning cracked across the sky and the rain fell with sharp, cold spikes mixed among the hard drops. Jadaya put on a burst of speed and reached the door of Kol's home as another flash of lightning slammed into the harbor with an explosion of sparks and steam as it heated the water.

Kol and Ola looked up as she raced in, relief clear on their faces, though it disappeared quickly as all of them looked out at the storm suddenly raging above the city.

"What in the world?" Ola stood with her hand on her throat as her silver fine hair floated around her head with all the energy in the air.

Jadaya looked at the sky and the storm that existed only over the city. Off to the north she could see clear night sky, Percit's broken halves visible. "I think Note is talking to your gods."

"Note?" Kol looked at her, his eyes dark. "You met him?"

Jadaya nodded and explained her day. They had been aware of the raiders helping with the cleanup, but neither had been involved with the fighting as they lived far enough out. No raiders had come their way.

"Ah," Kol said slowly, looking at the raging sky. "We had long wondered what happened to him. I hope the storm is a reflection of the gods' anger toward those that hurt him, not Note."

They had closed the door and taken the dryn into the kitchen area. Jadaya and Ola set to work cleaning and butchering the meat. "Can you tell me about Note?" Jadaya asked slowly. "He is the only Aoisan with hair that is not silvery white. And he fought. Fought well."

Ola looked down, focusing on the meat as Jadaya looked back and forth between them. "Did I say something wrong?"

Kol took the hide they had removed and set it up on a frame to stretch and clean it. "No. He is a reminder of our failure, worse now that we have failed again."

"Failure? This makes no sense," Jadaya said slowly. Her hands were busy with the meat as they cut it into roasts and steaks, some going in the cold box, others to be seasoned and dried.

Kol began to scrape the hide, removing all remnants of the flesh and membranes that stuck to the inside. "Were you not told this has happened before?" He, like Ola, avoided looking at her, appearing to give all their focus to the dryn they were processing.

"It was mentioned. Note was very vocal," Jadaya said slowly.

Kol nodded. "Note was one that was taken suncycles before, when they last came. He is the only one to ever return home. He simply said their captures killed none of the children, though some died of disease, but he refused to answer to his name anymore, saying he was Note."

Jadaya nodded, as she thought it odd he had a word for name. None of the other Aoisans had a name like that. Most of them were simple sounds, but Note was a word related to song. It had struck her as different.

"He warned Lir and Ijo that Pelisic needed to prepare for more raids from the Char. But they did not listen, saying they had talked to the gods and that the risk was low." Kol paused to glance out the window. The storm had lessened, but thunder and lightning still crackled across the sky, as if the sadness had turned just to rage. "I now am thinking the truth may not have been told. He has since been an outsider here, with his dyed hair and refusal to sing. No one has heard a single note pass his lips since his return."

Jadaya jaw dropped in shock. The Aoisans sang all the time. Even now Ola had a low hum as she worked, not enough that she drowning out Kol, but a soothing sound that matched the pace of their labor.

"Has he ever said what happened?" Jadaya asked as she thought about what she knew of Charinsky. It was a country on the other side of the deeps from Wysko. Ships rarely crossed the deeps as the monsters that patrolled there, guarding the prison of the Usurper, the one that killed Perci, were without mercy. They tolerated little to cross their waters, leaving only the foolhardy or the desperate to sail through those waters. These monsters made the route for trade circuitous, and the journey to Charinsky arduous, though you could see the mountains of Charinsky from the Wysko capital on a clear day. The Chars were a reclusive people with a single god as Percit had been Xyl's wife, dead all these long hundreds of suncycles. She knew very little about Xyl, their remaining deity.

"No. Well, yes. He said they were taken to Charinsky and turned over to the temple. That their purpose in life became to sing to Xyl and keep him from attacking." Kol shrugged. "He never explained, at least not to my knowledge, what happened there. Why he has such rage or what caused him to try to not be one of us?" The sadness in his tone made Jadaya want to hug him, but blood covered her hands. There had been enough blood on bodies for today. She had no desire to see any more.

The Aoisans she had met were anxious when there was imbalance in their relationships. None of them thrived on conflict like many she knew in Zuyika. But it made little sense that they ignored setting up some guards if this had happened before.

"How many times have you been raided before?" She finished putting the meat into the brine or the cold box. Ola would sell some of this tomorrow. She took the brain and put it in a pot, adding some water to make brain liquid for the hide, though it would be a day or two before it was needed.

Kol tilted his head as he finished scraping the hide clean. "My grandfather mentioned them. As far as I can tell, about once every twenty-five to thirty cycles, though these are by far the most children ever taken," he whispered.

Jadaya jerked up from her task of liquifying the brain. "They raid you every twenty-five cycles and have since your grandfather's time?" She did the math in her head. Most Aoisans lived well into their late hundreds, if not two hundred. That meant these raids had been going on for a very long time.

"That sounds about right, though he admitted he remembered hearing about them as a child."

Jadaya just looked at them, unable to understand. "And you never put up guards or walls or went after them?"

"How would we go after them? We have no sea ships, only fishing." Kol gave her a questioning look, and she shrugged. It was true their vessels were not created to go far into the ocean, but to not set up guards and restrictions to their city made little sense to her.

"But why not post guards or change the entrance?" The idea of children being captured for unknown purposes made her sick. Why did the Aoisans not fight back? The image of dead Aoisans lying on the ground answered that question. They were fishers and crafters. She had seen no armor since she opened her eyes here.

Kol finished cleaned his tools, not looking at her. "I know not. That is between the priest and priestess to decide."

"Oh. Lir was killed," Jadaya said, as they would not have heard.

Kol jerked his head up to look at her, while Ola sank even further into herself. "Is Ijo well?" His voice shook a little.

Jadaya shrugged helplessly. "No? Yes? She was up and talking, and she received jars of tears and water from Rian and Pel. She is functional is all I can say. The death toll was thirteen. The bodies are at the temple now to be prepared." The names of the dead were ones she was unfamiliar with, and if Note had known, he kept that information to himself.

"Ah," Kol said as he pulled the scraped hide down and took it over to a basin to wash it out.

Jadaya felt caught in a trap. The storm outside had faded and now just big sad drops of rain hit the roof with a desolate plop. She found the lack of guards or ways to protect themselves inconceivable. In Zuyika they had Chosen guards everywhere, and no ship could come into the harbor without being inspected. And to lose children, yet not go after them? She shook her head.

Ola finished up the brine for the jerky and dumped strips into it to sit overnight. Tomorrow she would put them in the oven to dry slowly. Kol rinsed, focusing entirely too hard for what the task required.

"I shall go outside and let the rain clean me off," Jadaya said into the silence. The blood from the dryn, raiders, and her own wounds had dried to a sticky film that covered her. She covered the few steps to the door and was outside before either of them responded. Jadaya lifted her head to the sky and let the rain fall down over her as she mourned both her former life and the lives lost here.

The question that plagued her was, "why were the children taken?"

The anger that kept her fighting when the ship she had been exiled on went down sparked back up. Letting gods just throw away children, like she had been thrown away, created a ripple of anger through her. But what could she do? How do you go against gods?

CHAPTER SEVEN

LAZUL

The throne room was chilly with the ever-present gloom. High walls of carved stone were broken up by tapestries that did nothing to alleviate the somber feeling. The last of his petitioners were leaving and Lazul sighed as the last of them disappeared out the doors. Torches lit the room brightly, but it still felt dank.

When was the last time I saw the sun? Felt direct heat on my skin?

Lazul was unable to remember exactly when it had been. At least two mooncycles and it was only Reaping season. That knowledge led to the next unwelcome thoughts, lower crop yield and hungry people. He felt one more piece of pride rot and fall off. If he could make it better, he would, but his options were limited. The steady click-clack of his steward's footsteps heralded news. The question was if it was news he wanted to hear.

Probably not. It rarely is.

"King Lapis, Cantor Zayn-" Actin started, but before he could finish, the person in question spoke.

"Is here to speak to you. Begone, Actin. This is no business of yours." The contempt in every word echoed across the chamber. Lazul lifted his head to see Zayn sweep by Actin as if even being in his vicinity would spread contagion.

Actin, a spare man dressed in elegant, fitted robes that made Lazul feel underdressed or overly pompous, stiffened, but his face remained blank. "Is there anything else I can get for you, Your Majesty?" If there was an extra stress on the word "majesty", Lazul found no fault in that.

"No. I am well, Actin. We will head to my office." Lazul rose from his throne, an uncomfortable chair at the best of times, encrusted with gems that sparkled in the light, and implied he was wealthier than he was in reality. He needed to see about getting more padding for it.

The stiffness in his body faded as he walked to his office, ignoring Zayn, who followed him, his footsteps rapid to keep up. It was a point of pride that he walked fast enough to make it uncomfortable for the priest. The warmth from that moment of pettiness that would fade fast enough, so he enjoyed it while he could.

Lazul pushed open the door to his office, ignoring the man lurking behind him. The roaring fire warmed the small room, and he took off his robe of office. He kept the sign of relief to himself as he hung it on a robe stand. The rich robe had thick, soft fur imported from Vykland, silk from Wysko, and wool from Agrina. It looked impressive, but weighed almost one hundred sixty tellaweights. Too much to wear at any other time.

The expensive silver dressing mirror in one corner of the room reflected a distorted version of himself, or at least he hoped his nose was shorter than it appeared. But the blond hair, pale skin, red nose, and florid skin seemed accurate. He sat down at the desk with the fire to his side and then turned his attention to Zayn, if only to remove his presence that much faster.

The priest had already arranged himself in the chair facing the desk, not bothering to ask permission. One more volley in the game they played. It was a constant question as to who had more power, the king or Xyl's priest?

A game I suspect he is winning, for all that he acts pious.

Lazul longed for a large glass of the special mead he had hidden away. But if got some now, he would need to share it with Zayn. Social strictures demanded it. He had no desire to give the cantor more than he already had.

Zayn has more than enough luxuries he pays little for.

Trying to delay whatever news the man had, Lazul examined him. The silver-blond hair was luxurious as always, falling to his shoulders, and the rich robes of black and red had to be woven with wool as fine as the king's own robe of office. It was the jewelry on the fingers and the smirk on his face as Zayn waited for Lazul to speak first that slid slivers of annoyance under the king's skin. The temptation to sit and start going through reports and make him wait bubbled to the top of Lazul's mind, but that meant tolerating Zayn's presence even longer. The price would be too high.

"Well?" Lazul said, lacing his fingers together so he could refrain from fiddling with things. Giving away his level of discomfort only gave Zayn points.

Zayn all but preened as Lazul gave in. "The ships arrived this morning. Xyl obviously helped them sail here quickly. We have new singers." The smugness in his voice soured what spurt of joy leaped up in Lazul's soul.

"How many?" How many children had been ripped from their homes to play servant to their insane god was the question he really wanted to ask, but that would expose too much, and you never knew when Xyl might be paying attention.

"Twenty-nine made it back. We lost one ship. Per the captain, they had someone in the city that put up an organized fight, killing multiple men. We might need to think about that in the future, but this group should be good for another twenty suncycles, and the breeding program promises to fill out the ranks, though at a slower rate that is desirable." The priest shrugged. "They did well with obtaining mostly young ones. In a few suncycles, this will be the only life they remember."

"How many died on the voyage?" Lazul feared the answer, but ignorance was unacceptable. It took effort, but his expression remained placid as he watched the cantor.

"Only two. More than acceptable losses. The rest are properly terrified and as a consequence, keen to please. I am sure my priests will get them in line quickly." At this point, Zayn licked his lips like a feline contemplating cream, all but purring. Lazul had to fight to keep his gorge down. He avoided any thoughts about what the priest looked forward to with such gluttony.

"Then we should expect some sun soon?" The hope in his voice gave him away, and from the pleased smirk, Zayn had caught it.

"Yes. I expect next tenday should be sunny. The children will be taught the songs starting tomorrow and we make very sure they are eager to learn." Zayn smirked again. "We have found that both reward and punishment work extremely well, especially if there is someone we can make an example of. That lesson always sinks into their minds extremely well."

"Zayn," Lazul said warningly. "We are skirting the edge of what is acceptable. You know their gods will not tolerate slavery." He still was unsure why their gods allowed this at all, but given that otherwise he was sure that his kingdom and people would be dead, he tried to not complain too much.

Zayn waved his hand. "They are not slaves. They are fed, clothed, kept in pleasant rooms, and all we ask is that they sing. No one could call that slavery. Many of our citizens would love to be as pampered and coddled as they are. It is a life of luxury." Once again, a smirk flickered across his face.

"Except that they are not allowed to leave." There was no way the nation of Charinsky could allow them to leave, but if they were treated well, Lazul could convince himself that they had a better life. It was that or destroy his people.

"Who would want to leave such luxury? To go back to a life of fishing and toil? This is a reward. We will have to leave a few boys untouched to ensure they can breed. Find one or two with good bones and a pleasing voice. As soon as it changes, we will pull them for breeding the others. Luckily, the girls keep their voices with no intervention needed."

Only the fact that his fingers were laced tightly together kept Lazul from rubbing his face. He knew what Zayn spoke about and hated that it was something he had to allow, but the cost of not doing this would be too high. But did the man have to look like he enjoyed it so much?

"Whatever. Get them singing, put Xyl in a better mood." He looked at the priest, trying not to sneer. "Is there anything else?"

"No," Zayn said as he rose, his voice like oil. "Just reminding you that the tithe is due soon. We want to ensure the children lack for nothing, yes? After all, our very kingdom depends on their ability to sing. I would hate to see what might happen if they caught chills or something like that." He nodded his head in a mockery of respect to Lazul.

Gritting his teeth, Lazul nodded. "I will see that it is delivered." More money taken from his people. Hopefully, after talking to Actin, he could find a way to get the money needed.

"Excellent," Zayn purred and swept out of the room.

The door shut behind him and for long heartbeats Lazul considered getting up and barring it. He slumped back in his chair, pulled off the crown, and stared at the portrait on the other side of the room. It displayed a man who looked much like him, with a tall, elegant woman standing next to him. It was obvious she was born some place other than Charinsky, but she must have accepted his father's gods at marriage. Her curly red hair mixed with her height, which Xyl left unaltered, marking her as an obvious foreigner. If he remembered correctly, it had been Delcona. "How did you do it? How did you manage to live with this? All the things I was unaware of as prince. Back when I wanted so much to be like you?" Lazul stared at his parents, not expecting an answer.

With a sigh, Lazul pulled his mead out and poured himself a large cup. Taking a sip, he turned to look at the fire, drink in hand. The theft of children had been going on for ages. As a child himself, he once thought they were volunteers or visitors or something. It had never occurred to him they were captives. Torn from family and home. How many died so they could live?

"More would die if Xyl were to rage. You know this. Even if the death toll was in the hundreds, it is less than what would happen here. My citizens would die by the thousands. Surely the imprisonment of a few children is a valid price to pay?" His voice sounded thin and querulous in the room, and it left another mark on his psyche. How many before him had justified this?

As king, his duties involved ordered executions, prison sentences, and forced marriages to keep tempers down and the realm together. All of those seemed like nothing compared to knowing about the Singers.

That was what all the Char called the children that made up the Choir of Percit. They sang to Xyl, telling him of her love, never ending and eternal. That someday she would return. They sang the songs daily and lifted voice to special paeans during festivals. This music brought ease to their god. The clouds would clear and the sun would shine. It was part of the reason the raid had been authorized. Two mooncycles without direct sunlight, and the crops were perishing. His people needed the sun, and his loyalty was to his people first.

Lazul was unsure why the Aoisan's gods had not interfered. On good days, he convinced himself they understood the needs of Char and allowed this out of their understanding. On bad days, he wondered what they would leave of his country if they ever realized what was going on. He repeated the words over in his head - pampered, coddled, treated well. They have no reason to leave.

He could almost believe that except that near the end of his father's reign, some *had* left, led by a boy that fled. A few had returned, crying that they could never go home. A few had died, killed by the priests. But to his knowledge, the boy had never been caught.

Lazul took a gulp of mead to push the thoughts away. It occurred suncycles ago. The boy probably died on the sea. He had a kingdom to rule and that meant letting the temple do what was needed. For a long moment, he wondered what it had been like when Percit was alive. Had Xyl ever been happy? There were stories, old ones, of their land being full of sun and joy. But that all changed longer back than there were records kept in the royal archives.

He shied away from thinking how the cloudy days were more common, and more and more songs were required to keep Xyl from his sadness. A knock on his door pulled him from staring at the fire and Lazul shook his head.

How long have I been stuck in this rut?

He refused to dwell on trying to decide if he meant the last bit of time or for his reign as king.

"Enter," he said, turning to look at the door. As he expected, Actin pushed it open.

"Sire, here are the notes from the latest council. You asked to review them once completed." Actin matched his words by placing the notes on the desk. "Would you prefer dinner here tonight?"

The asking was a mere formality as Lazul looked at the pile of work awaiting him. "Yes. And send someone to prepare my chamber in three fingers. I want some sweets for when I retire."

Actin nodded and backed out of the room. With a sigh, Lazul picked up the paper and groaned as the first item was discussing his need for an heir, which meant a marriage. It would be a long evening.

CHAPTER EIGHT

JADAYA

The last of the funeral rites were performed a few days later, returning the bodies to sea. Pel stood offshore on top of the waves and pulled each Aoisan to him, honoring them. The dead Chars were sent to the deeps as Pel refused to touch them. Jadaya had no idea if the monsters that patrolled those parts of the ocean ate them or if the dead simply sank to the bottom.

Life had returned to normal in Pelisic, though she remained more aware of Note and the possibilities of raiders coming in. She found herself staring at the horizon, searching it for signs that there were ships approaching, but all she ever saw were the fishing ships of Aois.

Note confused her. All the Aoisan men that Jadaya had seen filled out, maturing into broad shoulders and lean waists, suitable for a life where you spent much of your time casting out and pulling in fishing nets. None of the Aoisans had hair anywhere other than their heads and eyelashes. Their brows were a ripple of darker colored skin, not hair like she had. Often she envied their lack of hair elsewhere, as it felt like her body hair was long enough to braid. But Note still retained the litheness of a young teen, though he obviously was much older. Subtle questions let her know he had seen at least forty suncycles, making him much older than her, yet he looked different from the other adult Aois.

Maybe other gods have touched him?

It was the best idea she could come up with, but it still felt wrong.

No one talked about the attack, which Jadaya found rather odd. But she knew as the outsider they might not feel comfortable talking about it with her. She tried to push it aside, but she had kept some of the swords from the fallen, and took to practicing outside. She spent fingers working herself to exhaustion in the evening trying to regain some of the skills she had let fade. It seemed important to get back to her previous level of expertise. Just in case.

After helping Kol in the mornings, she headed into the city and aided in their rebuilding and repairing. It amazed her how much damage men could cause when they were rampaging through a city. Doors torn off, walls broken, furniture destroyed. More than a few had stolen what they could find, others had been more focused on the children. She still feared for them, and felt guilty she had returned so late, but there was little she could do now.

In the middle of holding up a door while the Aoisan homeowner reinstalled the leather hinges, a child of about ten ran up to her, a cut on her arm still healing. The ring of bruises above the cut stood out in gray and yellow, indicating someone had grabbed her arm with force. Yet another reminder of the raid, though this one would heal. "Jadaya, the priestess and the council, would like to talk to you now, if you please."

The girl rattled off the words so fast it took Jadaya a moment to unravel the words and translate them. Her command of the language improved every day, but she still needed to translate in her mind.

"Ah. I see." She looked at the Aoisan, but he simply tied the last hinge and nodded at her.

"Let go."

Jadaya did so, and the door hung once again. "Bless, Jadaya," he said, bobbing his head with his gratitude. "Go on with the child. No need to make them wait."

She looked at her clothes, a simple pair of leggings and a shirt with a binder, both scuffed and dirty with streaks on them, though through diligent scrubbing, the blood had all been removed.. "I should wash first??" The idea of appearing looking like this made her intensely uncomfortable. Her gods never allowed that.

But they are no longer your gods.

She flinched from the thought and focused on the child, distracting herself.

"No, lady. They said immediately." The child bobbed up and down as if remaining still was an impossibility.

Jadaya nodded gravely to the child. "Then take me to where I am bidden." Like a hound released from a rope, the child spun and raced back up the street. Jadaya's long legs kept up with the girl as she wove through the city to a building Jadaya had seen but never entered. Kol had mentioned a town hall once, but in the mooncycles since she arrived, she never heard of one happening —which really meant little. Between healing and hanging outside the city, there was much she missed, or maybe she had no energy to care. The ache from losing her home, family, and gods still occupied most of her thoughts. Though the familiarity of her new daily routine gradually eased that ache. And dealing with the anger still at her core, one with no outlet.

The white building had less ornamentation than most of the dwellings, and the metal doors had a more serious look. While the building was only two stories like most in town, the temple was taller than all of them, it had more of a presence with thicker walls and stairs that were decorated instead of white maub. The song of Pelisic had returned, and it felt like an aura of normalcy had reattached itself to the city. The door swung open at their approach and a man stood in the shadow.

"Ah, Aryix bless, Iki. I will take her from here." The kid bobbled her head and then turned and headed back to wherever children disappeared when adults were occupied. The man turned to Jadaya. "I am Councilor Rek. Please come with me." He stood taller than Kol, but his hands were soft where Kol had hands as weathered and scarred as Jadaya's back. His robe was of a pale blue she knew came from one of the ground up seaweed dyes. The same dyes that were prized even in Zuyika.

"Am I accused of something?" She could think of no other reason than she had offended or hurt someone to be called here, but nothing jumped to mind.

"No, no. Nothing like that. Ijo and the councilors would like to speak with you." His voice sounded reassuring, but the nervous timbre convinced her there was more going on. Her hand ached for the familiar feeling of a hilt in it, but that would be inappropriate in this place. She followed him into the building and directly toward a large room where something lay on the ground with multiple people around it, including Ijo and Note. There were two statues in the room, one of Rian, the other of Pel, and Jadaya would have sworn they were following along with the conversation, though she could never catch them moving. It still intensified the need to have a weapon in her hand.

All of them looked up at her as she entered, and she felt the hair on the back of her neck rise. If this had been training with Master Halke, her instincts would have her diving to the floor to escape the blow coming at the back of her neck. Her muscles stiffened as she fought those instincts and walked into the room. The object they were all peering at was a map of the known world and Jadaya was stunned by the detail. Most countries only had their coastlines, and the deeps marked out. While the Ged could sail across them safely sometimes, it was best to know where they were so your own ships could avoid them. Almost all countries had some level of fishing fleets, the oceans being too rich to ignore.

She came to a halt at the edge of the map, realizing only then it was an enormous piece of cloth and all the markings on it were embroidery. The amount of work it entailed left her stunned. This was a masterpiece, and the embroidery allowed it to be updated as you could pick out the existing threads and add details as they were discovered.

"Ah, you must be Jadaya, the refugee that washed up on our shore only to save so many of our children. We were blessed when Pel brought you here." A woman walked forward to her with open hands reached to her. Jadaya allowed it. The clasping of both hands in a square between visitors was an old custom to show no weapons or poisons were in your hands. It gave her time to inspect the woman whom she had not met previously. Her silver hair was in more braids than she saw most wearing. Usually Aoisans went for tails or twisting their hair up on their head. The braids were different than the ones the Zuyikans used, thinner and with only three strands, with no other hair feeding into the pattern.

Maybe I should offer to braid Kol or Ola's hair. It might be interesting.

She dressed in the same pale blue as Rek, but her hands had more calluses and her eyes were sharper, peering into Jadaya and seeing more than she might wish.

"Bless," Jadaya whispered in response to the comment. What else could she say to that, even if it never occurred to her to do anything else?

"I am Councilor Eha. Now that you are here, we can continue the discussion," the woman said with a wide smile, revealing her slightly pointed teeth, a trait of Aoisans.

Jadaya looked around, assuming the two other men in pale blue robes were also councilors. That left an older man with thick arms, scars across his arms and face, that looked like healed cuts to Jadaya's experienced eye. He met her gaze with a sharp nod, one warrior to another.

"As we were saying, how do we get to Granite to retrieve our children?" Eha leaned over and peered at the map.

The older man shrugged. "In theory, sail up around Fivika and then you will be there. But you refused to listen," he said with an exasperated air. "Getting there is a minor problem. Rescuing them and not getting them or yourselves killed is the challenge. Are you going to invade the country with fisherman? The streets will run red with our blood. All it will do is to decimate our people. The best way would have been to stop them from getting here. Now that it is done, there is no realistic way to get them back."

Eha waved his protestations away. "That is why she is here. Jadaya, you can go get our children and bring them back." Eyes of pale gray stared up at Jadaya with an entreating look.

"No," she blurted, looking at all of them. "It is impossible for me to do it. One person would simply die."

"But you cut through them like hot metal through fat. They were simple for you to kill," Eha said, a hint of desperation in her voice.

"Yes. That was what, ten, fifteen of them? This is a city full of people, and I have no idea why they took the children." Jadaya looked from face to face, noting the only ones trying to not mimic a small child denied a treat were the old warrior and Note.

"You are saying you would fail?" Ijo asked, as if seeking clarification.

"I am saying I would die without ever reaching them. If you wanted this, you would need a team of at least ten people, all experienced warriors, and a Ged ship waiting at the harbor. There would be a chance that they could get in and out, but their skills would have to be better than me, silent, and have the gods on our side. Otherwise, we just die. I have no idea where you could find people like that. What am I missing? Why the worry now when you knew this was possible and made no attempt to stop it?" Jadaya felt too off balance to be politic in her questions. But that rage, the rage that had been simmering deep in her, flared up more.

The statue of Rian moved, and Jadaya had to lock down her immediate attack reflex. Statues should be stationary.

The statue spoke, though the lips remained still. The head, however, rotated, peering at the small group. "We know now what the fate of our children would be if they were to continue to be subjected to Xyl's hospitality. For the sake of our sibling, we were willing to allow the use of children over the cycles, though they were normally taken with trickery, distracting us. Now that the lies have been exposed to us, it is no longer tolerable. They must be rescued and soon, before the consequences are irreversible." The statue went back to its previous position and the group of people glanced at each other, though Note leaned against the wall, his eyes closed, jaw locked.

Jadaya narrowed her eyes, the rage and need to do something bubbling up, but she shook her head. "Unless you are coming with us, there is no way to do that with the people here." The idea of a death march held no attraction for her, and these were gods she owed no fealty to.

Do I even have gods anymore? Do I want to have my gods back? Can I live with no gods?

The thought shook her. She had assumed some land would take her in, their gods accept her, but she did she have to? Zula and Yika had thrown her away, even with all her suncycles of service. Elike, the woman she had loved, had betrayed her to maybe save her. Not only did the gods dispose of their faithful, they let their children be stolen. How dare they treat them so badly? She would not have treated a pet the way her gods had treated her. The rage that had been building blazed even higher as she focused on what the other were talking about. There were low mutters and gestures as they talked about what the captured ones would face. Still, the statues seemed to follow or watch, which made it even more uncomfortable.

"I might have an option," Ijo said into a lull in the mutters. Everyone turned their attention to her. "If Jadaya was willing, she could go to the old gods and beg their assistance."

CHAPTER NINE

NOTE

Note barked out a laugh as he ran his hands through his hair. The black dye was unfaded, though it would soon. He thought Rian might have finally understood his need to have his hair so different, that or his last threat to shave it off finally curbed her urge to meddle.

At least with my hair, why not meddle now?

"If you want her dead that badly, why not just ask me to kill her?" Note said into the sudden silence at Ijo's remark. "It would be faster and less painful."

The dark woman, at least a hand taller than everyone else in the chamber, shifted into a more active stance, her brown eyes lingering on Note as if judging her odds. He was neither stupid nor arrogant. In a straight fight, Jadaya could carve him into pieces. Note rarely allowed for straight fights. Winning was the important thing. Honor just got you killed.

"What? It might work," Ijo said, her voice coated with desperation. Too much desperation.

"Ijo," Note said slowly. "Was your grandson taken?"

Ijo hid her face, but her head bobbed up and down and everything became clear. She wanted to prevent her grandson from experiencing what he had. From being damaged like he was. The conflicting emotions were clouding his reasoning right now, so he just nodded and focused on the map. "The big problem is the aftermath." His voice carried in the overly quiet chamber, and he looked up to see all of them watching him, like felines watching prey.

"Aftermath?" Huk looked at him, frowning. "What do you mean by that?"

Note sighed and wondered how such a naïve people had survived as long as they had. The deeps surrounding them was probably for the best. Otherwise, he was relatively sure they would have been turned into chattel for another country and their gods. It was obvious their gods would avoid fighting for them.

Have they ever fought for us?

"Let's say we get in there, kill who needs to be killed, and now we have the Aosian's to save. Not only are there the new children, there are the ones taken previously, and any Aoisans that were born." Note held up his hand, ticking off the list of victims. His mind raced as he tried to lay out the possible paths.

"Wait, new Aoisans?" That comment burst out of the mouths of multiple people and Note sighed.

"Did you think they would stay children forever? And live a life of celibacy? Us?" He waved at the Aoisans standing there and the councilors nodded with a hint of pink rolling over their skin. During young adulthood, partners changed almost daily as personalities settled in. Few made long-term partnerships with those they dallied with in their youth. Those that did tended to be together for life, like Ijo and Lir. His stomach twisted as he remembered lifting the dead body of the high priest into the wagon.

Do I feel sorry for her, or envy that she had what I never will?

"There were breeding programs when I was there. The priests would select one or two boys to use as studs. It exempted them from other duties, and they only occasionally sang. Most of the songs Xyl prefers have no need of tenor, baritone, or bass voices. They do love soprano, though." Another bitter smile slipped out.

Maybe I am enjoying this too much, watching their preconceptions get shattered?

"They encouraged all women to have children once their moon flows arrived, though only when having sex with other Aoisans. They wanted to avoid having mixed-race children." He smiled sardonically. "If they were mixed, the ability to sing may not be present." A soft chuckle slipped out as he watched the reactions of the people in the room. "Here is where our low childbearing has been a blessing." He avoiding mentioning how those boys were treated or that most copulation involved little consent on either side.

"That is also because we have always required both to truly want the child. It helps make them more loved and less resented." Rian's voice floated through the chamber and Note shrugged.

"However it works, there were only a few that were pregnant. But there are some. Again, we have killed everyone in the local vicinity and now have at least fifty, if not a hundred, people looking for rescue. How?" He threw it out there, waiting for responses. Everyone avoided his gaze.

"Then comes the next part." At this, everyone stared at him, waiting for him to break their hopes again.

Why did I come back? I can never fit in here again. Maybe I should join the Ged. Would they accept me?

Note ran his hands through his hair, trying to keep his temper. He ignored the color transferred to his hands from the dye, making them look as bruised as he felt. "We will have stopped the songs. What happens when Xyl wakes and expresses his rage?"

All of them flinched, even Jadaya. They all had stories of the gods in a rage. And those were of gods who were angry, not one that was insane.

"We will deal with that," Pel said, his voice hard. "We are owed by all our siblings. But I am unsure if they will assist." The words carried a note of finality and Note did not have the energy to argue with it.

"Ged. We can ask the Ged to assist. That many could fit on one of their bigger ships." Huk offered slowly. "They could wait offshore a ways and only come in at a signal. Even the youngest of us can swim a long way."

Note hummed, then stopped the second he realized he had made music, the bile stinging his throat. He coughed and turned to hide his face from the others. The white stone seemed so uncaring. He wanted to fill it with color to give himself something else to stare at. Coat it in pain and anger. What color would that be? Red, brown, purple?

"Maybe. If the youngest were born in water. Most would have been born in a bed, secured in the temple." He ignored the gasps of horror and the strike of lightning that hit the building. Pel and Rian were having their understanding of the world destroyed with his words. Good. Maybe something would change. He continued. "So be it. Maybe it is possible. But you have no skilled team. You have no one that could do that."

"The old gods," Ijo insisted. "They still have powers and relics. Surely, they could assist. They are not bound by the agreements of the gods now. Xyl has broken them."

Note shrugged. "Xyl has been breaking them for hundreds of suncycles. If we want to be fair, the agreements were broken when the Usurper killed Percit and drove Xyl mad. They still remain imprisoned."

"It is true the agreements were broken long ago," Rian said, her voice but a whisper he had to focus on to hear. "But to wake them might kill us all. Our siblings will not assist in this, they fear our brother too much. Yet I will no longer have my children be abused as they are." The last words had the force of a storm, implacable and uncaring about the death left in its wake. "I am willing to take the chance."

"Rian?" Pel's statue turned to look at her, the carved face immobile. "Are you sure?"

"Cassix has much to answer for. But maybe he will help. Maybe our siblings will help." Rian's whispered words carried hope and doubt.

"And maybe they will destroy us all?" Pel sounded unsure.

"Then maybe our siblings will quit hiding, pretending Xyl no longer poses a problem to us all. I may take the chance." Rian sounded wistful. "Besides, I have missed talking to Lyx."

"Your mother is more reasonable than your father," Pel pointed out.

The mortals watched the gods argue. It felt like watching your parents have a fight. Note wanted to laugh, but their decisions affected too many for him to be amused.

"True. But maybe the time has softened him?" Rian sounded like a child wishing for a pony.

"That I doubt, but I will not gainsay you." Pel turned the statue's head to peer back down at the map. "You have our permission. They are located at the Mount of Aryix, what you call the Mount of the Old Gods. There is a path from Vykland to there, but the way is difficult. But if you gain their blessings or assistance, they would ensure your success."

"There is no way to win," Jadaya said softly, but there was an underlying anger that confused Note. "Unless they provide an army. Or do you believe the gods will walk with us? They are more likely to toy with us if we release them. Treat us as broken toys." Her words were nothing but truth and Note was unable to argue with them.

Ijo knelt next to the map and looked up at Jadaya. "I beg of you. Go get the assistance of the old gods and rescue my—our children."

Jadaya sighed. "I would do nothing but die. There is no hope of me succeeding." She stared at the map, her mouth in a hard line. "There is little hope of success."

Note watched her fingers twitch, searching for a weapon, but her voice was considering, not defeated.

"There is no way for me to just walk in there and rescue them. It requires much more preparation and why would captured children listen to me?" She gestured up and down her body with two fingers. "I would be more of a stranger to them than the ones that took them."

"We would provide you with anything you need. Please?" Ijo was begging now and Note looked away, unable to bear the naked grief on her face. Her husband dead and grandson gone, while he no longer remembered what his parents looked like. They had been killed when he was captured, and he never could remember their names. How could he know what she felt?

"Ijo, I am not a warrior from the old stories. Was I more skilled than the raiders, yes? Am I good enough to take on anyone that comes for me? No." Jadaya seemed exasperated, but something smoldered behind her eyes that drew Note to her. An anger he was familiar with. Anger at the world that would dispose of them so easily.

"We would offer you a reward, former Zuyikan." Pel's voice broke the stalemate as the mortals stared at each other, unsure where to go.

Jadaya looked toward the statues. "A reward?"

"Yes," Rian said with a burst of hope. "Two. One is a favor from two gods. Anything you might ask that we can deliver is yours."

Jadaya went so still, Note wondered if she could disappear into the night if no one was watching her. "And the other?"

"We will talk to Zula and Yika on your behalf," Pel said, his voice echoing through the chamber like a clap of thunder. "We will request that your exile be undone."

Note watched the woman as her skin lightened to an unbecoming dark gray.

"And if I die during the attempt?" she asked with her voice soft, hands twitching again. Note wondered what she was reaching for.

"Then we will deliver your spirit directly to them and petition them to accept you on our behalf." Rian spoke with a clarity that Note had rarely heard. Each of the gods collected the spirits of their people, or at least they said they did. While Percit was still the goddess of death, with her death the afterlife had broken, and the gods did not or would not say where you went.

Not that it mattered to him. Nonexistence with no more pain or guilt sounded wonderful. It was the guilt that kept him alive. Remembering those who had been too scared, too young, too weak, to come with him. The memory of each of the four who had died as they tried to get home. The last images of their faces haunted him, and ensured he would never quit trying.

Jadaya looked at the sky and a fierce smile crossed her face. "No. I want something else." She looked directly at the two statues. "I will prove they should have never disposed of me. I will wake the old gods and demand their assistance. I want you to rub it into their faces at every turn how the one they had no use for did what the gods were too scared to."

The statues stood there like the immobile marble they should have been, then twin grins spread on their face. "We can do that. We will laud your adventure, regardless of the outcome. You will be known as the one to overthrow the gods." They turned and looked at Note. "Both of you."

The smile that crossed Jadaya's face had a level of anger and even a touch of cruelty that Note was pulled to. She focused on Ijo. "I will go, but I will need much assistance."

Note jerked his head to look at her. Had he heard her correctly? She was agreeing to go on this insane venture? She wanted to prove her gods wrong so badly? He looked at the statues. But then, his motives were similar.

Why not go? At least then you will have done something. Maybe made a difference.

Ijo collapsed in a grateful sob and Note felt his anger against her ebb. Maybe if his relatives had still been alive, there might have been a rescue planned. Or maybe they would all be dead anyhow. He would never know.

"I shall go as well." The words slipped out without him choosing to say them. But the moment they left his lips, they felt right. His anger now had a focus. "You need someone that knows where they are imprisoned. And your supposition is correct. They would fear you just as much. Me, they might talk to and listen to my commands." He looked at the councilors, who seemed all too relieved he would be leaving. His presence in the council meetings and constant argument for change had proven a thorn under their scales. Perhaps he would return alive. If not, his conscience would be appeased and he would be able to face the dead with a peaceful heart.

Jadaya looked at him as if weighing his usefulness and Note was unable to find it in him to get annoyed. They would be together for a long while. It was best they got used to each other now.

"Bless," she said, nodding her acceptance. "That will make it easier. But there is much to be done and best case we are looking at multiple mooncycles before we get near them. Look." She held out her hand for the ornate pointer that Huk carried. He gave it to her with a touch of reluctance, as if she might use it as a weapon. Note would have enjoyed watching that.

The quiet, almost self-effacing woman had disappeared. Now he saw a warrior, a general, and a spurt of hope bubbled up in his heart. She moved the pointer from Aois over to Fivika. "We need to go here first. I need armor and weapons that suit me, not to mention supplies. Then from here to Vykland." She moved it up to the land that took up the northern part of the map. Then across that country to where the access to Mount of Aryix stays. Then…" she trailed off and shrugged. "I guess if we are still alive, we shall see what the gods grant us and how to proceed."

Note looked at her proposal and nodded. She was right. He also needed more weapons. Knives were easy to lose, and he would need to find more throwing weapons.

"Do we have that much time?" Ijo said, her voice think with emotion.

Note shrugged. "Maybe? How old was the oldest male?"

"Eleven suncycles," Huk responded immediately.

"And your grandson?" Note's shoulders relaxed at that news. They probably had time, as Aoisans started maturing when they reached at least fifteen suncycles. Maybe they had time to do this.

"Ten," Ijo said.

"Then we have at least one suncycle worst case." He let his eyes drift over their path, calculating the time. It had taken him two cycles from when he escaped to make it back. Suncycles of pain and doing things he never wanted to think about again. "But maybe we can, depending on the gods."

The gods were suspiciously quiet as the mortals worked on figuring out plans.

CHAPTER TEN

JADAYA

K ol and Ola had been both upset and relieved she had agreed to rescue the children. Upset because they knew she could get killed, relieved because all the Aoisans ached over the stolen children. Jadaya just smiled and let them talk about how wonderful it would be for the children to come back. She avoided pointing out that it was much more likely she would die trying to do this, but she saw no other option.

The idea that Rian and Pel force Zula and Yika to see what they threw away. To laud her in front of them was the first balm she rubbed on her heart that helped. The other issue, the punishment Yika had laid on her, the removal of what had made her Zuyikan, was just another piece of kindling in the fire they had started in her.

The lash marks across her back had healed, and she just needed to make sure they were supple enough to not pull when she moved. Jadaya was reminded of Yika's punishment every time she glanced at her skin, but the frustration at losing her ability to see distances, and whatever else had been taken from her, were what drove the rage. She had believed they loved and cherished their people; her eyes were being opened to the fact that they were instead just toys.

Jadaya continued to make a list of what she would need. They had raised the idea of hiring mercenaries, but they were few and all too many were Char. People seemed to run from that country. But she thought she had her list ready and headed to the council with it. Note intercepted her path.

"Note," she acknowledged, while slowing her pace a bit. If this man would travel with her, she should know him better. Know if he was someone she could trust at her back.

"Night warrior," he said in a mocking tone as he nodded in greeting.

The mocking amused her, as there was a level of respect in his look, but she responded in kind. "Maybe, but given that you all but glow in the dark, it is better that at least one of us will be able to sneak in and not give away the entire mission." She kept her tone light, trying to figure out where his limits were. To her delight, he barked out a laugh.

"Valid. I must remember to cover up if we sneak around at night. Is that your list?" He nodded at the parchment she held in her hand.

"Yes. I believe this will at least get us started. But they do realize this will take a large amount of money? Armor and weapons are not cheap. And using subpar equipment will ensure our failure." Jadaya looked around the city. While the pearls were worth something in other countries, while she served Yika, she saw how the pearl necklaces were some of her favorites. They would have to have bags of them and that would drive down the value.

"They have more than you think. You forget how well we swim and dive. Pel has been pointing out wrecks to our better divers for tendays now. There should be enough to get what we need." Note sounded confident as they walked.

Money was a language, in that every country had their own, but there was also a global currency in the basic coins. From most valuable to least, they were platinum, copper, silver, and gold. But each country's coins were stamped with their symbols and vendors always preferred local. Currency exchanges were near city gates, but you could always purchase coin with valuables like lead, gems, or pearls. And barter was alive and well. Most farmers had no use for baubles, but hide, rope, or other trade goods could get you food and supplies.

"Have you been to Fivika?" She kept her eyes straight ahead. The ship they loaded her onto upon her exile had been the only vessel she ever experienced. They had gotten caught in a storm between the deeps and Vykland, and the ship had been torn apart. Her arrival here still astonished her as none of the Ged on the ship had arrived with her. She spared a moment to send gratitude to them. They had taken care of her when they were not obligated to.

"I skirted it. I traveled through that country, but I entered none of the big cities. Instead, I headed down to Delcona and worked through there to Agrina. Then managed a ship back here." His voice had zero emotion to it. "Then I worked my way from the bottom back to Pelisic."

"Do you think the old gods will help us?" She kept walking, but both of them had slowed to an amble, avoiding the end of a conversation that they were unsure now how to continue.

Note snorted. "I think if they notice us at all, we are dead."

"Then why did you agree?" This time she did look at him, interested in what he had to say.

"Because I am unable to think of any other way to do this. And if we die during the attempt, then maybe that will stir Rian and Pel to do more than send mortals on tasks they should do." His bitterness coated the words, and she laughed internally.

"Do you not fear them?" She remembered the whipping and the pain. But that had been done with mortal hands. Yika's punishment that would echo through her life. Maybe that was the one favor she could ask for. Returning her body to her, all of it. The sight, the fertility, her skin color, and whatever else they ripped from her.

"Fear?" He tilted his head, slowing to a stop as the steps into the city hall awaited them. Note "The worst they could do is kill me. They may not be as protective as many of us wanted to believe, but they are rarely needlessly cruel. They would just kill me." He shrugged. "I survived worse. Trust me, death is not something you always avoid. Sometimes it is the reward you ache for." On that comment, he moved up the stairs and pushed open the door. "Are you coming?"

Jadaya nodded, processing his words. She knew Zula and Yika were crueler than Rian or Pel. If anyone had ever talked to them the way Note talked to his gods, they would have been dead before the echoes of the words had stopped. Just another example of how little they thought of their people. They also were in almost every aspect of their people's lives. They visited even the smaller villages regularly to ensure their presence would not be forgotten.

To ensure we feared and worshiped them.

Together they entered the building and Jadaya kept looking around at the lightness of it. Their city always seemed pristine and serene to her eyes. Where Zuyika had colors everywhere, with grey or brown muddaub creating walls. Here, the pale consistency provided her a sense of peace.

She felt stress slough off and pulled her shoulders back, enjoying the stretch. Note curled into himself more as they walked to Rek's office. He was the one that would try to get what they asked for and help with figuring out how to get them there. He seemed torn between fear and glee at this, but Jadaya realized how many moving pieces there were. And how many of those pieces were outside of her control?

Note whistled outside Rek's office. An Aoisan way of knocking that she still fumbled with. She never learned to whistle and sometimes when she tried, it came out flat. At home, or what had been her home, people clapped. Many places both there and in Pelisic had cloth for the doors. Rapping your hand on muddaub or coral walls just hurt your hand.

"Yes, enter. I have someone for you to meet," Huk called out.

Jadaya had already seen the figure standing next to Rek. The curtain was more of a sheer indicator of privacy, not fabric that would block ears or eyes from being aware of what happened in his office.

Note pushed aside the drape and with a flourish indicated she should go first. Jadaya glanced at him as she walked through, but his face told her nothing. Setting her thoughts aside, paper still clutched in her hand, Jadaya faced the man that stood next to Rek.

He stood half a hand shorter than her with curly brown hair to his shoulders, light tan skin, an engaging smile, muscle layered with fat, and nails bitten all the way down. She watched him, cataloguing his abilities. But simply standing there told her little, other than he was relatively fit. His coloring gave him away as Ged, which meant the insanity of doing this was that much more real.

"Note, Jadaya, this is Rylix. He is a trader that has been coming here for a few suncycles and is willing to help us with our situation." Huk nodded to Rylix, whose grin spread wider.

"Welcome, wondrous warriors. It does my heart joy to assist in a mighty undertaking such as this. I am sure the story will go down as legend among our peoples." He said with a smile and a nod of his head. "As your esteemed councilor has said, I am Rylix. I shall help with obtaining travel to Hearth, the main city of Fivika, and then to Vykland to ensure the gods will bless this endeavor."

Jadaya blinked and fought a smile. "Rylix, well met." The man exuded charm and personality.

Note just nodded. His eyes narrowed as he looked at the man, then over at Rek. "Why him? I know we need a guide and a ship. Is there a reason he already knows so much?"

Huk shrugged. "Keeping it from him when he is the one to secure the ships and inns seemed unwise. But he has earned my trust over the suncycles."

Jadaya examined Rylix again. Her first guess had been he must have been under twenty-five, but a close examination revealed fine wrinkles at the eyes, calluses on the hands, and an ease that spoke of suncycles working with strangers.

"Have no fear. I will never divulge what your plans are here unless you say it is allowed. My word is my bond, but we need to share some information, as you need to know where you want people to take you. But then that is my job, is it not? Which means we will set sail for Hearth in two days' time. My relatives will be here then."

"As to the question about Hearth," Huk said, holding out his hand. "Your lists please?"

Jadaya placed it in his hand, and Note pulled a worn piece of parchment out of his pocket and dropped it on the desk. Huk shot him a glare, but picked up both lists, taking more time on Jadaya's. She cringed as she had written it in Ged and her penmanship had never been beautiful. Her time had been spent in the practice yards, not in the classroom.

"Ah, yes, it is as I thought. These are why you are going to Fivika, and Hearth specifically, your lists." He sounded simultaneously tired and relieved.

An odd mixture, Jadaya thought.

"Explain," Note demanded. He held his arms across his chest in a protective stance, yet the body language said he was merely waiting for action. Jadaya wanted to know more about this man full of contradictions, but it would be rude to ask questions like that to a stranger and he still was that to her.

"Weapons, armor, clothing, supplies—we are lacking much of this." Huk looked down at the list, then picked up another list on the desk. "Then here is the list Rylix submitted. Shelter gear, tents, snowshoes." He looked up at them, his eyes wide. "Snow has rarely fallen here. We have no way to provide this. But if you are to succeed, and we want you to succeed, you require these items."

The depth of sincerity surprised Jadaya. It slipped out in her words. "Why now? This has been happening for generations. You lost generations of children. Why do you suddenly care now?" With a force of will, she kept her arms at her side. She might go after these kids, but she doubted she would return here alive.

Note snorted. "This I am very interested in hearing. After all, you never answered me when I asked." His still face set off alarms in Jadaya, but she had no sense that he wanted to attack her. She still turned her body slightly in case she needed to get out of the way or block an attack.

Huk focused on his desk, avoiding the man's accusatory glare. Jadaya was unsure who she felt sorrier for, Note who had obviously suffered at the hands of these people, or Huk who seemed to answer for everything. Either way, it made her feel like she was witnessing something intimate, and that made her even more uncomfortable. If there had been an easy way to leave, she might have, but the answer also seemed important. After all, if they wanted her to cross half the world, she needed to know why now, why her?

"When the gods refused to stop it, the council met, many times over the suncycles. We decided that if they allowed this, it must be something that had to occur. Much like storms bring the wrecked ships here, it had to be part of the flow. When you returned, angry, contained, different, we met again." At this point, Huk raised his head, staring at the other man.

The guide, Rylix, all but faded into the background, letting them squabble. Jadaya understood that as she tried to not draw any attention to herself, either. Though at this point, it was likely that the two Aoisans were oblivious to them.

"This time we questioned what had happened, but the information you provided gave no explanation for your anger, your difference. We waited to see what the gods would say. We thought there were a few more cycles before the possibility of the raid. They came earlier than we expected. The council sent multiple letters to Charinsky, but we have never received an answer and there is no easy way to travel there. We let it be, thinking it would be what it would be. Now the new information has thrown us into disarray, and we are desperate to undo the damage we allowed. Children have died because we trusted too much." The last words were laced with so much pain that Jadaya could hear it in the way he breathed. The pain created when you realized your gods protected you less than you thought.

Note turned his head to the wall, not responding, and she was unable to see his expression to have any idea what he was thinking.

Jadaya broke the tense silence with one last question. "If there is no easy way to get there, how did their ships get here and presumably back?"

Note's head tilted at the question, but he said nothing.

"I can assure you with no doubt in my mind or heart they were not captained by Ged," Rylix said, his voice strong and confident.

"I believe that. There was no sign of Ged on the ship. They were crewed by the same people that raided looking for children." Jadaya nodded at him. If the Ged had turned their hands to this, it might break her faith in the world. She focused on Councilor Rek, waiting for an answer.

He just shrugged. "I assume either their god or a path we are unaware of through the deeps. But it is nothing our fishing boats could traverse, nor have the Ged ever mentioned a faster way across."

Rylix looked thoughtful at that comment, but kept quiet.

Note broke the standoff. "Then we procure supplies from Hearth and go to the Mount of the Gods."

CHAPTER ELEVEN

RYLIX

Rylix stood back and watched the discussion. They all agreed to the plan, heading to Hearth. When Huk first approached him with the plan, Rylix had refused. His exile from the Ged was almost over. Even now, the memory of his actions made him cringe. But just last tenday a note from his madar saying his error had been forgotten, and he had permission to find new trade routes.

The small trading he performed up and down the island chain that made up Aois had given him experience and solidified his reputation with Ged, who did not know his story, but it was nothing fulfilling. Aoisans were a pleasant, if boring people, which limited the potential profit and experience. The last five suncycles spent traveling up and down, usually only with a wagon he could pull or float, provided little opportunity to do anything truly interesting or gain the sort of reputation he wanted.

Among the Ged, possessions tended to be fleeting. When you were a nomad, either on land or sea, there were limited spaces to keep belongings. Other than a few heirlooms, your real wealth was your reputation. And his reputation would need years to recover. While he had been a promising new trader when he was twenty, his stupidity had erased that.

While the fact that he could go back to his parents meant the mistake was no longer on the tongue of others, it did not mean he had anything to go back to. The trade here in Aois was decent, but it only added to his reputation as quiet and boring. Neither of which would make up for what he had done. Rylix longed to be someone who made a difference and ensured safety and prosperity for the Ged. And maybe a way to erase a mistake.

When Huk begged, he pulled back and thought about it. He was technically no longer exiled here, but he had nothing waiting for him. But if he agreed to guide them through towns and lands he'd traipsed through dozens of times as a child, he could create a new trade route from Aois to Fivika.

After much hesitation, Rylix agreed, which was how he found himself here. Listening to them talk about rescuing children from another country. Deep down the kernel of an idea that maybe if he was part of saving these children, it might make up for Kryx's death. Or at least help defray the eternal cost. If they succeeded, he would have gone far to create a new name for himself. The next Gather he went to would see how or if he had been redeemed. Of course, if they failed, he would be dead and his choices would be something for his family to debate. Though he knew his name would not be a popular choice for a long time.

Rylix shrugged to himself. Death was always a part of life. It just came to some earlier than it should. Hopefully, this journey would find him with more stories than wounds and a start on repairing his life. He sent a quick prayer to Aryix and Quas to watch over this venture and promised to do a special offering to them when they reached their prison.

"I have reached out to my family with news of the need for travel. There should be a ship pulling into this harbor in the next tenday, given favorable winds and the gaze of Lyx on them. Given than it is the first step on our voyage, the fare for transportation to Fivika is what I would regard as extremely reasonable." Rylix kept his voice assured, as if he was confident his family would help. He let loose the smile that assured them he was only looking out for their best interests, which was true. You rarely lied while trading. Exaggerated, of course, used wild analogies, flattered and cajoled, but you never flat out lied. That could damage the trust people had in you. And he of anyone knew how hard it was to regain trust.

There was a perception of the Ged. They were the lovers you had when you just wanted to have fun. They were guides when you wanted to create new trade routes or infrequent ones. The ships you used to transport your most precious cargo were most often owned and crewed by Ged. The storytellers who still knew the old tales and followed the ways of the old gods. But they were also indifferent to local laws, would smuggle things in and out of various countries, and would charm the pants off you, only to sell them back to you for a kiss. But they were not liars, thieves, pirates, murders, or rebels. Those Ged that were never showed their faces at Gathers, because they would never leave. Not alive.

"As you say," the one called Note responded with a sharp jerk of his head. "When the ship comes, I will board it." He turned with nothing more to the others and walked out. Rylix watched him go. A strange one, this Aoisan. He masked his silver hair with dye, was rumored to never sing, and avoided all relationships. Sitting at the local bar and listening to gossip while tipping well was always the first move in any new venture. Everyone had secrets, a past, and memories they ran from. The information you gained was always worth even the subpar drink. Lucky for him, the coconut liquor they made was strong and delicious enough to make him forget for a time.

"I do not have funds to buy what I will require," Jadaya said. Rylix had no idea if it was an apology, excuse, or confession. Her words could have been any of those, and her body language shed no light on her.

It had surprised him to find a Zuyikan here in Aois. They were an almost xenophobic culture, and their own gods were very possessive. Little was known of the 'night warrior' as the locals were calling her. That she washed up on this shore and had been tended to by a couple was given. But the rest of the information was rumor and speculation. Was she cursed by her gods? An exile? Did she flee her gods? Were they cruel to her? What did the brand on her cheek mean? The questions were nonstop, but the attitude after she carved her way through the invaders and saved children and adults alike was definitely positive. She had cut her way into the hearts of the people of Pelisic, even if she remained unaware.

"We know and we will gladly cover the costs," Huk said with a nod. "You and the others are risking your lives to save the children. This is literally the least of the things you can ask of us. We will do what we can to give you every advantage."

The woman smiled, a sharp fierce bearing of her teeth, then she nodded to Huk and Rylix, and headed out the door. The Aoisan, Note, mimicked her actions, fleeing the chamber. Rylix waited until he heard the front door close before moving to take a seat in front of Rek. "They are fascinating people you send on a quest from the tales of old. Skill and pain making up a band of ragtag people headed to beg favors of the gods. Will there be songs about this?"

Play it carefully. Be what they expect, your scars do not matter.

"Only if you are planning on writing them. We have failed our people so badly, there is no way to make it up. Our gods know that too. I have no insight into the minds of gods, but whatever allowed this travesty to occur will not happen again. They have said so."

Rylix leaned back at the absolute certainty in the man's tone. "They have spoken then?"

What it was like to talk to your gods?

The Ged still worshiped the old ones, the ones their children had overthrown and imprisoned. Of all the peoples, only the Ged remained true to the first gods. Their gods were prevented from talking to them via normal means, but some of his people still spoke to them in dreams or visions. Rylix had never been a mystic, so for now, the fact that his gods never meddled in his life was perfectly fine. It sounded safer in the long run.

"Yes. To Ijo and the council. There will be changes, so be unsurprised if you no longer recognize this place when you return." Huk wore a pensive look and Rylix tilted his head, amazed at the drama in what was normally a boring country.

"Then it is best we are ready to leave when my relatives arrive. We have settled my fee." That had been handsome enough. Ten sets of dyes in colors only they could achieve, ten tellaweight worth of pearls, and a tiny vial with three of Rian's tears. That alone could command a hefty sum. Healing by the gods could cure almost anything. He could either sell it, trade it at the Gather, or save it in case of emergencies.

"Yes, we have." Huk smiled knowingly. "But we still need to discuss the trade goods that will get you passage into Vykland. Traders are almost always welcome, but you will require goods that are of value."

Rylix smiled, falling back into who he had once been was better that wallowing in his guilt. "The pleasure of working with a connoisseur who understands that trade is a living, breathing thing and varies by area is a genuine pleasure." He meant every word of that.

Often, people were unable to understand why what they had to trade was less valuable than what they desired. And some goods needed to be traded far away from their originating country. But that is why the Ged existed, to keep them all from becoming isolated nations that interacted only via fighting.

"So, what do you have to offer?" Rylix had most of the valuable trade goods sought by every nation in his head, yet he pulled out a small journal. Wrapped in waterproof cloth with pages sewn into a leather cover, he jotted down the date after thinking a moment.

All the countries used the same method of tracking the seasons, with ten mooncycles to a suncycle and five tendays in a mooncycle. It would let him easily plan how much they would need per mooncycle. Numbers were just as consistent, because even as languages changed, dates and money never did.

The other wonderful thing about his little notebook was the first page contained his notes on the seasons. No one had ever explained why, when the countries near the bottom of the world seemed to be the opposite time of growing from the top. When Fivika was starting planting season, Agrina was starting harvesting Season. Even Aois, a long country that seemed to go from one end of the world to the other, would have the capital city in shelter, while the remote islands at the bottom were in ripening. At the end of the day, it was just something to remember for trade. If a country would be entering ripening, you would sell nothing if you showed up with fur coats. A good trader kept track of all of this, and Rylix planned on being a fantastic trader.

"We have been discussing that extensively. Have you verified the equipment that will meet you in Calin?" Huk asked.

It was a good question. Calin was the harbor they would land at from Aois. From there, they would travel to Hearth. Hearth served as the hub of Fivika, where each of the four regions brought their goods to trade and sell. Fivika was unique among all the countries. Rather than trade goods that were standard across the entire country, it had four major regions. Every region had its own specialties: glass, ceramic, metal, shipbuilding. Things they needed.

Rather than going to each individual town, which could take mooncycles, they needed to go to Hearth so they could buy everything in a few days, then head to Betan and hopefully find another Ged ship willing to take them to Vykland. If they were lucky, he would find someone willing to sail that far down the coast, but worst case, just going directly across would be possible. If they ended up in that situation, not only would they need viable trade goods as they crossed the country, but appropriate clothing. In a few tendays Vykland would be starting shelter and they received much more snow than Aois.

Rylix consulted his notes. "From what others have told me, we should expect the trip from Calin to Hearth to take at least two tenday if we are pulling a wagon and not racing. The best option is to trade as we go, though not fast. It is up to you which you believe would be more beneficial in the long run."

Huk leaned back, his eyes slitted as he thought. Rylix let him. It was difficult planning this for people when you were unaware of their tolerance for camping as they traveled.

"For now, subtlety is more important than speed. From the information gathered, all the temples are on high alert with the festivals coming up. The last thing we want to do is give them reason to believe something might happen. Slow, with valid reasons for being in that area and then going to Vykland would be best." Huk gave Rylix a twisted smile. "In this case, Note's penchant for dying his hair will help diffuse attention. Many will believe his gods have either abandoned or exiled him. Same with Jadaya."

Rylix nodded. Outcasts were uncommon, but they existed in almost every country. It would make an interesting cover, but it raised other questions. "Do you have reasons to believe that anyone will attack us as we venture toward Charinsky?"

Huk sighed and rubbed at his temples. "We have come to the attention of the gods, and they are meddling. What do you think?"

Rylix winced and nodded. There was a reason the Ged still followed the old gods. If they did interfere, it was subtle, almost unnoticeable. That seemed a safer way to live.

"Very well. Then I will arrange for two sets of jacks to be waiting for us and two caravans. Then at least two more for riding and two mustangs, just to give us more power if we get stuck or need to dismantle the caravans." Rylix scribbled as he talked, his book filling with his own notes. Jacks were the most popular work animals capable of pulling large wagons. They were docile with wide ears and cloven hooves, with tails that could sting like a whip if they got annoyed. Mustangs were made for speed and power. Rarely were they harnessed to wagons. They were ridden and used for scouting or pleasure riding. Though he had heard of some of the upper classes connecting them to light two-person wagons.

Huk winced. "Do I want to know what that will cost us?"

"The wagons are mine, just in storage. I will make arrangements to have them waiting for me in Calin. My family owes me the use of two mustangs. It will be the jacks that will need to be dealt with." Rylix ran some calculations. "Even with a family discount, plus the need to transport to Vykland, it will cost at least six tellaweight of pearls and one tellaweight of copper." Rylix hid his wince here.

There was currency, though trade was the lifeblood of most, as it was easier to change what things were valued depending on where they were. Gold was the most common currency, as almost every country had it in their soil. The coins were generally valued via weight, plates being the most valuable, followed by copper, silver, then gold. All currency was broken out by tens, as how else would you do it? The gods had given all of their people ten fingers. But mustangs and jacks were not cheap.

Rylix sighed and looked up at Rek. "There are ways to make this cost less, but it would require a higher percentage of goods remain mine to keep than normal. Though, as always, I would endeavor to earn the most out of any trade."

Huk huffed a laugh. "You enjoy this more than I. What is the cost?"

Rylix smiled and leaned in to haggle. Huk was correct. This was his life and repayment.

CHAPTER TWELVE

ZAYN

Z ayn stood on the balcony, watching the new singers mill around in the internal courtyard. They would be isolated for the first mooncycle. That moon would involve training, both their voices and songs, and an introduction into what would encourage obedience and avoid pain. He had found that a treat and a punishment worked well on children. They were so pliable.

He leaned against the thick railing, admiring its solidity. The blocky style of the temple made it look like a fortress, but the inside of it created a world of beauty devoted to Xyl. The courtyard he looked down at had been sanded and polished to a high sheen, with the carving on the inner walls displaying stories of Xyl and Percit's life. While the area contained trees, grass, and paved areas, it only had one entrance. It was their refuge, their exercise, and their reward for good behavior.

A woman, dressed in the same style of robes as he but in black and gray, came up on his right. She had streaks of ash drawn down her face from under each eye, marking her as one who believed, bordering on zealotry, but he made sure there were few of those left. Those that remained were in distant temples where their excesses were easy to ignore. But zealots had their purpose, and they turned a blind eye to anything that threatened their belief.

What is her name? Ah, yes. Algoi. Easily led, moderately shapely under those robes. I believe she has been popular among some of the priests.

"How are they doing?" he asked, not watching her, but the children. Zayn honestly wanted to know. The health and relative happiness of the children reflected in their voices, though there was something sweetly potent about despair when you were singing to a god mourning his beloved's death.

The priestess stood rigidly, her hands clasped together in front of her. "Well enough. There is the expected crying, but sweets and the occasional switching is cowing most of them. They are already clinging to each other and regarding the older singers as refuge." She had twisted her blond hair back into a bun on her head and her blue eyes had the fervor of total belief.

How long has it been since I bothered to care about what Xyl actually wanted? Oh well, at least she will ensure the children remain healthy, for their voice if nothing else.

Zayn shook his head at his foolishness. Xyl was too wrapped up in his despair to pay attention to the short lives mortals had, and it served Zayn's purposes well.

"How many older singers do we have left? And which ones?" Try as they might, the breeding program was nowhere near as successful as he implied to the king. For as long-lived as the Aoisans were, they had short lives as captives, and that frustrated him to no end. The worst time was between seventeen and thirty. The number of singers that died trying to escape was infuriating. They were provided with everything and so little was asked of them. And their fertility was so low, no matter how many times they were bred. He had only two children out of the last ten suncycles, and one of them had died for no reason any of his priests could tell him.

"We have seven females left and five males, only one of which is intact. He, of all of them, is the happiest at being able to serve our god." Her voice contained only pious faith and part of Zayn rolled his eyes at anyone being that blind. The man was content because his primary job was copulating, not singing. "The older singer is Iko. She had one child, but it died at birth. She was the one who implied they died because there was no sea to receive her babe."

There is no chance I would give Pel an opportunity to realize what his people are subjected to. Just another aspect to consider. Would a tub of saltwater work?

"I assume you encourage sex often and give them the right incentives?" Zayn knew the best option would be if they could breed their own singers, but with only one child, though they were old enough to join this crop, they would never have their own string of Aoisans for that. If they could have a strong breeding set, it would make it easier to provide bodies to all the temples and make sure they kept Xyl happy.

And complacent. The last thing I need is a god investigating the temples.

"Of course, but even though both parties are showing every evidence of enjoying it, we have seen no signs of pregnancy," Algoi said with her head bowed. She moved closer to peer over the edge. "We may need some new blood. Perhaps his seed is too weak?"

Zayn tilted his head, not answering. She was closer than truly acceptable, but her pose retained the proper respect, and it was the easiest way to watch the children without being obvious or uncomfortable. "Are there any possibilities for a new stud within this batch?"

She bowed her head, and he read the negative before she spoke. "Not at this time. They chose mostly children under ten, but in a few suncycles we may be able to see more."

Zayn hummed as he thought, watching the scene below. It never ceased to amaze him how resilient children were. A few gathered around the older girl. Woman really. She had to be at least thirty. He wrinkled his nose at that. But what were the proper breeding ages? For a Charinsky she would have been well past her prime, but Aois? He had no information to make a judgement on.

"Set them up for review this evening. We need to prepare for both the inspection in a few tendays and the Day of the Fall in two mooncycles. How many fully trained singers remain?" That number changed often enough that he no longer bothered to monitor it. When he first came into the position of cantor, there were twelve singers for each lesser temple and the high temple had twenty-four. Prior to this latest raid, they were down to thirteen for the high temple, *his* temple, and only six for the four lesser temples. That was barely enough to create the songs of grief and harmony. While the high temple would get enough song out, they were in a precarious position. Even now the clouds that covered Charinsky implied Xyl was thinking too much, grieving too much.

"If we have three suncycles to train, we will be full at fifteen per lesser and thirty at this temple." Her voice was smooth, but even so, he heard the tension underlying it. He could get furious, punish her, but why? She carried no fault in this situation, and it would undermine his standing here in the temple. No, better to use her zeal to his own means.

"Does that mean we will be below full song strength for this Day of Death?" His voice was silky smooth, and she stiffened even more, pulling back from him. Zayn hid. A smirk. It was good that people remembered you still had claws.

"Yes," she whispered, pulling back even farther from him.

He had expected that answer. It was part of why he authorized this raid, though the king believed it had been his guiding hand. Though he still worried, just the smallest amount, that the gods might pay more attention to the lives of their people. It was always a risk.

"Call in the other priests and priestess, tell them they will provide a harmony with the singers." His voice was firm and sure, as if he had planned on saying it all along, instead of deciding in that moment.

"Yes, Cantor," she said and started to pull back.

"Algoi?" He said, his voice deceptively calm.

She stiffened and stopped moving, her eyes firmly on the ground. Zayn suppressed his smile. Instant obedience never failed to provide a thrill that washed through his body, leaving pleasure in its wake. "Make sure both Xyl's and Percit's clergy are ready for this. Surely they their practice and their worship is current and active, yes?" His voice was dangerous, and he enjoyed her trying not to flinch at his words. All who entered the temple were required to have perfect pitch and be able to sing all the songs to their gods without missing a note or a word. They were also supposed to practice and sing in worship a minimum of ten fingers a day. For those in the ranks, at least. But all too often, the clergy, himself included, regarded it as unneeded.

It would be, if we could keep the singers alive. Getting another raid in the next suncycle or two might be impossible.

He kept his thoughts hidden. The cantor normally only sang on holy days, but he would need to make sure his voice was still rich and the songs perfect. He had a wonderful voice, though never as perfect as the Aois.

"Yes, cantor. I will ensure they are ready. We would never want to disappoint our divines." She never glanced at him, though her knuckles were turning white.

"Excellent. Please send the primary conductor to me. I want to discuss the disposition of the children." He had turned away, watching the new singers frolic below. Already they were losing their fear and the amount of tears had lessened. The older singer kept them moving and eased their fears, though the sadness on her face annoyed him.

They are fed better than most and have very little toil in their lives. Why do they never understand what a blessing this is, with the small amount that is asked?

"Yes, cantor." The scrape of robes against fabric and stone faded as she moved away. Zayn watched and his eyes alighted on two of the children. They were like other Aoisans their age, but even watching from above, their spirits were bright, and they ran, laughing in their joyous tones. It was enough to melt the hardest heart, or incite a desire to hold and control that spirit, that energy.

"You called for me?" The unctuous tones of Conductor Chalc slipped into his thoughts. Zayn straightened, annoyed his pleasant thoughts had been disrupted. Yet, this was the person he needed. Chalc loomed over him, something he detested, but the man was one of the most effective conductors he had. He also controlled the children better than most.

As their headmaster and choir leader, Chalc controlled their songs and bodies. A cadaverous man, Zayn resisted the urge to tell him to eat, but the sharp beaky nose, sunken eyes disguising gleaming dark blue windows to his greed, shaved skull, and lanky frame were just part of who he was and nothing that could be altered. But his singing voice was music to the gods' ears and his ability to guide the singing of others was nothing short of divine.

"Yes. Those two, right there," he pointed down to the two little boys. "I want to reserve them for my special lessons."

"Of course. I will earmark them to remain here." Chalc's voice remained smooth as he watched the ones Zayn pointed at.

"Have you determined which one we will reserve for breeding? I think given the dismal results our current stud is producing, it might be good to change that up." They needed more children and right now, the project was all but failing.

"Unfortunately, our current males were rendered incompatible with that goal and from cursory inspections, the current batch requires at least five suncycles before we will be able to see which ones will be most valuable." Chalc shrugged, the movement similar to the rise and fall of a wave. "We are still assessing their voices and ranges. It will be another tenday before all of them are categorized and marked for the various temples."

"As I thought, hence me making my desires known now, instead of later." Zayn went quiet, watching them for another few heartbeats. "Is the older girl down there one of your selected ones?"

Chalc nodded. "Yes. She is quite biddable and is tolerable in the bedchamber. Not as good as some in the past, but they rarely survive the experience." Chalc was known for his extreme tastes with the older girls, and Zayn sighed.

"You need to watch how harsh you use them. They are a very finite resource. If necessary, find a priestess to keep yourself occupied. But regardless, she has everything she could want: food, dresses, your attention. Tell her to smile more. She looks like she is preparing to attend a funeral. If she is to help with the new singers, having that depressed look on her face is not conducive to easing them into life here. Though remember to keep them from the male singers. If we make them fear the future, they are harder to control. They have enough to work on right now, fearing the inevitable is a waste of energy."

"I shall remind her of just how lucky she is this afternoon, Zayn." Chalc's voice was snide, almost mocking, but he let it go. The man had as much to lose as Zayn did, creating tension between them was annoying for both of them.

"Good. But remember that the inspection is in a mooncycle. Make sure there is nothing visible remaining from your reminders. We need them to be happy, joyful even, and have their voices lifted in remembrance." For a moment, the self-serving attitude faded. "We need sun and to pacify Xyl for a few moons, or the king will reduce even our tithe portions to the level we will need to surrender some of our luxuries."

"That is at the forefront of my mind. I will endeavor to make sure our resources are in perfect condition."

Zayn cast a sideways look out of the corner of his eyes, but Chalc seemed sincere and he let it be, though he made a note to look for another to take the role of conductor during the temple review. This one might become problematic.

"See that you do." Zayn turned and headed back to his apartments, thinking of the fun he would have later that evening.

CHAPTER THIRTEEN

JADAYA

J adaya stood glaring at the ocean. The dark waves were hungry mouths waiting to devour her. And she agreed to get on a boat and cross those again. A shudder ran through her body, followed by annoyance.

People travel the ocean all the time. We will avoid the deeps and get to Fivika.

The reminder provided no reassurance. The ocean still looked like a ravening maw that would savage any being foolish enough to step out on it. Sighing, she turned her back on the water and the dangers hidden in its depths. Her steps took her back to Kol's house, and she paused at the entryway. It had provided her refuge these last tendays, but now she needed to find her place in the world. Maybe that had driven her agreement to embark on this journey.

Or that if I die doing this, my worry about my gods will be gone.

The hole inside her where her gods used to be throbbed and the desire to scream and cry ripped at her. Her clothes felt too small. The apartment Kol and Ola shared with her felt cramped and strange. The food, the manners, everything was just wrong. For a moment, her breath caught in her chest and the world spun and distorted in ways that made her want to scream. The need to run, to find somewhere she fit again, battered against her mind and heart, and she had to force herself to breathe, to fight the blackness at the corner of her vision.

"Jadaya?"

The voice pulled her out of her spiral of frantic thoughts, and Jadaya forced herself to stand up straight as she pivoted to see Note standing there, looking at her. She was still learning to interpret Aoisan facial expressions. The lack of eyebrows and perpetually smiling faces left her confused. But Note had almost no reactions. He never smiled, spoke flatly, and touched no one. As if Note learned the hard way to never show emotion.

"Note," she said, forcing the emotions down. It took a heartbeat to shake off the feeling of being a square piece trying to fit into a shell, but she did it and even managed to smile.

"Rylix and Huk want to talk to us. They are setting aside money for the trip. While they have our lists, neither knows enough about traveling to ensure we can afford the basic gear." He turned as the words left his mouth.

He got four steps away before she realized what he meant and caught up with him. "I have no idea what I need. I have never traveled anyplace. Well, here. But that was unplanned." The last words were said with forced cheer, and she wondered if he believed her.

From his sidelong glance, she figured not. It had been worth the try, though most knew her story. The scars on her back itched with sudden ferocity, as if thinking of them caused the skin to pull tight. This trail of doubt would serve only to make her weak. She refused to be weak. She swallowed past the worry and looked at him. "You said you traveled across the world, so you have experience with this?"

Note snorted. "Yes. I traveled extensively, you could say."

She nodded. "Then I bow to your knowledge. I know how to fight. I know how to care for my weapons and gear. But I am unsure how to prepare to travel, especially sea travel. I thought Rylix would help with that."

"He will. But he needs our input." Note kept his gaze on the walls ahead, not bothering to look at her as he walked, just headed into the city and the building that still seemed so foreign.

Jadaya bit her lip, the desire to be back where she knew everything, knew the bells, the smells, the sounds, the people. Where she looked in faces and saw similar eyes and hair and teeth. Another swallow, and she berated herself as they climbed the last few steps.

Your former life is gone. Get over it. Take this chance. Worst option you die. Best option…

Her mind trailed off. What would be the best way for this to resolve? The children returned, obviously, but for her? What did she really want when it was all said and done? Did she even *want* her gods back, want their forgiveness?

Her body moved on instinct, following Note into the room where Huk and Rylix waited. Jadaya let the questions swirl in the back of her mind, unsure how to address them.

"Are you listening, lady of charcoal?"

She blinked, aware everyone stared at her. Jadaya read the room, but they all just looked impatient. With her face heating, she focused on Rylix, who had been speaking.

"My thoughts were on what we face. Please repeat your comment?" She kept her chin up, trying to hide her embarrassment.

"All is well, lady warrior," Rylix said with an engaging smile that confused her. "We are discussing what supplies will be required. At this point, you will, unfortunately, be the only female to travel with us. What moon preparations will you require to stay comfortable?" All the men in the room looked at her and she blinked, taking a moment to process their request.

"Oh. My blood cycle was stopped suncycles ago. The gods detested the smell of blood, so they altered all the Chosen to not bleed. You need to petition to bear a child. Only then would your womb be made fertile again. It also makes our lives easier, as we never worry about supplies." That much had not returned, both a blessing and a curse. If her bleeding never came back, there would never be children. But that worry would be faced at a later time.

"Ah, then we shall be blessed with fewer medical needs. Are there any other supplies for a long journey you would require?" Rylix still had his friendly, engaging smile, though he took a moment to draw a line through something in his ever-present notebook.

Jadaya shrugged. "I am unsure. I have never traveled outside of with other Chosen and the trainers always took care of logistics."

Note seemed bored by the conversation, but he kept still, leaning against a set of shelves, eyes closed. She had little doubt he heard every word and processed it. He reminded her of an asp, waiting and conserving energy until it was time to strike. The asps were known for their ability to be overlooked, as well as how deadly they were when they struck. She found herself glad his venom would find targets other than her.

Rylix nodded. "Then it is good there are towns along the first part of the trip. It will make it easier to acquire anything that I have missed in my preparations. No worries though. My family is very skilled and may have already planned for this."

Jadaya decided mentioning that her few forays outside the city had been practice for their squads to use weapons against creatures that would fight back served no purpose. For the Chosen, the large sabers and ursoids were excellent opponents for you to practice with your sword, as their claws were as fast and deadly. For most of the warrior Chosen, it was a rite of passage to fight a creature one on one and win. She had proven herself in that arena multiple times. Looking back, she realized she had few skills outside of knowing how to kill. That would have to change.

"We will need to get proper clothes in Fivika and again in Vykland as the weather there is much colder than is common in either Aois or Zuyika. But those we can obtain as we go." Rylix looked down at his notes. "I have a caravan ready to welcome us at Calin. We will get supplies there and then head out on our own, though the wagon we will use has been created for me." He had an odd smile on his face when he said that. "However, we will need to watch for bandits and other dangers on the road."

Jadaya nodded. Even though the gods tended to take care of their own, there were always those who felt they had too little or had forsworn their gods and turned to a life of thievery.

Or maybe their gods abandoned them.

That idea that this might happen to others shook her to the bone, and she pushed it away. Trade was needed for all countries, even Zuyika and the risk of attack would be good practice for her skills and keep her too busy to think. She hoped.

"That leaves us with the last details. A ship should be here in the next tenday. We are gathering trade goods, but anything you think you might need or wish to bring is advised. Aois uses little from other countries, so we will need to be strategic in how we approach trading. I implore of you now, please leave that to me." His face lost his customary smile, and he looked serious for once. "If we are to obtain the best value for what we can carry, we risk everything if even a speck of gold is left on the table. For any purchase over a few gold, please let me be in charge of it."

Jadaya shrugged, not too worried about that. She had rarely bought more than a few sweets or gifts at the market when she had a coin or two, usually a gold someone had left behind. Most of her needs had been filled as a Chosen, and now she had not been of the mind to think of treats or trinkets. Knowing the value of items in the marketplace had never been a skill she required.

Huk spoke, and Jadaya forced herself to pay attention. "Pel has been assisting with that. He has directed divers to numerous wrecks, and they have pulled up more valuables than we expected. Not only copper currency, but some gems, weapons, and even some sealed honey."

Jadaya lifted her eyebrows at that. There were many insects, birds, and rodents that pollinated, but the bees that created honey were vicious. Deadly in ways that many overlooked, and they would follow raiders of their hives for miles. Even as little as three stings could kill an adult male. But if you avoided their hives, they would ignore you. Few bothered to raise them, as the risk was too great.

"Good. We can get a lot for sealed honey. Make sure that is well hidden." Note pushed himself away from the wall as he spoke. "Is there anything else or more we should bring?"

"As usual, please bring anything that you find necessary in your day-to-day life. We will travel light, so remember that." Rylix smiled. "Though small luxuries will make the journey that much faster."

"Jadaya, Note," Huk said, his tone apprehensive. "We have cleaned the weapons and wanted to give you first choice to see if any of them would suit you. We have none here experienced in making weapons like the ones you use or would suit you. Most of our smiths focus on hooks, arrow, and spear tips, or the occasional pan."

That much was true. The Aoisans utilized the sea to the point that many of the basics in Jadaya's experience were unknown or unused here. Their cooking pots and pans were giant shells or grills constructed of bones or made of their coral clay. Their fibers were collected from seaweed, ground coral created their muddaub, their pipes were coral clay baked in giant ovens until it was as hard as rocks. Even the furniture they used was created out of seaweed, trees, and shells. It left them with few trade items of great value.

"Show us," Note said, standing in the middle of the room. "Though my knives are still what I prefer."

Huk nodded. "We figured as much, but you shall have the best we can offer."

Jadaya hoped they had something that would suit her better. The curved swords of the Charinskys never felt right in her hand and were shorter than she was comfortable with.

Huk led them to a room, Rylix following, though Jadaya felt it was more out of curiosity and a desire to value what was there. On a table lay an assortment of weapons. All clean, polished, and oiled, but she could tell some were ancient and others had only been there a few suncycles.

"Any that were overly damaged or had structural flaws were pulled and even now are being melted down into ingots," Huk explained. Jadaya just nodded absently, as that was the only thing to do with weapons damaged beyond use.

She wandered over and quickly ruled out any of them that were too short or curved. One even had a wavy blade, which made no sense. Then she wrapped her hand around the various hilts. If it was too short to fit her hand, she let it go, or if it was so narrow her fingers overlapped her thumb, she ignored it. That left her with three. None of them were perfect, but upon lifting them, one was heavier than was comfortable, which meant it would be a great training sword. The other two swords were shorter than the ones she trained with, but the weight felt right in her hands. The length was close enough to what her muscle memory expected that Jadaya knew she could adapt.

Note did the same perusal, but he was more selective. A small pile of sharp little knives grabbed his attention, and he fondled them, the point drawing blood from his finger. "I think I will keep these. They might come in interesting."

Jadaya nodded. "I would like these three if you would. Not perfect, but better than what I have now."

"As you say. Then Rylix, I believe the rest is up to you and the Ged."

Rylix just grinned. "This will be a trip to tell your grandchildren."

"Assuming we live that well,'" Note said, the knives having vanished from the table.

"Well, it makes telling your grandchildren stories easier, yes. But either way, our trip will be the subject of tales."

Rylix's smile was so big Jadaya let him have it, as she went to see how to carry what she needed. And figure out how to say goodbye to Kol and Ola.

CHAPTER FOURTEEN

NOTE

Note had spent the last tenday watching his new companions. He arranged things so he intercepted Jadaya in the oddest places, giving him a reason to talk to her. If he was going to risk his life at her side, he wanted to make sure he had her measure. Her facial expressions and feelings had resolved for him, and he was caught between envying her naivety and being frustrated that she had no control of her emotions. All her feelings were writ large on her face and body for all to see. It meant she would be all but incapable of deceit. What kept him amused was she thought she concealed her feelings. If only the child knew. To him, she *was* a child. His own childhood had vanished when he was taken. The luxury to be whole vanished as he dealt with things that had forever changed him.

Then there was her exile. While he doubted her gods even thought of her once dragged from their presence—and with whip marks like that, dragging was the only option. Plus, her brand was a siren call to any who recognized it. But that meant he needed to see who recognized it. And if it would change how people treated them. Hopefully, most would think the nut sized brand was a strange beautification choice. The Vyks had a version of branding, so it was rare, but not unheard of. The other advantage was most Zuks were isolationists, as the deeps and the mountains limited most of their trade to just Wysko.

He shrugged. It would be what it would be, and her skill with a sword or bow was undeniable. He needed to make sure they were sparring once they started traveling. Both of them would need to stay in shape or get into shape. Note ran his hand through his hair again, the seaweed dye already fading. He would update the color before they traveled. Maybe, this time, there would be tella dye available. It might stay longer. At least from how badly it stained teeth it should be more permanent.

He stood outside the house and whistled. It took a moment, but soon enough the man he was looking for pushed it open, giving him a warm smile that sent frissons of stress through him. No one should be that welcoming to a stranger unless they wanted something. "Rylix, do you have a moment?" Note tried to sound friendly, but that emotion had been burned out of him a long time ago. People were to be used or were looking to use you. Best case, your existence was immaterial. If he had his way, no one would ever notice him. It was the only way to survive, to be unnoticeable.

So you yelled at the gods in the middle of the street?

His cynical inner voice refused to let him avoid his own hypocrisy. But no one else needed to know his conflict.

Rylix's smile, if anything, increased. "Why would I not have time for my future traveling companion? Please enter and be welcome." Still overly friendly, the man led him back to a table where his notebook and stylus lay next to a pile of counting beads. The council had provided him with an empty house. The previous occupant had not survived the attack.

Note settled into a comfortable stance, as these walls were still prickly, unlike the smooth interior walls of the council hall. "I wanted to check on the planning and see if you needed anything, as well as verify if we should bring our own goods for barter and trade."

Rylix sat back and looked at Note, his face open enough to convince a child of his honesty. Note met his gaze, trying to see the man underneath. He seemed well formed and intelligent. His hair was a long mane of curls that made Note glad his hair was short and straight, only requiring the occasional touch up of dye. He would never have silvery hair again if he had the choice.

"It would be helpful, though the city and your gods have been extremely generous." He waved at the counting beads and his notebook. The stylus, a shaft of graphine wrapped carefully in leather, lay next to it, obviously well used. "Even with my most pessimistic calculations, I believe we will be able to get all the supplies we need at Hearth, and pay for transport to Vykland with our wagon, mustangs, and jacks. But no one can gauge how sweet an individual's traveler's tooth will be or their need for luxuries." He smiled again. "But rest assured, as long as you have no desire to travel in a panoply and have servants catering to you, we should be able to journey in relative comfort."

Anyone who traveled kept a small pouch of gold or pearls to trade. They usually were worth so little, no one would steal it. Now a pouch of copper, that could you get you killed. Enough copper and it could be melted to make weapons or tools. Gold was mostly useless, though pretty. But having the ability to buy your own trinkets made life easier.

Note snorted at the idea of him being lugged around like a high priest or rich landowner. "Very well. And is there anything you need?"

Rylix tilted his head, watching him. "I do have a question. I feel you are well-traveled outside of Aois, even to Charinsky?"

"Depends on your definition of well-traveled," Note said, still trying to understand this man, though the question raised alarms. "Why?"

Rylix shrugged and gave him that disarming grin, so friendly and warm that it set Note even more on edge. No one could be that nice or easy going. "Because my parents traveled most in Agrina, which is why I was able to earn this route. Aois is simple compared to other countries, as the needs of most Aoisans are easily met. Your people are so self-sufficient that outside pots and pans made of metal or some fabrics that are warmer for those at the other end, you want little." Rylix waved his hand around the room. "Even here, few pictures, tapestries, or rugs. What you have is woven from seaweed, and you press what you find beautiful into the walls in designs that are pleasing to your eyes. While it has taken persistence to make a profit here, I fear that there is too much I am unaware of in the other countries."

Note watched him as he spoke, and while friendly there was nothing that made him think he was lying. More, it was a man being honest, and unforced honesty was relatively foreign to Note.

"I see." Note nodded and moved to sit down in the other chair, thinking. "My travels involved little luxury or trade, but surely you have information from others." It was a prying question, but if this man was so new, they were all at risk of failure. Besides, travel still contained danger from others. Not all exiles were so clearly branded as Jadaya.

"Yes, much. I have compiled the data they have sent and compared it by season and route. I have little fear that I will make this a successful trip, ensuring there is funding to take you all the way into Charinsky and then back. But to assume I know everything there is to know would be the height of arrogance. And what the Ged see is not what others might see." His warm smile invited Note into the joke, and part of Note wanted to lean in and accept the friendship. The memory of another child, neck broken laying on the ground while red and black robes loomed over him, telling him it was his fault and there would be more deaths if he was unable to learn his place, flashed into his mind, snuffing the warmth Rylix generated.

"Then it is good you are not arrogant," Note said stiffly, regretting the weakness of taking a seat. He swallowed, shoving the memory back into the darkness where it needed to remain. He tried to let some of the stiffness fade. It gave too much away. "I can tell you that what I saw of Fivika was a wealthy land with creativity and new things at every corner. Even the little villages I traveled through had wonders I had never seen before. If you were going there to bring things back here for trade, I could talk for fingers. But from here to there?" Note closed his eyes trying to think, but then he thought he was being hunted at every step and took little time to explore the countries he slipped through. That had been arrogance, to assume he was important enough to waste the time to chase once he crossed the border. "I will think about it, but for now I would say bring a multiple bags full of crushed oyster shells."

Rylix tilted his head. "Oh?"

Note shrugged and stood. "Just a thought. They can use it in smithing and for gardens and it is what we add to our muddaub to make it white and strong. I doubt most of the people over there have access to the amounts we have." That was an understatement. All shells were delivered to a few families that ran that industry. They were boiled and then either planted in existing beds to provide homes to fish and young oysters, or ground up and then used in a variety of ways.

"That is something I had not heard of, bless. I will see how to include some of that in our supplies." Rylix flashed a smile. "Is there anything else you will need for this trip?"

Note snorted as he headed to the door. "A blanket to lie on and one to cover me will be more than I had before. I am sure I will survive." He left before Rylix could say more. The sheer charisma of the man grated at him. Having friends made you weak. It gave those in power ways to hurt you.

Who is going to hurt you now? You escaped.

The words provided no comfort, and he headed to find Jadaya. He needed to make sure he knew how she fought. He had seen her during the invasion, but at the time, making sure he remained alive seemed more important than inspecting her style.

His own fighting techniques had been hard learned. Fingers spent watching the guards drill from a tiny window in his room. A window they blocked up when they discovered he was mimicking their movements. Then he learned from the groups he fell in with as he fled across multiple continents. More than once, he broke laws and traded favors. One of them involved teaching him how to fight.

Those had been lessons he threw himself into, needing to learn, needing to have control of his own life. Part of him wanted to be captured again by the priests. His voice would make him a target, but if they came for him, they would be the ones begging for mercy and bleeding on the ground, not him.

Rage shook him and he pivoted, heading down to the water, letting it wash over his feet as he tried to regain his equanimity. Right now, if he fought, he might be tempted to kill, and Jadaya had done nothing to earn his ire. The salt in the water washed over his skin, pulling away some of his anger as he stood there. He would need to remember to grab a few pounds of salt. Having baths with freshwater tore at his skin. Another lesson learned early, but at least that had not been a purposeful torture and salt was available to them. They just had to learn to add it.

"Will you ever forgive us?"

"No," he said, not lifting his head to look at the being standing on the water in front of us.

"We swear we were unaware. And Xyl speaks to no one anymore." The words were said as an explanation, but Note quit caring a long time ago.

"That is what I find unforgivable. That you let us be stolen and yet assumed we were happy? Why would you think that? Especially with care being given to your brother, who is insane with grief. What good can come of that? You cast away the most vulnerable of your people and expect me to care that you are sorry. No. I am still Aoisan. I fought too hard to come back here, but I will never kneel and beg your love again." This time Note looked up and Pel stood on the water watching him, his face impassive.

"Even you, the longest lived of all our creations, die so fast. We miss out on suncycles because we sleep or are involved in something else. We assumed when you arrived on Charinsky's shore that Xyl would cherish you as we had and then we…. Forgot." Pel shrugged. "We prefer those who are our children because they want to be, but others are not so…understanding. Do not assume our sibs will be as kind as we are."

Note just gave him a look. "If they dare to stand in front of me and justify what was done and have issues with my rage, they are welcome to kill me, and I will try to kill them." He turned and left the water, trying not to enjoy the look of shock that graced Pel's face.

CHAPTER FIFTEEN

LAZUL

Lazul stood at the entrance to the stable and hid a sigh as Actin spoke. "Your Majesty. It is improper. You need to have a carriage and at least a twenty-person escort. It is only fitting, as the people will come out to see you." He sounded as if at any moment he might die from the shock of the king being seen without a proper entourage.

"Actin, enough. It is sunny outside. Look." Lazul lifted his hand and waved it toward the sky. Blue shone down, with only a few clouds in the distance. "It has been mooncycles since the sun has been this warm. We are in my own country and the inspection will take at least a tenday to complete. I want to be outside, let people see me, and feel the sun on my skin. There will be a carriage following us, but the point is to *let* people see me, not hide."

That last thing Lazul had any desire to do was sit in a stuffy carriage for days as he traveled through the kingdom inspecting temples. It was bad enough that his primary traveling companion would be Zayn. All he could do was hope that the man would choose to ride in his own carriage. A twinge of sorrow as he thought how much he envied his parent's relationship. They at least had each other to talk with. Everyone in Lazul's life was looking for a way to use him, undermine him, or control him. It was enough to make him want to scream.

Actin clamped his jaw shut and did a sharp nod. "Very well, your majesty. I will ensure the carriage contains what you need for the inspection. But you will still need an escort."

"I know. A five-man squad. Led by Captain Malac." At least Malac had common sense, and Lazul thought that if he had been born a noble, they might have been friends. As it was, most of his lords thought they could do a better job. There were days when he was tempted to let them.

"Of course, sir. I have arranged stops with the lords at the various cities for your overnights. Do not forget to address your need for a wife."

Lazul almost groaned. Instead, he managed a wan smile. "Yes. Who will be presented to me again?"

The look Actin shot him made him feel like a misbehaving child, but he ignored it. This trip was turning into a nightmare between Zayn and a parade of women controlled by their fathers being thrown at him. "You will be introduced to Lord Garnet's daughter Merel, Lord Epidote's daughter Eosphor, and Lord Felspar's niece Cupri. All of them bring stronger ties to those areas, and Lord Felspar especially, as he is at the far end of Charinsky."

Lazul nodded. "Yes, Aryix bless for the reminder, Actin. Now if we can get on the way?" He itched to be away from the castle and its gloom. If he was lucky, there would be a few fingers of quiet, before Zayn met up with him.

"Of course, sire. Captain Malac is here with his men."

Lazul narrowed his eyes at Actin, feeling like he had definitely handled him, if the Captain was already ready to go with exactly four men behind him. A headache started to form behind his eyes. At this rate, he would be ready to come back and hide in his chambers before he even left. Rather than responding to the efficient, if annoying, manager of his life, Lazul wheeled his mustang around and headed out. The carriage, wagon, and his escort of five followed him out the gate.

He had just enough time to tilt his head back and smile as the sun caressed his face before it was disrupted by a voice.

"I see you are ready to head out, your majesty." He knew the voice all too well, and the mocking tone carried to everyone in the train. Lazul sighed, his face still tilted toward the sun, though it had become cooler with the unwelcome presence. Had a finger of time to himself been so much to ask?

"Zayn," he replied, not looking at the man yet, trying to siphon the last few moments of pleasure from the warmth of the sun. "I take it you are ready?"

"I look forward to inspecting my temples. To make sure they are at the height of productivity for their worship of Xyl and making sure they sing the songs properly to keep him quiescent." Zayn smiled a smug, supercilious smile that slid under Lazul's skin.

I want to enjoy this trip. Surely I can ignore him.

Lazul let his face drop from the sun and forced a smile that felt false, if not more of a snarl than a smile. "Very well. Captain, are you ready?" He turned his attention back to Malac, a younger man with the trademark coloring of most Chars, blond, pink flushed skin, and stocky bone structure.

"Yes, your majesty," he replied, his tone full of respect. "Men, ride out."

Lazul smiled when Captain Diam Malac paced his mustang next to him and spoke. "Sire, with the four wagons and the mustangs we have, we will take the full tendays to reach the last town. I am assuming you do not wish to spend a tenday traveling back. Do you wish for me to arrange a ship to carry you back once the inspection is completed?" The captain kept his voice formal, but Lazul thought he detected a hint of sympathy in the man.

Or it is wishful thinking because I want to be rescued from Zayn at any cost?

"Yes. That would be preferable. My royal ship, please," he stressed. His royal ship only had a single bedchamber with facilities, as it was meant for quick jaunts, not overseas trips. While normally it would take at least six days to sail from one end of Charinsky to the other, on the west side of the country was a strong current that rippled from the bottom to the top, making the trip in less than two days.

It also ensured he had two days without Zayn, as even that man would balk at claiming the bedchamber for his own. At least he hoped so. If not, well, there would be some emergency that required his attention.

Captain Malac nodded and waved at a young man who trotted his mustang up to him. A few short orders, and the man whirled his beast around and raced back into the castle. Moving through the city was slow enough that he would be able to catch up shortly.

They rode out, with people around the palace ignoring him. He came down into the city center two or three times a tenday, often on foot, though always with an escort. The act of him leaving the city proper was uncommon enough that people would come out to see and wave at him once he left the center of the city. Most around the palace knew they were starting the temple inspections today. All except the main temple, as Lazul could do an inspection there whenever necessary. Though he was unable to remember the last time one had been done.

"Captain, I believe you are in my spot," Zayn said from the side as his mustang, all black and trimmed in red, pulled up beside him.

Malac nodded and pulled back. Lazul searched his mind for a reason to keep the Captain there instead of Zayn, but nothing occurred. And while having the priest as a nuisance was frustrating, making him into an enemy would be too dangerous. Talking to him for the entire trip might tilt that balance, however.

"Yes, Zayn?" He asked, trying to keep his voice politely interested as they left the market area.

"How are you faring, your majesty? Did the sun help improve your day?" Zayn said in a tone that implied Lazul had been unwell.

Lazul kept a smile on his face with effort. "I believe the sun improved everyone's day. The songs helped Xyl, so he blesses us."

"Yes, I thought the new singers I arranged for did a wonderful job for their first songs. I need to keep training them, though. They can only achieve true excellence via constant practice. Why, even some of our priests sang, just to provide harmony, you understand."

Lazul gritted his teeth at the smugness. The singers were captured children. A desperate measure set in motion hundreds of suncycles ago. Something he loathed, but until there was another way, the cost of not having these singers was too high. But the arrogance of Zayn to take all the credit—as if the original idea had been his. And the idea that he had anything to do with the care of stolen Aoisans was laughable.

An idea, based too much in spite and annoyance, raced through Lazul's mind. Before his brain could convince him to ignore it, he spoke. "I believe we should start by inspecting the high temple this round. It has been a while since I performed a full review of the primary temple to Xyl and Percit." He matched words with motion and turned the head of his mustang toward where the temple squatted, chunky and immovable, at the other end of the city.

"You what?" Zayn sputtered as his mustang almost ran into Lazul.

The surprise and discomfort in his voice was the sweetest thing Lazul had heard in ages and solidified his decision. He had no memories of the last time he felt like he had the upper hand with the man. It felt good. As if sensing his amusement and general good mood, the mustang kicked up its pace, with Lazul enjoying the sun and the sputtered comments too far away for him to make out.

He never came this way, as there was a quicker route that was direct from the castle, and it was interesting to look at the buildings as they approached the temple. Further away, the city bustled with energy, people going through their day—though more than one stopped to feel the sun on their face as well. But the closer he rode to the temple, the sadder it felt. It was not just the low song that came from it, but a miasma that seemed to spread sorrow and discontent.

Lazul frowned as he actively looked around. He admitted to himself part of it was to find fault with Zayn, but now it was driven by paying attention to his city. Something he often forgot to do. It seemed like the world battered at him for decisions constantly until he lived in a fog of his own inability to move forward. The bright sun and blue skies went a long way to clearing his mind and now he looked forward to the ride back, alone. He needed to get out more often.

All the thoughts rambled through his mind as he stopped his mustang at the entrance to the temple. He had dismounted as Zayn and Malac caught up with him.

"Why are you wasting time with this? There are many temples that never feel my presence and that need to be inspected first. All I can rely on is the words and letters of the priests and priestess, and that is rarely good enough." Zayn managed to not snap out the words, but the fact that for once he annoyed the cantor created injudicious bubbles of joy for Lazul.

What is the good of being a king if I ignore my occasional whims?

He smiled at Zayn with an absentminded manner and turned to the entrance. "All I ever see is the worship courtyard. I think I would like to see the living quarters of the order, the singers, their hygiene facilities, and the cooking facilities for both." Zayn struggled to dismount, wearing robes that, while impressive, were not practical for riding, as Lazul strode into the entryway.

The temple, like most buildings in Charinsky, was a series of blocks, square and rectangle that created the layout. The covered main entrance hall was where worshipers mingled and anointed themselves with ash ground from the pieces of Percit that had landed. When she had been killed and the moon broken, chunks had impacted the land, creating craters of death. Over time, those chunks had been collected, ground up, and brought to the temples. There were even teams of roving priests that went to other countries to find and bring back the pieces of Percit.

During services, all worshippers would draw streaks from the center of each eye down to show the tears of grief. Some of the truly devout would mark themselves daily with common ash. Lazul had never been that devoted. Few rulers could afford to be, but at the same time, angering a god that could destroy your land ensured a measure of worship.

Instead of heading to the ash chalice, he stood looking at the temple with fresh eyes. Seeing it not as the temple to Xyl but as both a home and prison.

"Really, sire. There is nothing to see here and we are wasting time." Zayn stood as if to block the way further in, his robes flaring around him in an impressive display of overt wealth.

Lazul gave him his blandest smile. "It would be good for me to have a reference, to see how living conditions are here. It provides a basis as to what the other temples might need or how they could be improved." Zayn glared at him and Lazul suspected he would be dead right at this moment if Zayn had the power.

"Why the reluctance? Is there something you are uncomfortable with me seeing?" He kept his bland smile on his face, but the change that rippled over Zayn had Lazul's attention.

Zayn went from angry and about to cross a line, to smooth and unruffled. If Lazul had not been paying attention, it might have seemed like Zayn was two different people. It also implied there was something Zayn very much wanted to hide.

What could he hide? He is more untouchable than I am.

The question lingered even as Zayn walked behind where the shallow dishes of ground stone were kept and opened a door that Lazul had not realized was there. "Sire," Zayn said, his snideness back in full swing.

"Captain Malac, please accompany me. The rest can wait outside," Lazul said, following Zayn. He enjoyed that flicker of irritation too much, but it was one of the reasons Malac was the captain he usually chose. The man also had the ability to take notes and Lazul knew from experience he would have a notebook in his pocket as well as a graphene stick.

With that Lazul followed Zayn into the parts of the temple previously unknown to him.

CHAPTER SIXTEEN

JADAYA

Jadaya heard the crunch of leather on shells from Note's footsteps before she saw him. They were scheduled to leave in two days, and she felt off balance. She had almost no possessions, and what little she had were gifts from Kol and Ola. The small pack held two spare shirts, a binding, three loincloths, one pair of pants, a wrap, her ajo oil, a small packet of beads for her hair, a blanket, and her weapons. It was more than she had when she washed up on the shore, but it seemed so little. Ola had included a few small things for her to trade, but they fit on her waist and barely seemed like anything.

"Any advice, or are you going to judge my lack of possessions?" She longed for the nice kit she used when she marched out on training. Then she had little reason to worry. Her pack would have rations, two blankets, head scarfs, bracers, boots, insect repellent, clothing, and everything else. What she was unable to carry, the supply wagons would.

"More than I had when I started out," he said.

She turned to look at him. Kol and Ola were out collecting fish and seaweed. She ached to do something for them, to show her gratitude. Maybe that was part of the reason she was agreeing to rescue these children. It was as good a reason as any.

"Does that mean I worry over much? That I what I am unable to procure will not be needed?" She watched him, still unsure what to make of this strange man.

"No. You will miss all the things you are unable to bring. But we have money and trade goods. If you find you need something, it would surprise me if Rylix is unable to find it." He stretched his arms behind him. "I came to see if you would like to spar. It would do us well to create a habit of practice as we travel."

Jadaya nodded. "It would be. But your style of fighting is one I never learned." She moved to the door, the recovered sword in her hand. It will felt slightly off, which added weight to her need to practice.

"My style is… not so much one as something I cobbled together," he admitted as they walked out the door, heading to the empty headland.

The view from there encompassed the sea and if she looked carefully, she could see the darker water of the deeps. The lack of her telescopic vision bit at her once more, but crying over that which was gone only wasted energy. She needed to focus on what there was to do.

"You were not trained?" The idea seemed foreign to her. All the Chosen were trained. Their skills were assessed early and then they were sent to the appropriate duties. Hers had been weapons, though if that would turn out to be a blessing or a curse, she still was unsure.

"Trained?" He snorted out a laugh as they stopped, staring out at the water. "Not in the way I think you mean it. I traded with a few… people I met on the way to learn how to fight. Knives are easy to get."

His face shuttered as he said that. Jadaya tilted her head, questions bubbling in her mind, but she avoided asking those questions. "How do we spar? Our techniques are very different."

Note continued to watch the water, looking out at the sea with something oddly like longing on his face. It felt like she watched something intensely private, and she looked away.

"I want to see how you train because, at some point, I need to be able to fight someone like you. The idiots that attacked us were slow and left themselves open. My speed allowed me to dart in and out. But I think trying that with you would only get me killed."

Jadaya frowned, looking at him. He was so slight compared to her, almost childlike. But she remembered the men he had killed as easily as she had. Learning how to deal with his skill would be best. "This is a standard routine." She settled into her stance, closed her eyes, pushing the world away and felt the weight of her sword, her body, the way it moved, all the little things that had changed. She accepted them and pulled them into her, then opened her eyes and moved.

Block, strike, follow through, block, parry, strike. She lost herself in fighting the invisible enemies, seeing the attacks in her mind. The first half-finger of practice was slow as she adapted to the sword, but then she moved faster, the smoothness coming back and a hint of joy flitted through her as she continued to fight her ghosts.

A finger passed before she stopped, taking deep breaths of air, feeling it fill her lungs, and for the first time in too long, she had a sense of peace. Jadaya let herself focus on Note. He had watched her but not done anything to draw her focus away as she found her patterns again.

"You rely much more on static responses to basic moves?" He asked it as a question.

Jadaya nodded. "There are only so many ways to attack with a sword, but there are more sword types than I had realized." She frowned, thinking of the different ones they had shown her. There had only been four weapons available for her training: long sword, short sword, spear, and bow. Halke had decided with her height and reach that the long sword and bow were the ones she would learn. Days spent standing in the sun, repeating the strikes over and over; or sending quiver after quiver of arrows into the targets to receive a nod. She swallowed and pushed it away. "You learn the strikes and their counters. After enough practice, it becomes muscle memory, not thought."

Note nodded, his pale eyes and dark hair still catching her off guard given the pastel colors of all the other Aoisans. "I would like to try a half speed spar and see. I suspect both of us need to learn more and there is no one here to teach us."

Jadaya nodded, a slight crease in her brow. "Do you believe Rylix would know?"

"Know how to train us or weapons?" Note had pulled out his two blades and stood in front of her.

"Yes?" She settled into her stance, the sword held in front of her, while she rested most of her weight on her back leg.

"The Ged are known for slings, throwing darts, and staffs." He lunged forward, his knife aiming for her groin area.

She stepped back and batted his hand away with the flat of her blade, but that was out of choice. If it had been an actual attack, she would have used the edge.

"Throwing darts?" She had not seen that on the ship, but then she had spent what little of the voyage she remembered on her belly, delirious and in pain. They could have been calling down lightning and she would not have been aware of it.

"Yes. Different clans have different types, but they can bring down brigands and large moelks with them." He spoke as he moved around her strike, making it seem slow and obvious, then darted toward Jadaya's neck with his knife.

Jadaya had heard of moelks before. They were huge herbivores that lived in more mountainous areas. Zuyika had hiros. The Chosen occasionally hunted two or three of them, large creatures with wicked horns that could kill the unwary. The scent of dust and sweat rose up from her memories. The thrill of the hunt, the risk of life and limb and knowing you could count on the person next to you.

All gone.

Hit with a thrust of grief, she flipped her sword up, rotating it quickly so the flat of her blade batted away the strike. It felt odd to not do full strikes, the way she would have done in practice, but the priests of Yika were always there to heal them. Even a broken bone only took a day to heal.

That is gone now.

She cleared her throat, trying to sound as if nothing was wrong. "Those sound interesting. Having another weapon, especially one not as obvious as a sword, could be helpful." This time she lunged straight at him, and he jumped backward, avoiding the strike, but it left him exposed to another lunge, then another. In less than a heartbeat, he was at the edge of their practice area.

"This is annoying. I had no chance to close in with you," Note said. His eyes narrowed as they both came to rest.

"You seemed competent during that fight against the attackers?" She asked, a lilt in her voice, trying to remember the fighting, but it remained a blur of panic, excitement, and her own muscle memory. Anything to get away from the memories ripping open her heart.

"They were not expecting a fight, left openings, and preferred large swings. You keep up your guard, hold your weapon close to your body, and use your height to keep me away." He studied her and the sword, colors cycling across his skin like the lights in the sky in shelter season. "If I come up against anyone trained like you, they will gut me like a fish," he said, his lips pressed together.

Jadaya cleared her throat, and he looked at her with cutting eyes. "With the daggers and this mission, it would be better to take out our opponents before they realize we are there." She tilted her head toward the bow that stood against a wall. "If we can obtain decent bows, it will help with our success."

Note titled his head as if changing his perspective or looking somewhere else. "The guards and priests that I remember only had swords or pikes." He looked at the bow again. "We have no need of that sort of weapon here, as we rarely hunt with more than nets."

Jadaya nodded. Watching them hunt waterfowl with nets had been an enlightening experience. They also had some spears they used underwater, but she had experimented with them, learning they were unwieldy on land.

"You know the odds are we will die less than a finger after we reach Charinsky," she said, her voice soft, but calm.

Note pulled his eyes away from the weapons and glanced at her, a smirk pulling up the left side of his face. "I will be surprised if we survive until we get to Vykland." He looked directly at her, not the normal side glances or quick little flicks of the eyes he gave her. "Are you sure you want this? You are young. You could have a family, a life, do something your heart yearns for."

She stood there, analyzing him. He was a decent-looking person, though the gills on the sides of his ribs were odd. But she felt no attraction to him, not that it mattered. His abilities in bed were immaterial. What mattered was would he guard her back?

"There is no reason not to," she finally said, turning away to stare at the ocean, trying very hard to not think about going back out into the eternal hunger that was the sea. "I am Exile. I have no home. Why not spend my life to correct something that I know is wrong, corrupt even? Nothing calls to me, so this is as good as anything."

She could feel him behind her, but stayed watching the sea.

"That is a sorrow, but one I will make use of."

At this, she turned to look at him, brows furrowed.

"Losing one's gods is hard. Having them throw you away is even harder. But I will gladly take what they cast off and if your life, your death, helps end the abduction of the children, I will ensure Aois remembers your name for multiple lifetimes."

There was no smirk on his face and he seemed more sincere than any other time.

"Then that is enough." What else was there to say? A journey awaited and maybe some place along the way she might find things to fill the holes in her heart.

Or I die and there is no more pain.

That thought actually gave her hope, and she turned to finish packing for their trip.

CHAPTER SEVENTEEN

LAZUL

The inner walls of the temple were polished as smooth as those in the worship areas. But the walls in the sanctuary were covered with carvings of Xyl and Percit. The long ago artisans depicted Xyl with his blond hair falling to his waist, bearded jaw, and delineated muscles, always offering tokens to Percit. She looked at him with her own hair wrapping around her feet and an expression of sadness that never went away as the moon hung above her. In these images the moon was whole, though not even books contained memories of before it broke. Before they needed to sing songs to her for Xyl.

The way Xyl had looked at her had always struck Lazul as more obsessed than in love, but then he had no wife. What did he know of looks?

Shaking off the thoughts, he followed Zayn. One or two of the priests stuck their heads out. The red robes and gray streaks of mourning on their faces only highlighted that he never saw Zayn wear the ashes outside of services.

"And you can see this is the back way. Over here we have the courtyard for the singers and the practice rooms and dining area to the right." Zayn waved his hands, barely slowing as he strode down the length of the hall.

"I think I will inspect the practice rooms," Lazul said, turning to the right. He heard the squeak of leather on stone floors behind him. In a moment, Zayn was in front of him again.

"There is little to see in there. Tuning bells, musical instruments, and tonal devices." Zayn was dismissive of the areas, as if he was inspecting the laundry, not what allowed their country to avoid starvation.

Lazul just nodded and continued walking down the hall, keeping the attitude in mind. He opened the first room, and it was what Zayn said. The bells for tone, reed flutes, even glass bowls to match your pitch. The second was similar.

"See nothing. The next room is an infirmary." Zayn sounded bored and annoyed, as if this was beneath him.

"You are welcome to have a priest or even a conductor show me around," Lazul said mildly. This was more reaction than he got out of Zayn in a mooncycle. There was no way he would end it early. It was too much fun. He kept walking and opened the next door. It was set up as a basic infirmary: splints, bandages, poultices, needles, even a birthing chair.

"I fear they would be unable to answer your questions fully. Would you like to see the priest's quarters next?" Zayn's voice was hard, cold even, and Lazul fought a smile.

"We will get there." Lazul moved to the last room, the door had a bolt on the outside, and opened it, lifting an eyebrow at the room with an enormous bed, rich blankets, a small needs room and not much else. There was no window. He glanced over at Zayn, who shrugged.

"For anyone that needs to be isolated if sick. For the breeding pairs so they can have some privacy," he said in a dismissive tone.

Lazul was unable to repress the flinch at "breeding pairs", but all he said was "Ah." Something about the room rang false, but he just shut the door and turned to walk back up the hall. Vague feelings provided no ground to ask questions. But it was one more thing he settled into his mind.

Zayn heaved a sigh, but stepped up ahead of him. "Here is the dining hall for the singers and the conductors that oversee them." He opened a door to a simple room with tables and benches. Not fancy, but not any worse off than what Lazul had in the servants' quarters.

"What are they eating?" Lazul sniffed the air, and it smelled not at all like edible food.

Zayn gave him an affronted look. "They eat the same as we do. Singers require high-quality food and I would never risk Xyl's anger by not making sure they could sing."

Lazul believed that. You could hear hunger in voices and Xyl responded unfavorably. But that answer still left the awful smell. It made him want to gag. Lazul turned to look at him. "You eat that?"

"What are you talking about?" Zayn sniffed the air and sighed. "That is not food. That is the cleaning oils. Look." He strode over and yanked open a small cupboard. One of the small jars of oil had fallen on its side and was dripping everywhere. "I will insure a sing—*someone* cleans it up shortly. Are you satisfied?" Zayn had an annoyed expression on his face that amused and delight Lazul.

"If this was any other temple, we would check out the singers' rooms, needs rooms, and their practice area. Should we do less here?"

Zayn gave him a tight-lipped smile that Lazul knew was as false as his politeness. "Of course not. Let us proceed." Zayn led him back out of the dining area, passing a room that, from the risers and bells, Lazul knew was a practice room. It was full of singers at the moment with a conductor in flared red and black robes leading them in song. He glanced at them as he walked, but Aoisans were so oddly colored compared to his own skin that the glimpses of pale faces told him little besides sadness. The other room was obviously a composition room. New songs were required to keep Xyl placated, so the creation of music never stopped.

As they walked toward the back, Zayn spoke in a voice that carried. "Back here we have the singers' rooms. They are grouped by age and gender," he said as he pointed at the rooms. "There are needs rooms on either end, and the older singers are fewer to a room." He pushed open a door revealing three-level bunk beds in rows of four, dressers, and small slit windows that let in breeze and light. It looked barren but comfortable. It was cool outside, but they kept the air in here at a decent temperature.

Lazul nodded, not saying anything. What could he say? The rooms were clean, there were blankets on the bed, dressers for clothes, and a few personal items scattered around. The needs rooms were the same. Water spouts for washing, the pump nearby, and waste holes that would go into the fertilizer system most cities utilized.

While nothing was fancy, it also was better than a lot of his people had, certainly nothing like the prison. Most of his poorer citizens still had to pull water from their outdoor pumps and bring it in. Here the water to bathe in was heated in large cauldrons. His own bath chamber simply had servants that brought in the hot water. In the back was a large tub that he knew contained salt water. His great-grandfather had found out the hard way that if Aosians were not able to soak in salt water at least once a tenday, they died quickly.

"The stairs lead to the second level," Zayn said and strode toward the spiral stair.

Lazul stopped to glance out into the enclosed courtyard. There were a few children out there playing and an older singer, though he knew that only because of her height. The Aoisans hardened rather than getting wrinkles. Their subtle scales getting harder and more inflexible, but that was something that only happened after a hundred suncycles or more. Aoisans of that age were rare, and not something he ever witnessed. Which meant the story might not be true. He bit back a sigh at what was one more example of what he was unsure of.

He caught up with Zayn at the top of the stairs and glanced at the bedrooms of the priests. The rooms were laid out in a similar fashion. There were needs rooms at the end of both halls and the men were on one side, the women on the other. There were only one or two to a room here and the bedding, furniture and over all supplies were nicer, but not substantially different. Zayn walked him through the dining hall, which while much nicer, less crowded, and contained a kitchen, there was little difference from the other one. The stairs leading down to the singers' dining were obvious, and he had no doubt they were fed well.

Prisoners, but ones that are well-treated.

He stuck his head into the library, which was where they researched songs and wrote them. At the last section of the second floor, Zayn halted, his forced smile on his mouth. "These are my quarters and storage areas. Is there a need to look at them?"

The desire to make him squirm as Lazul pawed through his possessions ran hot, but they were already opponents. There was no need to make him an enemy.

"No. I have seen enough. I now have a baseline for what the other temples should have." Lazul smiled, a bland smile.

There was a flicker of something in Zayn's eyes. Relief? Resentment? It went across so fast all Lazul could tell was that there had been an emotion, but what he was unsure.

"Very well, your majesty. I will meet you back outside shortly." His voice was back to its normal smoothness.

Lazul left him, heading back down, but a murmur of voices pulled him to the open courtyard. He stood watching as the older singer spoke to the children. They were sitting quietly rather than running and playing and all of them had their faces turned up to listen to her as they spoke quietly, but there was an intensity to her voice that caught him, even if he could not understand Aoisan. One or two of the children had tears running down their faces, but at a sharp gesture, they wiped the tears and nodded.

The clack of steps coming down the stairs had him pulling back. He had the feeling Zayn would not like what they were doing. But all prisoners had a right to grieve. Lazul shook his head, a sick feeling in his stomach as he headed back out into the greeting area.

"Is there an issue, your majesty?" Zayn said as he approached.

Lazul put on a smile this time. "No. I was simply taking in the unusual sounds. I am rarely here when there are not worship services being conducted."

Zayn nodded, a smugness under his smile. "Yes. But the next set of songs to Xyl should start in three fingers. We are the only temple with enough singers to have songs every six fingers all day. It is a new schedule that we are hoping will pacify Xyl. With his blessing, the weather should improve."

"The singers sing at night?" Lazul was surprised, though in retrospect he should have expected this. Everyone had suffered from the lack of sun lately and Xyl was notorious for changing what made him happy tenday to tenday. It felt like managing a toddler from the behavior of the children currently at court.

"They will for a while. It is a good way to train the new singers. The reaction to mistakes or off-key songs are not as drastic as it can be during the day," Zayn said slowly, but the flicker of a smile on his face implied there was another reason.

Lazul's thoughts centered on the storm that had happened last year. The singers had faltered, their numbers too low to keep up the harmony those songs required, and Xyl has gotten upset. The twisting winds had taken fences, livestock, and multiple roofs. It had been part of the reason he agreed to the raid. No one wanted to see another storm like that.

"Yes. We should get back on our flow. Each city is a minimum of a day away and we have a tenday for all the inspections."

Captain Malac waited for them outside the doors. Lazul nodded and rattled off what they had inspected at this temple as the captain took notes. Then, with a feeling of having missed something, Lazul mounted his mustang and turned its head toward the gate, giving one last glance at the building. Even from the outside, the amount of sorrow in those walls made him want to cry.

Will we ever be free of our god's grief?

The question haunted him as they rode out to the next stop on the inspection. Though more likely, he needed to worry about Zayn just as much. The man planned something, but what? He could not be king, the laws would prevent that. What did he want?

CHAPTER EIGHTEEN

JADAYA

Jadaya stood on the dock, looking at the ship. They had finished loading the supplies and most everyone was on board, but all she could see was the wind blowing, the waves crashing, and the horrid sounds of the ship breaking apart around her. She fought down a wave of nausea. It had all been theory, but now she had to get on a ship and sail. The white sails provided no relief. When she raced onto the ship to get the children, her focus was on the invaders, and she knew she could jump off and swim back before it got out of the harbor. But now. To spend *time* on a ship?

Panic beat at her, and she forced herself to breathe. Pel would watch them. Make sure they lived to reach Fivika. She would show the gods that not even her own fears could stop her. She fed her righteous anger into the fear and felt the foreboding shred before her rage.

"Ready to board?" The friendly voice of Rylix pulled her out of her internal battle, one her anger was winning. Jadaya forced her lips to smile instead of snarl. This man had done nothing to her.

"Not really, but no other way to get there." She tried to keep her tone light, but suspected the death grip she had on her pack betrayed her.

Rylix tilted his head and his eyes darkened. "I take it the sea and your stomach are not friends?"

Jadaya blinked, trying to remember. She had been in so much pain she had no idea if she had been sick. "I believe I am uninjured. It is more..." She trailed off, not sure what to say.

Last time I was on a ship I almost died?

Rylix just watched her, waiting, which was almost more uncomfortable. With a smile she wanted to be real, she shook her head. "I am well. Thinking of the challenges before us."

"Ah, but they shall come with glory, acclaim, and perhaps wonder," he countered, his smile real and bright.

"Or death, sorrow, and pain?" she parried back, her smile becoming more real.

Rylix shrugged. "It seems to me if life did not contain those negatives, how will you recognize the positives? After all, what is light if there is no dark?"

She looked over at him, paying attention to more than just his words. Where she stood with her body tense, waiting to attack or flee, he was relaxed and loose. The way she should be. With an effort of will, Jadaya forced herself to relax. Just the act of breathing and letting her muscles drop the tight, coiled feeling, helped.

"Do you feel better now, Night Warrior?" Rylix had a note in his voice Jadaya recognized as teasing. When had anyone last teased her?

She pushed away the stab of emotion, not even bothering to identify it. Warrior, that is what she was. "Perhaps. But that still does not relieve my concern about being on a ship."

"Ah, now that is something I can assist with, Night Warrior. Come and I shall introduce you to the captain and the first mate." Rylix grinned and waved her toward the gangway.

"Jadaya is my name, you know." She kept an iron grip on her bag as she followed him.

"Yes, but nowhere near as poetic and mysterious as Night Warrior. I can see the song written about our adventure, and the cornerstone will be the night warrior, the dark lady who cut through enemies as if they were but stalks of grain." He spoke in an expansive voice, and the grin on his face encouraged her to laugh with him.

Jadaya managed to not laugh, but she was smiling by the time they walked onto the deck. Waiting for them was a woman clad in the normal trousers and loose shirt, with breasts that sailed forward ahead of her. It was the first thing Jadaya noticed, followed by the mane of dark curly hair bound by a ribbon of brilliant blue and eyes that matched the brown of the wood of her ship.

Bindings can do that?

"Rylix. This is the Zuyikan you were talking about?" Her voice rang with power and Jadaya had no doubt the crew could hear her commands from bow to stern without an issue.

"Capitan Jolyx, this is the warrior lady known as Jadaya," Rylix said with a bow, as if offering Jadaya up on a plate.

The woman only came up to Jadaya's shoulder, but she had a force of personality that made her seem taller. "You will definitely stand out in this crew," Jolyx said, looking her up and down. "Are you any good at working on a ship? I need to know if you are helpful or pure passenger."

Jadaya shrugged, the woman's brusque tone oddly like that of her trainers. "Pure passenger, unless you want to teach me. The only other time I have been on a ship, I was injured and unconscious most of the trip. Until the end," her voice dropped at that last bit.

"Ah. Yes. Well, *Starguide* is unlikely to be pulled apart by anything. Getting you trained should be easy. You look like you know how to use those long legs of yours." She shifted her attention over to Rylix. "Get her situated in the berth, then make sure we have everything of yours loaded. I want to be out of this bay with the tide." With that, she spun on her heel, headed up toward the bow.

Rylix grinned. "The captain is a force of nature, which ensures we will be well taken care of. Come." He led her into the hold and over to the right. "We are traveling fast and light, so nothing fancy. You know how to sleep in a swing net?" He gave her a look that had an unexpected around of worry.

Jadaya nodded. "Yes. We used them in our rest areas."

"Then everything should be well. The needs room is there, and you can hang your possessions here." He pointed to a room off to one side, that if it was like the other needs room she knew, it had a single hole that dumped into the ocean and a basin of water pumped in to wash with. There was a hook near her swing net, two large baskets attached to the hull in her area, and pegs for her to put her weapon on. The pegs looked new compared to the wear and tear on everything else, but it was all well cared for and neat.

A man was walking toward them, a patch covering one eye. He could have been the father of Rylix with the same grin and easy manner.

"Ah, Tylax, this is Jadaya, the Night Warrior."

The man came over to them and looked her up and down with a quick assessing glance. "It will be hard to see her in the dark, that is for sure. But watch your head. This ship was built for short people, not ones with heights such as yours."

Jadaya nodded, the fight on the other ship and her impact with several struts still fresh in her memory. "I hope I would not be rushing through here in the dark. That seems to be when I have issues with my height."

An issue I never had at home.

The Zuyikans were all tall and lean, and she ached inside, missing things that were built for her height, but that no longer mattered. Frustrated, she fed her resentment to that feeling and took a deep breath as it burned the ache away.

"Never can tell. Learn to duck," Tylax said with a wry tone. "Trader, we ready to go?"

"I need to double check on the last of the trade goods. They should have been loaded about four fingers ago. As long as Note is on board, and there is nothing else we are waiting for, yes, according to my calculations." Rylix fiddled with his notebook, but Jadaya figured it was too dim in here to read it.

"Then we should let the captain know," Tylax said, and headed to the stairs.

"There are three staterooms on this ship, the captain, the first mate, and cook, and then the maps room. That is where we meet to decide on the pattern and verify the currents remained steady. There is the mess hall and the kitchen. But there are no other sleeping rooms on this ship." Rylix spoke in a low voice. "This is how everyone is treated. Please take no offense."

Jadaya craned her head to see him in the dim light and low beams. "Why would I expect a room? The last time I only had one because…" she trailed off. Because the Ged that ran that ship had feared she would die and knew her exiled status. "Do all Ged provide assistance to the exiled?"

Rylix blinked at her with the change of topic. "Let us go above deck. There are a few things I need to make sure were completed. You brought some trade items?"

She noticed he was avoiding her question, but she needed this answer. However, she waited until the sun was back on her face and she relaxed. The dark, cramped area of the ship had affected her more than she realized. At least up here on the deck, she could see the sky, feel the wind, and see the shore. Fear wrapped around her throat as she realized soon that would change.

Zydrah! When did I become a coward?

Her internal anger at herself pushed down her fear. "Yes," she said with forced cheer, patting the bag at her waist. "But only a few dyes. Ola makes a unique hue that no one else has copied. She gave me a few vials." Jadaya reached into the bag and pulled out a stick about three inches long, twisted with fabric in three colors that grabbed the eye. One was the color of the sun's first light in the morning reaching across the sea, a pink that was warm and bright at the same time. The second was the blue of the sea on a calm day during ripening. The third Jadaya caressed with her fingers. "She created this one just for me, when I mentioned missing the mature grains at home." It was a rich golden brown that seemed to glimmer in the light.

"Is it shimmering?" Rylix asked, leaning closer to look at it.

"Yes. She crushed gold into flakes and mixed it in with the dye. She used something to make it bind to the fabric when you dye it. It should last a few suncycles, though eventually the flakes will fall out."

"That is ingenious. I suspect you will get a good deal for that. Will it work with silver?" Rylix watched the shimmer of the fabric, almost like someone entranced.

"She said yes, but silver was too expensive to make it worth it. Gold she can find on the beach after a good storm." Jadaya shrugged. If it caught on, Ola might make more, since gold was easy enough to obtain.

He nodded and looked out to the dock. Jadaya followed his gaze to land on Note walking up the gangplank. On his back, he carried two bags bigger than hers, his knives strapped to his waist, and a loose coat over his normal gear.

"Coat. I am lacking a coat," she said with a touch of worry. It had been so warm since she was here, bindings and a light shirt with a wrap had been plenty of clothing. She had an extra wrap or two, and her loincloth and bindings, but that was it really for clothes.

"You will survive until we reach Fivika. The weather should be warm enough, and I suspect you are not prone to burning from the sun's rays." Rylix soothed, his eyes still on the dock, but now all you could see were the Ged getting ready to set sail, jumping down to release the moorings. "Oh. This is… Interesting." His voice had taken a hollow, shocked tone, and the Ged on the dock also slowed down, turning to look at the two beings walking on the water from the open bay toward the dock. "I guess the gods have come to say goodbye?"

"Trader, what in the name of Aryix have you gotten me into?" Jolyx's voice hissed harshly behind them and Jadaya almost jumped. The woman had moved with such silent grace she had been unaware of someone coming up behind them.

"Exactly what I told you, my darling captain. An adventure." Rylix's voice sounded the same, but he kept his eyes on the two beings approaching the pier.

"Adventure rarely includes gods sticking their fingers in," she growled as she settled down next to Jadaya, watching them as they stepped off the water onto the deck. All the Aoisans on the dock had cleared their path, watching the two figures with a mix of reverence and worry.

Jadaya had a jumble of emotions raging through her, but for now she watched Note pivot at the top of the gangplank, heave a sigh, and drop his bag. With a blank look on his face, he moved back down and headed toward the divines.

This will be an interesting trip.

CHAPTER NINETEEN

NOTE

Note approached his gods, wondering why they were here. His emotions still rocked back and forth between rage and guilt at how he had addressed them. Deep down, it amazed him he was still alive. If one of his worshipers had treated him that way, death on the spot might have been too merciful of a response.

Yet here I am alive. Why? Why so many things?

Note bowed his head as he came to a stop before them. "Pel, Rian."

They looked at him for so long he wondered if they had not been coming for him, but for Ijo. His frayed patience had almost reached the snapping point when Rian spoke.

"We want to let you know we will watch and help when we can, but there is only so much we can do," she said, sounding apologetic. Her eyes were kind, and he wanted to fall at her feet, but refused to show weakness.

"Just as no prayer would reach the ears of my siblings, your words will rarely reach us once you set foot on their lands. But know this, I am the god of the ocean, and if you set foot in my waters, I can hear you. It is all I can offer besides my blessing." Pel looked at him with eyes that Note expected to see rage in, but instead he saw sorrow and that made him more uncomfortable than anger.

"We gift you with this," Rian said and held out a wrist cuff to him. With hands that wanted to shake, he reached out and took it from her. At first glance, he assumed it was leather, but it had scales and was supple. He lifted his head to look at them, frowning a bit.

"It is from one of the deeps monsters. It is laden with my magic and Rian's." Pel said, his voice serious and oddly tired. "Our parents kept the secret of how to truly enchant items. We lost that knowledge when they were dealt with. But with this on, you should heal rapidly and if you soak it with your tears, you can call upon us. But be aware, we have only the abilities within our realms of influence in other countries and all of us hoard our realms jealously. Mayhap our parents can provide you with more assistance. They are bound, not powerless."

Note bowed his head. The problem with meeting your gods is they were rarely as powerful and all-knowing as you had believed. Wanted to believe. Which meant you had to rescue yourself.

"Bless," he whispered. Then, in a stronger voice, "Can you tell me if the children are still alive? Or are we going to seek vengeance for the dead?"

Rian went silent, her head tilted back, then sighed. "Some still live, but how many I am unaware. My tears still find their skin on occasion, but until now I had paid little attention to where my people were. I will try to be more aware."

Note remembered that courtyard, the one he could see the sky from. Most of the priests and conductors avoided the rain, but every so often Note would feel the drops of her tears on his face. There was little more he could say. He looked up to see them watching the ship. Feeling quiet, he just waited, though his body vibrated with tension.

"The Exile. Her gods will not acknowledge her existence," Pel said. "We would take her; however, I think her path is not with Aois. She is not of the personality to live our lives." Pel turned his sea-colored eyes on Note. They changed with his mood ranging from clear blue to stormy black. "But neither are you."

Note felt his heart catch in his throat. Was he about to be made Exile as well? He locked his jaw and knees and just waited.

"And that grieves me. But Note, you are ours as long as you will have us. You will always have a home in Aois." Pel paused and looked at Rian as Note tried to make sure he remained standing, shocked at the words. Though was he sad or relieved that they still wanted him?

Rian reach out a hand but stopped before touching him. "If you find another whose path fits you better, you are free to follow that path, but you will not need to forsake us. It is the least we can do for what we have allowed to happen to you and the others. Even if it means releasing our parents."

It was the first time they admitted guilt, and he wished they had refused to. It was easier to be angry when that person was denying responsibility. And now, they said he could find his own path, belong to multiple gods. The idea filled him with both fear and wonder and an odd sense of sadness.

"You should go. I will do what I can to make your voyage to Fivika a safe and calm one." Pel turned away, then stopped and looked back. "But when you find our people, feel free to mete out vengeance for what you suffered. We will deal with Xyl if he dares to complain."

With those last words, Rian and Pel walked back to the end of the deck and onto the water. Then, between one step and the next, they were simply gone. Note turned to walk back to the ship and saw everyone watching him. The Aoisans moved aside as he walked by, an uncomfortable mix of fear and awe on their faces. But the Ged watched him with something closer to suspicion and worry.

Both expressions made his stomach twist, and he clenched his hands tight around the bracelet. Holding his head up, he strode up the plank and picked up his packs. "Where do these go?" If he pretended there was nothing strange about his gods visiting him, maybe they would lose these looks.

The Ged he understood. They followed the old god and as far as anyone knew, none of them walked Aria any longer. Locked away by their children. He froze for a second at the wording Pel used: 'dealt with'. What had that meant? They were headed to ask these same gods for assistance, assistance his gods were unable to provide. He spun to look for them, but of course, they had already disappeared. Just one more question that he would discover the answer for himself.

Will they refuse to help us because I belong to some of their captors?

Even more questions sparked, but he locked them away. This was stuff he would address in the quiet of the night, when no one was looking at him like he might hold the answers to something. Anything.

"Of course, my Aoisan friend. If you would but follow me, it would be my pleasure to show you to your palatial quarters," Rylix said with a grin that told Note the quarters were anything but palatial. He was correct. It took but a moment to hang his possessions in the baskets for that, their laces tied in a way that would tell him if anyone took liberties with his belongings. Then he headed back up to the deck.

The fresh air helped, but the sharp look from the captain made him wrap fingers around the hilts of his knives as she strode over to him.

"Do I need to worry about them sticking their meddling fingers into how I run my ship?" Jolyx stood over him, her eyes dark with annoyance. Rylix greeted her when she docked, so he already knew she had little interest or patience with the gods. None of the Ged cared about the new gods and they were regarded with suspicion.

It must be odd to live a life without feeling your gods' presence at all.

" Pel will do his best to ensure a smooth trip for us. Otherwise, I think they will not interfere. Or at least they should be quiet. I can address none of the other gods." He kept his voice steady and his feeling tamped down into submission.

Though expecting the divines to abide by their word might be the height of foolishness.

"I see. And that?" She pointed at the band he still held in his hand.

Note glanced at it and with careful movements put it around his left wrist, taking care to make sure it felt comfortable there. He refused to admit it felt as right as the knives on his thighs.

"A gift. A way for me to remember they do care, at least enough to do this. What more can anyone ask of a god?" He looked back up with a patently false smile. The one she gave him back was more teeth than lip.

"Keep it that way. Though any assistance on a sea voyage is not something I ever dismiss out of hand." With that comment, she spun on her heel and shouted at her crew to finish pulling in lines.

Note went over and joined Jadaya leaning against the railing. She gave him a nod and a smile. He realized she lacked the look of almost everyone else. Not fear or awe or even suspicion. Just a smile tinged with stress. But given how she wrapped her hand around the handrail, he figured she was more worried about the ship going out to sea than the gods.

In a rare moment of sympathy, he offered conversation. "You seem to be the only one that is unbothered by the gods coming to talk to me."

Jadaya turned her head, looking at him with a frown. "Why would that bother people?"

Note snorted in derision. "Look at them. Even my countrymen are wary or scared." He watched her gaze at others, the Aoisans on the dock, talking in quiet huddles, the Ged giving him wary looks. An honest smile slipped on to her face.

"I see. I thought little of it."

Note gave her a look, eliciting more information. If nothing else, it would help him figure out how she thought.

"I was trained as a warrior. Selected to help defend the temple and the divines. But about three suncycles ago, Yika selected me to be one of her guards. Her personal honor guard. I saw her almost daily for cycles. She was always polite, but we held her in awe. Her beauty, grace, even how she spoke, was what most women longed to be like. I know her bed partners were usually released from being Chosen or put on messenger duty when she tired of them. But someone talking to our gods was expected. It is one of the things that still confuses me about Aois, how remote your gods are. Ours sat in on the laws, the discussions, meted punishment, and oversaw harvests." She gave him another sad smile. "You talking to them was the most normal thing for me. The yelling you did, however…" She trailed off, shaking her head with a wry smile.

Note's curiosity rose. "No one yelled at your gods?"

Jadaya's eyes widened, and she laughed as she shook her head. "Not and lived, that I know of. It is unthinkable. Even now, I know of no one brave enough to yell at them." Her brows furrowed. Note still had reservations about the fuzzy lines of fur on faces above eyes, but it was better than the clumps of hair the Chars had on their chins and cheeks. "I only remember the divines raising their voices once and that was to each other. To be honest, it sounded like a lovers' quarrel, and I focused on something else so I would not overhear."

"Interesting. Though no one yells at our gods either. Just me." He found no shame or guilt in his heart. They had earned it. But it probably scared a tenset off Ijo and she had lost too much already.

"You had no fear?"

"Of?" He looked at her, trying to figure out where they were in the conversation.

"Them striking you down," she said with a look of surprise. "Zula would have killed anyone who approached him in that manner, much less the yelling. Yika would have ordered me to kill you where you stood."

"Would you have?" Note was curious now. His previous travels had been as an escaped slave, fearing at any moment someone would grab him and return him to the Char. He realized now it had been a false fear. No one would have ever returned him, but it had taken until Agrina before he fully believed it.

"Yes. Without hesitation," she replied immediately. "They are my gods, and I would have never even thought about it."

"*Were* your gods, Jadaya. Now you have the freedom to find new ones." Note wondered what made him say that, but from her flinch it had not reassured her as he intended.

CHAPTER TWENTY

LAZUL

Lazul enjoyed the ride to the next city. It took most of the day and the lord should have a room ready for him and his staff. Zayn, of course, would stay in the temple. It had been a delightful trip with Zayn barely speaking to him the majority of the ride, either still sulking or annoyed. Either way, there had been sunshine, blue skies, and pleasant temperatures.

Captain Marcel rode up next to him. "Sire, it looks like rain is coming. It is advisable we increase our speed."

Lazul looked behind him and sighed. Clouds were building, a sign that Xyl's good mood had vanished.

What would it be like to only have seasonal weather?

The question seemed idle, but other than the few days of unexpected clear skies and sun in the middle of shelter season, Xyl's moods made everything more difficult than they needed to be.

"I agree. Tell the rest to pick up the pace." Putting his words to action, Lazul slapped his mustang into a canter, knowing they would most likely get wet, regardless. The mustang heaved a sigh but sped up. The first crack of lightning behind them had him picking up his pace. Lazul looked behind them and saw the massive clouds with lightning crackling across them, and growled.

What has angered Xyl now?

Zayn was not next to him, and in the next finger or two, talking became almost impossible between the crack of thunder, the noise of the harnesses as all the animals had decided they wanted to be inside, and the wagon full of supplies chattering and groaning as the jacks pulled it.

They had reached the city gates as the rain started. It opened with a soft drizzle, not the downpour Lazul had expected. The guards recognized them, not that gates had been barred since before Lazul's great-grandfather's time, and waved them in. With a path cleared for them, it ensured they made good speed to Lord Garnet's house, but they were still soaked to the bone by the time they made it. To Lazul's relief, the skies only opened up moments after they stepped into the covered stables. Stablehands were waiting for them and in no time at all, Lazul found himself, Captain Malac, and Zayn in front of a warm fire with hot drinks in their hands.

"Sire, is there anything else you need?" The housekeeper asked, her hands clenched tightly in front of her, as if expecting him to rage.

When did my people learn to fear me? I believe no one has seen me lose my temper since I was sixteen.

"No. Bless. But I am well," Lazul said, sinking deeper into the comfortable chair and sipping at the hot fruist.

"That will be all, Bismu," Lord Mandar Garnet's voice came from the door.

The person in question, Bismu, dropped her head in a quick bow and scurried out. Lord Garnet walked in, looking almost as worried as the housekeeper.

"Sire, I am glad you made it here intact. When the storm swept up on us, I feared the worst. Is there anything else I can do for you? Your possessions are being put in your room as we speak." He moved to where their small group was. Malac still stood, while Zayn had sunk into the other chair, looking as cold and miserable as Lazul felt.

Lord Mandar Garnet followed the normal body type for the Charinsky. He had a blocky build, blond hair, pale rosy skin, prone to putting on weight around the middle, and thick fingers that always appeared swollen. But by all accounts, he was an excellent manager of this city and area, and he was capable of interesting conversations at the dinner table. Or at least Actin praised his reports on a regular basis.

"A hot bath after dinner this evening would not be turned down," Lazul said with a smile. The heated fruist was chasing away the chills, and he knew Lord Garnet had installed a heated water cistern system a few suncycles ago. Meaning he could pull a bath in peace. The one for the castle was still being constructed. Apparently having stone a hand thick made it more complicated to put in the water system.

There are days when being a king is much less opulent than people would assume.

"Of course, sire," Garnet said, a huge smile on his face. "I know you will enjoy it." He had a right to be proud, as it had been a new idea when he had the system installed, but the invention had caught on quickly.

"I, however, would beg a favor of you, Lord Garnet," Zayn said in a tired voice. Lazul glanced at him, eyes narrowing, but then he relaxed. He bet himself five copper that Zayn would ask to stay here. A crack of thunder underscored that thought.

I will have to endure his presence, but sending any man out in this storm would be cruel. Even him.

"Of course, Cantor, how may my house assist you?" Lazul let the words, which were not quite as enthusiastic as the ones for him, soothe the idea of having to spend dinner with Zayn. At least he had a bath to look forward to.

"Given the weather, I would impose upon you to spend the night here instead of the temple. I fear I might catch my death if I attempted to brave the outsides right now."

"That is easy enough. I will see that a room is set up for you. The cook will serve dinner in two fingers. I hope that meets with your wishes."

"That will be acceptable, Mandar." Lazul waved him away. "Let me sit with my fruist and two fingers will be about right for it to have calmed my temper and warmed my body."

"Of course, sire. Please call out if you need anything." With that, Lord Mandar Garnet headed back out.

"Is there a reason Xyl is this angry?" Lazul asked into the quiet. The room was filled with the crackling of fire and the occasional thunder that breached the walls of the house.

When Zayn was slow to respond, Lazul pulled his attention away from the fire and looked at the man. A frown of concentration pinched Zayn's face together, making him look older than he was by at least ten suncycles.

"Zayn?" Lazul asked. Malac stood at one side of the fire, letting it warm his back as he monitored the rest of the room, guarding him as was his duty. There were vague noises outside the room, telling of people getting dinner ready, but otherwise they were alone.

"I am unsure. And this confuses me. This storm," Zayn waved his hand above his head, the frown still on his face. "It is similar to what I have seen when songs were missed on important dates or the singer's voice was flawed. Not in the middle of a random tenday, when the Day of Remembrance is less than a mooncycle away. The songs were sung correctly, and the sun shone clear in the sky for the last few days. I know not where this rage is coming from." His hands were wrapped around his cup, the steam wreathing his face.

"Could that have been natural?" Malac's input into the conversation had Zayn lifting his head and sneering at the young man.

"The clergy of Xyl make a study of weather that puts even the poorest farmer to shame. We know how and why the weather works and when the gods interfere. There is no way that was a normal storm. Though at this point I have no idea if Charinsky has experienced normal weather in suncycles." Zayn's sneer faded halfway through, and he sagged a bit. "I will request an extra set of songs to Xyl when I reach the temple tomorrow. It would be good for our inspection, regardless."

They all fell silent until Lord Garnet appeared to let them know dinner was served. With both regret at leaving the fire and dread at knowing what was ahead of him, Lazul let himself be led to the dining area. It was a large room with stone floors, walls of wood sanded to a sheen, and a table that was set for six.

Lazul sat one end of the table, while Mandar took the other end. A young woman, maybe twenty suncycles old, sat at his right, while Malac was to his left. Lazul took comfort in that at least he would be unable to easily talk to Zayn all evening, and worst case, Malac was intelligent conversation.

"Sire, let me introduce you to my wife, Mali, and my daughter Merel." Garnet's voice was filled with pride and Lazul hoped it was not just because of the beauty that Merel obviously had taken from her mother. Mali had long blonde hair with streaks of silver through it that made it shimmer in the soft light, a full figure of someone settling happily into their fifties, and bright blue eyes that seemed to sparkle with happiness. Her daughter had inherited her eyes and curvy figure that would resemble her mother's as she aged.

"Sire, it is an honor to meet you," Merel said with a curtsey and a little girl's voice that made him wince. After they were seated, and fruist was delivered, the food came out. No one spoke as the servants laid out the feast, steam rising from it, and a fresh cup of hot fruist went a long way to improving his mood. They all waited until he had been served, before serving themselves. The first finger of dinner they spent serving and asking for condiments to be passed.

Then the real torture started.

"Merel, tell King Lazul about your accomplishments," Lord Garnet prompted.

Lazul set his face in a welcoming smile and turned to the young woman, who flushed. Unfortunately for her, it was an unattractive reaction. Her skin mottled going down to her chest, where her cleavage was clearly displayed.

"Yes, Father." She still spoke in the high falsetto of a false girl, and he wondered who had told her to speak like that. It grated on his nerves. "I have been weaving and learning to manage household budgets. My mother has taken me as an apprentice to learn how to manage large homesteads."

Lazul tilted his head. The voice still grated, but the knowledge was interesting. He glanced over at Mali.

"My father was Lord Quartz, sire," she said as an explanation. "I helped my mother run the employee side of his mining operations."

It took him a moment to find the information in his brain, but then he remembered her father ran one of the larger mines in Charinsky. The mine produced tons of gems, stone, and coal. It also had hundreds of workers, along with healers and the kitchens needed to feed them. It was a good skill for any queen to have.

"Are you enjoying the lessons?" He asked, but focused more on the steaming meat. The dish was meat wrapped in a flaky pastry, and his mouth watered as he lifted it up. To his delight, it met his expectations of flavor, and he only paid partial attention to what Merel said.

"It is interesting, and I like to think I am good at it. But my genuine passion is in my weaving." She spoke quietly about it, going into excruciating detail. "The weight of thread is so important. There have been multiple times I needed to shred and re-spin to get the correct weight. Or even combine threads for the patterns I create."

He nodded and kept a smile on his face as his eyes glazed over. As she spoke about her accomplishments and her passion, he thought that in many ways Actin would be the perfect husband for her. He cared nothing about weaving, other than having enough blankets and clothes to keep him warm. But her passion was at least enough to keep her from being too boring.

Malac earned his pay by occasionally asking a leading question of her mother or father, while Zayn ate, his face and brow furrowed in concentration. Lazul suspected his mind was on thoughts that had nothing to do with their dinner conversation.

When the dessert had been served, a wonderful berry compote mixed with whipped cream, Lazul ended his torture. "Lord Garnet. The meal has been wonderful and the company engaging. At this point, I would dearly love to experience the bath you have touted." He allowed exhaustion to creep into his voice, not feigned, just normally suppressed.

"Of course, sire. If you would follow me."

One finger later, Lazul lowered himself into steaming water, a smile crossing his face as he closed his eyes and let the heat soak into his bones. Merel was a nice girl, but she was just that: a girl. She was barely twenty. He had seen over forty suncycles. He needed someone he could talk to, and she would be bored by life at the castle.

Another inspection tomorrow, then we ride on. For now, I will enjoy this bath.

He let his mind drift as the heat relaxed him wholly.

CHAPTER TWENTY-ONE

JADAYA

"W*ere* your gods, Jadaya. Now you have the freedom to find new ones."
The words Note had said rang in her ears like a peal of bells and she found herself unable to ignore them. She was unable to imagine herself looking different. This was the body she saw in the reflecting pools and in her mind. How could she abandon who she was?

The first bounce of the ship as it left the shelter of the bay jerked her back to the present and her eyes locked on to the white mouths coming up to devour her. Her hands tightened on the railing so hard she felt it splinter under her fingers. The sharp wood jabbed into her as Jolyx yelled from behind her.

"Get the sails up and head out. We are going to Fivika!" A roar of approval filled the ship as the crew went about their jobs.

In an effort to run from her own thoughts, she turned her back to the hungry sea and watched the Ged run about the ship. They resembled Rylix in coloring and hair, all of them with sun-kissed brown skin, curly brown hair, and quick smiles that seemed to come so easily to them. There were multiple women on the ship wearing the same as their male counterparts. They all wore wrap pants, loose tops, though the women had colorful bindings across their chests.

I need to ask how their bindings work; they are more supportive than what I wear.

Their movements were organized like a dance, and she rarely saw a misstep. Before she realized it, the harbor had receded into the distance and the wind filled the sails with a bright sun above them.

She had almost forgotten that Note was next to her until the crew burst into a song that went with the motions of the ship and Note flinched. Jadaya turned to look at him and saw a face set into remote lines. He still faced the sea, letting the music wash around him. Even she found her fingers tapping to the rhythm as the song ebbed and swelled. Note was a stone it swirled around leaving him untouched.

"What do you see when you look at the sea?" he asked.

"Danger, challenge, the unknown waiting to swallow us," she said quietly, focused on the waves that crashed against the hull of the ship. Her mouth opened to ask why he remained silent, but instead she turned back to the sea. "This is a rescue mission we are certain to die on. So why does it feel more like an adventure?"

Note's shoulders unclenched the tiniest bit, and he cast her a side glance from his pale eyes. "Because this time you are choosing to leave and go someplace new? Besides, it will take us mooncycles to get to the Granite no matter how fast we go."

"About that," she said, looking at the coast of Aois as they went up. "You act like they already have the children, but it will take us mooncycles to get there. Why not just go the way they went?" Jadaya hated looking like an idiot, but she was curious.

"Gods," he said with a bitter twist to his mouth. He must have seen her expression, because he heaved a sigh and continued. "Besides the fact that we are going to plead our case with the old gods, hopefully for something to assist this fool's errand, getting from Aois to Charinsky involves the gods meddling." He touched a new wrist band on his left wrist as he spoke.

"What does that mean?"

"Have you seen maps of the world?" He still watched the sea, not her.

"Only what I saw in the council chambers. I know Zuyika well, but outside that land I am unsure of much," she admitted, trying not to sound as pathetic as she felt.

Rather than laugh at her lack of knowledge, he only nodded and spoke again. "You saw the deeps that run between our two lands?"

She nodded. The deeps were both fact and legend. The places where monsters lurked and would gladly destroy a ship. Legends said the deeps were created for the monsters to guard the Usurper, to prevent him from ever escaping his prison.

"Well, there are ways across that. If you have a god that will distract the creatures that live there, or you are crazy enough to attempt crossing in the few shallower areas. Those are possible. The ships the Chars take dart across that area and pray the captain is right and that the gods that aid them are paying attention." There was a level of bitterness there she was beginning to understand.

"That is only half of the issue, children," Jolyx said from behind them. Jadaya turned to see her standing there watching them. "Come on. I can show you and we need to talk about our route anyhow." She motioned them to follow her with a wave of her hand and turned. A quick whistle got Rylix's and Tylax's attention. They all followed her into what was obviously the map room.

A large table took up the center of the room with strange equipment laying on it. Along the walls were scores of rolled up parchments. There were lanterns in every corner filling the room with a warm light. On the table, held in place by clamps on each corner, was a large map.

"We are here." Jolyx stabbed at the map with a finger along the coast of one of the land masses. "The deeps are here and here." She pointed to a series of dark blobs running between the Aois land and Zuyika, and then between Wysko and Charinsky. "It is not possible to get from one side to the other because of the deeps. They would need to deal with the currents. It is entering ripening, so these are the active currents." Jolyx pointed to fainter arrows that pointed up along the coast of Aois. There were also arrows that pushed from Fivika toward Charinsky.

"Once harvest sets in, they will change to this." She pulled another map and this time Jadaya realized they were labeled "Ripening Currents" and "Harvest Currents". This map showed arrows coming from the deeps toward Aois and down along Aois to swirl around at the bottom of the land mass. While the currents that had led to Fivika and then Charinsky were now pointed toward Aois.

Note leaned over, his pretense of uncaring gone. "I have never seen this. Is this why they raid at that time of year?"

"Yes. They probably go down and around, then dart in and out. Those currents only last for about six tendays. We already missed the strongest part. If we had left a tenday ago, this trip would take about seven days. That is how fast they are. But that is pushing a crew, especially with children on board. Honestly, I wonder how many actually survive." Her words put a damper on everything.

"Quite a few, but then I am unsure how many were taken." Note said quietly, his face passive.

"Well, we are going to assume most of them survived," Jadaya said with a forced smile. "And those who are there we will rescue."

Jolyx raised her hand. "That is all on you. As far as I am concerned, my job is to get you to Fivika." She looked at them with stern eyes. "I am not a hero, nor am I interested in being one. Regarding Calin," she said and reached to pull out another map. This one had Aois on right side of the map instead of the left. She tapped the top of it. "You can see the currents going up and out, then back down. It is the reason Calin is the preferred harbor for anything coming from Aois, Zuyika, or Wysko."

Jadaya let her eyes travel along the path and could see the currents that drove the directions of the ships. From what she knew, Zuyika had fishing boats, but that was it. None of them were involved in sailing across the sea, happy to live within their own world. For the first time, she wondered how much her fellow Chosen were missing out on by not getting to see the world around them.

"I estimate the trip will take us two tendays. We stop at the tip of Aois to resupply fresh water, but then it is a solid tenday plus across this stretch." She pointed at the wide gap of water. "Straight across would only be about seven days, but the harbor is down the coast enough that it will add a few days." She straightened and looked at them. "Any questions or concerns?" Her eyes went over each of them, but Jadaya saw no questions on anyone's face. "Good, then dismissed."

Tylax was first out the door, his voice echoing as he started shouting at people whose performance was not up to his standards. Rylix followed him, a bounce to his step that implied excitement. A feeling Jadaya wished she could share. The idea of going back out and looking at those rolling waves, all dying to pull her down into their depths, made her stomach twist. In an effort to delay going back out there, she turned to Jolyx as Note headed to the door.

"I did have a question, though it has nothing to do with the ship or our journey," she said, looking at Jolyx.

"Oh? And what might that be?" Jolyx rolled up the maps, but gave Jadaya a side glance with an arched brow.

"It is about your bindings—how do you do them to get that effect?" She moved her hands out away from her chest in a curving motion.

Behind her she heard Note choke on what sounded like laughter as Jolyx blinked, then laughed.

"You are asking about my bindings and how they support my breasts?" she asked, like she had trouble understanding the question.

Jadaya nodded, almost welcoming the censure or amusement, if it delayed having to go back to watch the sea. It was more relaxing watching it from on land than on the flimsy planks of wood that were the only things keeping you from its belly. "Yes. The only bindings I know of flatten and secure. They do not provide for any roundness. I knew some who would be in pain at the end of the day because of their bindings. Yours bindings make your breasts look more like…" she struggled to find the word then shrugged. "Breasts, not fat men."

Jolyx laughed, a sound that filled the cabin, but it was a sound of amusement, not mockery. "I see what you mean," she said after she stopped laughing. "Come by my cabin this evening and I can show you." She gave Jadaya a hard look. "Though unless you are tightening your own bindings to the point of discomfort and providing extra padding, you will not achieve this look." She grinned and thrust out her chest a bit. "But I am willing to show you."

"Bless," Jadaya said, and then realized she was out of things to say. She nodded and headed toward the door, leaving the captain to put away the last of the maps. She walked back out and found a corner of the ship where she was relatively out of the way. Once settled, Jadaya watched the Ged move through their jobs and tried to forget about the monsters out there. The sea that had already tried to eat her once.

Note joined her after a while, sitting down and just watching the crew, they watched and let the music, chatter, and activity wash over them, a part of it, yet somehow separate. Neither of them moved until the bell for dinner sounded, and then she gladly retreated to the mess and away from the never-ending water.

CHAPTER TWENTY-TWO

NOTE

It had been so long since he found himself out to sea that Note had forgotten how much he loved the water. The never-ending, ever-changing waves soothed his heart and let his mind flow. He had also forgotten how much the sea Ged loved to sing. Not the same way the Aois sang. Those songs were sang in specific harmonies or as single songs that meshed with all the other songs people were singing. They were rarely the same song, though often in the same key. They would weave in and out of harmony, and no one noticed if you were silent.

Not so on a ship. They all sang the same song, all the voices rising in chorus, letting the beat move them through the chores and their days. It pounded on him as if his body and mind were a drum. Their beats and friendly encouragement were enough to make him want to scream. They had even coaxed Jadaya into singing, and her voice was rarely in key, much to his annoyance. Actually, few Ged had the ability to remain in key or tune, which meant all the singers had flat areas, off key notes, and generally were jarring to an ear raised on perfect voices. It was torture. And they wanted him to sing with them.

Even the idea of letting a single note of song out of his mouth caused bile to rise. Memories of rewards, punishments, songs that were breathtakingly beautiful, and the feel of hands on his skin roiled around in his mind. He avoided everyone, hiding from the songs and the memories. His swing chair in the depth of the ship's hold let him remain obscured from most everyone. Except when they came seeking him.

"Note. Is everything well?" Jadaya's voice broke into his seething need to get away from the songs, from the memories that corrupted what he had once enjoyed. These songs that pulled at him to join them in a way the Aoisan songs never did.

"Yes. Is there an issue?" He kept his head resting on his arms, swaying with the movement of the ship. Keeping his eyes closed, he tracked her movement by the creak of wood and the whisper of cloth.

"You are down here, not on the deck where the weather is beautiful and even the sea is clear." Her voice carried no accusation, but still there was curiosity there.

They had stopped to top up the water and supplies at the tip of Aois. Now they were on the run to Calin. He ached to be off the ship so there would be silence instead of song. Surely, no other group of people had the annoying habit of singing while they worked.

"Too noisy. Easier to think down here." That was a flat lie. It was stuffy and smelled of unwashed bodies and whatever goods were being hauled for trade. But the wood surrounding him muffled sound, which left him alone with his own thoughts.

"Ah." She stood there for a moment. "You dislike the singing?"

"That obvious?" He figured that fact that he never sang, and left when anyone started, had to be expected behavior by now. But he would put the knife to his throat first before asking anyone else to quit singing.

"All the Aoisans I have met sing. But you avoid it." The question hung there in the air, unasked yet heard.

"What do you think happens to the children that are taken?" He avoided the subject, his eyes still closed, but even thinking about that time made him want to gag or scream.

There was a rustle and creak, and he figured she had sat in the swing chair across from him, though unless she had lit the lamps, her skin would make her all but invisible down here.

"I am unsure." Her voice was soft as she spoke, the darkness adding a strange intimacy to their conversation. "I was taken as a child too, or offered up depending on your perspective, when I was Chosen. I was trained and provided everything I could want. But we, both the Chosen and our parents, saw it as an honor. There was no force. Maybe that makes the difference?"

Note fell silent, he had been unaware of what Chosen encompassed. "Could you leave?"

"And go where?" Her voice held confusion as she responded.

"Home?" How could she not know where to go?

"The temple was my home. I supposed I cried at the beginning. But there were others there, friends, Elike." She had a strange hitch when she said that name, like it hurt, but she fought it. "We were educated, trained, given jobs, provided with everything. Why would I leave? If I remember correctly, my parents had little, and losing a mouth to feed benefited the entire family. The reward of having a child Chosen is a lower tithe for ten suncycles. I was never hungry or cold in the temple. I figured these captured Aoisans lives must be horrible if you are so desperate to rescue them."

Note fell silent thinking.

What was the difference between us? Is it just attitude?

"You regarded your being taken as a good thing?"

"Yes. We were told by our teachers and the caretakers. Over and over, so by the time we were almost adult we knew how good our lives were. Besides, we made regular trips out to assist others and saw the children who were not Chosen. Our lives were better." She paused and hummed a bit. "I also saw the Offering Day. Hordes of parents there with little ones, all hoping they might be Chosen. The joy and relief on their faces assured me it was good."

"No one ever argued or feared it?"

"Maybe?" Again that soft hum as she thought. He gave her the time. "Perhaps the more wealthy resented it? But I suspect, looking back at the things I ignored then, that it was still to their benefit. Some of the Chosen had extra treats or possessions the majority of us never had. But we were not hurt?" Her voice lilted up on the last word as if it was a question, as if she no longer knew what was the truth.

Note heaved a sigh. "Maybe they were similar, but for me it was always a prison with punishments and the corruption of singing. That might be what I can never forgive. That it made me hate song." He could still enjoy music, but voices lifted with that music sliced through his heart like a knife.

"We were punished when we broke the rules," she said in a hesitant voice. "But we knew what it was."

"What was your punishment?" He was honestly curious. Their punishments had not been minor things.

"Run laps, push-up, no dessert with dinner, occasionally extra chores like cleaning out the needs rooms." Her response was immediate, and he sensed no lies in her statement.

"Ah. Maybe they treated the other singers better than I. All I know is my experience and those of the ones I was kept with."

"Will you tell me? There is something that is driving you, Ijo, and your gods. Something more than being honored prisoners." If there had been sympathy, he might have lost his temper, but all he could hear was confusion in her voice.

Why not tell her? Get it out there. The darkness will make it easier.

With his eyes closed, he spoke. "I suppose the first few tenday were tolerable.

We were unhappy and wanted to go home. The lack of ocean water hurt more than I realized until later. But we had to sing. At first we refused. Until they whipped one of the older boys in front of us." He heard her gasp, but kept on talking. "He died of his wounds, as they said only singers get treatment and he refused to sing. So we sang. Morning, noon, night we sang. Then there were the holy days where we sang for ten or twenty fingers at a time. All to keep Xyl happy.

"Some of the priests and priestess, and trust me, the women were no better, had special friends among the singers. If you caught their eyes and made them happy, you would get extra rewards. Sweets, new clothes, extra time in the salt bath. We learned to pretend to be happy. It was an odd sense of having to do nothing but sing, but causing any trouble could mean death."

His words faltered, and he sucked in air through his nose, trying to focus. "Some of the older girls were encouraged to spend bed time with the one intact older male singer. I could never decide if I envied him or felt sorry for him." He could feel Jadaya's gaze on him.

" When the boys were about twelve cycles old, the conductors started watching us carefully. The older ones just looked sad. We were confused." If he spoke about it as a generic term, maybe he could get through this. When talking to the gods and Ijo, he had been blunt, wanting to shock and hurt them. Jadaya. He just wanted her to understand.

How odd is it we were both taken from our parents, but her experiences were mostly positive and mine was mostly negative?

"They wanted to make sure the boys kept their high voices. Xyl rarely enjoys bass. He prefers the light voices of women. We were told it makes him think that Percit is singing to him. At the time I just thought they wanted us to singer at a higher note. Then I was taken away for 'special' training. The conductors took me to the infirmary and make me drink something horrible. It smelled so bad, but from the look on their faces, I knew I had to drink it."

He was no longer talking about it happening to someone else but him. He had no idea how to stop, as he only had his experience. "You felt dizzy, then you fell asleep. A hard, deep sleep. I heard more than one boy never woke up from that. But maybe that was preferable. Because when I woke up," he paused and swallowed. "Part of my body was gone."

Note forced his voice to remain stable, crying now would prove how weak he was. He would never allow himself to be weak again. "They had cut off my balls." There was a slight intake of breath from her, but he kept going. "I still have a penis, but the part of my body that lets me father a child was removed. It kept us from becoming adult men. My voice never changed and my body remained like a boy's. It happened to all the boys except one, the one that was encouraged to have bedtime with the girls as soon as they achieved their fertile cycles."

A long, slow sigh escaped from where Jadaya sat. "Note," she whispered.

"So yes. I hate singing, all of it. I had to do it day in and day out, or they would not only punish me but others. The price for disobedience could be someone else's life. We were given things. We never went hungry or cold, but our job as boys was to sing. The girls were to sing and have bedtime with our intact singer. And most of us learned to tolerate, if not enjoy, being the special pet of a priest or priestess. It is amazing what you can tolerate when there are no options."

They sat in silence in that dark hold until she moved. "I do not pretend to understand what you went through, though I now I understand the pressure to get there. Most of the boys taken were too young to be maimed so, correct?"

"Yes," he responded, his voice thick with unshed tears. The words he used with Ijo and the gods had been harsher. Raped. Cut. Abused. But he had no knowledge if for Jadaya, given she was raised by gods, if those acts would horrify her.

"Then we will rescue them. I was taken, but no matter what I feel for my divines, no child was ever maimed, and our punishments were never that severe. The one child I knew who refused to be Chosen, they returned to his parents. And bed times with children would have resulted in death." She gave a funny laugh, half sob, half humor. "I was made Exile and branded because I dared to be intimate with a woman. I chose poorly. It was one of their laws, no same-sex intimacy, and I broke that law. But even so, I was whipped and branded, but I was not maimed as part of my service. And I was not a child. Note, I—"

"Bless." His voice was low and thick. "It is enough that you know. I would ask you, Jadaya, not to share. I have no desire to be seen as less than I am, regardless of what I am lacking."

"You are still Note. With or without body pieces. But I will tell them you have reasons to avoid singing, the rest is yours to tell." Again he heard the sounds of her standing and moving away. In the darkness, he let tears run down his face, ones he kept locked away for over ten suncycles.

CHAPTER TWENTY-THREE

ZAYN

Zayn sat at the latest dinner trotting out prospective wives for King Lazul. It provided him with amusement on a trip that contained too much annoyance to be enjoyable. The latest offering was a girl barely in her teens. He thought her name was Cupri, maybe. While he knew a conductor or two that would have enjoyed having her in their bed, it was obvious Lazul cringed at the very idea.

It is inconvenient having a king with morals.

The thought drifted through his mind, and he grabbed it and pulled it back. That was the root of the problem. Lazul had morals. Not just those behaviors that Xyl and Percit taught were right, but other concepts, most likely put in his head by his Delconan mother. And those ideas were putting the singers, the people, and his own pleasures at risk.

"Do you agree, Cantor?" Cupri asked, her voice so innocent and naïve that he thought of all the ways he could use her. Ways to break her. It would be fun. With effort, he kept those thoughts off his face.

"I do apologize, my lady. I was thinking of the inspection tomorrow and my thoughts were elsewhere. What was the question?" He kept his smile innocuous.

"I wanted to know if you agreed that the songs of remembrance were better than the songs of mourning?" Cupri was so serious, he blinked.

They are songs. They keep Xyl pacified. What else matters?

"You are right, of course. Those songs were written by masters in the later suncycles and have proven to make Xyl remember how happy he was with Percit." The glib answer rolled off his tongue. "But on that note, I believe I need to head out to the temple. Sire, we will be ready for you by five fingers after dawn."

Lazul nodded, a complacent look on his face. Did the man have to look like a sheep all the time? That was the problem. They needed a wolf as king, not this sheep who was unable to see how his courtiers were herding him.

"Very well, Zayn, I will see you in the morn. And my dear Lord Feldspar, I believe it is time for me to find my chambers. The travel today has left me most exhausted." Lazul rose as he spoke, signaling an end to the dinner for all of them.

The moue of disappointment on the girl's face made the relief on Lazul's more amusing. Zayn left them with his farewells and headed to the temple. It was only a finger's walk from Feldspar's estate, so rather than taking his mustang, he had walked to the temple, and now walked back to the estate. It gave him time to clear his mind and process.

This was a medium-sized temple in the city of Quartz. He would stay in the visiting quarters tonight. They had known this was coming, so they had quarters ready for him, but his reason for coming back as dinner ended had more to do with the treat waiting for him in the temple. However, it was not something Lazul should see or would approve of.

He slid into the temple, glad to see the head priestess waiting for him. He had selected her specifically many suncycles ago. She shared his predilections, though she preferred them older, at least twelve. By that point, he felt they were too old, though occasionally a unique flavor added some spice to his treats.

"Cantor," Cire said with a nod to him. She had reapplied ash below her eyes, though he knew she cared little for Xyl or Percit, simply the power of her position.

"Cire. I trust everything is ready for tomorrow?" They walked towards the quarters for the priests and he scanned the areas as he walked.

"Yes. All the singers were promised rewards of sweets and an extra five fingers of outside time once the inspection is completed. They have also been informed that if there are any problems, all of them will be whipped and one will no longer need to worry about Xyl." Her voice was smooth as she kept up with him. Her blond hair had hints of red in it, suggesting one of her ancestors had been from Delcona.

"Good. And the play areas?" They both knew he referred to the rooms where the priests took rewards for their service, not the standard walled courtyards for the singers.

"Cleaned and set up to mimic the visiting room like what you have. All toys that are inappropriate have been locked in my personal chest, which, from what you have said, Lazul would never think to look in." She had a sneer in her voice at Lazul's name that mimicked the thoughts Zayn had earlier.

"Good. And the refreshments?" He had given no orders, more curious as to what she would come up with than any worry the evidence would not be hidden.

A slow smile stretched across her face. "I think you will enjoy this. You mentioned Lazul prefers white fruists?"

Zayn nodded as they continued a circuit through the temple, seeing if anything remained to be cleaned or altered prior to tomorrow.

"I recently came across an additive. It makes a person more agreeable and less likely to worry about things. I put a tiny amount in the white fruist. The amount will be small enough. There is no risk of making him act obviously different, but he will be easier to distract and will sleep very well the next night. Higher doses just make you giddy and uninclined to move." Her voice was soft, barely carrying past his ears.

Zayn paused to look at her. "Is there a reason? He has been remarkably easy to distract over the last few suncycles."

She shrugged. "Extra precautions. There are a few singers that looked too mutinous for my comfort. I would prefer to be able to blame any inappropriate behavior on something innocuous and have him be easily persuaded to ignore the disruption. If you are concerned, it is easy enough to change out the fruist."

He shook his head. "No. I am encouraged by your initiative. Are you sure you have no desire to come serve as my assistant in Granite? We could control almost everything in the country."

Cire shook her head. "I am honored by the offer, but I prefer to rule over my small territory. The amount of effort it would take to convince the others to fear me would distract me. The constant politics would be most annoying."

"Ah. Yes, I can understand that." He remembered his younger days and the constant scheming for position and power. It had taken him ten suncycles to get to the position of assistant to the cantor, then another suncycle before he arranged an accident to eliminate the man. One of the few things the former cantor had done that impressed him had been the removal of Lazul's parents, King Jet and Queen Malaia. It had been impressive. An accident that no one suspected had been sabotage. But it was also why he wished she would take the position. As she could not be the cantor, Xyl decreed it had to be a male, therefore it kept him safe from her. As it was, he would never dare allow himself to have an assistant.

"Is there anything else I should be aware of?" They had climbed to the next level, and he looked into a couple of the singers' suites. One or two heads raised as he opened the door and glanced in, but there were few new singers here and they knew anyone opening the door in the night usually meant there was an issue. Most heads remained motionless, pretending to be sound asleep. The rooms were neat, well-appointed, and only the fact that no window was large enough for even a skinny child to slip through provided any indication of it not being a normal room.

"No. They are scheduled for normal songs tomorrow. Their harmony is perfect. The only thing we have to worry about is any surprises. But I have done everything possible to ensure that does not happen."

Zayn nodded, believing her when she said that. The last stop was the needs rooms, and he blinked. "You have put in the new water cisterns and the heat?"

"Yes. Though for the salt baths, the water remains cool. But we installed the upgrades in both their needs rooms and the priests'." A slight tone of smugness filled her voice, and he understood. He had tried for two suncycles to get those improvements put in, with no luck.

"How? I see all the ledgers. I know there are not enough tithes to afford that." It was a valid question. Each town gave about one twentieth of their taxes to the temple in each town. The town itself kept a quarter for their own infrastructure needs. Another tenth went to his temple, the rest went to the royal treasury. It paid for the roads, guard, king, and to buy food in the suncycles Xyl could not be convinced to allow enough sun in. Those cycles were why few complained about the taxes. When your children had no food, food from the king made you indebted.

I need to remember that and start a fund in the temples to provide food and other supplies to those that are without. It would be a good way to endear the populace to us even more.

Cire smiled. It transformed her into a stunning woman and for a moment, Zayn wondered why he had no desire for her. He let it go. The desire for power and the power to take what he wanted was more than enough. "No, we did not. But we have an experienced master craftsman in the city, and he was willing to trade his labor in exchange for one of the singers to go to his home and sing for him."

Zayn opened his mouth to protest, anger filling him at the risk, but Cire raised her hand, stopping his instant rage.

"He actually wanted the songs, not anything else. You know all music is prohibited unless it is sung to Xyl. He used to travel in his youth and was exposed to other music. As such, he missed having it in his house. One of our older singers, a male if it matters, goes once a tenday and spends five fingers singing to him. They are always songs to Xyl, but often the older ones or ones we rarely sing. It makes the craftsman happy and does no harm."

"And if the singer tries to escape?" He still remembered the boy that escaped when he was still a conductor. One of his favorites. The memory still rankled after all these suncycles and he rarely allowed the singers out of the temples because one of them—actually five of them—had fled the temple. They never returned. It had not been his fault. He had been in another city at the time, and the priest who left their door unlocked was punished. Zayn always assumed the punishment was death, as he never saw the priest again, but he could be wrong.

Another smile, this one cold and lacking all compassion. He saw that smile in his reflection occasionally. "He tried once, suncycles ago. Both feet were broken. He walks with a permanent limp and requires canes. It was a horrible accident, of course. He fell from the second level and the breaks were unable to be set properly." She smiled the entire time she spoke, and Zayn wished he had more priests with her perspective. With a force made up of women like her, maybe he could be king. "Besides, a priest that can run always escorts him."

Zayn let his anger go and stared at the advanced plumbing, greed washing through him. "I am impressed. That is a most creative solution. I shall have to see what I can find in Granite."

Cire nodded and escorted him to the visitor rooms. "Then I will leave you here. Your treat is inside. Please do return him prior to dawn without any marks."

He shot her a hard glance. She had the audacity to lecture him?

Cire just looked at him. "The inspection is tomorrow. The last thing I want is anything such as the marks from bed play to explain."

Zayn fought to keep from flushing. She was correct, and it galled him. But this was why she ran the second largest temple in Charinsky. Because she would do what was needed, even if it meant staring him down.

"You are quite correct. Aryix bless for the remember."

"Aryix grant," she said in response. "Enjoy." With that, she spun and headed back to her own rooms and possibly her own entertainment. But somehow he doubted that. He required the stress relief. She would most likely not indulge until after they had left the city.

He pushed open the door and nodded to himself at the nicely appointed room, but mostly at the young boy who sat on the bed waiting for him. A smile spread as he shut the door and the evening he had in store.

CHAPTER TWENTY-FOUR

SHINALA

The winds that swirled around the prison were always cold. The liquid rocks, heated by the rage of the gods, created warm dry caves. The creation of the mount, through Aryix's fury, had left pools of hot water, freshwater springs, and land for prey to graze. The sandy beaches and grassy plains made it a comfortable place to exist.

Shinala, an enormous white saber, yawned, her belly full from a fish one of her males had caught earlier that day. She lay stretched out in the sun, enjoying the mild day. The splash of the waves was a sound she had become immune to eons ago. The scent of hot rock, feline, salt, and rotting fish were so expected she barely noticed them anymore.

The mountain behind her rumbled, sending a tiny shock through the ground. It was enough to make her open her eyes, but the sun, with clouds in the far distance, seemed as normal, boring as always. Her lids slid shut, seeking slumber again. She slept most of the time now. Every so often, a day might pass as she slept. There was little enough to do and time seemed endless. It was at the point the storms were the only thing of interest and what they might wash ashore.

A nudge at Shinala's head finally roused her, and she lifted her head to see Lev looking at her, his red ruff and green eyes a callback to his father. Could she even remember what her mate had looked like? For a moment she tried, but aside from the impression of power and intensity, his image faded away like mist. Lev lifted his head and pointed toward the chamber. That was unusual enough it sent a spike of curiosity through her.

She rose to her feet, licking the side of his face in thank you as she passed with a purr that faded as she padded toward the opening into the mountain, tail drifting back and forth. There was no hurry. Time had little meaning here.

Over the suncycles, boredom had become the bane of her existence. At first, the sentence to guard her masters had seemed like a vacation. To laze around and relax, let the heat seep into her bones. To frolic with her males and chase silly moelks and catch the fish foolish enough to come near shore.

But she soon tired of it. Her partners and the others under her command were fine Leonaids: strong, skilled, proud, flexible in body, mind, and spirit. The first few suncycles, they relaxed, letting themselves enjoy the break from guarding, fetching, serving, protecting, or spying all at the whims of their gods, their creators. But even vacations become tedious.

That thought elicited a growl as she padded into the large chamber. They had all gone in and talked, raged, begged, and pleaded with their gods, to no avail. Now guarding the entry was just the one duty none of the Leonaids could let fade into the past.

Like her memories.

"SHINALA. IT IS GOOD TO SEE YOU. IT HAS BEEN A LONG TIME."

The voice echoed through her mind, but she sat, licking her white fur as her senses took in the room. The narrow path she trod to come in widened to a flat area, polished smooth over the multiple visits to this spot. A river of liquid rock, so hot she could cook over it, if she or any of her people had the need to cook. Just out of reach, separated by the river of magma, were her gods. As always, the six alcoves carved into the stone, five of them were filled with figures encased in crystal. In front of each crystal figure on the stone peninsula, sat a black bowl with high sides for the offerings Shinala had brought, long ago.

The reddish crystals held an inner light that swirled and eddied through the figures. Each god had a slightly different color. Where Aryix was blood red, Quas had silver touching the currents. Gela had green while Lyx was coated in blue, creating a hue closer to purple. Stari's eddies were all the colors and by far the most hypnotic. When they had first been sentenced here, Shinala had lost days watching the currents of power run through these tombs, waiting for her gods to come back.

"SHINALA, WILL YOU NOT SPEAK WITH US?" This time the voice was Quas, but she ignored it, still working the dirt out of her paw.

The largest cocoon contained Aryix. He had always stood taller than all the others, handsome in a way none could ever quite replicate. Even after all this time, she could easily tell their voices apart, though in her mind they had no sound, only flavor. Those voices, their essences, were seared into her very being. They had created her.

The old stories were both true and false. She and Raja had been created by all of them. Aryix had donated his blood, Quas his quick thoughts, Stari her fluid grace, Lyx her tears, and Gela had breathed life into them. Their existence was in her very bones.

After a finger of time, her paw clean, Shinala lifted her leonine head and her body rippled. Bones shifted, fur receded, and flesh rearranged. With a shake of her body and mind, she assumed the shape of a mortal. Now she stood about six hands tall, her skin the same white as her fur, her eyes emerald green, with her hair in long, matted twists, as if all her fur had gone there, covered her back like a cloak. It had been a suncycle since she last shifted to this form. The greatest advantage was the ability to talk, though she missed the warmth of her fur. She sank down on the floor, enjoying the heat down near the liquid stone.

"There is no time here. If you wished to talk, I know you can speak wherever I am." There was no anger in her voice, it was just a statement. Even her emotions seemed distant and pale.

"YES. BUT SEEING YOU REMINDS US," said Aryix, his voice softer.

"Is that wise? Do you wish to be reminded?"

"SOMETIMES." That was Lyx, a note of wistfulness in the mind's voice.

"IGNORE THEM, SHINALA. THEY ARE BEING DIFFICULT. WE HAVE BEEN ARGUING AND THEY AVOID THE SUBJECT. I DO NOT. WE WERE NEVER PERFECT AND MADE MISTAKES. MORE THAN WE SHOULD HAVE. OUR CHILDREN..." Quas fell silent and Shinala tilted her head, curious. Of the children, three had been born before her creation. The others came after and she had sometimes been nursemaid, playmate, guard, or teacher to them as they grew, but never an equal. They were the children, she but the creation.

"Argue?" This was interesting. Different. It also said they were more awake than she suspected.

"WE MADE MISTAKES. NOT LISTENING TO OUR DAUGHTER WAS ONE OF THEM. NOW WHAT XYL DID MIGHT DESTROY MORE THAN ONE LAND. THE MORTALS ARE HURTING. THAT PAIN MIGHT CAUSE THEM TO CHALLENGE EVERYTHING AND YOU WILL BE NEEDED." Stari's voice rippled like a creek through her mind.

"And? Am I to be given rein to fix your error?" To get off the prison, to do something? She still hungered for revenge on the children for the insult they did to their parents. For the deaths they dealt to her family, her people, her mate. That was enough to wake her mind. A challenge.

"YES. NO. MAYBE. NEVER. IT MUST." The words spoken by all of them crammed into her mind and she winced, pulling back. Obviously, the argument was still going.

"What do you want me to do?"

There was only silence to her question. It hung there for fingers, and her boredom grew again.

"WAIT," Aryix said finally. "WAIT."

Shinala growled and stood back up. "Why disturb me for this? What else do you think I do? I wait for death. If it was not for my vows to you, I would have already sought it. Others of mine have."

Shinala had quit counting the days, the mooncycles, even the suncycles she had been imprisoned there. The ticks for each one filled an entire cave, only adding to her depression. If forced, she could tell you the number of suncycles by putting together multiple words. It held over four zeros and served only to send her to the height of the mount to howl out her frustration. Already at least three of hers had walked into the ocean and never returned. They may not be mortal, but that provided no protection from loneliness and lack of stimulation. Nor did it heal the wounds the uprising had caused. Wounds of the heart took more to heal than ones of the flesh ever had.

"SHINALA," Gela said, her voice soft and rich. Of all of them, Gela was the one who had been the mother. The one whose absence still hurt, even now.

Shinala paused in the tunnel, looking out toward the sun-filled sky. Looking out to where there was nothing for her but more of the same.

"THE LEONAIDS WILL BE NEEDED. WE ASK THAT YOU BE READY WHEN THEY ARE."

"Ready for what?"

They never answered her question, and in disgust Shinala shifted back to her saber form and headed for her men, seeking comfort and an anchor to the here and now.

Once again, the gods were meddling. If only that would mean something to do. But a tiny ember of hope had been kindled deep in her heart. Time would see if there was more to fan it into a fire.

CHAPTER TWENTY-FIVE

LAZUL

Lazul yawned as they approached the town of Amyet. A large area, one of his five main districts, and in charge of some of the most profitable mines. The temple here was also one of the bigger ones and, according to Zayn's boasts, had singers that were better than even his. They sent the youngest boys here to ensure they never lost their perfect voices.

There was something about how Zayn mentioned 'ensuring' that always made Lazul squirm in the seat, but he would never elaborate, saying only it was a temple ritual and only for the young boys. Then he would change the subject.

Lazul shook his head. At this point, he just wanted food and a nice bed. Though the food part meant dealing with whatever young thing they wanted him to marry and would shove in front of him now. Oh well. He had survived thus far; the odds were he would survive this.

"Are you looking forward to Lord Nephrite's offering?" Zayn had ridden up next to him and asked the question in a teasing manner that seemed overly lascivious to Lazul.

"Not really. Most of them are too young. Do they think I want a child?"

A flicker of a smile curved Zayn's cheeks for a moment, a smugness that for most of the trip had not been in evidence. "Do you not want someone young? A wife you can mold to suit your…tastes?"

The way Zayn said the words felt like oil in his ears. The impression it left made Lazul vaguely nauseous.

"Not like that. If my choices matter, I need a partner. Someone that can help with the decisions that need to be made. Not a child I need to cater to or comfort.

Do you really think I have time to deal with a young woman fresh from her mother?" He gave the cantor an incredulous look.

Zayn tilted his head. "Now that you say that, no. I had not been thinking of the other aspects, only the heir issue. Which would cause issues if you die without one. Given your parents, we know accidents can happen."

The lasciviousness had faded away, leaving thoughtful consideration. That aspect of Zayn was someone Lazul could talk to. Of all of them, Zayn had laid out very vehemently why he had no desire for the throne. You could not hold both positions, and his current role in many ways had more powers than the king did. Lazul had to get agreement from his councilors, the lords, and even the populace.

Zayn just needed to say 'Xyl said' and most of his requests would be fulfilled. In many ways Lazul was the only one that could block him, but even that was only in matters of treasury or tapping into city resources.

It must be nice to have power with so few checks.

The thought made his mouth twitch, but he brought himself back to the conversation.

"I am unsure why they keep focusing on the ones that have not even settled down into adulthood. If it is simple comeliness they worry about, a woman of sixty and of thirty look very much the same." His voice held frustration as being a queen took a sharp mind and strong will, not just a pretty face.

"True. One of the gifts of Percit. Beauty never fades, staying with us until the moment of death," Zayn said with a touch of superciliousness. "But their fertility does change."

"True. But is it not true a woman in her late twenties still bear a child as easily as one in her teens? Just give me a woman with a mind to talk to." He let slip a bit of exasperation, but Zayn already knew it was there. He had witnessed a few of the dinners and had been entertained by how frustrated Lazul grew as the meal progressed.

"I think you might be at the mercy of what your councilors daydream of. A young thing to do their bidding, not a queen to sit on the throne with you," Zayn said thoughtfully. "And that means the rest of this trip will be more of the same. Maybe when you get back, you could beat into them what you are looking for?"

"The biggest issue is Mother came to the crown a young woman, growing up with my father, and she is the only queen they remember; a young woman who learned as she aged. They forget I am already a tenset older than she or my father was at their marriage."

"I had not realized that. Why?" Zayn seemed genuinely curious.

Lazul was quiet for a while as they rode, trying to figure out if Zayn was safe to tell what he thought the real reason was. Finally ,he shrugged. Zayn was the one person that might be able to help.

"You will argue with me, but I think most of it is because of X-" he broken off, his lips thinning. Lazul continued, but pointed at Zayn's robes and the symbol of Xyl. "Him. The weather is more and more unpredictable and the disasters that happen with tantrums have ramped up over the last tenset. I believe this is causing other countries' rulers and their gods to back away. Not wanting to risk interacting with us."

Zayn opened his mouth but stopped when Lazul raised a hand.

"I also spent time reviewing all our records and interactions with the other nations. Granted, we, Aois, and Vykland are the only countries that exist by ourselves on our continent. The deeps that surround us also make it harder to trade with us, but that explains only a part of the distance. There is something either about us or him that makes them reluctant." He lifted his eyes to the sky on "him", making it obvious who he spoke of.

Zayn's mouth opened and closed for a moment. Then finally he replied. "I will take what you said under advisement. But I fear...." He stopped eating, looking down the road at the town that was growing closer. "That you are closer to the truth than I might like."

That ended their conversation until dinner. Captain Marcel had sent people ahead, and Zayn had been invited to dine with Lazul and Lord Nephrite. The conversation was not forgotten, but pushed to the side. If they were lucky, it might be brought back up this tenset.

Lazul sat at the head on one end, while Lord Poll Nephrite sat at the other end. The eight-person table had them at the ends, while three more sat on each side. To Lazul's right was a pretty young girl Lord Poll introduced as Chryso, his daughter. She had the typical blond hair going toward a fiery gold that glistened in the firelight, and blue eyes that were the deepness of the sea.

Lazul could see where Chryso got her looks, as already she was a reflection of her mother, but brighter. Mora had the appearance of someone who had much on her plate and little assistance.

To Lazul's left was Lord Poll's estate manager, Anyo Gate. A boring man from what Lazul could tell so far as everything he said was a fact and had little opinion on anything, even the food, which was excellent.

Poll had placed Zayn to his right, which Lazul was perfectly happy about. Uncomfortable conversations were exhausting.

That left a woman between Zayn and Anyo. She was at least older than her twenties, though she could have been eighty, as looks said little. Poll had introduced her as Hauyne Tupite, his widowed sister. There had been a tightness to his words that made Lazul wonder about the story behind her presence. Where

Mora and Chryso were bright sunny blondes with dark blue for eyes, Hauyne was a silver blonde with icy blue eyes that could almost look clear in the correct light.

But best of all, she had a mind.

"As I told Lord Nephrite, the number of opals coming up that are of exquisite clarity or above had increased by fifteen percent. But our sales are down by thirty-five percent because of lack of external trade. We have the highest graded opal and amethysts in all of Charinsky, but until we expand our external trading partners, we will not see commensurate profits." Anyo spoke each word as if setting it down in stone.

Chryso smiled. "Amethysts are my favorite, but sapphires match my eyes." Her eyes flicked to the simple circlet he wore with only a sapphire and ruby carved as two halves of a circle in the middle.

Mora, Lady Nephrite, chimed in. "Yes, she is gorgeous in most of the darker gems. But not only is she beautiful, she has brains. Chryso is working on her gem assayer certification. She has a test in a tenday." Mora looked at her daughter with smug pride. The test for assayer certification was difficult and was recognized as a measure of expertise across Charinsky. An impressive achievement for someone her age.

"Yes, with study she should pass," Hauyne said with no expression, however, but both Mora and Chryso flushed.

"At least I will have a career," Chryso said, with her nose in the air.

"Yes. But will you be able to find a job? I know from painful experience, few are willing to hire from the family of nobles. There is the fear that if you are disciplined or let go, they will be punished," Hauyne said, spearing a piece of coopbird meat with her fork. Poll's lips tightened at her comment.

"What do you mean? Are you looking for work?" Lazul was more interested in what Hauyne said. His words made her flinch the tiniest bit and her eyes shut and opened so fast most would have thought it a blink. He suspected it was something else.

"I apologize, sire. My frustration and an old argument slipped out at a time and place that was inappropriate." Her face and smile were both tight, and he could see frustration in the clenching of her jaw.

"What work would you be looking for?" he asked again, now even more curious.

She looked away and blindly stabbed at something else on her plate, this time creamy white tubers in a butter sauce. It crumbled under her stab, causing her to bring an empty fork to her mouth.

"I am certified as a diamond assayer, and I have both MSI and EM certifications, also at diamond levels." She looked at her fork in surprise as there was nothing on it and set it down. "But even with that, no one here is willing to hire me, because of my status."

"Because of your sharp tongue," Chryso muttered. Mora flicked her fingers at the girl with a sharp hiss.

Lazul arched an eyebrow at that, ignoring the byplay between mother and daughter. With the gems that Charinsky produced, being able to assay them in a consistent manner was paramount to preventing charges of fraud or shipping gems to trading partners that were the wrong grade. Which was why, ages ago, one of the rulers, he never could remember who it was, had created a gem assay certification. There were three levels to most certifications: Topaz, Sapphire, Diamond. Diamond was the highest and if he remembered correctly, there were under a hundred people with that certification, whereas people with topaz were well over a thousand.

Mine Safety Inspectors, or MSIs, were valued as well as they understood how to dig and keep the mines safe even with Xyl expressing his displeasure with anything and everything. It was suncycles of training to earn even the first level and the grueling exam for the Diamond level had more people that failed it rather than succeed.

The last certification was for Estate Management, which meant she could easily do Anyo's job.

"Indeed. I have found her insight most helpful. With her assistance three areas where there were shortfalls were addressed, and she analyzed another issue where discontent would have created a major problem." Anyo said all this with a smile, but Lazul noted he still took most of the credit.

Hauyne sighed. "I talked to people and looked at the numbers. Most problems can be addressed with the application of a little good sense."

Poll snorted. "You extorted me out of five plat to solve a 'problem'. They would have been able to work without the new shed and lighting for sorting."

Hauyne's lips thinned. "And production is up by at least twenty-six percent because of those changes."

"It will still take over a suncycle to recoup that expenditure," he resorted.

Hauyne just shrugged and went back to eating, her lips thin.

Zayn caught his eye from the other end of the table, nodded at Hauyne and smirked. Lazul bit back a sigh and turned to Chryso, who was currently talking to him about worship services and how the songs had been so boring lately.

"I must direct you to Cantor Zayn for that. The songs are not chosen because of our interest," he said, and Zayn nodded at the girl with a smile that looked forced.

Zayne answered the unspoken question. "We sing the song in celebration and love of Percit. If you have a new song that you have written, please bring it to the temple. We are always looking for new songs to worship with."

"You mean appease?" Hauyne said. Poll and Mora both paled and Hauyne sighed. "We sing them not in celebration, but appeasement and praying they sate his need for either guilt or penance. Then we hope he ignores us at best or only hurts us a little at worst. I have never been able to decide if it is the worship or the fear of his reaction that he craves more."

Lazul and Zayn looked at each other in surprise. This was a truth that few knew and fewer understood.

"Hauyne, you will not speak like that under my roof. Is that understood?" Poll was white with rage and fear and instantly turned to Zayn. "I do apologize. My sister's thoughts are often aired when they should never leave her skull. Rest assured we revel in the worship of the love Percit had for Xyl." The words tumbled out with a touch of fear in them and Hauyne ducked her head.

"He is right. My thoughts should stay mine. If you would excuse me?" With that, she rose and left, her cream dress revealed to be long loose pants with a matching blouse. For the rest of the meal, Lazul ignored the looks from Zayn and Captain Marcel and focused on the charms of Chryso, but his thoughts never left Hauyne. Her strong face, sharp words, and intelligence, all in the body of one that he found attractive. Though if he was honest with himself, her mind and tongue interested him more.

CHAPTER TWENTY-SIX

RYLIX

Rylix held absolutely still as Note talked. He had been taking a nap in his swing chair and their voices had woken him up. But until Note relayed his story to Jadaya in the dark of the hold, Rylix had not realized how personal and intimate of a moment he had stumbled into. Bedroom activities would have been easier to excuse himself from. Instead, he just lay cocooned in the sleep sling, trying to be silent, as they shared their childhood and held back tears at what they had both suffered.

Even after Note and Jadaya left, he remained quiet, letting the thoughts and emotions battle through his heart and mind. To think his own past, the death of Kryx, and what he had regarded as his exile had been so horrible. It was nothing. He had been a nominal adult when sent here. His needs were taken care of and his 'punishment' had been forcing him to grow up and take responsibility for his actions.

Now he was part of a rescue for more children. Retribution for the suffering Note and others had experienced. His hand drifted down to cradle his balls, reassuring himself they were there and giving one last thought of sympathy to Note. He would help to the best of his ability and maybe prove to himself his worth, as well as to his family.

Then he pushed the emotions away and rose. Dwelling on the past changed nothing. All he could do was to ensure the future was better. Rather than exiting the main stairs, he took a back ladder that led up to the kitchen. It was a shortcut that ended where supplies were stocked in the hold, so the cook could send the cabin boy down for supplies without having to go halfway across the deck.

"Rylix, what are you doing coming up my supply ladder?" Sylx asked as he poked his head up through the hole. Sylx was an enormous woman that some would assume was fat. But Rylix had seen her pull up the anchor by herself and he knew it was all muscle. She was also an excellent cook, making the constant food of fish seem exciting each day.

"Testing out alternate escape routes, of course. What sort of Ged would I be if I was caught unprepared?" He smiled at her and lifted his nose. "And what delicious repast have you created for us this day?"

"Flatterer," she said, flicking her knife at him. "If you have messed up any of my storage, I will use parts of you for the next meal." She grinned and shook her head at him. "But since you are wandering through, would you let Jolyx know I need some blue seaweed for dinner tomorrow?"

"Oh? What are you making tomorrow?" Rylix leaned on the wall, enjoying the flirting, letting his new knowledge settle into his brain. If he even indicated he was aware, it would cause issues with their little group, and he had no desire to make this journey any more fraught with danger than it would be. At least his portion of the trip was over once he got them to Granite.

"Fish wraps, but the blue seaweed needs to sit in the air and dry for a full day before I can pound it into edible food. So get. I have work to do."

"But of course, master chef of the sea, I leave you to your artistry." He bowed to her with a flourish and headed out of the galley, through the mess hall, and then back onto the deck. The bright light caught him unaware, and he stopped for a moment to blink until his eyes adjusted to the brightness. He turned to scan the deck, looking to see where Jolyx was.

He found her up by the wheel and trotted up to her. "Ah, my captain, the master chef Sylx has a request to be made of you." Rylix added a lyrical aspect to his sentence and was rewarded with a glance skyward and a slight smile.

"And what would that be?"

"She requests blue seaweed for tomorrow."

Jolyx's eyes brightened. "Oh, she is making wraps. That is easy enough to do. Anything else?"

Rylix hid his laughter. Jolyx had no time for anything that unrelated to the ship. But he wanted to sift through her impressions. "What do you think of our two guests?" He moved up near the wheel, leaning on the railing, looking over the rest of the ship. Note and Jadaya were in the middle of a clear area of the deck. This time, Note was teaching her to fight with knives. It was going, not that he could tell if it was well or poorly. But neither was bleeding too much, and they had looks of concentration on their faces, not anger. He read that as everything was normal.

"Who is asking? Rylix the trader looking for more profit or Rylix the Ged making sure he stays out of the paths of the gods?"

Her response surprised him, and he looked back at her, arching a brow. "Is there a difference?"

"For a Ged, you are throwing yourself directly into the gods' business. That is very unGed like," she said. There was no condemnation in her voice. Ged let a person follow their own path as any path could be the right one. But they rarely had any interaction with gods. And avoided the notice of the other gods when possible.

No, I simply attempt to pay a debt for abuses done to those who could not fight back.

Rylix kept his thought to himself, leaning on his charm. "Ah, but this leads to our gods and has the chance to reap a great profit. Not to mention the acclaim that will come with it if we succeed." He kept his voice light, but her response concerned him. Was he going too far? Already gods were showing up and meddling.

"Ah, then this is about reputation and standing at the Gather?" Her eyes were locked on the sea, not him, but he knew she was watching.

"Partially. It also is an opportunity. The trade goods I have and the ability to take them from Aois to Fivika to Vykland, then on to Charinsky? No one has ever done that specific route. Parts of it, yes, but all of it? No."

She shot him a look that plainly said she knew he hid some of the truth from her. "And?"

Rylix sighed and turned back to look at Note and Jadaya. "And it feels right," he breathed.

"Ah. In that case," she paused, and he saw she was looking at them too. "I think one is too naïve for all she carries scars that should have taught her more about the perfidy of people. The other has scars that are invisible and drive him past logic or sanity."

He has scars that you are unable to see, deep ones that would change any man.

Rylix kept the thought from his face, even though he still shuddered at the idea. Castration. Even the worst punishments never included that. "Anything else?" He asked as he let his eyes drift over the sea. Far to their left were the mountains of Aois. While he knew in the distance to his right Vykland lay, there was no indication it was there at all.

"I think," she said slowly, as if each word had weight to it. "Someday I will say I held those two on my deck and started them on their journey. I am still unsure if I will be lauded for that or condemned. That thought has kept me up in the small fingers of the morning. But I am putting faith in Aryix and Lyx that they will see further into the hearts of them than I can."

Rylix tried to hide how shook he was, but his look must have revealed something and Jolyx laughed. "I would not spend my time worrying. There is much in store, but I have little doubt your trade shall be successful. I hope to hear the full tale at the next Gather."

It was as much a dismissal as anything, and Rylix nodded, turning around, trying to think. Hiding back in the swing chair held no appeal. Being near either of them felt unwise at this juncture until he had a better handle on his reactions. "Is the spy's nest free?"

Jolyx nodded. "Have fun. If you fall, I will charge your family the full amount."

"I would expect nothing less, Captain," Rylix said with a laugh. While he was land Ged, his childhood had seen him on many ships and climbing the ropes offered little challenge. Moments later, he was on the large platform that served as a lookout post for the *Starguide* when there was a need. Piracy was always a possibility, but they were usually independent rebels, outcasts, or misfits that crewed them. Few nations had ships, and the Ged had more than the rest of them put together. Most often, the lookout post was used to track storms, monsters, or land in poor visibility. Sometimes from here, you could see over the fog and let the crew know if there was a danger approaching.

For now, he settled down and pulled out his notebook, but nothing that he had learned affected his plans. Those were always of trade, goods, costs, and other things for his reputation. Not secrets that belonged to others.

Gods. It kept coming back to gods. Rylix still followed the old gods, but they had been locked away for generations upon generations, and few other than their mystics could claim to still speak with them. The Ged kept to the old laws and other than offering prayers in the morning and evenings, they lived their lives, not worrying about what their gods might think.

Rylix had no desire to follow another god, but seeing Pel and Rian walk up and talk to Note made him wonder what would it be like. He settled down on the platform, legs crossed and hands in his lap, and he closed his eyes. Of all the gods, Quas had always been the one he felt the closest to. The traveler, the one that had come from the stars and helped create the world of Aria. Quas was the stars in the sky, and he was the one who called to Rylix. All Ged said a prayer to Quas as the evening fell, but for now Rylix sat and thought about this god, one that was still imprisoned in the Mount of the Gods.

Why had the Ged never tried to rescue them? The old stories gave an answer to that. Aryix had raged, threatening to break the world. Rylix had no illusions that anyone would survive his rage if he was free. It was best to leave him sleeping forever. But would Note and Jadaya be waking him? Could Aria survive that? The story of the Downfall was still told at the campfires of the Ged, but in all his listening, both as a child and an adult, he had never heard the story told anywhere in Aois. Maybe they had forgotten it?

Did forgetting the old stories make their actions better or worse? That Aois only remembered that the old gods had magic weapons. Yes, the old gods, or at least the Leonaids, knew how to create things that could kill the gods. Did anyone want or need a weapon that powerful? But even more concerning, if Jadaya and Note were unaware of the old legends, did they have any idea what they were walking into?

That thought had his eyes snapping open, and he realized that once they were off the ship, he needed to have story time. Jolyx would toss him off her ship if he told the stories onboard. No one wanted to risk the Usurper hearing about the gods' defeat and getting ideas. These old stories were only told on land around a fire, when everyone was well protected. Where, hopefully, only Aryix and Quas could hear the tale. Fire had always been their element, the fire of the stars and the breath of life.

Yes, he would tell stories. And maybe these young adventurers would understand what they actually sought. Remind himself of the risks.

He stayed up on the platform thinking of gods and heroes until the stars came out and the bell for dinner rang.

His dreams were of a new god looking at him as if seeing him for the first time and stirrings of the mountain behind him.

CHAPTER TWENTY-SEVEN

JADAYA

The waves were almost friendly this morning. Jadaya stood on the deck, a mug of telcha in her hands. Telcha was something the Ged cook, Sylx, introduced her to. Made from roasted and ground tella nuts, it produced a brew with kick, but with the narcotic properties gone. With the addition of beet powder, it was a pleasant way to wake up.

Note hated it, but everyone else on the ship depended on it. Rylix had assured her he had enough packed for their trip. But most places in Fivika and Vykland served telcha. Jadaya had only drank tea prior to this, as telcha had never become something she had seen or tried in Zuyika.

She rarely missed home at this point. Her anger and the excitement of a chance to prove she was valuable had driven away most of that feeling. This entire trips was new experiences: helping sail the ship, sparring with Note, fighting her terror of the sea, and just marveling at the way the weather moved over the sea. Watching sunsets was not something she had often, always too busy or trying to get back to Elike, to her lover. Now she watched the sun rise and set. It was breathtaking.

She leaned against the railing, looking out at the endless sea.

A presence to her right had her tilting her head to see Note standing next to her. In the days since he had shared the truth of himself with her, he had been prickly, as if she might use that knowledge against him. Inside, Jadaya still twisted in anger and frustration at what was done to him. That level of brutalization, just to retain a singing voice, horrified and enraged her. She had known no one that had been maimed in such a way. Yet it changed nothing about who he was, and she absolutely knew to keep this information to herself. But it explained his rage and in that, they had become closer, both of them having something to prove to the gods.

"Morning," she said in a quiet voice, then looked back out to sea. He had a cup of seaweed tea in his hand. Something she found more bitter than was palatable.

A soft grunt was his only response. They stood there together as the sun painted the sky with green, violet, and soft orange as it rose into the skin in all its bright orange glory. The sea was calm, but a decent wind, though not in the direction they needed it to blow. But it made the sea less ravenous looking, and that was always to her preference. Tracing the edge of the horizon, Jadaya squinted as another ship broke the line. Tall sails of cream, not black, and a different shape than what this ship was.

"There is another ship," she said, more to herself than to Note. This entire voyage had felt like they were alone in the world, to the point that she wondered if the land had disappeared.

"Where?"

She pointed, and he grunted with a half sigh. "Probably should tell Jolyx. Your eyesight is better than mine."

Jadaya repressed a snort. If she was still fully Zuyikan, her vision would let her tell how many people stood on the deck and their gender. She felt blind half the time, missing the eyesight she used since birth. But rather than say anything, she turned and headed toward the mess hall, where most of the crew still was. She found it too claustrophobic in the mornings with everyone eating breakfast, needing the fresh air above her after a night inside the ship. Rylix was still asleep. He had mentioned that he enjoyed sleeping with a roof above him while he could. She was still pondering what that meant.

Jadaya made her way back down to the mess hall and found Jolyx. The captain of the *Starguide* was sitting at the small table in the back with room for three people. Right now it was her and Tylax, the first mate.

"Captain?" Jadaya had enjoyed their discussion about the different bindings. After learning that you could wrap them in different patterns and even buy ones that would cup your breasts as opposed to flatten them, she had resolved to purchase new ones in Calin. While they were friendly, Jadaya still treated the captain formally. It was better to err on the side of formal than casual.

Jolyx looked up, a smile on her face. "Morning, Jadaya. Is there an issue?" Her voice was casual and her cup of telcha half gone.

"I spotted a ship on the horizon and Note thought I should tell you." She had no idea if it was something the captain would want to know or not, but either way she could get a refill on her telcha.

The captain stiffened and stood up. "What color were the sails?"

Jadaya shrugged. "Cream, I think. I know they were a light color."

"Tylax, get Duas up to the spotter and see what you can see. Get everyone else up and armed." Tylax nodded and was yelling out orders as the mess hall cleared out, with the crew leaving at a run.

Jadaya stepped back, surprised, and tried to get out of the way as the crew flooded out. She stayed in the corner until everyone had left, then made her way over to the pot of telcha as Sylx peeked her head out.

"What is this? Did my cooking go bad?" the chef demanded, putting her hands on impressive hips.

Jadaya shook her head, as she added a touch more red beet sand to her telcha. "No. I told them there was a ship on the horizon."

Sylx went still, then nodded. "Go get your sword, dark one. The odds are it is time to fight." Jadaya had noted almost none of the Ged ever used her name. What they called her was never rude, just not her name. Then what the cook had said sunk in.

"My sword?"

Sylx gave her a grim smile. "Pirates. There will be a fight soon." The woman locked everything down as she spoke.

Jadaya blinked, then smiled. "Oh, that sounds like fun." It would give her a chance to stretch herself and provide an outlet to the rage that had taken possession of her heart for herself, for Note, for the children currently prisoner, and the child he had been.

She headed out and slipped down to the crew quarters, weaving through the crew rushing back up to the deck. It took her but half a finger to finish her telcha, strap on her sword, her bracers and rebind herself. She rarely slept with bindings, but having unbound breasts in the middle of a fight was unwise and painful.

Armed, she headed back up into the chaos orchestrated by Jolyx. "Tilt the sails some more. If we can get within sight of Calin, they should back off." Her voice was clear as men and women responded to her orders.

"No good, Captain. They have the winds behind them. Intercept estimated in four fingers," Tylax called out from the wheel.

"Quas take them. Scum of the seas. Not even the Usurper would want them," Jolyx cursed. "All hands prepare for battle!"

A roar of agreement as the lines were secured and weapons appeared almost out of thin air as the crew prepared to face the vessel bearing straight for them.

"You ready?" Note asked next to her.

Jadaya glanced down at him and smiled. "Oh, this should be fun."

Note snorted. "You are a warrior through and through. I am simply hoping no one is killed."

Jadaya shrugged. For her, the thrill of fighting for her life, having the blood pound in her ears, and feel her body moving with a purpose, would be better than the sweetest telcha.

The two of them leaned against the outer wall of the captain's cabin, staying out of the way of the crew as they waited. For the last finger, the ship was quiet, everyone watching the pirates draw closer to them. Rylix joined them a heartbeat later, a pipe in one hand and darts in the other. The corner of his vests hung heavy and Jadaya wondered what was pulling them down.

"No quarter, my crew. The *Starguide* shall be richer today by another ship," Jolyx roared as the pirate ship drew close enough that they began throwing grappling hooks to link the ships together.

It surprised Jadaya that the crew left the lines alone. Instead, they stood back and waited, dark grins on their faces. They all held the funny curved swords like they knew how to use them, while Tylax had wooden batons in his hands.

"They want this fight?" she asked as she stood up, ready to dive into the battle to come.

"Jolyx has one of the best trained crews among the Ged. And they get the ship if they capture it. There is excellent motivation to win, besides the avoiding a watery grave part." Rylix smiled at her, and she saw the sword at his side.

"Maybe you should join the sparring Note and I do."

"My lady warrior, believe that I would, but my skills are in a different arena." He patted the sword. "This is a last resort only and mostly I block, in an effort to keep my head on my shoulders, you understand?"

"That is where most people prefer to keep it," she agreed and rolled her shoulders. "Time to see how I measure up." It was the last intelligible words she had time to say.

The attackers threw planks across the railings and rushed the *Starguide* crew. They responded with a yell of primal rage and the fight was on. Over the last tenday, Jadaya had learned the names and faces of everyone, and they all knew who she was, so she had no fear of attacking the first person to throw themselves at her.

A white-skinned man, reddish blond hair sticking up wildly, swung a sword at Jadaya, while yelling. She lifted her own weapon, blocking the swing, then trapped his sword, bringing it down and under, exposing his belly and letting her sword slide right into his jiggling expanse of flesh. He fell with a surprised gurgle, falling off her blade. With a grunt, she brought it up to block the next attack. That man, almost as tall as her and twice as hefty, roared as his axe came down at her.

Fearing it might break her blade, as she had no expectations of quality on these found weapons, she turned, letting the blow slide down her blade, then her arm rose back at him with a slash of her sword. He leaned back with a smile, exposing teeth that were as dark as her skin. Tella stains.

That is not the right color for teeth.

The thought was full of revulsion as she blocked another blow. She hit him with a glancing slash across his shoulder, and he grunted as his shirt turned red with his blood. He pulled back with a roar and launched himself at her. She skipped backward, letting him keep up the charge. As her back heel hit the railing, she crouched down and lunged at his waist.

She caught him in the middle, and with an oof, his body folded over her shoulder. With a grunt of effort, she heaved up and backward. He flew over the railing with a splash into the water below. Jadaya turned back to the fight. She was on the far side of the ship from the attackers, and she took a second to get a lay of the battle.

Note was drifting through the fighters, his knife slashing in and out, cutting tendons from behind while the pirate was occupied with the person in front of them. Rylix had stashed his pipe somewhere and was moving in and slapping little darts into people. After first, it looked like it did nothing as most of them seemed unaware he had touched them, but she saw them start to slow and wobble, and that meant their death.

The crew of the *Starguide* were fighters, but all she could see were the flaws. They all needed to drill more. She would have to bring that up to Jolyx. After. With a smile, she dove back in and proceeded to use her height and reach to carve a red path through the attackers.

CHAPTER TWENTY-EIGHT

ZAYN

Zayn bit down on his anger and took the message from the priest. The annoyance almost slipped out. "What do they mean, they need two more singers? This is from Amyet. They are a tenday away best case. The Day of Remembrance is in three days."

The priest shrank in on himself, and Zayn sighed. "Well, they will get their answer by no one being delivered to them. I have no way to even get them a response before they need the singer." The priest ran away and Zayn rolled his shoulders, trying not to rage. Everyone knew this was coming. He went down there less than three tendays ago. That had been the perfect time to request more resources.

Not that I know if I would have had one to spare.

He stalked down to the practice room and slipped in. The singers were on the benches and, to his relief, so were most of the priests and priestess. The new Aoisans were too unfamiliar with the music to risk having them sing this day. He stood there, the music washing over him as he ignored it and listened for notes that were flat, breaths at the wrong time, or anyone that flubbed the words. The number of errors he noticed did nothing for his temper. The worst part was that the clergy were making the most mistakes. That was not acceptable. Though he knew he would be just as awkward if he were singing right now. The reason he fought so hard to rise in the ranks was partially to not have to sing. Zayn might have perfect pitch and could sing a variety of ranges, but he hated singing. It was stupid, an inefficient use of time, and the songs were boring.

Not that I would ever admit that, even under torture. The scandal would be time consuming to stomp out.

He waited until the song was done, and the conductor turned to him. Zayn moved over and murmured in his ear. "Reward them. They are doing well. But the clergy should be better. They can skip lunch and dinner for all I care. Remind them exactly what happens when Xyl gets annoyed."

The conductor, one of the junior ones, paled, swallowed, and nodded. "Yes, Cantor."

Zayn cast another glance, enjoying how all of them paled as his gaze rested on them. Then he swept out to head to oversee the decoration of the worship area.

He got there and stared around, his jaw dropping at what he saw. The area was normally a grass- and gravel-filled open courtyard, set so broken Percit hung directly above during worship time. Everyone stood in the gravel areas, letting the grass act as dividers for the rows. They were to concentrate on their sorrow for the loss of Percit and pray to Xyl and the dead goddess for their favor. The walls, carved with pictures of Xyl and Percit, would remain pristine except for the Day of Remembrance.

The wall carvings were supposed to be painted for the day to come. All the bias reliefs were normally colored until they looked like living paintings. It was breathtaking, as master painters would come in and pour their devotion onto the carvings. It was one of the few aspects of the Day he actively enjoyed.

But rather than having the paintings done, the entire courtyard looked like a group of younglings had played with the paint and smeared it everywhere. It was an explosion of colors that jarred and revolted. There were young singers, priests, and even some of the street kids scrubbing with brushes and buckets of cleaning solution.

"What is going on?" his voice roared out as the magnitude of the damage registered.

One of the priestess jerked her head up and came racing over. "Cantor, there was an incident last night."

"I see there was something. What happened?" He was too busy glaring at the damage to his temple to even pay attention to who was talking to him.

"As best as we can tell, dissidents broke in and spilled all the supplies and ruined what the masters had done so far. We are trying to clean up, but the likelihood of us finishing and the masters being able to get the courtyard up to standards is, um, low, Cantor."

Zayn realized his hands had clenched into fists and the priestess had shrunk into herself even more. With a force of effort, he relaxed his hands. "I see. We can forego the painting this year. What Xyl hears is more important than what he never sees. Get it back to pristine and let me know." He managed to not snarl as he turned to dash off a note to Lazul. These dissidents had gone too far. Watching their disruption of the kingdom's functions, like the diverting of refuse collectors, the destruction of all the cabbage coming into the city, even the sinking of the king's boat—after he returned from the inspection—had been highly amusing.

This was not.

He jerked to a halt at seeing one of the female conductors standing waiting for him. His eyes narrowed as he stepped into the entry section. "What?" Zayn resented the touch of wariness in his voice. He was the cantor. He should not be getting hit with surprises like this.

"I wanted to let you know most of the new children are sick," she said. She raised her hand before he could explode. "We have verified they do not have one of the spreading diseases. Instead, they have food poisoning."

Zayn felt his stomach clench at that. When he told Lazul they shared the same food, it had been the truth. While the priests, him especially, might receive the better cuts, they still came from the same roast, pot, pan, whatever. If they were sick… He swallowed.

"Everyone else is well. It turns out the younger ones had been given an old pie as a treat for learning their songs so well. No one realized it had gone bad. They will all recover, but extra cleaning and salt supplies will be required. Most of them are confined to the needs room for the boys. Only two girls were affected, and they are all young enough that using the needs room in front of each other, especially at this level of sick, is not an issue."

Zayn just looked at her. He took three deep breaths. "Bless. You are handling this correctly. I will authorize whatever you need."

She nodded, a look of relief on her face.

"Have you informed the cook yet?"

"Yes. All old food has been purged, and a thorough cleaning will start shortly. He said to let everyone know the food tonight will be porridge, as that can be started quickly without risk."

Zayn closed his eyes. They could all eat porridge for one night, even him. And pushing his priests away would accomplish nothing.

"Very well. Carry on."

She fled from his presence and Zayn stood there, wondering what would happen next. As if in response to his thoughts, there was a horrible crash from the practice rooms. He sprinted up the stairs, his robes pulled up to his knees.

He entered the practice room he had been in not two fingers ago to see singers and priests laying on the floor groaning, the risers they had been standing on, in pieces on the floor. "What by Percit's Tears is going on?" Zayn had no energy left to roar at this point. He just looked at the disaster.

"The risers just shattered. They have had much more weight on them prior to this. I have no idea," the conductor stammered out.

Zayn resisted the urge to pull his hair out. Instead, he leaned out the door and roared in a voice that carried through the temple. "Get the healers here now!" He then raced over to the infirmary, grabbed bandages, splints, and pain drops, and headed back. By this point, others were arriving and diving in to help. He handed out the bandages and splints as they identified the ones that were severely hurt versus minor injuries.

Whomever went to fetch the healers must have run the entire way. Not one finger later, there were two healers there, dealing with those with active injuries. The rest of the day disappeared in a wave of taking care of those that had been hurt, then dosing them for their pain.

By the time it was done, Zayn was unsure if he should be grateful or incensed. There were two broken bones. One singer broke their left arm, and a priest had a broken leg. They had three with head injuries that would be kept awake most of the night until their eyes were reacting equally. Four that needed stitches. Pain drops were handed out freely and half the occupants of the temple were in drugged sleep or watching over those who had been injured.

He had sent a message to Algoi to meet him in his quarters at four fingers to dusk. He had managed to wash his face and strip out of his robes by the time she knocked on the door. Her face was streaked with ash, blood, and the same bone weary exhaustion he felt.

"Wash your face, then come sit." He said. Part of it was him being nice, so her guard would lower. The other part was he had little desire to look at a blood- and ash-streaked face for this discussion.

She used his needs room, then came out and sat down in the chair he waved at. He had long ago created a little seating area with a table in his apartment, hiding his bed behind simple wooden screens. It gave him an area to relax and talk to his subordinates without being in his bedroom.

"Here, drink," he said, pouring them both generous glasses of fruist. He had considered adding the fascinating herb that Cire had shared with him, but right now he needed his brain working and hers.

Algoi had to be tired, because she made no protest, just taking a large drink of fruist, then setting it down to look at him.

"How bad is it?" He asked. People were hiding problems from him, and normally he preferred it that way. He had little time or inclination to deal with the day-to-day issues. But if the Day of Remembrance was going to be affected, he needed to know.

She took another drink before replying. "The courtyard will be clean, though not painted. Only two, the ones with broken bones, will be unable to sing. They will need at least a tenday on pain drops to function. The kitchens are still shut down for scouring. The singers are scared, but we ordered food from a few shops and treated them, praising them for how well they are doing. We will have the number of voices we need. My worry is that they will not be focused on their songs, but will be distracted."

Zayn winced. Distracted singers could spell disaster. Already most of the temples were putting up the bare minimum, even with the clergy singing with them. He took his glass and drained it, then refilled both of theirs again.

"Any ideas?"

Algoi looked down at the table. "Today is a bad day. If we were not looking at the Day of Remembrance in two dawns, I would not suggest this." He fell silent, her hand fiddling with the glass.

"Say your words. I have no anger left after today," Zayn advised, weary to the bone.

"There are a few faithful that sing with voices that almost rival the singers. They are not quite as polished, but they contain a level of commitment that only our priests can rival. I suggest extending a 'special' opportunity to them and pull them in for the next two days of practice. Their faith might balance out the distractions of the rest." Algoi refused to look at him as she spoke and he sat back, sipping on the fruist. When she finished, she looked up at him, her face drawn.

"That is a brilliant idea, Algoi. Implement it. Today. That way we can get them in here and practicing tomorrow. All practices will be moved to the worship area, so that will help. I am also going to get the masters to only high-light with gold various parts of the carvings and have priests walking the area tonight and tomorrow."

Algoi smiled at him, relieved. "I will." She paused, playing with the glass. "Do you think it will be enough?"

Zayn forced a smile. "Of course it will. Xyl knows how hard we try. Now finish your fruist and get messages out to your faithful. We only have a day to train them."

She nodded, and after a last gulp of fruist, was gone. Zayn leaned back and thought.

How bad is it going to be? If Xyl is not assuaged, what happens?

For the first time in life, Zayn wondered if the kingdom would survive Xyl's rage.

CHAPTER TWENTY-NINE

NOTE

The attack by pirates surprised Note, but when Jolyx came up shouting orders, he found himself with knives waiting with a level of anticipation that should have worried him. Instead, he dove into the fight with a newfound glee. His practice with Jadaya helped in the first few seconds.

A man came rushing over the planks, his coloring so close to Char, that any doubts Note might have felt dissolved. The curved sword came slashing down, much slower than how fast Jadaya could move. He spun to the left, letting the blade slice through the air where he previously stood. At the same time, he swung his right hand toward the face of the pirate, blade pointed at his eyes. He reacted by pulling up his sword to a high guard position, leaving open the underside of the right arm.

Note drove his knife in with a quick flick and cut deep into the artery that ran under the arm, then spun out of reach. With a grunt, the man dropped his arm and swung the sword hard at Note. If it had connected, it would have cut Note in half.

With a wicked smile, Note dropped to the deck, letting the blade sail over him, and jabbed up, this time into the groin for a deep cut, severing the artery there. He then rolled away, tripping another pirate before springing to his feet. His original attacker had blood covering him from the cut to his foot and it got darker with every beat of his heart. When the sword fell from fingers unable to hold it, Note dismissed him and turned his attention to the man scrambling to his feet from Note's tripping.

"I will cut you into fish bait!" the man shouted, diving toward him. This one had a sword in each hand, meaning he could negate Note's advantage. Note danced backward, avoiding the controlled strikes, his mind racing. Jadaya and he had practiced this and prior to this mission, he might have let himself get killed. Now he had too much to live for. Too much to prove.

He waited until the man lifted both arms up, getting overconfident as Note had found no opening so far. That was what he needed. He darted forward, faster than the man could swing, getting inside his range. One knife slit across his throat, the other across the man's belly. The swords fell with a clang to the deck as the man grabbed at his throat.

"See who is fish bait now," Note said with a grin.

He resisted the desire to howl in delight and instead found another foe. Time disappeared, there was only strike, duck, feint, dodge, kill. Flickers of Rylix fighting, throwing small darts that sank into eyes and throats. The man danced on the railings and stairs, even climbing up the rigging to hang upside down and cast his little missiles of death. There were also flashes of Jadaya, her tall, dark figure obvious as she cut through the attackers like a mad goddess. It all combined into one massive tumult of impressions, reactions, and emotions.

Then he turned, and there was no one lunging at him. Another turn and he could see men on the deck, dead and dying, and Jolyx's crew on the other ship. Nowhere did he see a blond head, or anyone fighting. He kept scanning and saw Jadaya standing there, her clothes as blood splattered as his, but not obviously harmed. Rylix was combing through the dead, pulling out his darts and dropping them in a bag with a look of distaste on his face.

He looked at himself, but other than a cut on one leg that was long and shallow, he was unharmed.

"Sound out! Who needs assistance?" Jolyx's voice boomed from the top deck and he snapped his attention to her. There were a few cries of help, but not many. "Tylax, get them taken care of. Let me know who we lost. Then you take the other ship. Pick your crew."

It all went so fast, as the crew seemed to know what to do. He, as well as Jadaya, had been learning to help. Raise the sails, clean the head, even how to process the seaweed that made the food edible. But this was outside what little he had learned, so he stepped back, leaning against the cabin to stay out of the way.

A finger later, Jadaya found him, and the grin on her face told him she enjoyed the fight as much as he had.

"What does it say about us, that we court death?" he asked, his voice low as the crew killed any pirate not already dead and aided their own as best they could.

"That we like to live? That we delight in using our skills for the reason we learned them?" Jadaya said, her eyes on the sea. "I think it is enjoying living and being willing to fight for it. And the fight is so much fun. Knowing I am good enough to come out alive in a battle to live."

Note grunted, unable to disagree. They assisted the crew in cleaning up the blood, as dried blood created fall risks. Then they helped wrap the bodies of the two that died in the fight. Note assumed more would have died, but Jolyx had a good crew. There were also three seriously injured. He glanced at his leg and saw the cut had already closed. His eyes narrowed, and he focused on the wrist cuff.

"Captain, who is worst off?" he asked as he went down to the mess hall where the wounded were laid out on the tables.

Jolyx nodded at the man on the table nearest the door. "Him. Two bad stab wounds. Why?"

Note moved over to him and pulled off the wrist cuff, placing it on the man's wrist. "No idea if this will help, but the odds of it harming are low." He tied it on and stepped back. It was always possible what Pel gave him would work only for him, but if it would work for others, he would risk it.

Jolyx looked at him, then shrugged and continued working on the sailor she was mending. Note just moved back against a wall, not sure of anything else he could do. He watched people work and managed to not think, just wait.

"Well, he is still alive and has stopped bleeding. What did you do?" Jolyx's voice pulled him out of his empty state.

"Gift from the gods. They said it would heal. Took a chance it would work for more than me." He tried not to look shamefaced, but he had put little faith in it. Maybe this was an actual enchanted item. It would be very helpful if it really would heal.

"Huh. Gods being helpful. Will wonders never cease?" She looked at her crew member for a long time, then shook her head. "Grab the lady warrior and meet me in the map room." She was walking out the door as she spoke, so he had no time to ask questions.

Note pushed off from the wall and headed back into the fresh air. The burst of salt and freshness made him realize how the scent of blood and dampness had permeated the air.

I hope they can air that out before we need to eat in there.

The idea of eating anything in that room right now made his stomach churn. He searched the deck for Jadaya, but no tall black woman stood there. Note headed down into the hold and toward the crew berth area. He found her seated under her sling chair, running a whetstone over the sword.

"You hurt at all?" The words he spoke surprised him. Caring was dangerous. But she was a companion, one he needed if they were to have a chance at success. It was only smart to make sure she was uninjured.

"No wounds, though I am sore. A few lunges that I was off balance for. My legs are telling me the technique was incorrect." She kept her attention on the sword as she spoke, checking it in the light coming through the porthole. "You?"

"Same." He watched for a while longer. "It would be easier to see on the deck," he pointed out.

"Yes. But I was in the way, and they have no need of a stranger watching as they take care of their dead." Her voice was calm, but he noticed how hard she held the sword.

How often has she been in fights? There is a difference between warrior and enjoying battle.

That thought sank into him, and he resolved to think about it—later. "The captain wishes to see us."

Jadaya nodded. She slid the sword back into its sheath and rose. He turned and headed back up, hearing her follow behind him. Her steps were soft, but the creaks of the wood under her were constant.

The door to the map room was open with Jolyx, Rylix, and Tylax already in there, along with another man, Drix.

"Good. You two made a big difference today, and the battle would have been more costly without you. How much do you know about Ged and pirate rules?" Jolyx started right in as they walked in the door.

"Nothing?" Note's comment was echoed by Jadaya, but Rylix looked smug about it.

Jolyx nodded, a sour look on her face. "As my cousin here reminded me, if you are part of those that fight to repel or defeat pirates, you are entitled to a portion of the value of the capture."

Note blinked, surprised. That was unexpected. "What exactly does that mean?"

Jadaya had a frown of concentration on her face as she listened.

"We will sail the ship into Calin with Tylax and a minimal crew on board. We have already gone through and looked at their cargo. Other ships are rarely as well defended as ours. If you add the value of the ship to the value of the cargo, which might be more or less depending on what the rates in Calin are, you are entitled to a share. While it is only about five percent each, it should net you close to three plat a piece."

Note found his lungs forgot to work as he stared at her.

Three plat?

Note had never seen that much. Even in the temple, the offerings rarely contained more than one or two silvers worth. He could buy anything, *everything*.

He just blinked, unable to process what that meant. She talked about the fact it would take a few days to get the money together, as she knew the value of the ships and the cargo, but rarely had that much currency on her. Plus the fact that the crew would receive the same cut as they did and the dead crew member's family would get their portion.

Note finally managed to get words out. "And how will we receive that?"

Jolyx's face had lost her sour expression. Instead, a sort of wry amusement sat there. "You have a few choices. If you wait another two tenday in Calin, we can give it to you in coin." Note noticed a subtle shake of the head from Rylix. "Or we can deposit it into the money holders for Fivika and give you a writ that you can pull from a bit at a time as you travel the country. But the writ is only good while in Fivika. After that, you would pull it all out or leave it there for your next journey."

"Does Vykland have the same sort of money houses?" Jadaya asked, and Note thought it was a great question. This situation was the exact opposite of how his life had been last time.

"No. If you need it there, take the cash now," Jolyx said. Her eyes bounced between Note and Jadaya as she waited.

"Can I tell you when we get to Calin? There is much to think about," Jadaya said, just when Note thought the silence had grown too long.

He almost sagged in relief and spoke up immediately. "That would be my preference as well. There is no reason to decide now, is there?"

"No. Let me know before you leave so I can place the funds in your accounts." Jolyx gave them a sharp nod and Note took that for the dismissal it was.

He and Jadaya both left, leaving Rylix behind as they wandered out in the sun.

"I have never had that much money," Jadaya said when they reached their normal talking spot. It let them see the ocean, but they stayed out of the way of the crew. "I remember on a few holy days being given two silver to spend on treats or a bauble. The most I was given was two copper when Yika needed me to run an errand. But three plat?" She shook her head and kept talking. "Yika spilled her coin purse once, and she had some in there. It was a white metal that felt lighter than the gold or copper, but so much harder. And now I have three?"

Note nodded, his feelings about the same as hers. "We can buy a mustang for that. Or our own wagon."

"We could save it for other adventures," Jadaya said, an odd tone in her voice.

Note turned to look at her and said slowly. "Other adventures?"

She shrugged, and a smile crossed her face. "I mean, if we live, we should have plans, right?"

CHAPTER THIRTY

LAZUL

Lazul let Actin fuss as he straightened his robe and made sure the crown sat properly on his head, anchored discreetly by pins in his hair. It would be a bad sign if the proof of his rank fell off while in worship today. The gaudy diadem was platinum, and the gems were mined from his country, the blues and reds vibrant, while greens set along the sides. His robe of white, blue, and red made him look too much like a peacock in his opinion, but he could not deny it created a presence.

"There, your majesty. You look like a proper ruler now. Are you sure you want to walk, rather than take a carriage to the temple?" Actin had a wealth of disapproval in his voice, and Lazul swallowed his smile.

"Actin. My parents walked to the temple to show Xyl they shared his grief. Do you think it would be wise to change that precedent now? With as emotional as Xyl has been?"

Actin's lips thinned into a line, then he sighed. "Your majesty is correct. It would be unwise to anger Xyl at all. The weather has been unpleasant of late."

Lazul gave Actin a sardonic look. "The weather is about to send my country into a famine. You are as aware of the reports as I am. If I have to crawl on my knees to get us a few mooncycles of decent weather, I will."

A flicker of emotion raced over Actin's face, something Lazul might have identified as respect. "Very well, sire. Then I believe you are as ready as I can make you."

"Bless," Lazul said with a nod of his head. He turned and headed out of his quarters and down to the common exit into the city. There were the formal great doors at the front of the palace, and for almost any other day he would exit that way, with the courtiers creating a grand spectacle. There would be pomp and circumstance, and he would feel like a fool for the next day or so, as everyone looked at him and critiqued everything.

But not this day.

Captain Malac waited outside, along with a few other guards and all of his senior staff. Actin had followed behind him, a coat appearing in his hands. This day everyone went to the temple. The past had taught them that skipping the Day of Remembrance had consequences for everyone.

"Are we ready, Captain?" Lazul looked at Malac, who, like everyone else, was dressed in their formal uniforms or best clothes. In many ways the Day of Remembrance was more important than your own wedding, as that might only make your life miserable. This could tear the country apart.

"Yes, sire." Malac bowed formally as he spoke.

"Then lead the way." Lazul allowed them to put him in the center of the entourage as they headed to the temple. The road down had been cleared of people and wagons. Even the jacks had been put in their stables today. Everyone walked. Why had Actin wanted him in a carriage? Lazul suspected it had been a test, but who knew? Actin was very protective of the monarchy, much more than Lazul was. Or what he remembered his parents being like.

The temple would have the outer gates to the courtyard open today, so the music would encompass the city. He would be in the front, of course, making sure everyone saw him. All he wished was that he was a better singer. He could sing, but it was barely in tune, and he worried sometimes that his voice distracted from the purity of the song. His mother had an excellent voice, though the only times he heard it was singing for Xyl.

All other song was forbidden. The only songs you could sing were to Xyl and while they were beautiful, they were songs that required concentration to sing. Once when he was a child, they had gone to Hearth, and he had listened to a bard passing through. The fun, jaunty, energetic songs had captured him, but even then he knew better than to ask for songs at home.

The walk to the temple was a short stroll, though with all the people, it was slower than normal. As they walked, Lazul tried to go through all the contingency plans that were set in place if Xyl refused to be placated by their offerings. The last tenday had been decent. The sun, in all its orangish glory, peeked through the clouds regularly, but it was too cloudy to see the skies at night. Today it was perfectly clear. It always was on the Day of Remembrance. Percit's broken halves hung in plain view. They were singing their sorrow at her death and Xyl would make sure she heard.

Lazul pulled his mind back to the contingency plans. He had been pulling a tenth of all the tax money into an emergency fund for suncycles. If needed, they would send a ship to Fivika to get food and anything else they would need to survive the year. But if the worst happened? He fought down a shudder.

How old had he been, twelve suncycles? Thirteen? It was a blur, but he remembered what happened. A disease had swept through the city, the country really. Singers had died. Chars had died. And those that showed up to the Day of Remembrance all had scratchy throats, stuffed noses, and a cough. The songs had been thin from the singers and mangled from the populace. His parents had stood at the front, singing with all their might, but Xyl had raged.

Funnels made of the air had burst out of the clouds, sweeping across the land, destroying crops and buildings with ease. The lightning that followed had killed people in the street, animals in the field, and set multiple trees on fire. Then it had rained. It rained for two tenday. By the time it quit, every house had a hand of standing water in it. The cost to livestock and his people had been astonishing. He remembered his mother taking some of her jewelry; the platinum crafted rings and bracelets, and using that to buy food and new herd stock.

A shiver rippled through him, though he kept a calm, cheerful smile on his face. The singers had to ensure they were on tune and calm Xyl's ire. By themselves, the people of Charinsky were not skilled enough.

A turn and the crowd reached the temple doors. Many of them headed to the back, where the enormous gates had been opened. The temple backed up to the square where the markets were held. Today, it was full of people. He glanced at them briefly, taking in the stress on the parents' faces, the confusion on the older children, and the troubled expressions on the youngest. Even the children realized this event, while a celebration, held little fun.

He entered the entryway and dipped his fingers in the Ashes of Percit. At this point, he suspected half of it was charcoal powder mixed with flour. Could there have been enough pieces found to create the amount of ground powder needed? He brushed the question from his mind as he drew double streaks of gray tears under his eyes, then turned and headed into the worship area.

Captain Malac and his squad ushered him to his position in the front, two steps up from the ground, so all could see him, know their ruler cried as hard as they did. Lazul took a breath and pulled on a devout face. While the face might be false, the emotions he would put into the songs would be real. Hopefully, Xyl would feel that.

He had been here less than half a finger when a bell sounded and the singers flowed into the area. They had risers at the very front, so all could see and marvel in their song. They wore the same colors as the priests, but rather than the gown that was belted and another robe over the top, they wore billowing loose smocks that were in black with red rings at the bottom. It made them look like a series of bells with silvery handles standing on those risers.

Once they were all situated, there was another bell and Zayn strode out, followed by the rest of the clergy. Lazul knew every priest would be here, regardless of their normal sleep cycle. All the temples would start at the same time. It was part of why there was an inspection. Part of Zayn's job was to make sure they were all on the same time.

They moved into their places with a smooth efficiency that Lazul had to admire. Some, the conductors, Lazul realized, positioned themselves at the base of the risers, so the singers were above them. Zayn took his place at the center of the stage, while the rest of the clergy were to his left. Lazul took a deep breath and tried to center himself and move into the proper mood. Xyl needed to know they mourned with him, because his people needed sun and dry days.

A bell rang, and Zayn lifted his hands. The throngs instantly quieted. Lazul allowed himself a quick glance back and saw people out past the walls and the open gates into the city. A sea of blond heads, all facing Zayn, ready to plead with their god with songs. Lazul pulled his attention back as Zayn spoke.

"City of Granite, my fellow Charinskys, we gather this day across our country to mourn with our god Xyl for the loss of the beautiful Percit." He paused for the refrain.

"Forever will she be remembered," the crowd responded.

"Today, the anniversary of her death, her moon shattered, as the Usurper killed her."

"May he remain in torment forever," the crowd responded. Lazul let himself add heat to those words. That god had almost destroyed his country by killing her. May he scream for all eternity.

"We will lift our voices to honor her memory, beauty, and love for Xyl," Zayn said with his voice carrying through the temple. It had been tuned for perfect acoustics, and Lazul let himself be carried away by the words.

"Forever will she be loved," they all responded.

"Let us sing our first song, Loss of Percit," Zayn said, and the bell rang as he stepped back to join the other priests getting ready to sing. It was the cue, and the singers tilted their heads back a long low note that raised the hair on the back of Lazul's neck. The sound was a cry of mourning, sorrow, and grief that could not be contained. Emotion that was real, and he knew it came from their own pain. Then they began to sing.

He knew the words, and sang them, but he felt his own less than perfect voice damaged what they created, but the power of the crowd, the familiar words, swept him away. So many voices singing the same words and tunes, any imperfections were smoothed out, and the city rang with power, grief, and love.

Clouds gathered overhead, and he knew they were over the entire country, but the rain that fell was light, like tears down a mother's face, the grief old and comfortable, love mixed with sorrow.

As the last notes of the song died away, Zayn stepped back up. "We all mourn the loss of our beloved Percit, but memories should not be sad. They should be filled with the joy and love of the one now gone." Another bell and a sound that rang with lightness and joy, but Lazul frowned as he watched the singers. Was it him, or was there a tinge of sorrow under it? They started into the song, which was a one of the standard set of five that were sung on the Day of Remembrance. It started off fine, but the first verse in, he heard the anger and sorrow lacing into the notes. Rather than an uplift in the music, there was a descant.

He saw Zayn's head snap to the singers also as all the Aoisans downshifted the notes, making it rather that a song of lightness and joy it became a paean of loss masked with false joy.

The crack of thunder as lightning hit the temple was the first warning as to how bad this was going to be.

CHAPTER THIRTY-ONE

JADAYA

The last day had been calm, and the port of Calin was but eight fingers out, the harbor warm and welcoming. But far in the distance, she could see clouds that heralded a storm that Jadaya wanted nothing to do with. She wandered up to the helm to ask Jolyx. She had adapted to being on the ocean, but she feared going into another weather front, no matter the last one had good ramifications.

"Will we hit that storm?" she asked Jolyx, who stood with her far viewer looking at it. Even if they made it to harbor first, the idea of traveling through that on land was unpleasant.

"No. It is hanging over Charinsky. The odds are it will remain there. Which has implications that worry me, and should worry you."

By this point Rylix and Note had shown up to listen. It was as if there was a feeling of when the three of them needed to be somewhere. They always turned up when something interesting was occurring.

"Why?"

"If my calendar is correct, today or yesterday, one of the two, was the Day of Remembrance for Percit. It is something the Charinskys celebrate—though that is probably the wrong word—every suncycle to ensure Xyl is kept relatively happy." She gestured at the clouds that hung so far away. They should have been only wisps, but they roiled hard and tall, going so far up in the sky that they disappeared. "If that is hanging over Char like I believe it is, they are about to have a terrible suncycle and will be desperate." Her voice was grim, and Jadaya found her eyes drawn back to the storm hanging in the sky. "Keep it in mind for what you said you are going to do." Her dark gaze turned to Note. "They regard the singers as the only way to survive, remember that."

She turned and started calling out instructions to the crew as they headed to the harbor. Jadaya had learned how to be helpful during the trip, but for this she got out of their way knowing she would slow them down. She let her eyes linger on the clouds and wondered what else lay in store for them. And just how bad could those clouds be?

In her little corner, Note showed up. They had spent the last few days sparring with the crew, as their performance during the attack had made all of them eager to learn. The pirate ship, *Wavebreaker*, followed in their wake. They had pulled an extra set of sails from the *Starguide* to avoid confusion. The Ged sails were white, with a blue band across the top. Ged blue was a special dye only they had. It remained dark even when exposed to wind, rain, and sun. It also made all Ged ships easily identifiable, and Jadaya knew she would never see black sails again and be able to rest easy.

She and Note leaned against the railing as the ship was expertly brought into the harbor, and men ran alongside to grab the ropes tossed to them as they were secured to the dock. She was aware of it, but her mind was spinning with thoughts about journeys, adventures, and seeing the world.

"Are your thoughts that engrossing?" Note asked from her side, and Jadaya glanced at him, but then sent her eyes back to the activity on the pier. The raised voices as the second ship came in, and she recognized more than one Ged waiting for them.

"Maybe. If we succeed, what do you plan on doing next?"

Note laughed, a bright peal of music, more than she had heard from him before. "Jadaya, if I live, if my people are rescued, at that point I will worry about what to do after."

"You can accept there is nothing awaiting us after this life?"

His smile faded, and he shrugged. "More I never thought I would live long enough to see even this much. If I raise my hopes, there is more to lose." His voice was dark, and she thought about all he had already lost: his family, his childhood, his manhood. It was a lot, and maybe losing more was more than he could handle.

"Maybe. I think I would like to dream about the future. A future I control. Have something to look forward to. Prove to the gods, all of them, that nothing can stop me." Her voice became fierce again as the banked anger slipped through.

Note was silent as the last ropes were secured, and the ship came to a stop. "Ask me when this is done. If we live. Ask me then."

"I will," she said and shifted her focus to the chaos that was the Calin harbor.

She watched, fascinated, at the variety of people. For the most part in Zuyika, she saw her own people, the occasional Ged or Wyskan. Here, she lost track. There were people with hair as black as her skin, people who looked like they could pick up jacks and walk with them, some with designs on their face and arms, and even some with hair that was a bright red. It was a jumble of life and people that was as fascinating as it was overwhelming.

The harbor was alive with the movement, shouting in multiple languages, animals and cargo being pulled off the boats and heading to what looked like a vast market in the distance. The shudder of the boat as the gangplank was tossed down signaled the end of the trip.

Jolyx walked up to the three of them. At some point, Rylix had joined their observation of the harbor. "If you would wait for about three fingers, I will have the scripts needed for your portion." She pointed to the three people walking up the gangplank. "I need to talk to them-" She was cut off before she managed to say any more, as one of the men stormed up to them, anger radiating off him to the point Jadaya found herself reaching for her sword as it was so aggressive.

"You were going on a trade run for family. What is that?" He jabbed a finger at the Wavebreaker that was secured to the dock next to them.

Rather than getting upset, Jolyx crossed her arms under her breasts and arched an eyebrow. Jadaya wondered if the lifting of her breasts was intentional or a side effect. Either way, the man's eyes would flip down to glance at them occasionally.

"Looks like a ship to me. Do you see something else?" Her voice was mild as she looked at him. "Do we need to find the glassers for you and see if they can help with your vision? I hear they have some that can help both with reading and distance sight."

The man was obviously Ged with his dark curly hair and tanned skin. Red flushed his face and cheeks as he gritted his teeth. "I can see it is a ship. Why do you have it? This was a trade run, not an acquisition. We did not authorize you to spend that level of money."

"Good. Because I would have never paid that price. It cost me the lives of two men. It was almost three." She kept her eyes on the man, but Jadaya felt the glance. Note had retrieved his cuff from the wounded man, and he had lived. No one was sure how much it had helped, but they were sure he would have died without it.

That stopped the man, and he blinked at her. "What?" his voice was much more reasonable.

The two who had come up with them sighed. The woman stepped forward. "I told you that purchasing a ship was unlikely. Jolyx, what happened?"

Jolyx relaxed, dropping her arms to her side. "I think we should start over," she said with an icy voice, but her face had relaxed. "Good afternoon, Elder Gilx, Elder Smoy, and Elder Myilx. I assume you are here for my report."

The woman, Myilx, tried to keep her mouth in a straight line, but the corners of her lips kept turning up. "Good day to you, Captain Jolyx. Yes, we are here for reports and have some concerns about the ship that not only came in with you, but seems to be captained by Tylax?"

"Yes. The previous owners of that ship were foolish enough to think they could take us as free goods." The three elders all snorted at the idea.

Jolyx shrugged. "It was a closer battle than I would have preferred. They are getting better at killing. Part of the reason we succeeded are these three standing here." She turned and gestured at the little group and Jadaya found herself standing straighter as their surprised glances fell on them. "The lady warrior carved through the attackers as if they were wheat heads to the scythe. The Aoisan accounted for a fair number with his knives. And as for our trader kin," she said, pausing to look at Rylix with narrowed eyes.

Jadaya turned to glance at him and was surprised to see a flush heating Rylix's cheeks.

"He is both very effective with his little knives and darts, and far too interested in giving away profits." There was still a touch of dark annoyance in her voice.

Rylix shrugged. "I was simply ensuring that the rules were followed both to the letter and the spirit. Without the efforts of myself and my companions, the cost would have been much greater." He smiled in his charming way, eliciting rolled eyes and a sigh from Jolyx.

"He is not inaccurate. As such, they are being accorded a full salvage share of five percent."

The ripples of surprise, annoyance, and acceptance that went across all the elders made little sense to Jadaya. She was still trying to process having that much money.

"Speaking of which, have you decided how you would like your earnings? And please remember, that was an estimate. The final amount will be based on the value of the ship and the cargo." Jolyx turned that arch look on them and Jadaya found herself trying not to squirm. Jolyx was beautiful, smart, capable, and could make you feel a child who had taken a sweet.

"I would prefer to take two copper to spend now, and have the rest put in the money house. You said we can take it out from any city in Fivika with the script, so if we need more, I should be able to draw it from in either Hearth or Betan?" She wanted to verify, as the idea of carrying that much money terrified her. She had studied the maps that Jolyx carried in the map room and knew Betan was the city they would leave from to get to Vykland and the mount of the gods.

"Yes. You will be able to pull money out there," Jolyx agreed.

"The cities have updated their agreements," an elder said. It was Gilx, the one who had stormed up to them furiously. "You can now pull the money out from any money house in Delcona, Agrina, or Fivika. Last I heard, they are working on creating a partnership with Vykland, but that is still suncycles away."

Jolyx raised an eyebrow. "That would be convenient."

A smile of pride crossed the elders' faces. "Yes, it would."

"I believe I shall take the majority of my portion," Rylix said. "I would rather purchase more trade goods for both Vykland and Charinsky when we get there. But please put one plat in my name and half a plat in holding for my family."

The three nodded like his comments made sense. Jolyx looked at Note. "And you?"

"I believe I will follow Jadaya's example. Some money to spend will be nice, but the rest can stay safe."

Jolyx nodded. "Very well. You are free to stay here this evening as we will not have the ship evaluated and cargo priced until tomorrow at the earliest."

Rylix nodded. "That is what I supposed. For now, I at least am going to go explore the market. It has been a few suncycles since I visited."

The elders nodded at them and then followed Jolyx to her cabin, leaving the three of them standing there.

Rylix smiled at Jadaya and Note. "Well, what are you waiting for? Go explore. Do you have some gold to spend?"

Jadaya shook her head, and the glimpse of black hair tossing in the corner of her vision let her know Note was in the same situation.

"I figured. Here." He dug into the small bag on his waist. "Here are two copper each. I know you will be receiving handfuls more than that once the money is deposited. Go enjoy." With that he left Jadaya standing there with two copper, looking out at the sea of new things to explore.

CHAPTER THIRTY-TWO

LAZUL

Lightning hit the top of the temple, where the thin spire of the steeple reached up into the sky. It was set so that when Percit rose, that line cut between her broken halves. The steeple *melted*. That was the only word Lazul could come up with. The light from the streak of power that slammed into it remained in his vision as he looked to where the line had split the sky. It sagged and fell apart as he watched. Then the screams pulled him out of his stunned fixation on where the spire once stood.

He whirled to the screams coming from the back of the worship area, where the gates had been opened into the streets to make sure everyone was included. People ran as a funnel of air dropped down in the middle. Oddly, Lazul was relieved. This funnel was only about as wide as he, and barely as tall as the gates. The ones he remembered from childhood had reached into the sky and been as wide as his royal barge was long.

"Sire, we need to get you back to the castle," Malac urged, pulling on his arm.

Lazul shook it off. "The castle will provide no protection if Xyl continues to rage. Protect the singers." He pointed that them. They had fallen quiet, looking up at the sky in horror and fear.

"Sire," Malac protested.

"Go," Lazul ordered as he headed toward Zayn. The cantor was staring at the damage to his temple in astonishment and an odd expression of affront.

"Zayn?" Lazul asked, having no time or energy to deal with formalities. Zayn was unresponsive, his head still tilted up as various priests were cowering or had fled. Lazul grabbed his arm and shook him. "Zayn!"

"What?" Zayn snapped, turning to glare at him now instead of the temple.

Lazul managed to not hit him, though his hand curled into a fist. "Look around you. We need to get them singing before Xyl destroys everything." As if in response to his words, hail began to fall. The small pellets of ice were not deadly yet, though already they were proving annoying. But Lazul knew, from painful experience, they would get larger and larger. Already they had moved from a quarter-tella sized to half.

"Selfish, ungrateful, louts," Zayn muttered. "Yes. I have it." He turned away from Lazul and pulled the nearest priest to his feet. "Get them into the entry chamber. Start the hymns with *Percit My Love*. Go!" He turned and grabbed another clergy that ran by him. "Get outside and start the populace in *Percit My Love*. Everyone you see needs to be singing."

Lazul nodded. *Percit My Love* was a simple tune listing of all her attributes. It was one of the first songs you learned in the temple, and it was something usually sung in rounds. A howl of wind caught his attention, and he backed away from Zayn, to look up and out toward the sea. Granite was set at the top of Charinsky with the harbor to the east. While from the city proper you were unable to see the sea or the ships, it was only about two thousand hands from the temple to the edge of the seawall.

The towering funnel of water, wind, and raging grief that reached past the clouds was visible against the darkening sky.

"Xylicat!" Lazul swore as he flinched when hail struck him. The hail had increased to bigger than his thumb.

"I am planning on skinning them alive," Zayn swore, glaring at Lazul. "Come with me," he ordered, storming into the entryway where the rest of the singers were gathered. There were more now, even the youngest ones, as well as the majority of the clergy that remained, as opposed to being sent out to get the populace to sing.

With a shove from the cantor, Lazul found himself with the milling singers and priests. Zayn stepped up to where a conductor would normally be. "Listen to me, all of you," Zayn yelled in a voice that boomed through the room. Lazul flinched back as much as the Aoisans did. "You will sing. All of you have been taught *Percit My Love*, so I will start, and you join in. Focus on love, eternal faithfulness, and joy. If I hear a single sob, I will flay the skin from your bones. Now get ready."

Each word landed like a blow and Lazul fought not to act like a scared child at Zayn's words. Only the fact that there were other clergy around prepared to sing along with him allowed the resentment to fade. It also helped that outside the open door, he could see that the hailstones had increased to the size of eggs and hear the sound of buildings breaking and tearing in the distance.

If we are unable to improve his mood, he will destroy my country.

That drove him more than anything else to focus and when Zayn started, they all joined in at the first refrain.

Percit, oh Percit, wisdom's embrace,
In starry realms, your kindness we trace.
Goddess of moon and death so divine,
In your glory, our hearts entwine.

The simple song continued and Lazul latched on to it as his focus and poured out every ounce of love and need into it. This particular song was more from her followers' viewpoint than her husband's, but for now, it was an easy way to get everyone singing. He silently prayed his people were not sent to her door this day. At this moment, his mood was very devout.

In the silence of the night,
Percit's presence, a guiding light.
Through the veil of death, she leads,
Wisdom's path, where love succeeds.

Even as he sang, his heart fully in the meaning, he kept his eyes on the cloud in the distance. The song echoed from the streets, not in rhythm with them, but still it was singing. The sounds were more amateur than the singers' offering, but it was honest.

Zayn kept directing them, but Lazul saw him tilting his head to pay attention to the sounds coming in from the street as well. But the hail still fell, now the size of round fruit. He could hear the occasional crack as it went through ceilings next door, and felt the thuds as it hit the temple.

"The populace will continue to do the rounds of *Percit My Love*. We will switch to *The Love of Xyl & Percit*."

Lazul choked and looked at Zayn. The man wanted them to be killed. That song, while it was one of Xyl's favorites, was also one of the hardest to sing. It required a range that most Charinsk's were unable to reach. Lazul could, but it had been suncycles since he had sung it. He scrambled for the words as more cracks of thunder and lightning struck, leaving the streets white with the bright light.

"If you are unfamiliar with the song, learn it fast. Jump in with the chorus as soon as the rest of us start it. Because if we fail, we die." Zayn's words were barely audible over the noise of the storm.

Lazul felt his jaw drop as Zayn launched into the song. All priests had to have perfect pitch and be able to sing, but he had never heard Zayn single in a solo manner. It had always been with the overlapping voices of others. His voice was *stunning*. As good as the singers.

Oh, Xyl, to Percit, my love profound,
In realms of stars, your beauty's crowned.
Through moonlit nights and wisdom's grace,
I sing to you in this sacred space.

Then he started in on the chorus. A few joined him there, including Lazul.

Oh, Percit dear, my heart's delight,
In realms of wonder, day and night.
Though distance parts our cosmic dance,
Our love transcends each fleeting chance.

They got stronger as they sang, the difficult transitions flawless. The hail had turned to rain, and for a moment, Lazul thought maybe they had a chance. The song lifted higher, chronicling the love of a husband for his wife.

A hiss and roar dashed his hopes as he clenched hard on his bladder. He knew that sound. It was that of a koxylitic lizard. Lazul kept singing, but his attention darted back and forth between the door to the worship area, unsure where it would come from. He wanted to go check out and make sure everyone had gotten to safety. He had no illusions that the hail could have killed people, as could the funnel in the harbor, but death by a koxylitic made the rest of those seem like preferable deaths. The venom it carried dissolved you slowly from the outside in, leaving you screaming in pain as you died over days. No drug or solution was strong enough to block the pain. Usually, you just killed the victim to assuage their misery. Xyl was the god of all reptiles, and the fact that he sent a Koxylitic into town, into his temple, showed how enraged he was.

If he kills me, maybe he will let his anger go.

It was a frantic thought. If his death would satisfy Xyl, he would offer himself up with joy. But deep down, he knew Xyl would never be done with his grief and rage.

Malac and his squad of men had remained to guard him, and they had their weapons drawn and were looking back and forth even as they sang. The hissing roar came again, this time from the left. Everyone, even the singers who could have never seen a Koxylitic before, had their eyes locked on the wide-open door as the splashing and roaring got larger.

Zayn made a face and pointed at Lazul, then the door, his gestures clear, but he never lost the song that spiraled up in perfect harmony, though over the rain, thunder, and roaring wind it was almost impossible to hear. Almost.

Lazul nodded, knowing he and his men had to deal with it. Lazul never had any desire to be a hero, a military man, or even fight in wars. But he still drilled daily with his guard. It had a twofold purpose: it let them practice and familiarize themselves with each others' movements, and kept him in shape. That being said, a sword was normally not part of the official uniform.

I am adding that to my royal outfit, no matter how much Actin protests.

The dark thought grabbed him as he looked around for a weapon. He refused to grab one from the guards. That would be unacceptable. His eyes grabbed on a glint of metal. In the corner was a long staff with a wick on top. A lighter for the higher lanterns in areas. He moved over to grab it, still singing. Though in a moment, breathing would become much more important. Nodding at Malac, they moved over toward the door, but they were too slow. The head of the koxylitic snaked around the door, looking in. The song faltered as a few people screamed. Zayn clapped his hands and snapped their attention back to him, and he gestured, moving them back into the worship area, ignoring the rain that was still coming down, though it had lessened.

Lazul nodded, and he and his men turned to face the monster coming in the door. Koxylitics were about as long as a man and their body at the shoulder was only mid-thigh on most people. But it could move faster than a man could run, and it seemed like it had a head full of teeth. With a long, flexible neck, it could almost bite directly behind it. And that was where the problem came in, the venom that lived in its saliva. How it managed to live without poisoning itself, Lazul had no idea. But he knew they had to kill it, and quickly.

With a whisper of relief and regret, he quit singing and turned his attention to the creature. "Malac, let me get its attention, as I have the longest reach. You all stay behind and stab it. If we can make it bleed enough, it should die."

"Sire!" The word burst out of the mouth of all his men and for a moment Lazul felt proud to be their leader.

"We have no time. Right now, the singers, the priests, everyone who has their voice lifted in song are more important. Now!" He lunged with the point of the staff. The lighter was a pointed metal with a wick in it. The metal jabbed into the head of the creature, and it whirled on him, hissing. He backed up, jabbing as it snapped and followed him. Lazul knew the room was only so long and if he got trapped in a corner, he would die.

You said you would die for your people. Prove it.

Rage at the situation, the singers stolen from their homes, Zayn for being such a conceited asshole, and Xyl for asking more than his people could give, override fear, common sense, and self-preservation. With an inarticulate scream, he slashed and jabbed, using all his power and strength to keep the koxylitic occupied. His squad dived in and out, their swords slashing and piercing. Every time the creature turned to attack one of them, Lazul dove in with the stick, jabbing at eyes, nose, mouth, anything that would pull its attention back to him. The screams of rage and frustration of the creature filled the room to where all he could hear was his own breathing and the creature's noises.

Then his stick broke in half when teeth clamped down on it and it shattered like it had been made of eggshells in the koxylitic's jaws. With a hiss of annoyance, it turned to attack the men behind it.

"No," Lazul growled and lunged. He tried to grab the head and wrap his arms around the mouth, preventing it from biting anyone else. The attack missed as he tripped on his robes of office. Another thing that had to change. With a hiss, the koxylitic whipped its head around, and its fearsome teeth clamped around his thigh.

He screamed as lances of fire penetrated his thigh. Lazul's body hit the floor as his men attacked the creature. Only the fact that it still had its jaw locked on Lazul's leg prevented it from turning to attack them. With a cry worthy of a koxylitic itself, Malac slammed his sword through the creature's brain, killing it.

Then they all stood and stared at their king, the creature's teeth still embedded in his leg.

CHAPTER THIRTY-THREE

JADAYA

Jadaya headed down the gangplank, the two copper tucked into her bindings. Jolyx had shown her how to wrap her existing binding to create a pocket. It was almost impossible for that to be picked as you noticed if someone slipped a hand between your breasts. Note and Rylix followed.

"I will return, but with this new largess, I must talk to my family and see what they can change for our trip. Enjoy the market, stay aware of the people around you, not everyone will trade fair. Yet I have faith you will find wonder and fascination in the market." Rylix waved at the bustling area in front of them, then disappeared in a different direction.

Jadaya looked at Note. "I would enjoy company." It seemed safe to say, as telling him this was intimidating seemed unwise. The markets she had visited in Zuyika had been a quarter of this size and everyone had looked like her. Here there was a bewildering array of skin tones, heights, smells, languages, and sounds. If she had found herself her alone without companions, she might have fled.

"Sure. You have anything you want to buy?" Note sounded easy and relaxed. She kept reaching for her sword, which she left on board. Per Jolyx, walking around with a sword was asking for trouble. Note had left his daggers on the ship, but she knew he had his smaller knives. She needed to find something less obvious. Maybe while they traveled, she could get Rylix to teach her knife throwing. In the flickers of time between the attackers, she had seen his skill and his rapid throws, usually ending in death.

"I would like to find some of the different bindings Jolyx showed me and maybe some of those small throwing knives Rylix had. I know we had spoken of finding weapons here. Is that something we should look for?" They walked into the market proper as she spoke. It was hard to keep her attention on Note when there was so much to look at.

The market was a series of canvas and wooden frames. Signs hung from poles in front, often with images rather than words. The fabrics were every color in nature, and she wondered if Ola's dyes would find any buyers. But that was a worry for tomorrow. Today she would explore. She lifted her nose, sniffing the air, trying to place the various scents. The sounds of trade, barking of dogs, and the flashes of movement belonging to cats darting through the throngs all seemed almost overwhelming.

"That sounds like an excellent suggestion. I might get some too. The ones I found on the wrecks are weighted for fighting, not throwing. But that might be something we should wait for Rylix on. I am not positive how they should be balanced as I have had no chance to play with his." Note smiled as he watched a dog begging for treats from people purchasing kabobs from a stand.

Jadaya shrugged as a scent caught her nose. "I smell cinamint," she said with a slow smile.

"Cinamint?" Note asked, looking at her.

"It is a favorite from home. A ground spice we use." She knew she was smiling, but just the smell reminded her of good times. The Chosen as children getting treats, the cakes and cookies on holy days, the smells of the kitchens. Without conscious choice, she followed her nose toward the smell. She was a full hand taller than most people and she ignored the looks she got, enjoying the ability to move through the crowd as people tended to move out of her way.

"There, that sign is in Zuit." Her joy leaked out, and she resisted the urge to run. It was too crowded, but now the crowds made her even more impatient. They wove through the crowds until they reached the booth. A tall Zuyikan was working behind a counter, making dough cooked in boiling oil, then dusting with cinamint and white beet juice power. He was the dark black of charcoal and his hair was in tiny braids instead of the twists that Jadaya did her hair in. His lanky muscles and the way he moved almost made her want to cry in familiarity.

"Zalo," she said with excitement, slipping into Zuit from Ged.

The man's head jerked up, dark eyes searching for the speaker, and his eyes found her as she closed the last few steps to his counter. A smile spread across his face, then his eyes locked on the brand on her left cheek. He blinked, then his face lost all joy, and he went back to cooking, not even looking at her.

"Zalo?" she said again, this time slower as pain wrapped around her heart, slowly climbing up her throat. No reaction.

"Am I missing something?" Note asked, stepping forward. "Hey, she is speaking to you."

The man raised his head and looked at Note, a smile crossing his face that Jadaya knew had no joy in it. His eyes were blank. "Morning. Can I interest you in a cloud dough? I have cinamint, a specialty from my country, red and white beet juice powder, ground tellanut spread both types, or even some fruit preserves." Not once as he spoke did he even glance at Jadaya.

Note looked back and forth between her and the man. "She is the one who wants something."

The man just widened his smile a bit, looking only at Note? "Are you sure there is nothing here that calls to you? They are the best cloud dough in the market and the only one with cinamint."

Jadaya blinked rapidly to keep the tears back. The rage at what she had lost helped push it back. "Exile, Note. He will never acknowledge my existence. I am nothing. I no longer exist."

Note actually snarled, and for a moment Jadaya thought he might attack. Instead, he turned on his heel and strode away. Jadaya turned to follow him, giving one last glance back at the cloud dough maker, but the man was resolutely looking the other direction. They walked away from the area and the sparkle and joy of the market had been snatched away from her. At that point, going back to the ship and doing routines until she dropped with exhaustion sounded like the best option.

"I need a drink. And while I love my home, they are lacking in variety and taste when it comes to alcohol. It is one of the few things I miss about Char. They had some good booze." Note spoke in a voice that sounded cheerful, but Jadaya wanted to scream.

They took even my countrymen from me. Elike used me. They threw me away.

She went back and forth between rage and grief, keeping her in an odd balance that let her move, but anything else seemed too hard. The market changed as she followed Note almost automatically. The vendors seemed random to her, and she tried to find something to grab her attention, but the pain lashed at her, making everything blur into a wash of colors and sounds.

"Here. Come on," he said, as he turned into a fenced off area. She blinked and tried to look at where they were. It had tent-like material above it, providing shade to the multitude of tables and stools that crowded under it. Servers were darting around the seated patrons, serving drinks and food with cheerful abandon. To her unspoken relief, she saw no dark skin, no possible rejections.

"Grab a seat anywhere. Someone will serve you shortly," one of the waiters called as they stood there.

Note moved over and got a small table on one side, providing a view of the busy market. "Jadaya, look at the board and see what you want." He pointed to the board on the wall above what looked like a busy kitchen with a counter. She could see grills going behind the counter, jugs of drinks along a wall, stacks of produce, hanging meat, and people back there chopping, cooking, pouring. It smelled good, if unfamiliar. The names meant nothing to her. She had eaten whatever Ola had placed in front of her, not caring about what it was called, other than it was food. The primary drink of Aois was spring water or tea. Their one alcoholic drink could remove dye from cloth, it was that strong.

"I am unsure what any of that is," she admitted, using the confusion to pull her out of her whirl of emotions. The smells, however, caused her stomach to remind her she had not eaten yet that day.

"Anything you dislike or will make you sick?" He asked. His voice was still wary, or perhaps concerned. She was unsure of the difference or if it mattered.

"Not that I know of," she said. She had always been an open eater, liking the flavors and spices.

"Fine." The waiter came by, and Note ordered. Her attention drifted to watching the people, both eating and flowing past the booth. Zuyika was a society that had few strangers. The Wyskans from the other side of their mountain range and the Ged. Other than those, she rarely saw foreigners. The occasional one would visit the city for trade, but they were not trusted and stayed near the docks. Here she saw everything. Though she only saw the rare glimpse of Aoisan, obvious from their silver blue skin and silvery hair, or Zuyikan with their skin so black that it called to her. To her relief, none of the few she saw glanced at her or noticed, letting her lie to herself that they would not have rejected her.

"Jadaya?" Note's voice pulled her from her people watching and she realized her pain was fading. She had known it would happen, but the reality of it had shocked her.

"Yes?" She turned to look at him and caught the look of worry in his eyes. "I will survive. It was a shock. But also something I knew to expect on our travels." She reached up and traced the scars on her cheek. "Will this cause us problems?"

He shrugged. "That is a question for Rylix, but plenty of people have noticed you. It is hard not to, and only that fish bait reacted that way."

Jadaya nodded and closed her eyes. She took in a deep breath and let it back out, then opened her eyes, feeling more centered. "So, what did you order?"

He looked up and leaned back. "Here it is, take a look."

The waiter dropped two plates containing sticks with meat, vegetables, and fruit skewered on them, and two mugs full of a dark red liquid. He also dropped change on the table, seven silver and eight gold. "Enjoy."

"I ordered fruist, as the beers are not something I enjoy. If I remember correctly, their fruist is sweet and strong as some liquors." Note lifted his glass and took a swallow, a smile crossing his face. "Yes, just as I remembered."

Jadaya shrugged. "I enjoy it, but the Chosen are unable to get drunk, so it is all the same as water to me."

Note's eyes widened. "You never get drunk?"

"No. We had the occasional contest with each other, but it is just liquid." She poked at the food. It smelled good, with the meat nicely charred and the vegetables seared and juicy. She wiped her fingers on her skirt and picked up the skewer, pulling off the first bite of meat. The flavors were rich, explosive on her tongue, and the taste of red meat was a welcome change after mostly fish these last mooncycles.

Note was eating with the same evident approval. She took a drink of the fruist and smiled. The fruist was strong, as was the hit of alcohol in the back of her throat, warming her spirit as it slid down her throat. They wasted no time talking, instead enjoying the food.

"You want another drink?" Note asked, a slight flush on his cheeks.

"Yes," she said. She felt lighter and happier than she had in a while. If sitting here eating and drinking gave her that feeling, she had little desire to disturb it.

Note held up two golds at the waiter and pointed to their glasses. A handful of heartbeats later, two more mugs were set in front of them. And Jadaya drained the last of her first drink.

"You want anything else with that?" the friendly server asked.

Note tilted his head and pulled out another gold. "A tray of cheese bread?"

The gold disappeared, and the man nodded. "Quarter finger, it is being pulled out of the ovens now."

Jadaya tilted her head, following the outline of the kitchen and saw the chimneys of large ovens. This place had a variety of different cuisines. Maybe she could come back and try more of them. She took another drink.

"Where to after this?" she asked, back to looking at the people and the wares. There were so many things. She wanted to go see the stall across the street. It looked like they had different hair clasps. The urge to dispose of anything Zuyikan ate at her. If she bought some new beads, she could redo her hair. Maybe create a different hairstyle.

"We still need to look for bindings and knives. I think the signs said there were weapon makers further down the street. As to the bindings, the clothes makers are in the blue section. We entered via the jumble section, red."

Jadaya blinked her eyes as she took another drink. "Yes, bindings." She frowned, looking at Note. "Why are you leaning to the side?"

He looked back at her and laughed. "You are the one leaning. Not me. I think you might be drunk."

"But I am unable," she protested as she looked down at the cup and realized it was mostly empty.

Note rubbed his nose, unable to hide his smile. "I think that is one of things you lost. Welcome to the rest of us mortals. Where you can get drunk. But since I have no desire to deal with a sick drunk, that will be your last drink."

Jadaya found herself pouting, but the warm fuzziness that enveloped her was one of the best things to happen in a while.

CHAPTER THIRTY-FOUR

ZAYN

The crack of lightning was the embodiment of his worst nightmares. Xyl was angry. At that moment, if Zayn could have skinned all the singers alive, Aoisan and Char alike, he would have. The change in the music had caught him by surprise, but he had no way of stopping it. Now it was a disaster.

He looked up at the sky, trying to figure out the best way to fix this. They needed to get Xyl pacified. But how? Could he trust the singers to sing the songs correctly at this point?

"Zayn?"

If he could get a solid group going, one of the simpler songs that the populace could sing, maybe. That was assuming the populace was still around and not cowering in their sties like pigs.

"Zayn!"

"What?" He snapped, turning to glare at the king. How could the man not realize he was busy?

"Look around you. We need to get them singing before Xyl destroys everything."

Zayn wanted to slap the man. Of course, they needed to get them singing. What did he think he was working on? Which song round?

"Selfish, ungrateful, louts," Zayn muttered. "Yes. I have it." He turned and grabbed the nearest priest, pulling him to his feet. "Get the singers and the other priests into the entry chamber. Start with *Percit My Love*. Go!" He looked and saw another clergy grabbing him. "Get outside and start the populace in *Percit My Love*. Everyone you see needs to be singing."

A familiar howl of wind grabbed his attention and for a moment he flashed back to many suncycles before when Xyl had become enraged. That wind had roared then and erased entire buildings from the earth. It had taken suncycles to recover.

All of this was because those idiot Aoisans were unable to recognize a blessing when they saw it.

"I am planning on skinning them alive," he snarled, switching his attention to the king. The king that could sing, if not as well as the singers. "Come with me," he demanded, then headed to the entryway where the ungrateful wretches were milling around.

"Listen to me, all of you," he barked out, standing in front of them, pulling on their automatic obedience when a conductor stood at the front. "You will sing. All of you have been taught *Percit My Love*, so I will start and you join in. Focus on love, eternal, and joy. If I hear a single sob, I will flay the skin from your bones. Now get ready."

Zayn took a deep breath, pulling on his suncycles of training to start it off right. Not only did the pitch have to be perfect, he needed to sound like he was gloriously happy and faithful. That was hard enough on normal days. Now with the rain, hail, and wind, he had to reach deep and swore if he lived through this, others might not.

"Percit, oh Percit, wisdom's embrace," he sang, projecting his voice and smiling as he heard the sound bounce in the chamber. Then the singers lifted their voices up to match his. He snapped his hands at two of the priests that were not quite perfect and gestured them to the door. They knew to grab more people to sing. For this specific song, having it being perfectly synced up was less important than singing. If the priests in charge of the other temples failed in doing something similar, they might all die. And if they lived, he would be finding new priests to run things across the country.

The singers joined in as he directed them to go up an octave and tried to ignore the hail that provided the wrong type of percussion for this song. He would need to do something different. His belly twisted as he made a decision. This song was rarely performed because of the difficulty level, but he could sing it and the singers had better be able to match him, or they would provide extra fertilizer to the already lush gardens in back.

"The populace will continue to do the rounds of *Percit My Love*. We will switch to *The Love of Xyl & Percit*."

The blinks of surprise and choked sounds annoyed him even more. Did they really think he lacked a complete understanding of what was going on? This was his job and the reason for him to be in this position—knowing how to pacify Xyl.

"If you are unaware of the song, learn it fast. Jump in with the chorus as soon as the rest of us start it. Because if we fail, we die." He did not try to disguise the annoyance and contempt in his voice. With a deep breath, he opened his mouth and sank into one of his favorite songs. While beautiful, he loved it for the complexity and richness. It took skill and passion to sing it well. He had both.

"Oh, Xyl, to Percit, my love profound," his voice lilted up to hit the notes and double catch breathing patterns. At the chorus, others joined in, and he could all but feel them catch Xyl's attention. As the song grew in power, only the fact that it was impossible to smirk and sing at this level kept the look off his face.

The lightening of the rain was proof Xyl's rage and grief were lessening. Then he heard the roar. Only long practice kept him in tune as the sound of a koxylitic registered.

Xyl, you misbegotten waste of a god. You should have died instead of Percit. At least she would have only given us her tears.

He kept singing but glared at Lazul and pointed at the door, trying to increase the emotions in his voice. If he was lucky, maybe the actions of the lizard were started before, when Xyl was still raging. He had to get Xyl to calm down, so he kept singing, pulling the singers' attention back to himself as Lazul and his thugs fought the monster. He kept his back to them. Either Lazul did his job or they all died. And even if he killed the monster, Xyl's rage might still erase the city from existence.

The fight seemed to take forever as he went into the last verse of the song, mind racing to come up with a new one, one that Xyl loved. The problem was he got bored with songs after a few suncycles. This was why they were always crafting new ones, but it had to be new music as well as lyrics. An entire enterprise had sprung up around it, but when you were only allowed to have songs sung by temple singers, it put a damper on truly creative music.

I might need to lobby the king to change those laws. Maybe more song is needed not just focused song.

The scream and sudden silence broke his concentration. Zayn whirled to see Lazul laying on the floor, the beast's head clamped around his leg. The wind and rain had completely stopped. The only sound he could hear were people in the city still singing *Percit My Love.*

That is unexpected. Who is going to rule now?

The thought flittered through his mind as more screaming broke the silence. The king's guard, Malk, Malac, something like that moved over to the king, face gray.

"Sire," he all but sobbed. Zayn just looked at his king. He had a good handle on how to control the man. This complicated everything.

Lazul panted as he grabbed his leg. Pain screamed in every word as he spoke, "You know there is no cure. Give me a knife."

Zayn processed that and had to admire the man. Apparently, King Lazul was made of sterner stuff than he expected. He was unsure if he could be that strong if he was laying there with the koxylitic biting into him.

Tears running down his face the captain handed over his dagger and Lazul, biting down a scream lifted it up to his neck, the dagger glinting in the sudden sunshine, and pulled the blade to the right, only for a hand to grasp the blade and stop it before he did more than nick his neck.

A person stood there, holding the blade of the knife against Lazul's straining arm with little effort, long blond hair cascaded over his shoulders, clothing of a style not worn in hundreds of suncycles around his waist, and eyes that belied any modicum of sanity. With a hand clenched white around a blade and the only blood was the drop from the nick in Lazul's neck.

Xyl is here.

Even as the words reverberated around Zayn's head, he dropped to his knees, bowing before his god.

He is here. The last time he was here....

Zayn had no memory of any texts that talked about Xyl being manifest. All of them were of what they did to placate him, based on the effect songs had more than anything else. But he had never expected to see Xyl in the flesh. His mind almost blanked as he realized his god was looking at him.

"How interesting. A king that cares. It has been a while. Percit would have enjoyed you." The last words were said in a croon that sent ripples of terror down Zayn's spine. He knew Lazul would not have enjoyed Percit's attentions. For the first time, he wondered just what Percit had been like. The songs only talked about her beauty and the love Xyl had for her, but now his mind quivered in confusion.

"I admire your courage. It is more than I expected. The songs almost soothe the ache in my heart, but this, a king fighting to protect others? Why, that is interesting." Xyl leaned forward to peer at the head of the koxylitic. "I like interesting," he crooned again, and Zayn considered fleeing to Vykland. Knowing your god is insane, and *knowing* were two different things.

Xyl effortlessly pulled the knife from Lazul's grip, though if the man were as shocked as Zayn was, a child could have done that. The god dropped the knife and reached down to pry apart the jaws of the creature, then tossed the head aside, looking at the mangled leg. "Looks like that hurts. Does this hurt?" He jabbed a finger at Lazul and the strange frozen tableau snapped as a scream of pain broke past Lazul's lips. "I guess so."

Lazul had his teeth clamped closed, but still muffled whimpers and grunts of pain slipped through. Zayn gave up trying to pretend obedience and lifted his head to watch.

"Oh, pain. Yes. Now you understand pain. This is what I deal with every day. The pain that burns from the inside out. You can live with it, you know. It becomes so sweet that its absence almost hurts, so you open up the wound anew. Sweet, sweet pain." Again, that croon which ranked as the most terrifying thing Zayn had ever heard.

The king had more courage than Zayn expected, or that he possessed himself. Lazul looked up at the god and gasped out, "Xyl, we honor you. Please do not take your anger out on our people any longer. I am going to die. Please accept that as the price."

Xyl tilted his head. The crazy eyes were now green, though Zayn would have sworn they had been blue when he showed up. "Die. No. I like the idea of you being the king, suffering a portion of what I suffer daily." Zayn kept flicking his gaze back and forth between the two and saw Lazul go even whiter, if possible. "Yes. Suffer." Xyl flicked his hand and Lazul slumped back to the ground as if the energy supporting him had been violently removed. His leg healed, but the red scars of the teeth stood out bright against his white skin.

Zayn went cold as Xyl turned to look at him and walked over, crouching to look him in the eyes. The gods' eyes were now black and the smile that crossed his face revealed teeth sharper than any Char had. "My cantor. Oh, you and Percit would have been so good together. The toys she would have used on you. After all, you enjoy your little treats, do you not?"

Zayn had never been as terrified as he was at that moment. Even breathing seemed unwise. Xyl reached out and stroked an impossibly smooth hand across Zayn's face, tilting his chin up to an agonizing level, but Zayn made no sound. He could barely breathe or think.

"Yesssss. I am happy. Write songs celebrating her darkness. She was glorious in her anger, her depravity, and I want to hear those songs as well. Dark, angry, full of power, like my goddess was." He stood, removing his hand so quickly Zayn's head dropped, hitting his chest, and he fought not to sob in relief.

Xyl walked to the door of the worship area and looked. "Time has made your memories soft, pure. Let me fix that." He stared out at the doors for another ten heartbeats, then turned back to them. "I am watching. Disappoint me at your peril," he said sing-song voice. Then he started to laugh, a crazy, mocking sound, and Zayn smelled the scent of urine in the air as multiple people lost control of their bladders. Then Xyl was gone and blue skies let in the warmth of the sun.

Zayn crumbled down for a moment, wrapped around himself like a child. Then he forced himself to stand and looked around. The king was laying there, panting slightly, his men still kneeling and trembling, the singers were curled into balls and crying, while some of the priests looked terrified, others were rapturous.

He had to know. With legs that shook, Zayn forced himself to go to the door and look out at the worship area. Shock hit him, and he had to hold on to the door for support as he gazed over the changes Xyl had wrought.

"Just who was Percit?" His words were quiet, but he knew everyone else had the same question.

CHAPTER THIRTY-FIVE

RYLIX

The market at Calin promised delights, wonders, and some of it was true. It was one of the two major ports for Fivika, meaning there were always ships coming in and out and a plethora of goods to be bought and sold. But the unwary could easily be swindled. He had given Note and Jadaya two coppers each, figuring with the payout they were getting from the captured pirate vessel, even if they lost it or were swindled by an untrustworthy merchant, it would not harm them. He, however, headed toward the family encampment.

There were advantages to being Ged. They were welcomed in almost all areas and cities; they were regarded as trustworthy, and they had no gods demanding much of them. The Ged still worshiped the old gods, mostly Aryix and Quas, but a few worshiped Lyx or Star or Gela. Rylix gave honor to Aryix and Quas at dawn and dusk and had never worried about it outside of that.

Now, he worried about seeing his family again.

The Ged encampment was a permanent tent city outside of town, full of children, animals, and family. The Ged were all related and tracked their connections almost obsessively, both for marriage and because knowing how you were connected to the world mattered. Even the sea Ged were related. Jolyx was his third cousin's wife's sister's brother-in-law's fourth cousin. Though for anyone past immediate family, they had two terms, close-cousin (not eligible for marriage), or far-cousin (eligible for marriage). After that, only the matriarchs kept track of the details past fifth cousins.

He waved at people as he walked through, a false smile on his face. Though to his relief he recognized almost no one. In the last five suncycles while he traded up and down Aois, his contact had been Jolyx, who brought word from his parents and siblings.

Rylix headed toward the main building, avoiding a few dogs seeking attention or food. It was the only actual building there. All the homes were tents, or soft-sided wagons. As he entered, the familiar smell of kalcha tea caught his nose and he felt a small amount of stress bleed off. The front was a large counter with three people working on ledgers at it. One of them, a woman roughly his age, looked up and nodded at him. "Morning. Name?"

"Rylix Gelzason," he said as she grabbed another ledger and looked him up.

"Ah, you are the one they are waiting for." She smiled, her gaze more interested. "I am your far-cousin, Lanyx."

Relief at no flicker of recognition made his charm all the more real. "My dear far-cousin, that I should meet you only adds to the beauty of this day." He continued letting his charm beat down his worry and stress. "You said they are waiting for me?"

Her interested smile stayed as her eyes roamed over him. "Yes, elder Dylax, Betryx, and your mother Gelza. They are in Green."

He swallowed hard at that. Elders waiting for you was never a good idea. "Aryix bless," he said in gratitude as she gestured toward one of the many large rooms in the building. This building was primarily used for business and at the back, it had a large kitchen that opened to the huge patio. It let the Ged traveling through eat with others, and not have to cook. Permanent residents would share the cooking chores in the communal kitchen or sample the wonders of the market.

He pulled out his notebook as he strode down the hall, pausing to clap outside the green door.

"Yes, enter," said a female voice.

Rylix pushed open the door and walked in, revealing his mother and the two elders at a table covered with maps and various notebooks.

"My wandering son," Gelza said, rising from her chair and coming over to hug him.

He leaned into the hug. Five cycles without her hugs were too many. After a moment, he pulled back and looked at her. There was a touch of gray at her temples, giving her an imperial look, but the rest of her hair was still the vibrant chestnut his father had always loved. Her curves were healthy, and the flush of excitement looked good on her. But best of all, there was no trace of anger or blame in her gaze.

"You are, as always, the embodiment of lovely grace, Madar." The endearment for "mother" was heartfelt, as he had missed his family during his exile. He kissed her cheek, feeling better with her here.

"As always, you could charm the feathers off a bird. Come, sit. This is Dylax, the current trade coordinator for Fivika, and this is Betryx, council elder." She introduced the two others. His smile stiffened as he nodded to them.

Dylax was a lean man with skin so weatherburned he looked like leather, but his eyes smiled, and his long dark hair was plaited at the back of his head.

Betryx was older than Gelza, but not by much. Her eyes were a light brown, and they weighed and measured him as if he were a sack of tellanuts.

"Sit, boy. We have received your requests and have questions about the route," Betryx ordered, her voice not unkind, but businesslike.

"And I have information for you, elders," he said as he took a seat. "And mine should be shared first, but I still want to take this route. To see if I can succeed."

To see if I can make a difference in the world and atone.

"Oh? And what is so important that your information might change our minds?" This time Betryx's voice contained wary contempt. That told him Kryx had not been forgotten. Which was only proper.

"The gods are involved, personally. They have touched both of my traveling companions. One of them is Exiled from Zulyika, the other is …. tasked by Pel and Rian to attempt this journey, this rescue." If he had thrown a boulder into a puddle, the reaction could not have been greater.

"What?" burst out of all three mouths. His mother and Dylax paled, making their brown skin look sickly gray.

Betryx placed her hand over her chest as she gaped at him. She recovered the fastest. "I think you need to explain further," she said, her voice low and controlled. Her comment acted as a command, and he settled back with a nod, arranging his thoughts.

Rylix explained the raids, the stolen children, being approached by Rek, and then the gods and the discussions they had been involved with. He covered every detail up to arriving, including their leaving from Pelisic with Pel and Rian speaking to Note. He avoided any mention of Note's wrist cuff or the abuse to the children. That was his business alone.

There was silence when he was done, and the three elders looked at each other. After what seemed like ages, his mother turned to look at him. "Are you sure you wish to do this journey? You realize it will be less trade and more danger than we would knowingly send you into." Her eyes were worried as she looked at him.

"It also will not support the trade routes that we thought to send you on. There are other routes we earmarked for you to ease back into this life with. You have proven your skill, paid your debt, and there are two routes that have opened up. Your far-cousin Paxil has given birth, but it was difficult, and she has elected to move to our Delcona compound until the child is weaned and walking. And your cousin Malyx was in an accident and his leg had to be removed from the knee down. Everyone decided his skills would be better used teaching youngsters the use of the blades and stars." Betryx had recovered from the shock and her voice was back to a matter-of-fact tone.

Rylix closed his eyes at the mention of the debt. Could he ever really pay it? Both of the routes they suggested were prosperous and would enable him to visit various Ged enclaves on a regular basis, even the ones that were shared with the sea Ged. Those had houses that floated on the water so they were able to sleep. It was an offer he had not even thought of being eligible for. Not after Kryx.

Do I want to turn this down?

Everything about it said it was the logical choice, but the reluctance that coated the very thought of walking away from this quest made the choice obvious.

"Aryix bless you for the offers, but I think I will stay on this journey. If nothing else, I might meet Aryix, Quas, and Lyx." The idea of seeing them filled him with a rightness, reassuring him this was the correct choice, at least for him.

Betryx breathed out slowly. "Just remember, they have been imprisoned for a long time. My rage would be absolute at the betrayal of their children. They were never known for being forgiving. I would advise you to review the legends and tell them during the evenings. Your companions should understand what they are going into."

"I will. But this is what I need to do." There was a slight emphasis on need, and he caught his mother's eye. Something flickered across her face and she nodded.

"I agree," Gelza said. "Rylix should take this trip. I give him my full support."

After a moment, the elders shrugged, agreeing with his mother, and they got down to hashing out the final details. The extra plats from the capture of the ship caused smiles to cross his mother's and Betryx's faces. It gave the expedition more buying power, though he put a half plat in the family pool. There it would earn interest and give younger members loans to buy their own supplies. It also meant he needed no loans for this adventure, which put him many hands above most of the Ged his age. By the time he left, he felt well satisfied. They promised to have the wagons and goods ready by the morning after next. It would be enough.

Rylix had promised to come home for dinner the next day, but for now, he wanted to get back to the ship and verify all the goods were moved off. He would spend this last night on the ship, be at his mother's for dinner, and then they would start their adventure.

He was still turning over the things he wanted to do as he walked back to the ship. A swaying tall, dark figure wobbling down the dock grabbed his attention. Jadaya's swinging hair twists almost made him seasick as she wove back and forth. Note was next to her with a grin wider than Rylix had ever seen on him. He kept the woman from falling off into the water.

Rylix sped up his steps to meet them. "You went out drinking?" It was not what he would have expected of either of them, and it was information that might change how the journey went.

Note chuckled as Jadaya tipped her head back to look at the sky, the sunset painting it in colors of green, blue, and pink. "Not exactly. We had an unpleasant experience, and I needed a drink. We had two mugs of fruist. I drank it just like she did." His lips kept twitching, and he looked amused at her antics. Not the annoyance of a friend with a drunkard. "She said the Chosen of her people were immune to alcohol. I suspect when some of her Zuyikan aspects were revoked, she became extremely susceptible to drink. She has been babbling about the beauty of everything for the last two fingers."

"Ah," Rylix said, turning his eyes toward the woman. She was younger than either of them, but her scars, both internal and external, often made her appear older than she was. Now she appeared to be a young woman, drunk for the first time. It was oddly endearing.

"Indeed. I figure she is about ready to sleep, though tomorrow we would appreciate your assistance in locating vendors for some knives and stars like you use, and we never got around to buying the bindings she wanted."

"That I can do and easily. Assuming she does not have fruist head in the morning, we will go do that. Assuming Jolyx will have our payouts by the morning the of the day after that, we should be ready to start the journey."

Note's smile faded, and he nodded. "We are unable to acquire the weapons and supplies we need here?"

Rylix walked with them as they moved up the pier. "We could. But what they offer here are the castoffs, not good enough to sell at Heart, usually apprentice made. While we do not have the time or money to request custom blades, I would prefer they be the best possible." He gave Note a side glance. "For both of you." Rylix smiled as Jadaya spun in a circle. "For now, I think it is best we get her to bed, and we shall head out in the morning."

Note nodded, and together they got Jadaya to bed. After she was tucked in the swing chair, Rylix went and knocked on the captain's door.

"Enter," she called out.

Rylix pushed the door open and Jolyx sat at her little table in front of the wall bench. "Coming to check on the money, are you?" she asked with a grin and a lift of her mug.

"I thought it would give me something to dream about tonight," he said with a smile as he leaned against the wall. "From your smile and the scent of," he sniffed again, "honey fruist, I take it the talks went well."

"Turns out that ship had taken out more than one of ours." Her voice turned dark, then she let it go. "There were bounties, cargo presumed lost recovered, plus the ship, which was not Ged, but a captured Vykland ship."

"Interesting. What I am hearing is a delightful bonus?"

"That and I need a new first mate," she said with a fake pout. "Mine is the new captain of the Waverider. He is taking three of my crew, those looking for new opportunities. And multiple of mine decided to retire with that windfall. I will be in port for a while. As to the bonus, I have scrips for all three of you. You can pull out what you want in cash from the money house."

Rylix fought down a grin. She was enjoying teasing him too much.

"Oh? Perhaps enough for us to purchase our own ship?"

"Only if you decided on a sailing life, but I doubt the dark warrior would enjoy a life on the sea. It is not where she fits."

"No, it is not," he admitted. "I doubt she knows where that is at this time."

Jolyx tilted her head with a rueful laugh. "The trials of the young."

"Yes, elder of such advanced age," Rylix said back with mock sincerity. Jolyx had made forty suncycles. She had zero gray hair, and he knew she could run him into the ground.

Jolyx snorted. "Enough trader, I have the numbers. Each of you, each of my crew, earned four plat, eight-three copper, six silver, and seven gold."

Rylix was glad he was leaning against the wall. A good wagon could be purchased for seventy copper. And there were a hundred copper in a plat. The *families* had that much money as a whole, not a single person. At least, not that he personally knew. The rulers of area and lords might have that amount.

"I see you are as shocked as I was. But yes. I could buy another ship, but then where would I be? As it is, I will install some upgrades on the *Starguide* and enjoy a mooncycle of luxury here in Calin." She took another drink of her honey fruist. "You will be gone in the morning?" It was both a question and an encouragement for the answer to be yes.

"We will. I bless you for your excellent care of us, my Captain." He pushed off the wall and gave her a bow that was both mocking and not.

Jolyx snorted. "Begone, young trader. Go live and I hope I hear of your exploits from your own lips, not as a memorial."

Rylix grinned and her and bowed slightly. "That is my wish as well. Good night, captain."

CHAPTER THIRTY-SIX

NOTE

The next morning Note stood at the railing, his packs next to him. Jadaya was still packing up her things. To his amusement, she was embarrassed at getting drunk. She woke up with a clear head, but her mortification provided levity to the morning. He knew he was nowhere near as pleasant a drunk. His moods turned to anger and cruelty, but it took much more to get him drunk than two mugs of fruist. It was something to keep in mind, especially for those drinks that tasted like fruit but had more alcohol than a whole bottle of fruist.

Rylix, to his surprise, walked up the gangplank from the dock as Jadaya came up the stairs.

"Wondrous good morning to you both. Are you ready to hit the market, then to the Ged enclave so we can start our journey?" His smile spread across his face, warm and charming.

How did the man always seem so excited by life?

"Yes," Note said, simply looking at Jadaya. She had her peacebound sword on her hip, her bag with the extra sword, her blanket, and her belongings in a tidy bundle.

"Yes," she said with a smile, ducking her head and Note fought the smile. She reminded him of a small animal with oversized feet and eyes. But he had the feeling she would become someone to be respected, maybe even feared.

"Then let us away into the marketplace. But first here is an advance on your earnings." Rylix gave both of them five coppers, then led them into the maze of tents and booths with a sureness that Note had to wonder about. The man had been on Aois for most of five suncycles. How did he know it so well?

"This booth has the best binders in the marketplace, at least according to my mother, and given that she and the captain are of similar endowments, I trust her recommendation." Rylix waved Jadaya into the shop, and she nodded, going in, as Rylix stood outside with Note and a few others.

"Your mother?" Note asked, watching the people around him, looking for any Char, though they seemed sparse.

"She was amused, but happy enough to recommend someone," Rylix said with a shrug. "After that, one of the merchants who carries the weapons I use is only a few rows away."

"Yes. How do you know this place so well? Jadaya and I rambled for a while before finding much of anything."

Except the man who shoved a sword in her gut with nothing but his silence. Note blew out his anger. Their gods might be more vengeful than his. He would try to not make assumptions. Rylix's laughter broke his spiral of anger.

"I grew up here. My mother is waiting to meet you. I spent most of my childhood racing among these vendors. While some of them have changed, for many, these shops are family owned, so my memory is still accurate." He looked around. "It is wonderful to be home, but I am ready for the road. The walls of the ship were nice for a change, but I ache for the fresh air."

Note looked at him in confusion, but before he could ask more Jadaya came walking out of the shop apparently more endowed than when she went in. He tilted his head. "That is different."

"Yes. It will take me a while to get comfortable without the constant pressure, but I think I like this," she said with a funny smile. "Though still going back to the other bindings prior to a battle. These wobble more than I am used to."

Note choked down a laugh and heard Rylix doing the same. "Then to the next merchant?" Rylix was smiling as he guided them through the streets to the next merchant. True to his word, there were a variety of small knives, stars, and needles. "I am skilled with the throwing knives. The stars require a wrist movement that I never mastered, and they do not sink as far. The needles are powerful, but unless you place them exactly where you want—say the eye or throat—they are easy to ignore in the heat of battle."

Rylix spoke with the confidence of someone who had learned all this the hard way.

"I would like to play with the needles and knives. While I believe you regarding them as weapons, would they not be better for small game?" Jadaya fingered the long needles. They were about the length of her hand, from palm to the tip of her middle finger.

Note imagined that spearing a bird or hare and nodded to himself. Those would kill game. He had other targets in mind.

"As you wish, my dark warrior," Rylix said. She shot him a glance and Note fought to keep the smile off his face. The man was overly flowery in his words, yet he never got a sense of mocking. Just an odd way of showing respect.

They let him haggle for the weapons they both wanted, and by the end Jadaya got her needles and knives for five silver and two gold, while Note used ten silver to get multiple sets of knives, a case, and sheaths for them.

"Now if you would, my fine compatriots, it is time to visit my home, my family, and see to our wagon. If all is ready, before we leave, we can sup with my family."

Note and Jadaya followed him, leaving the market behind, yet not heading into the city. Instead, they went to the west side where one enormous building stood, surrounded by tents, canopies, and various cooking areas. The tents ranged from small, like what Note had acquired during his run across the world, barely enough for one person to sleep in, to larger than many houses he had seen. These larger tents were often connected to others, and the impression was you could walk from one to another without ever going outside.

Rylix led them to one of the larger ones. They followed him into a tent with a wooden floor, pillows on the wooden surface, and a small stove in the corner next to a table with tea and snacks. "Madar, I am here with my companions," he called out in a voice that carried as he moved to the small stove.

Note turned around, looking at everything. The rigid tent prevented the light breeze outside from coming through the walls, the small stove heating it easily. Rylix put the kettle back on the stove to heat as a woman came striding through a flap on one side.

While she was Ged, and they all had similar coloring, Note could see she was where Rylix got his eyes and his hair. She was about as tall as Note, with curves, a smile, and sharp eyes that probably calculated the value of everything they wore with a single glance.

"My favorite son, introduce me to your companions. Though I would venture I can guess who is who," she said in the same lyrical way of speaking that Rylix had.

"Favorite, am I?" He asked with a smile as he turned from his tea preparations.

"Of course. You are the one leaving," she said with a mischievous grin. Note tried to remember if his parents had acted like that. But the only memories he could pull up were vague and involved screaming. He shook his head to dislodge the images. Not now. Later, after the Char had been dealt with, he could remember.

"Madar, may I introduce Jadaya, the dark warrior and Note of Aois," Rylix said, waving at each of them in turn. "Companions, this is my Madar, Gelza."

"I see now why my son was so taken with you," Gelza said, looking at

Jadaya, whose head came perilously close to the top of the tent ceiling as she was still standing.

"He is?" Jadaya looked back and forth between them. Note wanted to laugh at her bewilderment but kept a bland face, though he laughed to himself.

"Of course! A woman of such height and majesty, any man would be honored to travel by her side." It was said with such a straight face that Note was unsure if she was being honest or not. Then she turned to him and smiled. "You, the swimmer, are the one to watch. You would yell at gods? I am not sure if I should beg my son to run far away from you or hitch his wagon to your bonfire."

This time, Note gave in and laughed. "I would advocate running the other direction, but then if the fire is large enough, it can be seen from anywhere."

Gelza smiled to match his grin. "Well said. Come, food is waiting. Rylix, leave the kettle. The heat is low enough it will not boil." She led them out the door and turned going toward an open kitchen and tables with others gathered. Her introductions of the Night Warrior, the swimmer, and my favorite son, were mixed with far cousins, near cousins, and uncles and aunts. It was a bewildering array. But the food was good, the questions and discussions lively. To both his relief and amusement, they talked more about trade goods, discussed what Rylix had procured, and argued about what they would have done were they the ones leading this adventure.

But no one tried to slip in and go with them, nor was there anything other than family amusement and teasing. It was a glimpse into a world he had heard of but never experienced. Jadaya, he noticed, avoided the fruist that flowed freely, white and red, and instead stuck with tea or water mixed with juice. All in all, it made Note wonder why Rylix would ever want to leave, but the more he watched there was a twitchiness about the man, as if he was keeping himself tightly bound to fit in.

What would he look like unbound?

The thought nagged at Note until lunch was over, and Gelza took them out to the staging area. It was a seven-day trek to Hearth with multiple little towns in between. While their goals were not a secret, they also needed to avoid looking like a war party. Char would be difficult enough without giving them more warning or time to prepare. There was a difference between preventing people from escaping and preparing for an assault.

A wagon, if you could call it that, along with two jacks and four mustangs, waited for them. The jacks were low, powerfully built creatures, with broad chest and withers, both in a dull brown color with short coarse hair. Aois had little room to feed jacks or mustangs, so they were rare enough. While he fled Char, he spent little time with animals as they noticed him when people were oblivious. The mustangs were at least a hand higher at the shoulders than the jacks, each with a slightly different colored coat. They had long ears that drooped over at the tips, narrow faces, and thick legs with cloven hooves like the jacks. But they seemed curious, not aggressive.

"Here we go. This is what will get us from one end of Aria to the other. And all these creatures are ship trained as well, so we can take them to Vykland and Charinsky if we decide." Rylix looked proud as he patted the side of the wagon.

"'What is that?" Jadaya asked, her eyes locked on the same thing Note fixated on.

Rylix grinned, the constraints that Note had seen on him cracking a bit. "My new creation. We are going to test it and see if it works as well as I planned. Take a look. It has tents on either side, swing chairs, a stove, sleeping areas inside, and all the goods we are carrying." He explained as he showed them. The wagon was on four wheels and longer than Jadaya was tall. It rose to a good head taller than her, but still Note could have touched the top if he stretched, and it had a solid roof. All four sides of the wagon had cleverly rolled up canvas that unrolled and could be supported by poles that were tucked into the side, providing shade and protection from the rain when stopped. Then a section of the front, underneath the bench where the driver would sit, which also had built in sun and rain shades, slid out like a long drawer, and unfolded into a nice kitchen area. A basin, cutting area, dishes, knives, a leather flask to hold liquids, spices, and a grill, pan, and pot to put over a fire with the struts to support them.

When that slid in, Rylix showed them the swing chairs carefully wrapped up and stored on the outside, so if they were in a tree laden area, they would be easy to set up. Each of them came with a tent to protect you while sleeping. Then there was extra canvas to create dry areas for the animals. When Rylix showed them the inside, Note was amazed. The two side walls unlatched and came down, creating counters to display goods, while inside the wagon was a collection of cupboards, drawers, baskets, and storage. There was even a section that pulled out full of pads, blankets, and tiny tents if the swing chairs would not work.

"Then you can put all of your belongings here." Rylix pulled a drawer out of the back that seemed to slide most of the way to the front that was empty. "It should easily hold all of our possessions. The other two drawers are full of food supplies and charcoal, should we be unable to find firewood."

Note just blinked. He had expected something much more basic. This would be like traveling with a store and all his own possessions.

"We could have tripled what we brought and still not have used all the storage," Note said as he slipped his belongings in there. There were also carry bags for each of the mustangs. "You said you designed this?"

Gelza laughed. "He has been sending us ideas and sketches for suncycles. We were worried it would be too heavy, but the top is packed with lighter items, and the heavier pieces, like the charcoal and kitchen supplies, provide a solid weight at the bottom. The expanding tent areas have already been copied as additions for multiple wagons as they watched this being created. We can but hope it performs as well as he believes it will."

Jadaya had moved over to the mustang and was petting its nose. "The only issue I can see is I will not be riding one of these."

"What?" Rylix turned to look at her and then blinked. Note fought not to laugh at the look on his face as he turned, looking at Jadaya.

"Oh, huh," he said as he actually looked at her standing next to the mustang. Her waist was above the mustang's back. It took little imagination to see that her on the back would have her legs all but dragging in the dust.

Rylix had a poleaxed look on his face. Note could see the frantic thoughts as the man tried to adjust to this new information. "I suppose you could steer the wagon."

Note could almost hear the defeat in the man's voice, knowing he had hoped to drive what he had spent so long designing.

Jadaya laughed as her eyes went over the bench, obviously designed for someone Rylix's height, which was almost a head and a half less than hers.

"Bless, no. My knees would be up to my ears. Walking will be fine." Her smile spread across her face.

"That will make our trip very slow," he warned.

Jadaya shook her head, still smiling. "I will wager my pace is faster than the jacks at a fast trot. I may need new soles for my boots come Vykland, but I can promise I will not slow us down."

Rylix bowed to the inevitable. Note would ride one, the other would be laden with feed for the four animals. After a round of goodbyes, more food pressed upon them and stored in bags, and two mustangs being left behind, they finally managed to set out, about five fingers later than he had hoped. They set out, the sun slowly headed towards its rest in the west as their direction.

His visit had reassured him the Ged thought his debt had been paid, but he still felt the guilt that wrapped around his throat. This would make it right.

I hope.

CHAPTER THIRTY-SEVEN

LAZUL

Lazul lay in his bed, the light from the dawning sun creeping into his eyes as it rose. He took a shuddering breath as pain ripped through him. Xyl had not been lying about the pain and there were days when he wanted to take enough tellanut that he forgot who he was. As it was, his teeth were acquiring the stains that indicated his use. It was a weakness he hated.

Forcing down the whining, Lazul forced himself out of bed and to the basin of water waiting for him. The reflecting glass showed he had lost weight over the last tenday. He felt like an invalid, but when you looked at him, there was nothing wrong. His leg healed fully, though the scars left behind proved how horrific the injury had been. The healing had been so perfect there was no reason to limp as all the muscles worked. The bones were solid, his tendons flexible. There was nothing wrong. Except for the pain. It lived inside him. Nothing made it better except alcohol, tellanut, or stronger painkillers. He had already ordered Actin to find stronger drugs, though he suspected many thought he was becoming addled. How did he explain there was no joy in the feeling, simply relief that brought the pain down to levels where it felt like he had merely walked too much? Instead of feeling like he wanted to run a knife across his own throat.

Quit feeling sorry for yourself. You are alive. Xyl saved you.

Yes, his god had saved him and revealed something that he had never suspected. From the shock on Zayn's face, it had been a shock to the cantor as well.

Lazul washed and dressed, breathing deeply as pain rippled through him, stealing his breath sometimes. From finger to finger it changed, sneaking up on him and slicing through his ability to function, then other times it was just there, low and slow. That he could deal with. The rest sent him seeking relief.

"Sire?" Actin called from his door as he finished his morning toiletries. The only sanity saving aspect was it had no effect on his ability to do things, just his ability to tolerate everything.

"Enter. What is on the plan for today?" Staying polite, being kind, not losing his temper required all of his attention of late. The pain ate away at everything, and no one believed how much it hurt.

"You have the court of lords to discuss the damage done during the Day of Remembrance. They have their estimates ready." Actin hesitated. Even if he doubted the pain, he was at least still assisting. "There is a new additive I found that might lower your pain. Would you like to try it with your morning meal?"

Lazul fought down the laugh. Like to try it? At this point, if you said another koxylitic biting him would help, he would try it.

"Yes, bless. I will attend shortly." He forced himself to stand up straight and curve his lips up slightly as he nodded at Actin.

"Sire," Actin said as he slipped away.

Lazul finished dressing in robes that were lighter than what the hall required, but he found the pain kept him warm as he fought through it, at least until he was so exhausted all he could do was shiver.

I need to expedite getting the heated water cisterns installed. It is the only thing that provides any amount of relief.

Another thing on his list. It grew faster than he could remove items. He moved out to his private dining area, food waiting for him, still hot. If nothing else, the servants held him in greater esteem than before. The story of the fight, his sacrifice, and Xyl's actions had swept through the land like wildfire. He, Malac, and Zayn were heralded as heroes and people whispered the gods honored him.

If this is how Xyl honors you, next time let the koxylitic kill me.

He looked at the small bag of powder near his plate. Did he drink it, put it on food, or just eat it? Lazul sighed and dumped the drug into the fruist with his breakfast. It mixed easily, and he took a sip. There was the slightest taste that seemed somehow familiar.

Lazul ate his eggs, meat, and fruit in between sips of the fruist as he tried to place the taste. It was similar to the white fruit he had been served in Quartz. Why? That memory swam up as he thought about the entire inspection trip. Something felt off to him when they were doing the temple inspections. To be honest, they had always disturbed him, but he had assumed it was because of their position as both hostage and hostage taker and the amount of power they had. They rode the line when it came it Xyl, and it was a precarious place to be.

A place he never wanted to be, even though it gave them power even he as king was unable to use.

Lazul became aware the pain had lowered to a dull roar, lower than he had felt since that day. It was still there, but it was behind everything, and he realized his shoulders had relaxed. Just like that fruist had made him feel. The visit, the head priest Circe offering him fruist at every turn, and the smiles and easy way they went through the temple. He had stayed relaxed and incurious, not worrying about anything during the visit.

They drugged me.

The realization should have shocked him more than it did. What he now needed to figure out was why. He was alive, so it was not a plot to kill him. The sparkle of light off the fruist caught him and he smiled at it, admiring the shine and color.

Distracted. This makes me easily distracted.

He wanted to cry. Something that worked, that pushed the pain down, and it made him too easily manipulated. His throat locked as he rang the bell. Actin appeared like magic.

"Sire?"

"Actin, this new additive is wonderful, but please note I should only have it in the evenings or on days when I am not involved in any meetings or rulings that require interacting with anyone not trusted. Which at this point is you and Malac." He gave the man a hard look and, to his consternation, Actin flushed as he nodded.

"It is my honor, sire."

Lazul pushed away any doubt. At this point, if Actin had wanted him dead, he could have killed the king a hundred times over. "That being said, can you please ask Malac to assist me? I have to attend the council session and I need both of you. If there is anything you find I am missing or oblivious to, note it and call a recess due to my 'illness'." If there had been an excess amount of sarcasm in his voice, he was unconcerned. "I will need telcha with pure tella juice in it. Make sure my pot is filled and keep my cup warm and full." Telcha normally had no narcotic effects, as roasting seemed to remove that, though it made an excellent boost to your morning. Hence the addition of tella juice. Now if there was something he could do about his teeth.

Worry about it later.

"Of course, sire. At once. And I have taken the liberty of adding a charcoal paste with mint to your needs room for your morning teeth cleansing. It helps to get the linens white and the healers have assured me as long as you spit it out, it is harmless." Actin nodded at him before turning to leave.

Lazul glanced at his seneschal, wondering if the man had learned to read his mind. Before he could follow up on the comment or thought, Actin left the room, and Lazul returned to his food. He wanted more of his tainted fruist, but it would be unwise. With that unwelcome realization, he drank only his telcha and luxuriated in having his pain so far down. It had only been five days and already he was unable to remember what it had been like to not hurt. Something had to change. The idea he had suncycles of this ahead of him? Depression slammed into him like a living thing and a sob burst out of his throat.

"Sire?" A servant was at the door, looking at him with wide eyes. "Do you need assistance?"

With a swallow, he pushed his feelings down and set his mouth in a straight line. "No, bless. I am fine."

With a doubtful look, the servant pulled back. Lazul finished his food, drinking the telcha and staring at the fruist. How long would the effects last? For now, he savored the reduction of pain and would see how difficult the council meeting turned out to be for him.

"Sire? You requested me?" Malac was at the door and Lazul let an actual smile slip out. Of the people who believed him, who understood, Malac was primary. To his surprise, Zayn had been another, but that he would deal with later. He had been there, heard the god, and witnessed his madness.

"Yes. I need you at the council meeting. One of the new drugs works, but it makes me easily distracted. I have Actin who will be there as well. But I want you to listen quietly, and then discuss it with me."

"Of course, sire." Malac's eyes darkened as he looked at Lazul. "How are you, sir?"

Another moment of wishing that this man had been a noble. It would have been wonderful having him as a genuine friend, not just a trusted servant. "I will survive. The new drug is very nice. Makes it so I am just sore, not in pain. I had another question for you. After the inspection at Quartz. Did I seem odd to you?"

"Odd?" Malac had a thoughtful expression as he stood there, eyes narrowed. "You were unusually relaxed. After most inspections, you come out quiet and somewhat depressed. This time, you were almost chatty. But you gave me none of the signals and did nothing that could be regarded as worrisome. Did I miss something?"

"I am unsure. I suspect I had this same drug there, in my fruist." Malac's eyes darkened, but Lazul waved it away. "If they want me dead at this point, that is their choice. Then they get to deal with all of this." He waved around the room with a sigh. "But it makes me wonder what they were worried about me noticing and how often I have been influenced in such a way. "

Malac rocked back on his heels, a small swaying motion as he thought. "As to how often you were affected, that was the only time on the trip you were unusually happy or chatty, though most of the time you regarded the temple visits as a nice escape from the matchmaking."

Lazul groaned. "I forgot. That will also be brought up in the meeting today." He gasped as a wave of pain spiked through him. He took a shuddering breath as it faded away. "They will want a decision."

"Do you have one?" Malac sounded curious.

Lazul forced a smile. "Yes, and no. I have decided to invite Lord Nephrite's sister Hauyne to visit me in the palace for a mooncycle."

Malac arched a brow. "Oh. That will send them into a boil."

"I can but hope. They will be unable to deny her lineage, but will argue her age, and that she bore no children." Hauyne was a widow and about five suncycles Lazul's junior. Of all the single women he had met on the trip, only she had not been presented as an eligible bride, instead she was living with her brother and had joined them for dinner. She was smart, funny, and had a passion for city infrastructure he found fascinating. Their conversations had been lively, and he found her attractive and smart. The question would be if she was interested and if she could deal with his changed circumstances. Right now, the idea of any intimate time made him shudder.

"If it helps, I thought she was nice, and she made you smile." Malac offered the opinion with self-effacing charm.

"Maybe, at least I know she would be good dinner company."

Actin stuck his head in. "Sire, the lords are here."

Lazul nodded and rose from the chair, enjoying the still dull levels of pain. "I should do this while I can think and not sob. Can you give me the rough overview of the tallied destruction?"

Malac did not need to ask what Lazul referred to. Xyl's rage had swept over the area, with only the city of Quartz coming off with almost no damage. That struck him again. Why was that city with so little torn apart, while other cities were still tallying the dead? Quartz had some livestock killed, some trees toppled, and roofs needing repairs, but that was it. Per the reports he had read, Circe's temple kept singing until sunset, even after Xyl's rage had died.

Why?

That thought rang through his mind as Malac rattled off the latest damage totals. The harbor had lost all the docks and piers; they had to be rebuilt, as well as five ships that were destroyed in the funnel. In Granite, three houses had burned down from lightning strikes, twenty people were killed due to debris flying at high rates of speed, at least a hundred head of livestock, doors, roofs, and fences were destroyed, and flooding. The flooding was throughout the country, but they had plans for that and it was being diverted quickly. Temples were damaged, homes destroyed, and at least one city had their walls broken. That would take suncycles to rebuild, if ever.

Lazul made plans as he walked, trying to keep his reactions to the spikes of pain down to double breaths. It helped at least a little. It was easier to let people assume he was winded from walking, that they could understand. As he entered the council chambers and found the lords already arranged at the large table, all he could do was hope the new drug kept the pain down until he could finish up this meeting. His doctored telcha was waiting for him and Actin poured it even as he sat and forced a smile.

"Lords, let us begin with the damage estimates and tax changes." It would be a long day and he still avoided thinking about what Xyl said. The changes to their understanding of their gods.

CHAPTER THIRTY-EIGHT

JADAYA

Jadaya leaned into the lope. It felt so good to stretch her legs, to be able to run. Aois had been all hills or small beaches, and she had to watch her step, or it was climbing. This was *running*. She far outpaced the wagon and the mustang that Note rode. After a few days of working out paces with the others, they had determined how far to go each day and she would run ahead, scout out places and towns they were coming near, then head back.

It made for extra wear and tear on her, but she loved it. Her body felt like her own again. It also gave her time to think. Her rage at Zula and Yika was unabated, and she felt her lip curl in a snarl at the thought. She had finally shaken off the shock and was tired of being led. She would prove to the gods that she was not someone to discard.

Up ahead, under one of the wide banak trees, a man sat. She slowed as she approached. As they moved through Fivika, she had learned that they imported most of their grain from either Delcona or Agrina, and Fivika focused on manufacturing as their primary source of commerce. The homes all had small gardens that were used to provide vegetables for the households. The majority of the trees in the area bore some sort of edible fruits or nuts, but the country as a whole created things, not agriculture. All of which made finding a traveler, one that seemed to be alone, an oddity.

Jadaya slowed to a walk as she approached, casting a glance behind her. The wagon was at least six fingers behind her at the rate they were going. They kept the animals at a brisk walk, but the chances of breaking trade goods if there were going faster than that was too high. Note had found the drier air here as annoying as she found it wonderful and he kept his mustang in the shade of the wagon as much as possible.

For the moment, she was on her own. With her sword on her back, strapped to prevent bouncing, she could grab it quickly if there was danger. As long as the stranger had no ranged weapons.

Why are you assuming he will attack?

She shrugged to herself. Assuming attack was safer in the long run. By now, she had reached the area across from him and he looked up at her.

"Bright morning, Zuyikan. What brings you so far from your home?" His voice was mellow, but the words sent shards of anger and pride straight into her heart. The snub from the man in the market still rubbed at her.

"Not Zuyikan," she replied, her finger tracing the scar her former gods had branded her with. Jadaya yanked her hand down as soon as she realized what she was doing. Since the man's shunning of her, she was much more conscious of the scar, resenting it.

"Ah. More fools they. What brings you on this path? With your companions so far back?" He nodded toward the far cloud of dust being created by the jacks and wagon. It had been a while since the last rain.

"What makes you think I am with them?" Her mind was throwing out alarms, but he rested under the tree. His long shaggy brown hair implied Ged, but his light pale skin was closer to that of the Delconians she had seen, yet his eyes were a pale gray and she suspected he would only be slightly shorter than her when he stood. She had no idea of his country or his gods.

That was rarely a good thing. Some were like her, outcasts, but many just left their gods, or renounced them, and from the discussions with Note and Rylix, this was because some were like her old ones, harsh or distant or not what the person wanted in a god. Others found themselves on the wrong side of a god's temper and were tossed out without notice. The children from those offspring could and did possess a blending of the traits from their parents, but who knew which gifts—if any—they would inherit? That meant they had fewer consequences for their actions in some ways, depending on the gods they were from and the gods whose territory they were in.

Which is the situation I am in.

She let her shoulders relax and hated that she had an in-built prejudice she had not realized. But the question was still valid.

The man smiled, a cheerful one, but to her eyes it seemed like he was unused to his face moving in that way. There was something about the stiffness that implied disuse. For all that, it was a welcoming smile. "Simple logic, nothing magical, I must admit. You have no bags, yet carry weapons, and your gods rarely let their people travel. It only makes sense that your companions are behind you."

His voice was rich and smooth Ged, but she had no idea what his native tongue was. Jadaya nodded. "That makes sense. But it raises the question, why are you sitting here on the side of the road? Is this to be an ambush?" She let her eyes drift both ways and even up into the tree, but the short grass would not have hidden a mortal and the tree, while large enough to provide shade, was not big enough to hide multiple attackers.

"Ambush?" The man grinned at her, showing strong, perfect teeth. "No. I am but a traveler and was taking a meal break here in the shade. Would you join me?"

He waved at the cloth spread before him. On it was some cheese, bread, and a few fruits.

Why did I not notice that before?

The scent of the bread, fresh according to her noise, drifted to her as the wind swirled one direction then another. She hesitated. Offering strangers food was common hospitality, but from a simple traveler?

"I have water," he said, pointing at the flask.

That grabbed her attention. Her dry mouth agreed that liquid would be welcome. And what harm was there in joining him? She looked back and saw the wagon was still at least five fingers away. Taking a break and waiting for them would cause no issues. They would still be traveling for fingers, as the next town was still ahead of them.

"I would be honored," she said, walking over and settling herself down on the ground opposite him. It put her back to the road but let her see on both sides of him and she should be able to hear anyone approaching.

"No, it is I that am honored by your presence. I wander a lot, but rarely in Zuyika. Tell me your name, lady?" He spoke as he tore off a chunk of bread and cheese, then offered her both of them with the flask.

Jadaya took the flask and the cool, clear water tasted better than the best fruist. She had to force herself to stop drinking, knowing all too well that was a good way to make yourself sick.

If I am that thirsty, I need to be drinking more water.

"Jadaya," she said after setting the flask down. "And you?"

He tilted his head, watching her. "You may call me Cass," he said finally.

Jadaya was unfamiliar with that name structure. If it had been Ged, it would have had an "x", "y", or "z" in it. But it would have multiple syllables, like hers. But her experience with others was still new. For all she knew, the Agrinans or Delconians had names that followed that pattern.

"You said you are a wanderer?" She took a bite of the cheese and had to restrain herself. The cheese was rich and creamy, with a hint of herbs that were unfamiliar in cheese.

"I like seeing the world. Exploring the people and places. I do minor tasks for people, but my needs are simple. Mostly I travel." He pulled out a small knife and proceeded to cut one of the fruits in half, handing it to her. "And you?"

Jadaya had added some bread in between the bites of cheese. It was fresh and crusty. "Where did you get this food?"

"Oh, here and there. Lots of farmhouses will pay with food for small assistances," he said with a wave of his hand, dismissing it as immaterial. "What are you doing so far from," he hesitated for a moment, as if changing what he was about to say. "From where you were born?"

Jadaya avoided his question by taking a bite of the fruit. It was at the peak of ripeness and the juice dribbled down her chin as she tried to swallow it, not letting the sweet nectar slip away. After she swallowed every morsel of the fruit, resisting the urge to ask for another piece, she answered, being oblique as they had discussed. "Just helping a Ged friend set up a trading route. We are headed into Hearth. It sounded like something interesting to spend my time doing."

Cass nodded slowly. "That is more interesting than…" Again, he paused and changed what he was going to say. "That sounds like a horizon broadening thing to do. Stretch your legs and your mind. I would like to see more young ones do that. Experience other cultures than their own."

Jadaya thought about it. Would she have been different if she had seen other places before she had been exiled? It was a thought. The distant jingle of the wagon coming toward them pulled at her attention. "My companions are almost here. Would you like to meet them?"

"Not right now, I think," Cass said, standing. "But I am sure as we are both wanderers, we will run into each other again." He packed the food and cloth with fluid, efficient movements, then tucked them into his sack. "But here. Keep the water. You might need it." He handed her the flask as she stood with him, confused as to his quick actions.

She started to refuse, but he had already stepped back onto the road. "I will see you again, Jadaya. May the path you take lead to the end you desire." He smiled that odd smile, as if it was something he had to think about doing, then he stepped on to the road and continued to walk to the next city.

Jadaya stood there in the shade of the tree, watching him for multiple heartbeats. Then she glanced back down the road where she could see the jacks and the wagon coming into view. She turned to watch Cass, but there was no one on the road. With a frown, she stepped onto the road and did a quick jog forward, looking for him, but there was no one walking and no hills or bushes to hide in.

In the far distance she could see the next town, as the road from Calin to Hearth was rather flat, only gradually rising for small hills.

Cass had vanished.

Jadaya slowly walked back to the tree, arriving about the time Note and Rylix did, the harness on the jacks and the straps on the other mustangs, creating enough noise that anyone in the vicinity could have heard them.

"Anything wrong, Jadaya?" Note called out as they approached.

"Did you see a man walking down the road?" She asked, stepping forward to pet the mustang, tall enough that Note only looked down a little.

"A man?" Note looked ahead and then glanced at Rylix. "No. Just you standing here."

She frowned and turned back around, the water flask still in her hand. "That is very… Odd. I was talking to him, shared food, and he headed out, but then was gone. You are sure you saw no one?"

Note looked at her, then back at the road and shook his head. "Your vision is still better than mine, but no, I saw no one."

Jadaya frowned and then let it go, slinging the flask across her back. "What now?"

Rylix had jumped down from the wagon seat at this point and was stretching. "We have two more towns before we get to Hearth, but setting up outside of the towns seems wise. There should be a spot before the next town where we can camp, then trade early in the morning. It is a clearing near a stream, specifically set up for overnight travelers. Do you want to go ahead and prep?" He had finished stretching by this point and was checking on the jacks, but they seemed unaffected by the weight of the wagon or the days of walking.

"Yes. If there is any game, I will see if I can get it." She had been practicing with the needles and was getting pretty good, at least for small game hunting.

"Excellent, then we shall see you there." Rylix sprang back up on the wagon seat and clicked the jacks into moving.

Note hung back a moment, looking at Jadaya. "Are you sure everything is well?"

She shrugged. "I guess I miss my distance vision more than I realized. I will see you at the campsite." With that, she waved at him and took off at an easy jog, passing Rylix and the wagon in ten heartbeats. The movement helped to soothe her, but still she kept an eye out for Cass. She saw no sign he had existed, except the memory of food and the water skin on her back.

CHAPTER THIRTY-NINE

RYLIX

They reached Hearth a whole ten fingers earlier than Rylix had expected. Their travel had clicked along perfectly, and after the first few days, they became a seamless group when it came to traveling. Jadaya ran ahead, scouted out locations, and often had rabbits or tree-hares skinned and ready to cook by the time they got there. Rylix did most of the cooking as neither she nor Note had learned those skills, both for distressingly similar reasons, but he just took it in stride and showed them ways and options for food as they traveled.

Rylix figured neither of them would ever be skilled cooks, but at least at this point, they would eat more than charred meat on a stick. The camp setup and take down were just as smooth. From his point of view, their biggest flaw, and for a Ged it was a huge flaw, was their inability to sell anything. Every time he watched them, he wanted to groan. They had no idea how to point out an item's usefulness, how it was better than the rest, or even the rarity of it. If he had depended on them making money, this trading trip would have been a disaster.

The Fivika people were straightforward, but they, like anyone, could be persuaded to spend more and they had a weakness for anything not made in Fivika. As a people they were slimly built, with straight black hair that was smoother than oil, and eyes that were completely black, without whites like the rest of the peoples. They had nimble hands that were used in their craftsmanship. Their olive skin worked well with yellows and reds, so he prioritized those colors as well as finger puzzles. They loved flavors in their foods, so the spice packages were also set out. Now if only he could have convinced either Jadaya or Note to wax rhapsodic about them or get Jadaya to display some of the cloth that worked with her coloring as well as theirs, something about the undertone of their skins matched.

As it was, Note would package and deliver goods purchased, while Jadaya stood tall and looked imposing. With her quick reactions and eyes, few dared try to pilfer anything and just her attention alone stopped more than one pickpocket. With luck, they would get better, but they found no joy in the give and take or the ability to find just the right item for the right person.

Other than that glaring flaw, they were good travel companions. But who knew how that would go when it became more than a simple walk in gorgeous weather? It was ripening season, so the weather was pleasant, people friendly, and the roads well maintained. But that would change. The question was, could they adapt?

You worry too much. Let it be until you need to worry over it.

Rylix still fretted over the various scenarios as they approached the town gates to Hearth. Here was where they would obtain the armor, weapons, and trade for different goods that would be in demand in Vykland. It was also where he would sell the honey. Only here could he get the proper price for it. Honey was precious and hard to come by, and he had three jars, three! That alone could have financed the trip.

Nice to not have to stress about money, but still I need to prove this is a viable route, without the presence of rare items.

"Halt." the guard said as they reached the front of the line. Note was on his mustang and Jadaya was walking alongside the wagon. They would find a booth to rent for the next tenday as they sold their wares, and hopefully that would be enough time to find her the sword and all of them armor. "Name and purpose?"

Rylix kept his friendly expression, but internally he called the man an idiot. He was Ged. What other purpose would he have? "Rylix of Ged, here to trade for a tenday."

The man looked at him, then scanned over to Note and Jadaya, and to his surprise, the man's brows furrowed. "Your presence is requested by the Chancellor and the Steward. You will be escorted there." The man turned his head and barked out an order, "Jensen, escort them to the hall."

Another man, at least ten cycles his junior, snapped off a salute and turned to them. "You will follow me."

Jadaya and Note glanced at Rylix, and he shrugged. This was new to him, but this was his first time trading in Fivika. There were always nuances to everything. They were led through the city, and Rylix was very aware of the four extra guards that appeared with their escort, Jensen. It was obvious this was not an optional visit.

Upon reaching the hall, a large building with many people going in and out and connected to what he would have termed a palace, they were directed to a courtyard with stables to one side. Two young Fivikians came out.

"Take care of their animals. They are seeing the Chancellor and Steward," Jensen said. The young ones bobbed their head, reaching out to grab reins and traces.

Jensen then turned to them. "Place all your weapons in your wagon." There was no arguing with the flat stare or the command, so Rylix put his obvious knives inside, while Jadaya and Note did the same with theirs. He kept his throwing knives and needles in their hidden places, as did Jadaya and Note. At least they would not be completely disarmed.

"Come. They will have been notified of your presence by now," Jensen said, herding them toward a door.

Rylix was very aware of his travel rumpled clothes, dusty appearance, and the lack of a bath in the last two days. His first priority had been to get to a Ged friendly inn so they could bathe and enjoy a night on a real bed. The swing chairs were nice, but he wanted a solid place to sleep and a chance to get clean with hot water..

They went with Jensen and were deposited in a room with two doors. "Wait here," he ordered and stepped back outside the door they had walked through and shut it. Rylix knew he or someone else was on the other side, guarding it.

He sighed and sat down in one of the chairs. Jadaya looked around the room, but it was plain with beige walls and six chairs and nothing else, not even pictures on the walls.

"What do you think this is about?" Note asked as he perched on the edge of the chair, looking like a squid about to squirt ink everywhere.

"I am unsure. This is not something I have heard of, but that means nothing. Maybe they require passes to sell?" Rylix doubted that, as usually the owner of the booth would charge them for a license and let them know the tax rate. All areas demanded a cut of your profits, usually five percent, but some areas had been known to try to overcharge Ged. It would not go over well if Fivika was implementing that policy. He would need to let his mother know immediately if that was the case.

Jadaya kept looking at the walls, and her hand going to where the sword should have been. At least she avoided playing with her knives or needles. Note was unsure where she had them all hidden. They should create a game that helped them spot weapons. Challenge each other with how many weapons could they hide on their body without others being able to tell.

And now I am afraid to be without weapons? This trip is changing me more than I thought.

They waited for what seemed like multiple fingers, but Rylix figured less than one finger had passed before the opposite door opened. A woman about Jadaya's age stood there. "Come, they are ready for you." She wore dark slacks, a shirt of red silk material, with her hair twisted up into a tight bun on the back of her head. Her liquid black eyes were unreadable. She led them down a hall to a large conference room, where two women and two men sat at the table waiting for them.

"Aryix bless, Mayia. You may leave us," one of the older women spoke. The girl bowed and went back out the same door she led them in via, but Rylix saw one more door behind the Fivikans waiting for them.

They studied each other in silence. The four were dressed in a similar manner: slacks, blouses, hair either at the nape of the neck or twisted up. Spectacles hung from a chain on the eldest woman. She had touches of grey in her sleek black hair, but her face showed few signs of it. Their eyes just looked like empty pools of darkness and it made it hard to have any idea what they were thinking.

Rylix broke the silence. "You wanted to see us? May I ask why?" His smile and charm seemed to bounce off the four of them.

"You are the one called Note? The ex-singer?" the eldest asked, her dark eyes peering at Note.

Noter stiffened, every muscle in his body locking up. Rylix considered saying something, but he had no idea what to say.

"I am," Note said, his voice tight and clipped.

"You are the Exile," she continued, looking at Jadaya. Over the days of travel, Jadaya had talked to them about her exile and branding. Over time, she had come a long way to accepting who she was now and what she was learning. Things that would not have happened if she had stayed where she was. They had even run into one other Zuyikan while traveling, and the shunning had not affected her. She let it roll off of her.

Jadaya just touched her brand and nodded.

"That leaves you, the Ged, who is on this foolish journey." The last comment was directed at Rylix.

Note bristled and Rylix hoped he was not about to use any of his weapons. They would all get slaughtered and that would ensure failure.

"What is a fool to one is a wise man to another," he said mildly.

One of the men snorted a bit, then went back to standing silently.

The eldest sighed and looked at the other woman. "I am the Chancellor of Fivika, Lydia. This is Corela, the Steward of Hearth. This is Jontan, Steward of Calin and Orand, Steward of Betan. We were warned about you coming here." There was a lack of emotion that was disturbing given they had been pulled in here to talk to these people.

"Warned?" Note said. His eyes narrowed and Rylix resisted glaring at him. Their lack of subtly now might get them killed.

"Your gods sent word to Joven and Sinka," she said dryly, still watching all of them.

"I see," Note said, but he backed down from the edge of jumping into battle. Rylix wanted to tell him good job, but was afraid that would be even more problematic. Everyone's stress level was spiking.

"Yes. Pel let us know you were on a mission authorized by them and asked for assistance if Xyl needed to be killed. This was a shock. Sinka even went to talk to her sister Yika." Lydia's gaze went from one to another, but her eyes were so dark, only the shifting of her head let him tell what they were watching at any given moment.

"And did Yika say anything?" Jadaya asked. She had a curious look, but Rylix heard no yearning, simply asking what the weather was.

"Only that she has no child named Jadaya," Lydia said, but this time there was a touch of sympathy in her voiced.

Jadaya grinned, a move that made Rylix want to hug her at the sign of growth. "That is acceptable. I have no goddess to honor." She left Yika's name out entirely, and Rylix wanted to cheer. Instead, he sat and waited for the next obstacle to be thrown in their way.

"It sounds like your gods and their gods have had fun discussing the status of their siblings and our journey. What does that have to do with us?" Rylix inquired gently, trying to make sure his voice was calm and friendly.

"We know you are going to kill Xyl," Lydia said, her words hard and her body rigid.

"What?" The word burst out of Rylix, Note, and Jadaya all at the same time. They glanced at each other with a mixture of surprise and panic.

"That is not the plan," Rylix said softly. "Do we look like we could kill gods?" He waved at the three of them, travel-worn and young. None of them had thought about killing a god.

Another glance between the four, and he cursed himself for not being better at reading the Fivikans. He needed more practice. If he lived that long.

"We can call Pel and Rian here if that would help," Note offered.

Rylix had not known Fivikans could pale so drastically. All of them went gray.

"No. We can avoid that," Lydia snapped out, her hands shaking.

"Then we seem to be at an impasse. Where do we go from here?" Rylix asked, looking at them, trying to glean some information about what was going on.

"I believe I will talk with you," a voice behind them said.

Rylix whipped his head around. He had not heard the door open, but the whispered comments of "My lady" let him know the goddess standing there had most likely not walked through the door.

CHAPTER FORTY

ZAYN

In the tenday since the day of Remembrance, Zayn had hardly sat still. They were still cataloguing the changes to the bas reliefs in the worship area. Comparing them to the carvings that had previously adorned the walls. There were a few priests with excellent memories and the carvings had been meticulously recorded, but now they needed to see all the changes.

Before, it had always conveyed the worshipful, pure love between the two gods. With Xyl worshiping Percit, and she accepting his gestures. Now it was explicit, arousing, and disturbing. It showed Percit with chains on her as she cried in ecstasy from Xyl touching her. There were some where she was the one using whips on Xyl, or others, and the obvious pleasure on her face gave you no doubt that she enjoyed it. Pain, lust, desire, and suffering were all wrapped together.

More than one priest had quit, but Zayn had little doubt there would be more to fill those slots. His problem was trying to figure out how to inform the populace of the change without losing them. They had hung sheets over the carvings for the last two worship sessions, but people were already talking, and he had no idea which way to guide it. And that was the root of his issue. Which way to drive the nation so that it was best for him? Which in many ways meant best for Charinsky.

Zayn knew if Xyl's wrath destroyed the kingdom, his life would be short and not very pleasant. But did he want to encourage the debauchery and darkness? Or point out that it was only for the gods to do, as there was no point where a mortal was anything other than worshipping at their feet, though sometimes used for sexual pleasure.

He had spent over twenty candles in the library looking for anything to explain what the gods had been like before her death. Part of him worried that this was yet another sign of Xyl's madness. Maybe he was trying to create something that never existed.

Zayn snarled to himself, as he hid in his room with a cup of strong fruist at lunch. All he wanted was some luxuries, to have his toys, and be able to watch people fear him. This was much more work and responsibility. Before, he just needed songs to be sung and stay aware of basic household management. Now he needed to figure out the best way to guide the temple and country, so a god remained happy, he remained powerful, and his country remained rich enough to pay taxes.

"I have to go talk to Lazul," he muttered as he drained his cup. The man was useful. Maybe talking to him would help give him some ideas about how to manage this. With another grumble he rose, changed his robes, and headed out of the temple. The walk would give him a finger to figure out what he wanted to say.

At the palace he strode in, only to be blocked by Actin. "I need to see King Lazul," he ordered. "Now move."

"You will wait in the small conference room," Actin said, not blinking as Zayn loomed over him.

Zayn pulled back, frowning. Actin had never stood up to him before. The act shook him. "Why? I can talk to him in his office."

"You will wait in the small conference room," Actin repeated and this time a guard stepped up behind him, his face uncaring that Zayn was the cantor.

"Very well," Zayn muttered. "Go scurry off and tell him. Otherwise, I will go find him." He glared at the servant in contempt. The man knew exactly who he was, so why was he interfering?

Actin ignored him completely. "Take him to the small conference room," he said to a nearby guard. Then the seneschal turned back to Zayn. "I will let him know you are here and requesting to speak with him." Actin nodded to the guard and then turned away, heading deeper into the palace.

With little ceremony, the guard ushered Zayn into the conference room and shut the door firmly behind him. He was so shocked he just sank into a chair and tried to figure out what he had missed. With everything going on, he had paid little attention to the activities of court or rumors about the palace in the last tenday, too focused on the damage done to the temples, the singers, and trying to figure out the consequences of Xyl's words and actions.

A servant came in with telcha, but only one cup setting at one end and giving Zayn a stern look. "This is for the king. Would you like some?"

Did I walk into another palace? They have never spoken to me like this.

"Yes, with whitebeet and cream," he managed to say as the servant lifted an eyebrow, waiting for him. A quick nod and the servant was gone. Zayn stared at the tray. It was obviously telcha, he could smell it. It had a small bowl of redbeet powder, a pitcher of cream, but there was also a small pitcher of something else. He was just about to get up and look when the door opened and Lazul walked in, followed closely by Actin.

"Gryst!" The curse slipped out of him as he looked at the king. In a tenday, he had aged suncycles. His normally pudgy build and swollen face had thinned, and gray was creeping up at his temples. He moved like someone had worked him over in the training yard. "What happened?" Zayn was glad he remained seated. At this point, his legs might have given out. His entire world had changed.

Lazul settled himself down while Actin poured the telcha and added the liquid from the small pitcher in it, along with the creamer. But Zayn could barely take his eyes away from the king. It was like looking at the carvings. All you could do was compare him to what had once been.

"Zayn. You needed to see me?" Lazul's voice was quiet but sharp as he wrapped fingers around the mug. Zayn saw them go white as he clenched, then released, lifting it to take a careful sip. Actin remained in the corner, quiet and unnoticeable, if not for the fact that he never remained. Before, he had always vanished as if eager to escape any notice.

"Yes, but first, what is going on?"

Lazul lifted an eyebrow. "Do you not remember?"

Zayn blinked as his mind spun, but nothing leapt to his mind. "I guess not?"

The smile held a touch of cruelty to it that reminded Zayn of the new pictures on the walls. Of Xyl's smiles as Percit writhed in pain and pleasure.

"When Xyl healed me from the koxylitic bite, he cursed me. Or blessed me. It depends on how you look at it. He said, and trust me, these words have been seared into my very being—'I like the idea of you being the king, suffering a portion of what I suffer daily. Yes. Suffer'." Lazul said the words, caressing each one in a way that was distressingly like how Xyl talked. A hint of silken madness under the words.

"You are in pain?" Zayn asked, trying to put all the pieces together.

Lazul blew out a breath that once upon a time might have been a laugh, then took another mouthful of telcha. "That is one way to say it. If this is only a portion of what Xyl feels, then I would have already slit my throat. It is no wonder he is mad. Now what did you want? I have something to discuss with you as well." The slight edge of cruelty and madness had faded, and he just sounded tired.

Zayn's eyes flickered over to Actin and back.

Lazul shook his head. "He remains. He has proven his worth a hundred times over at this point. In some ways, he and Malac are running the kingdom. And yes, I do need a wife and quickly. There are plans being made for that, even as we speak. So talk."

In all the suncycles Zayn had talked to the king, cowed him, and overridden him, he had never felt power from the man. It had been one of the many reasons he had been happy with Lazul on the throne. The man was so easy to manipulate. Now he saw a king that he might have to respect, no matter how much he despised that idea. His mouth went a little dry as he reworked what had planned on saying, coming at it from a different angle.

"It is mostly about our god, though some of it is what direction to take the temples." He wanted to be careful and not say his name. The last thing he wanted at this juncture was Xyl getting more involved.

"Explain," Lazul ordered, but the lines in his face relaxed as he drank his telcha.

"Are you aware of the changes that were made to the temple?" The changes their god made to the temple more accurately, but in this case, being discreet seemed wiser.

Lazul closed his eyes, and Zayn was unsure if he was thinking or enjoying whatever was in his telcha. His words startled him as Lazul spoke with his eyes still closed. "I know there were some changes to the carvings. And If I remember correctly, he mentioned that She may have been … darker than we believed."

Zayn could hear the capital "She" and was relived the king had avoided using their names. "That might be an understatement."

Lazul opened his eyes and caught Zayn in a piercing gaze.

When did his eyes get so blue?

"And your question or concern is?" There were no emotions to the word, but the eyes were sharper than Zayn remembered them ever being.

Zayn leaned back and realized the world had shifted more than he thought. "You have changed," he said, both as a way to stall and to pull out information from the king.

That cruel smile appeared again. "It is amazing what sheer agony can do to focus your attention. And removing any illusions you might have possessed."

That comment sent Zayn's thoughts scattering as he realized just how much more deadly the king had become. This new man had no patience and the risks of him seeing too much were real.

If he learned about my treats, what would he do? Would he even care?

Zayn took a long breath, mind racing, looking at the king who had closed his eyes again, drinking the cup of telcha that Actin had refreshed, but Zayn knew the man was aware of his every breath.

He would. He would probably order me killed. But now that he has changed, what options does that leave me?

It also changed nothing about the current issue of which way to lead the country. And he needed Lazul's help. If the king agreed with what he proposed, then the people would follow. Then later he could decide what to do about the man.

"If I simply reveal the true relationship between them," he said. There was no mistaking which "them" he spoke of. "The land could descend into debauchery and cruelty. That would not be good for either of us." Though he doubted Lazul cared about his luxuries as much as Zayn did.

"That seems likely. Is it that bad?" Lazul's voice was mild, but there was steel underneath it that Zayn had never heard before.

"If you believe the changes in the carvings, yes. Lots of violence in the sex, mortals used as toys, pain and pleasure mixed." Talking to the king about this felt unnatural, but there was little choice.

Lazul heaved a sigh. "I hear something else?"

"I am still not sure that is accurate. None of the texts, not even the oldest of them, mention anything like that. It is possible, but I have nothing to base my assumptions on. And whatever we come out with will guide the populace and I am running out of time to decide."

Every word fell like bitter ash from his lips. The idea that the king would have power over him was the worst part, but if they promoted different things, the country could fall into chaos and that did neither of them any good. Zayn would rather keep his luxuries, and that was best done when the populace was happy and compliant.

The silence went on so long that Zayn poured himself a cup of telcha, enjoying the heat and wondering if the syrup was the pure narcotic of the raw nuts. If the pain he saw on Lazul's face was real, that would be the most likely answer.

Lazul opened his eyes, setting the cup down. "Doing both would be easiest. Tell people what happens in the bedroom between consenting partners is private and not for us to judge. But in His rage and grief it twisted in his mind and it was distorted to be the crux of their love. It provides fact to both. Stress that what happens behind closed doors with consent is between those two people. I will work on talking to a few vendors of more adventurous, intimate items to spread the word on how to handle it. Then we see. If He reacts badly, then we can change direction. But this gives us the best of both worlds. If the plan I have in place works, there may be a few other options." By the end his hand was shaking, and he reached again for the telcha, Actin watching him with a frown.

Zayn leaned back, thinking about it. If they did some creative draping on the carvings, it would look less violent and more sensual. With a little shading of paint and muddaub, it would lessen the shock value but remain true to the gods.

"That would work. And then we see if we can placate Him. We are working on new songs, but given the weather the last few days, I think the rage wore him out."

"Yes. Much of the construction and clearing of damage has been completed," Lazul agreed, his hands still on the cup. "Is there anything else of concern?" There was a darkness to his words that told Zayn there had better not be anything else.

"No, sire. This gives me the path to follow." The respectful words burned on his tongue, but the ruler and the cantor had always had to work in tandem. Xyl would allow nothing else. And the histories made very clear that Xyl expected the cantor to concentrate on him and Percit, not ruling a country. Taking over the throne would never be an option, but the breaking of the reins he thought he had on the king disturbed him.

"Excellent," Lazul said with a nod. He set the telcha cup down and looked right at Zayn. "Now, I would like you to explain exactly why you were drugging me with the fruist in Quartz."

Zayn felt his blood drain from his face as Lazul's cold eyes locked on him.

CHAPTER FORTY-ONE

JADAYA

The last tenday on the road, the settling into her new identity, and the endless motion, allowed Jadaya to grow up and out. As they traveled, she stretched outside her experiences as Chosen and saw life around her. She realized just how coddled and blinded she had been. The joy people showed in getting trinkets or things to make their lives easier highlighted how much she had been given and what she had never received. In Zuyika, there were no celebrations or unexpected presents, nothing just for fun or because you wanted to look pretty. She, the Chosen, never wanted, but she had no memories of the giggles she saw in other children or the joy at getting a sweet. At the end of the day, she was unsure if she missed that life or not.

She loved the new foods, faces, and experiences. But her rage became sharper and more defined as time went on. Not only at what her gods had thrown away, but at what they had denied her. Family. Watching parents with their children, the running and playing of little ones, the kisses of those who loved you. She had never had that as a child. Everything was training, classes, instructions. No cruelty, but no love. If you got hurt, the minders tended to the wound, and then you were sent back to training. The hugs and affection she saw between people made her realize just how barren her childhood had been. And let her know why she had drifted toward Elike so much. She had pretended to give the affection Jadaya craved.

And now she saw just how much she and Note had lost.

The need to rescue the children, to save them, had been rising in her. As well as the simmering desire to maybe rescue other Chosen. But that still was only a kernel of an idea.

Sitting in the room and turning to see a goddess standing there made her wonder once more about the relationships between them and the gods. And wondering if they did more harm than good.

Rylix rose and bowed. "My lady. How may we ease your fears?"

Jadaya studied the goddess. She had the same flawless skin all the gods seemed to, with a sheet of black hair that whispered at her ankles as she moved. Her eyes were the same endless darkness as her people, but in hers glints of light moved, as if she had a rainbow buried in the depths. Her face was not cruel, but the frown on her brow signified this visit contained little frivolity.

"Sinka, we would have dealt with this for you," Lydia protested, a worried look on her face. "Have we acted wrong?"

Sinka shook her head, her hair ripping like water. "No. But there are things you do not comprehend. And I would seek clarification." She turned her attention to Jadaya and her companions. "Can you kill a god? Can you kill my half-brother?"

Rylix looked at them with wide eyes. Note's lips were pressed in a thin line. But Jadaya found her mouth opening before better sense kicked in.

"Our intention was not to kill him, but to rescue the children. Though if he is as mad as people say, it may be the only way to protect everyone." The idea of going up against a god made her stomach flip up and down.

Sinka lifted an eyebrow. "Rescue the singers? But why?"

Note managed to keep his words civil, but Jadaya could hear the venom in his voice. "Did your brother not tell you what they do?"

Sinka had three full siblings, Zula and Yika—Jadaya's gods—and Pel. If Pel had spoken to her and Joven, surely he had let her know why they were doing this.

"He mentioned it, but surely he was exaggerating. The priests of Xyl would not allow that to happen." Sinka had a look of doubt on her face and Jadaya cringed as Note took a step forward.

"Really? Take a good look at me and tell me it was an exaggeration."

Sinka looked at him and for a moment all Jadaya could see was rainbows in her eyes. There was no darkness. Then she flinched. "They would do that to *children*? That has never been acceptable. If that is what he is allowing, why is it only now we know?"

"Because you have no desire to know. Look, now, can you see any of your people in Char?" Note's voice was harsh.

"My people..." Her voice trailed away, and she closed her eyes, only to open them again with a shocked look on her face. "I am blocked. I see nothing but the land."

"Then how would you know?" Note said, his voice bitter. "Xyl is hiding everything from everyone."

Sinka looked at the three of them. "What do you plan on doing?"

The three glanced at each other, and then Jadaya shrugged. "What needs to be done? First is to visit the old gods and beg for assistance. Especially as it seems none of the new gods will step in."

"We are unable-" Sinka started, then broke off. She tilted her head as if listening to something else. Then she looked at the three of them for a long time. Jadaya was blind to her thoughts, as her face remained impassive, but the silence stretched long enough all of them were uncomfortable.

"I see. Xyl is a step. Others are involved. The world is changing." The words fell from her lips like drops of water on a steel pan, ringing with more force than seemed possible. "So much starts with you." She turned to look at the council sitting at the end of the table. "Hear my words now. They are the start of our salvation or our destruction. What will come to pass rides on a knife's edge. Let them make their own choices with neither help nor hindrance."

From the bowed heads, Jadaya knew those words were going to be law to them. But before anything else could happen, Sinka turned back to them.

"You will either save us or destroy us, but I will not risk tipping the scales. Travel through my lands quickly. May my parents give you what is needed."

With that, she was gone.

Jadaya just stared at the spot where she had stood. The words made no sense, but they filled her with a queasy yet glorious feeling in the pit of her stomach.

Lydia stood, pulling Jadaya's attention back to her. Her face was gray and the lines around her mouth now looked like crevices. "You heard her. She has spoken." Her eyes were fathomless dark pits as she let her gaze roam over the three of them. "You will be returned to your possessions and animals. You may do what you need in our city, then leave. As she said, we will neither hinder you nor help you. I do not know what salvation you might be the beginning of or what destruction, but that is not my problem. Go." She flicked her hands and Corela stood, her face just as pale. Even her black eyes seemed to have gone gray.

Corela opened a door. "Escort them back to their possessions. Let them have what they want. Treat them as if they were any other merchant that has traveled to our city."

The three of them moved to the door. For her part, Jadaya's worldview was still shaken by all of this. Prophecies were things of stories, not something involving her. As they reached the door, Lydia spoke again.

"Do not get in trouble or break our rules. I want nothing to do with you. And I will hope that you make the right choices." Her voice was hollow, and Jadaya shivered, still remembering it as they were shown their wagon and beasts, both untouched from what they could tell.

"That was interesting," Rylix said slowly as they headed out the gate. All of them were walking, leading the animals, as the market space was not far away.

"Interesting?" Note said, his hands tight around the reins. "All I wanted was freedom for those captured. Are we setting out to change the world?"

Rylix shrugged. "That worries me not at all. Every person changes the world every day. The question is how far-reaching the changes are."

They fell silent as they wove their way through the city to the market square. Fivika was laid out with an easy to understand system, and the obvious planning that went into the design astounded her. Zuyika had been more haphazard, with new buildings and gardens being developed at the gods' whims. Here, it was methodical and organized. It was both nice and boring at the same time.

Rylix found the marketplace director and obtained a location and tax chit for their setup in the morning.

"There should be an inn one street over you can check into. Hopefully, they will have an area for a tent," he remarked as they headed back through the city. The wide streets made it easier than Jadaya would have thought with the wagon, jacks and four mustangs.

"Tent?" Note asked as they stopped outside an inn.

"Yes. This business was recommended to me by a far-cousin. I will go see if they have a room. Will you watch the equipment?"

Jadaya nodded even as Rylix disappeared through the door.

"Why would we need a tent? Sleeping on the ground was acceptable, but a bed and a bath would go a long way to making me feel better." Jadaya's eyes followed the disappearance of their travel companion.

Note nodded vigorously. "Oh, yes. A bath. I need to grab the salt and soak. My skin itches from the lack of water and salt in the air. I was too busy being scared to pay attention last time. The freshwater rivers and lakes did little good. It was why I went down the coast, so I could dip in the ocean and revive myself."

Jadaya nodded. She had seen how saltwater was required by Aoisans while living with Ola and Kol. For her part, a bath, and a chance to oil and twist her hair would be welcome. Even though she only washed it every tenday or so, it needed a good wash to remove the road dust. They waited outside, watching the people drift by, the sea of straight black hair looking lifeless and flat to Jadaya's eyes.

"We have a room. I assumed you would not mind sharing. And they have a bathhouse and a place for the animals and the wagon. I am looking forward to the bathhouse for one." Rylix smiled. "As we will be staying for a few days, I convinced them to lower the price of the room and the baths. I am ready for a good soak. This way." He led them around the back of the inn, where a large stable, a fenced pen, and a series of tents were set up in the back.

"Tents, why tents?" Though Jadaya had to admit glancing at them, they were the nicer ones, with beds and wash basins in them.

Rylix glanced at them, a frown flickering across his face. "You are truly unaware?"

Jadaya shot a look at Note, but he looked as clueless as she felt. "I am not sure what you are talking about."

Rylix laughed. "Let us get the animals and wagon secured and over our meal I will tell you the story of the choice the Ged made, and why to this day the land Ged are unable to sleep under a roof and the sea Ged are not allowed to sleep on land."

They took care of their animals, then, grabbing their packs, they all headed in for food and the promised baths. The bath house had hot and cold running water, and individual stalls with tubs and showers. It was glorious as Jadaya washed her body and hair, then sat in the tub, letting the heat sink into her bones. Only then did she allow herself to think about the possible meanings of Sinka's words, as she carefully oiled her hair and twisted it tighter. The familiar ritual was one of the last things to tie her to the land of her birth.

Now, as the words reverberated in her mind, she wondered what the home she carved out for herself would look like. And if it would be stained with the blood of a god.

CHAPTER FORTY-TWO

RYLIX

R ylix woke before the sun, the tent letting in the sounds that told him the day had begun. He allowed the others to sleep, too excited to wait for them. Instead, he hooked up the jacks and moved the wagon into position in their leased marketplace spot, returned the jacks to the stable, then got to work setting up for the day.

As the sun peeked over the buildings, people were drifting into the market, looking for everything from produce to clothing to weapons. The noise was a chatter of Ged, Fivikan, with the occasional Char mixed in. Already the smells of fried foods, grilled meats, and sweet beetroot were making him hungry. While he set up, he took the time to speak to the nearby vendors. They were friendly enough, especially as he had goods that were not the norm. Aois was distant enough that the products he brought had the air of the exotic about them. It was like being home as the trading day started in earnest.

By the time Note and Jadaya arrived, he knew where to send them for what they would need.

"Morning. You enjoy your sleep?" He asked as they came over less than three fingers after sunrise.

"Yes. The bed and the baths were nice," Jadaya said, looking at how the wagon's walls had dropped to create a wide area to display everything. "I thought only the small part dropped?"

"No, all of it is set up to open and close. But in the small towns, there was no need to open it up fully. But as you can see, this morning has been profitable." There were already gaps in the goods they had brought, and people were obviously spreading the word as more customers headed their way.

He stopped to sell salt to a woman who had walked over. Aoisan salt was a pale blue and had a lighter taste than the salt gathered in other areas. He had watched them prepare it and figured the rain from Rian was the reason it possessed that delicate taste.

"I have found out where to send both of you. Jadaya, the sword maker is deeper in, with a permanent black smithy. Go to the money house and get a writ from our account." He handed her his ring. "This will authorize you. Pull out one plat. Then head to the blacksmith. From what I understand, he should be able to find the right blank for you and then customize it within a day. It is fine if you add a copper or two to increase the speed."

Rylix's good humor faded a bit. "The council is not going to interfere with us, but they are watching us closely." He nodded across the street to a city guard that leaned against a building, switching between watching them and the entire area.

"I saw him. But you think we will be left alone?" Note was staying in the shadows, but there a few Char that were here shopping and more than one did a double take at seeing him.

"By them, yes. But I would not like to stay here longer than needed. Here is five copper." Rylix handed the coppers to Note. "Go get the clothes you need for the deep cold. When I close up the wagon, I will find my own."

Rylix saw more and more Char glance at them and watched the guard talk to another that had wandered by, eliciting sharp looks in their direction. This complication was not one he had thought of beforehand, and he had no plans in place to deal with it.

He said nothing to his companions, but smiled. "Now go, enjoy. You have money to spend, feel free to purchase items, if you find something you want. You know the capacity of the wagon." He needed them gone. Between the rarity of Jadaya, both taller and darker than the rest of the people in the market and their closeness to Charinsky, the word of strangers might spread faster than was desirable.

His two companions headed out after his directions, and he continued to charm and sell to anyone within reach of his voice. He also put the word out for the Tears of Rian, the Tears of Pel, and the honey. Those were items that could not be sold at the marketplace.

If only both Zuyika and Aois were not such isolated countries. Their people stand out among the other mortals and draw attention.

He let his eyes drift across the milling people. The Fivikans with their straight black hair and black eyes, Wyskans with their hairless heads blue or green patterns across their skulls, along with Delconans with their hair the color of fire against skin the color of milk, and the Aggies with their dark brown hair and tan skins paired with green eyes. But as long as he watched the milling crowd, Jadaya had been the only Zuyikan seen since Calin. And Note was still the only Aoisan.

How can a race with a sea god have little more than fishing boats?

He pushed the worry out of his mind as another customer came up. Sales were going better than his most optimistic predictions and it was freeing up a lot of storage. Even with him planning on restocking for the trip to Betan and from there to Vykland, he should have room no matter what Jadaya and Note might purchase.

Jadaya came back around noon with a smile on her face. "I found the smith. He measured me and pulled out a sword that needed only to be shaped. It was the right length and weight. He added a sheath for another two coppers. Barring any issues, he said he would finish it by tomorrow evening."

"That is good. The cost?" Rylix still kept his eyes on the way people around them reacted, noting the amount of attention she garnered.

She winced a bit. "I feel you would have gotten a better price, but it cost eighty-five copper."

"That is a good price. Maybe not what I could have done, but still worth the money. Now if you will watch the wagon for a bit, I need to take my profit and deposit it in the money house and then grab some lunch. Do you need some?" He placed the money in a pouch inside his tunic, making it harder for anyone to steal.

"Yes, please." She handed him back his ring. "Here. They were surprised by me, but still let me have the money."

"They should. I put yours and Note's descriptions and names on this account. If they had denied you access, I would have demanded to know why." He glanced up at her with a smile. It would be hard for anyone to match their descriptions in Fivika.

Jadaya laughed and then turned to help someone coming up to look at the goods.

He left her knowing she would do fine, if not as well as he would. As he stood in the line to the money house, a street child approached him, in clean clothes, which meant the child was not as abandoned as he wanted people to believe.

"Are you the man with the honey?" The child spoke in passable Ged, and he responded in such.

"Yes."

"My master is interested. Would you meet with him?"

"I can. It will be after dark, and I will bring guards," Rylix responded.

"Of course. Meet at the weaver hall," the boy said, eyes darting back and forth.

"A finger after sundown," Rylix agreed. This was normal. He had listened to his father talk about how these sorts of trades went down. Selling the honey would give them a nice influx of money, though between the ship and the goods he had sold already today, he had evidence for the profitability of this route.

Depositing the money, he swung by a kitchen selling thick meat stew in bowls of bread. He grabbed two and headed back to the cart. Jadaya was selling to one person, and he stepped in as more customers approached upon seeing he was back. To his concern, the number of people watching them had increased.

The Ged taught their people how to notice watchers and the children even made games around it. You needed to know when people's eyes were on you and make sure you did not give away information you wanted to keep secret. But the number disturbed him. Aoisans were rare, yes. But even the Aoisans had wanderers.

He paused mid-transaction, trying to think if he had ever seen one off of Aois. But spending the last ten suncycles there, it was hard to remember being elsewhere.

"Trader?" the woman said, and he shook himself with a smile.

"I must apologize, my dear lady. I got lost in my memories for a moment." He finished packaging up what she had purchased.

The woman, well into her seventies, laughed. "Just wait until you have reached my suncycles. Sometimes memories are the best parts of the day."

He sent her on her way with salt, shells, and some of the dyes. They were almost out of the salt and the shells had been popular among those with any metal working. The dyes were colors not usually found in Fivika, and Jadaya's had sold for fifteen coopers each, to her delight.

Note wandered up, smiling, a look Rylix regarded as strange. He so rarely smiled that it looked odd. "I found the coats and they will be able to quickly make ones that will fit Jadaya. I already dropped mine back at the inn. What else is there for today?"

Rylix flicked his eye from watcher to watcher and forced a smile. "The next few days will be busy. Go enjoy soaking in the baths while you can. Once we hit Vykland, they use natural pools that have water, but it is not salt."

Note's smile had faded slowly and Rylix noticed him shifting uncomfortably. Rylix suspected he could feel the gazes on him. "Sounds good. See you for dinner?" Note glanced around at the words.

"Yes, I would say about four fingers after sundown. My lady warrior, would you be so kind as to escort me to a trade prior to our supper? I may have a buyer for the honey, but no one goes into an unknown situation alone."

Jadaya nodded, busy eating the last of the soup, and tearing the bowl into bite-size pieces.

Note waved and headed out, but to Rylix's discomfort at least three people followed him. Worry tore at him, but he pushed it down.

Either I believe the man can take care of himself, or it is better we die before we start.

The thought rattled around in his brain, but it only made him worry more. By the end of the day, they had sold over sixty percent of his stock, and he determined he needed to increase prices. Jadaya went and fetched the jacks, and together they got the wagon back to the inn and secured. Not only would the guards the inn hired keep watch, but no Ged would allow someone to break into another's wagon. And there were at least two Ged that were traveling through, though not on a trade expedition.

Together, Rylix and Jadaya headed to the weaver's square, an Aoisan-retrieved sword on her hip and the vials of honey in a padded case that he carried across his body. Trying to steal it from him would only result in broken jars and wasted honey.

They reached the area almost exactly a finger after sundown and the boy was waiting for them.

"This way," he said and headed to one of the large warehouses. Looms met his eye as they stepped in, the security guard nodding to them. "Boss is waiting for you," he said, waving to a section of the room with tables and papers scattered on it.

Rylix smiled, feeling less apprehensive, as they headed toward the back. A small man, dressed in high-quality linens and wools, looked up as they approached, two guards behind him in the shadows.

"Ah, you are the trader with the honey?"

"Yes," Rylix said, carefully removing the case from around his body. "There are two jars. They have each been verified. They weigh ten tellaweight each." As he spoke, he pulled out a tiny silver spoon, broke the seal on the jar with his knife, and carefully dipped the spoon into the honey. The amber thick liquid glowed in the light of the flickering lanterns. He handed the man the silver utensil.

Anyone who wore clothes like that could afford the honey. It was worth almost two plat a jar, though if the man bought both, he would sell them for three plat total. That alone would pay for passage to Vykland for all of them, the wagon, and the animals.

The man held it under his nose and sniffed, then let his tongue taste a drop and sighed in pleasure. "I want them both. One plat."

Rylix set the lid back in and pulled out a small stick of wax. "A lantern please and four plat."

The grin that crossed the man's face as he nodded at the guard to bring the lantern over set off their haggling. Rylix resealed the jar as they reached an agreement. Three plat and twenty copper. Money exchanged hands, and he slipped it into an interior pocket. With that sale and the recovery from the ship, their trip had been funded three times over. While honey and tears would not be the normal trade goods for the beginning of a trip, it was an excellent start.

"Rumors spread like wildfire about you today. Where are you headed?" The boss said, still savoring the honey on his spoon.

Rylix shrugged as Jadaya stiffened beside him. "Just testing out a new trade route. So far, it has been successful, but there is a long way to go until I know."

"Yes, testing is the best way, but it is not often I have seen a Ged travel with a former Zuyikan and an Aoisan. Neither of those stray far from their homelands." The look on the man's face was too interested.

"You know the Ged, we attract wanderers," Rylix said with a smile, though he had alarms going off in his mind. "We try different routes, though so far this one has some promise to it, even if it needs refinement."

The boss nodded. "True, true. Ah, well, if you have anything else of this quality. Let me know." He nodded in dismissal, and Rylix tilted his head in a gesture of respect that let him keep his eyes on everyone.

"I will." He turned and walked out, every sense on high alert, but to his relief and puzzlement, they exited the warehouse with no issue.

"What was that?" Jadaya said in a low voice.

"I am not sure, and that worries me." Rylix said as they kept to the busy lanes on the way back to the inn.

CHAPTER FORTY-THREE

NOTE

Note noticed their agitation the moment they walked in. He tensed, but there were no sounds of trouble following them.

"Is there an issue?" He asked even as he stood, making sure his daggers were at hand.

Jadaya looked at Rylix, a crease between her brows. "There were questions."

That told Note nothing, so he looked at Rylix for more information.

"Too many questions. We make an odd group of travelers and it has people curious." Rylix sighed, seeming preoccupied with his own thoughts.

Note leaned back and closed his eyes, thinking. "I am not telling people what we are doing."

"No, but I would be very surprised if what occurred in the meeting was not spreading through the city at a rate of speed the winds would quail at," Rylix said with a twist of his lips.

"Ah, yes. So what do we do?" Note kept his eyes shut as he thought. What options did they have?

"Do? I think continue as we are. We need the supplies we have ordered. It will take us another day or two to be ready. We stay on our guard and proceed." Rylix sounded assured, so what else could Note do but agree?

He opened his eyes to see Jadaya still standing there, pensive, but not arguing. "You are correct. There is little they could do. Hopefully, the idea of three people taking on a country will be laughable."

Rylix smiled, his wide grin full of amusement. "Indeed, it is. If you had told me, I would find it most amusing. I imagine most will agree."

They agreed to not worry about what the managers of Hearth would do.

There was little they could do to affect it either way. After a dinner, Rylix headed out to a tent, while Jadaya went to use the bathhouse, something Note understood the lure of, but he had other plans.

Note pulled on a cloak with a hood and headed to the nearest bar. There in a dark corner, he ordered fruist, why anyone would drink the awful mess they called beer he had no idea, and he listened. Suncycles of living in the temples, he had learned to listen to everything, both the sounds of voices, the weight of steps, and even how the songs were sung.

He could hear pain, sorrow, and joy all in the same tune. Worse, he knew how to make all those emotions appear in his voice on command. He hoped, in the deep part of his heart, that someday he might be able to sing again without every note being wrapped in pain and anger.

Note shook the thoughts away and listened. There were talks of shortages, rising prices, the storm to the west, complaints about spouses, everything that he expected to hear. If his group was being talked about, it was still controlled information. Maybe letting the gossip spread would count as hindering them.

Who knows? The gods never make sense.

He had just about decided to leave when someone sat down on his left at the table he was at. "I thought the Aoisan never left their homes unless by force."

Bitter anger mixed with a fear that he wanted to deny wrapped around his gills. His lungs stuttered and froze as he was torn between fight and flight responses. The language was Char, and it contained every terrible memory with those words. He turned slowly to look at the man who had sat next to him. The pale blue eyes and the blond hair removed any touch of doubt he might have had. An older man, one who would have been a staunch worshipper.

Note swallowed, trying to restrain the anger that flooded him, but killing a stranger in a bar would do nothing and the odds of him even feeling better were low.

Remember who the real enemy is, the king and the priests.

"And you are talking to me why?" he managed to say, while keeping a tight grip on the cup of fruist. It was that or pull his knives.

"Curiosity. Why is an Aoisan not safe and secure in his islands?" There was honest curiosity there.

"Those islands lack in safety, and why should I answer your questions?" The instant rage had faded and now he wanted to know why this man was here.

"I am curious. All Aoisans I met were prisoners. It interests me to see them as people, not singers."

The tone of the man's voice was even, not sarcastic or even predatory, but Note kept his guard up. "Singers, no. We were slaves, in all definitions of the word."

The man bowed his head, then lifted his mug to drink. The odor of sweet mead reached Note's nose and the noise in the bar rose as a musician started to play. It was a common song, one even Aoisans played in their bars.

"This is why I travel," the man said. Note looked at him and the man gave a half smile. "We get no music that is not worship of our gods or the songs of grief. There is no fun or laughter, it is always hymns to gods that use us as whipping boys. But away from Charinsky there are funny songs, sad, rousing, ballads, and stories. So many types. I travel because there is a world outside the one I thought I knew."

Note watched him, unsure why he was telling him this.

What am I supposed to say?

"I wanted to let you know, there are rumors about you, but if they are true, and you do attempt to rescue the singers, not all Char know how they are treated and those that do are not always in favor. The cantor and the king decide how it goes, not the people." He drained remnants of drink in his mug and set it down. "Remember that when you are there. If you need help, mention a broken song chain. Those who agree will do what they can." Without another word, he got up and left, leaving Note sitting in the corner thinking.

Rumors mean trouble. But who would believe something so crazy?

He stayed a while longer, but the clientele were heading to bed and he had heard nothing new for fingers. With a mental shrug, he stood, leaving a few gold for the fruist. He stepped out of the bar, heading back to the inn. He was about halfway there when three men stepped out of the shadows.

"We were beginning to think you were going to sleep there, Aoisan," one of them said in a thick Char accent.

Note paused, his hands drifting to his blades. "What do you want?" He scanned the area. Most people had departed and outside of the three men he saw no one, but the inn was too far away, and the bar meant turning his back on them.

"Aoisans bring nice finders' fees. Char is always willing to take in Aoisans. Your kind rarely leaves the shelter of the islands, but when you do, it means money." While the man's face was obscured, the sneer in his voice came through crystal clear.

"Ah. There is a bounty on us?" Note kept his voice noncommittal, but he pushed back the cloak he wore, making sure his arms were free.

"Yep, and I never heard of one that sounds like a croaking leaper, so we can sell you." The men moved closer and Note sighed.

"I suppose you are not willing to walk away?"

"Would you leave found money on the street?" Laughter followed the reply, and Note was torn between being annoyed and looking forward to what was to come. Worst case, he died, and he never had to worry about this again.

"I think you might find me difficult to pick up." The memory of the rules the council gave them—no help, no hinder—made him hesitate just a moment. Almost a moment too long.

The men moved in quickly toward him. Note whipped out both arms, sending small knives flying from them. But he still needed more practice. One bounced off the chest of the man to the right, and the other nicked the center man's leg.

"If that is all you have, this is going to be easier than collecting eggs," the center man sneered, not even bothering to look at the nick.

I need to remember to poison the blades.

The thought whispered across his mind as he drew his daggers and danced back. He looked for openings to strike and cursed that there was no water here. It was a truth few disputed. Aoisans were the best swimmers around, but on land they were just mortals. If there had been water, he would have just fled via that.

He took two more steps backward, then in a fluid motion he had practiced with Jadaya, he thrust forward, a dagger in each hand. A thrust, then a sweep to the left, and it worked perfectly. Part of him wanted to celebrate as the center man fell to the ground, his throat ripped open from the dual swipe of blades.

"Fish bait," one of the men snarled. Note just smirked. While many Aoisans would have regarded it as a horrible insult, he realized words were just noises a long time ago. They both rushed him, and he twisted hard to the right and backward at the same time. It let him put the building at his back, removing one attacker from immediate threat, and placed him fully in reach of the other. But he had blades ready.

Good thing they are lacking armor. That would make this more difficult.

The lack of armor let his knives slice straight to skin, and he slid them along that man's gut, the whiff of feces telling him the man was dead though he might walk for a while yet. A scream of pain came a second later as the man registered what Note had done. Alarms, bells, and whistles started going off as his attacker crumpled.

The other man, eyes wide, looked at him, then at his two companions laying on the ground. He snarled. "Next time I shall bring more and as long as I avoid crushing your throat, the Char are uncaring about the rest of your body. I suppose you can sing while missing fingers or a leg." He turned and ran as the city guard came pounding down the street.

"Hold your place. The Guard is here." The man running away kicked up his speed a notch, but three guards took off after him, their leather-soled boots hitting the pavement in a pace at least a third faster than the ruffian's.

The other guards surrounded Note, leaving the man with a star on his leather armor and another with a red knife on his tunic to investigate the two downed men. One was already dead, the other was holding his intestines in and screaming in pain.

The red knife was the symbol of healers across most of Aria. Note was unsurprised when the man looked up at the leader and he subtly shook his head. The leader sighed, giving the healer a quick nod, then turned to Note, who remained against the wall. Meanwhile, the healer slipped out a knife and, in a swift practiced motion, slit the man's throat. The cries ceased, and the man cleaned his blade and stood up. There was a reason the knife was red.

"What happened?" The gruff question came from the leader. Note assumed the symbol meant officer of some kind.

"They wanted to capture me and turn me over to the Char. Apparently there is a reward for any Aoisans they turn in. I declined their offer, and they took offense to it." Note shrugged, but other than that he remained still.

"Take him in, get someone to collect these bodies, and we shall let the captain decide."

Note thought about saying something but decided silence was the better choice. Now, if he could figure out how to let his companions know, that would be good.

CHAPTER FORTY-FOUR

RYLIX

Rylix paced back and forth at the booth. Note had not returned last night, and he was not here this morning. This was unlike the man, and Rylix did not like unknowns.

"Where do you think he is?" Jadaya asked, worry evident as she kept fiddling with the small knives she had placed around her. Her skill was getting better, but she would never give up her sword.

"I am unsure, and that means there is a problem." Rylix stood near the wagon, staring at the river of people flowing through the marketplace. He had zero idea where to go. "Jadaya, go pick up everything we ordered." He pulled the slips with the confirmations of payment on them and handed them to her. "I will close down and go check the courts, then…" He trailed off, and she nodded.

"Then you will call on the house of the dead?" she asked, her face grave.

He nodded slowly. All cities had a house of the dead. It was where corpses were taken for burial, disposal or otherwise. Letting bodies lay in the streets encouraged disease and despair—which was a disease itself.

"I believe he is well. Surely he would not allow himself to be killed so easily. His rage at injustice is too powerful."

Rylix gave her a smile. "I will believe that also. Now go on your errand. I will go on mine." She headed out at a quick walk while he sealed up the wagon. It would be safe left alone for a few fingers. Then he headed toward the city courts.

He found them easily enough and made his way to a long counter where three people sat answering inquiries. Once it was his turn, he went up to speak to the older man, his black eyes uncaring. "Yes, I am looking for a companion of mine. An Aoisan that goes by Note."

"Oh, that one. We have him." The person at the counter seemed uninterested in the request, marking something on their list.

Rylix kept the sigh of relief inside, but it did him good to know their trip had not been sabotaged so early under his watch.

The man lifted his head and called out, "Carisen, take this Ged to the special disposition room."

A young man, his face still red with pustules of teenage growth, waved at Rylix who followed him through the maze of hallways.

"Here you go. They are going through last night's pickups now." He left with a nod, then headed back the way they came. Rylix went in the door to find a large room with benches, and a lectern at the front with doors on either side. It was full of people waiting like him. There were a few guard officers and two people at a table with ledgers in front of them. He took a seat on a bench and watched, trying to figure out what was going on here. And how he would rescue their friend.

"Next," the man at the lectern shouted. The door to Rylix's left opened, and another guard walked a man into the room. "Charges?" the lectern man said.

"Bar fight, one man injured, owner says fifty copper of damage." This time, it was one of the people with a ledger in front of them, the woman. She had her hair pulled back into a high tail, and she only glanced up to verify the person before speaking.

Rylix cringed. That would take one man at least five tendays of work to earn as a laborer.

"Liar. It was maybe five silver of damage. I can pay for it now. And the man deserved it. He dumped ale on my head because I bumped him coming in," the man protested.

The lectern man looked at the woman at the table. She, in turn, flipped a page on the ledger on the desk. "The officer's notes are here. Per them, multiple witnesses verified it was retaliation for the aggression on the other patron's side. Guard reports estimate the damage at maybe one copper."

"The fine will be one copper for the bar owner and five gold for our expenses. Payable now." Rylix figured the man standing at the lectern was the local civil authority. He knew he was supposed to memorize all the legal systems for each country but had not worried about that part. That was a mistake, it seemed.

A woman rose from the benches and walked forward. "I have the fine." The guard moved the man over to a table where a different clerk sat with a different ledger. The money exchanged hands, and the prisoner was released. As they walked out, the woman looked like she might kill him and prevent him from getting into any more trouble.

Rylix sat through three more of these. The pattern being similar, charges were read, information about the case presented, and a fine declared. One of them was a murder, and that one was referred to a tribunal and taken back through the door. Then Note was brought in. He looked tired, but uninjured. Which eased Rylix's stress level.

"Charges?" asked the lectern man.

"Death of two men in self-defense. The Aoisan says they were trying to kidnap him. One was apprehended running away. That one swears they were set upon without reason and he lives only because he ran while this man was killing the others." The guard rattled all of this off while Note stood there silently.

"Thoughts?" the man asked, looking at something on the lectern. Rylix suspected it was a book with the list of people being brought in today.

"None of the three were known as good citizens, but there is no record of them attacking anyone. He is a visitor, but I have no information about him other than he was seen with a Ged and a Zuyikan." The guard shrugged. "There is no trustworthy information as to the actual incident."

The lectern man looked like he was about to say something, when a woman on one of the front benches rose. All the guards went silent. Rylix looked at her, but she was unfamiliar. He had no idea which way this was going to go, so for now, he waited. Worst case they could break him out? Maybe?

"The Chancellor sent me," she said in a clear voice, though from the reactions of the people that worked here, they seemed to know this. "This man is known to us. It has been said Fivika will neither help nor hinder. Here is our verdict: you have ten fingers to leave Hearth. You have a tenday to leave Fivika. It has been said."

All the guards murmured back, "It has been said." The guard holding Note marched him to the other man at the table who reached down and handed Note a satchel which Rylix assumed contained his possessions. He stood as Note turned, and he could see the relief on Note's face as the guard pushed him toward Rylix.

"Go. You have heard was what was said. You have ten fingers, then we will throw you out," the man at the lectern said. Note wasted no time walking toward Rylix.

"I think we should go," Note said, his face a blank mask.

"Already working on it," Rylix said, his voice just as quiet. "I sent Jadaya to get everything we ordered. We should be ready to depart, though I need to close our accounts with the inn."

Note nodded. "Good. I will explain once we are away from people." His eyes indicated everyone watching them as they headed out.

"Ah," Rylix said, then fell silent. They remained that way, unspeaking until they reached the wagon. Jadaya was there, putting the last of the purchases into the wagon. "We need to go. If you will collect the mustangs, I will settle our accounts."

Jadaya's eyes flicked to both of their faces, but she said nothing, just nodded and they set about their various tasks.

It took them three fingers to get the jacks and mustangs saddled, hitched, and their possessions cleaned out of the inn. They were outside the city in four fingers, and Rylix felt the eyes of the guards on their back the entire time. As they got far enough away from the city that the sensation of being watched faded, he turned to Note.

"What happened?" Worry and curiosity burned in him.

Note rode one of the mustangs on one side, while Jadaya was walking along the other side of the wagon, her new sword strapped to her hip.

"Yes. I was concerned when I woke this morning and you were not there," she said, glancing at Note.

Note sighed, rubbing his face. Rylix noted he looked even more exhausted than when he was first brought into the court. "I was concerned about the meeting you had with your buyers. I wanted to see if there were any rumors or stories about us. So I went to a pub to listen. I barely finished a single cup of fruist."

Rylix nodded. It was how he gathered a lot of information, so that made sense to him. "Did you learn anything of interest? And how did that lead to your being arrested? "

Note was silent long enough that Rylix almost prompted him.

"Two things of interest. One was the Char that sat at my table uninvited. He said he traveled because he liked the music. Then he mentioned that of those Char that understand what the singers are, not all of them support the practice. He implied heavily that there might be help there if we were to rescue them."

Rylix leaned back against the wagon at that. The news was unexpected and an array of possibilities opened up with that.

Note started speaking again. "After he left, I listened for a while longer but heard nothing useful, so I headed back to the inn. I was about three streets from the pub when three men, Char I believe, though the lighting was low, stepped out to intercept me. They postured, but the gist of it was they wanted to take me prisoner and take me to Char to sell or trade me. I declined their generous offer." His voice was heavy with sarcasm.

Jadaya snorted at that, and Rylix agreed with her.

"The aftermath was two dead, the guard there, and me spending my evening in jail where I slept not at all. You saw me this morning." Note shrugged. "Nothing else to tell in regard to that."

"Huh. I wonder how they knew you were in jail to have a representative there, but I suppose they were watching out for us. Is there anything you did not get that we needed to obtain in Hearth?"

Note shook his head as did Jadaya.

Rylix relaxed a bit. "Excellent. Then we are ahead of schedule. If I have it planned correctly, a Ged ship should be in Calin in nine days, making it so we can get out of Fivika on schedule and prior to the deadline." Rylix settled down, feeling better. While the deadline was concerning, they should just be able to make it. They would be in Calin for two days and then the ship would take them near the Mount of the Old Gods before dropping them in Vykland. Then they would have to figure out how to get across. That part he still was unsure of.

They bypassed the first town they came to, not wanting to bother since most of the people only lived about four fingers from Hearth. When you were that close, no one was going to buy from a trader. They spent the night under the stars and Rylix lay there for a long time, watching the night sky and thinking. With the gods involved, it made all of this riskier than he had assumed.

Am I happy with this choice?

The answer disturbed and excited him. Originally, his assumption had been it was only the Aoisan's gods and Xyl they had to deal with. But now that the other gods were involved, it made all of this much more deadly.

And more exciting.

If this worked, if they somehow survived, they were in an epic saga, like the stories the Ged told around the campfires. Which reminded him. He needed to tell the histories to Jadaya and Note. They needed to know the old tales. He would start tomorrow. But for tonight he watched the stars from his swing net and let motion carry him into his dreams where the gods were immaterial and Kryx still lived.

CHAPTER FORTY-FIVE

JADAYA

They were two days out from Calin and Jadaya looked forward to the city, hoping they had baths like Hearth had. Even one night to soak sounded amazing. She felt like dust coated every inch of her body and no matter how thoroughly she scrubbed when they camped near a stream or a river, she still had the sensation she road dirt covered her. There was only one more small town between here and Calin, and they would stop at it in the morning and then hit Calin in the evening. Hopefully, then she could get that bath.

She had regained her tone and strength in the days since they started on this journey, so for now she was moving at a ground eating trot, looking for a place to spend the night. If she was lucky, it would be near a stream. Up ahead was a series of small groves in a line, implying the existence of water. She veered that way, lifting her head to sniff the air as she approached the trees.

"I see you kept the water flask," a voice came from her left.

Jadaya pivoted, drawing her sword in a fluid motion as she braced on her right leg, left leg bent, ready to lunge as needed. She had sensed no one in the area, so the comment was unexpected.

Cass was leaning against a tree, smiling at her. "Excellent reactions. If I was a brigand, I would definitely be regretting my choice of victim."

She lowered her sword a bit, still wary. The aforementioned flask hung on her hip. The water always seemed impossibly fresh and cool from it, even if it had been stale and warm when she refilled it.

"Why are you here?" The question came out unkind, but she cared more about how he had just appeared than anything.

"Traveling like you. I assume your companions are behind you?" He nodded toward the road, never taking his eyes off her.

"They are," she said, slowly sheathing her sword.

"Wonderful. Then you can camp with me." He waved deeper into the trees. "There is a good place for setting up camp." His eyes traced back to her and then down to her hip. "I am happy to see you got a better sword, though it still does not quite suit you, like it should."

Jadaya pulled back, looking at him. "It is well balanced and matches my height and strength. Why do you say it does not quite suit?".

Cass shrugged, turning to walk deeper into the trees. "There is a path over here wide enough for the wagon." He waved her to head in his direction, and after standing and listening for anything or anyone else that might be there, Jadaya followed.

He led her to a wide, clear spot with a deep pond filled by a burbling spring. "The water is warm enough to swim in. The source of the spring over there is pure and tastes better than the finest fruist." Cass pointed toward a path that wove the other direction. "And your wagon should be able to fit. There is even plenty of grazing for your animals."

She inspected the area, noting everything he said was true. It was almost as perfect a site as she had ever seen. Even the trees were spaced far enough apart to make tying the swing chairs to them easy. On one side, on a slight rise, she saw he had a pack, a swing chair, and a small ring of stones for a fire set up.

"This is an excellent spot. I will bring them here." She wavered for a moment, watching him. "Were you following us?"

"Not exactly, but your ousting from Hearth definitely garnered notice. I was not opposed to running into you again and thought it might be interesting to meet your companions this time." His smile was amiable, and she sensed no deception in him, but at the same time something ran false, or at least odd in his words.

Not able to think of anything else to say, she followed the path to the road and waved at Note and Rylix. She had only been three fingers ahead of them, so they were easily visible when she stepped out of the trees.

They reached her in short order. "There is a good campsite in here, with a pool to bathe in. And the man I met before we reached Hearth is here." Cass relaxed and confused her at the same time, and she disliked not being sure as to her reactions. "I am unsure of him," she admitted as they turned into the path.

Note stiffened, and Rylix did a subtle check of his weapons. "Dangerous?" Rylix asked.

"I think not, but he is odd. And right now, anything odd concerns me," she admitted. "But you will need to decide for yourself."

Note nodded and slipped off the mustang. Fighting from the back of the animal was not something he had any experience with, therefore being on the ground was a much wiser choice.

Together the group moved through the trees into the clearing and, to Jadaya's relief, Cass still sat on his little hill, a pot hanging over the fire. He looked up with a friendly smile. "Afternoon. Please set up your camp. I was brewing some tea. You are welcome to share."

Jadaya let Rylix jump off the wagon and walk to Cass. The Ged had the social skills she lacked and at this point, she wanted to see what someone else made of the man. "Well met. We have been mostly alone on this trip. It is nice to see another traveler out here. We are scouting out a new trade route. What brings you this way?" Rylix's voice was friendly, but Jadaya stayed to his left behind him with Note on his right, watching the man.

"Ah, but that is not all you are doing, is it?" Cass said with a gentle good humor that made Jadaya want to sit at his fire and talk to him. But his words made her stiffen.

"What exactly could you mean?" Rylix asked, still the grin and easy manner, but his hands were near where he kept some of his little knives.

"Rumors spread fast, and really if you wanted this little adventure kept a secret, it would have been best to leave him in Aois." Cass nodded to Note. "And made Pel and Rian promise not to talk to any of their siblings. None of them are good at keeping juicy rumors to themselves." Cass kept a smirk on his face, but Jadaya felt frozen in place.

How does he know so much?

"Who are you to tell us this or know so much?" Note stepped forward, the dagger drawn and his body a taut bowstring ready to be released.

Cass laughed, a sound that made Jadaya flinch as it sounded louder than should be possible. Then he smiled. This time, it looked like something he was more familiar with. "I believe Rylix knows who I am. Or at least he should."

Rylix had gone so still Jadaya thought he might have stopped breathing as he stared at Cass. Then he sighed and his entire body relaxed. "I apologize for being so slow. I should have guessed the first time Jadaya mentioned you. Cassix, is it not?"

Again, that quick smile and a laugh that sounded like thunder lived underneath it. "Indeed. I knew I placed my trust in the right man. Please make your camp. I will talk to you over the evening meal, assuming you are willing to share? The life of a traveler means my provisions are slim and not what most mortals require for sustenance."

Jadaya's eyes were locked on the man, or the god. Why had she not suspected? She looked back at the flask. "This is enchanted?"

Cassix laughed. "Yes. A minor one, but yes. Someone I knew crafted it a long time ago. Any water put it in it purified and cooled. Not the most powerful enchantment, but Aryix thought it would be useful at the time."

Note's hands were still locked on his daggers, but he had a resigned slump to his shoulders that Jadaya found odd. "So, are you here to stop us?" Note looked at the ground as he spoke.

"Stop you?" Cassix sounded surprised and tilted his head. "Why, by Aryix, would I stop you? This is the best thing I have seen in what feels like eons."

Note's mouth dropped open a moment before he snapped it shut. "Then why are you here if not to stop us?"

Cassix looked at the water and the spring, whose burbles filled the air. "That sounds like something to be discussed over supper. You have animals to care for. Go and do that first. I think I will search for something to act as my contribution to the meal." With that, he rose and stepped into the trees, disappearing. Though Jadaya could not have said if it was a trick of shadows or the god using his powers.

Note shot a look at Rylix. "I feel like this is somehow your fault."

"Mine?" Rylix said with a laugh. "How is this my fault?"

"You are the one that tell us stories each night. I feel like they called him here," Note said, but she could tell he was mostly joking.

"If it was my stories, then they have been paying attention to us already, and I would like to point out you are the one who yells at gods in public." Rylix looked like he was trying not to laugh.

Jadaya cut into the bickering the two of them had created to pass the time on the road. "It matters not, but being rude seems unwise. Animals, then dinner, and then we see what he has to tell us."

The men looked at her and nodded, almost relieved that she was providing direction, which she found amusing. This meal should prove entertaining if not informative.

Long practice had the animals secured for the night with food, water, and a grazing area. The grass in fact was rich and full of seed heads she thought were slightly out of season, but none of them complained as it let them save on feed for the animals.

Soon enough they had a fire ring created, at least twice the size of Cassix's ring. Bread was cooking in a pan, and a stew of dried meat, vegetables, and seasoning was going in the pot. With only another day to Calin, they might as well use the rations. With unspoken agreement, they offered the better of what they had as opposed to the plainer fare they normally ate.

Cassix stepped out of the woods, his hands full of mushrooms and fern heads. "Ah, wonderful, these will add to the stew." He offered the supplies to

Rylix, who inspected them, then rinsed and added them to what was currently cooking. Rylix would know if they were safe to eat. Jadaya had learned much on this trip, but mushrooms remained delicious but mysterious in her mind. One would cure, one would kill, and one just tasted good, and she was unable to tell the difference between them.

"Aryix bless. These will indeed make the meal heartier. But it needs at least two fingers to cook. I have a few flasks of fruist. Would you like some?" Rylix had his salesman smile on, all teeth, no eyes. Jadaya had watched him over the days and could tell now when he was putting on a front versus really involved with the conversation. This was the calculating Rylix, watching and weighing everything.

That is good. He has the legends my upbringing lacked.

"Ah, that would be wonderful. I must admit that the creativity of mortals when it comes to food and drink has always astonished me," Cassix said. His smile, Jadaya saw, involved both eyes and body. It was interesting to watch the two interact.

Rylix pulled out the flasks and cups, though Jadaya stayed with water. After the incident at the market, she was not about to drink unless it was with friends and in a safe space—this was neither. When they all had a glass of fruist or water, Rylix raised his glass. "To the road ahead."

They all raised and took a sip. Then Rylix—to Jadaya's amazement—looked directly at Cassix. "Why are you here?"

Cassix smiled, but this time a shudder crawled down Jadaya's spine when she saw it. "I want your little quest to succeed, of course."

CHAPTER FORTY-SIX

ZAYN

"Say that again?" Zayn looked at the man, unable to believe what he had heard.

The man cleared his throat, legs shuffling as he spoke again. "We ran into an Aoisan, a Ged, and we think a Zuyikan, who had rumors surrounding them and their mission. From what the word on the street was, they are coming here, to Charinsky to rescue the captured Aoisans and strike down the people in power that allow this. The gods have been talking and Joven and Sinka declared they would neither 'help nor hinder' this group in their quest. There is also a rumor that Sinka made a prophecy, but those stories range from they will destroy everything to they will be our salvation. So my trust in that information is lacking." The words tumbled out as if they burned the man's tongue. Then the traveler dropped his eyes, focusing them on the temple floor.

The information rattled around Zayn's mind, but he forced his face back into a calm visage. "Aryix bless you for this information. Does anyone else know?"

The man, whose name he could not remember, shrugged. "It was the talk of Hearth for a few days, so yes and no. Most thought little of it, but there was a scuffle. Someone tried to grab the Aoisan to bring him here. Two died. It got the three kicked out of the city and country."

"Do you know where they are headed?" Zayn wondered if they were already here and the world was about to crash around his head.

"Not really, but they headed out toward Betan, which makes no sense if they are planning on coming here. I left Hearth not four fingers after they did, and I was here in four days. The currents are swift between us and Fivika right now."

The currents, the bane and salvation of all those with ships.

"This information is very welcome." Zayn reached into his purse and pulled out two copper. "Take this as a token of my gratitude. I ask that you keep this quiet. Panicking people would do little good."

The man took the offered coppers, his eyes wide with gratitude. "Of course, Cantor. I saw what was done by Him," he said in a quiet tone, nodding back toward the worship area. "Getting Him riled up would be bad for everyone."

"That it would. Go and Aryix bless." The man scurried out and Zayn sat in his little office.

Algoi stepped from around the divider that separated his living quarters into two sections. "Do you trust him?"

Zayn shook his head. "It matters little. If the rumor spreads, eliminating him would not stop it. All I can hope is that it remains a rumor that the singers will never have the opportunity to hear." He fell silent, his mind going over options. In the days since Xyl's revelation, all of Char worked to repair the damage. But the change in the worshipers worried him. They were darker, bruises were more common, the favorite songs were new ones that talked about the pleasure of pain, and the death rate of wives had spiked. In all his reading, there was no hint that Percit and Xyl had any sort of relationship besides the normal one between husband and wife. The depictions that were now on the walls, the implications of what Xyl said, and the new songs created from dreams had no basis in anything he could find.

Which makes me wonder just how insane our god is.

"With as precarious as everything is, though the sun has been nice, if they do come here, it could cause…issues." Algoi's words were slow and careful.

Zayn snorted a laugh. "Issues is one way to describe it. Rumor travels faster than the wind. If they show up and remove the singers from even one set of temples, the word would spread. You and I both know that while most Char understand and support the necessity of singers, most is not all. These travelers may very well find support here, if they have not already connected with that aspect of the population."

"True," she murmured, more to herself than to him. Then, to his annoyance, she bowed her head. "What you would like me to do, head priest?"

For a moment, he really wished she had more backbone. A subordinate he could actually talk to would be nice. Too bad Circe still resisted his requests to come here. She would have had ideas and plans. But wishing for the past was a waste of time.

"At this point, nothing. We need to keep up the songs and ensure we get the harvest in. I will deal with this."

"Yes, Cantor." With that comment, she left his room, shutting the door quietly, leaving him with the mess in his hands.

No matter how he twisted or turned the information in his head, he had neither the resources, connections, nor knowledge to deal with it. "I need to go talk to Lazul," he muttered to himself. A thought that he dreaded. The bumbling king had faded, and he almost feared this man. After the king had raked him over the coals regarding the drug in his fruist, Zayn felt like he had barely escaped with his head. The lie he had managed to sell was that some of the older singers were seeking sexual partners among the clergy and that they had a pregnant singer they had not wanted him to notice, as until that point they had never had a child that was born to both. In all honesty, he had no idea why that had not happened, but either the fertility levels of the Aoisans were almost nil or something else was at work.

Lazul had bought the explanation, if barely, and the only consequence had been asking for more of the drug. Zayn received it just yesterday. The bundle sat on his desk for a delivery he had been avoiding.

"Now is the time, I guess." With a mental sigh, wondering how much more Lazul had become like a ruler of old, which he was unsure if it was a good or bad thing, Zayn changed his robe and shoes, then headed to the palace to deliver both drugs and news.

Normally he would have just strolled through the palace and gone to find Lazul wherever he was, but not anymore. Not only were the servants less cowed by him, but they seemed to care that Lazul was only disturbed if the matter was important. Zayn was both impressed and annoyed. For now, though, he saw no other option but to give into the new patterns of governing.

He was shown in to meet Actin, who also seemed preoccupied and uninterested in the fact it was the cantor standing in front of him. "You wish to see the king?"

Zayn almost snapped at him, the tone of voice was as if he was some petty merchant seeking to sell the king wares, but then he looked at the man, actually looked and registered the shadows under his eyes, the rumpled clothes, and the unwashed hair. In other words, Actin looked nothing like Actin.

"What am I missing? Why are you so exhausted?"

Actin lifted his head to peer at Zayn and blinked. "Oh. Cantor." He stared at him a moment, then nodded. "Yes, he will want to see you. This way." Actin rose from his chair and moved stiffly for the first few steps, then limbered up as they walked, but not to Lazul's office. Instead, they went into a section of the castle Zayn had never entered.

"Wait here," Actin said, then knocked on a door and slipped inside so neatly Zayn was unable to glimpse the occupants. Instead, he looked at the hall. It was brighter than most, with multiple arrow slits letting in the light of the day and giving proof of the continued wonderful weather since Xyl's fit. Zayn was about to start fidgeting when Actin opened the door. "Enter," he said, waving Zayn in. "I shall return with refreshments, sire," he said, then shut the door behind him.

Zayn looked first at the room he was in. For some reason, he was unwilling to look at the king quite yet. It was cozier than the king's normal office, with a fireplace at one end, a sitting area, and at least two comfortable chairs, with lanterns hung on all the walls to give light. With reluctance, he looked at the king and, to his surprise, a woman. They were both watching him with expectant, if slightly amused, looks.

To his relief, Lazul looked better, though still drawn and focused, but he looked like he might be capable of smiling. The woman looked familiar, but he was unable to place her or recall her name.

"What is it Zayn? More complications with Him?" Lazul avoided the name just like Zayn had started to. The last thing he wanted to was to summon Xyl's attention.

"No, more like complications with other things. Is your pain less?" Zayn did actually care. A pain-free king was easier to deal with than this new one.

"No, but I suggested some alternate methods that are at least assisting him," the woman said, and Zayn peered at her, still trying to figure out why he knew her.

"Sit down Zayn. I detest looking up at people, and it puts an added strain on my body. Surely you recognize Hauyne? Lord Nephrite's sister?" There was a touch of amusement in Lazul's comment, but Zayn ignored it.

"Ah, Hauyne," he said, settling down in a chair, his package still held snugly in his arm. "I admit I was unable to figure out your identity. You look... different." And she did. When he had met her eating dinner at Lord Nephrite's house, she had her hair pulled back off her face, was dressed in the shapeless garb that was considered proper in noble houses, in a color of pink that made him think she was about to spew food all over the table. Now her hair was cut to shoulder length and lay in rings of curls around her face. Her blouse and vest were tailored to her, revealing a womanly body, and the color of indigo flowers made her look healthy.

"Given what I was required to wear that night, I will not hold it against you. In fact, I would prefer it if all of you erase that night from your memories," she responded with a wry smile. "The reason I wore that is a tale I will not bore you with." She looked like she was about to say more, but bit back the comment and glanced at Lazul.

They looked at each other for a moment and Zayn was amazed to realize they already had silent communication down. Impressive for less than two tendays.

"What was the information and the reason you are clutching a package?"

Lazul asked after the briefest amount of time. Hauyne was watching him also, a curious look on her face.

"Ah." Zayn cleared his throat. "This is a shipment of the drug you had asked about. The temple in Quartz has promised to send this much at least once a mooncycle." He still detested the fact that he had been caught drugging the king, but at least the only price had been more of this drug. Zayn sat it down on the small table next to him.

Lazul's eyes lit up, and Zayn saw both him and Hauyne relax across their shoulders. "Aryix bless, Zayn. That will make the evenings easier." He closed his eyes, and the light flickered over lines in his face that had not been there a mooncycle ago. For the briefest of moments, Zayn felt a twinge of guilt but brushed it away.

While he is sharper and less easygoing now, he is also more distracted and will not stick his nose into my business if I keep everything quiet.

As the thought went through his head, Lazul opened his eyes and Zayn noted that Hauyne never seemed to pay attention, but he doubted she missed much. With that reminder, he sat up straighter and smoothed out his face.

"You had mentioned another thing?" Lazul was looking at him, but his eyes flicked more than once to the packet of drugs.

"Yes," Zayn said slowly. The walk here gave him no insight into how to broach this issue, so he just said it. "I had a visit from someone that was just in Hearth. They said there is a small group of travelers that has rumors surrounding them. One of them is that they are coming here to rescue the singers."

Both Lazul and Hauyne locked eyes on him, but they waited, not asking questions. "One of them is Aoisan, the other Ged. The greater concern is that Fivika was ordered to neither help nor hinder them and Sinka made a prophecy that they will destroy everything."

The only sound in the small chamber was the crackle of the fire, and he waited.

"I see," Lazul said after an interminable wait. "This is good information to have. I will think about it. Is there aught else, Zayn?"

"No, sire. But I thought you should know," Zayn said as he rose.

"Yes. Let me know if you hear more."

It was clearly a dismissal and Zayn let it be, turning and fleeing the room of a man he no longer knew how to control. Going back to his own little domain was far preferable.

CHAPTER FORTY-SEVEN

NOTE

Note looked at the god. "And what does success mean to you?" He wracked his mind for information about Cassix, but listening to the tales of gods had never interested him, and the tales Rylix told in the evening had not addressed this god. He knew Cassix claimed no people, no land, but he was one of the new gods. It was frustrating to not know where someone stood.

Cassix tilted his head. "That is an excellent question." He took a sip of the fruist that Rylix had poured and considered it. "For me, freedom of your people and peace for Xyl."

Note tilted his head, trying to parse that comment out. "What does peace mean?"

"Ah, now that I am not sure. It could be death, it could be healing, it could be something else. But I am sure you are the ones to bring it about. Besides, Pel and Rian have been extremely lax in the care of their people. No one else has had what is theirs so freely stolen."

"They said they were convinced to let it be, and they mentioned you," Jadaya said with a quiet voice that carried, her hand twisting her cup of water.

"Ah," Cassix said, falling silent as he looked up at the sky. "I suppose they are right. That was a long time ago." He lifted one hand to brush it away. "In my defense, then I thought it was a onetime thing, and after a suncycle or two, Xyl's grief would ebb. The first group of singers," he stopped and looked at Note. "My apologies. The first group of captured Aoisans were treated like royalty and they sang the songs with willing hearts. I also think, though it has been a long time, that adults were the ones captured and many of them enjoyed the stay. But over time…" he trailed off and then shrugged.

"Over time, my attention drifted to other things and how the situation has devolved was only recently made clear. You are free to regard my actions now as penance for my mistake, then." He gave them a brilliant smile then took another drink of fruist.

"But are they?" Rylix said, dark eyes still locked on the god even as he stirred the fragrant stew.

"Are they what?" Cassix looked at him, the smile that danced on the corner of his lips reminding Note too much of one of the priests who enjoyed special times with him. Note's mouth filled with bile and he took a large gulp of fruist to wash it down.

"Are your actions penance?" Rylix faced the god with a calm expression that Note had to admire. Yelling at Pel and Rian was one thing. Cassix was an unknown quantity.

A low, rich laugh filled the clearing. "No. My actions now are…" the smile faded from his face as Cassix stared at the moons overhead. "An attempt to fix something before the consequences become more than one country in misery. Add in a touch of guilt, a modicum of curiosity, and a hint of mischief, and that might cover it. Or have nothing at all to do with any of my actions. My actions are a mystery as much to me as to you most days." His grin was self-effacing, and Note felt the urge to smile with him. He fought down the urge to give in to Cassix's charm.

Jadaya laughed. "Basically, you are bored?" She seemed less upset by the god than Note was, but then she had served her gods day in and day out.

Cassix shrugged. "Maybe? More like I believe that you three are a catalyst."

"A catalyst for what?" Note asked.

"Change? Healing? Destruction? I am not sure. I never agreed with what my siblings did to our parents, yet I offered no obstacle. Maybe it is guilt? Maybe I want to see what happens when people are not chained to a belief." His voice was light and almost nonchalant. Note swore there was another emotion hiding under it, but he was unsure what it could be.

"Food," Rylix said in the silence that fell. With efficient movements, Rylix dished up portions for all of them, handing out the plates as if this were commonplace, eating with a god.

Note ate, not bothering to taste the food as he watched Cassix.

"Mmm. I think this is one of the reasons we spend so much time with mortals. They do things with sensations that we never thought of. Like this. Textures, tastes, heat. It is so much better than just eating a piece of fruit." He lifted the fruist. "Or this. The idea you can change what it is into something different, intoxicating. Never will you cease to amaze me, I think."

Note wanted to scoff, but he thought about it. As horrible as being captured and abused in Charinsky, he had tasted food, seen things, experienced things, that otherwise he never would have. Did that mean he was glad he had been captured? Never. Even the thought made him want to snarl. But maybe there was some good that could be gleaned from it.

Cassix opened his eyes and looked at Note. "Note, you are one of those amazing things. Most of your compatriots died. Some just gave in and lost the will to live. Others wasted away, pining for what they lost. The Aoisans were never intended to be warriors, but you fought. You struggled. You escaped. Do you know how rare that is? Think about it. In the tensets of suncycles this has been going on, only you escaped and made it back home."

For a heartbeat, Note wondered if the god had been reading his thoughts. "Which should prove how horrible this is and why it needs to be stopped," he said, but the normal heat was lacking.

"Oh, I agree. But think about the entire situation. You. You alone, out of all the Aoisans captured over the suncycles, escaped and came home. Why you?"

Before Note could answer that, not that he had an answer, Cassix turned his attention to Jadaya, who froze with a spoon halfway to her mouth. "And you. Zula and Yika like to use exile as a punishment. At least a handful a year. It is their stick to the carrots they offer for acquiescing to their rule. Most of you just die. More than one stood outside the gates begging to be forgiven, refusing food and water, until they passed out, then died. Their bodies dragged to the burn pits as if they were nothing more than a stray piece of rubbish. But you are here."

She shrugged. "I was rescued."

Cassix laughed. "You fought. You struggled when the ship came apart, floundering in the water, refusing to drown. You kept fighting until a piece of wood came within your grasp and you clambered on. Even as the Aoisans took care of you, you fought to get back into shape, to make the scars a memory, not something that restrained your abilities. Most people would have refused to move, letting that tissue twist them inside and out. And now, rather than living a life where no one hurts you, where you can hide, you are here trying to right a wrong that even the gods turned a blind eye to."

His smile was wide and brilliant. "So yes, I am waiting to see what else you change as you are the outliers and I always love those that challenge the existing balance."

Note had no idea how to respond. What do you say to something like that? As it was, he focused on the food, not wanting to see the watching eyes of the others.

"So we are like the gods of old?" Rylix asked. "Like Kalina when she fought the dragon to build Hearth?"

Note tilted his head thinking about that. Rylix had told the story as they neared Hearth. She had been a god, married to a mortal and determined to protect her family and country..

"No. Kalina was the child of two gods, and would have become a god if she had not chosen to die with her mortal spouse. No. You are something new. People who chose to do something against the will of the gods. People who might change the world."

Note shuddered at the excitement in Cassix's eyes. He was all but delighted at the idea that they were challenging his fellow gods.

"There are those to walk their own way," Jadaya protested. "The pirates, robbers, those who walk away from their gods."

"Bah!" Cassix shooed the thought away with a wave of his hand. "They are the ones who chafe at the rules, but they only want it to change for them. They want the power, the luxury. They would never lift a hand if there were no reward for them. You? There is no reward at the end of this for you, at least not a material reward. You might die. You might destroy a country. You might kill a god." The smile got brighter. "The change may be no more than a leaf floating to the right as opposed to the left. Or it might be that a tree falls, changing the course of a river. Or the forest might fall at your feet."

Nausea rose in Note's throat and he set aside the stew, unable to finish it.

Is that what he wants us to do? Be champions of destruction?

"So that is what you want? Us to destroy everything?" Jadaya said with a quiet voice. Note jerked. Too many people were thinking the same thoughts as him, and he had no idea if that was a good thing or a sign of something terrible.

"You misunderstand," Cassix said, scraping the last bit of stew onto his spoon. "I want nothing." He looked up at them with a grin that eclipsed the fire. "I just want to see what you are capable of and what happens next. And if I can provide a modicum of support to enable your quest, well, why not?" He finished the bowl and set it down. "Aryix bless for a wonderful meal. May your journey generate more than you ever dreamed." He smiled at them one more time, then headed back to his little swing chair and slipped into it. A moment later, soft gentle snores emanated from the area.

Note looked at the other two. "My fear level just increased by untold amounts."

Jadaya shrugged. "I am unsure why he thinks we have the power to change anything. The odds still say we die before we ever rescue even one child." Her voice sounded firm, but Note saw her hand tremble as she lifted the spoon to her mouth.

Note took another swallow of the fruist trying to wash away the foul taste in his mouth. He turned to look at Rylix. "Do you have thoughts?"

Rylix had finished his meal, and his gaze went back and forth between the fire and the sleeping god. "The Ged refused to take part in the overthrowing of the old gods. I fear now that I may be involved in a coup of overthrowing the current gods. I am not sure if that is a good or a bad thing. But either way, he is not wrong. Our legends are of the gods - I have never heard one of mortals changing the world. Have you?"

Note thought hard about it but finally shook his head. "There are stories of tragic loves or lovers across countries who gave up one for the other. Stories of following your heart to another god. But there are no stories I can think of where mortals challenged the gods or changed more than their own life."

He looked at Jadaya, who had put her empty bowl down, but her grip on her water was tight. "We have some, but they are teaching stories. Going to fight a feline or a horned one and winning or losing depending on the tale. Saving a village by running to warn of a flood or sacrificing yourself to get the attention of Zula. But always either things believable or asking for help."

Rylix nodded. "Ours are about being honest in trade or smart Ged who trick thieves. A few love stories or adventures - avalanche, flood, brigands. But they are always something plausible, if difficult. I know of nothing where the heroes challenge the gods."

They were all quiet until Rylix stood. Note look at him as the man smiled. "I wanted to make a name for myself. Why not become a legend that changes the world?" He laughed and Note felt something deep in him unkink as Jadaya began to laugh and he joined in. Why not? After all, change had to start somewhere.

CHAPTER FORTY-EIGHT

LAZUL

The door closed behind Zayn, and Hauyne reached for the package. "Do you want some now?"

Lazul glanced at the window. "No. There is still too much time until I can be guaranteed no claimants will need to see me. Tomorrow, I have nobles to appease and judgements to make for petitioners. So tonight, before I head to my bedchamber." He looked at the door where Zayn had gone. "Thoughts?"

"About the cantor?" she asked, looking at him. Hauyne was his height, and she had inherited from her parents a generous bosom and wide hide hips as well as a clear rosy complexion and gloriously golden hair. He still had not figured out where her sharp tongue, fast mind, and iron will came from. But he was enjoying getting to know her. While she had barely been here a tenday, Actin already had declared her the best decision Lazul had ever made. The king found himself leaning on her more and more as the days went on. Which meant there were other things he would be unwise to put off much longer, but he wanted to make sure she understood what she would be walking into.

"He is off balance, especially compared to the dinner during the tour. His foundational beliefs have been shaken, and you have changed enough that he is unsure how to manage you." Her tone was cool as she watched him with light blue eyes.

Her words registered and Lazul pulled back, affronted by her statement, then winced as his body punished him for the fast movement. "What do you mean, manage me?"

Hauyne gave him a pitying look. "He has had you dancing to his whims for suncycles. You ask a question and he distracts until you have forgotten it. Sometimes by an attack, other times by mentioning something he knows you care more about. Now, you are focused and have no energy, so it is harder to confuse you. So he is unsure."

Lazul wanted to protest, but he closed his eyes as he panted through the pain and thought about it. To his chagrin, Hauyne was correct. Had he always been such a fool?

"I think this curse of mine might be a blessing," he finally said. "But go on."

Hauyne tilted her head. "He is not a good man. There is a cruelty and greed in him that are dangerous in a person with power. But for now, he cares more about solidifying his base as the rumors of the god's words are rippling through the land."

Lazul narrowed his eyes at her. "You are good, but you know far too much. How?"

Hauyne laughed. "Right now you have me in a fascinating position, and I have decided to leverage it as much as possible."

The king shook his head in amusement, and she grinned.

"You may be the king, but there is much you are unaware of. I am not the queen, though people suspect—maybe—that is why I am here. Neither am I a noble's daughter, just a sister. I work well with Actin, but I grew up with few servants for a large estate, so I understand their workload. They also have seen how you are easier to handle with me here."

Lazul tried to decide if that was a compliment or insult or both. "Go on," he finally growled. Her smirk widened.

"Which means I talk to everyone, and they talk to me. I have established myself as gossip center and a confessor, as they know I will keep their secrets. As such, I am developing a good sense of what is going on in Granite, and to a certain extent, the country. It is rather fun." She smiled as she talked, her eyes sparkling.

Lazul settled down, his gaze drifting to the drugs, but he tamped it back. "So you are becoming a spy master?"

Hauyne blinked, surprise evident on her face and he took a moment to study her. She was not the young beauty most of the nobles or his council had thrown at him, but she had a striking face and a nice body. In the end, it was her mind and humor that made him ask her to come up here. He had been brutally honest when she arrived that this curse from Xyl had changed him and she would need to decide if she wanted to deal with his curse. To his astonishment, she had nodded. She requested to be set up in the visiting quarters and he gave her full run of the palace, but the late afternoon rests had quickly become their thing and part of him had hated having it interrupted by Zayn, yet that was someone he could not ignore.

"Spy master? I am not sure I would go that far, but maybe the pulse of the land?" she suggested, but she looked rather pleased at the title.

"Very well, spymaster," he said with a teasing grin. "What do you think of the information Zayn brought?" He already had his own opinions, but was curious to see her thoughts.

"I shall have to come up with a better name than that. Besides, would it not be Mistress?" she teased back, a soft smile gracing her lips. It fell away as she considered his question. "There are two problems with the information he brought," she said in a thoughtful tone.

He lifted his eyebrows, encouraging her to continue as he hid a wince as pain arched through his body. He had become very good at not crying out or even reacting. Though the sweet ease of the drugs was something he longed for to an extent that it worried him.

"One is if it is true and they get here and succeed. What happens then? As it is, the last incident could have killed hundreds if not thousands. We need the singers to survive, though I think we are going about this the wrong way, but while I have ideas on what should be done, I have no ideas as to how to go from the current situation to a more sustainable one." Her words were slow and thoughtful as she stared at the crackling fire. He found himself always cold of late.

Lazul tilted his head, wondering what her ideas were, but he stayed silent. Over the last tenday he had learned she put thought into her words and rushing her resulted in her shutting down. All he could figure was her father had not been a patient man.

"The second problem is if the news reaches Him." She jerked her chin up to indicate Xyl. "If he feels we are not reacting appropriately or worse, that we no longer care about his grief to the extent that we would allow the singers to be rescued…" she trailed off and shrugged. "By the time his rage was spent, Charinsky would no longer exist."

Lazul sighed. He had thought of the first one, not the second, but she had hit key points. "There is also that fact that a certain segment of our population has always had issues with the singers. It is not unreasonable that these rescuers would meet with support once they were here and their mission became common knowledge."

Hauyne tilted her head, acknowledging his comment. "What do you think we should do?" she asked in a quiet voice.

His smile was bitter as he looked at her. "I see little option. We can never allow them to reach our shores, which means they must die."

Hauyne's face paled a bit, but she took a breath and closed her eyes for a moment, then opened them looking at him. He had always thought her eyes were just a pale blue, but now they were like icy blue diamonds, deep, hard, and something that was stronger than it should have been.

"This is the price of the crown?" Her words were a question, but there was certainty in her tone.

He nodded, a grim smile on his face. "Yes, it is."

She took a deep breath and held still for five heartbeats, then she released it and looked at him. "How exactly do we do that?"

Lazul blinked, then barked out a short laugh. "I have no idea. There may be something in the records, but the palace guards have no skills in this. But if we let them get here where, in theory, I could affect it..." he paused, swallowing hard.

"Then He might find out about them. Then He would create a huge issue," she finished somberly.

"Exactly." He pulled a discreet cord next to his chair. "I think we are done for the day," he said, glancing at his fruist. "Make me a small glass to sip on while we talk, please?" He held out a hand that shook with pain. "I believe I have met my limits." He could almost taste the relief the drug would bring as his body fought to be stronger than the pain. A night of sleep made it so the mornings were almost tolerable, but the longer the day was, the more he did, the higher the pain crept. He laughed a bitter laugh to himself. At the rate this was going, there would be no heir, as he had no energy or even desire for sex the majority of the time. Yet another issue he needed to discuss with Hauyne.

A knock at the door came as Hauyne was making him a glass of fruist with a small portion of the herb. They had discovered the hard way that the potency of the herb varied, so it was always better to start off tiny and increase it until it reached the right level, pain relief but still in control of his facilities.

"Yes, sire?" Actin said as he stepped in.

"Close the door, please, and take a seat. I need to speak with you," Lazul said as Hauyne placed the fruist on the small table next to him.

Actin looked slightly worried as he sat down, looking at the two of them. His majordomo had confided that he fully approved of Hauyne and would do everything possible to support her. Lazul looked at the man and made a choice.

"Actin, you worked for my father, and I need to know that I can trust you implicitly." He took a sip as he watched Actin's face. Confusion, insult, then worry all flashed across it, landing on caution. The man would never make a good ambassador. He displayed his emotions too easily.

Or maybe he trusts me enough to show them? I have heard others complain that he is less emotional than a statue.

"Is there an issue where you think I have not been loyal?" he asked, his body stiff.

"No. But I am about to ask you a question that if you spread the news around the nobles or the temple, I would be dead in a mooncycle." Lazul kept his voice casual as Hauyne sat back down, but she kept a rigid pose as if she was ready to spring up at any moment and he noted the small dagger she wore at her waist had been freed from its bindings.

That is interesting.

He focused back on Actin, who had stiffened. "Sire. I promised your father a long time ago that I would ensure you would be a proper king. Few realize how hard you work, and as much as it pains me to say it, the curse has honed and sharpened you into a man I am honored to serve. I await your question." Actin lowered his head after he spoke in a small bow.

There was a level of sincerity that stunned Lazul, and he bowed his head in response. "I regret it took this to make me a better king, a better man. Maybe it is less of a curse and more a blessing I realized." He laughed softly. "Though if the pain was to stop, there would be no complaints from my lips."

Actin allowed himself a commiserating smile. "I believe that might be the best way to look at it, but no one doubts your pain, at least not those of us here in the palace. At times, it is distressingly obvious." He raised his hand before Lazul could speak. "And that is for the good. The nobles need never realize, and it should be kept from them, but us, the servants, we know and admire you. Lesser men have crawled into bottles or other things to escape the pain. You manage it and we see it. Your question, sire?"

There was nothing but respect and loyalty on Actin's face and Lazul felt ashamed for ever having doubted the man.

"We need to have some people killed. Do you have any idea how to hire an assassin?"

CHAPTER FORTY-NINE

RYLIX

When they awoke in the morning, Cassix was gone. The only proof he had been there was the circle of stones on the ground with the remnants of a fire and the marks on the tree where a swing chair had been. Rylix stood there for a long time, looking at it before walking back to finish making the morning meal.

The three of them were quiet as they decamped and headed back out. Jadaya kept fiddling with the water flask, while Note rode the mustang. They each seemed lost in their thoughts. Rather than moving ahead as they planned to travel until they reached Calin, Jadaya stayed nearby, occasionally sitting on the back steps of the wagon.

When they stopped for lunch, Rylix broke the silence. "Did Cassix's comments last night make you waver in your decisions? Knowing what this journey might accomplish?"

Note chewed at the bread and cheese he held, as Jadaya munched on an apple.

Rylix waited for them to respond, tearing off a chunk for himself. This was a serious question and deserved to be answered with thought.

"Not for me," Jadaya said when the fruit was gone. "I fear what he thinks we can do, but I would rather try than spend the rest of my life drifting, searching for a place I fit. What has happened is not right and I have little desire to pretend it is. People should not be objects, to be discarded when no longer useful." She stopped to take a breath, then looked at them, a hardness in her eyes he had only seen glimpses of before. "I would rather die trying to change everything than live doing nothing."

Her words sounded like a challenge to the gods, and Rylix could not help but smile. He turned to look at Note, who had an odd look on his face.

"Be careful, Jadaya, or we might think you are a poet, to write our stories in the stars." Note gave her a sad twist of his mouth, before looking back at the bread in his hands. "His words disturbed me, but not because I am doing something or willing to, but because no one else has. That makes me want to weep and scream and rage. So if I can be someone for others to look at, to realize they can change what has been done to them, even if the cost is death, I would rather die that way than live as an escaped slave."

Rylix flinched at Note's words, but he agreed. The idea of living as a slave made his skin crawl and provoked a spike of anger at Note's gods. It was why the Ged only worshiped the old gods. They knew their gods were locked away and were mostly unavailable. So whatever trouble you found yourself in, it was up to you and your family to get you out of it or, as he had done, pay the price for your stupidity. It also meant you had no reason to fear them meddling in your life. Or at least that was what he had believed until he realized they were talking to Cassix last night. That god obviously had every intention of meddling, and it made him nervous.

They cleaned up their camp, took care of the animals, then re-hitched them to the wagon and headed toward Calin. At the rate they were going, Rylix figured they would be there about eight fingers before sundown. That would give them plenty of time to find an inn and set up connections to sell in the marketplace. They still had a few days before the ship would arrive. Though as ships depended on the waves and currents, that estimate could easily be one or two days on either side. The sea ignored everyone and cared not for the worries of mortals or gods.

They were right on schedule as Jadaya came back from her roaming around the area to enter the city with them. They waited in the entry line with others, watching the flow. The guards, dressed in their trews and tunics with the symbol of Calin and their rank on their chest, checked people in with a speed implying suncycles of practice. The control and efficiency of Fivika had always amazed and annoyed Rylix. That level of control provided rewards in the ways of data and screening out problematic elements, but it was also a control that most Ged chafed at. Maybe that was why there were only a few trade routes that went through the major cities in Fivika, most of them staying outside in the smaller towns that were less regulated.

"Names and purpose?" The guard asked, looking at the ledger he held.

"Rylix of Ged, Note of Aois, and Jadaya," Rylix said, watching the flow and trying to decipher what the people coming in might require. The sudden stiffening of the guard yanked his attention back to the man even as he saw Note and Jadaya react to the guard's body language.

"Hold there," the guard barked, then turned to look toward the small shack on the inside of the gate. "Collins, the traders on the sheet are here."

Rylix glanced at Note and Jadaya, who were both tense. He had no idea what this could be. Worst case, they could deny them entrance. At that point, he would have to regroup and figure out how to get to their ship. The docks were only accessible via the city and while they could use a small boat to get to the Ged ship, docks made loading a wagon much easier. Was it even possible to get the wagon on a ship without a dock? A group of five guards came trotting over to them, led by a man who was at least ten suncycles older than the rest of them.

"Rylix? You just came from Hearth?" he asked. His sharp eyes had no animosity that Rylix could see, but then that probably meant nothing.

"Yes," Rylix said slowly, all too aware of the fact that they had become the center of attention. If he was lucky, it would translate to sales in the market as people came to talk about why he had been stopped.

A hard nod. "Collins, go tell Lady Elise." The man, Collins Rylix figured, gave a nod and took off at a run toward the center of the city.

"You will come with us." The man ordered and before he could even make a protest, the reins of the mustangs, and harness leads for the jacks that pulled the wagon, were in the hands of the guards. One of them walked next to Jadaya and gestured in the direction they were being taken.

Though Rylix cast glances at the others, there was little they could do without risking their lives. So he rode his wagon peaceably, mind spinning, as they were personally escorted through the city.

What is it with this trip and everyone knowing about us? Are the gods meddling again?

All he could do at this point was hold tight and wait to see what happened. The fact that no one had weapons drawn made him feel marginally better. He still needed to make sure his family knew how much the gods gossiped. He could recall no records that mentioned this. It was more than a bit aggravating.

They kept walking, people occasionally glancing at them, but the all-black eyes made it hard to see reactions. Who would have guessed pupils told you so much about a person's state of mind? His confusion rose as they went through the middle of town and he could see the walls of the other side approach. As they passed through those gates to the docks, Rylix had no idea what the issue was, as they stopped at none of the city offices.

Their little procession came to a stop at the docks. The hive of activity was alive with ships being boarded, fishing ships coming in, people buying the fish as it was coming off, and piles of goods awaiting their ship. Their little group came to a stop at what Rylix figured was the harbormaster's building. The man who was obviously in charge looked at them, then at his men.

"Wait here," he said, then headed into the building.

Rylix leaned over from his bench, his attention directed to one of the guards that stood near him. "Could you tell me what is going on? I am sure there must be some sort of mix-up." This made no sense and worried nipped at his heels.

The guard shrugged. "I go where they tell me go. If you want answers, talk to the captain." The man just kept staring ahead and paid no attention to anything else.

Rylix sighed. Why were Fivikan guards so well trained? Almost anywhere else, you could get people to gossip and tell you what was going on.

The creak of the door to the harbormaster's office heralded the answer to his confusion. The captain walked back out, followed by a woman dressed in a severe jacket and wide-legged pants. For the most part, women wore whatever they wanted, but Rylix had never seen that style of dress before, it struck him that his mother would love wearing flowing pants like that. He was about to ask her who designed them when the woman started talking.

"Hearth warned about your presence and as a whole, Fivika has decided we have little desire to be involved in this venture. As word has passed down that you are planning to go from here to Vykland, we have expedited that process. The fish trader will take you, three of your animals, and the wagon to Vykland. You have two fingers to deal with the animals that will be unable to be transported due to cargo restrictions."

Her eyes stared at them, the Fivikan flat black emotionless as the night sky.

Rylix stammered, his orderly throughs thrown into disarray. "Wait. We have a ship coming for us. It should be here in a few days," he protested. As he spoke, guards were stepping back to look at him, their fingers dropping to the swords on their hips.

"That is not acceptable. You will load your supplies on to that boat and be gone in two fingers." Her words were flat, uncompromising.

"Good mistress, that is unreasonable," Rylix started with his winning smile and charm, looking down at her.

She cut him off. "If you do not take the offer I have made, you will be put on the ship with nothing except the clothes on your backs." She turned to the captain. "Ensure this is done. The *Salt Fish* is waiting."

"Yes, ma'am," the captain said. She nodded once and turned to head into the city, leaving Rylix on the bench of the wagon trying to figure out what happened.

"You have two mustangs and can only take one. Choose which one and I can offer you a decent price for it," the captain said. Rylix was still trying to process everything as the guard moved forward and started disconnecting the animals. His mind was spinning, as he had no plans or contingencies for this absurd set of events. Even gods showing up had left him less confused.

After a moment of looking at each other, Jadaya heaved a sigh laced with resignation. "I will get the extra supplies off the mustang and cram them into the wagon," Jadaya volunteered and went to do it.

Rylix shook his head and forced himself to focus on the now. "The one she is unloading." He jumped off and went about double checking the wagon was as sealed up as possible. He pulled out their coats as Note jumped off, handing one to each of them. Vykland was colder than Fivika and on the deck of the ship, they would want them. The captain handed him ten copper with no comment and part of Rylix felt a surge of appreciation at that, but the desire to throw a fit clawed at the back of his throat. Rylix knew the decision had been made, so the best he could do would be to go with the flow and make sure they arrived in as good a shape as possible.

Things were moving so fast that as the guards were leading the jacks down the dock, he finally saw the ship that had been referenced. It was a fishing boat with a huge flat deck. Some far back part of his mind filled in the information that they pulled up some of the huge sea creatures and harvested them on that deck. The guard captain waved and pointed and men on the deck nodded. Within a finger, the wagon was on the deck and the animals tied to railings.

Rylix made his way up, trailed by Note and Jadaya. "Can you get us all the way to Resin?" he asked, confusion showing in his voice. The captain, a gruff man with black eyes and a shorn head, hawked up a clump of mucus and spat it into the bay.

"Nah. I was ordered to take you to Vykland. That means leather. I can cross and be home before full dark sets in," he said in a gruff voice, pointing across the channel. In the distance, you could see the continent of Vykland.

Rylix pressed his lips together as he pulled up his mental maps. Leather was the city furthest east, while Resin was across the bay from the Mount of Gods. It would add a tenday or more to their journey, but they should be able to make it. Rather than argue, as he knew he would lose, he nodded and stepped back toward Note and Jadaya. Both of them were leaning on the railing, Note watching the docks, Jadaya focused on the sea.

"What do you see in the water, Jadaya?"

She glanced at him and shrugged. "It changes. There is fear, promise, and the danger of the unknown. But still death."

Her words chilled him, and he turned to follow Note's gaze. It took him a moment to see who Note was so concentrated on. But following the Aoisan's gaze, his eye alit on two people standing on the city wall. "Is that..." he whispered, hoping for a negative answer.

"It's Jovan and Sinka," Note said quietly. "I saw them watching earlier."

"Ah," Rylix said and let everything else remain unsaid as they pulled away from the dock, getting deported from Fivika.

CHAPTER FIFTY

NOTE

They had been at sea for four fingers and both coastlines seemed remote and impossible to reach. Note leaned against the railing and stared at the water and the shapes moving way deep down. Large shapes. "Rylix?" He asked, his eyes locked on the water.

"You requested my presence?" Rylix said with a smile that even from the corner of his eye Note could tell was fake.

"I know you are no expert, but are those normal?" Note pointed down into the water as one of the shapes kept getting larger.

Rylix bent his head to look where Note was pointing. Note saw him go a sickly green gray—a color that did not look good on him. Rylix tilted his head back. "Deeps guardian!" The scream was at the top of his voice and everyone on the ship froze for a split second, then the crew dove into action as Rylix raced for the wagon.

"Deeps?" Note said, his eyes wide as he followed Rylix. Jadaya appeared at his side as they raced to the wagon. Already the jacks and the mustang were becoming agitated as something bumped into the ship.

Rylix cast him an astonished look as he pulled open drawers with frantic speed. "You live in Aois. How could you not know what they are?" he asked. "Grab your packs, your coats, and whatever small things you can shove in here." Rylix held out a large black bag that seemed to be made of a shiny, thick black material. "And put this on over your clothes." He had ripped open the wagon door and had grabbed three things that were buried in the one of the deep inner drawers. They looked like fat weird belts that stretched as Note strapped it around himself.

Note wanted to ask more questions, but just then a monster's head rose over the edge of the fishing ship. It went up and up and up. He froze, following it until his eyes landed on the head full of teeth and eyes that he swore saw them. The head came down toward the deck, then whipped sideways. Its head and neck crashed into the mainsail, snapping the mast about five heads above the deck as if it had been a twig. As the mast flew into the air, tangling with the other ropes, a large clawed foot came up and grabbed one of the jacks. The huge hand wrapped around it, as it screamed in terror and pain, some of the claws gouging into it. With a casual moved it lifted the terrified animal, tearing it from the straps that held it to the deck. The jack flailed and screamed as the monster lifted it in the air toward the gaping mouth and sharp teeth.

"*Move!*" Rylix screamed as he slammed into Note, knocking him to the side as a tail slapped down where he stood only a moment before. Note tumbled to the deck and watched with frozen wonder as Jadaya moved faster than the serpentine tail and slammed her new sword through the last third of it. The monster screamed, part of the tail tumbling across the deck. Note was unsure if the scream was from rage or pain. It whipped its tail away, coating the deck in a spray of thick, oily blood.

The calm part of Note's mind puzzled over this happening. It was buried under the part that was guiding him to scramble up and grab a few more things for the bag, then letting Rylix seal it as they fought to remain standing on the deck of a ship that was being torn apart.

The deeps monsters were things of tales as few ever survived meeting them. Created by all the gods to guard the deeps where they entombed the Usurper. Everyone knew the rogue god was still alive and the damage he had done besides breaking Percit's moon and killing her was only a part of the destructions left in his wake. He had gouged fissures into the oceans, seeking to break the planet like he had shattered the moon.

The gods had wrapped him in seaweed, iron, diamond, and granite, creating a sphere of imprisonment. They then placed him in a chamber surrounded by magma that would break if the egg that surrounded him so much as moved. Then the creatures that had come with him, the monsters he had as pets, were set as guards against him and ordered to kill any that came near the depths that they had created.

This was known. It was part of the reason why it took ships so long to go from one country to another, as you had to catch currents and avoid the deeps. But Note's mind threw up map after map, and there were no deeps here, at least not close. So why was there a monster here?

He grabbed onto a railing as Rylix handed him the bag stuffed full, bulging at the edges. "It will resist water. You are unable to drown. Take it. It will give you some trade goods and access to my accounts if you make it back to someplace with Ged alive."

Note just stared at him, confused. From the time Rylix had screamed, the warning to now had not even been a finger. Yet the deck was splashed with blood from the creature, there was one dead—and half devoured—jack, and sailors were screaming as another claw came down for them. But Rylix had organized them and set it up, so if they survived they had a chance to make it home.

Panic grabbed him in a way that he had not felt since he was a child and was ripped away from his parents on that dark day. The day the gods let his world be destroyed.

The memory grabbed him, and he glanced at his wrist, the cuff. The words from Pel drifted back into his mind and he held up the cuff to his face. Tears streamed down his face, and he wiped them into the cuff. *"Pel!"* He screamed the word out to the wind as the severed tail slammed down and shattered the ship, throwing them up in the air. And then into the churning ocean.

The cold water was a shock to his system, but it helped clear his head. The water was his element. All Aoisans swam from birth. Even though the water was cooler than the water along Aois, it was still saltwater and his body sang with delight. The device around his waist pulled him up and he turned around, looking for shipmates. The nictating membranes that protected his eyes underwater slid across his eyeballs, and the world around him jumped into clarity. He could see the legs of people in the water, the pieces of the ship, the wagon bobbing up and down. If he had realized that what Rylix handing him would prevent his swimming, he would have resisted it. For now, he spun, trying to decide. The wagon was lost. What they had in the bag and on them was all. So, the bag was important. The flailing legs of one of the animals got his attention and an idea. Swimming fast, he moved toward the animal. Once he reached it, he unhooked the strange belt from his waist and, after struggling a bit, managed to lash it around the mustang with the ties still attached to its harness. The mustang was much heavier than he was, but it lifted the animal's chest up and he pulled it to the distant opposite shore as he looked for his companions.

The darkness that was settling across the ocean and land made it hard to see and there was the monster that was still attacking the ship. Splashing grabbed his attention, and he saw Jadaya swimming toward them, the device keeping her up and moving. He grabbed her when she got close and pointed her to land, the mustang still swimming strongly. It was a swim, but if the monster forgot about them, they might make it.

Where is Rylix? Where is Pel?

As if his thoughts pulled the god to the forefront, a column of water rose with

Pel standing upon it. He seemed three times taller than Note had ever seen him, and for the first time in a long time, Note was very glad to see his god.

"What is the meaning of this?" The words echoed across the skies, rolling like thunder. The monster froze, looking up at the god, then it let go of everyone, launching itself into a whirl that threw it up in the air, then it pivoted to dive into the water. A cord of water wrapped around it, halting it in midair. The creature writhed as the cord of water dragged it closer to Pel, the tail still spraying blood as it thrashed back and forth.

Pel looked at it with an expression Note had never seen before. The god stood on the column of water like it was a pillar of marble, the creature dangling in front of him. Now, with it hanging in the air, Note got a complete view of the creature. It was long like a snake, with a sinuous neck and tail, but it had legs, ridges down its back, a broad head, and a forked tongue that flicked around as it struggled in the god's grip.

"You know the rules. This is not the depths. Why are you here?"

Pel spoke the words, not shouted, but there was a power to them that made Note curl up inside. If the question had been directed at him, he would have been babbling an answer. Instead, the creature hissed, spitting at Pel in defiance.

"You dare? So be it." Pel pulled his arm back, and the water contracted in two different directions, taking the creature and ripping it in half. The water rope dissolved, and the monster fell to the surface of the ocean with a splat like a thunderclap. Pel turned and looked around, then his eyes locked with Note's. A moment later the water underneath them hardened and Note found himself standing alongside the mustang with Jadaya on the other side as Pel emerged from the water next to them.

"What happened?" Pel asked, looking at the mess.

Note opened his mouth, then stopped looking at the sailors clinging to the ship. Part of him wanted to throw them to the anger in his god, but he knew they were not the ones to blame. "We were crossing to Vykland, and the creature attacked. The ship and the sailors belong to Fivika. Do you see Rylix?" Anxiety coated his voice as he stood on the water, looking for their friend.

Pel sank into the water, though their stable surface remained. A gigantic wave of water picked up the remains of the ship and the sailors, lifting it up and away, headed toward Fivika. Less than a finger later, Pel came back to them with Rylix and the water-logged wagon. "Come, I will get you to Vykland." The water under their feet undulated and with a speed that Note had never experienced sent them to the shore. The water stopped as the ground appeared under their feet, leaving three mortals, a mustang, and a damaged wagon next to them.

"Are you injured?" Pel asked, looking at them.

Note followed the god's gaze, but other than wide eyes and shivering from the cold, he saw no wounds on either of them.

After clearing his throat and modulating his tone, he was more respectful of Pel now. "What happened? Why was there a monster here? Have the deeps changed?" The worry and fear leaked into his voice.

To his shock and vague horror, Pel sank to the sandy shore, holding his head in his hands. Note made a half step forward before he halted his motion. He looked at Rylix and Jadaya with wide eyes, but they just shrugged and stepped back, giving them room.

"Pel?" Note was unsure what he was asking, but gods, his god should not look like weeping was an option. Anger was so much easier to deal with.

"We thought everything was contained. But the Usurper is stirring. We think he has corrupted Xyl. That is why his rage and the twist his love has taken are so dark. Someone has to be helping him, but we are unsure who. Everyone proclaims their innocence, but already things are changing, changes outside our initiations." At no point did Pel look up at him as he spoke, but instead focused on the ground, his wet hair clinging to him like a web of sorrow.

"The creatures were sent, broken away from the commands they were given. If this continues, the world could become surrounded by deeps isolating our peoples more than they already are." He looked up and locked eyes with Note. "At this point, you might be the only chance Aria has. You need to talk to our parents, get them to help you. Stop Xyl, even if this means his death, and then find out who is behind the corruption in our world."

Note swallowed, fighting not to let his knees buckle at the idea. "What makes you think we can do this? We are just mortals."

Pel smiled up at him even as the water rose to surround the god. "Because no one else can break the chains they put on themselves."

What? The chains? They did that to themselves?

The god was almost gone and Note shoved that thought into the back of his mind as he rushed to ask one more question. "Could it be Cassix?"

The water stopped rising, swirling around Pel as if undecided about rising or falling. "I think not. He never favored our choices, but he would never destroy or harm this world. He fought the Usurper the hardest and would have killed him had it been possible." With that, Pel was gone, leaving them alone.

CHAPTER FIFTY-ONE

LAZUL

Lazul made it through the last meeting of the day, a discussion about contingency measures if Xyl lost his temper again. The council hammered out some basic options, but none of them would stop a god if he lost all control. Which left them with hope and prayers, neither of which would stop Xyl, as they knew all too well. He moved through the halls slowly, every joint hurting, though he was getting better at not hunching over. It provided no ease to his body, so why not walk tall and proud? He was learning that if you acted fine, most people believed you were fine.

The small chamber that had become a haven for him and Hauyne to discuss the day was deliciously warm and he sank into the chair with relief. While his acting skills were improving, his body was burning resources, trying to balance out the pain yet keep him moving. He chose to make his days shorter. All meetings or audiences were complete by the time the sun came within six fingers of the horizon. After that, he was only available to Actin or if there was a true emergency.

As if sinking into the chair summoned the man, Actin walked in carrying a tray while Hauyne followed him. Lazul's eyes tracked the tray with a longing painted clear on his face. The tray held a carafe of fruist, two glasses, and round gels of the drug. Once the kitchen cook realized how much Lazul suffered, she had taken to boiling the strange herb that Zayn said was called graes, in liquid and bone marrow and making little candies he could eat. The concentrated drug was amazing, dampening the pain without making him as susceptible to suggestions as mixing it with liquids. It let him drink less, though he still used the fruist to make life easier. No one thought it odd for the king to drink multiple glasses at dinner.

"Evening meal will be ready in about three fingers, sire. Do you wish to eat in here or in the dining rooms?" There was nothing in his words to tell Lazul which to choose, so he asked as Actin poured glasses of fruist for both him and Hauyne.

"Is there anyone I need to appear for that would require my presence in the dining room?" He hoped not. The idea of moving again made him want to sob.

"Besides the Lady Hauyne? No, sire."

Lazul fought to not smile as he popped one of the jellies into his mouth. It tasted like honey and green herbs.

"Then if the lady will agree, I believe I will eat in here." He turned his gaze to the lady in question. "Lady Hauyne?"

She chuckled. "In here would be wonderful, Actin. Please ask the cook for extra fruit for both of us?" It was the middle of Ripening and the weather had allowed the fruit to come to full flavor. Everyone was taking advantage while they could, and he knew every extra fruit was being dried and preserved as fast as possible.

"Very well. Milady, sire," Actin said as he left.

Lazul took another drink of the fruist. His eyes closed. The mix of the alcohol and the jelly was already taking effect, as if his pain was water in a bucket, slowly draining it away until the level could be managed. He opened his eyes to see Hauyne looking at him.

"Yes?" He asked, wondering if he had offended her. His temper was shorter of late, but he had thought he was keeping it under control.

"Nothing, just thinking. There are times you astound me," she said, her brows furrowed as she watched him. She picked up her glass of fruist, looking at it. "I was betrothed once. I believe my brother told you that?"

Lazul nodded. "Yes. He said the young man died?" Lord Nephrite had only mentioned it in an aside with no more information.

"You could say that. He liked fruist. The more aged, the better." Her voice was dry. "He could drink five or more carafes a day. I know some men are mean or cruel when they drink. He was none of those. He was just stupid." Her voice had an odd note of bitterness in it. "Which is a blessing, I suppose. He decided to go down into one of the mines to find a seam of emeralds that someone had said they had found. He took no equipment, no guidelines, and only a single candle."

Lazul flinched. The mines were dangerous, which was why miners were paid so well. Not only was there the risk of a collapse, but over the suncycles they had become a maze of tunnels. Miners always attached a guide rope to their belts when they went in, so you could follow it back out with your bag of ore or gems.

And all of them would bring multiple candles and light boxes. The dark in the mines was absolute and sound distorted oddly, turning you around in a second. His father had done a tour one time and, as Lazul had been looking at the mines with too much interest, his father had arranged an example. Deep in the mine, the guide blew out the lantern and plunged the cave into darkness. Only his father's hand in his kept Lazul from panicking, but every breath, every sound had magnified, and he had no idea where to go. It was an indelible memory, and it told him what the outcome had been before she said it.

"They found him a tenday later. He had fallen and broken his neck. I still am unsure if that was a blessing, to die so quickly as opposed to the slow death of thirst and fear." She twisted her lips in a bitter smile. "All of that is to say, you are not him."

Lazul blinked, unsure of where this was going.

Hauyne's smile warmed a bit. "When you explained what happened and your use of fruist and drugs, I almost turned and left. But your blunt honesty kept me here. You are different. You take what you need to function and avoid it if the effects would make you unable to govern effectively. Most I know would rather be insensate than experience a moment of pain. You accept the pain, but rather than let it control you, you treat it like an annoying aspect of life."

She fell silent, and Lazul was unsure what to say. "Aryix bless?" he said uncertainly, fiddling with his own glass. "Why are you telling me this? You know you are free to leave at any point."

A warm smile broke over her face, making her beautiful instead of striking. "I know. But I like it here. I like you. I am more than willing to welcome you to my bed. And I will even agree to be your queen."

Lazul's heart leaped in his chest and a smile spread across his face, but it halted as she raised her hand.

"But only after we have dealt with the issue looming over us, threatening everyone," she said with a serious gaze, the smile fading and revealing a warrior in the lines of her face.

If someone had kicked his knees out from underneath him, he would not have fallen as hard as he had for this woman. Her strength and intelligence roused his mind in ways his body refused to. But she was right. Xyl and the ones coming for him were more important than anything else. Lazul sighed and took a larger drink of fruist. The pain had dropped to a level that he could almost ignore, and his head felt only slightly fuzzy.

"That issue is terrifying. What do you suggest we do? Actin has looked for anyone we could hire, but there is no hidden association of assassins. Or at least not that he could find." He felt the familiar wave of hunger hit him as the pain receded to the point his stomach was no longer in constant turmoil.

She set the glass down and twisted her fingers, but still watched him unflinchingly. "I think we let the strangers come."

"What?" He sat up with a jerk, wincing in pain as his body protested loudly.

Hauyne raised her hand. "Hear me out. All we have are rumors and those are bad things to base decisions on. But I was thinking, why not help them? Get them here. If they can defeat Him, stop Him, it is worth it. Unless you have devised another way to rectify this situation?" The lifted brow caused him to sigh and feel like his tutor had called him out for making up an answer to a question.

"No. It has been obliquely mentioned to the nobles, but since the last thing we want to do is say the name, it makes it hard to talk about it. Besides, how do you defeat a god?" He heard the whining in his voice and it annoyed him. A king should not be ready to let his people suffer. Lazul knew if his death was required to rid Charinsky of their god, he would die. But that option did not seem viable. Right now, there were no answers about how to stop Xyl.

"That is my point. We let them. We help them. They must have an idea of how to stop him or there is no reason for them to be on their way here," her voice dropped to something like pleading. "Surely there has to be a way."

Lazul drained the fruist in his glass. Taking a deep breath to try to control his breathing as fear and excitement raced through him in equal mixtures. "If there is, I am unaware of it. My father died before these sorts of questions occurred to me. But what if they fail? What if the only thing they manage to do is either rescue the singers or simply annoy Him before they fail?"

Hauyne shrugged and lifted her glass. "Then we do what maybe we should have done when our goddess first died. We go to war against a god."

The words fell into the room, and Lazul was sure he felt the world crack. Go to war against a god. Was it even possible?

Hauyne sat there calm and composed, but as she lifted her glass of fruist to her lips, he saw the slight tremble. As king, he had every right to order her executed on the spot. Rebellion against Xyl was a capital crime. She risked her life even speaking the words.

"I think I might have just fallen in love with you," he said the words without thought, but they were honest and from his heart.

Hauyne choked on her mouthful of fruist, covering her mouth, coughing as she set her glass back down. "What?" she managed with a rasp.

Lazul gave her a long lazy smile, being happier in that moment that he had been in mooncycles, if not suncycles. "I thought you might suit. Someone I could work with, enjoying talking to, and hopefully be compatible in the marriage bed. The best I had hoped for was someone I could trust and rely on as a friend. I never expected to find a woman I could fall in love with. And you are that." He reached over and pulled the bell as she stared at him, her blue eyes wide.

Actin reappeared in a moment.

Did the man stand outside waiting for that summons? Or is my time perception that bad?

"Actin, would you go get me the box?"

His majordomo arched a brow and allowed a slight smile to cross his lips. "Of course, sire." The man slipped back out as smoothly as he appeared.

"You know if he ever decided to betray you, you would be dead before you had a chance to scream," Hauyne said as Actin stepped out.

"Why do you think I pay him so well? The biggest advantage is Actin is loyal to the Charinsky, which means me. In a moment, that loyalty might be tested. Do you trust me?"

The smile that blossomed on Hauyne's face made him smile. She smiled rather than answer, just took another drink of fruist as Actin stepped back inside with a small box. When he made to leave, Lazul stopped him. "Wait, please. This will involve you."

Actin froze for a moment, looking at both of them with a frown, but he closed the door and took up a post next to it, waiting with the eternal patience of a servant.

"Hauyne, will you do me the honor of becoming my wife, to rule this land, and protect its people? I ask you this with the knowledge that you will not be joining me in marriage until the god of our land is defeated and our people safe." Lazul's eyes were locked on Hauyne who blushed, making her radiant, but he heard the sharp intake of breath from Actin near him.

"Yes, I accept," Hauyne said, holding out her hand. With his body flooded with so much joy that the pain was pushed away, Lazul slipped the bracelet on her hand. It was as golden as her hair and had tiny insets of gems that mimicked what would be on her crown. A sign to all she would be the queen when she took the crown.

Lazul turned to look at the majordomo, who had not moved, but his face was white as he looked at them. "Well, Actin. You are privy to everything that happens in this palace. Will you help us destroy a god or at least help those who can?"

Actin closed his eyes, inhaling through his nose, then letting it out again. Just when Lazul wondered if he would have to call for the guards to kill someone he regarded as a friend, Actin opened his eyes. "Yes, your majesty. I will be more delighted than you could ever know to assist you in this so you can marry the Lady Hauyne." Actin cleared his throat, bowing slightly. "Now, are you ready for me to serve dinner?"

CHAPTER FIFTY-TWO

JADAYA

Jadaya stood looking at the place a god had all but cried in front of them, then took a deep breath and surveyed the area. It was a sandy shoal that led up to a gently sloping hill. In the distance was the promise of a city, if the smoke rising was anything to judge by. Shivers wracked her body as a cold wind came down from the north and wrapped around her.

She moved toward the lone mustang, using it to break the wind. "We will not be able to use the wagon with only one animal, and the mustang is not suited to pull it," she said while petting the trembling animal.

"That and one of the axles is broken, so it would not move anyhow," Rylix said, moving over to look at the wagon. "But the good news is the craftsmen that made this did an excellent job. We only have a mustang, so we will all be walking, but we can salvage a large amount of goods if we work at this."

Jadaya nodded, willing to accept that, but did they have enough to make this work now? Only the intervention by Pel allowed them to survive. Note would have lived, of course. She had no idea if it was possible to drown an Aoisan, but it was unlikely the rest of them would have survived. She spared a thought to the sailors that had been on the ship with them, then moved to assist Rylix with the wagon.

It took all three of them to wrest open the back door, releasing a deluge of water that drenched them again. Rylix sighed at the disarray in the caravan, then he crawled in and started going through everything that was salvageable. Jadaya left him and Note to going through their possessions and went further up the hill and set up camp. They were not going anywhere tonight and already the cold air was making her clothes stiffen and fingers and toes numb. When the sun sank into the ocean, the aching cold would become dangerous.

She got the fire going, with the mustang grazing nearby, and sought more driftwood or other fuel for the fire. The sun had disappeared by the time Rylix came moving up the small hill with Note in tow. They both had bags full of stuff, including the odd watertight bag he had insisted they bring with them into the water.

Note followed Rylix loaded with the camping equipment and a pile of food. "It will be salty, but we might as well cook it now as it will rot," he said as he spread out a blanket and set his load down near the fire.

Jadaya nodded. If the towns in the distance proved unfriendly, they would be in trouble.

Rylix dropped his load. "I salvaged what I could. If I can figure out for sure where we are, there may be a Ged encampment somewhere, but I only know of one in Vykland. And it is the opposite direction we need to go." He looked back mournfully at the wagon. "The work my uncles and cousins did on that was amazing. I am bereft by the very idea that anyone might break it into pieces. A bit of love and some work and it would be as exquisite as it had been for us." He heaved another sigh and stared into the fire.

Jadaya sat down and handed him the dinner she had made. They ate in silence. Her mind was full of the information Pel had imparted, and she trembled at the idea they might change the world. But her rage at the gods who exiled her, who let this situation happen in the first place, mixed with the need to prove that she was a person, not an object you could throw away, adding to her mix of churning emotions.

"I think we should do it," she said. The words were spoken without conscious intent, the end result of her whirling thoughts.

"It?" Rylix said, raising his head. The dark curls, encrusted with salt and sand, reflected in the light, making him look like he had little stars in his hair.

"Change the world. Become heroes of legend. Defeat a mad god." The words sounded so incredible, impossible even, but the idea was grand enough to supplant her rage. More accurately, her rage mixed up in it. To change the world so no one else ever suffered what she did? That was worth dying for. After all, mortals died for less on a daily basis.

Rylix shook his head. "How? We are shipwrecked. Most of our supplies are gone. We only have a single mustang. We could get home easily enough, but to get to the Mount of the Gods, then to Charinsky? Much less cross the country to rescue children and get them home? And when that god attacks? He is a *god*. We are mortals."

Jadaya tilted her head, hearing both his words, but more the plea to give him a reason to not give up here.

"We keep dividing everything into gods and mortals," Note said quietly. "We all know we are mortal, we get injured, we age, we die. But..." his words faded into the crash of the waves on the shore, his face a carved relief. "But we know gods can be killed. Look at the reason we are here. Because a goddess was murdered."

Jadaya nodded as he, like the rest of them, avoided using their names. The mad god was too sensitive to use His name and the last thing anyone wanted was His attention. But Note was right, gods could be killed.

"Yes, by another god," Rylix said, looking at the sky. Above them the two halves of Percit hung, jagged and broken, while Shio kept circling around them, pulling the currents with her as she floated across the sky.

"So?" Jadaya said softly, a smile spreading across her face. "We are going to the old gods, the ones you tell us tales about. They have weapons that can kill gods. If we gain their assistance, how can we not at least try?"

"If," Rylix said. But he sat up and put another piece of wood on the fire. "If." He heaved a sigh. "Most of the stories are of the gods. Maybe we need to have stories of men and women. Of those who challenge the gods and succeed or fail. Maybe we need to provide a reason for those stories to exist, even if we die in the process." He sounded more like he was trying to convince himself rather than them.

"It is probable we will die," Note commented, but there was no defeat in his voice. "But if just two of the captured are rescued and the raids stop. I would be happy to die with that as my legacy."

"Go down as a legend?" Jadaya asked, her smile growing.

"Live as an example," he countered, looking at her. "Proving you can say something is wrong, even to the gods, and make them listen."

"Proof that power, even being a god, still contains the ability to make mistakes. To be wrong," Rylix said.

"Oh, they are wrong often," said a voice from the shadows. Jadaya jumped to her feet, sword drawn as someone stepped into the circle of their firelight. "But the real question is: who are you and why are you on my shore?"

Jadaya stared at him. Her gut reaction was this stranger was not an immediate threat, but that meant little. The speaker was a man, at least a two hands shorter than her, and he looked like a standard Vyklander. He had bare feet that seemed impervious to the cold ground, dark body hair that was visible on the tops of his feet, forearms and from his chin down his neck. Tanned skin and dark eyes, and thick black hair bound in a tail at the back of his neck. He stood with arms crossed, looking at them. There was no obvious anger, but there was an aura of immovable patience.

She sensed the movement behind her more than saw it, but a moment later, Rylix was at her side. He snorted out a half laugh. "Ord. Please join us," he said with a wave of his hand.

Jadaya widened her eyes as she looked at the god, then put her sword away. Starting this part of the trip attacking a god would be unwise. And if this kept up, she would have met all the gods of her world.

The realization that meeting gods had become commonplace distracted her as the man, the god, moved to enjoy the warmth of their fire. At this point she had met Cassix the wanderer, her gods Zula and Yika, the Aoisan gods Pel and Rian, and even Fivikan gods, Jovan and Sinka. Now one of the Vykland gods: Ord. Had anyone else ever met this many gods besides her companions? Shaking her head at her own meanderings, she moved back to the fire. The wind coming from the north cut through their wet clothes and she shifted her concentration to drying out their footwear. The icy kiss of the cold could cost toes or fingers, making getting their clothes dry a priority.

"Would you like something to eat?" Rylix asked as Ord settled down next to them.

The god sniffed the food and shook his head. "Your offer is kind, but no. Now, who are you?"

The three of them glanced at each other. It seemed like their life kept getting more complicated, but lying served little purpose, especially given how much the gods seemed to gossip.

"We are headed to the Mount of the Old Gods to ask for assistance and weapons to rescue my fellow Aoisans. And possibly deal with their mad god," Note said, his chin tilted up as he watched Ord.

Jadaya wanted to sigh. She would never claim she was the most diplomatic of them. That was Rylix. But even she could present information in a manner that was less challenging. Perhaps in a way to request assistance. A glance at Rylix and she saw his shoulders slump at Note's words. But they both let it go, waiting for the response. Though she was relieved he did not say Xyl's name. They had enough issues as it was.

"Ah. I see Pel and Rian finally started paying attention to their people and not their pet projects." Ord snorted out an explosion of air. "I suppose they are leaving it to you?"

Note gave a nod at the comment.

"So why here? While the area around the Mount is all but unsailable, there are many days of journey between here and there." He struck her more as a merchant verifying what color you wanted, interested but unaffected by your choice, than a god examining mortals.

Note let a growl slip out of his mouth before he replied. "The managers of Fivika kicked us out. Tossed us on a ship to dumps us here, though I believe they would have preferred to come to port. A monster of the deeps attacked us, shattered the ship. Pel showed up and put us and our belongings here. He mentioned—" Note broke off and shook his head. "As you can see, we are here and are trying to recover."

Ord's dark eyes inspected them. He let his gaze flick from them to the wagon sitting on the sandy inlet, then to their wet clothes as they huddled around the fire. "I see. So, what are your plans?"

Again, the questions, but only passive interest. Were all the gods so different? As a child, she had always assumed that the other gods were as involved in their people's lives as hers were. It turns out the amount varied widely. It made her feel like every time she figured it out; the ground shifted again under her feet.

This time Rylix spoke, his smile and charming manner focused on the sale, though of permission instead of goods this time. "We are going to recover what we can, set up as a trader and work our way toward the Mount. We will buy and sell as we go, though as you can see, the wagon is no longer capable of coming with us on our journey."

Ord nodded, looking at them for a long time, then shook his head. "I warned them all when we held the farewell for Percit, that Xyl was unstable." Jadaya flinched at the mention of those names, seeing the same reaction from the others, but Ord continued on, either unnoticing or uncaring. "But they rarely listen to either of us. So their problems are theirs, not ours." He rose back up, shifting as he gained a comfortable stance. "I will neither bless nor curse you. You are free to travel across Vykland and see if you reach the Mount. But it is none of my business if you fail or succeed. But neither will I make any effort to impede your path. My people are free to make their own choices. What you achieve may change everything or nothing. I am sure that Qian and I will watch with interest. Travelers," he said with a nod, then turned and headed back into the darkness.

The three of them looked at each other and finally shrugged. Of all the reactions from the gods, maybe this was the best. As the sun set and the whole moon shone between the halves of Percit, Jadaya shivered and worked on getting food in her and their clothes dry enough to start the journey to the west.

CHAPTER FIFTY-THREE

ZAYN

Zayn was so exhausted that he lacked the energy to be surprised as the man in front of him finished speaking. "I see. That is unexpected."

The man, a servant in the palace, bobbed his head. "I overheard when I was cleaning. They were unaware I was there. It was the king and Actin talking in the council chambers about how to destroy our god. I stayed hidden until nobles came in, then slipped out when other servants were bringing in refreshments for the meeting." His eyes were wide, but he was waiting for something.

Zayn had avoided flinching at the word 'god'. At least the man had avoided saying his name. The last thing he needed was Xyl's attention. Zayn rose, turning his back on the man as he poured two glasses of fruist. "That is good. Have you mentioned this to anyone else? Your wife? Best friend? Another priest?" Zayn mixed some opi into the fruist while he asked the question.

One of the advantages of the king asking Zayn to bring in a large supply of drugs meant it was easy enough to have some reserved for his personal use.

"Of course not!" The man appeared shocked at the question. Zayn doubted he had, but he needed to make sure no one else knew. "I waited until my shift was over and came here. It took much to convince your priest that I needed to see you, not anyone else."

Zayn nodded. "I apologize for that. They are rather zealous about protecting me." He turned, offering the man the drugged glass of fruist. "Here. It is a wonderful vintage I am sure you rarely get to try."

The man colored in pleasure and took the glass. "Aryix bless, Cantor, I am honored."

Zayn tried to hide his flinch, but ever since Xyl showed up, even saying the names of other gods made him nervous. The idea of having anyone else poking their fingers into this mess was enough to make him scream. "What else do you do at the palace?" he asked with an absent air, his attention on the man enjoying his fruist. He was pretty sure he had put enough opi in there to drop a jack. Opi was a new substance, gathered from flower seeds in Wysko. It made you see your dreams with small doses, but in large doses, it stopped the heart.

"Cleaning mostly. I enjoy making the floors and walls go from dirty to clean. It makes me feel like you can see how good of a job I do." The man spoke with a smile as he sipped at the fruist. "This really is excellent. An interesting aftertaste."

A thread of guilt trickled through Zayn. This might qualify as a good man, but he was now too dangerous. He set his own glass down, the fruist untouched.

"That sounds excellent. Too bad you are not one of my priests," he said, his eyes locked on the man who was tilting to the side.

"Nah," he slurred. "My singing is more like croaking." He blinked and shook himself upright. "Sorry, I am more tired than I…" he slumped against the wall and slid down it.

Zayn rescued the cup. Blown glass from Fivika was expensive and looked down at the man, his lips in a tight line.

Should it say something about me that I went immediately to killing him?

A finger later, the man had stopped breathing. Zayn still watched him a little longer, more because it gave him something to focus on than anything else. The question that ran in circles around his head was what to do with the information. There were so many options.

He could tell Xyl. He knew with absolute certainty that if he called for Xyl with the addendum that he knew information about people trying to stop the honoring of Percit, Xyl would be in front of him in moments. And then what? The king would be dead, they would need a new king, and Zayn thought the only other person with royal blood was a teenager somewhere. The laws of the land would not allow him to be both king and cantor, and honestly, the king had too many people watching him, tying his hands more tightly than Zayn's. When it came to power in Charinsky, the cantor had more; with fewer restrictions.

He could tell the king he knew. Order him to stop and make sure to dispose of these people with the threat of Xyl or even turning the populace against Lazul. And then what? The king would treat him as an enemy and nothing would change. They would still have a god that was dangerous and unstable.

He could help the king. Take the risk that if Xyl was killed, everything would be better. And then what? A new god? No god? Either way, Zayn would lose the power and benefits he enjoyed now. The odds of him still having singer children to enjoy were low.

Or he could pretend he knew nothing. Never mention it again and let the king do what he wanted.

What is more important to me? My power or the people?

That question was the truth of the matter, and every time it came back to the people. He had nieces and nephews, cousins, siblings. Most of them were far to the south, and he rarely saw them. But he had no desire to have them die from the temper tantrum of a god. But for his use of the singers to be known? That had just as many risks.

Zayn rose and went to the door to the suite. He threw it open. "I need help in here!" he bellowed out. As the footsteps raced toward him, he ran his hands through his hair and mussing it up and widened his eyes to convey panic and stress.

Algoi and one of the senior conductors were the first to reach him. "Cantor, what is wrong?" They asked, their eyes casting about for danger. Zayn was inwardly amused to see Algoi and the conductor clutching the knives that were under their robes.

Do they want to protect me that much?

He snorted as he whirled to point at the man lying on the floor.

Odds are they have no desire to be cantor right now. No one would want to deal with Xyl. I have no desire to deal with him.

"He was in here talking to me. He had concerns about Xyl and making sure he could help pacify him. Then he groaned, clutched his chest and fell to the floor. I think he quit breathing?" While the death of the man was necessary, he had no issue channeling his own internal quandary to make him seem more upset and anxious. Algoi was already in next to the man checking him over.

After a moment, she looked up at him with sad eyes. "I am sorry, Cantor, but he is dead. It sounds like an issue with his heart. We have seen this happen to others."

Zayn nodded, letting his shoulders droop and his head fall, hands clutched together. "I see. Will you please contact his family? I feel so bad that this happened here in the temple. Tell them we will cover the funeral costs." He went over to his purse and pulled out four copper. "Please give this to his family with my sympathy."

Algoi took the money, nodding. "I will see that it is done."

Zayn stepped back and let them deal with this. He mentioned the chest grabbing as that was something they had seen in the temples more than once during worship. It was a known indicator of death and there were rarely any warnings. And he felt guilty. The man had done what he thought was right. Hence the money toward the family. It would help them out.

"Please also send a note to the castle. I believe the man worked there. I would not want them to think he was shirking his job when this is the reason he does not return." He kept the serious and sad mien on his face, even as his mind raced around like a trapped rat.

"At once." Algoi nodded and Zayn let her do her job. One of the best things about that woman was her absolute faith. It was also the most annoying. But he knew the family would get all four of the copper and she would get a message to the palace. But he still had no answers to his quandary.

Once they were gone, he carefully washed out the fruist glass the man had used. He re-secured the opi in a hidden drawer, then he poured himself a large glass of fruist, in a different glass, and sat back down to think. Even the idea of one of the boys to come distract him held no attraction. The idea of killing a god occupied his mind.

Could they do it? Do I want them to succeed?

The layers of possibilities lay there, but everywhere he looked, his destruction was either guaranteed or probable. If Xyl continued as their god, this tightrope of uncertainty would remain, with his insanity getting worse every season. If he died, then they had no god, and that idea made him just as uncomfortable. Would they essentially become Ged? That life held no appeal. Or would another god absorb them? Change them? The obvious choice would be Deox and Iryx of Wysko. Zayn shuddered at that thought. The Wyskans, or Snakes as most mortals called them, were the strangest of all the lands. Even the gills that Aoisans had seemed normal in comparison. Though the Fivikans' black eyes were still strange. Snakes had smooth skins with subtle scales. They had no hair, not even eyelashes. Instead, they had scale-like markings that acted as measures for their beauty. When you added in the wide feet, extra flexible joints, and long pointed tongues, it took little imagination to believe they had been created from serpents.

Zayn toyed with the fruist in his hand, taking another sip. The options spread out like multiplying rivulets of water from a broken pitcher. And all of them collected dirt and created new messes. He had no idea which option would be the best to put his power behind. Only the knowledge that hurling the glass across the room would waste fruist, shatter a glass he liked, and give away too much about his frame of mind, kept him sitting and drinking quietly.

What do I do?

The question hovered in his mind even as he headed to bed, alone. The time available to make a decision was disappearing like the sun into the ocean, and if he avoided the issue much longer, the decision would be made for him. His bitter wish for a god to pray to or someone to talk to rippled through his mind as he sank into sleep, wondering if the choice had already been made.

CHAPTER FIFTY-FOUR

SHINALA

The gods had mentioned something was coming, but was that in a mooncycle, a suncycle, or even a tenday of suncycles. Hope of change was not a change. So the repetition of sleep, eat, sleep still existed. Meaning there was nothing that could alleviate Shinala's boredom.

"Change is coming," a voice whispered next to her.

Many millennia ago, she would have cut the throat of the person before they moved within a tail's distance of her. Even a few hundred suns ago she would have sprung up, enraged at the arrogance. Now she flicked a tail at him, not even opening an eye.

"Come talk to me. You always enjoyed our conversations," the voice cajoled her. Shinala yawned, showing the speaker her teeth, but then she stood and shifted, taking the two-legged form that was never quite warm enough. She settled back into the warm sand, not looking for the speaker.

"Change never comes. We are out of time. Left to let the wind destroy our sanity one finger at a time. We are the forgotten." The words whirled around her like the unceasing winds.

The voice laughed and settled down next to her. She could feel the heat coming from the body, not that she had not known who it was even before he spoke.

"This might be massive change and a chance for you." Amusement and assurance filled the voice, enough to spark a teeny amount of interest.

Shinala lifted her eyelids, revealing green eyes that locked onto Cassix sitting across from her. Someday she would find out what he tasted like. The blood of the gods always had a zing to it that lingered on your tongue and in your systems for hands of days.

"Why speak in riddles, betrayer? There is no change outside the blowing of the wind, the caress of the clouds, and the tears of the sky." If only there was. Something different to do, to experience, to survive.

Cassix smiled, exposing pitiful teeth. How did he eat with those? Long ago memories of her in mortal form crushing through a piece of fruit flickered through her mind and she pushed it away. Even the clothing she had once worn in that shape had crumbled to dust. Perhaps that is what she should do. Dissolve into the passage of time and let it take her away.

"This is a change that might shake the foundations of our world. It might even release your prisoners and reshape Aria." Hope seeped into that voice, the voice of the one who had not actively participated in the betrayal yet had not stopped it either.

This comment pulled Shinala up and she shook her head, letting long white locks tangle around her. "What is this you prattle about? The last mortal to visit us was so long ago, even their bones have become sand." The comment was sharp and hard, and if she had been in cat form, her tail would be lashing back and forth in agitation. Or was it hope? That would be more dangerous. If Cassix gave them hope and it drifted away like smoke, she would see how long a god could survive as her Leonaids fed on him.

"A trio of heroes come to seek the weapons of the old gods, of my parents. They are seeking to rescue those the people of the mad god have captured. To change what has been going on for many suns."

Change? Could anything change? "Mad god? Ah, the spouse of the moon goddess. She died ages ago. Why depose him now?" She wiggled the toes of these feet. Useless. They had no claws, though the thumbs on the hands were useful. Her body was still strong, but it was stiff in ways it had not been only… her mind avoided thinking of the time and went back to Cassix's comment. Mortal servants would not be amiss here on this island or, more accurately, mortal tools. The Leonaids were unable to slip off the chains of this island, and all the comforts they had brought with them had faded away so many suncycles ago the memories of what they were no longer existed. Mayhap mortals would bring brushes? She remembered liking when someone brushed her.

"There is one who finally had enough rage to threaten his own gods. He wishes to change things," Cassix said with a glee that Shinala found exhausting and annoying.

"So? That is one. One person never affected the world," she said, flicking sand at him, though she knew that was untrue. One mortal could start a landslide or a war.

"Really? And here I thought one person started everything. But there are two more. An exile from Zuyikan and a Ged."

"Ged?" Shinala lifted her head. "They still exist and are faithful? And why would Zula and Yika kick out one of theirs? They are greedy about their possessions." The mention of the Ged interested her. There was a period of many suns after the imprisoning of their masters, and them as well, though she had not realized it at the time, when Ged ships came and traded with them. The memory of trading both goods and the pleasures of the flesh stirred in her memory. But slowly they had quit coming as well.

"I know not, but the woman, Jadaya, is a great warrior, and the rage is building. As to the Ged, this one knows the old stories. He shares them with his companions. He is becoming one that might-" Cassix broke off and shook his head. "I suppose you are right. There is little they can do," he said with a sigh.

Shinala lashed her tail at him. "If you believed that, you would not be here." She yawned, closing her mouth that had no sharp teeth. How did they survive in this form? "So, why are you here?"

Cassix laughed, though he shifted away from her a bit. "Never change, Shinala, you were the most dependable of all of us. Why did you agree to be here with them anyhow?"

Lifting her left hand, she wiggled her fingers, then used them to comb through the tangled mess that was her hair. "Why are you here?"

Another round of laughter as Cassix stood looking at her. "Because maybe they can be what changes everything. Or at least the start of it. And because…" he sighed, turning to look out at the sea that churned with monsters in the distance. "Xyl has to be dealt with, and no one else will."

"You could," Shinala replied, fighting with some serious knots. She would need to see if Mace could make her a coom? Comb? Something to drag through her hair.

"No. I tried once. It only served to make him fixate more on the loss of his wife. I suspect now there is no other option." To her surprise, he sounded remorseful and worried. It was odd to hear the light-hearted god care about something.

"I see," she murmured, though it still sounded like gods were being silly. After all, if her gods were imprisoned, why could they not imprison Xyl? "Ah, that is your plan. You need me to help them so they can put the mad one here."

He shot her a look with smugness in the glance. "Maybe."

She focused on her hair. The knots seemed to be growing. "No."

Cassix turned to look at her. "No. What do you mean, no?"

"No, you will not be imprisoning that lunatic with our gods." Even from here, the taste of Xyl's insanity was a bitter thread that wafted through the world. How the others could not sense it astonished her.

To her intense amusement, Cassix's shoulders slumped. "But then, what can we do with him? If he stays in Charinsky, if he stays unchecked, not only that land but all the lands could suffer. We have to do something and if they fail, we all lose." The note of pleading surprised her.

"So kill him," she said as she finished stretching.

Cassix blanched. "Is that really a precedent you wish to set?"

Shinala lifted her lips to bare all her teeth in a mockery of a smile. "Remember who you are talking to. Your siblings betrayed my masters, of which Xyl was one. Do you think I would have any issue feasting on their bones? On his bones?"

"They left Aryix and the others alive," Cassix protested.

"Because they feared what their deaths would cause. I have no fear of killing my master's offspring. Of all of them, you are tolerated because you tried to warn your parents and took no part in the matter. But do not think that makes you a friend." Shinala gave up and stood. Maybe one of her Leonaids had a comb. Stretching, she turned to head toward where her pride waited.

"Will you at least talk to the mortals if they make it here?" Cassix called back, his voice urgent.

"I will not eat them on sight. That is the most I will promise," she said as she headed down the beach, dismissing him.

Mortals here again? This could be interesting.

CHAPTER FIFTY-FIVE

RYLIX

They rotated watch the next morning, with Rylix standing it in the dark of the night. He spent most of his time watching the sky. This far north, the stars looked different, and he wondered how he had arrived here with these people. Oddly, that was not the part of his situation that really had his attention. Rylix tried to decide where he wanted to go from here. The possibility of just going to the nearest harbor, waiting for a Ged ship and heading back to Calin was possible, or Delcona, or even setting up a new trade route here. He knew there was a small enclave near a port in Vykland. He had options, but what did he want to do?

That gods seemed to show up every time they turned around was unsettling, to say the least. He knew of no other Ged that had met any gods, and he was up to six? It was enough to make him nauseous. Most gods were insular, caring only about their land and then their people. While they might meddle, they normally left the Ged alone, as his people still owed allegiance to their parents, not them.

It had gone past the being part of the group who would create a legend. Now it was killing a god. Did he want to be part of this? It would not change the fact that Kryx was still dead. The Ged had no need for other gods and no need to kill them. But what had been done to Note and other children like him made him sick. Why would any god allow it? Maybe this was why the Ged stayed true to the old gods, because they were not involved in anything that happened in Aria. But the idea that any god would sanction sex with children made him sick and furious at the same time. And by saving them, maybe he could forgive himself.

"So what do I want to do?" he asked the stars. Rylix flinched when he realized he spoke the words aloud and he looked around, tense, wondering if another god would pop up to talk to him. No one appeared, though he remained watchful until it was time for Note to get up and take his watch. Rylix headed to bed, wrapping up in the still damp blankets, his mind still racing. But the fire was warm, and he fell asleep, only to be woke up what seemed like moment later. But the sun crept up over the sea and the fire was roaring with cafe in the pot and the last of the provisions being made into food.

They nodded at each other as Rylix rolled up his sleeping blankets. Obviously everything was being arranged on the mustang's back, so he added his to the load and looked around. The beast ignored the packs secured to it, still grazing placidly. "So, my fine companions, have we decided on the plan for today?" To his amusement, they glanced at each other, then back at him.

"We are headed to the Mount. But if you do not wish to accompany us, we are prepared to drop you off at the nearest town in our path." Note looked resolute, Jadaya concerned.

Rylix ducked his head, mostly to hide a smile. It seemed their thoughts were all running in the same direction, but he had found his path while he slept. "I believe I shall be your companion in this endeavor. While you will be the heroes, at worst case I can be the bard to ensure that your tales are told far and wide. Besides, I speak Char and Vyk much better than either of you."

Jadaya smiled at him, the wide grin creating a splash of white across her dark face. "That would be helpful, as I speak neither. Learning Aoisan has been interesting."

"And she still sounds like she is gargling water," Note teased. But Rylix consoled himself with the flash of relief that crossed Note's face.

"Then we should set off on the journey to free the singers and face a mad god," Rylix said with a gallant wave.

It took them two fingers to go over the wagon one more time and ensure they had packed everything that could be salvaged. Then they redid the packs on the poor mustang to create a balanced load. But with the three of them walking, the goods did not seem to bother the animal, and now each of them carried a pack with their own possessions.

The walk to the road helped to loosen up the saltwater soaked jackets and stiff limbs. By the time they headed east, all of them were warmed up and moving easily, even in the brisk air. Vykland was cold most of the time, and Rylix knew the snows came early and stayed longer than in any other country. Hopefully, the next large town would have leggings and thick coats, as those had not existed for them to buy in Hearth.

As they walked, Rylix took in the sights of the strange landscape, rolling fields that headed north to where a huge mountain jabbed up into the sky, white and almost gleaming. He knew it had to be at least a tenday away, but even so, it was huge and made him very glad they would not be required to climb that to reach the Mount of the Old Gods. He directed his gaze to the east, but the clouds and trees in the distance obscured any glimpse.

From what he had looked at on the maps, he figured it was at least a tenday to get to the closest point of land to the Mount, but then they would have to figure out how to cross. Here was where he hoped the old stories he knew would help or that they could rent a boat. But after the last boat ride, he was reluctant to get back on the water. The smell and sounds of that creature would remain vivid in his memory and adding any new terror of the sea did not seem wise at this time.

"I think I see a town ahead," Jadaya said, breaking the companionable silence. They had been walking for at least nine fingers without a break, though the pace had been easy to maintain. The road they were on was more of a trail between one town and the next, but still Rylix could hope it was a big enough town that a bath was available and hopefully a Ged tent, though it was promising to be colder tonight than last.

He watched as they walked and sure enough it was a town, or, more accurately, a village. They were met with curious smiles as they came in, but it had no inn or bath houses. A few items were purchased, but there was little enough to buy.

"Promise ye, I do. Next town over there are baths to be had. There is even a place to rent a bed or room," one of the women said, holding her salt-soaked fabric that they had sold for a fraction of what Rylix had hoped for, but the sale at least covered the goods they had purchased with a bit left over. The other things sold were some of Jadaya's dyes, spices, and metal arrowheads. But the rest had been of little interest to the town.

"Aryix bless, my good woman," Rylix said with a becoming grin. "Would you have any idea how far it is?"

"Ah, with your young legs? Before the sun sets arrival, though not much before. So do not play as you move as you will not be allowed in past dark." The last part was said with a flat assurance that told Rylix something happened that towns locked their gates after dark, but this small town did not have any. What danger existed that a village was untroubled, but a large town could not ignore?

"Is there something they fear to lock gates at night?"

The woman burst out laughing. "Nay, they just want to make sure they charge all who enter and if you leave the gates unmanned at any finger of the day you miss out on money. Yet, having more than a token guard in the evening is more than the jarl can bear."

Jadaya laughed and even Note hid a smile. At least greed was one constant that seemed to cross all the countries. If only some of the more positive traits were as common.

"Aryix bless, my lady," Rylix said again with his own laugh. With those words they set off to the next town with an extra step to their feet as the idea of baths was enough of a lure to make him wish he could run with the wind like Jadaya did. But even as they walked, Rylix kept an eye on their surroundings. This weather was strange to him and he worried they might not be ready for the changes it could bring.

His worries seemed unfounded as they reached the town. It was half the size of Calin and they were indeed charged as they entered, but the fee of a gold each was less than he had feared. Their coppers were safely tucked away between the three of them, and the gate guard directed them to where the nearest inn stood.

Upon arrival the innkeeper assured them they had beds for Note and Jadaya, as well as stable space for the mustang, but he looked doubtfully at Rylix.

"There is an old building set up for a tent roof, but it has not been used in suncycles. The stove here may or may not work. Ged rarely travel here." He looked almost worried at the idea of anyone staying in it.

Rylix smiled. "If it has four walls, the rest I can make do if you are willing to let me make some changes to the stove and structure?"

"Nah, do as you wish. As for the baths," the innkeeper spoke, his chest swelling up with pride. "There are hot springs baths, a sweat lodge, cold showers, and a woman down the way does small washings for guests at a reasonable fee."

"Spring baths? Lodge?" Jadaya asked the questions as Rylix tried to remember what he had heard of those.

The innkeep grinned. "Yes. Water from the mountain is heated by the liquid fire held deep in the mountain. It has healing properties, and the sensation is wonderful. It is mixed company, though. Nudity is common but not required." This last part, he said with an apology to Jadaya. "Few here have ever traveled far enough to meet a Zuyikan."

Jadaya graciously smiled rather than correcting him. "That is not an issue, as long as they understand touching may result in the loss of fingers."

A dark grin flashed across the man's face. "Good. That is not acceptable and my daughters use the pools. Anyone that touches without permission has no need of fingers." He shook his head and grinned. "As for the lodge, it is a room full of steam with fragrant oils. It seeps into your skin and removes your worries of the day, letting you sleep deeply."

They all agreed that sounded delightful. The innkeeper offered to let Rylix stay for free if he updated the Ged space. While Note hunted for a place to go shopping the next day, Rylix and Jadaya fastened down the tent canopy they had salvaged, repaired the little stove, and made a quick muddaub to seal the cracks in the building. By the time full night fell, the little shelter was cozy, if not warm, and would be comfortable enough once he curled up in his own blankets.

Note had reported back there were stores that supplied clothes and would be able to alter some for Jadaya and him. With that done, they went to enjoy the hot lodge, something Rylix fell in love with and Note hated with a passion. Jadaya said it reminded her of the hot ripening days in the field. But the innkeeper had told the truth. After a soak in the water from the mountain, then the hot lodge, Rylix found himself asleep in seconds after climbing into his blankets and closing his eyes. Deep inside, he wondered what else would happen along the way.

Even further down, he wondered who he would be when it was done.

CHAPTER FIFTY-SIX

LAZUL

The last of his responsibilities done for the day, Lazul found himself moving down the corridor, but every step caused pain to ricochet through his body and he kept falling against the wall, which just hurt more. He was panting and only ten steps from the door to his chambers when Hauyne found him.

"Ah, a bad day, I see." Her voice was mild as she came up and set his right arm over her shoulders. It pleased him somewhere in the depths of his mind that she fit so perfectly against him.

"I wish I had found you when I was younger. Pain free," he slurred.

"A terrible day. You can barely talk, and I know you have had no meds yet today. Come on." Her voice was brisk, but underneath it was a note of empathy. Not pity, just an acknowledgement of his suffering. It felt nice to be seen and not have the pain dismissed. Most of the nobles assumed he was being dramatic, as did the hangers-on at court, though their number had decreased greatly as he had little time or patience for their prattle.

"Smart, kind, caring. Should have found you sooner," he muttered as she pulled him into his chamber. As soon as she was inside, she grabbed for the bell cord and yanked. The rings for the servants registered in his brain, but mostly he paid attention to her, trying to focus.

"This worries me. Come on." She led him further in, turning the corner to where his tub was located. At least a fire was already going, warming the room up. The large tank with water also had a fire merrily going. "Aryix bless," she murmured, and he agreed. The idea of a hot bath sounded wonderful. Now, if he could get some food and pain-killing drugs also, it would be even better.

With a grunt, she sat him on the bench, leaning him backward as he swayed.

He cracked open his eyes to watch her. There was something about this woman that amazed him. She moved over and cautiously touched the tank about halfway up. "It's good. Good," she said, as if talking to herself. She did that often, and he found it endearing. Before she could do much more, Actin came bustling in.

"Oh, he does not look well," he blurted when he saw Lazul.

"No. What happened today? Was there something I was unaware of?" Hauyne started emptying the tank into the tub, nodded as it steamed. She tossed in some scented oils, then touched the water, hissing at the heat. A large bucket of cold water stood in one corner of the chamber.

"Not that I am aware of. I left him about six fingers ago with the council of nobles to finish up the damage reports and compile an agenda to discuss with Zayn. I have no idea what happened. Let me order some refreshments." Actin darted out of the chamber as she added water to the tub until it was hot but no longer scalding. The metal the tub was made of both retained and bled heat, so it was best to pour in boiling water first then add the cold after the tub had warmed up, leeching off some of the high temperature.

"Now for you." Lazul raised his head at her words and summoned his strength. He let her help him strip, the pain disposing of any modesty at this point, and it was better to have his future wife see him like this than a servant. They had the bad habit of gossiping.

It took the rest of his energy to step into the tub, hissing in pain and relief as he sank into the heated water. The water covered him up to his shoulders and he let loose a soft whimper.

"Lazul? Are you well?" Hauyne was kneeling next to the tub, and he turned his head to look at her.

"No. But this helps," he admitted, wishing she never had to see him so weak. He cursed his god and this affliction that Xyl placed upon him because he dared to help his people. Maybe he could have been a better ruler, but he thought his rule had been good. Or at least decent.

Or does it matter at all? If Xyl did this just to be cruel, nothing mattered.

That thought had been working through his brain for tendays now. And it felt like a truth he had been avoiding.

He opened his mouth to speak when Actin rushed in, a large carafe for fruist on the tray, along with gels and a small jar of white powder. "I brought your normal supplies, but I also added some of the powder from Wysko. It is called mophe. It is what the doctors use when they need to remove a limb."

Lazul shuddered. He did not know if he hoped that amputation hurt more or less than this. "The gels and the fruist for now. I would like to think I am not at that level of pain."

Actin nodded, handing him two plum flavored gels and the glass of fruist. Then he left them to talk. Lazul chewed on the gel. At this point, the flavor was almost a distraction, but he would never tell the cook that. He found it worked better if he let it dissolve in his mouth. Then he sipped on the fruist, closing his eyes as he let the heat and the drugs push the pain away.

Lazul had no idea how long he sat there, locked in his own mind, before Hauyne spoke. "What happened today to make it so bad?" Her voice was soft with worry and a touch of steel in it. He opened his eyes to see her in the chair near the tub, watching him. The fire made the room warm, and he saw the touch of sweat on her brow. Guilt lanced through him and he sat up, drinking more fruist before replying.

"Me. I was stupid. I thought I was getting a handle on the pain, so I only took a half amount at breakfast, and skipped it at lunch. It has to be like walking, right? The more you do, the easier it becomes." He looked away from her, embarrassed. "By the time the afternoon sessions were done, it was all I could do to sit up straight. I think I remember what we talked about. I know I was not persuaded to do anything stupid, but for the life of me, I have no memories of what we discussed."

"Actin was not there to monitor you?" Her voice was mild, but he still felt the sting of rebuke.

"There were some logistics he needed to deal with today, so one of the scribes was with me, taking notes, which I must review. But I made myself act like nothing hurt. Even when the pain was pounding in my brain. Why have I not learned to tolerate this pain?" There was a mixture of whining and a plea for relief in his voice. He closed his eyes and sank back down into the tub. Already the water was cooling to his regret.

Hauynes' cool hand touched his arm. "I think you are asking over much of yourself. The difference with most other pain, even the pain of labor, is that it has an end. Yours does not. It might rise and fall, but it is always there, beating against you. Even the rocks of the land give way to the constant attention of the waves. Do you think you are stronger than rock?"

The image of the cliffs eaten away by the endless attack of the sea flashed into his mind, and he snorted in laughter. "No. But I had hoped I was stronger than pain."

"Not this. I understand the need to try, though I think you will not try it again?" Her voice had a touch of acerbic amusement to it.

"No. I will not try it again." He sighed. "A bit more hot water, please?" The kettle had been refilled at some point, so she let more into the far end of the tub and he moaned in pleasure. "Aryix bless," he murmured.

"Are the gels helping?" she asked.

"Yes, but if this continues, unless the mophe makes me pain free and interested, begetting a child might be difficult." He kept his eyes closed, hating yet one more weakness being displayed.

"I had suspected. Few men would have been as gentlemanly as you have been." Again, that acerbic amusement in her voice.

"I would have been delighted to be less of a gentleman and more of a sex fiend, but while the spirit might have been interested, the flesh has not been."

"Yet one more crime to lay at the feet of a god," she said, her voice bitter, and he cracked his eyes open to see her face. There was sorrow and frustration and he laughed, painful and bitter, but it was a laugh. "Do I amuse you?" she said, her face smoothing to a bland expression.

"No. It is just nice to know my attentions were wanted and amusing to realize this situation has made me incapable." Lazul smiled at her, the drugs making it more subtle than he wanted.

Her mouth twisted in a smile. "Yes, I will welcome your attentions, but that brings us to the next aspect." She stood, looked outside into his chamber, then shut the door firmly to the needs room and sat back down. "What are we to do to ensure the success of the strangers?" Determination filled her voice and at that moment Lazul realized his heart was hers, as was the crown. She would make a better ruler than he, but he would like to raise a family with her. None of which would happen if they did not deal with their mad god.

"I am unsure. They must succeed, but we have no knowledge of where they are. They could have already failed or died on their trip," he pointed out, the relief from pain almost making him giddy.

"Can we trust Zayn? Would he be for or against this?" Her voice held hope that he hated to dash.

"No. I have no idea if he would support them, but he is the head priest. He will never be anything other than for his god, no matter what he might feel. The best we can ever hope for is that he might turn a blind eye." Lazul watched her through slitted lids.

"Ah. I had hoped for a moment Zayn might find a shred of compassion." Hauyne seemed oddly relieved and depressed by his response.

"Do you think we could trust him?" It was very possible his own judgment was as unsteady as his emotions these days, but he did not think so.

"I have never liked the man," Hauyne admitted. "But the version that just left seems different from the man I met at dinner in my brother's home. Less arrogant. More unsure of his place. But that means little when it comes to this. Unless you are unwavering in your thoughts to tell him, I would not. I have people looking for the three, but until they land on Charinsky, I will know little."

"Very well." Lazul sat up. "Then help me to bed, my love? It will be a busy few days. I will not interfere in your spymaster duties. I only ask you to put the country first. My survival is immaterial." He managed to stand, the heat and drugs having made an incredible difference. Hauyne helped him out of the tub and wrapped him in robes. It took another finger for him to crawl into bed.

"I disagree greatly with your survival not being paramount. But I understand what you mean. If the country dies, then we are as good as dead," she spoke as she assisted him in laying down. "I hope this has proven that you should take the drugs each day, yes?" Her voice was sharp as he lay down with a sense of relief.

"Yes. No more arguing and I will take it as needed each day. But we still need to figure out what can be done." Lazul let his head hit the pillows and closed his eyes.

"Do you trust me?" Her voice seemed distant.

Lazul cracked his eyes open and whispered his response. "More than I trust myself."

"Sleep."

He let darkness claim him and promised to be a better person and king when he woke.

CHAPTER FIFTY-SEVEN

JADAYA

They spent two days in town before they left again, as well supplied as they could manage. There were a few things, like the honey, no one in the towns on their path would ever be able to afford, but other things sold well, and they made a few more gold promising to pass on letters at each town.

In the various villages they traveled through, the people were polite, if quizzical, at their presence. No one chased them out, yet they also provided no encouragement to linger. A single night was all that the townsfolk expected them to stay. The trio plus one mustang found themselves approaching the forest between them and the rumored path to the mount of the old gods.

"How much information do we have about this section of Vykland?" Note asked as he stared at the trees.

Jadaya understood his concern. In Zuyika, there were long rolling plains, mountains with scrubby trees, and sandy deserts with various dangers. The lands they had passed through had been either foothills, farmlands, or cities with occasional copses of trees. She had never seen trees like this. The tall stately trees in Aois had seemed almost friendly with the open spaces beneath them as the sound of the leaves and ocean created a symphony of songs that welcomed you.

The dark line of trees that lay ahead were brooding, angry almost, as if they stood as a guard to what lay beyond. They hunched over the land like a hunting bird over its prey and she shuddered to think what might hide in the shadows.

"I talked to a few villagers in the last place. There are no cities beyond that line that they know of, though there are rumors of a few villages. If there is a large town, it has to be almost completely self-sufficient, as there is no trade that could reach them." Rylix sounded calm, but his body was tense as he looked at the foreboding line of trees. "My primary worry is that." He pointed up toward the gray sky that hung over them, making it feel like they could touch the heavy sky if they were only a hand taller.

"Only way out is through," Jadaya said with false cheer. She hefted her backpack and started toward the trees as a light snow started to fall. They all had the proper clothes now, so the harsh cold was no longer an issue and hopefully inside the forest it would be warmer.

That was a false hope.

As they stepped under the trees, the light snow almost vanished, but a deep cold crept into her bones, lonely, dark, like the depth of the sea. Jadaya shivered as it washed through her. They walked single file with Rylix bringing up the rear and the mustang and Note in the middle. He was suffering more from the cold, as the ocean never reached temperatures this frigid. As they walked, the snow continued to fall, pushing down branches and falling on them in clumps.

She had hoped with the branches laden with snow, it would be lighter, less foreboding in here. That hope was dashed. It was even colder and more alien. She had seen snow one or twice as a child, but it had always been something fun to play in, then go back inside and have a hot drink. This had no aspect of fun. It was wet, heavy, tasted of ash, and clung to them, slowly soaking through the water-resistant leathers and furs they wore.

"We need to make camp soon," Rylix called up from the back. "This is taking too much out of us and the darkness will fall fast with the heavy snow."

"Yes, please." Note's words came out in a chatter and she glanced back to see he was more blue than normal.

"Yes." She looked around trying to orient herself, but the snow, darkness, and trees made it into a maze where not even the sun peeked through to give her any guidance. "Rylix, do you have any idea? Or do we just make a camp?"

She looked back to see Rylix looking around with a frown on his face. They were too far in to back out and they needed to shelter before it got worse.

"I guess we will try a technique one of my uncles told me about once. We need a section of trees with overlapping branches and minimal snow underneath."

"Very well," Jadaya said and kept walking, now looking for something specific. It took another two fingers of moving forward before she found something. There were four trees in a cluster while a fifth had fallen to one side, almost creating a shelter. There was only a scattering of snow as these forest giants had branches so interlaced not even the snow could force them down.

"Rylix, will this work?" she called out. A moment later, the crunch of shoes through the snow sounded and Rylix materialized next to her.

"Oh, that is excellent. Come, let us get the mustang and Note in the middle." He moved as he headed back to pull the others up to her.

It took a bit of coaxing, as they had to convince the mustang to climb over the tree, but they were soon all in the little protected area. Just not having the snow on them helped, but Jadaya wanted to get warm and fast.

"Here, help me," Rylix said. "Note, if you would gather as much fallen wood as possible and bring it inside."

Note, his face gray with cold and exhaustion, nodded and disappeared over the wall, while the mustang lipped at some plants that were nearby.

Rylix, for his part, had pulled out their tent fabric and ground covers, as well as a collapsed pile of sticks. Jadaya had paid little attention to what he piled on the mustang, trusting he would bring what they need and had taken all of their personal belongings as her burden to carry. It let them get more out of the wagon than she would have believed.

Four of the sticks connected to create a tall pole almost a hand taller than she was. While the others expanded in a latticework that she had seen in some of the Ged tents at Calin. It was about five hands high but expanded to triple her height.

"We are lucky with the fallen tree. It will provide a wall. Come help me and hold this here." Rylix pointed to where he had one edge of the lattice on the ground and she held it there as he expanded it to reach in a big arc around them, using the fallen tree as the base of a rough arch. Once secured to the ground, he grabbed each of the tent fabrics and slipped the hole at one end over the tall pole and the other ends to the lattice. All their tarps were large triangles, and most of the time they used two that overlapped to create a protected space. This time they spiraled out from the center pole and he attached them all to the lattice, creating a layered tent faster than she would have thought possible.

He then took the long ground cover they usually put down in wet areas and ran it around the lattice, tying it to the flexible wood. The difference was almost immediate. While Jadaya could only stand in the center, the temperature rose quickly.

"If you can take the saw and go cut some of the boughs, the softest you can find, we use that as a floor. It might be lumpy, but with the blankets we have, it should be warm."

"What about the mustang?" she asked, looking at the animal that already looked like it was snoozing.

"All Ged animals are trained to be in tents for cold weather. We just need to put it near the door and it will help keep us warm." He seemed more relaxed with the icy wind cut off from them.

There was a scramble of sound, and they looked up to see Note climbing in at the opening that attached to the fallen tree.

"Impressive," he said as he came in, arms full of wood that, while damp from snow, was mostly dry. "I put more just on the other side of the tree." He piled it to one side, the opposite side from where the mustang stood. "But I really need to sit."

Jadaya looked at him and he seemed like he had darkened at least two shades, and here a darker blue was dangerous. "Sit," she said. "I can get kindling for the fire, then more branches to feed it." She climbed out and shivered instantly at the renewed attack of cold. Steeling herself, she moved out and found branches, cutting them off with the jagged tooth saw Rylix had packed. The green branches of fresh growth were soft and flexible. Hopefully, they would help distance them from the cold ground.

With the lack of sun to give her an idea of time, she headed back, boughs in multiple bundles, tied together with leather strips, unsure of how long she had been gone.

From the outside it looked little different, but as she stepped through the flaps, a wave of heat slammed into her, and she moaned in surprised pleasure. Inside, Rylix had a fire going, and it warmed the entire inside of the shelter. The kettle was on the fire and food was being cooked. More wood had been brought in. Between the mustang and the fire, the inside felt like the warmest embrace compared to the brutal cold outside.

"Excellent. Come on and I can get these set up into beds for us." Rylix bustled over and grabbed all the boughs while Jadaya stepped forward to enjoy the warmth of the fire. Note looked better with the heat and was drinking something that steamed.

"Tea," he said in response to her look. "Want some?"

"Yes," she said, and a moment later, had a warm drink in her hand. The heat flowing down her throat warmed her from the inside, and she felt much better after that.

"If you would take the spare pot and grab more snow, we need it to cook in a bit," Rylix muttered, still fighting with the branches.

Jadaya did that. It took only a moment, but the cold outside had either deepened or the finger of warmth made it feel more intense. She ducked back inside with a shudder of relief, setting the pot near the fire to melt.

"All done," Rylix said with a smile. "Given the temperatures, I figured we will want to share heat. Note, you will be in the middle, as you are suffering the worse."

Jadaya thought it was a measure of how miserable Note was that he made no attempt to argue, just nodded. Rylix set himself to preparing food and Jadaya finished laying out bedrolls. Whatever Rylix had done created a softish bed that allowed the warm air to get underneath and prevented the earth from leeching their heat.

She fed the mustang while the two men finished getting the food ready, then they all ate in companionable quiet, too tired to talk. With the blankets and coats layered on top of them, shoes still on and facing the fire that had been banked to burn slowly for the night, they let each other's heat and companionship spread as they let sleep take them.

The shaking of the tent and a roar of rage ripped Jadaya out of her dreams. Dark dreams full of water, storms, and a feline scream. Snow fell on her as she sprang to her feet as the supporting pole cracked, bringing the tent down on top of them. The last thing she saw before the fabric blocked her view was fur and claws.

CHAPTER FIFTY-EIGHT

NOTE

The roar of something large and angry yanked Note out of dreams of freezing to death. Even with Jadaya, the mustang, and the fire, he was still cold. He never enjoyed shelter season, but this was crazy. Why so much snow? He hoped the next part of their journey would be warmer.

"Watch out!" Jadaya's shout grabbed his attention. With a yelp, he rolled backward as the tent collapsed around them.

"What is it?" he called out, grabbing his knives and trying to find a way out that kept him away from the creature.

"Hungry?" Jadaya said as she ripped at the lattice still somehow attached to the ground. The tarps came undone and floated down around them, revealing gray skies, snow-covered trees, and a gigantic creature staring at them like they were lunch.

"This is going to hurt," Note muttered.

"I need my spear," Jadaya snarled, though he suspected that was mostly to herself. She had drawn her sword and braced as the monster approached.

Rylix's head popped up, eyes wide as he stared at the brown shaggy animal. "Keep it occupied. I have an idea." His head ducked back under the fabric.

The mustang was going crazy as it smelled the creature. The musky thick odor was overpowering. Still covered with the fabric, it was unable to see what was attacking it, but it still tried to get away. Note agreed with the mustang's reaction.

"*Alliakka!*" Jadaya yelled and darted forward to shove her sword in the monster. Note still had no idea what it was, but its shoulders were at the same height as his head. Covered in dark brown fur, it had long black claws at the end of all four legs, long pointed ears, and teeth that could double as daggers in a long snout. The creatures in the sea suddenly seemed much friendlier.

The creature turned its attention to Jadaya as she came in to attack it with her sword. She darted in and back without drawing more than a swipe from the creature, mainly because the monster kept focused on the mustang. That changed the instant her sword sliced into it. It roared and turned, now locking its dark brown eyes on her.

"The coat is thick, but it is just muscle and bone underneath it," Jadaya called.

Note tried to move to a place where he could attack, but the boughs under the collapsed tent, the wiggling of Rylix trying to do something, and his own bone deep cold made moving hazardous. He growled to himself and tried to throw one of his daggers, but it hit the dense fur and bounced off. Jadaya moved in again, blindingly fast, like a viper striking, and stabbed the creature again. But if it was worried or scared, Note saw no signs of those reactions. All he knew was it was getting closer, and the growls told him nothing other than it was hungry.

"I almost have it," Rylix called out from under the fabric, but Note was too busy trying to move as the creature charged at Jadaya.

She jumped back. Her feet landed on pine boughs and she slipped, falling, The monster lunged toward her.

"To the deeps with you," Note muttered and leaped forward. What he tried to do was get to the side of the creature, stab it, and then leap away again. Fear must have given him extra strength as instead he ended up landing across the back of the creature. That distracted it, and it turned, trying to see what had happened. The act of turning pushed Note up, so he took advantage and straddled it. His legs clamped around its ribs behind the shoulder blades. Note had never squeezed so tightly with his thighs in his life, trying to stay on and out of reach of those deadly claws. Whispering a pray to Rian, he took both daggers and slammed them into the monster's neck, right above the shoulders.

The roar that came out of the thing shook the forest. It lifted one giant paw and swiped at Note. The claws tore through the air toward the left side of his body, but he leaned away. Instead of ripping out his ribs, they tore furrows down and across his torso, shredding skin and muscle.

Matching the roar from the creature, Note screamed. It was a high and sharp sound, rending the darkness, born of pain and fear. He drove the daggers down again, this time at an angle, and they caught in the muscle and bone of the immense creature. The resulting roar was so loud his ears rang. The left hind claws came up, raking across his back as if the creature was scratching off an insect. They dug in, mangling flesh before they pulled back, taking Note with them. It sent him flying into the mustang, still trapped under the tent. He impacted the poor mustang with a *whumpf* that sent all the air out of his lungs, and his world became pain.

"Got it!" Rylix yelled, popping out of the tent. "Close your eyes and mouth."

Note rolled over, tears running from his eyes, and put his face down into the tent as Rylix did something. Strong spices assaulted his nose, but he could barely breathe from the pain, so it changed nothing.

The beast sneezed, coughed, and roared again, but this time it was quieter, confused. Another hint of spice, but Note could feel the blood streaming from his wounds.

"Now, Jadaya!" Rylix's words were sharp, and Note felt the fabric yank underneath him. A grunt, a roar, then a thud that shook the ground.

If I die, at least I tried.

The fuzzy thought wiggled in his mind as he felt hands turning him over. "Note? Note?"

The world went black, and he sank into it gladly. Anything to escape the pain.

CHAPTER FIFTY-NINE

RYLIX

Rylix swore. He now had a dead ursoid and a dying companion. This was ridiculous. Maybe the gods *were* against them, because they provided little assistance. "Jadaya, can you pull the tent out from under the ursoid? We need to rebuild it. I will calm the mustang, then we need to take care of Note." He was pulling his companion toward the gap in the tent as he spoke. If he was unable to get the mustang calmed down, it would run away and right now they needed its heat and ability to carry supplies.

"I think so," she said with a dubious tone.

Rylix looked up and saw the true size of the thing. In the fight, with the fear and stress pounding through his veins, it had seemed huge and shapeless. Now that he could see it, immense barely described it. And he had no time to worry about what they had just survived. "Lever it up if you have to. I know the creature is too big to move, but for now we just need the tent up. Grab a sapling too, as a new pole."

Between drugging the mustang with some herbs, getting Note under cover, rebuilding the tent, and ending up with the ursoid inside with them, time disappeared.

He hated leaving Note alone for so long, but the reality was if they were unable to get the shelter back up, he would die. Rylix made sure the leather cuff from Pel was tight on his hand, then raced to reconstruct everything. Maybe the cuff would help with the healing enough for them to get him somewhere better than this. He needed to get the fire going and start some hot water to clean the wounds. The trade goods and supplies had been tucked under the fallen tree, so they had been protected. He found the strongest alcohol he had, as well as bandages and herbs to make a paste.

At this point, Jadaya returned with a new pole and stuck it under the fabrics, lifting the fallen tent. The raised space made it easier to work, but also amplified the rank order of the ursoid. The ursoid and the spicy pepper mix he had blown at it. His mouth felt like it might burn for days, but he had dumped the pepper mix, usually used in moderation in food, into his blowpipe and blown it in the creature's face. It had been enough to distract it and let Jadaya get in the final blow, though from where the daggers still were, Note might have actually killed it. The ursoid had not yet realized it was dying before Jadaya shoved her sword through its neck into the skull.

Rylix laid Note out and started cleaning his wounds as Jadaya came over with the herb mixture.

"Oh, those are deadly," she whispered. Rylix looked up at her to see wide eyes staring at the wounds across the Aoisan's body. He pulled himself back and actually considered the gravity of the damage. Up until now he focused on the steps that needed to be done in the best order to keep Note alive, but now he pulled back and looked—she was right.

The first slash had ripped through his clothes and the claws had raked from his spine forward. Deep enough to expose ribs and tear muscle, but as there was no smell of bowel, Rylix assumed his intestines had not been punctured. The second wound was from the base of his neck to the top of his rear, tearing through muscle and at least one rib. Blood poured out of both wounds and Rylix knew he had to work fast. He was no healer, but if he could stabilize Note and stop the bleeding, maybe the cuff's magic could save him.

Together he and Jadaya stitched closed the largest lacerations across his body, then covered them with moss treated with some of the precious honey. He cut one of the blankets into strips and after putting the clean cloth on the wounds as bandages, he and Jadaya wrapped Note tight, trying to keep pressure on the torn flesh and give his ribs support. What worried Rylix the most was even after cleaning the wounds with hot water and the small amount of distilled grain spirits, the edges were already turning an inflamed red.

They put him down in the best place they could and wrapped him in the blankets. His skin was cold and clammy and already he shivered, though Rylix found the tent too warm.

"Will he live?" Jadaya's words were quiet.

"I am unsure. Without that cuff, the answer would be no. But perhaps it might be enough. I gave him enough medicine that he should not be in pain. But there is little I can do about infection. Either he can fight it off with the help of the god's magic, or he dies. I have no other resources." He sighed and got up to check the mustang. His medical kit had included some powdered morphe and tella. For Note, he mixed the morphe with some hot tea and dribbled it into the man's mouth, his reflexes swallowing it. Though it took forever to get enough into him that the unconsciousness had moved to drugged slumber.

For the mustang, he mixed the tella powder with a bit of sugar the animal had licked off his hands. After a finger of petting, the strong tella slipped into its system. Now the mustang sat on the floor softly snuffling, ignoring the dead ursoid.

"What can we do?"

Rylix rubbed his neck, staring at the dead creature. "We use that," he said with a definite nod. "We can use its liver to make blood soup, and as we are going to be here for a few days, we might as well make the most of the meat. The hide should be a good trade when we reach civilization next."

Jadaya arched a brow, but nodded. She pulled Note's daggers from the ursoid. They were best suited for butchering and skinning work and set herself to cleaning them.

Rylix prepared for the messy business of butchering a creature that weighed as much as all of them put together. He should be able to smoke the meat, make rich stews, and if he was right, there were some plants out there they could add to their diet. Either way, they would not be moving until Note went to the grave or returned to the living.

CHAPTER SIXTY

NOTE

He was so cold. He shivered and tried to call for help. But his mouth would not work. Then darkness came again. It felt like he lived in a world of cold and pain. Every so often, food appeared in his mouth, and he struggled to swallow. Rich, bitter, but he craved it. Then there was water, sweet but warm, and he wanted more, yet darkness reclaimed him before he could take more than a mouthful or two.

There were voices, but they only conveyed safety and concern, so he let them be as he drifted in the dark. Off to a side was light and not knowing what else to do, he moved that direction. The world resolved to be Aois and the city of Pelisic and he smiled to see it. They had not even been gone two mooncycles but already it seemed longer. He had lived off dreams of home once, only to find he no longer fit.

He turned to look at the port and cried out in horror as he saw black sails approaching. Frantic Note raced into the city to warn people, but no one saw him. Then he froze as his mother walked down the street carrying a child of about five.

"Mai?" He formed the words, but no sound came out. With mounting fear, he watched the men run toward his mother. They grabbed him, slamming a sword into her when she fought to protect her child. Protect him. She fell in the street, blood streaming from her, even as she reached for the child he had been. Her screams brought another man running from a house.

"Dai?" A man came sprinting toward the Char that held Note with one arm, as the invader cut down the man as easily as the woman.

He could barely remember what they looked like, but here in this dream world he saw them, crystal clear in a way his memories had lacked for suncycles. Now he saw what they had looked like before they died. And remembered their expressions as they died and their murders carried him away.

"Are all mortals killed so easily?"

The words were not Aoisan, but neither were they Ged. He should not have understood them, but he did. Note spun looking for the speaker, but all he saw were his memories rolling out before him.

"Who is there? Where I am?"

"These are your dreams, not mine. I was curious. You are dying and I thought I would like to meet you before you die." The words came again without stress or panic, just stating a fact.

"No! If I die now, no one will carry on. I have to stop this. Stop Xyl." Note's words were a confused protest, but he screamed them. The enslavement of his people must stop.

"Hush, idiot one. You may be dying, these maybe your dreams, but that does not mean the mad god will not hear his name and come see who calls him." There was a sharpness to the voice, but it still spoke no language he knew, yet he understood every word.

"Who are you?"

"Does it matter? If you die, will the knowledge of who I am change anything?" Again, just a mild curiosity, as if the life or death of Note meant little.

"I will not die," he snarled back. He was on fire and freezing at the same time and he was unable to change it, so he focused on the voice instead. It was that or watch those he had once loved die over and over again.

"You are so sure?" It sounded curious now.

"Yes. I will overcome this." He tried to project assurance into his voice, but he shivered at the same time. So tired of fighting and trying to stay conscious.

"I see. If you live, then I will see you later, child of Rian and Pel. Then we will see what you are worth."

The voice faded, as did the scenery around him. His eyes opened to see the fabric above him. "So cold," he chattered. Jadaya's face moved over him, her dark braids all but touching his face.

"I know. Just hold on. Here, can you drink this?" She held a cup up to him, steam rising from it.

Note raised his head, eager for the warmth. He choked, trying to swallow what she poured into his mouth. It was thick and bitter, like blood and herbs.

"I know. It probably tastes awful, but drink it anyhow." She must have read the question in his eyes as he forced down another mouthful. "Liver, blood, tea, and herbs. It should help. You lost a lot of your own blood."

He pulled his head away when he had finished the cup. The heat warmed him, even as his mouth revolted at the taste.

"Here," she said, offering him some candy. It was solid red beet dust mixed with some juice. The overwhelming sweetness helped to wash away the taste in his mouth. Note tried to ask a question but the darkness and cold pulled him back under.

This time he found himself in the temple, the stone walls cold and judging as he stood there with other children. Many of them were crying, but he knew his parents were dead. The memories were still bright in his mind at that point. So he just waited. Death would be welcome, but hate fought in him to make him want to live. To take vengeance. His heart leaped as an Aoisan woman walked in. But her words dashed his hope.

"You are singers now. You will sing. The price of resistance is death. Not always yours." There was something broken about her, about how she spoke. She faced them, but her eyes looked through them, not at them. "Learn well, and you will be rewarded. Resist, and pain will be the least of what you suffer." She turned and walked out, leaving the younger ones to cling to each other. Note just stood there as it sunk in: he was a slave and the only option if he wanted to survive was to make them think he was broken. With anger resisting every movement, he slumped his shoulders and dropped his head. Watching feet and learning tones.

"Interesting. Even as a cub you thought, and raged."

The voice was back, and it served to pull him away from the immediacy of the memories, distancing the pain. That was what these were. Memories? He hoped so, because maybe then he could forget. He watched them speed through his life in the temple, in slavery. The scroll of memories were a fast tumble, then it slowed as the first time he was called to a priest's room, ordered to strip and crawl into the bed, appeared in vivid detail. He could recall the smell of the room, the feel of those hands, his own confusion, horror, and then grief as the realization there was no escape sank into him.

Note turned, looking for the voice, needing something else to focus on. Those memories still hurt. Remembering the suncycles he endured until he was too old to be attractive anymore.

"Who are you? Are these my dreams?"

"They are what you keep hidden in your mind. What I find fascinating is what you are hiding from yourself. These memories and the emotions associated with them. You put everything aside to be what you think is needed."

"My wants and needs are unimportant. I must stop this from happening." His words were impassioned, but he flinched at the cry of pain and confusion from his younger self as he fought the attentions and was beaten for his rebellion. He had known even then to stay quiet, but sometimes the situation surpassed his ability to be the proper little slave.

"Yes, but your needs drive all of this. You gave purpose to the Exiled one. You have made a Ged look outside his own wants. If you succeed, what then?" A bit more curiosity in the voice this time.

Note laughed. It was a sad sound, but he tried. "Then I guess I get to be a hero. Jadaya said she would like that. Travel the lands and try to change things."

"Ah. Now I see the attraction for Cassix. Do you think you can succeed?"

"Cassix?" Note jerked his head back up, still looking for the speaker. "Is that who you are?"

"No. I am no god. Can you succeed?"

Note turned slowly and looked at the boy, older now, silent except when singing, the one who watched and memorized everything, like who enjoyed too much fruist when on evening duties. Who would accept the right type of bribe to look the other way? The faces he intended on killing.

"I have no idea, but that is the wrong question," he said, still watching the boy he had once been. The child who pretended nothing touched him, nothing mattered.

"What would be the correct question, then?" The voice sounded amused, but Note no longer cared. He was so cold that even thinking had become hard.

"Do I want to live if I do not at least try?" Darkness claimed him as the words were spoken, and all he heard was amused laughter as he fell into the blackness of nothingness.

CHAPTER SIXTY-ONE

ZAYN

Zayn led the song and made sure his face appeared joyful as the singers and the congregation joined him in singing. It was an old paean, meant to express the love between Xyl and Percit as if it was a real living emotion, but the words had always struck him as odd. Now the way people sang it made it almost salacious.

> *I kneel before you, worshiping you, the woman you are, the goddess I need.*
> *No other can replace the pleasure you bring. Your lips, your hands, your body are*
> *   my treasure.*
> *Within your body, I experience ecstasy.*
> *Once more, bring me to you, clasp me close, greet me with your lips.*

The grins and heated glances that slid between people as he faced them made him fight a shudder. Worship was to keep Xyl happy, not encourage an orgy. The worst part was, it seemed to be working. The skies glowed blue. The sun shone with warm rays; even the crops seemed to grow faster than usual. Everything was wonderful. Why did he want to scream?

It took five fingers before the last of the parishioners drifted away. He noted there were more swollen bellies than normal and bile rose in his throat. Instead, he praised the singers, his priests, then headed to his rooms, ostensibly to change clothes. In reality, a glass of fruist called his name.

In the tenday since the palace worker had suffered a 'heartstorm,' Zayn had felt like his world was spinning out of control. His decision to do nothing with the information had become an inertia he was unable to shake. The world, the church was changing, and Zayn hated every second. His god was a faithful husband who grieved his dead wife, not a perverse deity who enjoyed the crueler side of sex. Then there was the fact that he had proof, or at least information, that the king planned on helping the group coming to destroy his god, and he had done nothing.

Nothing.

The word shook in his head with condemnation and Zayn accepted it. But his mental list of options and consequences had not changed. No matter what he helped or prevented, the world was going to change. It already had, and he hated it.

A knocking at his door pulled his mind back to the present. After a quick review of his surroundings and his clothing, he responded. "Enter." He wore a day robe and while it might be early to be on his second glass of fruist, no one would dare comment on that.

Algoi pushed open the door and slipped in, shutting the door behind her. He noticed she was not wearing tears today. In fact, they seemed to have disappeared a tenday ago. Interesting.

"Algoi. Is there an issue?" Once again, he wished Circe was here. He needed someone intelligent to speak with.

She glanced at him, then at the floor, her hands shaking. "I am concerned about the way the worshipers are reacting."

He wanted to snort. Instead, he nodded. "As am I, but was there something specific?"

She lifted her head, swallowing hard, and his interest peaked, but he waited with feigned patience. "There are multiple parishioners that have approached various priests asking if they would provide either education or participation with them on the acts that are displayed on the walls."

Zayn blanched. While they had not dared destroy the carvings Xyl had placed there, he had hoped downplaying them and having some of the most explicit covered up would dissuade people from paying too much attention to them. Apparently, that hope had been wrong.

His mouth opened, then closed. It took the rest of the glass of fruist before he found an answer. "While the priests of the temple have never been required to be celibate, it has always been assumed they would not have families as their time was spent ensuring the worship of our god was paramount." He, like most others, was avoiding saying the gods' name. He certainly had no desire to speak with him again. Once had been more than enough. "They are free to participate as they feel comfortable, but we have no institutional knowledge to provide instruction as to what is displayed. I would remind them that what is possible for a god to survive is not always possible for a mortal."

Algoi looked relieved, and he had a fleeting thought about what she looked like under the robes. She was excellent at her job, and he rarely thought of priests in that way. " Aryix bless, cantor. Do you want a treat brought to you?"

The way she said the word, he knew she meant a boy from the singers. The thought did not even cause him to stir. That was supposed to be his treat, something forbidden that his rank let him enjoy. Not an accepted practice.

"No. I am still processing the service."

She nodded and left without another word, leaving him staring at the window. What was wrong with him that even the thought of that left him cold and flaccid? The words of Xyl came back to him. "The toys she would have used on you. After all, you enjoy your little treats, do you not?"

He wanted to scream. The idea of being a toy for Percit, the implications of the tastes she had, and the realization that his 'treats' were enjoyable because they were taboo and he had power. Zayn had always loved power. It made him feel safe. He no longer felt safe. The idea of being like his gods caused nausea to rise in his mouth. He had enjoyed being bad, being cruel, because ... because *why*?

Zayn wanted to sob as the world he had created cracked more. He wanted it back the way it was, with gods that portrayed a sweet and kind love. One where perversions were kept to the bedrooms as dark secrets. It was no fun to break the rules when it turned out no one cared. What good was power when anyone could have what you had?

He filled the glass again and stared sightlessly at the wall. All this time, he thought this proved his influence and that he could thumb his nose at his god and his society. No. The actions showed he was a sad man trying to prove he had control over someone that could never refuse him.

The realization as to what he was settled into him like an icy wall of fog. He abused children because he had the power to do so.

"So be it. But what do I do now?"

Nothing. He would do nothing. He could do nothing. If they killed Xyl, then he would see what remained. If they failed, he would see what remained. But either way, he would figure out how to control the fallout. He would get his power back.

Zayn smiled to himself as he turned the glass in his hand. He would make sure he came out on top no matter what happened, and the best thing to do was to start planning now.

CHAPTER SIXTY-TWO

JADAYA

Jadaya lay next to Note. Her long limbs wrapped around him, the blankets and coats layered on her, the fire as big as they could make it while still in the tent. Rylix had meat curing and cooking while she spent her time keeping Note alive. He burned with fever and shook with cold. They had agreed he needed to be kept as warm as possible, so Jadaya sweated as she wrapped him with her body, skin to skin, as he drank her heat like he drank the water they offered him, greedy and desperate.

"How is he doing?" Rylix's voice pulled her from the doze she had fallen into.

"Better, I think. He stopped shivering and the heat along his ribs was not as intense. Those claws must have been filthy." Everyone knew to clean wounds, but they had only water and distilled spirits here and it obviously had not been enough. If the cuff had not helped to heal him, Jadaya knew Note would have died.

"Good. I did some scouting. There is a stream of smoke coming from the west. I think it is about a day's walk, but with the trees it is hard to tell," Rylix said, chewing on his lip as he looked at the Aoisan.

"I think by tomorrow he should be able to ride if we wrap him warmly," Jadaya said, laying her cheek on Note's head. "I think his fever has broken," she said with a smile. "He feels normal."

"Ah. That is good news. Then, yes. Let us do that. I will work on repacking everything. It will increase our packs, but it should be fine." The lattice had been destroyed by the ursoid attack, leaving it to be used as kindling. Claws had shredded some of the tent, so it was not as nice as it had been, but Rylix and she recreated a decent shelter. The mustang had settled back down, but they were almost out of grain for it and the snow made finding fodder difficult.

They needed to leave and get to a place with walls and food. Hopefully that would be to the west. If not, Jadaya had no idea what their options were. A flash of humor slipped through her. She had craved something to make her needed. This filled that need. She was still enjoying herself, even with the fear and the cold.

Jadaya stretched and pulled away from Note, then pulled on her clothes. He did not protest her leaving, so she took that as a good sign. Previously, if she moved at all, he whimpered and his body chased after her, seeking heat.

Once dressed, she turned to look at Rylix. "I am going to make a needs stop, then see if I can find some fresh greens for both us and the mustang."

Rylix nodded, busy rearranging and organizing. "Be careful."

Jadaya just smiled and buckled on the sword. She stepped out of the tent, making sure to reseal it, then stood breathing in the cold crisp air. It hurt, but after the stifling heat of the tent and the sweaty Aoisan, it felt good. At least she knew now that sweating Aoisans smelled like the sea. From experience, she knew there were worse options. With that thought making her smile again, she moved through the woods with care, glad for the snow. It crunched as she walked, leaving a clear trail back. If it started to snow, her return would have to be quick or her path would disappear. She found some sprouts the mustang would enjoy. A wild onion peeking through the snow was added to her collection. She found an asprik tree in a small grove and cut off a branch. The bark could make a tea that helped with pain, so it was always good to have.

"Nice to see you know how to not abuse a tree."

The words were gruff and in Ged. She spun to see a man dressed in skins staring at her, but his expression contained curiosity, not hostility. He was obviously a Vyk, the lack of shoes proving that if nothing else. Her feet ached just thinking about walking through this snow without shoes.

"Hurting it only hurts those that follow. It is a waste," she replied in Ged, looking at him. "Are you from the nearby village?" If not, she had a bigger problem.

"Closest might be more accurate. Not often I see Zuyikans in this area. Especially not lost in the trees." His glance took in the surrounding area.

"We had to stop for the snow. Then one of my friends was hurt." She looked at him again. He had the squat power of most Vyklanders and was dressed warmly. If he knew where the village was, it would make getting Note some place warmer much faster. "Would you be willing to assist us to get there? We are traders." She added that as she saw his wariness.

His face cleared. "Ah, traders. I should have guessed. Yes, take me to your friends."

Jadaya turned and backtracked to their tent, definitely looking the worse for wear. As she approached, she called out. "Rylix, I have a Vyklander with me. He came from the nearest village."

Rylix stuck his head out of the tent, a smile blossoming on his face as his eyes landed on the man next to Jadaya. "Ah, friend. How wonderful it is to meet you. I apologize our circumstances are not as congenial as usual, but between the snow and an upset ursoid we seem to be unprepared for guests."

"Ursoid?" the man asked gruffly as Jadaya led him toward the tent. "By Ord! You were serious. You killed him?" The man stopped outside the canvas wall and looked at the immense creature. Even after two days, Rylix had barely made a dent in the meat available on it. If not for the cold, it would have rotted. But Rylix expertly dressed it, removed the innards, and kept it packed with snow, inside and out. The snow on the outside, and around the hide, protected it from scavengers and kept it preserved.

"Yes," Rylix said with a smiling shrug. In the time Jadaya had gone, he had repacked their belongings, leaving only the tent still standing and the blankets surrounding Note. The mustang was in a corner eating what Jadaya assumed was the last of their grain. "As you can see, it did damage to our tent and our companion. We believe he is past the worst of it, though not well by any means, but a house and access to water would be very helpful."

"Do you want to keep the ursoid?" The man's eyes kept drifting back to where the remains of the creature lay, mostly covered in snow. It had to be worth something both as food and for the hide, but that was something Jadaya had no desire to deal with, nor did she really have the skills to treat the hide the way it should have been.

The bargaining smile slipped across Rylix's face and Jadaya shook her head and went over to check on Note, while Rylix set out to trade the ursoid for shelter for them and feed for the mustang. As she crouched down, Note's eyes flickered open.

"Jadaya?" It was a croak of sound. She held the cup of melted snow to his lips, letting him drink what he needed.

"Feeling better?"

"Should be dead. So yes?" The croaking words made her smile.

"That is an accurate statement. We are going to move you. You think you can handle that?" She eyed him carefully, noting that while his fever had broken, his wounds were still swollen and tender.

"Anything for an actual bed," he said with a twitch of his lips, but his eyes were already sliding back closed. In the last two days he had dropped weight, putting him at risk, as Note had little extra fat. They needed to get more food into him, and soon.

She turned back around to check on the men. "It is a bargain, then. Let me call my kin." The Vyklander, whose name she was still unsure of, stepped outside. Rylix nodded.

"That was a stroke of fortune. He is calling kin, and they will get us to the town we need. The one that faces the Mount of the Old Gods." A sharp whistle with a series of trills sounded out. Loud and sharp enough that Jadaya winced as it felt like a shard of ice was piercing her skull. Faintly, she heard another whistle in obvious response. The man stomped back in.

"They come. I am Krosto. My sons are coming." He cast an eye back at the tent and Jadaya got the distinct feeling that the ursoid carcass was worth the energy they were expending. It was less than a finger when three more men came out of the forest. Jadaya was watching carefully, and she swore one moment the forest was still, the next moment they were there. Their coloring and the light-colored hides and fabric they wore mimicked the colors of the trees and bark.

"Da?" the first one said.

"Let's help the traders pack up their camp. There is a ursoid they killed that we will get in exchange for putting them up."

There was a glance between the men, then they shrugged and set to. Before Jadaya would have believed it, given the effort it took for them to set up the tent, it was down, packed up, and the mustang out eating the greens Jadaya had found.

Krosto held Note in his arms. The Aoisan looked small and fragile compared to the very solid man who carried him. Rylix had the reins of the mustang, while the three boys carried the ursoid and the meat that Rylix had been preparing. A single glance around to make sure everyone was ready, and Krosto set out, his large feet crunching through the snow.

They wove through the trees as if each one looked different and their feet had no issue with the snow, either for traction or movement. Jadaya was not quite as lucky. Here in this land with snow up to her knees, everything about this place felt too pointy, sharp, long, and cold. She towered over all the men by at least two hands. If you had asked her, they could have been going in circles, except the snow was unbroken. Wading through that snow was more exhausting than she realized, especially when going at a steady pace and not the slow meandering she had done the few times she went out before. The only other creature that seemed to struggle as much was the mustang. But even he walked in the steps of Rylix, who walked in the steps of the men carrying the ursoid, making the snow more compact and supportive.

Jadaya was just about to give up and try walking behind the mustang when they broke out of the trees and into a wide clearing. She stood there and just stared. The clearing itself was unimpressive, simply being a wide space with obvious room for crops during ripening, and a village with multiple houses and lodge barns.

It was the view that grabbed her attention. A small bay with a few two-person boats lay in front of the Mount of the Gods in the distance. It rose into the sky, a perfect cone reaching up into the clouds. It had brown and green around the base, then as it climbed it turned silver, then white, then at the very top she realized it was smoke issuing from it, not clouds surrounding the summit.

Krostos must have seen her look as he boomed out a loud laugh. "Impressive, is it not? I, for one, am glad they are there, secure and not disturbing anyone. Though having the volcano spit them out might be entertaining." He ended that statement with a loud laugh.

Jadaya shot him a look, worried that they might delay or try to stop them. "You would be at risk if the mountain erupted?" Everyone on Aria knew of the volcanos, most lands still had a few. No one lived near them, though the crops grown in that soil would be some of the best. Their rage when they exploded could cover unbelievable distances.

The man laughed, shaking his head. "No. We would be fine. We are still a full day's walk from there and, besides, it would have to cross the bay to get to us. The Mount is farther than you think, and our bay has wave breakers. Now come. Let us get your friend to the taphouse and get him into bed." With that, Kronos led the way to the small town, and Jadaya followed, now wondering if getting the help of the old gods would involve the Mount exploding in rage.

CHAPTER SIXTY-THREE

SHINALA

Shinala lifted her head, nostrils flaring. Something new had entered the town on the other side of the ocean. The breeze brought unfamiliar scents to her and her tail lashed as she considered what she had been told. Cassix was not the most trustworthy of sources, yet he rarely lied and she was so very bored. Even her males, after ages of being here, could walk the entire island with their eyes closed. It was to the point the only interesting thing was battling the waves. They were never the same.

She looked up at the sky and huffed. Best-case scenario, they would be here in less than a tenday. Worst, they never came. Did she disturb the prisoners for this?

Amusement twisted her muzzle. Why not? They had to be more bored than she, though they only occasionally rose to the level of consciousness. She stopped at the spring-fed pool, this one of icy cold fresh water, and drank her fill. Waiting for them could take days sometimes. It was best to ensure you were not thirsty when you went in.

"I am going to talk to them. I will be back whenever they are done," she said to the guard who lay outside the entrance. A lifetime ago, maybe a fingerset of them, she would have torn him to shreds for being so lackadaisical on duty. But in thousands of suncycles no one had ever tried to talk to them. It was like guarding a piece of dung. No one knew it was there and if they did, no one wanted it.

He flicked his tail at her, lying in the patch of light. While the ground around the base of the volcano was warm and the heat stayed constant, pure sunshine was rare and most of them took advantage of it when they could. The clouds created by the volcanos' rumbling kept the springs and plants well-watered, but few Leonaids enjoyed being rained on.

With an internal huff, Shinala padded into the side of the mountain. It looked no different from any other part, but here she walked through a wall of dirt as if it was not there. The tunnel she stepped into stretched out before her and she walked down it, the heat that seeped into the very air sinking into her bones. It felt good. The older she got, the stiffer her bones and muscles were. Though by this point, her age was more in her mind than her body. It was yet another sign that she was out of shape. She had forgotten how good this heat felt. Another half finger of walking and she stepped into the prison chamber. Emotions long worn thin still roiled up at seeing her creators, her…*lieges* like this. They should be free to roam the world they created. That their own children dared to do this was something Shinala never understood. She would have killed any of hers that turned on her like that and left them for the scavengers.

"PEACE MY SERVANT. WE ARE AT EASE WITH THIS STATE." The words echoed in her mind, her body, even her bones, and Shinala leaned into the voice with a half purr. It had been too long since she felt Aryix speak.

It was an old argument, one she still did not understand. She stopped in the middle, sitting down and wrapping her tail around her, glancing at the five chambers. Legend had it their children had chained them to the stone of the mountain. That was not the truth. They were encased in crystal and magma surrounded each crystal, rubbed against it, scoring it, but since the crystals were directly tied to their essences, their godhood, it constantly regenerated, repairing every scar.

She could still see their faces, eternal and with a look of peace and acceptance that had driven her to rage. But that was ages ago. Now she just felt sad and oddly betrayed. The need to challenge them to make them want to come back scratched at her heart, but she had tried. For hundreds of mooncycles, she had tried. Argument, pleading, begging, and none of it had gotten them to release themselves from these cages their children had put them in. Children who were a fraction of what her lieges had been. Her gods. Her creators.

Shinala felt them stirring, turning their attention to her. It was as if the sun had realized you were there and focused all of its heat on you. She bowed her head in joy at feeling them again, and grief knowing this was but a shadow of what it should feel like. It was one of the many reasons she had pulled away. It hurt too much to feel only a tenth of what something should be. Doing without was easier, but oh, she had missed this.

"MY LIONESS. YOU HAVE RETURNED. ARE YOU WELL?"

The softer voice of Gela washed through her and Shinala wanted so badly to be at her knees, to lift her head for a scratch, that it felt like a knife was being driven into her. In an effort to lessen the pain, Shinala shifted. In her place, where once had been a lioness of gleaming white, now stood a woman. Her glorious white hair was in braids that twisted and turned like living things, her skin as white as the lioness's fur. Shinala knew from reflections in the water she had a broad nose and her eyes were a white that most would assume meant she was blind. She stood twelve hands tall, a body rippling with muscle, claws for nails on her hands and feet, and teeth that even in mortal form belonged to a predator.

This form honored them. Wearing the form of the mortals put a distance between her heart and her creators. It made watching their imprisonment less painful. It also let her speak.

"I am well. I come because Cassix has told me that changes are happening. How much are you aware of?"

She never knew what they paid attention to, or why they were allowing themselves to be imprisoned. Maybe someday she would understand. Today was not that day.

Aryix spoke, and she swiveled her head to peer at his chamber. The crystal cleared a bit, allowing her to see him standing there. Through the facets, she could see his waving red hair and skin the color of the dark earth. His eyes were closed, but she sensed his attention on her. "MUCH. XYL HAS LOST HIS WAY AND THREATENS MORE THAN ONE LAND WITH HIS PAST ACTIONS. CHANGE IS COMING AS WELL AS JUSTICE."

She tilted her head. "A group of mortals are coming this way. They plan to ask for help in their quest, though if they want to simply stop his predations or to stop him, I am unsure." She also had little reason to care. Why should she help these mortals, when they had done little to help her people? Not that she needed much, but she still missed the occasional Ged visitor.

"AND?" She was unsure who spoke this time. Quas and Gela were more wild and unpredictable than the others. Then there was Stari. The god was different in their perspective depending on which form Stari inhabited. The male form was always more direct and harsh, while her female form nurtured and cared, yet was more vindictive. Personally, Shinala preferred Stari when male. He was less complicated.

But then she had been the leader of a clan of males for suns untold. She had never had a daughter and never had to deal with other females under her command. Some of her sons had birthed daughters with the mortals and the Leonaid blood always came true, but none were her or her dead mate.

"What do you want me to do?" she asked, her eyes scanning over their muted faces, familiar and yet strange after all this time. Only Quas had his eyes open, the darkness radiating out more than the silver of his hair.

They locked eyes for a long time until her heart pulsed in her eyes and Shinala realized she had quit breathing. With a desperate wrench of her head, she broke eye contact and took a deep, shuddering breath. So much information had been passed to her in those long moments, but Quas forgot she had been created with the need to breathe.

"You are in agreement with what he told me?" Her voice shook as she filtered through what Quas had given her. Information that might take a while to fully understand and some that she thought useless.

"YES." They chorused. "BUT YOU WILL NEED MATERIALS FROM US. ONLY OUR ESSENCE CAN HURT OR DESTROY OUR CHILDREN." Aryix continued, and Shinala tilted her head to focus on him.

"Do you want him dead?" She would gladly kill Xyl. His treatment of her Leonaids had often brought them into conflict, and one of her males still held a grudge.

"HE IS BROKEN. HE SUFFERS AND WILL NEVER HEAL. ETERNAL PAIN IS DEADLY. THERE WILL BE A PLACE HERE FOR HIM. HIS MADNESS SHOULD HAVE BEEN CHECKED LONG AGO BUT OUR CHILDREN FAILED HIM AND PERCIT." Shinala shuddered as Stari's voice washed through her and then the mountain groaned.

"I see," she said slowly, though she felt she was missing much. What did the long-dead goddess have to do with now? Shinala looked down at the five bowls sitting before the crystal tombs. They looked like shining black glass, but she knew they were a type of stone, rare and sought after. Here were five bowls that, once upon a time, you could have asked for a kingdom for one of them. They were big enough that it would require two hands for her to carry them out. It was what they contained that was truly valuable.

"SHIN, MY CHILD?"

Shinala closed her eyes as Gela, the one who had breathed life into her and her mate all those cycles ago, spoke. She turned to look at the one she had avoided, the one she wanted a hug from, the one she wanted to cry on, the one she had hid from not wanting to add to her pain. The green eyes locked on hers.

"Yes, my mother." They had all created her and her mate, all added to what they were, but Gela had been the one to bring to her life, to hold her and Raja as mewling cubs and nurse them until they could hunt for their own food. Gela had shown them how to shift forms, and the pleasures available to the mortal and animal form. Of all the gods, the loss of Gela still bled.

"WHEN THE TIME COMES, THE ANSWER IS YES."

Shinala looked at her, but the green eyes closed. "What is yes?" There was no response as she scanned the gods in their crystal prisons, but all of them had their eyes closed. Shinala sighed, then crouched and stared at the bowls. The knowledge Quas had deposited in her mind telling her how to create weapons that would harm a god. If the mortals passed the tests to prove they were worthy. If not, well, there was time. The gods, old and new, were not going anywhere. And neither was she.

Each bowl contained materials to make weapons that had not been seen for eons. Donations from each god for her to use to forge a chance. A pile of red-gold hair from Gela, liquid silver blood from Quas, dark black ingots from Aryix, a pile of dust that shifted color in the light from silver to brown to green from Stari, and from Lyx a pile of metal nuggets the color of her hair.

What she needed to do coalesced in her mind. Assuming these mortals passed her tests. Deep inside, she had no idea if she wanted them to pass or fail, but either way, something in her had changed and she had no idea if she liked the change or not.

It took her five trips to take everything to the old forge, and it took days to get the forge to the point it could be worked. Several of her men shifted to mortal form to help, which led to the occasional distraction. Shinala had forgotten how much fun mortal bodies could be. But eventually, she was ready. Now to see if the mortals arrived.

CHAPTER SIXTY-FOUR

NOTE

Note woke. He was warm, there was a roof over his head, and he was hungry. Turning his head, he saw he was in a small room with Rylix in a chair, the fire in the fireplace burning merrily.

"Rylix?" he croaked, his throat protesting at saying even that much.

The man jumped from poking the fire and turned to look at him, a smile spreading across his face. "Note. You have returned to grace us with your presence once again. My relief knows no limits. We were worried for a while that not even the glorious cuff provided by your gods could assist. The wounds were both deep and the claws of the ursoid were filthy." As he spoke, he got up and brought Note a cup. It was full of cold sweet tea and Note drank it, letting the wetness soothe his throat. "How are you feeling after your fight with the fearsome creature?" Rylix sat back down facing him, his eyes full of worry.

Note closed his eyes and assessed. With cautious optimism, he moved his torso, flexing the ribs on either side. They protested, but it was weak and something he could easily ignore. The rest of his body's responses were similar. Everything ached, but nothing absolutely hurt. Note let his eyes open and looked at Rylix. "I believe I am well. Though I would like the use of the needs."

The brilliant grin flashed across his face. "Of course, it would be my pleasure to assist you in that endeavor."

Note arched his eyebrow at the man, who shrugged. "Very well, maybe not pleasure, but I am most relieved you are well again. Assisting you to the needs room is preferable to cleaning up your wastes. Again."

It took them a full two fingers to get him to the needs, let him do a simple cloth wash, then dress before Note was ready to ask any questions.

"Where are we? What happened?"

"Not much to tell, or at least for this rendition, it can be briefly summed up. When telling my clan of our glorious adventure, it will be greatly enhanced. I am sure you remember the ursoid attacking?" Rylix asked as Note sat at the small table in the room. He had determined they were at a house, but it seemed void of personal items.

"Yes. We killed it?" Note remembered the beginning, but the end was blurry, though the flash of pain when the claws had raked through him was vivid.

"Yes. Though whether it was you or Jadaya is debatable. We were tending to you when Jadaya went out to find some greens and, hopefully, some herbs. Instead, Krostos, the leader of this village, found her and brought us back. They had an empty house, so they let us use it. Jadaya has been working with them to repair some things, using her height to reach areas beyond them. As for me, I have been sleeping in a small tent area we constructed in the back, this time with stone walls to anchor the tent. With that and some hot stones for my bedroll, I am well pleased."

Note felt his stress bleed off of him. "And the Mount?"

Rylix grinned. "When you are ready, we can go look at it. It truly is an impressive sight."

Once Note finished dressing for the cold weather, they decided to go find Jadaya. Though weak, he followed Rylix outside and stopped to stare at the mountain far across the bay. The Ged was right; the Mount was impressive, an almost perfect cone with sloping, golden land at the base. Rylix had mentioned it was still days away, and it made him realize just how big the mountain was.

They found Jadaya assisting with holding a girder up as men swarmed around her, fixing a roof. One of them turned to look as they walked in.

"Ah. The pale one has survived. You are well?" A large man with a smile spoke to him in Ged.

Note glanced at all the shades of brown from light to black with Jadaya in the middle and laughed. His silver-blue skin definitely qualified as pale in this company. "I am moving and hungry, so I will take that as an indication of survival." The men met his response with laughter and drew a smile from Jadaya.

"Then it is time to eat. Come, Jad, you have assisted greatly. Already I can smell the soup and bread." The same man spoke with casual friendliness.

Jadaya glanced up and cautiously moved her hand down, but the girder stayed where they had secured it. From the damage and the tree branch laying outside, it looked like a storm had ripped through and thrown the branch through the roof.

Note glanced at the village as they walked through. It was laid out in a circle, with houses of varying sizes circling around an immense stone fire pit in the middle. It had to be wider than Jadaya was tall. As they walked by, he saw proof of use over suncycles in the well-set stones, the forked spits for roasting, and the small bread ovens inside the ring.

There were two large buildings, one obviously a barn, at the edge of the circle. He could see their mustang in the fenced pasture, as well as some small woolies, jacks, and some horned long-furred animals he did not recognize. The barn was big enough to store food and all the animals, plus room for their fodder. Built of long timbers, he suspected it held the villagers' livestock and extra food stores. As they walked, he heard the barking of the huge shaggy dogs in the fenced area with the animals. One of the woolies bleated at it and went back to grazing. The scene was simple and made him miss Pelisic for a long breath.

It was obvious the villagers had carved this space out of the forest. The trees they felled to create their clearing probably built most of the houses and the barn. He kept inspecting everything, feeling off balance as they all knew him, but he knew no one. The other building, the one they headed toward, was long and low, built with the same type of wood as everything else. The base was created from stone and mortar, laid with the same rocks as the fire circle. The Vyklander led the way into the lodge, the other following with good-natured talking behind them. Note had no understanding of the language, but he recognized the tone. The one you had after a good day of fishing and were ready to head home to your family.

Inside the lodge were long tables with benches and a series of fireplaces at the far wall mixed with large brick ovens. Cut into the logs were shelves upon shelves with baskets set partially into the ground. Pots hung in the fireplaces and the smell wrapped around Note's stomach and squeezed. When was the last time he had eaten?

It did not take long before the three companions and the man sat down at a table, each with a bowl of thick stew, dark rich beer, and a chunk of bread served with it. The man waved at the three of them. "Eat. I will talk while we eat."

Note took him at his word and dug in. The rich stew seemed to fall into the dark pit that was his stomach. He used the bread to sop up the remains of the juice in the bowl and he thought he could have eaten more. But already a wave of exhaustion was crawling up his spine. The others ate their food at a more leisurely pace, making it quiet for the first part of the meal.

The man who spoke prior to eating set aside his spoon and looked up at them, his gaze taking Note in, as if assessing his health. "I think the wolf of hunger has been sated, at least for a while. I am Krostos, chief of this village and head priest for Ord. My wife is the priestess of Qian." His accented Ged was easily understood, if fumbling, like he had not used it much until now.

An icy chill started in Note's stomach, and for a moment, he thought he might be nauseous. He and priests did not have a harmonious past.

"We have talked to the gods, and they agree we are free to help you as we see fit. They are unconcerned about your journey and told us to treat you like any other traveler. So be it. What do you need and what do you have to trade?" The comments were just dropped there as if he was saying it would snow tomorrow.

Note glanced at Rylix who nodded. He would let the trader take the lead, though now he rather wished he had some fruist. The emotional mood swings were exhausting, and he suspected he could lay that at the feet of his wounds and recovery.

"We already traded the ursoid for your warm hospitality." Krostos nodded at Rylix's words, and Note got the feeling that much had been a given. "But we also have fragrant spices from far away, some exquisite fabric that was protected from the water, and some fabric that was affected by the sea water. I am willing to part with it at a deep discount." Rylix continued to list what remaining trade goods they had. Oddly, they were money rich and trade goods poor. Note had no idea how that would affect the next stage of their journey.

Krostos grunted. "I am sure the women would be much interested in the spices as well as the fabric. Water stains are easy to fix. The next question is, what do you want?"

The three of them glanced at each other, and Note was the one to speak. "We need to get to the Mount of the Gods."

"That is what I expected. But you can no longer sail there, though you could once." He spoke in a slow, thoughtful voice.

"You could?" Jadaya asked, leaning forward. She glowed with pleasure and Note wondered at that. It took him a moment to realize she was filled with joy at being needed. It was something he would have to consider as time went on.

"Yes. The old stories say that before the moon broke and Percit died, ships would stop and there was even trade between us and the Leonids. I think there was an old story of that trade as the reason for this town existing. But when the moon broke, and the goddess died, the tides changed. They became violent and would dash any ship to death upon the shores. That was when the currents became variable. It was at the same time the monsters moved in, attacking any ships that came too close to the shore." His eyes were dark. "They are still there, and every so often we will see them outside the bay, looking at us with hunger."

Rylix leaned back, looking thoughtful. "Now that he says that, memories spring to mind. There were old stories about routes that were stable all suncycle long and the trade it spawned. Then they faded away to deal with the currents that shift in the seasons and placement of the moons. If anyone ever linked the two — the breaking of the moon and the currents — it was not a story I heard, but then there are many legends that I have not been privileged to hear." He shrugged, but the pensive look did not leave his face.

"So, there is no way over there?" Note asked. The idea that they were so close, yet blocked, ate at him.

Kronos titled his head back and forth. "It is always possible you could get a ship from here to there, but I would not lay money on it." He paused, his eyes distant. "There might be one more option, though it is but a slim chance. Let me see if it can be presented to you at dinner."

Note sighed. Nothing was ever straightforward, but for now it mattered little. He was still too weak to travel, so waiting and planning gave him the time to get stronger.

"In the meantime, we have food to gather and animals to tend." He rose, and while he was wide and stocky, he was barely as tall as Note. He called out in Vyklander and the men finished their beers as the women teased and kissed them before sending them out.

"Go sleep more, Note," Rylix said with a smile. "Now that you are past the danger, I can work on showing the women the trades while Jadaya helps the men. Her height and strength make a difference for them in fixing storm damage."

Note had a spurt of desire to protest, but the food had settled in and that creeping exhaustion had seized him by the throat, demanding he sleep. "I will. Wake me for dinner."

Rylix nodded. "Of course. Now come. I will make sure you are in bed before I set up what we have. I hope the noise in the main room will not disturb you."

Note crawled into the bed, the door between the bedroom and the rest of the house shut. He heard voices and people come in, but then he fell deep into a sleep that made him oblivious to everything else.

CHAPTER SIXTY-FIVE

LAZUL

Lazul was unsure if he had become inured to the pain or if the new balance of drugs and fruist had made it bearable. Either way, he was doing better, and Actin had quit hovering quite as much. Though the presence of Hauyne helped a great deal. The major damage from Xyl's temper-tantrum had been fixed. The mood of the people was still darker than he liked, though. But at least the crops were coming in and the harvest looked like it would be the best in cycles.

He walked down the hall, the day mostly over. The fact that he could move and was looking forward to a quiet evening with Hauyne was a bonus. It was the first time in a while he felt like he still had energy at the end of the day. Often he woke up to her next to him, but they had not enjoyed any bed time, though it was obvious all the servants and the nobles approved.

There had been multiple hints as to when a good time for a royal wedding would be. The servants made sure their connecting chambers were ready for her, though she still officially stayed in guest quarters. He wanted to marry her, but he did not want to sentence her to a life of caring for an invalid. It was the only thing that prevented him. He had even gone through the royal jewelry to find a crown for her, but he had no necklace that matched her strength. It was something he would need to discuss with Actin about quietly having a custom one made. A necklace suitable to show you were the future queen had to be both elegant and impressive.

It was yet another thing on his list.

He pushed into the room that had become their parlor. While not completely private, most servants did not disturb them and it would have to be important before Actin would call him from here to deal with an issue. They should have a name for this room, so servants could reference it. Another thing to deal with, at some point. Lazul sank into his chair. A carafe of fruist and drugs were waiting for him. He poured a glass, added a tiny amount of opi, as he could feel the pain creeping along the sides of his mind, and settled in to enjoy some quiet time to think.

The problem of Xyl and the possible heroes still hung at the forefront of his mind. But since they left Fivika, there had been no news of them. Were they dead? If so, what did options did he have? The slow but steady shift to darker emotions in his people, along with the rise of domestic abuse, concerned him, but as long as Xyl acted like it was acceptable, it created a massive conflict between the temple and the crown. Women were equals, not chattel. He could increase the punishment for violence against women, but if the temple backed the abuse, how could he stop it? The only way would be stopping Xyl or changing him. But how?

His spiral of frustration and guilt at not being able to better help his people was broken when the door opened. Lazul looked up to see Hauyne walk in. In one hand was a notebook, the other a basket. She had a frown on her face that worried him. She rarely let her emotions slip onto her face, at least not in public.

"Is there an issue?" He set his glass down and sat up in the chair, dismissing a flare that shot through his body. Pain was becoming something he could ignore, like breathing.

She glanced at him as if she had been so intent on her internal thoughts she had been unaware of his presence. "Ah, good evening, Lazul. Issue? Maybe." She settled into her seat across from him. Some days, he thought her chair was too far away, but it made it easier to eat at the small table and see each other while they spoke. Besides, he rather enjoyed getting to watch her. She was striking, and the more he learned about her, the more beautiful she became.

Hauyne set the basket on the floor, and he glanced to see a pile of letters in it, while she set the notebook on her own little table. "I have received missives from all over the kingdom, mostly from women or servants in noble households." She paused and rose, coming over to pour a glass of fruist for herself. Hauyne settled back down, sipping the glass, but her attention was internal. "The number of women being raped has spiked and too many of them are pregnant. The idea of consent, of the loving relationship between man and woman, is being supplanted by the violence depicted in the temples. And the men are refusing to marry the women they have been with. If this state of affairs remains too long, the women are going to kill men in greater numbers than they already are."

"Already are?" he asked, surprised, wondering why none of his reports had this information.

She gave him a bitter smile. "It is easy enough to slip a knife into the heart of the man next to you in bed."

"Ah." He swallowed and took another sip. "I do hope to never inspire you to those lengths."

A flicker of amusement crossed her face. "I have faith that you are not so stupid as to think what he portrayed is the correct path."

Lazul let a wash of humor go through him before he sobered. "That means we are back to something needing to change soon."

Her blue eyes were bleak in her face as she looked up at him. "Yes. Or there will not be a country left worth saving."

"I might be able to offer you some hope regarding that," a voice said from the corner of the room.

There was only one way into this room, and the corner of the room held the fireplace that crackled with heat. In that corner stood a man, dressed simply in Ged style and looking at them.

Lazul sprang from his chair, whirling to look at the corner of the room. He almost crumpled as a gasp of pain was ripped from him at the movement. With a grunt of effort, he grabbed the chair as Hauyne moved in front of him, blocking any potential attack.

"*Guards!*" she screamed loud enough that Lazul winced.

"Peace," the man said, raising his hands. "They are unable to hear your call, and I mean no harm. I only wish to talk." His eyes scanned over Lazul and he sighed. "My brother truly can be cruel. Sit, before you fall."

Lazul froze at the words, and Hauyne turned her head to glance at him. The king sighed. "We might as well sit down. It is not like we could do anything to him."

Hauyne returned to her seat after she helped him sit down, but her eyes remained on locked on the god. The man moved over to where they could both see him easily. He gave them a bright, cheery smile. "Good evening."

Lazul looked him over. Not any of the peoples he knew, which really only left one option, given he called Xyl brother. "Cassix?"

"Shhh," he said, putting a finger to his lips. "I am trying to avoid his notice. His insanity makes him unpredictable, where the rest of my siblings care little about my presence in their lands." Cassix shrugged and looked between the two of them. "Am I correct in stating you are not pleased with the changes in your land and people?"

Lazul snorted. "This pain is one thing. What he is doing to my people is something else. They are becoming monsters. We were never the best, but we loved our families and protected and cherished our families. Now? Now they are thinking what is depicted on the temple walls is how they should act." His mouth twisted in disgust at the words. That his people should have fallen so far hurt.

"That is what I had hoped. Now on to the little band of heroes."

"Heroes?" Hauyne asked, her mouth still set in a hard line. Lazul knew that any man who hurt her would end up dead in short order. Yet another thing he admired about the woman.

"I think they will be." Cassix shrugged. "That or martyrs, though I would prefer the heroes. The dead rarely get much done."

With his fruist in his hand and the pain having been pushed back enough, he could think, Lazul focused on the traveling god. Of all the gods, Cassix was one who seemed to have no set interests. He popped up in stories occasionally, usually as a trickster, but Lazul had no idea what to expect from him. Aid? Or betrayal? "So they are coming? Will they kill him?"

"They are. They have some challenges to face, but already they are growing, becoming. As long as Shinala lets them live, I expect them to be here in less than a mooncycle." He paused and looked up at the ceiling. "Or two."

Hauyne stiffened at something Cassix said, but Lazul sagged in relief. Then the rest of the logistics settled into his mind. Getting them here was only part of the challenge. "And then what? Can they kill a god?"

"Oh, they will possess the tools, but your job will be to convince them. Right now, they primarily want to rescue the singers." Cassix cast a dark look at Lazul. "For which I do not blame them. Really, not only do you steal them from their parents, but then they suffer that level of abuse? Why would you not think it would be discovered? The biggest surprise is that it took this long."

Lazul blinked, then looked at Hauyne, who looked just as confused. Turning his attention back to Cassix, Lazul chose his words carefully. "I admit stealing the singers was never the right thing, and I am sure being away from their families is difficult. But I am unaware of any other abuse. The inspections prove they are well-fed, given pleasant rooms, warm clothes. In fact, I am sure they live better than many Charinsky."

Hauyne nodded, though he could see it was reluctant agreement, still keeping her eye on the god.

Cassix tilted his head. "Word of advice, be honest. They are slaves, not singers. They are prisoners. All the other words are simply excuses to not face what they are. But that is not what I mean. Your priests are some of the worst mortals I have seen. It does not surprise me they have flocked to his temple in search of power and the opportunity to slake their perversions on those unable to protest, or if they do, they simply disappear."

Lazul ducked his head, focusing on the fruist. The god was right. They used the title 'singers' as if it was something to be proud of, an honor. It was neither.

Then the rest of the sentence registered. He snapped his head up to ask more, but the god was gone, leaving him nothing but questions.

"Hauyne?" he said in a soft voice.

"Yes?" Her voice was just a quiet.

"What do you think he meant?"

"I am unsure, but rest assured, I will figure it out." Her voice had a hard edge, and he nodded. As much as he wanted to fling himself into the search for truth, his lack of energy made that unwise. This would be one more thing he entrusted to her. How would he manage without her?

CHAPTER SIXTY-SIX

JADAYA

Jadaya strode into the lodge hall. After two days of working with the men, they accepted her as one of them, though they still had issues with her being female. It seemed like Vyklanders had relatively rigid jobs for the genders, but they had not given her any issues about her not being with their women.

The question she puzzled over was it her height, strength, or skin color that made her fit in with the men, yet not the women? The odds were she would never find out. Note and Rylix were already sitting at one of the long tables in the lodge and she sat down opposite them. She cast a sharp eye over Note, but it looked like the nap had done him good or the cuff had time to finish healing him.

"You look like you feel better," she said, watching the women bring food to the tables. Generally, they sat in family groups with each wife getting food for their family and a few of the single women feeding the bachelor males and their guests.

"I do. Even the stiffness in my side is mostly gone." He scanned the hall. "What do you think Krosto meant about there might be a way?"

Rylix shrugged and smiled up at the young woman who put food on their table. The meal tonight was stew, bread, and fresh greens. Everyone reached for the greens first. The crunch and spicy sweetness eased cravings Jadaya did not understand, but then she could not remember the last time they had eaten fresh vegetables and then it had been a seaweed salad.

The hall filled with the sound of low conversation and eating. Jadaya watched and let her mind wander to the mountain so close. It had taken much effort to get here, and now there was no way to sail there. But Krosto had promised them a bit of hope. All she could do was wait, and patience had never been her strong point. But the food and fresh greens helped distract her. The youngest girls had gotten up to pick up dishes and take them to the washing area. She listened to their chatter and realized it was a time for them to talk and gossip when no adults were around to overhear, as they were still at the tables talking.

She let one of the young girls take her dishes with a smile and a nod. That caused giggling, then leaned back, waiting. It was the hardest part of everything. And they seemed to wait so much for things. As she watched the Vyklanders, Rylix leaned forward, his voice low and, to her surprise, he spoke in Aoisan. "What do you think they have for us?"

She looked at him with a raised brow and saw Note doing the same. "Are you worried about something?" Her voice was just as low and given that he was speaking in a language none of the Vyk probably knew it heightened her stress.

"Too many gods. Too many reactions. We are going to face the old gods? For some reason the end of this journey and what it meant never really occurred to me. It was the adventure of the journey I focused on. But now…" He trailed off, looking pale and discomfited.

Note let a small laugh slip out. "You mean now that we might face them? I heard more about them from the stories you told us at night than I knew existed. And now you become worried? Who are we to ask them for favors when our gods imprisoned them? At least you still worship them, so they might not kill you on sight."

Jadaya laughed with abandon. It was a full, rich sound and half the room turned to look at their table. She spoke in Ged, not caring about what others might hear or think. "We have come so far. The gods have already made their decisions, though mostly it has been to abandon us. Now I am willing to see if these the old gods will accept us. The worse that can happen is we die. And that has been a risk all along." She shrugged. "And the best? We change the world." She left her fears behind a long time ago. After all, her gods abandoned her, so why would she expect any less from gods who owed her nothing?

A hush fell, and her words echoed into it. The Vyk looked at each other, then nodded as if it was something they had expected. Note and Rylix watched her with wide eyes, and she just wanted to wave her arms around and yell. If nothing they did mattered, then what *did* matter? If they lost their lives on the foolish quest, then why not here? Why not face the old gods? Maybe they would be better than their children, who were cowards.

Motion grabbed her attention and, ignoring the expressions on Note and

Rylix's face, she turned to see Krosto stand and walk to the front of the hall. There was a low stage there and in the last few nights there had been singers or storytellers up there entertaining while the young women cleaned and the young men restocked the supplies of wood and food from the back storage areas and the water from the well.

He stepped on to the stage and a hush fell over everyone, broken only by the rattle of dishes and the grunt of young men as they moved heavy cauldrons of water to where the dishes were. People turned to look at him, including their little table. Was this what Krosto had promised?

When the attention was fully on him, he spoke.

"Many of us have met the travelers, though I have talked little about their ultimate goal. Now I will share it with you." He glanced over at his wife, who nodded her head.

It had struck Jadaya that the one thing the Vyk were not, were gossips. In Zuyika, everyone would have known every detail of their quest by this point. But here, even if people had overheard things, they kept it to themselves. It was an interesting cultural change. Most small communities hungered for gossip, but here they rarely talked about what their neighbors were doing. Instead, it was of the future crops, good harvest places in the woods, new techniques, tips, and tricks. Even the young ones talked about things, not people, though anyone with eyes would see who was sweet on whom. Subtle, the young ones were not.

But for all that, the anticipation as he spoke could not have been greater.

"They have come here on a mission to find the old gods and beg a boon." A murmur of astonishment washed through the room and more eyes turned to them, but Jadaya kept watching Krosto.

"As we all know, the mount is no longer accessible via the sea since the death of Percit." As one, everyone glanced up, as if they could see the broken moon hanging there. It was a constant reminder of the long ago battle that had raged across the skies and resulted in the goddess's death. With it had come the Tears of Percit, chunks of the moon that slammed into the ground. Even now, a fingerset of generations after, it was still spoken of in hushed tones, though no evidence remained of that legendary battle.

"But once it was, by land and sea. We know this, though not how, as we, the Vyk have never had need to visit. The knowledge has faded from our memories and now we have only songs. With that in mind, I ask for Qonia to sing the song Two Moons."

"No!" multiple voices rose in protest. It caught Jadaya by surprise. As a group, they were very giving and calm. For this level of worry, it must be something big. There was a rustle, and one of the older women rose.

Where the young women had light brown skin, long black hair, feet that could walk through fire and ice, and stout but powerful bodies, this old woman was the reverse. Her hair was a cap of white that lay across her head like a scarf, with lines in her face so deep that if she cried, the tears would never escape. She was thin to the point that clothes were tents on her bones, yet she stood straight and you could see the remains of what she had been.

"That is one of the sacred songs. We sing it only on the Day of Destruction. When the tears fell and people died, the storms came, and the waves never calmed. Why should we break with tradition to let outsiders hear it?"

Krosto shrugged. "It was not always tradition. It simply reminded us of what had been, so it became less common, then it was regulated back to only that day. We are the Vyk. We adapt to what is needed. Are you saying that we should not learn from what has gone before?" He focused on the old woman, but his words were for everyone.

"And if we give it to them, then what? If they let the gods out? Or destroy them? Do we have that right?" Her words were soft but clear. Jadaya found herself holding her breath. Would their quest end here, or was there a chance for them to continue on?

"Then they make their own decisions. Who are we to remove their choice? Do we not have the freedom to act as we wish without judgement from our gods?" There was a murmur of agreement. Ord and Qian were odd. They lived in a house in the deepest part of Vyk. They would help as a neighbor, but they had no laws or expectations besides maintaining good husbandry, taking care of your livestock, growing crops, and placing families first.

"But they are affected as well. What do they say about this?" Her voice was still quiet, but the anger had faded a bit.

"We say share. They are the pivot that will change the world."

The voice was feminine, rich, powerful, and came from a side wall. Jadaya whipped her head around to find the speaker. There, against the wall, were a man and a woman. The man was the same who had spoken to them on the beach, saw Pel begging. It answered the question that he was Ord. The woman next to him could have been twenty or a hundred suncycles. Her hair was liquid silver that ran down her back, her skin luminous even in the torch lit hall. A strong body, with hips that curved and caught the eye, yet there was an air of warmth and motherhood that radiated from her.

The hall had dropped to silence, and the old woman ducked her head. "I apologize, Qian. No disrespect was intended."

"None taken. I am glad to see there is discourse and people willing to disagree. In this case, there is nothing to protect us from. We know their objective, their goal, and we feel it needs the opportunity to occur. We will not actively help, but if our people choose to, then why should we oppose?"

There was something about the way those words were said that made Jadaya narrow her eyes. They were joyful. About the route, the gods, or what lay waiting for them at the end. At this point, Jadaya had given up trying to understand the machinations of the gods. They made little sense and worse, trying to understand them resulted in contradictions and headaches.

A soft undercurrent of sound swept through the room and the old one sat down, her duty done.

Krosto looked at them. "So we shall sing "Two Moons"?"

Qian smiled and Jadaya fought the urge to go to her, curl up in her arms, and let her hold her for all eternity. "No."

A frown flickered across Krosto's face and Jadaya felt a protest rise to her lips, but then Qian spoke again.

"I will."

An expectant hush washed over everyone as Qian walked to the front and Krosto offered her the dais before he went back to his seat. Qian stood there in simple leathers, her feet strong and callused as they tapped out a beat on the floor. The soft thuds filled the air with more power than Jadaya thought a simple wooden stage could provide. The young ones gathered as a group, sitting on the floor, excitement filling their faces at listening to their goddess sing.

When the beat wrapped everyone in it, pulling their hearts in time with her thudding foot, Qian opened her mouth and began to sing "Two Moons".

Two moons dance through the sky,
the goddesses keeping their eye
On us from the mortal plane,
Where their tears are the rain,
Their joy the sun,
Their anger the storms.

Two moons dance around the mount,
Pulling the water with them as they go,
Waves crash, splash, and drive before
The fish, the weed, the lives of the unwary.
Their teasing the waves
Their love calm seas

Two moons dance across the stars

Disappearing into the dark
Leaving us bereft without their light
Yet water low and smooth is
Their promise to return
Providing a path to what once was

Two moons circle the old gods,
Waves and monsters circle the world
Yet dark is the sky that shows the path
Calm is the water where monsters hide
Their hunger great yet assuaged
When the road is passable.

Two moons now broken hang in the sky
No more dancing or joy.
Rage eternal drives the waves.
Higher, harder, deadly are the storms.
Their sorrow is faces hidden
The way torn and broken.

No moons grace the sky.
Darkness broken by the sun.
Yet one chance this to see the gods
And beg for what can not be undone
Their prison is a pretense
Their children are still loved.

Once the moons danced
Now they cry at the price paid
While one lies dead and others rage
Yet still their parents lay entombed
Their love patient
Their rage unabated.

See them only when the moons
Leave to cry for what was, what
Was destroyed by strangers and greed
Seek the parents only in the dark
The way is long, the time is short
The path in the dark.

Two moons still dance, the waves
Pull and rage at their command
Only when they hide their tears
Can mortals see the land, the prison
The isolation of Leonaids.

CHAPTER SIXTY-SEVEN

JADAYA

Jadaya stood, the packs on her back. The villagers had agreed to keep the mustang for them with the understanding if they came back, they would reclaim it, otherwise it was theirs to keep. As no one seemed to believe they would be back, it was a good deal for everyone.

They had pored over the song Qian had sung until their yawns were more prevalent than their words. But by the next morning, they thought they at least had an idea. One night a mooncycle, both moons were gone from the sky. For Note that was when you went the furthest swimming as the seas were smooth. For Rylix it was a night to remember the gods, old and new. For Jadaya, it had meant little, but now they were betting everything on it.

Now, a tenday later, they stood on a beach at least ten fingers away from the small town. The villagers rarely came here as there was only broken stone, unending wind, and monsters from the deeps close enough to hit with a spear. The broken halves of Percit were sinking into the sea and Shio, the other moon and one of Delcoma's goddesses, had already disappeared from view. Even now, the waves were settling down.

It was a long walk to the mountain and at best they had ten fingers before Shio rose again. Already it was darker than usual, so they all held torches in one hand and a prodding stick in the other. Krosto could only tell them what the song had said, as it was sung in Vyklander, but it was obvious from the glimpses of spine and tail that there were monsters on either side of them. Barefoot was nonviable for any non-Vyklander. The stone would tear their feet to shreds. They were wearing cobbled together leather wraps around their feet to give them more flexibility, yet still protect their flesh.

"Do you see it?" Note's voice was a whisper. There was no reason to be quiet, but Jadaya felt the same. There was something about this part of the journey that felt different. It meant something. There was no veneer of trade or anything else. Here they were going to find the old gods. Something she had never heard of happening.

"I do," she said, her own voice low. Just under the water, a thin path of tumbled rocks was visible. But not ten hands on either side were the monsters. The darkness of the water implied it dropped off fast. She had zero doubt that if they slipped or fell, one of the beasts would be on them within moments.

Rylix closed his eyes and inhaled deeply, then let it out. "We should start. It is a long walk and one with a time limit."

"I should go first, Note last. He can swim the best of us and, if needed, can stay underwater longer. So hopefully if either of us slip and fall, he can grab us." Jadaya glanced at her two companions, and they nodded in agreement. "It is time," she said as the moon disappeared and darkness blanketed everything. She lifted the torch and stepped out into the water. The stones of the path were whiteish and reflected the light, but she had to concentrate to see them, the flickering flame lying about their position. Instead, she used the stick to verify where they were each step. She could hear the other two behind her as they moved into the water. Together they started across the underwater pathway, the splashing of the monsters to the sides the only sound.

The silence of no waves, only the occasional splash from the surrounding creatures, and her own breathing was more distracting than she had expected. But she kept moving. Each step was a treacherous balancing act between the currents, the slippery rocks, and the fact that she was unable to see where she was going, regardless of the torchlight. But moving step-by-step, she walked forward into the water, occasionally glancing behind to see the shore receding behind her. They had talked about tying rope to each other, but decided that if one of them slipped and a monster grabbed them or they started to drown, there was no reason to take all three of them. So for now, Note was their safety line in the fact that he could get in and out of the water faster than any of them.

Jadaya sank into a pattern for walking on the submerged road. Prod, step, balance, prod, step, balance. It felt like weapons practice, consistent and repeatable. When the pole sank into the water with the next step, she stumbled, thrown off her rhythm. She paused and started prodding, but there was nothing there. She lifted the torch higher and peered at the water. It took her a moment, but there, about twenty heads away, she could see the barely pale rock again. But in between where she was now and there, the path was completely gone. She turned and looked back. They were quite a few steps behind her, so she pitched her voice loud enough so they could hear her, but not so it sounded like a scream. "The path has a gap that we will have to swim to get to the next section. " She heard Rylix mutter something under his breath, but it was too soft for her to figure out what he was saying.

Note called back to her. "Do you want me to come forward and cross first?"

She looked at it again, but there were no other options. They would have to swim across. A quick glance to either side proved there were still sea creatures occasionally bobbing up and down on the calm ocean.

"No, I have to do it anyway, so I might as well go first." She stood there longer than she wanted to think about, trying to convince herself she could make it to the other side. Going fully into the water meant she would lose the torch. Jadaya could swim, but not well enough to be able to keep the torch out of the water. "Note, can you swim and keep the torch?"

"Possibly. I will try."

She nodded and dropped it. The sizzle as it hit the water and the darkness that followed made it feel even more treacherous. As long as she kept the pole, she could continue. Still she lingered as the shadows from the torches that Note carried came up behind her. She had to go. It was that, or they turned back.

The packs on their backs had been wrapped and sealed against the water, while their most precious possessions were in the waterproof bag that Note carried. Other than their clothes getting wet, she should be able to swim just fine. The problem was that word "should". One more deep breath, and she stepped off the edge.

The shock of the cold water took her breath away, and she floundered for a heartbeat, splashing more than what she wanted to. But then she found her pattern and swam towards the other side, holding the pole in her teeth. There was still a current, but it was simply a nuisance, not enough to pull her off course, and she found the other edge, in less than a quarter of a finger's worth of strokes.

She set the pole across the path ahead of her, wedging it into a crack so it would stay. Then she tried to climb back up onto the rocks, but they were slippery. Her clothes were wet; her bag pulled at her. After struggling, she got one foot up on the path. As she lifted herself up, the side of her calf dragged against one of the outcropped rocks. "Ouch," she gasped out in sudden pain as the rock cut like a knife blade, slitting right across her calf muscle. The salt splashing into it was a constant burn to add to the agony.

She finished pushing herself out of the water, then twisted to look at the back of her leg. Blood ran down her calf, streaming into the water. She would need to bandage it, but not until they got across. Jadaya raised her head to look at the others. "I made it without much trouble, but it will take effort to get up. Let me stay here and help you out, so you avoid getting cut like I did."

As she spoke, she noticed that the noise level around them was rising, and she turned her head to look at the sides of the path. Now, instead of one or two sea monsters splashing around, more and more were coming, circling around, agitated. She looked at the blood running down her leg and followed the trail to the water. It almost seemed like she could see the blood she had lost rippling across the waves toward the deeps. Her heartbeat doubled as she watched the monsters. She knew what predators could do once they had your blood scent. It made sense the monsters in the water would be the same.

"You have to move fast. They caught the scent of my blood in the water." It was too dark, and they were too far away. They would not make it. Her heart raced as she looked. "Rylix, move fast. I can lift you up onto the path if you come in on the side. You as well, Note. Hurry."

Her mouth went dry as Rylix tossed the torch and jumped into the water. His swimming was more ungainly than hers, which meant more splashing, and the creatures were coming closer. She grabbed her pole and shoved it straight down in a crack, wedging it tight so she had something else to pull on. Of the three of them, she was the strongest, but on slippery rocks, with monsters all around them, she would take any advantage she could come up with.

Rylix came up alongside the narrow path and she crouched, one hand on the pole, the other outstretched. He grabbed her hand in a firm clasp, and she heaved. Between the water in his clothes and the pack on his back, he was heavy, but she refused to be stopped when they had gotten this far. With a grunt of effort, she rose to her full height, still pulling him up. His feet scrabbled along the path, then he found leverage.

"Good. Now keep going forward. Move fast, I have Note," she ordered. For a moment, Rylix looked like he would protest. She cut him off. "Go. We will be running."

Rylix nodded and turned, moving down the path as fast as he could in the near total darkness. Jadaya turned back to look at Note. "Are you ready?"

He looked at the monsters that were heading toward them. "Too many monsters. Take the torch. Catch," he called and tossed her the torch. It wheeled through the air and Jadaya reached out to grab it, just as Note dove in.

Where with her and Rylix there had been splashing and noise, Note just cut cleanly into the water, disappearing in the darkness. Jadaya turned, holding on to the pole, the torch held high as she looked for him.

"Where are you?" the words were a muttered question or maybe a prayer, though to whom she did not know. As she looked, a flash of green scales went through the opening in the path, so wide it scraped against either side.

Jadaya wished fervently for another arm, so she could hold the torch, the pole, and a sword. As it was, she kept looking for the Aoisan.

"Here, pull." A few feet down the path, Note's head popped up, silver-orange in the torchlight.

She wrenched the pole out of the crack and moved forward to his position. She had just reached him when an enormous head rose out of the water behind him. "No!" She shoved the torch into his hand, the other still tight on the rocks. She dropped the pole. Jadaya reached down and grabbed the arm that held the torch with both hands and heaved up hard and fast. Note was significantly lighter than Rylix and fear lent power to her movements. He all but flew up as the monster's head came striking down where he had been but a heartbeat before.

"Run," Jadaya yelled, as she let him go and drew her sword. The movement was so practiced that she managed it, even with the slippery footing and a pack in her way.

Note danced backward, the torchlight making him seem like a silver apparition on the water. It distracted the beast a bit. Jadaya swung the sword down, lodging it in the creature's neck. It screamed, a high-pitched oily sound that hurt her ears. But its convulsion let her wrench the blade free. She crouched, grabbed the pole, and ran. Each step was a nightmare of balancing on slippery stones, slime, fear, and following a flickering figure.

"Behind you!"

She dropped to the path, the water splashing into her eyes and mouth as scales went over where she had been standing.

"Run," Note called and Jadaya pushed herself up, sword still held tight as she returned to her mad rush across the path. All of her focus was on the stones at her feet, the sounds behind her, and the thudding of her heart. Time disappeared and all that remained was the constant effort of staying on the path and moving, the splashing of her own feet drowned out only by her heartbeat.

She almost fell when the next step was sand that moved under her weight. With a sharp inhale, she stood and looked around. Note was standing there with the torch, Rylix leaning against a small cliff, and behind them creatures were tearing at the one she had wounded.

Jadaya looked at them, then moved over to collapse next to Rylix. She opened her pack; the water seal having worked well enough, and took out a bandage. Cleaning her wound with more salt water, layering a salve over it and wrapping it tight all gave her time to get her fear and heartbeat under control. Finally, she felt in control enough to pay attention to the two men.

"Are you both well?" She had seen no injuries, but that meant nothing.

They both nodded, pale in the torchlight, but it had shifted. On the edges of the horizon was the faintest hint of the sun. Dawn was coming. She looked up the cliff. A faint path, suitable for the fleet footed caprils, wound up it.

"We go up?"

"Are you well?" Note asked, his eyes looking at her leg, then her.

Jadaya shrugged with a laugh. "I would prefer if there is another way to get back. Though running headfirst seems faster, if more dangerous."

The two men chuckled and Rylix rose as they looked at the cliff left to climb. "Nothing to do but go up," Rylix said.

"Ever forward," Jadaya responded and started off. The warmth coming from the island was a relief after the coldness of the water. But first, they had to find the old gods. They had come so far. What was one little cliff?

It took effort, but compared to the path across the bay, this was simply exhausting and difficult, not terrifying. Jadaya reached the top first and used her strength to help the others up. The three of them stood there looking around, trying to figure out where to go.

A voice rang out in the clearing, full of power, "You have come to the Mount of the Gods. What is your purpose here?"

CHAPTER SIXTY-EIGHT

SHINALA

"They have started the crossing," one of her males said. Shinala lifted her head from the sand where she had been sleeping in mortal form. The sun felt different on furless skin.

"Finally. I was thinking their hearts had proved too weak to make the attempt. Will they have time?" Shinala looked up at the sky empty of the two moons that normally danced across it. But soon the sisters would come back. This she knew, but still it was like the day Percit died and the moon exploded. Anything could change what you knew. Hopefully, this change would not be as traumatic as that had been.

"If they move quickly, yes. Otherwise?" He shrugged in a feline movement that conveyed everything.

She agreed. "Very well. You know what to do."

"We are ready."

With that, she stretched, arching her hands over her head, then headed to the path. The last part was a cliff had a tiny trailed carved into it. Even she had trouble climbing it, which was why the Leonaids guarded the path from the top, not the bottom. She settled into a spot that gave her good visibility, yet ensured even if they looked right at her, they would never see her. She yawned and closed her eyes, enjoying the sun on fur free skin, waiting for them to arrive.

The sun had moved far across the sky before she heard them on the rocks.

"Put your foot there, Note. Now hold still. Let me get past you." The words were in Ged, and she savored the sound of it as she opened her eyes and yawned again before refocusing on the little cliff.

Shinala watched as they climbed up the last few feet of the rock face. It had served to disguise the path to their sanctuary, their prison. Now it let something new in. A thrill of excitement, something she had not felt in suncycles, rippled down her spine. This might be better than a hunt.

As she had waited for them, she had thought of the challenge. It had to prove they were worthy, yet not destroy them. Show what they would need for the journey ahead, yet not make them feel like they could not succeed. But most of all, they needed to prove they were worthy of the gifts the gods would help her make for them.

Cassix showed up and helped. Using him as a conduit, something she had never known was possible, she created something new, different, challenging. It should show their worth and give her a glimpse into who they were inside, not the outer face they showed to the world.

They reached the top, and it was time for her to act. Though Shinala was still unsure if she wanted them to succeed or fail. She heaved a sigh. Mortal form meant mortal emotions. Her saber form did not worry overmuch about things like this.

"You have come to the Mount of the Old Gods. What is your purpose here?" She loved this little area. The old lava tubes made her voice echo so well. It was half the fun of setting up the first challenge here. It would add to the confusion.

The one with skin as black as new-fallen night, the female, the leader Shinala knew, as only women were fit to lead, turned slowly, looking for her. "We are here to seek assistance from the old gods," the woman called out in Ged.

One of the men, one of Pel's people, if Shinala remembered correctly, stepped forward as well. "We want help to free captured Aoisans. I am trying to free my people from slavery." They both were so different from the mortals she had last seen. Before imprisonment.

The third, a Ged, hung back. Him, she eyed. They had changed little in the thousand suncycles she had been here. It was nice to see something remotely familiar.

"So? The gods were imprisoned here. Why should they help? Why should they care?" It was a good question and one she was rather curious to know the answer to.

"Because one of their children started all this. And we must stop him. But fighting a god is a losing battle. Unless we have help. This terrorizing must stop. We need aid to stop it." The woman again.

The Ged stirred a bit, his eyes scanning the area. "We ask because the siblings fear. We ask because the balance was broken when Percit was killed. We ask because we still are their creations, no matter how much their children have altered us."

"Ah, but you are Ged. You are the same as you were in the before." Her voice kept that distorted, echoing sound. This was entertaining.

"We have witnessed. We have watched. We know. The old gods still created us. I ask now for their aid."

Ah, there it was. The old form and the one request she could never refuse. The only people that were still faithful to her creators, even if their gods no longer responded, or at least not often. Given what she had done and seen in the past tenday, she suspected the gods were not as trapped as she and the children had assumed. The amount of magic they provided her to set this up gave lie to their imprisonment. But that was a puzzle for another lifetime. Now she had something to do.

"Then find them. Enter the tunnels and make your way to the heart of the mountain. If you survive, you can ask them yourself."

Shinala faded back and watched. If nothing else, it would give her much to think about for a while. A distraction. The chances of them finding her were nonexistent. Her skills had faded a little, and besides, it was one of her gifts, to be invisible until she no longer wanted to be. Not even the children could find her. Back in the days when she and her Leonaids played with and taught them. That insult still stung. That they had locked their parents up here, when she and her family were as much parental figures to them as the gods had been. It was too easy for the children to throw away toys, something they had never learned to not do.

That was the past, and now there was a new future opening up. One that had grabbed her curiosity. And curiosity and her were an interesting mix.

CHAPTER SIXTY-NINE

JADAYA

Jadaya looked at the two men as the voice died away. "Onward I suppose?"

Note smirked at her, though she saw his hand tight on his knife. "It is why we came."

"Who do you think spoke to us?" Rylix was still scanning the broken rocks and jagged entrances to the mountain, a frown creasing his brow.

Jadaya froze and looked around. "That did not occur to me. One of the Leonaids? Did your stories not say they were trapped here, too?"

"But those were words, not growls and hisses," Note whispered, still scanning the area.

Jadaya blinked at Rylix. "What were the Leonaids?"

"Large sabers from the legends. But they were servants, pets?" Rylix looked troubled as he thought about it. "Maybe they have changed?"

"Them or the legends?" Note asked, a slight smile on his face.

"Both?" Rylix answered with a matching smile. "I have no legends to cover this. It is unknown territory."

"Then I suppose it is off to explore the unknown," Jadaya said. The bandage around her leg was red, but it no longer trickled blood, so it would suffice for now.

Note nodded and together the three of them approached the tunnels. They looked nothing like mine tunnels, nor like anything mortals had built. The passage was shorter than Jadaya, so she walked with her head bent. The ground was a tumble of rocks, sharp and jagged, but there was a rough round shape to it. They had left the lone torch on the beach, and none felt like climbing back to get it. A low light came from some lichen growing on the sides, barely enough to see by, but for now it would do. With Jadaya in the lead they moved into the tunnel, the only sounds their footsteps and breathing.

After they had been walking for a finger, a light glowed ahead, as well as an increase in warmth. Jadaya slowed her walk, but kept moving, regretting not having her pole. The idea to draw her sword niggled at the back of her mind, but until there was actual danger, she worried walking with it drawn would be seen as aggression. Which left her walking with her head ducked and trying to see in the faint light.

The tunnel widened into a large chamber, and she stepped in, breathing a sigh of relief as she straightened. She went in three steps and stopped, waiting for Rylix and Note. The tunnel she had come out of was shadowed, while the light in this chamber came from a few small cracks that let sunlight in. No one came out behind her. Frowning, Jadaya moved back to the tunnel and peered in, but no one was there.

"Rylix? Note?" Her voice echoed around her, but there was no response. Her pulse raced as she pulled the sword and turned, looking for something, but the worst part of it was there was nothing. No sound, no companions, just her in a cavern with two tunnels. One she had come out of and another ahead, just as dark and oppressive.

Now what do I do?

"Continue down your path, warrior. Your challenge awaits." The same voice that spoke earlier filled the cavern and Jadaya spun, looking for the speaker.

"Where are they? Where are Note and Rylix?" Her voice was low and dangerous as she tried to figure out what to do.

"Continue." The voice still echoed in such a way it was impossible to tell a direction.

Jadaya stood peering at the tunnel. She took a step in, but while she could see a short distance, much further back than they would have been, it was empty. Backing out, she looked around again, but it seemed to be the same cavern. The other tunnel, crack in the wall more accurately, loomed in front of her.

She could go back to the beach, but then what? At this point, her companions were gone and all she could do was hope to find them in the end. Taking a breath, she moved into the crack, the ceiling high enough she did not stoop. The light here was the same, but the air was warm and moist. Moving forward, the ground gave underneath her and she fell with a bone-jarring thud to the bottom. The fall knocked the breath out of her, but that was all. When she stood, Jadaya realized she was far enough down, that with the crumbling edges of the opening above, there was no way to get back up.

Growling mostly to herself, she examined her new location. It looked like a room someone had carved into the mountain itself. There was a rough table made of driftwood, a stone bed with a golden yellow hide on it, and two rooms with curtains preventing her from seeing into them. But she saw no way out. She looked again, but any exit must be behind the curtains or climbing back up, which would be difficult. Jadaya pushed away the curtain on the right and fought back a sob. It was a door back to Zuyika. The warm sand smell flooded her nose, the spices she had missed so much, the dry heat. On a chair in the room was her old uniform. The familiar grooves, color, feel of the leather. But what made her knees go weak was Yika walking toward her.

Part of her mind knew there was no way for this alcove in a mountain to open to Zuyika, but her heart told her it did. And her goddess was walking toward her. Jadaya fought back tears. She had believed she would never see her again.

"Jadaya. We were wrong. We need you again. Come back to us. Take your position again in my private guard. We were wrong to dismiss a Chosen like you." Yika gestured to the uniform laying there. "Let this silliness go and come back to us. It will be like you never left."

Her hand reached to for it, to be Zuyikan again, to be home. Halfway there, she stopped. "Never left?" she asked quietly.

"Of course. Everything will be the same. You belong here." The normal arrogance and assurance were there in Yika's voice. Jadaya turned her head, her body still reaching for the uniform.

"The same?"

"Yes, nothing will have changed. You belong here." Yika smiled. It was the warm, loving smile she had craved when she was serving. The smile that said her goddess had noticed her and found her pleasing. The smile that you leaned into when it was granted to you.

For a moment, the child she had been pulled at her hard. Then images flashed through her mind, the stories from Rylix, learning new skills, how to swim, Note's story, their journey, what they were going to do. To walk away from all of that. Leave the Aoisans as prisoners of a mad god. She would go home and it would be undone? What would that make her if she quit and walked away, knowing what happened to children under Xyl's disinterest?

"You can have your lover back," Yika said, and Elike walked up. Beautiful and smiling at her, the smile that welcomed her home.

Her heart spasmed, and she leaned forward, aching for Elike's touch. Then she pulled back, shaking her head.

"No. You made me an Exile. I am not Zuyikan anymore. You ensured that. You made my lover, Elike, betray me to save me. I am no longer yours." She waved at her body, her skin not the same shade as Yika's pure black but instead a charcoal, her eyesight faded, and the brand on her face telling the world her gods had rejected her.

Jadaya matched word to action and stepped back out. Shaking, she stood there a long time, but when she thought she had her emotions under control, she went to the second room and pulled back the curtain. There a single torch blazed away, waiting for her, and a tunnel, darker than Yika's skin, gaped open.

Jadaya looked once more toward the other room, toward her home and her former goddess. Then she picked up the torch and stepped into the tunnel, moving forward. Choosing the unknown.

CHAPTER SEVENTY

RYLIX

U p ahead, Jadaya stepped out of the tunnel into the light, disappearing for a second. He rolled his shoulders as he stepped forward into the cavern, only to find himself in one of the Ged tents with his mother, Gelza, sitting there, looking at him with the 'I know what you did' look that always terrified him and his siblings.

Shock stole his tongue as he stared at her, heard the noises of mustangs and jacks, of kids running around, of food cooking, the smell of his favorite meals, and the feel of the air in Fivika near the ocean. "Madar? What?" His world felt like it had been knocked askew and he turned, looking for the tunnel back, but all he saw were tent walls and two hallways.

"It is about time you got here. Are you quite through with your foolish journey? Trying to appease your guilt?" Her voice was sharp and exasperated, which threw him. He rarely experienced that side of her tongue.

"Foolish?" His pride was stabbed even as he flinched. "The information sent back was not enough to justify the new trade routes?" He had sent word back at Hearth and the first town in Vykland. He had hidden nothing in his notes and while the sea monsters had been unexpected, still the route would be a good one if it could be established without needing to ship the animals across from Fivika to Vykland.

"Yes, yes. It is, why do you think you are here? The Gather is almost on us, and then we need you to take that as an established route. Are you ready?" Her tone was still dismissive and as if he had been doing something stupid.

Rylix's eyes widened. "I am being assigned the route?"

Gelza lifted her eyes to the sky. "Of course. You set it up, now are you ready?

It will be announced at the Gather and a new wagon is being created for you." She gave him a dismissive glance. "The death of Kryx has been forgotten, so let it be."

Rylix felt like she had slapped him repeatedly. He had been aware vaguely that a Gather would occur while he was gone, but that had been fine. His fortunes were not established yet, so he had little to offer a prospective partner. "But I thought…" he trailed off. The normal scheme was to have the young ones, like him, try routes, see if they were steady, then set those with families and verifiable routes on them. His route in Aois had been given to a near-cousin with a wife and two children. But Kryx?

"Thought what? That you could mourn your own stupidity for all time?" She rolled her eyes. "It is in the past, and we need children to support the clan. It is time for you to find a partner. Now go," she said, pointing to the hall on the left. "Lanyx is waiting to get you set up and present your accomplishments at the Gather." She paused, looking at him. "Unless you still think the Aoisan's silly quest is worth your time and will remove your guilt."

Rylix bristled. "It is not silly. Those Aoisans are being stolen and made prisoners at the whim of a god that is going insane. How is wanting that to change silly? And I will always carry the guilt. My inattention let her die. It is my fault."

Gelza crossed her arms under her breasts and stared at him. "Please. You were stupid and busy showing off with friends. She decided to sneak out to play sea Ged and drowned. Move on. And since when do Ged care about the doings of the new gods?"

Her words brought back the image of Kryx washing up on the shore, after three fingers of searching for her, ever more frantic. He had been showing off, talking to friends about the idea he had, ignoring the little girl he was supposed to be watching. "It is my fault she died. My inattention. Helping the Aoisans will go a long way to making up for the loss of her future. The Charinskys are breaking the laws we all live by. No slavery. No hurting children." He avoided mentioning that these were the gods that had imprisoned theirs. Why should they let them do even more harm?

"Slave is stretching what they are. Prisoners maybe, but that has always been allowed. And children cry at nothing, most of their hurts are forgotten in fingers. And we all know if you break the law in another country, your gods will not interfere," she said with a dismissive air.

"And what law did they break? They were stolen. They are children. What have the Ged become that we will stand by and ignore something like this? Something that even in the before times was forbidden. When do we dismiss death and pain so easily?" Rylix had his fists clenched, and his heart pounded in his throat at the casual way his mother had erased the horror, dismissed his guilt. Was this how it had lasted for so long? Their people were unaffected, therefore it was unimportant.

Gelza shrugged. "What we have always been, neutral. The squabbles between the children are not our problem. We follow the old ways and our gods are imprisoned."

"There is neutral and there is willfully blind." The remembered conversation he had overheard, what the boys were subjected to, the abuse — emotional and sexual — to both genders made him sick to his stomach. "No person, regardless of their god, should allow this."

"Then begone with you," she snarled, flicking her hand to the left. "If you leave, I renounce you. I have no need of a child that puts strangers above his people. I should have known when Kryx died that you were worthless."

Rylix looked at her, part of his heart breaking. Something cherished and valued deep inside had just been shattered past all recognition. "And I have no need of a family that values money over the lives of innocents. One that ignores my own grief." Without looking back, he headed to the hall, blinking back tears that blurred his vision. Between one step and the next he was in a tunnel, the sounds and smells of life in the Ged a whispered torture that faded away.

Rylix sucked down deep breaths, trying to regain his calm. Neutral yes, indifferent no. The Ged were there for any disaster, often helping as much as the gods. There was something about a person feeding you when your house had burned down that meant more than the god replacing your house. He let out a shaky breath and blinked to reveal a tunnel with a room glowing red ahead. He turned to look behind him, but there was nothing, just a solid wall. Deprived of any choice, Rylix continued forward, but his heart still thudded with anger and pain.

CHAPTER SEVENTY-ONE

NOTE

Note watched Rylix step into the cavern in front of him, disappearing as the light blinded him. Note glanced behind himself one more time shaking his head. He saw no one, but it still felt like he was being watched. Too many suncycles of living under the control of others, and he could always tell when somebody's eyes were on him. Not that he knew who they were at this moment. Finally, unable to see anyone, he stepped into the chamber to find a Char guard standing there, leering at him.

"Oh look, here's one of the singers. They must have gotten away from us. Boy, get back to your bed. You should know better than to be out here alone." Rage flashed through him at a level he never remembered feeling before. Even hearing those horrible words, 'a singer', made him want to scream. His hands dropped to his daggers, and he lunged at the man, not even bothering to speak. All of his attention was on the guard, but from Note's memories, the guards had been in better shape than this one, or maybe that was just the view of a child versus an adult. Either way, the guard went down quickly.

He stood there over the dead body and heard the laughter of more men, accompanied by the clink of cups and dice associated with gambling coming down from a passage. A sneer crossed his face, and he took a step towards it. He held the knives, still dripping blood, ready to take vengeance when the smallest whimper had him turning his head.

In the small cavern's far corner were two children. They were all but invisible, huddled together, holding each other tight, with eyes wide as they looked from him to the body lying on the ground. Note stood there watching them.

Jadaya and Rylix should be here. There had not been enough time to take out both of them—Jadaya was too good. But he was alone, again. The laughter, hoarse, mocking, and all too familiar, drifted down the tunnel. His hands hurt from holding the knives so tight. But the children just whimpered and pulled back from him as he moved toward them. Taking a slow, controlled breath, he stopped to clean the knives on the shirt of the dead guard and slipped them back into their sheaths. With a single glance down the corridor where the others were, he walked over to the children and crouched, looking at them. They were so young. Had he been that young once? Those memories had been erased by time and pain. The time he spent as a singer felt like time out of a nightmare, something to be avoided. "Are you hurt?" He asked quietly in Aoisan.

They shook their heads frantically, their silver-blonde hair floating around them. Note looked around the cavern. There were three options. He could take them toward the other sounds, so familiar and so taunting for the opportunity for revenge they promised. He could take them back out to the beach, but then they were trapped between the sea and the mountain. Or this third tunnel that seemed to call with hope. Hope that was probably a trap.

"Do you know where you came from?" They both pointed towards the tunnel, the tunnel that he knew had to be the wrong choice. His distrust had no reason to it, and it was the only one with a nebulous outcome. They sat there for what seemed like a long time, unsure of what to do. But no matter how badly he wanted to go kill every single one of those men, of those women, of the priests and priestesses who hurt and used him, it was more important to take care of the two children in front of him now. Letting the dreams of vengeance fade away, he stood, holding out his hands. "Come. Come with me. I will get you to safety."

The children looked at him and looked at each other. Silently, one on each side of him, they took hold of his hands. He squeezed them tight, feeling the tiny, fragile bones in his grip. His mind raced as he tried to figure out what was going on. How did they get here? Where were his companions?

All he had were questions and no answers. With a sigh, he stepped into the tunnel, and their hands slipped away from his. Note spun trying to find them. Had someone grabbed them? Had they been taken from him? There was just emptiness in the tunnel with him. He took two quick steps back into the chamber, but now there was no third tunnel, just the one that he had come from and the one he stood in.

"What is this? Where are my companions? What have you done to them?" He stood glaring at the unresponsive walls, but other than the echoes of his words from the chamber, there was no answer to his demands. Note fought to get his emotions under control, but finally he turned and continued to walk down that tunnel, the tunnel that led away from the beach. The tunnel that had to lead him somewhere. But his hand still kept reaching for two tiny ones that were no longer there.

CHAPTER SEVENTY-TWO

JADAYA

Jadaya kept walking, and after another finger, she found herself stepping into a large chamber. Heat radiated out and sweat ran down her back. Liquid stone ringed the solid rock, flowing around it like a river. The heat coming from it was worse than a forge. If she looked up, above her was a glimpse of light, faint and far away. Around the solid stone, on the other side of the moat of liquid rock, were six alcoves, of which five held a crystal wall and it looked like something or someone was held behind the crystal. These details were all immaterial compared to the huge white saber that waited in the center of the stone peninsula.

In Zuyika, before being elevated to guard for Yika, Jadaya had done a hunt or two for sabers. They were fierce fighters; their pelts, claws, and teeth were highly prized. But they were rarely hunted unless they were attacking people, because even a group of twenty Chosen could easily lose half in the fight. But this saber made all the ones Jadaya had ever seen look like a kitten. With its forelegs stretched out before it, belly on the floor, and hindquarters tucked neatly underneath, the saber's head still came up to her ribs and Jadaya knew when the saber stood it would almost be able to look her in the eyes. It had fur whiter than the sands and eyes the color of green gems.

The saber glanced behind Jadaya and the scent of salt and smoke she associated with Note wrapped around her.

"Note?" she asked, unwilling to take her eyes from the deadly saber

"Yes. Is Rylix with you?" He stepped up next to her, so she could see him in her peripheral vision to her left.

"No. You all disappeared."

"Oh, excellent. This is the location you both ended up in. I will admit I was a tad … what in the name of Aryix is that?" Rylix's voice came from behind them and a moment later he was on her right as all of them stared at the white feline.

Jadaya had her hand tight on her sword. She knew she would die if the saber attacked them, but she refused to let her companions be hurt. When the saber stood, they all stumbled back a pace. Jadaya was disheartened to see she had been right about the creature's height. They were all dead.

The creature took two paces toward them, then its body flowed and shifted and a woman stood in front of them. Thick, white hair in braids was gathered at the back of her head, while her skin was a shade of pale white, the color of bleached bone Jadaya had never seen on a person before. She stood naked in front of them, at least the height of Jadaya and just as muscular. The only other oddity was instead of two breasts, she had two that were globular like a normal female, but then six more nipples, three on each side, ran down her stomach. And her eyes were white. Not clouded like the old might get, but instead of a brown or green iris, hers were white with a black pupil.

"You all passed the first tests," she said to them in Ged, her amber eyes tracing over them. "Now to pass the final test." She turned and waved at the crystalline walls over the alcoves. "The old gods are there. Imprisoned until Aria breaks. Call one of them out. Prove to me that you are favored by them."

Jadaya's entire body clenched at that thought. "What?" she managed staring at the naked woman. "You want us to awaken them?"

"How else would you prove they approve of your request, of your mission? Do you think they easily help those that want to kill their child?" Her voice was oh so reasonable, and Jadaya could detect nothing in her tone.

"Their child put them in here, tried to kill them," Note responded, his voice dark.

The woman tilted her head. "True. But you always love your child, even if you might not always like them. Call them."

Jadaya glanced back at her companions. While she had not thought it would be easy to gain the assistance of the old gods, part of her had assumed they would commune via dreams or something. Not actually wake them up.

"And if they respond? If they free themselves from their prison?" Rylix asked, his voice shaky.

She shrugged. "Then they wake and take their proper place again. Where they belong."

Rylix had a wild look in his eyes. Jadaya fought to keep her knees straight and looked at Note. For her, this was a quest, a chance to find her way in the world. For Note, it was personal. She pressed her lips together and nodded to

Note. In the end, it had to be his decision. They were his people who suffered. His childhood that had been perverted.

"And when they take their place?" His voice was so quiet only the amplification of the chamber allowed her to hear it at all.

"They punish their children and take back what was theirs." The woman's voice held no emotion. It was a statement of fact.

Rylix turned to his companions, placing his hand softly on Note's shoulder. "It would be war. God against god with all the peoples as pawns. They would destroy the world, the countries. By the time they were done, there would be no one left to rescue. And if the mad one is drawn up to fight? There is no telling what he might do in his grief and anger upon seeing his parents."

Note bowed his head, his fists white tight around his daggers. His head remained bowed as he spoke. "Is there no other challenge, no other way? I will give you my life here and now. Let you kill me with no word against it."

The woman shook her head. "No. You must call one out, prove they honor your attempt. It is their son you will need to kill to achieve your goal after all. Unless he is dead, the plight of the singers will never stop." Her voice was calm and remorseless.

Fear and panic beat a double tempo at Jadaya's throat as she looked at the figurines. Just the idea of waking them up made her sick. They were unable to wake the sleeping gods. Right?

Rylix reached out and squeezed her shoulder. She jumped at the sudden contact, but turned to look at him. "Let me try something first, please."

Beside him she could see Note, his face bleak. She glanced at him, but he nodded his assent. Rylix moved further out towards the woman. Jadaya wondered what he was going to do, as it looked like he had his eyes closed. He seemed to look internally, then about five hands lengths from the woman he knelt on the ground. Jadaya swallowed, but she made no protest as Rylix began to speak.

"Aryix, first of the gods, made from the land, I seek your wisdom. Quas, fallen from the darkness above, I seek your guidance. Lyx, of the sky and wind, I seek your vision. Stari, born of the sea, I seek your creativity. Gela, of the earth and flames, I seek your passion. I, Rylix of the Ged, ask that you hear me."

To Jadaya's mingled astonishment and horror, the five crystal cocoons glowed as if the being inside had awaked and focused on Rylix. It was an almost physical sensation, and she felt both honored and terrified.

Rylix's eyes were still closed as he continued to speak. "I and my companions are on a mission to save the captured Aoisans. They are ripped from their parents and exposed to things no child should ever experience."

Note, who had moved over to stand next to Jadaya, stiffened at those words, but he said nothing.

"We can not solely blame the Charinskys for this. They are driven by the madness of your son, Xyl." His voice was smooth and held a power that Jadaya had only heard from him when telling the old legends.

It felt like the chamber held its breath when Rylix said his name.

"Because of that, we may need to kill him to save the captured Aoisans. I beg your approval of this endeavor and ask that you bless it so that we may have a chance of succeeding." He ended by placing his hands and head on the floor for a long breath, then sat back up, his eyes finally opening.

Each of the crystals glowed with a flickering intensity and a warmth surrounded Jadaya, like a breeze from the plains on a cold evening. Warm and full of scents and promises of the Ripening season to come.

"I am impressed. It has been many, many cycles since I have heard the prayer of the old form. But still you must awaken one to receive the depths of their blessings." The woman's face told her nothing. She just watched them, but maybe her voice was softer, warmer now.

Rylix returned, looking both rejuvenated and despondent at the same time. "I hoped that would suffice. It seems not."

Jadaya turned to look at Note and saw Rylix doing the same. In the end, it had to be his decision. She would go with whatever he said.

Note stepped forward, his face a carved symbol of rage. He only moved a few paces in, close enough a leap could bring him back to them. "What you ask is the death of thousands. No matter my rage, I will not sentence even more of my people to death. I refuse." His words fell hard and empty on the floor and everything stay silent and unmoving. With a jerk, Note spun on his heel to face Jadaya and Rylix. "We are done. My people will live in captivity and slavery, but I will not have multiple countries' deaths on my shoulders."

Jadaya's emotions swamped her with a wave of relief and guilt and anger, all mixed into one roiling ball. Anger that they would ask them to do such a thing, anger that the Char would still be allowed their predation. Guilt that she was relieved that they would not be waking up the old gods. The war between them and their children would be devastating to everyone, but now. Now the Aoisans would always live in fear and there would probably be a war between those two nations. Everywhere she looked, she saw death and destructions. Something that if they had defeated Xyl, might have been averted.

She looked into the eyes of Rylix and Note, their own reactions mirroring hers. Jadaya set a hand on each of their shoulders. Words seemed too meaning-less at this moment. Their hands rose and mimicked her gesture, the three of them a solid triangle, supporting each other when there was nothing more they could do. Some prices were too high, no matter what.

As if reading each other's thoughts, they let their arms drop and turned to face the naked woman. Her head was tilted as she looked at them.

Jadaya spoke for them. "We are done. Let us leave."

Her voice echoed around the chamber, and the crystals glowed in a bright pulse that had her squinting. For a heart stopping second, she thought the gods in them would awaken.

"Interesting. It seems you have wisdom as well. The gods agree. You will receive their blessings. They especially enjoyed hearing the old prayers, Ged. It has been a long time since anyone prayed to them where they could easily hear." The woman's voice broke the tension, and Jadaya could only stare at her.

It was Note who found words first. "Does that mean you will help us?"

"It was all a test?" Rylix said almost before the last syllable had escaped Note's mouth.

"Everything is always a test. But you three passed. And the gods have given me permission to help you." She gave them a smile. "My name is Shinala. Follow me." With a small smile she turned and walked by them, headed to an opening that Jadaya would have sworn had not been there but moments before.

The three of them looked at each other, then Note's mouth quirked up on the left. "They are going to help. We are getting help to do this." The relief in his voice both elated and worried Jadaya.

They were going to do this.

CHAPTER SEVENTY-THREE

SHINALA

The three mortals followed her out of the cave. It amused Shinala to see them looking around with wonder as they exited and came out on the plain where she and her pride had existed for countless suncycles. Various males were sprawled out in saber form, enjoying the sun, flexing their muscles and showing their teeth.

Shinala kept her amusement to herself, but she approved of the mortals' automatic reach for their weapons. That was a good thought, if useless. She had no doubts they would fight well, but her pride had spent so long practicing they fought on muscle memory. Then there were the secrets that only the Leonaids still kept.

She headed over to the prepared forge. The materials provided by her gods were there waiting for her and the mortals. "Here." She waved at the forge, heated by the magma from the mountain. "This is where the blessings of the gods will be made physical." Her eyes traced over each of them. "You," she said, pointing to the female with skin darker than Aryix. "What is your name?"

The woman cleared her throat. "I am Jadaya. The Ged is Rylix, and the Aoisan is Note."

Shinala filed each of the names away. They felt right, and she watched them stare at her, wisely unsure if she was friend or foe. "Very well. Warrior, come here." The woman moved toward her, glancing around as if Shinala might shift and attack her. Which was possible, but not in her plans at the moment. "Lift your arm." She had Jadaya move through positions, measured the length of her arm and then her body. The weapon she needed to form was a sword that had a long enough hilt to support both hands but weighted such that she could use it one-handed. But she would require arm bracers and an earring to make it complete. But the bracer needed to be more than that. Ideas flickered through her mind as she ran through options. Each of the gods had their own strengths, and placing their gifts in weapons was not always the best option. She would force Cassix to help her enchant the weapons she made. He had to be good for something, after all.

"Aoisan. Here." She dismissed Jadaya with a wave of her hand as the pale male came up. "Show me how you use these knives."

His lips narrowed as he stared at her. She simply waited. Shinala knew what she was and her strengths. These mortals could not match her. Not until they had what she would make for them. He nodded and pulled them from their sheaths, lightning fast, then attacked an invisible enemy.

She watched for a moment, then spoke. "Hmm, can you throw them?"

The Aoisan stopped his fight and shook his head. "They do not fly well. The balance is wrong."

"Very well, go. Ged, here."

The three of them exchanged looks, but then the Ged, Rylix, came up and she studied him. "Blowgun and stars?"

He blinked at her, obviously surprised, but then nodded.

Those were hard to make with any value because they were easily broken or lost. Perhaps there was another way. The other two were fighters. The Ged was not. "Are you skilled with a whip?"

"As a young man, I used one for rounding up the jacks and mustangs. At that time, I was good with it." He sounded unsure, but they would have time to practice. It was the only thing she could think of as trying to train on something with no skill previously would take too long. And a bow, while useful, did not work well in close quarters. She always fought up close and personal. What type of fight was it if you did not feel your enemy's blood on your fur?

"Go." She lifted her head and stared at her males. "Show them where to stay, distract them. This will take me a few days." With that, Shinala turned, grabbed an apron that hung there and threw it on. While she was all but immortal, the burning embers and sparks still hurt and could cause her to flinch at the wrong time. The apron was created from the skin of one of the sea monsters, so it was thick and flexible. It worked well as a forge garment. That was something else she had no need of in a long time, garments. She snorted as she stoked the flames. What need had she for clothes?

As the images of what she needed to create bubbled in her mind and inspiration filtered through her, she piled up ingredients in different combinations. The last creations she had made lifetimes ago for the children of her makers had been lost or destroyed. The children sacrificed those items to create the prisons that held their parents. As far as she knew, there were only a few of her items still in the world. Cassix had the never-ending water flask, and the necklace of death was lost when Percit died. There might be one or two others somewhere, but they were small things.

A brief tremor of anger swept through her. As far as she was concerned, Percit's death was still unexplained and unavenged. While they locked up the culprit, there was no punishment. Percit had been nicer than most of the children. She had prepared the alcove for the Usurper, but instead they had locked him at the bottom of the sea. The logic behind that was still unknown to her, but if he broke out, she would not give them the option to keep her from the hunt. She would have revenge.

That thought was distracting, however. Instead, she went and pulled out her metal. Some were chunks of ore from the death of the moon. While the moon was not and never had been Percit, it had been her domain and her icon. It was only fitting that she should help stop the damage her death had caused.

Next, she needed the blood of the gods. It was not blood as most thought of it, but crystals that formed at their feet, created from the secretions of their bodies. When powdered and added to liquid metal, it made it almost shatter proof when the final tempering in salt water was done. Then she would need iron. She still had ore from what the mountain spit out when the gods were imprisoned. It would do.

Sword first, she decided. Long ago, when they made her, she realized she knew how to create things for a person. Be it weapon or jewelry, it was always one of a kind and somehow perfect for the person to use. It had been a long time since she got to stretch her skills. They were bound to be slow and rusty.

Lifting the enormous cauldron into the fire, she dumped the iron, a few titanium bars, copper, and the powder the gods had provided into it, setting the crystal aside. First, the metal needed to be purified from dirt and other material that had no business in a sword. While it heated, one of the Leonaids had smartly stayed behind to work the bellows. She went to her sandbox. When she had first created it suncycles ago, Xyl had laughed, asking if that was where she emptied her bladder. It was one of many reasons why he never received one of her creations. She went and pulled a bucket of water from the sea and dumped into the sand, spreading it evenly until it was wet and solid.

Then she began to cut, scrape, dig, smooth a shape into the sand, until she had the rough outline of a sword and hilt put into it. The final shape would resemble that, but her magic would make it into something special. For now, a piece of metal the right length and width made the process go faster. It would be enough to match what the woman needed.

Shinala replicated the mold for two axes. Something whispered in her mind, and she created a third, though she had no idea why. Then she dug out a shape for a dagger. Last was a series of curved shapes that mimicked a bird in the air. A flat square piece and an earring were simple metal shapes that she would shape later with finer tools.

Back at her crucible, she grabbed a long metal rod and stirred the melting slush, watching the chaff burn away. She had to move fast or what was in there would melt the rod. It was looking good. Soon she could pour, then shape. Heat and fumes wafted up in her face, mixing with the salt of the sea and the sweat of the male near her. For the first time in a long while, she felt alive and interested in her actions. Shinala, huntress of the gods, leader of the Leonaids, was forging again. Laughter rang out across the island, and she was surprised to realize it was her.

Maybe Cassix was right. Not that she would ever tell him. His ego was too big as it was. But it was good to know that maybe she could rely on his assistance. If this crazy plan had a chance of success, it would be because he helped. A sudden cry from the sea had her lifting her head to look. The monsters that guarded the deeps were active today. A coldness whispered through her body. The Usurper. Nothing they did would keep him contained forever, and she wondered if his imprisonment was closer to being over than they hoped.

With a soft growl, she pushed the idea away. For now, there were more important matters. That was a fingerset if not hundreds of suncycles away. For now, she would deal with the mad god. And her weapons.

She picked up the molded metal. Now it was ready to be forged. Time disappeared as her hammer matched the rhythm of her heart, the swinging of it as driving as the waves. She sensed the sun going down and coming back up, but that was nothing to a Leonaid. A tenday without rest they might have an issue, but a few days was nothing. She would sleep when done. The sword needed only sharpening when she had quenched it for the last time.

Now she moved to the weapons for Note that had been poured and molded the same way. Again, time disappeared, but not as long. The same metal as the sword, but shaping it, letting the magic that was one of her gifts guide her. It was ready for the final quenching, but Shinala needed a break. The mold that called to her and the weapon for Rylix. That one she still had to figure out how to make. She would need assistance for that one.

She stepped away from the forge, pulling the apron off and hanging it up while the fire banked, as if sensing her distance.

"You need food," Mace said next to her, and she turned to him.

"How long?"

"Four days," he said, handing her a plate. It was full of cooked fish, fresh and steaming with spices she had last smelled tensets of suncycles ago. Hunger slammed into her with the same force as the hammer she had been wielding for days. She grabbed the platter, shoving the flaky fish into her mouth. Spices and flavors burst in her mouth, and she had to fight back a moan.

"Good, it is," Mace said with a smile. "Maybe we need traders again. Had forgotten what spice other than salt does."

Over the suncycles her people had forgotten more than the taste of food. Even their way of speaking had become odd and broken. Why were they the ones that suffered because of the children? The gods seemed untouched by everything. Resentment for the first time in a long time spiked. Her eating slowed down as she considered the food. All this over some spices. What about clothes? How long had it been since she wore clothes? What she had were long turned into scraps. Their fabrics woven by the few who enjoyed handcrafts, beaten from seaweed and straw, then made into soft blankets that held up for suncycles. She looked around her domain with fresh eyes and sighed.

"I must sleep, but before I finish the weapons," she looked back at the cave. "I believe I will talk with some gods."

Mace, one of her favorite bed partners if she was honest, looked at her with clear eyes. "Change?"

She nodded slowly, still eating. "Yes, I think it is time for change."

His answering smile added to her guilt. How long had she been avoiding her responsibilities, her people? The answer was suncycles, but now maybe something should change.

CHAPTER SEVENTY-FOUR

JADAYA

The other huge sabers arose and came toward them as the woman, Shinala, focused on the forge. There was something oddly terrifying about having a creature that could look you in the eye and yawn, thereby showing all its very large fangs.

This one did just that. It had green eyes with tawny fur. After the yawn, it then put out both front feet and stretched before shifting into a mortal, just as naked as Shinala, who had donned a strange apron.

"Shinala busy is. You follow." He spoke in simple Ged, which sounded old and stilted. He turned and strode down a path worn into the rock.

Jadaya exchanged looks with the other two, who shrugged and followed the naked man down the path. Obviously for the Leonaids modesty did not exist, which made sense as animals rarely wore clothes. As long as her sleeping space was more than in a cave on bare ground, she figured she would be fine. That usually made for poor sleep and a stiff body. A bed of grass and a blanket made life easier.

The three of them looked at the area as they went down the path. They had been on a little rise that held the forge and entrance to the imprisoned gods. Now they saw the wide plains that spread out from the volcano turning slowly into white sand beaches. More than one of the big sabers was playing in the surf.

Not playing, Jadaya realized as it pounced and came out of the water with an enormous fish in its jaws. Fishing or hunting, depending on how you looked at it. The one in front of them did not pause but kept walking, leading them to a series of caves. He walked past the first four, then pointed. "Stay here you. Welcome is."

Jadaya closed her eyes in silent despair, but nodded her head. It looked like they were indeed subjected to floor living. Rylix went in ahead of her.

"Oh. This is nice," he said, his voice echoing oddly out of the doorway. "And as it is not crafted, I wonder if I will be able to sleep inside." He sounded thoughtful.

Jadaya and Note glanced at each other, then she looked over her shoulder at the shifter. He nodded toward the cave with his head.

She followed Rylix in and stopped a few paces in, giving Note plenty of room to follow her. Where she had really expected a rough hole in the hill with maybe an animal skin to lie on instead was three beds with mattresses over rope supports on wooden frames, a table, chairs, and even a back needs room. There was water coming from the wall in warm and cool temperatures. There were woven blankets on the beds, and an animal skin draped to block wind and light across the entrance.

"Hot water?" she said, amazed at the idea.

"Ah. Springs heated water. Drink no. Soak yes." The naked Leonaid said from the door. "Come. Food have."

Relieved and wondering what other surprises were in store, she followed him down a still-unexplored path. There was a fire pit and three fish laid out. "Cook we no. Cook you?"

Rylix laughed. "Yes, we can cook our own food."

Jadaya just looked around, oddly off balance. They had survived everything to get here. They had the blessing of the old gods, which were to be given to them as weapons? She still was unsure what that meant. But they had to wait until they were forged.

"It feels odd," she said, looking at the surf slamming into the shore, a violent difference from the calm surface they had crossed to the mountain in. "We have been striving to get here for tendays, and now we what, relax?"

"I know. But we have their assistance. That was the goal, right?" Note had come over to her while Rylix chatted with the Leonaids, Some were in two-legged forms, others still looked like huge predatory animals.

"True. But now?" It felt wrong to not be moving forward. To be waiting for reasons outside of their needs.

Note gave her an odd smile. "Now we wait and hope the weapons are what we need. But even with them, I do not know if we can kill a god." He looked exhausted, she realized.

Jadaya dropped to sit on the sand, watching the waves. They looked angry and taunting. As if daring her to risk her life on them, to challenge their wrath. "Neither do I," she murmured as the waves laughed at her. "But no longer am I afraid. And if the old gods think we can, then we will."

Note sat next to her, his toes buried under the sand. "What do you see when you look at the ocean?"

Jadaya smiled, her eyes never leaving the rippling water. "Now? Life. Challenge. A chance to change everything."

"Huh," he said quietly. "I see nothing except struggle. The ocean has always been my refuge. Now I almost fear it."

She looked at him with a flash of surprise. "Why?"

He wrapped his arms around his knees, pulling them close to his chest. "So much has changed. I think my anger was easier to bear than to understand how fallible my gods are."

"At least you have gods," she said softly. "Mine threw me away."

"More fool them," came a voice from behind. She stiffened, but had no time to react before Cassix flopped down next to them. "They never were the brightest of my siblings."

Jadaya looked at him and sighed. "If you can just appear out of nowhere, how are we to fight your brother?" She knew that the family connections among the gods were complicated at best, so siblings were the easiest way to define everyone.

"Ah, but I am not him and Shinala knows me. She might actually like me," he said with a puff of pride.

One of the nearby Leonaids chuffed out a laugh but did nothing more than roll over on his back and stretch, displaying numerous teeth and claws.

Cassix's lips twitched, and he shrugged. "It might be more accurate to say she tolerates me," he admitted with a wry smile. "But as for the rest," he said, his mood sobering, "I think it is possible. But to be honest, I have no idea how to do it."

Jadaya locked her eyes on him, then turned away. "If a god knows not how to kill a sibling, how insane are we to try?"

Cassix, who had mimicked Note's pose, stared out at the water, his profile giving nothing away. "I think the better question might be, how can you not try?"

"Does it help if we try and fail?" Jadaya asked, her gaze back on the waves coming in. There were flickers of fish in the motion and the blue waters seemed friendly and warm. But appearances could be deceiving.

"Sometimes, just seeing someone stand up, even if they fail, is enough to let others know they might be able to stand as well," Cassix said in a low voice. "Sometimes."

"Note, Jadaya, we have dinner," Rylix called out. Jadaya lifted her head to see where he stood, dishing up steaming slices of fish with more than one Leonaid lifting their head to sniff the air. She turned to ask Cassix if he wanted some, but there was no one there, not even an impression in the sand to imply anyone had been there.

"There are days when I wonder if I am still caught in fever dreams or if I died after my whipping," she said as she stood up.

Note barked out a laugh and easily rose to his feet. "I know I no longer reside in Charinsky. There is no song to drive me insane."

She let a smile slip out. "I notice you avoid song," she said as they headed up the beach.

He waved his hand. "Someday, maybe pain will no longer strike me when I sing, but until I have something worth singing about, it is all sour notes and false breaths."

Jadaya was unsure what that meant, but she let it go as they approached Rylix.

"Was someone else with you?" He said curiously. "I thought I saw three heads."

"Cassix," Jadaya replied. "He was trying to encourage us, maybe? Or at least convince us not to quit."

"He is a strange god, and not that good," Note said.

Jadaya laughed as she settled down with the plate of fish. Rylix, who had managed to keep spices with him, had sprinkled salt, some herbs, and peppers on it, and seared it to perfection. Her mouth watered as the scents wrapped around senses. "Maybe not, but we are still going, are we not?"

Note grunted and began to eat. A few of the Leonaids were still nearby, sniffing air. One of them, in mortal form, moved over. "Have enough? We eat?"

Rylix frowned. "I thought you preferred raw?"

"We no cook. We eat cooked," the man replied, his nose sniffing the air.

"Ah," Rylix said with a laugh. "Help yourself."

The others nearby shifted into two-legged form, complete with body hair and dangly bits. Jadaya noted again they really looked like Ged. They grabbed the large leaves that were being used as plates and in moments, most of the fish had disappeared. Low growls and grunts were the only sounds as they ate the fish at astonishing speed.

"Next time, I should ask for two fish, I guess," Rylix said, picking at a flake of his.

Note laughed, and Jadaya just enjoyed the sounds of laughter and eating. Who knew how long they would stay here? Until the weapons were finished, of course, but then how did they get to Charinsky?

That night in the small cave, she settled down on the bed, mind still tumbling over everything and wondering if they did kill a god, what would happen next.

That part worried her more than the idea of killing Xyl, it was the unknown because the world remembered the death of Percit. It was beat into you as a child and to this day, she still shivered when remembering the story.

Were they going to break the world in such a manner?

CHAPTER SEVENTY-FIVE

ZAYN

"Y ou do like your toys, do you not?"

The words sank into Zayn's brain, echoing deep inside as he rolled over on his bed.

"So many options for pleasure and pain, though you are predictable."

The voice kept crooning. Zayn shook his head to dismiss it, but the voice remained. Zayn swore he could feel the hot breath of another on his face.

"Maybe you would be a good toy? Percit would have loved to play with you."

That ripped him wide awake and his eyes flew open to see Xyl leaning over him, his handsome features smiling down in a way that had Zayn trying to crawl backward away from him.

"Ah, you wake. Tell me, what did you dream? Were you playing with your toys? Listening to their cries and whimpers? It is so nice when they beg, no?" The seductive tone made Zayn pull back even further, but the bed kept him trapped between the wall and the mad god.

Swallowing hard, Zayn grabbed his tattered attention and pulled it back together. "Xyl. How may this one serve you?" Most priests never saw the god at all. What had he done to get a personal visit like this?

Please, anyone, keep me from ending up like Lazul. I have no desire to live with that level of pain.

"Oh serve," the god said, drawing out the word that made Zayn shiver, but not in desire. His skin wanted to crawl off of him. "No, you are more what Percit would enjoy. I like them softer than you." Xyl pulled back after that, looking around the chamber. "So bright. Clean. You do not look like you are grieving the death of my beloved."

Zayn managed to sit up and scramble off the bed. He knelt before Xyl, his head bowed. His mind raced frantically. What did he want? And how did he make it through this unscathed?

"She lives in our memories. We celebrate her life and the love you shared." He wanted to point out the goddess had been dead for longer than he knew, but saying that would find himself begging for death.

"Ah, but she was more than just my love. She was my life. How can I enjoy the sun if she is not near me? Yet my people smile and laugh. They need to embrace the darkness that ripped Percit away from me. Her desires, the things I wanted her to want. What I was teaching her to adore. The things she would have become. But now, even in my temples, you pull people away from the richness of what she could have become. The depravity she should have embraced. All her people should know how creative she was with pain and pleasure. After all, did she not make me ache with her rejections?" His voice was pained, and he stamped his foot in frustration as if he was a child being denied a treat.

Wait, what is he saying

Zayn shied away from the ideas of the things he did with the singers, his toys, being done to him. He had the power, not others. Then what Xyl's said registered. The god's words made it seem like he had been corrupting Percit. His head spun, trying to understand what the god meant. Or at least what the words implied.

"How may I serve you, Xyl? I am your cantor and your will is my joy to perform," Zayn said, watching the god from under his lashes.

One moment he would smile, then his face would ripple as if in the throes of grief, then a smirk, followed by a grimace of pain or frustration. But the worst was when he looked at Zayn with clear blue eyes. The calculation and focus were enough to make him try to crawl under his bed and pray the god forgot he existed.

"Songs. I want more songs of the grief of her loss, and I want my temple to show the populace how she was. Her sweet darkness, the way she could make my pain last for eons. Denying me all I wanted. You shall lead them all in the ways of her darkness. Too much of her light has been celebrated and people no longer know she owned my heart and body in a way that none will ever match." He snarled. "And that I was denied keeping."

Zayn fought to speak, to keep his voice pleasant and subservient, not ready to scream in terror. "Xyl, we worship the light she brought, the passion she had for life, the light of the stars in the dark of the night, how she suffered to make our land prosperous, the peace she granted us in death. What else would you have us remember about her?"

Xyl laughed, and the sound rolled through Zayn's bones, hurting and feeling so good he almost gagged.

"She was light when she hid her darkness from me. There is no talk of the sweet pain she brought, how begging her on my knees brought the greatest pleasure, and how there should be no light at night, so that we may always see the stars to remember her sparkling beauty. The beauty she wanted to take away from me."

Xyl spun, the midnight black cloth he wore draped around his waist, threatening to slip at any moment. "Listen to me. Teach the people how to lean into her depravity, as that is all that is left for me. The memories of my loss. Everything else is gone, so I shall wallow in the agony without the pleasure she gave. Make their every scream of suffering, and beg of need, be a paean to me. I want tears as I cry my own for her loss. For only in misery do I find any pleasure. Those I bless will also find that sweet sensation, the only joy left to me. When the pain transforms, it is ecstasy like you have never known, and it is all I seek. The singers shall create the greatest harmonies the world has ever known." His voice went from crooning to demanding to glee.

Images flashed into his mind of things that Zayn had never considered doing to anyone and never wanted to, with the singers, the young ones, as the core of those lewd pictures. If Zayn had ever doubted it, he knew now that Xyl was beyond any measure of insanity. He was insanity itself. But warping the faith to match this madness was an awful thing to do. Already, just the changes wrought on the walls were changing the country to a point that it made him uncomfortable.

Zayn struggled to redirect him. He had no desire to be the receiver of those actions. The images that Xyl shoved into his mind made his own darkness seem like a planting day. "Xyl, my god, we need to remember that Percit—"

"No," Xyl roared. "Her darkness, her pain. I want everyone to feel the lack of the pleasure she brought with the sharp kiss of her love. Otherwise, I will drown this country in tears until all there is left is a dark mud hole fit for nothing but to build her tomb. There will be no sun, no relief. I will create the ultimate memorial to her. The king will do anything to escape his pain, so tell him my terms and together you will make this country a true legacy to her darkness." Xyl laughed. "In fact, tell him that publicly. If he bows down and becomes the leader in the depravity I crave, his pain will cease and he will rule as long as I am satisfied. He has a woman with him. Use her the way Percit should have used me."

Before Zayn could say anything, Xyl was gone, leaving him alone, kneeling on the floor in his darkened room with images of depravity and a new design for the temple services, as well as what he meant by some of his vaguer terms. Until that moment, he'd been unaware that Xyl had lit the room up with his very existence. And with him gone, the darkness seemed almost a relief. Sagging down, Zayn laid his head on the floor and fought not to cry. The only blessing he could see was that obviously Xyl was unable to read minds, though he could pour information in. If he could read minds, Zayn would already be dead. But that gave him no idea of what to do. Of how to mitigate or use the damage Xyl was causing.

After long moments of trying to get his heart beating regularly, Zayn struggled to his feet. He was no longer as young as he had once been and his days of being on his knees for any amount of time were long past. He made himself a cup of telcha and added tella syrup to it. The ability to mentally relax right now was paramount. He sipped on it with his eyes closed, mind racing as he looked at his options.

Darkness. Fall into it, embrace it. He knew he was more selfish than most and this way lay power and a life of hedonistic pleasure. The king would fight, but when pitted against a god, there were no options. If he, as the cantor refused, Xyl would destroy their land. If Lazul refused, the same thing would occur. And what life was there in a mud bowl with your people starving to death? Giving in to Xyl's demands would mean the pain would go away. Lazul was a weak man. He would cave. And if he caved…

Zayn shuddered and took a large gulp of the telcha.

If it was only him, even only his church, Zayn might have taken it with open arms. All the pleasure he wanted. But what Xyl wanted would turn the people of Charinsky into an entire population to be avoided. It would warp their culture, destroy the beliefs that had kept the nation together for so long. Their lives would shatter if they only celebrated the dark parts of Xyl, because without the good, there is no reason for any of the things that make life worth living. It would be worse than an opi addiction. All you ever wanted was the next taste, the next chance to run away. It would turn everyone into that, chasing the pain laced with pleasure. Nothing else would matter as Xyl only wanted that. And if everyone did that, the land was as good as dead.

Zayn glanced out the window to see the first traces of sun creeping up over the roofs of the city. There were no options. He would have to do what Xyl said, as the god would be watching. He needed to tell the king immediately. But he could still hope, deep in the depths of the heart, the conscience he thought he had killed, hope that it was possible to kill a god before he destroyed everything that made being a Char worthwhile.

The sooner he did this, the sooner he could keep control of the situation. There was no reason to avoid the required meeting, and he suspected Lazul was already awake, talking to Hauyne if nothing else. He dressed in his robes of office, the ones he rarely wore, but if he was going to do this, he had to make an impression. They were heavier than normal, made of long black silk, with red and silver stitching along the hem and arm bands. It had a high collar in lurid red, with a white stole he placed over it. The stole was stitched on one side with an intact moon and a shooting star, the other had the broken halves and a grave marker. He no longer remembered the last time he had worn them, probably at a formal event at the palace when they had other countries' representatives over. He stared at a mirror for a moment, not recognizing the man there, the man who would need to lie while telling the truth and hope that his god never caught what he was doing.

Needing fortification and the knowledge that some food might make this more tolerable, he stopped at the kitchens for a bite of bread. It tasted rich and warm on his tongue. The small pleasure made him want to cry. It turned out life was more precious than he had realized, and he had black marks on his life, but he was unwilling to destroy a country for his own pleasure. A life or two, especially when they were immaterial in the long run, yes, but a country? All of his people? No.

How do I make this work for me? I need congregation to enjoy my treats.

Zayn strode to the castle, trying to figure out how to give the most convincing performance of his life, while lying at every turn. If Lazul was too drugged up to catch his hints, hopefully Hauyne was as smart as Zayn thought she might be. He stumbled in his majestic approach to the castle, aware already of the eyes on him this morning. This needed all the pomp and circumstance he could muster. And hope that it worked. He had always prayed to a distant god. Now the god was here and what Xyl now espoused would ruin everything. Lazul had to see through what he would say and find a way to destroy Xyl. He would help all he could, but with the god watching him, he needed to be what the god wanted, yet be ready when the time came. Not that he had any idea how to help.

But, at the end of the day, was there any way to kill a god? Would he live if they succeeded? No, that was the wrong question. Would he live if they failed? The answer to that was no, neither would Charinsky. Mind made up, sorrow, rage, and a tiny bit of pride swirling inside him, Zayn strode into the palace demanding an audience with the king.

CHAPTER SEVENTY-SIX

SHINALA

Food, sleep, and a refreshing swim in the bay improved her mood greatly. But Shinala still had no idea what she was going to ask when she walked into the chamber. The crystal pillars, full of colors and shapes almost realized, seemed to glow extra brightly today. She stood there in her two-legged form, her white hair reaching her knees. She had Mace comb it out this morning before she came in. It had taken a while as she had ignored it for a suncycle or more and she almost cut it off, but she loved her long white hair that was as strong as silk and made her easy to find on a battlefield, though usually she had it twisted in up a braid and then a twist at the base of her neck.

The peninsula that led into the surrounding lava that the crystals stood outside seemed to pulse as she stood there watching them.

"I never asked, I assumed. Why were we here? At first, I thought it was to guard you, but if you had broken free, I would have served you as I always had. Then I thought maybe your children feared retribution from us, but they never understood why you let them place you here. But we do not age, we remain unchanged, yet still we are here. Why?" It was a question, a puzzle that needed satisfying. She was curious, but also the knowledge that so much had changed over the suncycles and what they had lost without realizing it ate at her. The gods were her first priority, but her Leonaids were her second. And she could do nothing for her gods but could do much for her males.

"BECAUSE IT WAS NO LONGER OUR TIME. IT WAS THEIRS."

There was only silence as she looked at them.

"Then what do I do? What is the next step?"

"LIVE. BE WHAT YOU ONCE WERE. BE MORE."

This time, there was an answer of sorts. She had returned the bowls that contained the original materials. From Aryix and Quas, crystal blood seeped into each of the bowls, luminescent and swirling. From Lyx, red tears oozed out in the general vicinity of her face, running down her crystal tomb to fill the bowl. While from Gela, she cried green tears. Stari's bowl filled with tiny pieces of crystal, each barely bigger than a grain of sand, but sharper than her claws.

"MAKE WHAT YOU NEED TO ENSURE AN END. BE WHAT THEY NEED. THE ANSWER IS STILL YES."

The word whispered through her and around her. Shinala frowned, still looking at the materials they had provided her. What she had already was enough to make the weapons. Why this? Yes, to what? Then it sank in, and her head snapped up to look at them. "Yes?"

"FIVE, NO MORE. WE WILL BE READY WHEN THE TIME COMES." The voice sounded resigned, and she felt her world tilt under her. Yes? Five? She swayed, standing there as her world restructured around her. Emotions battled inside her: joy, excitement, fear, anticipation, sadness. They all swirled around her, finally settling into a weird jitter that she had only felt before battle.

She swallowed hard, feeling more off balance than she had for suncycles upon suncycles. "Yes," she whispered. With the word still echoing in her mind, she took the bowls and their substances, her mind already filtering through the options and thinking. Shinala spoke to none of her males as she went back to the forge and pulled on her apron. She lost herself in what she made, the whip the most detailed weapon, but it was nothing compared to what she made for herself.

Once, long ago, she had used a sword and a spear. But both had been less effective than her claws in a pitched battle. But claws had limits. If her weapon did what she thought it might, there would be no limits. Heartbeats blended into fingers as she worked. Dimly she registered Mace and Katel checking on her, but her focus was on her work. The materials the gods had given her for her weapon were enough to make her tremble at what they gave her. She took a bucket of saltwater and shoved the sword into it. As the metal quenched, Shinala stood there facing the ocean, her mind quiet as what she had created steamed in the water.

"You understand?"

The voice came from behind her, but she continued to focus on her work. Cassix had always smelled of ozone and wood smoke with a touch of flower in it. It was a scent that oddly brought her comfort now.

"Yes," she replied in barely a whisper.

"I trust you. They trust you," he said, still behind her. Shinala almost turned to look at him, to see his face as he said that.

"Why?"

"Because you stayed. You could have left," he said and was gone. She stood and let the wind scour away the tears that crept down her face. The truth was, it never occurred to her. Her gods were here. Where should she have gone? Then she smiled. There were battles ahead, and that was a someday that she might still refuse. For now, she would focus on other things. Turning and leaving the circle of metal cooling, she grabbed a hide and laid it out. She picked up each finished weapon and set it down on the hide, then wrapped it up and headed to the beach where the Leonaids and the mortals were.

In the days while they waited for her to finish, they had made friends with many of her males. Note worked on creating new fishing implements and had often gone into the bay to collect things from the bottom where ships had crashed into the reefs. There was a way through the reef, but many ships had failed over the suncycles. Their collection of tools and other implements and even other items that had been protected well enough the sea had not ruined it had been retrieved by the Aoisan.

Jadaya spent her time sparring with any Leonaid that would, and the high fish diet in the last tenday seemed to have given her what she needed as she all but glowed with health and restrained patience. Shinala recognized the look, the need to be doing, but forced to wait.

Rylix had been his charming trader self, learning all he could, teaching her males how to cook, and what spices could do. He even figured out a way to make some sweets, something they had not had in hundreds of suncycles. He brought life and joy to a mountain that had lost it slowly, hair by hair, over the ages. It felt good to see the joy and interest in her males once more. Yet another thing they had lost and not noticed.

Shinala suspected Rylix knew all the names of the fifteen males that she had left out of fifty. While they were, in a sense, immortal in that they were ageless and never grew ill, they were vulnerable to weapons, accident, and murder. In the capture of her gods, twenty had died, as the gods had fought back at first. After their imprisonment and the assigning of the Leonaids here, their numbers had dwindled even more.

The first hundred suncycles she lost six to despair. The lack of others to interact with, the death of their friends, lovers, mates, and children, was too much. Most of the males had mortal women they loved, and those the god-children callously killed in the aftermath. It had been too much for them. There were also treacherous currents around the mountain. Now they knew it the way they knew the land, but at first, it took its toll. Five had been pulled under and lost. Even Leonaids needed to breathe. The last four were lost over the suncycles to simple injury. While they rarely got infections, falling into the lava that burst through every so often, or a sparring round gone wrong, or a deeps monster roaming outside its normal area, could still kill a Leonaid. It left her with fifteen, and the spurt of rage and grief caught her off guard.

Shinala stood there for a moment, watching them. The decision, the permission she had been given, rippled through her. Her gaze lingered first on one, then another of her Leonaids, as she decided. Five, they had said. Mace was obvious. Of all of them, he had always been her right hand and one of the few that never took mortals as bedmates, though he had graced hers often. A shock of red hair working on seaweed, pounding it into long thin fibers, grabbed her eyes. Lev, her only remaining child. He rarely socialized but could do more things with his swift fingers than many could do. With green eyes that matched wheat during planting, he could come with her. Still, she watched, unnoticed at this point.

A laugh drew her attention to where Jadaya and Katel were practicing with shield and spear. It was a common weapon pairing for the Leonaids, but Jadaya was still awkward, though as they practiced, she grew more comfortable with every moment. Katel, with his white hair and easy laugh, hid more than you would expect. He had been her weapons master, the one that trained and cross-trained the Leonaids. In the beginning, the female children had trained too, now she had only males left. In the before times, he had a lover, an adopted child, and they had been killed when Aryix was taken. Even now, his rage still burned, and she knew he would never stay behind.

First of those that would come even if she did not choose him was Paka. She found him watching, still holding himself apart from the rest. When they had been created, there had been her and Raj Lew. Then, over the suncycles, she had given birth to fifteen males and fifteen females. All of them were fertile and had children over the suncycles, but few of the children of the pairings with mortals had been female. Paka and Gesi had been one of the few pairs that never separated to play with others, to have children with others. They had been inseparable from the moment they saw each other, when Gela had breathed life into them. They had been defending the unconscious Stari when Xyl killed Gesi to grab the god and left the scar across Paka's face. Paka had never forgotten the death of his mate. She often was surprised he had not fled the chains of life here in this prison. From the moment the news of who these mortals were, his eyes had gained a new intensity. He would come.

That left her with one remaining. Who? She pushed the question away and walked onto the beach, her movement pulling eyes to her. All the talking stopped as her bare feet, soles hard as leather, reached the edge where sand turned into soil. The wind felt good on her bare torso after days of the apron protecting from the sparks. They would also have to learn to wear clothes again.

Ah, the things they would have to relearn. She knelt, all too aware of the eyes of everyone on her as the three mortals headed toward her. If she had called them, it would not have been any different.

She laid the hide on the ground and unrolled it. The mortals stared at what she had there. Shinala decided to start with the easy one, the one that had been a challenge to create, but easy to explain.

"Ged, the whip is yours," she said, pointing to it. "It is swiftwing." That was the name of a bird that dove hard into the water, coming up with a fish in its beak. The whip was a series of small silver links that had a handle wrapped in tanned deeps monster hide. The tip of the whip was a softly glowing crystal. Each link was shaped like a swiftwing soaring in the sky, with the tail and head connecting them together. "Put this on the tip." She handed Rylix a small leather cap. "Until you are ready to kill, keep it on. The crystal will cut through flesh or stone, even a god's flesh. And any wound will take three times as long to heal."

Rylix had a look of awe on his face as he lifted the whip up. The tip touched the ground when he held it out, arm above his head. "Katel can show you how to use it," she said, nodding at her former weapons master. Katel's eyes glowed with excitement as he looked at the weapon.

"Aryix bless. This will be a wonderful weapon," Rylix said with a stunned look on his face as he inspected each of the links.

"It should serve you well." Shinala took a deep breath and told him the rest. "The crystal learns when it slices flesh, and as long as you keep hitting that target, the power increases. But if you hit something else, it resets." She stared at him, hoping it would make sense.

"You mean it amplifies as long as I strike the same target?" He asked slowly.

Relieved, she nodded. "Yes, with cap off. Cap is special, made of treated deep monster hide. Hide remain uncut, but anything else shred." That had been difficult to make. To create the cap, she ground up some of the crystals to a fine power, then coated the inside of the sheath with those same crystals while putting her creation magic into it.

"This is amazing," he breathed, eyes locked on the whip, its design shimmering in the sun. "I will practice."

"Good." Shinala turned her attention to Note. "Now for the Aoisan."

NOTE

The hammering sound of Shinala's forge rang in rhythm with the waves and Note found it to be the first type of music he had been able to enjoy in ages. Time spent in the water, diving deep into the bay to bring up trinkets, food, and supplies, kept him busy and let his mind be quiet. He swam around the entire mountain multiple times and mapped out where the deeps were and the currents that were so deadly to any that required air to live.

In the evenings, they talked about how to get to Char, but no matter what, it would be a long trip back to Vykland and then hail down a ship. The idea of a ship and one of the Leonaid's comments about missing nice smelling soap had been chewing on the back of his mind. Swimming around the mountain for the fourth time, it finally clicked. On the side, almost exactly opposite of the under-water path they had followed to get there from Vykland, were the remnants of an old dock. If there was a dock, it meant they used to have ships stop here.

Note swam to shore and walked up to sit in the sand. The area here was more exposed to the wind, and the trees twisted and scraggly as they fought upward against the wind. Further down, near the base of the volcano, were a few stubborn fruit trees, fighting for life, lacking care. He had seen woolies that ran like caprils up around the rocks as if falling was not a possibility. Birds that called the mountain home sang in brambles thick with berries. Rylix had used some of those ripe treats to make an incredible dessert. Then there were the fish, rich in variety and plentiful. The Leonaids had gotten good at fishing in both animal and two-legged form.

With his toes in the gray gravel, Note looked at the cuff on his wrist. No one would expect him back for many fingers, so now would work. Closing his eyes, the enormity of what they would attempt hitting him like a storm surge. The idea of three people going up against an entire country, possibly a god, was enough to scare anyone. The tears born of worry and guilt leaked out of his eyes onto the cuff.

"Pel, I call upon you." The words were barely loud enough for him to hear, but they had no need to be. He sat and watched the water. Here there were only light blue waters, touched by hints of green at the deeper ends, but no signs of the deeps. The currents would pull you away from here unless you cut across them, and there was no reason to come here, to visit a mountain island all but lost in myth and shrouded in smoke and vapors. The odds were most of the time fog shrouded it from view and the deeps prevented much else.

The sun moved across the sky as he waited, the heat of the sand keeping him from shivering. A rogue wave rose and rushed toward him, thinning out and then fading to reveal the figure of Pel. The god stood before him, bobbing as if the water under him was an unstable floor.

"I see no danger," he said, looking around.

"No," Note said, his voice steady. "They agreed to help."

"The Leonaids did? Shinala agreed to assist?" The surprise in Pel's voice stung and Note's mouth twisted bitterly.

"Did you think she would refuse?" Had all this been a fool's quest? A task the gods set to help erase their guilt?

Pel glanced out at the sea, refusing to look at Note as he spoke. "She has been angry at us for a long time. After all, we imprisoned her creators, her gods."

"Your parents," Note pointed out dryly.

"Yes. That too." He refused to look at Note, instead focused on waves that seemed to respond to his attention by swirling and jumping around like a dog trying to please its master. Though Note suspected Pel was moving the water around.

Note fought back the urge to heave a sigh. That his god acted like a spoiled child being held responsible for his actions most of the time was yet another issue. "Be that as it may, she is forging weapons for us."

"What?" Pel whipped around to stare at him, his face pale. "Shinala is forging weapons for each of you?"

Note blinked at him, the change in attitude surprising him. "Yes."

"Really, brother, did you think if she agreed to help, there was anything else she would do? What did you expect, for her to rouse the Leonaids and rush off to fight a war?" The slow mocking voice of Cassix made Note start, as he knew the shore behind him had been empty.

Pel looked at his brother, who must have been behind Note, given the glare leveled above his head. "We expected advice. Maybe some of the old weapons she must have kept secreted away. Even ideas on how to contain him. But weapons made for them? How did she even get the materials? Are they free?" The fear that leaked into his voice at that idea caused Note's skin to pebble in reaction.

For the first time, Note wondered why the children had overthrown their parents. He had never really thought about it before, just accepted it as a statement of what was. But suddenly he was curious. What would drive that amount of fear? Or maybe he just feared their anger after more suncycles than you could count on being imprisoned. Note could imagine his anger.

"You would have to ask her. I can take you there if you like," Cassix said, moving around Note so he could see him as the two gods talked.

"No. That is not needed." Pel pulled away, deeper into the water, before he shifted his attention to Note. "What did you need? I assumed you called me here not to just give me an update."

The byplay between the gods was fascinating, and Note would have enjoyed seeing more. But rather than risk offending the god whose help he needed, he let it go. "The ship we took to get to Fivika. The *Starguide.* Can you push her off course and move the ship here? There is a channel that can be followed. If so, I believe a dock could be constructed here. Though having her moor out in the channel would be the easiest."

Pel looked around. "Yes. It will be done when I find her."

Note nodded. "Aryix bless. That will help us complete this task."

With that, Pel jumped up in a backward arc, diving into the water, his blue skin matching the colors as he disappeared from view.

"Ha! That was fun. I should do that more often." Cassix stood next to Note, his hands on his hips, grinning as he stared out at the shapes beneath the water. "I wonder if I could set them free."

A shiver of fear rippled down Note's spine. "Would that be a good idea?"

Cassix shrugged and looked at him. Of all the gods, Cassix acted the most like a mortal and when he contained himself, Note knew why they had not suspected he was a god at first. In reality, if he had said he was a far cousin to Rylix, they would have never doubted him with his curly brown hair, tan skin, and easy manner. Not compared to the others.

"Probably not. But it would be interesting," Cassix heaved a sigh, as if much put upon. "I believe it would be difficult at this point to release them. They have been imprisoned for a very long time. Oh, well." Cassix focused on him and Note rather wished he would pay attention to anything else. That intense look wiped aways all vestiges of mortality.

"Are you ready for this, mortal? The killing of a god? I warn you now, he is not what he once was. Before he worshiped her, would always check on her, even if she was gone a short time. Anything she desired was hers. All the other spouses talked about how he doted on her and ensured he was always there for her. Now, he is different. Harder, obsessive almost."

Note turned his head to look back at the ocean, something that was easier to bear than the attention of Cassix. "No. But he has to be stopped. *They* have to be stopped. I assume he is aware of what his priests do?"

"Very," Cassix said drily. "I am unaware if he approves or not, but he has never attempted to stop them."

Note nodded. He had figured as much, but knowing made it hurt even more.

Cassix turned to look back at where the Leonaids mostly lived. "You should go. Things are starting to happen."

"Happen?" Note turned to look down the shoreline. When he looked back, Cassix was gone. "Figures." He stood stretching and then dove back into the water, swimming toward where Rylix and the others were. As he wove through the water, the look of fear on Pel's face remained sharp and clear in his mind. That would stay with him for a long time. What could cause a god to be scared? How dangerous were the old gods?

He walked up the beach to where Jadaya and a Leonaid with white hair were sparring. The whiteness was also his mane color when he shifted, though of all of them, only Shinala was white as a saber. This one simply had a white mane over a tawny coat with a white tuft on his tail.

Rylix, for his part, was working on crafting small fishing hooks. The large fish the Leonaids seemed to catch easily. The smaller ones were savory and had a distinct flavor that Rylix had mentioned wanting for some meals. Note thought he should have learned to cook after he returned to Aois, but he never took the time. It had seemed unimportant. Food was just something you ate.

He watched them as he tried to figure out what Cassix had been talking about, when he saw Shinala approaching. The constant nudity of the Leonaids still caught him off guard sometimes, but the Aoisans wore fewer clothes than most. Jadaya worked on keeping her eyes up, but he had the strong impression this much male anatomy on display made her uncomfortable. For his part, Note was just glad that he had pants to wear. The idea of displaying his mutilation for all to see made him nauseous and angry at the same time.

They all headed over to her when she rolled out the hide displaying a king's ransom worth of weapons. She explained Rylix's, but his eyes were locked on what he knew were his weapons. An axe and a dagger lay side by side. They called to each other and to him. He suspected that was why she had asked for blood from each of them, to make these weapons theirs in all aspects.

His gaze snapped up to hers as she said, "Now for the Aoisan." She reached out and touched the axe. "This is Trinity. In your hands, it can be three or one. When all it is one, or all three have been thrown, it will return to your hand when you call. Its edges are thin enough to cut into most flesh like a hot knife through fat." She handed him the weapon, and he took it with an edge of reverence he had never felt before. It was the length of his forearm and hand, with the handle wrapped in strips of leather made from the one of the many sea creatures the Leonaids pulled in. If he looked closely at the handle, he could see the three shafts wrapped as one. Up the handle of the axe, the lines were there, but at first glance, they simply looked decorative. But as he examined it he could see where they became three. The head of the axe was a slightly curved blade with a hammer spike on the other end. It was balanced perfectly. Silver blade rippling with wavy patterns that remind him of the ripple of the sea, black metal handle, then the black leather woven around the handles. It looked as deadly as it felt.

"To split, simply think Trinity Three," Shinala said, watching him.

Note thought the words, but nothing happened. He looked back up to her, and she quirked up one side of her mouth at him. "It needs to taste you, to know you are its master."

That made perfect sense to Note, so he slid his thumb across the blade. It slipped through his skin so easily he almost cut himself overly deep. The blood poured out, and the axe drank it, shimmering for a moment in his hand. Then it went quiet. This time when he thought 'Trinity Three', the pieces disconnected, and he found three blades in his hand.

Shinala nodded. "The other commands are Trinity Return and Trinity One. You will need to practice, but it is weighted for throwing or fighting." She shifted to the dagger that lay there. It had the same metal as the blade and the handle was wrapped with the same leather, though this was a more blue shade than black. "This is Echo. It will return to your hand one second after it has impacted into something, unless your hand was on it when it went in. If it has tasted blood, it will pass through walls and stone if thrown toward that same target. It requires skill to use, but it will aid you for the kill shot if possible. It is unable to go around corners, but there should be no need for it to. You never need to call it. It will always return, but no one else can take it from you. This too, you need to feed."

He lifted the knife with hands that trembled and wiped his still bleeding thumb on the edge. It too absorbed it and shimmered, then went still.

"On both of these, if you throw, no mortal will be able to withstand, but only when they are in your hands will they cut a god. All weapons require your life force to damage a god. The whip, your weapons, and the sword. Remember this." Her voice was hard and Rylix nodded, still holding his whip, though the cap was on the tip.

Note wrapped his hands around the weapons with a possessiveness everyone could see. But he looked up at Shinala and smiled. "Aryix bless."

She laughed. "Literally in this case." Her head and gaze turned to alight on Jadaya, who stood watching. "Now for the warrior of no god."

CHAPTER SEVENTY-EIGHT

LAZUL

Lazul looked up from his breakfast as Actin knocked on the door and stepped inside. There was a frown on his face as he did a slight bow. Even after all this time, Actin still stuck to the formalities. He also was the only reason the crown remained a beacon of hope and Lazul knew it.

"Sire, Cantor Zayn requests an immediate formal audience with you." His tone was perfect and smooth and not matching the frown on his face.

"Formal?" Lazul asked carefully. While Zayn was an on again, off again opponent and ally, he was unaware of the man ever asking for a formal audience. In fact, he had no recollection of a single formal event since his coronation that Zayn had attended. For all his arrogance, the sheer spectacle a formal audience required was work for him and the servants.

"Yes, sire," Actin said, his lips together in a thin line.

Lazul sighed and glanced over at Hauyne, who had been silently listening. They were still trying to get more information and had scribes scouring the archives or royal records about anything regarding the gods and the death of Percit, but so far the results returned nothing.

"It means he needs witnesses and a show," she said, considering each word. "That means a performance, but for whom?"

Lazul nodded as he thought about it. A horrible thought struck him and he pushed it away. Xyl rarely talked to any Charinsky. Why would he appear twice in a mooncycle?

"Very well, I will see him first when the audience starts in four fingers. Send out the messengers to all the major houses now. They have a right to witness anything requiring a formal audience," he said, pushing away what remained of his breakfast. The pain was wrapping around him early today and he had been considering canceling for the day, but that was no longer an option. He had to make sure he avoided taking gris this morning as the drug would make him more susceptible. Instead, he took another swallow of telcha with tella syrup in it. That should give him some distance for a while.

Four fingers later, he walked into the audience chambers wearing his royal robes, not his normal working robes, and sat on his throne. To his relief, there was a cushion and a carafe of fruist waiting for him. From the nod Actin gave him, it had been doctored with what he would require.

Once he settled into his chair, he nodded at Actin.

"King Lazul's formal court is in session. Let the petitioners approach." His voice boomed through the hall and Lazul hid a wince. This particular room was vast, empty, and everything echoed. But formal meant the nobles were roused and here to witness the show. He had no idea if it was going to be a tragedy or comedy, but his money was on tragedy. But for whom?

Zayn strode up to the throne, his robes billowing behind him. Lazul fought to keep a somber face even as a twist of pain and worry flashed through him. These were different from his Day of Remembrance robes, which were solemn and elegant in blacks and reds. These were his 'I am very important' robes.

The black with silver and red stitching of the holy symbols on the sides fit him perfectly and made him look imposing and powerful. The last time Lazul could remember seeing them was at his parents' funeral and his own coronation.

He looks more kingly than I do.

The thought was wistful, but the worry deepened as Zayn approached. The look on his face was overly controlled. Similar to how he looked on the Day of Remembrance services when he wanted to be sure that he looked regal and imposing. But why this here? The worry twisted tighter in his stomach.

"Sire, our god, Xyl, has spoken to me and I am here delivering his message. Nay, his commands. I tell you as king of our country, so you might help to ensure his word is obeyed to the letter and none might be unaware of his decree." Zayn kept his eyes on Lazul, tight lines around them as his voice filled the hall.

The thread of worry tightened into a noose around his heart, but Lazul sat up straighter and nodded. "Cantor Zayn, tell us what our god commands of us." There was no other response possible, not if he wanted a chance to save his kingdom.

Zayn smiled, but there was no joy in his face and his eyes were dead as he continued. "As the light that was Percit has fled, so has the joy that Xyl once felt.

Now he lives in the remembrance of pain and the absence of pleasure. For without her, there is only darkness and the depravity of her twisted touch. He decrees that all should embrace this, the dark aspect of themselves, and our screams and pleas of pain and need will be the paeans to him. Let our people hurt and offer that pain to him as a thin shadow of what he feels. His need is all that matters. For a few, that pain will be pleasure and his touch will give them the surcease of pain transformed into the exploding joy of the heights of pleasure."

He paused to turn once, sweeping his hand to include the entire court. Then Zayn faced Lazul again. "All the things that are dark and twisted are an homage to her, and the pain and joy you feel when you give in to these acts are your worship of him. Be warned that this is his decree, and the cost of ignoring his commands will be high. Without his blessings, with his rage and sorrow, he will coat Charinsky in water and mud, and when there is no one left, then he will take this land and build a mausoleum to her. Xyl knows not what is in our hearts or minds, but hears our songs and praise to her, and requires this new ode to stay his hand." The words echoed through the silent hall as a death knell to what Charinsky had been.

"And he has one last word for you, my king," Zayn said, his tone almost mocking.

Lazul nodded his head, trying to not let any of his reactions show. Because otherwise he might start throwing up. "I would hear what our god commands of me."

The smile on Zayn's face was a mockery of everything a smile should have been, and the noose around Lazul's throat grew tighter.

"If you lead the change, show your subjects just what could be done to explore pain that can turn to pleasure. Take Hauyne and show the populace just what can be done with a little imagination and pain. If you become the icon of how you should follow Xyl's edicts, he will lift the eternal pain he graced you with. The king should be the leader in paving the way for how to act. After all, the king is the reflection of how our kingdom should go."

The words hit Lazul like a fist, and he tightened his hands on his throne. A relief from the pain, but to do that he would need to abuse Hauyne? Publicly? Not only was the idea of abusing Hauyne something that threatened to make him sick, but to do it in public as if that was an example of how men should treat their wives. Or worse, maybe he should have her abuse him, so wives would do the same to their husbands?

The worst part was the thread of temptation. To not hurt. To be able to function in the bedchamber. To feel whole again.

"I see," he said after he realized the silence had stretched on too long. "Is there anything else our god wishes us to know?"

Again that mockery of a smile. It almost made Lazul feel sorry for the man. "Only that the weak have always been those who please him the most. The temples will be changed to showcase just how the cries of pain and pleasure can be turned into music for our god."

Lazul tried not to flinch, but the noose around his heart yanked a little harder. "The singers?"

"They will be trained to sing in pain and in pleasure as our god demands. The services will show how the people can use each other to extract the greatest amount of pain yet still lift their voices up. After all, they are ours and there are none who would dare take them away, so of course their song shall be our gift to Xyl."

The phrasing caught at Lazul and he filed it away, still fighting with his reactions to the words.

"Your message has been heard. Aryix bless for sharing the words of Xyl." His voice maintained firmness for all that his body shook with revulsion and fear.

"It is not only my duty but my honor to serve our god." With that, Zayn gave another bow, this one barely respectable and spun, striding out of the hall, the robes billowing behind him as if flags for Xyl.

Licking lips that were dry enough to crack, Lazul addressed the court, though they were all looking as dazed and horrified as he felt. "Given the momentous information conveyed to us by the Cantor, no more will be heard today while we all take time to consider his words."

Retreat while we can and panic in private.

"Notice will be sent out as to the decisions about how we shall proceed." Lazul rose as he said the last words, and Actin preceded him out of the throne room.

He headed straight to the private chamber that he and Hauyne used, Actin leading the way. "I sent a servant to stock the room while Zayn was speaking, sire. And I saw Hauyne in the wings listening."

Lazul glanced at Actin, who was so pale he thought the man might keel over, but then everyone in the hall had looked as pale.

"Aryix bless," Lazul said fervently. At the moment, he was unsure if getting so drunk he was no longer able to think or running away screaming was the best option.

Actin opened the door for him and Lazul went in, finding Hauyne sitting there, her face white, a large glass of fruist in her hand.

He sank down. Actin nodded and started to close the door as he stepped out. "Actin, wait. I want you to join us."

His advisor frowned for a long moment, but nodded and closed the door, then pulled up a stool and sat near the door, but where both Hauyne and he could see him.

"That was unexpected," Hauyne said after they all had taken large glasses of fruist and drank some. Lazul had forgone any of the extra drugs, as the pain would keep him sharper and, for now, he wanted to be able to think.

"Very. But did you catch some of his phrasing? I think he hates this. But if he was visited, I suspect there is no choice for him." Lazul spoke softly, but the words were clear as he watched his fruist, not the people. The last offer still ringing in his mind.

"I did. But I also caught what he said. That was quite the carrot he dangled in front of you," Hauyne said even more quietly. "Will you do it?"

Lazul closed his eyes. He wanted to cry, scream, flee. But they had promised to be honest with each other. Opening his eyes, he stared right at her, the ice blue of her eyes locking on his. "No. I will not lie. There is a part of me that longs for the pain to stop and would do anything for the peace. But that is not the person I am. The person I want to be. I value you way too much to ever treat you in such a manner."

Silence fell until Actin broke it.

"I believe that is what the Cantor hopes you will do," he said thoughtfully. None of them wanted to use names at this point. The idea of summoning those of whom they spoke about terrified them enough to make them talk in circles.

Lazul turned his head, focusing on him. "What do you mean?"

Actin spoke slowly, as if trying to figure out each word as he said it. "He wants you to be the example. The person who is behaving as we know is right, even though you of all would benefit the most."

"Of course," Hauyne said, excitement in her tone. "He made it known you are in constant pain, pain given to you by that *thing*. If you act like that, your pain would be lifted, but if you continue to act like you, your subjects will see it. And he said that our thoughts and feelings are our own, so if we are careful, he will not know."

Lazul blinked, processing that. His mind had caught on the idea of no pain and had missed that implication or the relief of knowing Xyl could only hear their words, not read their minds. "There was also the aspect of stopping it. He said, 'there are none who would dare take them away' but we know there are. The three. They are the ones that could stop all of this."

Again silence, then Hauyne spoke. "So be it. I will place watchers on every port, every entrance into Charinsky looking for a Ged, a Zuyikan, and an Aoisan, or any one of them. The Ged that trade here regularly are known and I can count them. Any that is new or unknown, we will find, and we will help them deal with this problem."

"But will it be soon enough?" Actin's question hung in the air.

"All we can do is hope. There is little else we can do but wait. And hope they know how to kill a god. I would, but how?" Lazul's question left them all staring into their glasses and hoping for a miracle.

CHAPTER SEVENTY-NINE

JADAYA

Jadaya watched the handing out of weapons with awe, excitement, and hunger as she fought to pull her attention away from the sword that lay there. It was as long as her arm and rippled with the same wavy pattern as the blades Note currently fondled with a possessiveness she knew she would mimic. At Shinala's words, she moved closer and crouched before the hide, enraptured with the sword.

"This is Immunity", Shinala said, handing it to Jadaya. It was heavy, but not uncomfortably so. The hilt was long enough for her to wrap both hands around it easily. Wrapped in leather to prevent it from slipping out of her hand, it had a swirl of flames crafted at the end, long enough to cause damage if she slammed the hilt into someone. The quillons arched downward to protect her hands and were of the same rippling flames design as the pommel. Up from the crossguard, inset into the design of the quillons, which flowed up into the rain guard, were three clear crystals. They shimmered in the light and all of it had the water pattern on it, with both edges sharp enough to slice through flesh with ease. There was no taper as it ran straight, the blade being about the length of her arm.

Without being told, Jadaya gently pierced her thumb with the tip and it ate her blood with a shiver of glee.

Shinala smiled and nodded. "As this was made to fight a god, it renders the user immune to magical attacks, and every cut made to the flesh will have the same slowed healing effects that the Ged's whip does and will sluggishly bleed power."

Jadaya nodded, holding it up in the light. "This is amazing. I need to practice."

"Yes, but use care. I created a normal sword as well, the same weight as this. Use that one for sparring until the sheath for this can be created. If you hit one of my males with it, more than a glancing blow might kill them."

Jadaya swallowed hard. "I will." A grin wreathed her face, the compulsive desire to immediately start practicing making her squirm like a child.

"There is more. My crafting does not always make sense to me, but when I beat out the materials and imbue them with power, I know what they will do." Shinala reached down and handed her a bracer and an earring. "The bracer goes on your left wrist as you are right hand dominant. It will enable you to block even one of my weapons, but while it means your wrist will be protected from severing, it can still break."

Jadaya slipped it on, the blood still on her fingers from the sword. It drank it in, then it flowed and wiggled on to her, fitting perfectly, but with no opening. She gasped as it moved, lifting her eyes to Shinala.

The Leonaid was staring at her wrist with a puzzled expression. "I have never seen one do that before. The only other aspect that I know of is it will help you heal faster. Enough to make recovering easier, not enough to save your life on the battlefield. Then there is this." She handed her a gold hoop earring.

Jadaya took it with a nod. It was heavier than she expected. Without being told, she took some blood still seeping from the wound and smeared the earring with it. It too glowed and absorbed the blood. "Does it matter which side?" she asked Shinala.

"Left also I think." The woman watched her slide the earring in and then nodded. "It should allow you to sense gods if they are near you and make yourself more aware of their magic and what they are doing with it." She shrugged. "Sometimes my magic has a will of its own. And I think you may need this."

The earring slid into her left ear and after a moment, it felt like she had always had it. "Aryix bless. These are incredible," she gushed, carefully holding the sword toward her.

Shinala grunted. "I will get you the unenchanted sword. You will practice with fake until you know it better. A sheath will be made that can house Immunity. Then you can use it in practice." The woman tilted her head, looking at her, white hair spilling over her body. "These are the first weapons I have made in more suncycles than I can count. Use them well." Then she rolled up the hide and strode back up the shore to her forge, Mace following her with a wink at Jadaya.

Jadaya held the sword as if it was the most precious thing ever given to her, and it was. This was a magical weapon, forged by a woman who was all but a legend. And it felt so right. Glancing around, Note and Rylix had similar looks on their faces as they caressed and inspected their weapons.

Mace came trotting back with a sword that looked exactly like what she held, but without the stones or the details. "Here. For practice. Sheath I make." Another quick smile and he trotted back up to where Shinala had gone.

Hating the thought of not using the real sword, but needing to practice with the weight, Jadaya went to the room she had been sleeping in. For being a hole dug in the wall, it was cozy, comfortable, and provided an odd amount of privacy for the three of them, with their beds being in little side cubbyholes. Rylix had been right, and the mountain did not count as a roof, so he was sleeping well in his snug little bedchamber. She pulled out one of the leather blankets, harvested from animals on the other side of the mountain, then carefully wrapped Immunity in it. After one last look, she set it under the bed and raced back outside with the practice version of the sword.

The days disappeared in training. She fought with Katel, forcing herself to get better, be faster, until she was staggering with exhaustion. But never had she been more deadly. The sword felt better in her hands than any weapon ever provided. When Lev showed up with the sheath for Immunity, everything snapped together in her mind and body. The sheath barely altered the practice, but it meant she had no need to worry about hitting her sparring partner, which had dwindled to Katel and Paka. Katel, she learned, had been the weapons master for so long he was unable to count the suncycles. His skills were varied and what little rust had been on his abilities wore off quickly.

Paka was another matter. Rage, grief, and unwavering determination wove through his being. He attacked with power and only pulled back on killing blows. But he tested her in different ways than Katel and the morning light was their call to start their practice. Sparring with the Leonaids sharpened Jadaya's skills, and she fought better than she ever had. Note and Rylix were getting the same treatment and their skills were increasing just as fast.

The bracer already proved its worth. After falling into bed, every muscle screaming, she had expected to wake up stiff and in pain, but instead she woke ready to go again. A smile crossed her face as she dove back in, not needing to worry about the aftermath of pushing herself too much.

Jadaya had expected to die doing this, and if they were lucky, rescue some children, but now? She felt like they might actually have a chance if they went up against a god. But how did you get a god to show up?

She asked the question quietly one night, when they were all settling down to sleep. Each bed had its own little cubby, but in the middle was a table and chairs, and the other hall that led to a needs room.

"Do we know if a god is killable?" Her question hung in the air and Note and Rylix both stopped their evening routines to look at her.

"Given all this started because a god died, I would say yes," Note said with a sardonic tilt of his lips.

Jadaya waved her hand at that. "That was by another god, or at least another being. Can we?"

Rylix settled down across from her, a thoughtful look on his face. "The weapons that Shinala created make all the old stories I know seem weak in comparison. It was said she would create them for the gods when the world was still young. I am still awed by having one and I keep expecting her to ask for it back."

Jadaya laughed in agreement as Note came to sit down.

"So you think we can? Kill him I mean?" Her voice sounded more questioning than she wanted, but it was a valid question.

Note set his two weapons, Trinity and Echo, on the table. They were with him even as he slept. His hands traced their shapes as he spoke.

"I think, with these, we can. How much he is aware of I am unsure, but with these, he will bleed and I suspect he will die, or at the least be imprisoned like the old gods."

"Will that satisfy you?" Rylix asked, watching Note as closely as Jadaya was.

Note was quiet for a long time, but he finally looked up and met their gazes. "For him, yes. I still want consequences for the priesthood, the ones that carried out the abuse and the capture. But I think that will have to be decided after. Once he is dead and we have some leverage."

"Will we? Have leverage?" Rylix asked, his eyes hooded with worry.

Note shrugged. "Assuming we are standing over the body of their god, is there any greater leverage?"

Jadaya choked out a laugh at the audacity of it, yet it was true. If at that point they asked for the kingdom, it might be given to them. What more could they do if they tried?

"And if the other gods get mad at us?" It was a silly question she knew, given the gods had all but pushed them this direction, but somehow she thought the weapons Shinala made would terrify all the gods.

Note shrugged. "They kill us. And I am not sure I care."

Rylix fell silent and Jadaya looked inside herself. She had always known she might die, but now, when she finally felt like she was becoming who she had always wanted to be, the idea of losing it all seemed terrifying. She glanced at Note and thought about their different childhoods. Hers, while it might have been better, had seen no active abuse, just lack of love. But Note? No, that could not continue, even if it cost her a life she was just starting to live.

"It seems to me this is something worth dying for. After all, how many people can say they died while defying a god?" She gave them both a smile as she spoke.

Rylix let loose a soft chuckle. "Well, I promise you, if I live and you die, the Ged will write songs of your sacrifice and will ensure all who trade with us hear it." Another soft laugh. "In fact, knowing my cousins, I suspect that will happen even if I do die. We are changing the world, and the Ged have always made those events into stories and songs. I have little doubt that would be the same here."

Note looked at both of them, his pupils so dark they looked like the empty sky. "I am filled with conflict. You are both crazy, yet having you here is the blessing I never expected. Aryix bless you for going on this crazy quest with me. I am proud to call you friends."

Jadaya blinked as she looked at her companions. Friends. She had thought Elike was her friend, and more, but as soon as the opportunity rose, she threw Jadaya's friendship and love away like it was dung. But these two? Jadaya knew they would be beside her as they faced down a god. "As am I. Friends," she said the word the same way others might say the name of their god. In many ways, it meant more. She had friends who would be there no matter what came at them.

"Yes, friends," Rylix replied. "Prior to this I only had family, near and far cousins, but active friends, no. It is an unexpectedly agreeable feeling. To have someone who likes you for you, not for blood or obligations."

"Agreed. In the temple, you avoided more than knowing a name. If you cared, you risked having your heart broken when they died or were taken away. Looking back, I suspect they purposefully broke up friendships, to make sure we relied on the priests for everything." He looked at the two of them and Jadaya had to close her eyes for a moment against the pain she saw writ on his face. "This is new to me and rather wonderful."

Jadaya stretched out her hand in the center of the table. "To friends."

Smiling, both Note and Rylix gripped her hands, so each of them held the other. "To friends."

CHAPTER EIGHTY

SHINALA

Shinala watched as the three mortals spent the next tenday practicing with their new weapons. She could all but hear the pleasure of the metal as they learned to wield them. Mace and she had worked together, using yet more ground up crystals and impregnating a sheath for Immunity. It added weight, but Jadaya needed to be able to practice with it without killing her sparring partner.

Then there was the weapon she had made for herself. It had been so long since she had made named weapons. There were two, Justice and Weep, she had thrown in the lava at Aryix's feet when they were first imprisoned here. She knew there were a few pieces of jewelry still floating out there with magic in them, but it was all minor, like the eternal flask Cassix carried. The whispers in her magic that helped her forge it named it a dual chakram. It was called Eternity. It glittered in the sun, and she had used her own hair to braid the wraps around the handles, the white impervious to dirt and blood. The design that sprang from her created two half circles that had an S-shaped curve that snapped together or she could separate them as individual weapons, giving her a slicing blade in each fist. Her claws were amazing, but they did not neatly slice; they tore and gouged. When together, she could throw it by swirling it around on her finger and flinging it.

The magic of Eternity was different from battle magic like her other weapons had, instead it would flow into a bracelet she could wear in either form and no one but her could remove it. Though she supposed they could cut off her arm, but even then she doubted Eternity would let go. The deadly aspect of Eternity was the edges, ones she had to be very careful with. She coated the blades in ground crystal. The bowls provided by the gods were the only objects impervious to its power. She practiced in private, far away from the others, making sure she knew how to use it, aim it, and make sure she kept all her fingers. In fingers of practice, she had cut herself many times. For the first time in suncycles, she had to wrap her wounds as the Leonaids' accelerated healing was not enough, since the crystals prevented accelerated healing. She supposed there was poison in them; after all, they were created from the blood of gods.

One thing she had not told the mortals was the blood Xyl would bleed would crystalize and be the same thing she had coated into their weapons. If they survived, she would need to have her males collect it, make sure it was properly secured.

The screech of a bird pulled her attention away from the chakram and her own thoughts about the future. She turned to look back at the ocean, then the white sails grabbed her attention. A ship? Coming here? A wave of excitement mixed with frustration and wariness flashed through her. Why now would there be more mortals coming to this place? Even the Ged had abandoned them eons ago. Looking around, she realized she was where the dock once lay, a dock that no longer existed. If she was careless, the ship would get pushed in here and destroyed. Over the suncycles, she had enough blood on her hands; she needed no more.

Her skills had always been in crafting and battle. Being a diplomat, growing things, cooking, baking, even tending to animals had never worked for her. But creating things, killing things, those she was good at. But it had been a long time since the dock had fallen apart. The ship would be here in fingers. She shifted to her feline form and raced toward their little settlement. That was what it had become over the suncycles: a settlement. Though as the suncycles passed, they had lived more and more as animals and the realization that might not have been wise resonated in her bones.

Racing along the island in her feline form was faster than most animals, and she could maintain it longer than any mortal feline. She let loose a long, howling roar as she raced in, so by the time she arrived, most of the males were waiting for her. Their visitors were also there, looking confused and worried.

She shifted to her two-legged form as she hit the primary group. "A ship is coming in where the dock once was. If come all the way in, the ship will be damaged."

"Jolyx," the Aoisan said, and she glanced at him. "I asked Pel to bring her here. To get us to Charinsky," he said with a wince.

"At the speed at which she moves, she will sail in and bust open her hull, preventing all of us from leaving." Her eyes were on Note as she spoke. There was no way to repair the dock in fingers, which was all the time they had.

"I can go warn her." He turned to run toward the sea, diving in a stride into the waves. He had only been wearing shorts, so there was little to drag him down. She knew he could breathe underwater, but she still instinctually searched for his head coming up for air.

"We should go meet her. I know Jolyx will be more than a little annoyed," Rylix said.

"A little?" Jadaya snorted. "That is the least of what she will be."

"Then we should go and you explain to her, but it solves the issue of how to get to Char." Shinala still had not mentioned she would travel with them, nor had she talked to her males about it yet. That would need to be done soon. But for now, they had a guest to meet.

They all moved back down the island at a more sedate pace. All the males came with them, as something new was to be relished. She slowed down a step, letting Jadaya and Rylix take the lead, the ship in the distance proving an obvious marker.

She signaled the five she wanted, Mace, Lev, Katel, Paka, and Sher. The five fell back, letting the rest get up ahead. They looked at her and waited. "I have not told our guests yet, but I and five males will go with them on their journey to stop the mad god. I want you five to come with me." She kept her tone conversational as they walked, albeit at a much slower pace than they could have gone.

Paka flashed a hard grin, more of a snarl than a smile. "I would go with or without."

Shinala nodded her head. "I know. Which is why you are coming with me. You will get your chance."

Katel grinned at her. "Chance to stretch myself. Sounds fun."

Those two she had never worried about, nor Sher. "Sher go. Sher kill many. Bloodlust."

She flinched at that. It had been suns uncounted since any of them had felt the call of bloodlust and Sher had missed it the most of all.

"Yes. But I have no desire to lose my males to that."

Sher shrugged. "Life, battle, it is living."

With more interaction, their language skill would improve. She knew this, but still it was yet another reminder of her flaws. Shinala brushed it away. Now was not the time to worry over past choices. She needed to focus on her choices now.

"Lev?" she asked, looking at the green-eyed man. He was all she had left of Raj. She still remembered his birth. One of her children, of her males, and because of that, more isolated than most. Of all the Leonaids only two of her children still lived, Lev was one, Lovi the other. Their father, well, she still talked to him, but their coupling was so long ago she wondered if Quas even remembered.

With a shake of her head, she pushed the memories away. They no longer mattered. Instead, she focused on him, who watched her with those familiar green eyes.

"I go," he said, then looked ahead and continued walking.

That left the only one that worried her, more because he was better at catching subtle clues than missing him by her side. She looked at Mace who smiled down at her, the missing canine an odd gap in an otherwise perfect smile.

"Where you go, I go. Who else take care of you?" His words were simple, but the understanding in his eyes carried lifetimes of intelligence. He had been her favorite partner since their imprisonment. But she worried about her sons and Paka. They had no bed partners since the Ged quit coming. Yet another way she had failed them.

She rolled her eyes and bumped him with her shoulder, a common motion she used in both forms.

"Then I will let them know, but we should practice our warrior forms and let them see, so they are not startled at the wrong time." She had no memory of the last time she took that form, but to fight Xyl they would need it.

"Yes," Katel growled. "I shall do it when practice with the no god one. See how she responds."

The match between their language habits and the Geds burst into awareness as she heard his name for the ex-Zuyikan. Neither the Leonaids nor the Ged often used names. The Ged introduced you once, but then avoided it, as did she and hers. Was it a carryover from the old gods? She would need to think about it. The beliefs of mortals rarely registered with her back then. Now they might be important. Either way, it was something to consider later.

In the distance, the ship had stopped, and it looked like they were lowering a small boat into the water. "We should catch up."

The six of them broke into a light jog and caught up with the rest, who were waiting as the swimmer climbed onto the shore, the boat following behind him. The Aoisan shook his head, water flying off his dark hair, then he went over to where the rest of the group were standing.

"The captain and crew. She is coming in. She might be a bit … annoyed," he said with a smirk.

Rylix sighed. "In other words, I need to convince her to help us, not just sail away?"

Note shrugged. "Maybe."

Shinala turned to watch the small boat as they rowed through the shallows. As the bottom of the boat touched the sandy shore, one of the men jumped out and dragged it firmly up, then a woman jumped out. Shinala watched her stalk up to the three visitors, her hair loose and streaming behind her like a flag. She had more vibrancy than any Shinala had seen in suncycles and the words that flowed proved she was more than annoyed.

"What in the broken moon is this? First my ship gets grabbed by an uncharted current, pulls me across the deeps so fast even the monsters are left behind and throws me here? A mount forbidden for generations. And who do I find here but you three? I should have expected that, but mostly I thought we were about to die." Every word carried the weight of anger and command.

Shinala was reluctantly impressed.

The woman took her eyes off the three to scan the rest, and she stiffened. Obviously her attention had been on the Aoisan, then the others, but now she saw the three males who were still in feline form, and the rest of the Leonaids watching her in two-legged form, of which only three had any form of clothing on.

"Is there a reason no one seems to have any clothing? Because if this is a Char-inspired orgy, I will leave and take my chances in the deeps." The words implied something unseemly about an orgy, not that Shinala had often been in one. Usually, the attention of more than two males at a time was distracting and lowered the pleasure.

Her eyes locked on Shinala's and the captain's eyes narrowed as she flicked from her to the Leonaids in feline form, then back to her.

"I thought you were a legend. If real at all, you had faded into the mists of time." This time the anger had fled her voice. Instead, there was steel and a touch of fear.

"We were always real. It just became harder after the Ged abandoned us," Shinala replied, baring her teeth at Jolyx in what was not even close to a smile.

"My captain of grace and beauty and the powerful, wise leader of the Leonaids, let us not allow our emotions to drive us to unwise words." Rylix smiled as he spoke, his words tumbling out faster than normal. "May I introduce the wise leader of the Leonaids, the powerful and gracious Shinala?" He did a half bow and gestured between the two of them. "Mistress of the Mount of Gods, it is my greatest pleasure to introduce the captain of the *Starguide*, Jolyx."

Shinala walked up to the woman, taller than her by a thumb width, and nodded. "It is good to meet you, captain."

The woman took a long look at her and let loose a breath. "It is nice to meet you. I assume it was not sheer chance that I am here." She spoke politely, but her jaw still clenched and unclenched as she struggled with her temper.

"We need you to take us to Char," Note said with an easy shrug. "We have a god to deal with."

CHAPTER EIGHTY-ONE

NOTE

The explosion of words from Jolyx made it very clear she was not a fan of that plan. It took fast talking from Rylix, and the invitation from Shinala to come onto land and have supper, especially if she would bring some more seasonings, as Rylix's supplies were mostly gone, to smooth out much of the anger.

Mostly Note watched, having done what he could. He let Rylix and Jadaya take the lead, but he was aware of how much power Shinala controlled. From the subtle looks the other Leonaids gave her, to the way she spoke. She was a commander.

"So you need me to take the three of you and dump you on the shore of Charinsky? How exactly are you going to make your way into Granite? If you are going to trade, I see little that you have left. Your cousin is going to be very annoyed at the loss of the wagon."

"You will not only be transporting those three," Shinala said, pulling everyone's eyes to her. They gathered in the general eating area where Rylix cooked another large fish and used the new spices to season it to perfection. He also created a strange seaweed salad that tasted excellent. Jadaya had used the flask to make them all water, something that made Shinala smile every time she saw it.

All eyes had focused on Shinala as she sat down. The cross-legged position she sat in made it hard to keep your eyes on her as she still wore no clothing.

"Oh?" Jolyx said, watching her closely.

"Myself and five of my pride will come as well." Shinala pointed at the five.

Note knew some of them, but the one with the scar was unfamiliar. "We will be needed." She said it all as a statement, and Note could see Jolyx bristle.

"And what if I refuse?" she snapped back, her tone belligerent. Jolyx was still unhappy about gods messing with her schedule.

Shinala just smiled. And Note had to repress a shudder at that. He had little doubt as to her abilities and noted the minor cuts on her hands that were now healed.

"I see." Jolyx stared at Shinala for a long moment, and while the battle of wills amused him, Note kept his nose out of it. "Very well, but this is my ship, and I will not have naked beings on it. One, it is unsafe. Two, it distracts my crew, which is also unsafe."

Note watched all of this while eating the fish. Jolyx had provided some fruit, and it provided a tang that his body had been craving without knowing it. Everyone else must have felt the same as they were busy eating, not paying attention to the staring contest.

"Understood," Shinala said, to Note's surprise. At a certain level, he had expected her to refuse. "It was given at some point we would need clothing. But outside of loincloths, we have none. The Ged quit coming here, so we have no fabric." There was a certain amount of needling at that, and Note stuffed more fish in his mouth to stop his laughing.

"I will take no responsibility for the actions of those dead long before my ship was built. But I will say not even the oldest ever mentioned coming to this forbidden place," Jolyx replied, taking a bite of fish, still watching the Leonaid.

In some ways, it was better than watching a play. There, you often knew the plot, but not with this. Would they become friends, or would one attack the other? Was this the beginning of an alliance or a war? His amusement faded as he thought about what Shinala had said. Shinala and the other Leonaids coming would change everything. It might make it easier. But could they trust her?

Shinala was silent, then shook her head and waved her hand, shooing it away. "I will grant you that. It has been so many suncycles I have no words for their number. I would be grateful if you would provide us with some basics until we reach land."

Jolyx, obviously mollified, nodded. "There are enough that should fit most of your people, but he might be an issue." She nodded over the fish at one of the Leonaids and Note followed her gaze to land on Sher. The Leonaid was one of the largest, both in height and width, and not one ounce of it was fat. With a bright red mane of hair and a laugh that boomed, no one would think to cross him as he radiated a desire for a fight.

"Understood. We will see what we can do, prior," Shinala said. With that, the conversation was over, and the strange cat-woman focused on the fish. Jolyx, for her part, turned to spear Rylix with her gaze.

"You obviously have no trade goods. How are you going to hide your movement across the country? If I sail into Granite, you will be dead before you leave the docks. Best case would be the inlet opposite Granite, but there will be watchers even there. To survive, they need to see something other than those whom everyone is talking about."

Rylix put down the piece of fish and looked at her. "Until this moment, I was going to offer some of my money back in Fivika to you for some of your cargo."

"Would do you little good. At this time, I have barrels of oil and bales of cotton and wool. Not much that you could sell as small trinkets."

Note winced at that. He had hoped she would have more on her ship that they could sell.

"Ah, well then, my new idea is a bit … riskier." He spoke slowly and kept his eyes on the distant horizon. Note felt a chill as Rylix opened his mouth. "No one would expect to find us as a traveling show with sabers," he said slowly.

The head of every Leonaid snapped to Rylix like he was a quivering fawn in the middle of them. Note found his hands reaching for his weapons, wondering how many he could kill before they killed him.

Rylix raised his hands. "Now hear me out. Some of you, as mortals, are very noticeable. If we travel with you as 'trained' sabers, all the attention will be on you, not us. While it is exceedingly rare for someone to train one of the wilder animals, it would ensure access almost everywhere, yet we," he waved his hands at Note and Jadaya, "would not be what they are talking about. Though I still need to figure out a disguise for Note."

A low rumble filled the air and Note figured out the best trajectory to attack Sher first and wondered if Jadaya had her sword somewhere within reach.

"Interesting. What would we do?" Shinala's voice broke the tension.

"What?" Sher roared. "You would have them think of us as animals?"

Shinala flashed the most dangerous look Note had ever seen toward the redheaded Leonaid. "We are. We are Leonaids. We are warriors. We are servants. We are whatever we need to be to do the gods' bidding. And make no mistake, the gods want us to do this." There was something about how she looked at him along with the elbow Mace slammed into Sher's side that spoke to things she had not told them. The red-headed giant shrank back down and grabbed another piece of fish.

Shinala closed her eyes, and he wished he could read her mind. Then she looked at Rylix. "What is your idea?"

Rylix cleared his throat, his hand drifting to the whip that almost never left his side. Note understood that attraction.

"As I understand it, you are white when a saber, Sher is red, Lev has a red mane, while Katel has a white mane with brown fur, while Paka is all black, and Mace is the only normal or boring feline. Correct?" He watched Shinala, whose mouth had quirked up, but she nodded.

"Then my suggestion is Mace stays like us and acts as the 'caretaker' for you. Jadaya and I will be the 'trainers' and the presentation will be one of the sabers raised from birth with her in the wilds of Zuyika, traveling the world to show off their intelligence. Saying Jadaya hand raised them, will convince people why you are so big and can do the tricks. It should allow us to get information by listening to people and earn some money, as trade goods are scarce at the moment." He turned to look at Jolyx. "Speaking of which, I need to see if I can get a few copper from you for basic supplies. I can provide a writ from the bank for whatever I get."

Note had been listening, and the vision of what Rylix talked about sprang large in his mind. And from what he had seen of Char's life, Rylix was correct. Anything that was flashy or different would grab their attention. Especially if it had little to do with their insane god.

Jolyx heaved a sigh. "I can do that. And yes, my ship will assist, as long as the currents let us get there. Rarely do I travel that route, but if the charts remain accurate, I should be able to go around the deeps and dump you into the small port opposite the capital. They have limited supplies in that town. I am unaware if they even have a name. But you should be able to buy some more clothes...." She trailed off for a moment, and Note swore he could see Rylix's nose twitch as he focused on her.

"But? I hear something in what you are leaving unsaid, my glorious captain." By this point, everyone was looking at her and Drix sighed. On their first trip, his role had been second mate. But when Tylax took over as captain for the pirate ship they had captured, he had stayed with Jolyx and moved up to first mate.

"Ya might as well tell him. His nose is worse than a dog that has caught a whiff of a treat from his master's hand." Drix shook his head as he popped more fish into his mouth.

"Me and my big mouth," Jolyx muttered, looked at the leaf of food in her hands. Note waited to hear what she would say, but Rylix was all but vibrating. "We still have a few chests that were on the ship we captured. The thought was to take them down to Wysko to trade. They are full of clothing and fabrics that are the most gaudy things. Not even the most flamboyant of us would wear them. Some of it looks fancy, but after we inspected it, they were glass or paste, not gems." She pulled her head up and looked at Rylix. "I could be persuaded to sell it to you for two plat?"

Rylix laughed at that offer, and they settled into bartering. Note tuned them out as he gazed out at the sea. They were about to do this, with beings from legends by their side. If nothing else, it would be a much more satisfying way to die than at the hands of one of the priests that got too 'excited'. This he could accept.

CHAPTER EIGHTY-TWO

RYLIX

The crate of goods that Jolyx had was exactly what they needed and the more they dug through it, something others had not done in the confusion of dealing with the captured ship, the more he found. By the time he was done, he knew the value of the goods was such that he almost felt like he owed Jolyx money. Almost. But it let him create costumes for the three of them, and garb for the Leonaids to wear in both mortal and saber form. The saber garb involved neckpieces that added to their majesty, and he even found a special crown for Shinala that he secured with clips to her fur. It was perfect for walking around and looking gorgeous, but for any of the tricks, she would leave it off.

They spent three more days on the prison island, though Rylix had realized it was a prison for both the gods and those sentenced to watch them. He and Jolyx had a long talk about making sure the island went into the records as a place for ships to stop at with most food and some fabrics and home goods.

"I agree. We should have always been visiting here. But it is the cost that worries me." She waved her hand around. "What will they trade? Fish? That is something I can get anywhere."

"I might have a solution to that," Shinala said from behind them on the deck of the ship. Everyone was loading things, and they were getting ready to sail with the tide.

Jolyx spun, and Rylix had to fight not to jump. "I am about ready to order all of you to wear Usurper-blasted bells," Jolyx snarled. "This ship creaks and groans when a bird lands on the rail. How can you be so silent?"

Shinala grinned at them, showing overly long canines for all that she was in her mortal form. "Gift of the gods."

Rylix ordered his heart to slow down and nodded his head. "They gifted you with more than silence and grace. How can you assist us in our little trade dilemma?"

She pulled out a bar from the bag at her waist. "I have about twenty of these I am willing to trade."

Rylix reached out to pick up the bar. It was only about the length of his hand and the width of two fingers. It had a muted silver sheen to it and was lighter than he expected. "What substance would this be that you would trade for spices and goods?"

Shinala, for the first time, looked slightly nervous, then she shook her head. "Per Aryix, this is titanium. This is a metal that is stronger than iron, yet does not rust in water and is lighter than lead. It is what I used in the making of your weapons and some of the things I created long ago. It can be used in weapons, jewelry, mechanicals, anything really. As far as I know, this is the only place it can be extracted."

Rylix blinked as his mind stuttered to a stop. If it was what she said, they held a king's fortune. He exchanged a long look with Jolyx, then turned back to Shinala. "My knowledge of the ways of metalwork is lacking. Let us have but one. We will take it to the artisans in Fivika and give them a sample. Once they have played with it, we will know the value it could hold. I fear that as I am unaware of how useful it is, I may underprice or overvalue this. Would that be acceptable?"

Shinala shrugged. "That is fine. If it is not worth much, I will figure out something else to trade. My mal- My people deserve to live as civilized as they wish, not be forced to exist only as animals." She nodded, leaving the bar with Rylix, and strode across the deck to the ladder. Rather than climbing off, she dove into the water, acting as if she could breathe like an Aoisan. He heard the soft splash as she hit the water. With a shake of his head, Rylix turned to Jolyx, still holding the bar in his hand.

"If that is what I think it is, it will make what the pirate ship brought in seem like nothing." Her voice was so quiet he had to strain to hear. "You could keep it and become anything you wanted."

"Ah, but then, my dear captain, I would become what I have little desire to be. A thief and liar." He handed it to her. "In trust, for those that remain here. Give it to my mother. She will ensure its true value is weighed and you can know what to bring back."

"Are you so sure you will die?" Jolyx avoided looking at him as she tucked the small bar away.

"No, I believe I shall be the hero and save the day," he said with a grin he hoped looked real. "But I am not willing to let my arrogance endanger a possible profitable trade route."

Jolyx laughed, the sound drawing attention from the crew, who smiled in response, picking up their pace a bit. "This is why you are my favorite cousin. I will ensure that it is delivered to your inestimable mother."

He nodded at her and looked around. "Then are we ready?"

"Yes. It is a relatively short trip to the bay I have in mind, assuming the currents have remained in place." She glanced up at the moons, still visible in the sky. "They should not be changing for another few days."

Rylix nodded. The sea Ged lived by the currents, which were driven by the moons. Percit and Shio performed their dance across the sky in a manner that had seemed erratic, but there was a pattern to it. Shio moved in the same direction as the sun, her radiant face turning, letting you see all her beauty through the mooncycle. As the suncycle went on, she would come close, then back away. Percit, however, did not. Her broken face always looked down on Aria, tears still streaming. It never rotated, though she too came closer and then drifted away. Once a mooncycle, neither moon was visible in the night sky. Rylix had heard a Ged talking once about rotations and shadows, but he dismissed it. Even a goddess could take a night to sleep and step away from their people.

But all the sea Ged knew the size and position of the moons drove the tides and the currents. That meant they had to leave tomorrow.

"Very well. I will make sure everyone is ready." He turned and headed to the side, then stopped and glanced back at her. "Though I would prefer the boat to take me back."

Another bark of laughter from Jolyx and she yelled for one of the crew to row him back to shore. Rylix got back and headed to speak to Shinala and the five males she had with her.

"We should practice more while we have time. I know you are intelligent, so my worries are not you understanding my commands, but more what tricks and things we can do to excite and amaze people yet assure them you are safe." He had severe worries about egos getting in the way, but it seemed the most viable ruse for them to slip into Granite. And hopefully, no one would associate them with the trio in Fivika.

After talking to them, he had large rings made that he could hold up for them to jump through, they could leap over each other in a pattern, and listen to his commands like stand, walk, sit, and bow. But they were limited with what they could carry with them as props for the performance.

"I think with a few more routines, we can ensure their attention remains on your glorious performance. But you know your capabilities much more fully than I ever will, so what more would you suggest to showcase your skills?" He looked earnestly at them, knowing full well that some of them were not as enthused about the idea of being performing animals. All he could do was hope Shinala could keep them in line. If they wanted him dead, he was dead.

The males looked at each other, and he realized he was thinking of them the same way Shinala did. It seemed oddly more accurate than men, as they were Leonaids, not one of the races of the new gods. Shinala looked pensive, and he got the distinct impression she was trying to look into the past and remember things.

Paka almost never spoke, but this time he did, and Rylix realized his voice was lower and rougher than the rest. As if the scar across his face was only the visible wound. "We can do strength contests between us, rope and pulling. Sher win most, maybe against two or three?"

Their diction was getting better and Rylix wondered how long some of them had gone without speaking even to each other.

"That could work. I can get some of the ship rope, the one used for the anchors, to bring with us. I was thinking people love stories, and as Jadaya is supposedly who raised you, what if we do basic stories with her, mock plays?"

They looked at him with tilted heads, and he hurried to explain. "Have Paka be the stalking saber about to attack her, and the white saber, Shinala, rescues her, defeating the evil one?"

They shrugged in agreement and kept talking. When it was done they had decided on saber-on-saber strength contests, where they would decide ahead of time who would win. Rylix was surprised when they all mentioned Shinala would win, even over Sher, as she was the strongest of them. The question of why drifted through his mind, but he let it go. But she was the smallest of them, most of the males at least a hand taller than she was.

They came up with doing pyramids on top of each other, and then dancing to flute music, something Note could play and not be obvious he was Aoisan, as he could hide and have it come from behind the simple set they would design. As well as fetch, going and collecting things from the audience or handing out small things to them as well. While they would accept donations, their primary intention was to make sure no one suspected who they were.

That evening, the last one on the island, Jolyx and her crew were on the ship preparing for an early morning cast off. The Leonaids were acting odd, but he tried to make it better by creating a final feast using all his admittedly basic skills to create them something wonderful. The time here had been more relaxing than he expected.

When all were eating, and Jadaya and Note had returned, both freshly bathed as they spent more time practicing with their weapons than doing anything else, Shinala stood. Rylix focused on her, even as he tensed. This was unusual and, as such, he expected something bad.

"I and my males are ready to go with you. But there is one thing we have not shown you. You should know before the fight, so you waste no time reacting."

Rylix glanced at Jadaya and Note, but they seemed as clueless as he was. His eyes flickered back to her.

"Sher. Come." The huge redhead stood and walked over to her, not looking surprised at all. "Saber," she said, and he shifted in a smooth motion, what little he wore falling to the ground. Rylix tilted his head. What was he missing? "Warrior." Her voice was low and carried power and Sher shifted again. But this time, he became something completely different. He rose on his hind legs that warped into powerful thighs, with clawed feet. His torso and arms, while person-shaped, were covered with fur and muscles that were a mix of both forms. His hands ended in flexible paws with claws that could retract, as well as a thumb. Then there was the head. The saber's muzzle and shape made into a face that was similar and different to mortal at the same time. Together, the effect was awe-inspiring and made him clench his bladder tight as his brain told him to flee for his life.

"This is our fighting form and what we will use to help you against a god."

"Quas Destroy," Rylix cursed, swallowing the saliva that pooled in his mouth. That was all there was to say from the expressions on Jadaya's and Note's faces they felt the same, but for the first time he realized they might succeed, not just die trying.

The smile on Shinala's face was cold, and he saw the legends that spoke of her strength and leadership in that hard smile. "That is the form that ensured obedience and meted out punishment. We shall fight once more against the mad god, and Aria shall feel our might for the first time since before the Usurper."

The words rang with power and Rylix sat frozen as his mind screamed in terror. The legends had been true when they called the Leonaids the monsters Aryix created as his tools. What had they done?

CHAPTER EIGHTY-THREE

JADAYA

Jadaya sat in the stern, Immunity sheathed in her lap. The waves broke around the leading edge, creating wings of water that fish leaped through as they sailed toward Charinsky. The memory of the warrior form of the Leonaids lingered in her thoughts. Watching Sher change had reinforced that they had humored her, and it oddly hurt. If they had shifted at any point, she would have been dead before she could respond. For all her skills, she never had a chance. Did that mean her skill was nothing?

The blow to her worldview had driven her here with the crew flitting around her, still oblivious to the danger walking the decks with them. Right now, she felt almost afraid of Leonaids and that was a leeriness she had never felt before. How would she work with them knowing the monsters they changed into? And worst of all, when they were sabers, she was respectful, understanding their power, but never scared. Now she had images of her body gutted by those claws, lying there bleeding out.

"Scaring you was not our intent."

The voice had Jadaya spinning on her precarious perch, the sword in hand. She slipped on the wet wood and for a long moment she hung over water waiting to eat her as it had tried before.

A strong pale hand lashed out and grabbed her wrist, pulling her back in, and it was over. The terror pulsed through her for longer than the incident had taken.

Jadaya found herself face to face with Shinala as the other woman released her wrist slowly. As if nothing had happened, she continued speaking. "Will you be able to work with us, knowing now what we really are?"

"I dislike being played with." Jadaya said each word a bitter admission of weakness. "Katel, any of you could have disarmed me in a blink. Why this performance if you could just walk in there and do what you wanted?"

Shinala stared at her for a long moment, then started laughing. It was a rich, low sound, and Jadaya had never heard her laugh before. "Come. Sit, and we will talk." Shinala dropped to the deck in a cross-legged position.

Reluctantly Jadaya sat, but the memories of how fast the shift was gave her no rest. But she owed the woman enough that hearing her out was required. The sword sat heavy in her lap as a reminder of what she owed Shinala. She hated the idea of giving up Immunity for any reason.

"As for your statement, no."

Jadaya blinked at her, trying to figure out what she meant.

"You are one of the best warriors we have ever seen. Your pride is set aside while you learn. If any of us met you on the field of battle one to one, we would struggle, and you might win. Our speed is no faster in that form than what you already trained with. Our power is roughly the same as well. Of all of them, only I would put you down without issue."

Something must have shown on her face as Shinala raised a hand. "Know this. All the others are creatures of birth and much more mortal than I. Aryix and Gela created me and Raja Lew. He and I had many children." A sad smile flitted across her face. "At this point I remember not all the children I had, but of them, only Lev and Lovi still live of Raja's line. All the females died at the hands of the children of the gods, and they stopped me from ever carrying a live child again. But I was created and as such, I am not like them. But for those born of male and female, you would be able to go against them, and I know not who might win. Does that help?"

Jadaya felt a blush on her cheeks. Had she been so obvious? She focused on the hilt of Immunity, her hands tracing over the crystals embedded there. "I was not pandered to?"

"No. Katel enjoys teaching you. Training you gave him a reason to welcome the rise of the sun. We may not age, but we still hurt, grieve, and die. Of all the children left, of all my people, I have fifteen where once we numbered in the hundreds. Before the children rose against their parents, we lived and died as chance or stupidity took us." Shinala shrugged and looked out at the ocean, a smile pulling at the edge of her lips. "All I am saying is you, out of the very few mortals we have met, would be a challenge. Remember, we were literally created to keep the peace between the children and enforce the rules set down by their parents."

"Oh." Jadaya had nothing else to say, so they sat watching the sailors move around the ship as the currents dragged it towards Charinsky.

"What is it like out here?" Shinala's question was so quiet it took Jadaya a moment to realize she had asked something.

"What do you mean?"

"It has been so long since we walked among the mortals. What is life like?"

Jadaya was unsure how to answer that. Her legends contained no mention of the Leonaids, as enemy or friend. Her gods, her *former* gods, had kept the stories only to the things they had done. Isolating her people more than she had realized until this journey. So she would talk about what she knew. "The Aoisans are kinder than they have reason to be, given the Char's actions. They took me in and healed me, though they could have let me die with no one caring. Fivika is fascinating. So many things. Tubes that let you see far away, or glass that lets you see up close. They make dishes that look so thin and delicate, yet are strong enough to use every day." Wandering the market had been fun, and she saw so many things she had wanted to buy, not that she had a use for most of them. "I saw Aggies and a Wyskan, though I had no time to talk."

"The ships have become sleeker over the suncycles," Shinala said, looking around the deck. "The last ones I remember were square like bricks. You know who someone is by looking at them?"

Jadaya just blinked at her, at a loss. "Yes. Our gods changed us to match their desires." Not knowing what to say, she fell back on her teachings. "When they put their parents away for the safety of everyone, they took their people and changed them so they could better live in this new world. Zula and Yika gave us skin that soaked in the sun, but did not burn, hair that would twist like the wind, strong and fine, legs made for running the plains after game, and eyes that could see prey in the far distance."

"Ah," Shinala whispered. "I had heard a comment or two about that before the Ged quit coming. That people were changing."

The amount of time Shinala implied had passed shook Jadaya to the bottom of her heart. Shinala existed when there were only Ged. The woman had never met anyone from Zuyika, because when she was imprisoned on the Mount of the Gods, Zuyika did not exist.

Shaking it off, Jadaya smiled. "Then let me tell about them. Wait here a moment."

Shinala nodded agreeably, but there was a darkness in her eyes and Jadaya wondered how strange this world would be away from the mountain where she had been trapped for so long. With quick movements, Jadaya found Jolyx. "Captain, is there a map of Aria I could borrow for a while?"

Jolyx had been at the wheel watching the land still far in the distance. She quirked a brow but nodded. "Alyx should be in the map room. Return it when done. In one piece," she said with a warning tone. Jadaya just nodded and headed to the map room, where Alyx the map maker glared at her, but gave her the map of the world. Less than a finger from her leaving Jadaya was back, holding the map in her hands.

She dropped to the deck and unrolled the map, using Immunity to hold the top edge flat, and her heel and a whetstone to hold the other edges. "This Vykland, where the Mount of the Gods is." With that she spoke, tapping each land, and saying who their gods were and what the people were like. The Vykers with their thick layers of fat and feet impervious to cold and heat. The Wyskan with their smooth skin, long pointed tongues, and wide flat feet. Fivikans with their dark eyes and hair with no curl. She talked about the Aggies with green eyes, retractable claws, breasts that always seemed to be heavy with milk. The Delks who were ruled only by women and could eat anything a jack could, with hair the color of fire. Of course she had met Note and knew about the Aoisans, and the Zuyikans from Jadaya, that left only the Charinsky.

"What about them? The people that would steal others to sing for their mad god?" Shinala asked, eyes following the faint current lines that would pull them to that land.

Jadaya sighed. "I know little besides what I was taught. That he grieves the loss of his wife, that they have many gemstones in that land because she loved the sparkle of the stones, and that they have no old people. That I always thought was odd."

Shinala glanced at her, brows furrowed. "What do you mean, no old people?"

"Mortals age. In Zuyika, when you got older, you get wrinkles and your skin sags, your hair can turn white, and some grow smaller as their body ages." Shinala nodded with narrowed eyes.

"From what I know, and Note would be much better to ask, Char do not age like most do. All of their hair is blond and it might become more silver, but once you reach adulthood, you can gain or lose weight, get injured, but your skin remains the same, your body remains that of a healthy adult unless sick or badly wounded. How would you know who the elders are when you all look the same?" It had always disturbed her that with Chars, there was no way to tell their age.

Shinala blinked, then nodded. "She was always focused on the appearance she showed the world, and she hated the idea of aging, because even Aryix changed over the cycles. That sounds like something she would do."

Neither of them would mention the names of those gods. The others could listen in as they chose, but those two needed to stay as pronouns. You could never tell what He might be listening for.

"Now I have a question," Jadaya said slowly. Her heart quaked at the thought of asking this. It went against everything she knew, everything she had been taught.

Shinala just glanced at her, waiting for the question.

Jadaya took a deep breath, then let the words tumble out. "Are they really gods? And what can he do?"

There should have been a lightning bolt slashing down to kill her for daring to doubt, but the sky remained blue and the clouds were but white puffs in the sky.

"Assuming that a god is anyone that can do things you could never do in all the cycles of the sun, then yes, they are gods. Are they perfect, all-knowing, or all-powerful? No. Even Aryix and Quas were not that, and they were the first. Even the Usurper, who I suspect is related to Quas, was not that."

That revelation shook Jadaya down to her toes. Quas and the Usurper were related? How was that possible? But Shinala kept talking. "As to powers? He is faster than I am. Only the crystals I put in your sword can cut him deeply. He, like all of them, can be anywhere he wishes to be. But when I knew him, he had few weapons skills, relying on power to win. He can control the weather, and his rage makes the elements obey him. There may be more, but he was never one I served, and those of mine that served him all died when they attacked their parents."

The words had coiled tight around Jadaya's stomach, but the last part made her curious. "What do you mean, served?"

A bitter smile twisted Shinala's lips. "Raja Lew and I enjoyed sex, and we were fruitful. I had many children and they, in turn, had children. Aryix ensured there were no issues if they bred with each other, though many sought lovers among the mortals. That was what the Ged were called then. Just the mortals. Leonaid blood always bore out and my sons and daughters were as fruitful as I was. Many of them served the children in different capacities. They were slaughtered when the children turned, fearing where their loyalties lay. It is one of the few reasons I tolerate Cassix. He protected his Leonaids, bringing them to me when the children rebelled. But he only had five, as he was still more of a wanderer. Most of mine died trying to protect the gods." She shrugged. "It was long ago, but yes, the blood debt they owe me and mine is long and deep."

There was something in her face that Jadaya did not understand and, moved by that same something, she reached over and hugged Shinala with one arm. From the sudden stiffening of her body, it was not something Shinala expected.

"They have spilled a great deal of blood to get their way. You deserved better and your loyalty should not have been rewarded with prison." Jadaya's voice was fervent, feeling an odd kinship. Both of them had lost everything at the hands of these gods.

A low rumbling purr came from Shinala as Jadaya pulled back. "And your choice of lovers should not have cost you everything. Someday you will find someone worthy of you."

Jadaya flinched. "How did you know?"

"Cassix and I created the tests. I watched."

"Ah," Jadaya said, trying to shove her emotions down. "I may not find anyone, but that is at it may be. I may die soon, so it will not matter."

"Hmm…" was all Shinala said as they watched the waves bring them closer to Charinsky.

The waves crested and splashed, but her fears of the water of the future had faded. She felt full for the first time in ages. The hole that had been in her, created when she was made Exile was gone. Filled with Note, Rylix, this quest, these people. She might not have any gods, but she thought she might have something better.

CHAPTER EIGHTY-FOUR

SHINALA

The *Starguide* had made good time, taking only two days for them to reach the land that had seemed forever away only a tenday ago. The harbor had a largish town on the banks. It had a dock with mostly fishing boats, but it was still more civilization than Shinala had seen. Before she had been imprisoned, most people lived in small settlements and mostly worked with wood and mud. The stone buildings fascinated her. Jolyx explained Granite was less than a tenday walk away, with a huge harbor and currents that were more consistent. So only ships that got off course or were caught in odd currents stopped here.

They all shifted into their saber forms as the ship approached land. The breeze flung the sharp smell of mortal refuse and rotting waste into her nose. The smells were so different, even from what her new comrades had brought with them. Cooking, burning, sharp, sweet, spicy, and under all of it, the scent of mortals. On their prison island, the sea and the melted rocks from the volcano were the strongest scents. Here mortals and the mouthwatering aromas of seared meat were the strongest. She gave herself a quick shake to brush off the urge to find the biggest pile and roll in it. It smelled so appealing. From the sniffs the others were doing on the railing next to her, she knew they felt the same.

"Remember to sit there and look pretty until I call you," Rylix said, moving over to stand with them. A hint of fear sweat drifted from him and Shinala inhaled it like a fine perfume. It was good to know that the mortals still remembered that the Leonaids were deadly. Leonaids had never been pets, though the mention of a cat interested her.

She said nothing but sat down, wrapping her tail around her as she sat back on her haunches. Her males followed her lead as a rope was thrown to someone on the dock.

"Ged?" the man said. "You rarely come here. Granite's got better products."

"Just dropping off some entertainers. I hope you are ready to see something different," Jolyx said as the dock worker secured the gangplank.

"Entertainers? Well, that would be a sight." The Char tied up the board looking up at the captain and Shinala yawned, showing off her teeth. The movement caught the man's attention, and he paled. "Ya have sabers? Free?" There was a definite squeak at the end of that word and Shinala fought down the urge to purr in pleasure. It had been a while since mortals saw her like this.

"They are tame and most well-behaved bunch in the world. There is nothing like this, I promise." The sarcasm in her voice made Shinala fight back a snarl. They needed support, not subtle undermining.

Shinala heard the groan from Rylix, but the man stepped forward, a wide smile across his face. "Indeed. I must insist I give your town a free show as we stock up on our way to Granite," he called out with a joviality that sounded real.

Jadaya, already garbed as the great beast tamer, complete with her head wrap and silk blouse of red and yellow, stalked down the gangplank. She spoke in Zuyikan, as the odds were few Char spoke it, and the Leonaids picked up the language with ease. Most of the new languages still had roots in their original Ged, though even Ged had changed much over the cycles.

"Come in a line, please. Queen at the front." They had all agreed that using Shinala's name was risky, as she was mentioned in the old tales, but Queen was a good way to refer to her, and she had accepted the appellation with grace. The others she called by name as, after double checking with Rylix, their names had never been mentioned in the old stories. Even Shinala's mate had never been named, only her. There had been a pang deep in her heart when she realized no one alive remembered Raj Lew but her. Even her sons could not remember the face of their father.

With a soft growl, Shinala pushed the memories away and followed Jadaya's instructions, after reminding herself that she had agreed to this. The gasps and shrieks as she padded down the plank to the dock set her back in the right frame of mind. It was good the mortals feared her and soon she would remind the gods why they had feared her.

She sat on the dock, her males forming behind her in a triangle with her at the head. Katel was to her left, Lew to her right, while Paka and Sher sat directly behind them. Mace remained in two-leg form, watching with sharp eyes she snagged every so often. Of all of them, besides her, he was the most familiar with acting like a mortal.

"Excellent," Jadaya said, still in Zuyikan. She turned to look at the small crowd. It had to be at least half the town gathered at the dock. With a grim smile, she nodded at Rylix and he walked down in front. Garbed in the most outrageous of the outfits buried in the chest he bought from Jolyx, Rylix strode forward. Where Jadaya had red and yellow silks, Rylix shimmered as he moved in an embroidered shirt and jacket combination that went to his knees in greens, blues, and matching reds. The jacket also hid the whip coiled at his waist. That would also be used in their performance, helping to insure people thought it was only for show. They had added a snapper at the end of it, something he could easily remove.

"Feast your eyes on the sabers from the wilds of Zuyika!" He called out in a voice that carried to the shore where the crowds stood watching them. Guards were already moving toward them with swords and spears held in white grips. The wafts of fear were the best perfume to Shinala. "We will give a small performance after we have arranged lodging for the night. Is there an inn you could direct us to that we might set up and wash the travel off of us?"

While it was a misdirection, Rylix still told the truth. They needed supplies and Shinala was heartily sick of fish. It had been a staple both on the island and on the ship. The few deer they had were always treats and usually injured or elderly as otherwise they would decimate the population. That meant the idea of eating anything else sounded wonderful. While she could enjoy vegetables and fruit in mortal form, she still craved meat and could smell it cooking. The delicious scents made her mouth water and stomach rumble. Though the scent of fear was just as enticing.

"Hold!" one of the town guards approaching called out.

Rylix turned with his same smile, and Shinala yawned, knowing it made his job more difficult, but she lacked the willpower to resist. The change from marching to stuttering steps of the person approaching them amused her.

"My good man, wonderful to see you, as we need assistance. Is there an inn with a large yard we could rent for the night, and I believe we need to buy a milk grazer or two caprils for my fine furry friends here. We will need to purchase some supplies and have copper to spend." He spoke with the air of someone who knew he would never be refused. It was an odd self-assurance. Shinala rather liked it.

The words that came out of the approaching man were tense and stuttering. Obviously caught between competing needs. Shinala was glad she had to deal with none of this. Mortals had never made good eating, but the temptation to rip the man's throat out was high. And that was with the man speaking but a single word.

"Those are wild animals. They will slaughter people and livestock. They are not caged!" That last protesting had a bit of shriek to it and Shinala laid down, sensing her males following her lead.

"My dear guard. These are not wild animals, they are our family and listen better than your little ones ever have. I could trust them with a babe, and they would not leave so much as a scratch. Indeed, I could place a roast in front of them, and they would never touch it until my good friend here told them they could."

She watched those water blue eyes from the guard captain focus on her and she avoided the temptation to yawn again. Being in saber form always brought out her desires to play and toy with mortals. They were so easy to manipulate. Instead, she purred as Jadaya scratched her ears. That felt good.

"That is a risk we are unwilling to take. You must leave." He pointed at the ship and Jolyx leaned over the edge.

"They paid for getting here, and here is where I will leave them. Cast off. We have other ports to reach." Already the sailors were acting with alacrity. Shinala watched as Jolyx cast her eyes over all of them, her face tight.

Shinala sat up and waved at the ship, causing her males to mimic her actions and she heard Jadaya choking back laughter.

In a tone that meant good boy, she said in Zuyikan, "You just waved at her. Rylix is either going to strangle you or pet you to death."

Shinala laughed, though in saber form it came out as a low chuff. These mortals were fun. Hopefully, they would not die.

Discussion with the guard that Shinala tuned out continued. Worst case, they would pass through the town into the country, but she really wanted some of that food. The fear smell was boring her, especially as it was fading. She watched the people, letting the Char and Ged conversations wash over her. Mostly, she watched the young Charinskys play.

It had been so long. Children. All Leonaids loved them, and not to eat. There was something precious about them and seeing one for the first time since… Her mind stopped trying to remember the last time she had seen a child. Probably a suncycle or more before the imprisonment. They had been busy working. She and Raj had talked about having more. Normally, she had given birth to twins. But she had to remain in one form for the pregnancy, and they had been busy.

The information Note shared with her came roaring back with a power it lacked then. The people of Xyl had abused their captured young. Then it had seemed bad, but somehow distant. Distant because she had seen no young ones in thousands of suncycles. Now she knew and would shred anyone who had participated in the abuse.

She gave a low growl and shook herself, trying to calm down. The desire to wrap all the young ones in her arms and protect them fought with the grief she had dismissed for so long. When the god-children locked her there with her males, they had looked at her. Told her they could not risk her bearing more Leonaids and freeing the gods or coming after them.

To her credit, what tiny amount Shinala would allow, Qian had objected. The goddess of fertility and childbirth had refused. "My magic is to help life, not prevent it."

Xyl and Zula had been adamant. "She can not be allowed to bear any more cubs. In ten suncycles, they would have an army to free our parents, and we would be slaughtered."

Qian still objected. "This is wrong. If you feel that strongly, just kill her."

Shinala had agreed with that sentiment, but they refused to kill her. Maybe they remembered her taking care of them as babes, though it had not stopped them from slaughtering her family, her children's families. In the end, Qian agreed and did something. She refused to share what she had done, but never again did Shinala experience a moon time and she never quickened with child.

"Come on. We have found a place." The words said in Zuyikan cut through her memories and Shinala looked up to see Jadaya standing in front of them and Katel batting at her tail to get her attention.

Shaking off the memories, Shinala followed, trying not to watch the children too carefully. The silly mortals might think she wanted to eat them.

CHAPTER EIGHTY-FIVE

NOTE

Note found clothes that covered him from neck to ankle, then added a hooded brown sweater that he pulled up over his face. He slipped through the townsfolk, always looking at the ground so no one would see his face, and keeping his hands in his pockets. Over the years, Note had learned how to be invisible, and he used it to his advantage now to listen and watch but not garner attention. His job was to be no one of importance and while they were traveling to appear to be nothing but a lad for scut work.

Rylix had talked an inn into letting them have the Ged tent house and the stable yard. There were currently no guests that had jacks or mustangs. The man had also purchased two caprils which were currently roasting on outside spits as Rylix doctored them with herbs and spices. Those he had purchased almost immediately and the six Leonaids were all very interested in the process. That was probably half the reason for kids hanging on the fences.

The sight of five huge sabers sitting quietly watching two caprils roast was fascinating. If they had been wild, the animal carcass would have already been in their mouths. Rylix had even claimed the sweetmeats and was currently making a gravy with them, while he placed the heart in a pot with marinade for their morning meal.

No one seemed to pay attention to the smallest of their little band. Though Rylix and Jadaya were both doing their best to keep all the attention on them. Rylix was a natural at it and Jadaya was exotic enough that eyes followed her. It also helped she was still a hand taller than the average Char.

Mace acted as a nice foil, leaving Note to skulk in the shadows. That did not upset him at all. Being here had his skin crawling, and every moment he waited for a priest to clap a heavy hand on him and drag him back to the temple. They only had a small temple here, and he had heard the singing when they arrived, but he recognized none of the songs. That worried him. In the time he was there, the songs only rarely changed and there were a set of staple songs that were sung regularly. He had heard none of them.

In the shadows, he tried to calculate how many seasons since he escaped. The escape itself had taken more than a suncycle for him to finally get home, then once home he had hidden, paying attention to nothing, but the number should be no more than ten, maybe closer to eight. Would the songs have changed so much in that time?

None of the others had ever been to Char, so they were unable to sense the wrongness that coated everything. Though he rarely saw many Char outside of services, he had seen a few to know the normal dress was ankle-length skirts for women, no makeup, and hair kept up out of the way of household chores. The men wore pants and shirts with sleeves rolled up. Men and women had different but equal responsibilities and he had never seen any woman treated with anything less than respect, though he admitted people tended to be on their best behavior at the temples.

But now… He watched from the shadow where over half the women had raised their skirts to their knees, hair hung long and loose in ways that had to interfere with chores. They had eyes lined with what looked like soot and their lips were stained in a manner unfamiliar to him. Styles could change, but it was the behavior that really confused him.

Men leered at the women, they grabbed them, fondling bodies, and the women just stood there accepting it. The priests did too, and that almost caused him to fall out of his shadowed corner when he saw that. Gone were the long robes the priests normally wore and in their place were tight pants or short skirts and form-fitting shirts. The colors were still black and red, but now, rather than somber and serious, it came across as lurid and somehow twisted. It made no sense.

He hid in the shadows and watched and listened. Staying near a bar, which had more drinkers in the middle of the day, Note listened to the Char talk. They talked about the king and the cantor's relaying Xyl's demands. The changes, talks about the new images in the temples, and so much more that he wished he was the one drinking. It only took six fingers before he had figured it out.

Needing to get back to the others, he moved through the market, only to stop at the display in the middle. Where normally he assumed there would be musicians of some sort, instead there were wooden T shapes in a circle with Aoisans, bared to the waist, standing in front of them. They braced themselves as a conductor stood behind them, holding flogs. The Aoisans began to sing, and the priests, some with glee on their faces, others with horror, began to slowly and rhythmically flog them. The men and women, no children, he saw with relief, reached a perfect harmony, and it sounded like pain. His stomach roiled at what he saw.

The only thing that kept him from attacking was realizing the flogs were soft suede and they barely left even welts on their backs, though the priests that seemed to enjoy it left more marks than the others. There was something desperate about most of the faces, and he sank into the shadows even further.

Swallowing down bile, he slipped further into the shadows, making sure no skin showed, and headed toward their encampment. The others needed to know. He reached them after night had fallen and they and all the Leonaids, still in saber form, were in the tent, the small stove stoked to stave off the chill.

"Ah, you have returned, my friend," Rylix said, still channeling his showman energy. "What news do you bring us?" The words were too cheery and made Note swallow convulsively as he tried to find his own balance.

"Is there anyone near enough to hear me speak?" he asked in a low voice as he dropped onto one of the bedrolls near the stove. He felt like ice radiated from his heart outward, though the temperature was relatively comfortable.

His tone must have conveyed something as the smile dropped from Rylix's face and Jadaya rose to tie closed the tent flap. Shinala or Queen, obvious in her white coat, lifted her head and sniffed, twisting this way and that, before settling down and shaking her head in the negative.

"Their god spoke to the cantor and gave new commands. Telling them to lean into the darker aspects of sex. That is why everyone is dressed so oddly, and there seems to be a lot more rutting in the shadows." He had to hide twice during his surveillance near the bar as people had almost stumbled upon him as they had hard, brutal intercourse against the walls in alleys.

Everyone looked at him, their faces paling.

He continued. "The temples are changed. There is nothing about joy and love, only pain and depravity. Then there is what they are doing to the singers. Hurting them as they sing, making their songs nothing but pain. From what I hear, some of the bigger temples are having public sex with them as the worship services, forcing them to sing as they are—" His words broke off as even saying the words made him feel dirty. "Raped as part of the worship to him. Not everyone is behind this, even the priests are torn. And apparently the king is not giving in to the demand."

"Demand? What demand?" Rylix looked confused and all the Leonaids were intent on him.

"The cantor," Note would rather spit than ever say that man's name again. He was the one who had used Note the most as a child. "Publicly admitted that the king was cursed with unending pain by the god. But it would be lifted if the king would publicly act the way the god said he should. Even better if he used the woman everyone thinks will be queen as his toy. Lots of people respect him for his refusal, though an equal number think he is an idiot for not just going along with it."

"What happened here?" Rylix whispered. "Was it like this when you were here?"

"No," Note snapped out, then had to rein in his anger and fear. "No. Some of the priests abused singers. We were held here as prisoners. But," he paused and swallowed the words bitter on his tongue. "There was nothing like this. They wanted us cowed but healthy so we could sing. Even if they killed one of us as an example, I remember no torture. Some of the priests were kind, and the people were nice the few times we met them. But this? Something is really wrong."

Jadaya sighed. "That explains a few things. I had at least three offers of sex while I was fetching the items Rylix had ordered. I have never had that happen and from the reactions of people around me, it was normal, or at least not unexpected. At least there was no anger when I refused. Even the idea of coupling like that with someone I have never talked to before seems distasteful." From the expression on her face, Note figured the correct word was more like horrifying.

"This changes little, I fear, other than adding more pressure for us to get to the cantor as fast as we can." Rylix sighed. "The good news is we are only about seven days of slow travel to Granite. If we push directly there, we could reach the capital in four days. But if we avoid the small towns and giving shows, the word we need spread will not have time to grow. We need the king to want us there, give us space for a show, and then maybe we can see what is going on."

Note looked around. "Now would be a great time for Cassix to show up and tell us if we can trust the king or not."

They all waited a few heartbeats, but no god showed up.

"Figures. When we need them, they are absent. Calling Pel here would do no good," he muttered, for the first time wishing a god would stick their nose in.

"The land is probably blocked from most of their senses," Mace offered. "I know that happened often with the children when they were doing something they wished to hide from the others. As they got older, their powers let them hide more and more from their parents and each other. From what you have told me of Him, he would want no interference."

There was silence, though Shinala nodded in agreement with Mace's statement.

Note heaved a sigh. "From what I overheard, it has been at least two tendays since this happened. Even another tenday will make little difference." The words hurt to say. To know it meant another tenday of his people's suffering. Of everyone suffering. But the more he saw, the less he cared about surviving this, as long as Xyl and his worship were destroyed by the time they were done.

"Very well, then. We continue on our path, traveling slowly, giving shows, earning coin, and making our way to the capital, being anything except people here to change the world." Rylix laughed as he said that part. "If nothing else, we will have a bunch of excitement coming soon."

Note nodded and sank down on his roll, letting his head lay on the pillow. All he wanted to do was hide and cry for grief for his people, anger at the gods, and the guilt that he had escaped and they were still here.

Soon. I will rescue you soon.

CHAPTER EIGHTY-SIX

LAZUL

Lazul hobbled down the hallway. It was only early afternoon, but he had reached his limit. It had been two tendays since Zayn's proclamation and things had changed faster than he wished. The temple started shifting everything immediately and even the robes of the priests looked somehow provocative, though the general colors and cuts remained the same. He had refused Xyl's offer and on some of the nights, where he cried into his pillow with Hauyne stroking his hair, he suspected Xyl had increased the pain. Morphe and opi were what he leaned on after he finished his day, which he ended earlier and earlier, as tella no longer touching what wracked his body.

There were only a few beneficial aspects that he could see from all this. The primary one was that his nobles and courtiers believed his pain now. With that belief came the recognition of when he reached his limits. They were willing to end meetings and council sessions, letting him escape. The other one was the growing respect as he refused the god's offer. Being a person he could face in the mirror, though the pain and drugs were taking their toll, mattered to him.

Charinskys aged differently from most. Other races would sag and get brittle, their skin, bones, and hair all showing the life they had lived. His people were odd. They would have their hair turn colors, their joints become more painful, but a man at thirty and a man at eighty looked very similar past the wisdom in their eyes or the scars earned through their life. When they died, it was either disease, accident, or they simply dropped dead. There was very little in between. Percit had detested a long, lingering death and thought that looking old was ugly. So they never looked old.

But external factors could still change you. He had lost weight. Most of his people were stocky, tending toward soft, florid faces with thick hair. The man in the mirror was a stranger. A thin face, hair streaked with silver, gray skin, sunken cheekbones, and lines of pain around his mouth and on his forehead. It was bad enough he scared children because Charinskys never looked like he did, unless they were addicts and he wondered if that was what he was becoming. Or had already become. Though he never chased the drugs for fun or release, just to make the pain something he could live with. But that amount became more and more each day.

Their chamber was always kept warm as the cold amplified the pain. It was empty as he arrived and he sank down into his chair, both relieved and disappointed at the same time. Now he had time to think, but he missed Hauyne's presence and her insight.

A knock at the door and a servant slipped in, bring fruist, gels, and finger food. Looking at it, he realized he had not eaten since breakfast, which would make the pain worse. He sighed to himself. He should know better than to skip a meal. Blinking away the mental scolding, Lazul grabbed a gel, chewing on it as he assembled meat, bread, cheese, and a dressing. Chewing required energy, but painful experience had taught him it would be worse if he avoided eating.

Something had to change, but what? He would die before giving in to Xyl's blackmail, but his resistance was barely a candle in a storm. Crimes had increased. Those in the prisons were dying at rates his archivist had never seen, and female deaths had also spiked. The number of those that were with child when they died made him want to scream. Maybe he could appeal to the other gods. At this point, he would sacrifice himself if it would bring back a god to stop this madness. If they would heal his land, he would pay any price. But he had to be the one paying the price, not his people.

He ate two small sandwiches while his mind spun off of ideas. The only one that seemed to have any value was calling for either Cassix or trying to awake the old gods. If that was even possible.

The creak of the door and the cold it brought in pulled his attention from his inner turmoil and he looked up to see Hauyne settling down. His smile was instant at the sight of her. It turned curious at the smile on her face. There had been little to smile about in the last tenday, so anything that caused one was worth asking about.

"You are smiling. Do I want to know, or is this hush-hush spymaster stuff?" he asked, trying to tease a bit, though it came out more seriously than he had intended.

"Oh, this is hush-hush stuff, but I will share with you. Though for the love of Char, keep it to yourself," she said. Her voice had constrained excitement in it, but he thought he might have heard a touch of hope.

"Done. Now what has happened?" He picked up a few pearl fruits and dropped them into his mouth. Pearl fruits were what most fruist was made from, especially the stronger varieties, but crunchies made a nice cider, both alcoholic and non, and regardless of their green, yellow, or red skin colors, they all had the same flavor, though with varying degrees of sweetness.

"They are here," she said, as if sharing a secret.

He looked at her, blinking in confusion. "Who?"

"The three. They arrived. And I swear I think they might have Leonaids with them." Her excitement was contagious, but he struggled to get his mind to follow what she was talking about.

Then it clicked. "They? The ones? They are here? What do you mean, Leonaids?" That name sounded familiar, but for the life of him, he could not pull it to the forefront. His tired brain struggled to deal with the spurt of hope her excitement caused.

The smile that lit up her face took his breath away and, for a fleeting moment, all he could do was wonder how he had been so lucky.

"Do you remember the old stories? About the gods when they first created mortals?"

"Vaguely? My nursemaid read me a few stories. But most of my childhood was spent learning about Charinsky, not on the stories or legends." He fought to pull the memories out. It seemed familiar, but not enough that he could come up with it.

"You know I spent most of the last few suncycles living off of my brother's charity. To make myself as invisible as possible, when there was no work to be done, I sought out books and read. I suspect I read every book in the city and then some. But that also meant I read multiple tellings of the stories of creation. In them they mention the first one and she of fire creating two beings, crafting them to serve and protect, to be their hands and eyes when they could not be. They were gifted with the ability to change into a saber."

Lazul nodded slowly. "I remember. They fought against the children, and many of them died. Were they not sentenced to guard the imprisoned old gods forever?"

She shrugged. "That is what the old stories tell us. But that is why I think they are here. There is a Ged and a Zuyikan traveling with a bunch of trained sabers making their way here. It has to be them."

Lazul frowned. "No mention of the Aoisan?"

She frowned and shook her head. "No, but who else could it be? And trained sabers? Even the cats are untrainable. How in the world would you get a saber that size to follow your commands?"

"I could say the same thing about mustangs," he said wryly. "Given the number of times they have kicked me off."

"Even the most well-trained beast in the stables could not manage what the reports are telling me about these creatures. They have been moving toward Granite slowly, taking much longer than needed, but their shows are free, asking for donations if you enjoyed, yet they show no lack of funds for food. And those creatures are eating an old grazer or two caprils a day with no issue."

Lazul took a deep breath, his body aching with the movement, but at this point, the pain meant he still lived. "Then we must reach out to them. But at the end of the day, how do we support them?"

Some of Hauyne's smile faded. "That I am unsure. But surely they must have a plan. If they are really here to kill Him, then all we can do is support them, right?" Her words sought a reassurance Lazul could not give.

"Support I will. But unless they want to use me as a sacrifice, I am unsure what use I could be in a fight. Once maybe, but if I have no energy or strength for intimacy, my ability to fight exists even less." The words were bitter, but he'd had all his illusions stripped from him. If he already had a child, he would step down in favor of them ruling, regardless of gender. If he and Hauyne were married, he would step aside for her to take the throne. So many ifs. All he could do was work with what he had now.

"All we can do is ask. But I will get word to them and set up an area for both them and the sabers. The Ged in many ways will be the hardest," she said, almost speaking to herself at this point.

"Why?" he asked, confused. His brain was fuzzy, but they had often had Ged stay at the castle over the suncycles.

She arched a brow at him; her face changing from thoughtfulness to worry for him. "Because they are unable to sleep under a roof, remember?"

"Yes. And?"

Now it was her turn to blink, the worry fading and going back to confusion. "Then where will they stay?"

His brain finally kicked in. She had slipped into his life like the puzzle piece he never realized he was missing, so much so that he forgot she was still relatively new to the palace.

"Ah. Yes. Talk to Actin. The back courtyard? You know the small one, the size roughly twice my bedchambers?" He took another sip of the fruist, hoping the drink and the gels would even him out. He would have the morphe before he crawled in bed, but if he did it prior to bed, he would be insensate too soon. Though more and more, he found himself longing for those few fingers where nothing hurt, even if his mind had difficulty doing anything more than sighing in relief at that point.

"Yes?" She still looked confused.

"The walls are set so tent canvases can attach to them, creating a large room with the tent as the sky. That is why there is a fireplace at the far end, and we have moving dividers to create rooms within the space. There are ground cloths and feather beds specifically for that space. It is why it is rarely used, but yet always tended. If we have Ged visitors, they have a place to stay."

Hauyne looked at him, her eyes staring out as she worked through what he had said. "Oh. I had wondered about that. It was near the guest quarters, but outside of a table near the fireplace it seemed oddly placed and a weird location for an outdoor space with no gardens and two doors. Now I understand. I will get Actin making it ready. But how to explain it and not raise questions?" Her eyes were narrowed and Lazul smiled. He loved watching her think.

"That at least I can provide an answer. Just tell him you want to see how it would work and look if we had a large Ged contingent arrive, and you wanted to see it would work with the weather."

While Xyl had not been causing storms, the weather had become as changeable as his moods. Fingers of sun, followed by a rainstorm, then winds and a cold draft, yet then the sun would come out and the heat would rise as if it had never been cold. The reports coming from the farmlands were worrisome, but all he could do was listen. If these strangers…

"Hauyne?"

She looked up at him from where she was taking notes in her little book she carried. "Yes?"

"What if … what if they are unable to change anything or make it worse? What do we do?" Asking the words made it real and his heart tightened, fearing the answer, yet he already knew it.

Her blue eyes held his gaze as she answered. "Then Charinsky is dead and we give commands to our people to flee, asking for the other gods to take them. If we can get out of this land. Otherwise, we die slowly, trapped in his whims."

Char was surrounded by water and deeps on all sides. They would have to mobilize all their ships, beg assistance from the sea Ged, and work to evacuate the land. He would have to provide the distraction. Keep the god's attention until most of his people were safe.

"Will you start making plans for an evacuation? Start with the cities to the south. He seems to have his attention mostly centered here. Put out the word for any sea Ged ships to come to all our ports. The crown will cover the costs."

She looked at him for a long time and then nodded her head. "I will," she breathed, and he heard the death knell for his people in her words.

Let these strangers be the answer. Aryix. Save my people. Whatever price you ask. I will pay it.

CHAPTER EIGHTY-SEVEN

RYLIX

The trip through toward Granite went easier than Rylix had expected. People were desperate for a distraction and flocked to their shows. But even though he had never been to Charinsky before, he could see what had disturbed Note so much.

It hurt to watch people. The people of Charinsky acted as if their skins fit them like clothing made of burlap: itchy and too small. They smiled too hard, grabbed at any innocent joy with the greed of a drowning man, and lust and pain seemed to be the new normal. After five days on the road, his skin crawled and Rylix wanted it to be over. Even direct attacks by monsters seemed cleaner and less disturbing than this.

Standing up in the last town before the capital, he smiled and waved at the crowd.

"And that concludes the performance. I hope you enjoyed seeing our amazing sabers behave in ways you could never imagine. I bet you wish your children were half as well-mannered as these gorgeous creatures." Their closing act was the sabers fetching different objects out of the crowd. Little things they had handed out when people gathered, a red scarf, green bowl, yellow hat. Things they then asked each Leonaid to go find, which, of course, they did without issue. As long as it was not blue.

That had been an embarrassing lesson, but apparently in saber form blue was more of a gray and they had a hard time telling the difference. It had resulted in confusion, laughter, and their best take of the trip, so overall, the error had worked out in their favor.

He was passing the hat around while Mace helped Jadaya keep everyone away, and they finished packing up to get to Granite. They needed to find lodging there and then, hopefully, get to see the king. It was that or go to the main temple and simply challenge the god. If they had their preferences, they would like to only fight one side. If the throne was against them, it would make it that much more difficult. Though how much more difficult a mortal could be compared to a god was questionable.

They created their plan after the first few days of traveling through Char. Note came back with more stories of the king and his affliction, the woman at his side, the one that would be queen, and the growing distance between the crown and the temple. The cantor had not visited the palace since the day of his pronouncement, and reactions were mixed. Some blamed the cantor for not working hard enough to convince the king; others were relieved the king was refusing to do what the god demanded, though at the same time they feared it. It was amazing what people would talk about when they thought the only living creature near them was a saber.

What was obvious to everyone was the king's refusal to go along with Xyl's demands. After a few heated discussions, where even Shinala shifted to mortal form to weigh in, they came up with a plan. They tasked Note to find a way to meet with the king and test him out. Of all of them, he was the smallest and the one that could escape if captured. He had managed before.

With the last show finished, Mace walked around with a hat. Standing in front, smiling and nodding at people as they dropped coins and the occasional gem into the hat, Rylix was in full showman role. As the last few people left, one of the Char spoke to him with a smile so fake it hurt to look at. "I wanted to talk to you about a broken song chain?"

Rylix stared at him, trying to figure out what he meant, then finally the words registered. What seemed like suncycles ago, Note had told them those were the code words of the group that disagreed with the tradition of singers and the current religious leadership.

"Ah, my brilliant friend, how odd you should ask that. We have many wonders to show you, and just because you knew to ask, come see us in two fingers and we will have a special show just for you." His voice was jovial, but he dropped his volume considerably, directing it just to this man.

The man frowned but nodded and drifted away with the last of the other townsfolk. Rylix turned and headed to the others, who were cleaning up and getting ready to retreat to their rented space, a small area on the outskirts of town with an old milk grazer waiting for them. They would spend the night, then head out in the morning to Granite and hopefully the end of their journey. He could feel the anxiety ratcheting up and was glad that it was almost over. The stress of waiting was getting to everyone.

"My watery friend," he whispered as he got over to them. Note slipped out from the tent, his hood pulled low over his head.

"Yeah?"

"Broken song chain?" he asked, hoping he had not misremembered. Fivika and all that happened there felt like a lifetime ago.

Note stiffened and nodded. "That was what they said. Why?"

Rylix relaxed a bit, though he still held wariness. "Someone will be here in to talk to us. We can hear what they say."

Note grunted and slipped back inside. Within a finger they were all in the tent, the Leonaids with them, as anticipation rippled through the air. From outside, they heard footsteps approaching.

"Hello?" a voice in accented Ged called out.

Rylix stepped out to meet him. "My friend. Please come in. Wait until you see what I have to show you," he said in a tone so falsely jovial that he cringed. He also needed this over, or his voice might get stuck like this forever.

He pulled open the flap, and the man stepped in and froze. The five Leonaids all looked at him as he stood in the tent opening. Shinala grunted, and Paka rose and padded out past the terrified man. Rylix knew Paka would keep anyone away from being close enough to overhear anything.

Rylix waved him in. "I believe you wished to speak to us?" The joviality in his voice faded and Note stepped forward, pulling off his hood and revealing hair that was an odd silver-gray. The dye had been fading, and they had been unable to find a replacement in the towns they had visited so far. This meant a thumb length of his roots were the bright silver of an Aoisan, but the rest of his hair, reaching to his shoulders now and held back with a tie, was a faded dark gray that just looked dirty.

"Broken song chain?"

The man swallowed, his eyes darting to each of the huge sabers watching him the way they would a meal. He shifted back and forth on his feet, then closed his eyes.

"If you eat me, it might be better than living under this god." The words were more to himself than to them, so Rylix said nothing just awaited. The man's eyes opened, and he looked at them with the expression of a man who had lost all hope.

"I work for the not-queen. She sent me. I had seen you sneaking around." He nodded at Note, who just stood, waiting. Though Rylix suspected the man would be dead before he could make a move to flee if Note wanted. That was if the Leonaids did not get him first.

"I hoped the words might mean something to you. The throne supports you and they want to talk to you. If you come in via the harbor gate at night, they will sneak you in. There is a space waiting for you." He said the words in a rush, as if he expected to be interrupted.

"Why? Who is the not-queen and why do they want to talk to us?" Rylix asked, trying to put these new pieces together. He was unsure who this new player was. Not that he was sure at this point how much resistance their actions would be met with.

"She is by the king's side. She is trying to help. You and us. The gate is locked after dark, but if you knock five times and say 'broken song chain' someone will meet you and lead you to the palace." The man looked at them and shrugged. "That is all I know. Now I have to leave. I am expected two towns down, so the rest is up to you. But … you might be our only hope."

He stood clearly, waiting for permission to go. Rylix glanced at the others, who shrugged. He moved forward and opened the flap again. "Aryix bless," he said softly.

"If only he would," the man said in a tone of one with no hope left. He disappeared into the setting darkness.

Paka came back in, shook his head, then slipped out again.

Shinala yawned, stretched, and then shifted into her mortal form. Uncomfortable, Rylix handed her a single Ged robe. She pulled it on with a smirk in his direction. He shrugged. There was just something inherently distracting about a nude woman in phenomenal shape, with six nipples, that made it difficult to pay attention to the right things.

"It will be good to be in mortal form for a while. All the food is making me fat and lazy. This has been a surreal dream. What do we do?" She looked at each of them with the aura of a commander expecting a report.

They looked at Note, and he shrugged. "Hauyne is the not-queen, but I know nothing besides the rumors that she is well liked. We know the king was not going along with the decrees. So it might be a trap. Does it make a difference?" Rylix hated how flat Note had become. He had never been the most expressive person, but it was like looking at a shell of himself and Rylix hated it.

They all looked at each other. "Maybe," Jadaya said quietly. "If they execute us one at a time, even if the god was challenged, we would be dead."

Shinala nodded. "We would be difficult to kill, but as we learned last time we fought, we die when facing the children." A touch of anger coated her words. Rylix realized she was much like the Ged with proper names, in that she never referred to them as gods. They were always "the children" to her.

"Then we go. Worst case, we fight a god at the docks," Jadaya said, a sense of relief in her voice. "Either way, we will know."

"Tonight?" Rylix was surprised at the speed. But at the same time, a strong *yes* vibrated in his chest. It was time to draw this to a close.

"Why not? If we pack up and move, we can easily be there before the moon is high," Jadaya pointed out.

They had a single mustang, and they put everything on the beast so they were all unburdened. A slow trot would get them there quickly. Enough darkness had fallen that they could move without being obvious. Except for Shinala, her white coat would be like a ghost. Which could work to their advantage.

"I say yes. We need to end this before the country breaks or more singers are abused past surviving." Note's voice was hard. With every town, Note had grown darker and quieter as the extent of the changes were apparent. But none of them were crazy enough to attempt the rescue of any singers now. There was nowhere for them to go.

"Yes. I am tired of hiding and acting like a dumb animal," Shinala put in.

"The entire point is you are a smart animal," Rylix countered with a grin. "But I agree. We leave. Now."

Two fingers later, they were packed up, and they had everything on the mustang. They all set out at a fast trot, with Paka and Katel leading the way, while Sher and Lev brought up the rear. Shinala stayed in mortal form, running easily with them. The two of them looked like mirror images running together, black and white. One was almost invisible, the other a ghost of whiteness that gave Rylix shivers even though he knew who she was.

The road was empty as the sun had left the sky and other than the clatter of the mustang's hooves, they were almost silent as they ran. In his mind, Rylix constructed the saga that would be written about them and tried to describe this in his head, the way a storyteller generations from him would tell it.

And so the brave band, knowing some of their number would die, raced toward the gemstone city. Their fighters, the charcoal black Jadaya and the shining white Shinala, sisters in bravery and lethality, led the run. While the Aoisan, wronged so much by this land, loped near them, his name the one thing you never heard from him, a note of music. The foolish Ged, hitching his wagon to those who would surely burn like the tears of Percit falling to the ground, following along. They were surrounded by the four-footed forms of the Leonaids. Legends come to life. Now they ran toward the ultimate battle. Either the salvation of a country or the death of fools.

He could live with that as his epitaph.

CHAPTER EIGHTY-EIGHT

NOTE

The night run was oddly invigorating and Note found himself pleasantly tired as they reached the harbor gates. There was a small path that led around the wall to enormous gates that opened onto the docks. During the day they were wide open, letting people into the city. At night they were closed to prevent attacks from the sea. Note approved, given that was why his people had been captured so easily. The lack of walls to block out the harbor.

A small door was inset into one of the larger doors, and Jadaya approached it while the rest of them hid in the shadows. The five knocks sounded loud as explosions to his overactive hearing, but the door creaked open and soft words were exchanged. A moment later, Jadaya was waving them all through. The feel of Granite wrapping around him was the equivalent of diving into water fouled with sewage. Note had to fight to keep moving forward. Everything in him shrieked for him to run away, to get out. Fear beat at the back of his mind that the priests were going to capture him again, make him sing.

He locked his jaw and focused only on the white heels of Shinala ahead of them. Jadaya was all but invisible in the dark passages they wove through. Of all his new companions, Shinala was the most unusual with no place in his memories, so her brilliant white skin was a safe focus to lock his attention on. He almost ran into her when she stopped.

He looked around and found himself in what looked like a Ged tent set up for an envoy from the clans. It was warm and comfortable, with cushions and pillows. The smell of meat, fruits, and other savory dishes pulled at his hunger, but none of that could compare with his wariness.

Jadaya and Rylix were looking around with an expression of wonder. Rylix moved inside, touching the tent and dividers with an odd smile. Shinala and Mace just stood in the middle of the space looking around, while the other four Leonaids lay at her feet. Not panting, but they were not made for running for fingers upon a time and he could see their fatigue. A full finger passed as they explored everything, even the needs room behind small partitions.

The door into the courtyard that created the wall for the tent creaked behind them, and Note spun, Trinity up and ready to be thrown as a woman stepped in with another man, and two servants holding bedding for them. She froze as she caught sight of him and held out her hands, palms out, facing them.

"Quas grant. I mean you no harm. I am the one who sent for you," she said in unaccented Ged.

Part of Note was relieved she avoided the language of Char. The idea of hearing that tongue while he was fighting with both memory and emotion might be one thing too much.

"And you are?" he snapped. Then closed his eyes. He was too brittle. Note glanced back at Jadaya and Rylix, nodding toward the woman who looked at him with eyes that saw way too much.

To his eternal relief, they moved up, and he stepped back. He did not put Trinity away, but lowered it. He wanted to close his eyes and focus on trying to shed his reactions, but he had little time. What she would say was important. His own shadows of memory would wait until they had won, or he died.

With a mental shake, he forced himself to pay attention to the woman. She wore expensive clothes, but no crown graced her head. The necklace around her throat snagged his attention. A necklace like that meant something, but the meaning slipped out of his grasp even as he tried to think of it.

"I apologize. This all seems so odd both to me and I suppose more to you. My name is Hauyne. I am betrothed to King Lazul." Her voice was calm and clear as her blue eyes scanned all of them, lingering on the sabers, then Shinala, then on him. Her eyes darkened as she realized he was Aoisan and there was the slightest nod of apology. While more than apologies were due, later would be more appropriate.

"Ah, you must be the not-queen our contact spoke of," Rylix said with his normal smoothness. "That is one question answered, but not the other. Why did you seek us out and why are we here?"

She gave another tired smile. "I think you know, but the king must talk to you and that is impossible until morning. I invite you to stay here until then. Arrangements for food and a fire have been made. If you look, both doors are set so you can bar them from the inside. We, inside the palace, wish you no harm. Will you accept the hospitality and the promise of a discussion in the morning?"

"Is this not important enough to disturb his slumber?" Jadaya asked, her voice cool and Note was glad she asked his question. He wanted this over with, but then the idea of starting all this after a good night's sleep and some food would probably be wiser than jumping in after running for fingers.

"He would want to, but he is indisposed." The not-queen's gaze was cool and direct, but there was no possibility of compromise in her tone. "I promise he will see you tomorrow. Anything you need that I can provide is available at your request. This is Captain Diam Malac. He has offered to be at your service. He is trusted absolutely."

The man stepped forward, nodding at them. Behind him, the two servants came in with a bundle of blankets and pillows, offering all of them wide eyes. Mace and Rylix came forward to take them from the two terrified servants, efficiently depositing them on various bedding areas. Areas not on the ground, Note realized with a touch of relief. He was so tired of sleeping on the ground. His body ached, and he needed to get in the water soon. Maybe a quick dip in the harbor later.

There was something she was conveying with the comment about the captain, but Note had no idea what that was. They would have to see how it went.

"Aryix Bless. I believe it looks like you have accommodated all our needs," Rylix said, smoothly waving at the arrangements. "You even have our traveling hygiene rooms set up."

An oddly excited smile crossed her face. " It was interesting to set everything up and see how it worked. I have never been in a Ged encampment, but this is close?"

Rylix smiled at her and gave a small bow. "My dear not-queen, even the head of the clan would be honored to be hosted in such a manner." He laughed and gave her a smile guaranteed to charm her. "I would be delighted to offer this to my mother and fear not that she would find fault."

The woman, Hauyne, he thought, threw her head back and laughed. "Then I am glad your mother is a nicer one than mine. I feel sure she would not be silent unless she had found at least fifty faults." Another smile, and there was an odd mixture of hope and worry in it. "I leave you then to sleep. The captain will be outside the door if you need anything for the next four fingers. Then one of his trusted soldiers will stand there. No one has permission to enter until I and the king return in the morning."

With that, they both nodded and stepped out, shutting the door behind them. Jadaya wasted no time sliding the heavy bar over the door while Mace went to secure the back. There was the slightest creak, then a moment later a thud as he set the bar there into place.

"Door opens into an open courtyard. Can smell our mustang nearby." His voice was a low comment as the others prowled around the space sniffing, heads in the air.

They must have taken the mustang while he was focusing on following Shinala. Yet another thing he had missed. If his attention kept drifting away, he would be dead before he knew what was going to kill him.

After a moment, Paka went to lie by the door into the castle while the rest flopped at Shinala's feet.

"The only person near is the captain like the not-queen said," Shinala commented, walking around. "This is nice. Is this how the Ged live now?"

"Rarely," Rylix said with a shake of his head. "Maybe a few heads, but the permanent encampments are more likely to have these luxuries, like the fireplace stove and the solid tables. The ground is soft yet drains well. What lifts it up is the quality of the pillows and blankets."

The chatter annoyed Note. He tried to keep his anger under control, but it was a losing battle. "Enough with the accommodations. What are we going to do?"

They looked at each other, Jadaya, Rylix, and Shinala. He wanted to scream.

Jadaya took a breath and looked at him. "Note. You were hurt the most by those who live here. Do you want to stay here or go now?"

His mouth opened to say something stupid and risky. With a grunt of effort, his mouth snapped closed hard enough for his teeth to clash together. That was a good way to get killed and ensure more misery for his kin still in the priests' grasp. Struggling to be logical, he took a long inhale through his nose. That action brought with it the savory smells of the provided food, things that bypassed his mind and went straight to his stomach, eliciting a rumble of antici-patory hunger. They had not eaten before their run to Granite and now his body was making demands his mind had ignored.

He hung his head, acknowledging the needs of both body and sanity. "There is no reason to leave. We need the king's help, though I am curious why he could not meet now. But if the food is safe, we should eat and get a good rest. After all, are you not supposed to be well-rested and fed before you die?" There was a hint of mockery in his tone, but it was accurate.

Katel lifted his head and looked at the food, then nodded. Note realized he had seen the saber with the white mane sniffing all the food.

"It is safe to eat," Shinala said. That seemed to be enough to convince them. A finger later, after eating, their wave of hunger faded, though Shinala amused herself by tossing tidbits of food to Katel, Lev, and Sher. Paka refused to partici-pate. Each of the Leonaids, still in saber form, had eaten their fill, but in no way did it prevent them from catching what Shinala tossed at them.

"They are not animals, so why are they doing that?" Note asked after he had watched for a while, the weight of exhaustion pushing against him from physical and emotional stress.

She shrugged. "It is fun. No different from throwing a ball back and forth with a little one. But this way they get a tidbit fed from my hand. In some ways, it is an honor. But mostly it is fun." She shrugged and tossed one at Katel without looking. The saber reached up a paw and snagged it out of the air, then licked it off his paw with a rough tongue.

He gave her a disbelieving look.

"No? Watch." She tossed pearl fruit directly at him, her aim as always uncanny, and without thinking, he opened his mouth and caught it, his teeth crunching down on the cool sweetness. A surprised smile crossed his face.

"I see," he said with a little laugh, and the tension broke. A few other chuckles lightened the atmosphere as they glanced at each other.

"Tomorrow, we talk to the king. And then what? We see now that rescuing the singers will change the issue, not solve it. Do we challenge him? Dismantle the temple? What is the best option?" Jadaya's voice was calm as she asked the question.

Shinala shrugged. "Does it matter? We talk to the king, see if he is worthy of the name, though I greatly approve of his not-queen. Then we beard the cantor and the god in his temple. If we are lucky, the king and his soldiers, maybe even his people will support us. If not?" She gave a slow smile, showing teeth that were too sharp for a mortal. "Then we have the fight of a lifetime ahead of us. Well, your lifetime. I doubt anything shall compare fighting the children when we failed to protect the gods."

There was no anger, just amusement as she rose and stretched, then headed to one of the bedrolls, this one on the ground with another one pulled close to it and pillows surrounding it.

"You do not fear death?" Note asked as others followed her lead and stretched. They were also ready to sleep.

"What is there to fear? I have lived so long, death would simply let me move on to the next existence. How could I fear that?" She stripped and lay down on the bedroll. Mace stripped as well, crawling in next to her and pulling the woman into his arms. For all the gesture seemed protective, Note sensed the larger man sought reassurance and comfort more than trying to protect her. Around them the other sabers made themselves comfortable and with a swiftness that Note could only envy, they were soon asleep.

He followed their example, heading for the roll on an actual bed as Rylix dealt with the lights. Morn would come soon enough. The next one either would come, or he would be beyond caring.

Shinala was right. After this life, there was another one, be it here, or somewhere. All of them knew this with an assurance that made it a given. Death was the end of this life. Not the end of life. Maybe in the next one there would be more joy.

CHAPTER EIGHTY-NINE

ZAYN

The songs of pain surrounded him during the tenday service, with the voices occasionally breaking into a moan that Zayn hoped was pleasure. If not, well, at least they were all still alive. As he raised his voice in song, one of the new ones with a verse that hit notes to send shivers down his spine, not because of the beauty but because of the intent. The verse went on, a mockery of praise.

> *Let your hands make me scream, beg, and whisper your name.*
> *You hold my heart and my life at your pleasure.*

His smile felt pasted on his face at this point, a mask that covered his real thoughts. Two more visits from Xyl in the tendays that had passed since the first, each one worse than the last. How could a god who would never die visibly change so much? But every time Zayn tried to protest or remind him of Percit's sweetness and kind nature, rage bubbled to the surface, and the cantor backtracked as the threats of what he would do to Charinsky became more extreme.

"If you refuse to worship her as is proper, the storms I send will rip even stone from the ground, flinging the remnants of your cities as far away as the thresholds of my siblings." The miniature whirlwind that had formed in his office reassured Zayn that Xyl would do what he threatened. So he gave in.

The worship had gone darker, and he was only holding on to a thin shred of hope anymore as he tried to lose himself in the pleasures of the flesh. Maybe more than he should. Two of the singers had died from his attentions, boys under the age of thirteen. After that, they were of no use to him. No one challenged him. At least two other female singers had also died from the attentions of other priests. And he had word from the temples that some of the singers had taken their own lives rather than submit to the new performances required of them.

He felt no anger at that.

He rarely felt anything anymore.

If he took the time, those few rare moments in his room alone with opi and fruist, he could look at what they were doing and understood exactly what was happening in his church. If you could call it a church anymore. The priests were doing things their hearts and minds rebelled against, but like him, they understood that if they refused, everyone might pay the ultimate price. So they did things they would have never done in the light of day. Then, their own guilt at warping their principles drove them even further into their personal darkness, so they vented it on the victims within easy reach and disposable. The singers. Their slaves.

He no longer avoided the reality. They were slaves, but ones that were becoming less important as not only the priests changed, but the populace. Why not enjoy what you had at hand? After all, they were all dead anyhow.

Another long wail, but of pain or pleasure, it mattered little. The song had ended and Zayn turned to look at the congregation. The worship area was still full, though the makeup had changed. Where it had once been couples and families, here to remember their goddess and celebrate her life and the joy their marriage had brought Xyl, now it was different. He looked out at those gathered and saw no children, to his relief. Even in his most deluded state, he wanted no Charinsky children here, at least not those that their society's existence depended on. Instead, it was men with women cowed and broken, young couples hard and eager, and the teenage boys. The boys not old enough to be adults, but old enough to see the power the pleasure and the pain gave and to thrill at acts required to generate it.

It should have made him sick. He knew his proclivities made him a monster, but the access and temptation had been too much to resist. And in his position, there had been no one to gainsay him. He had always made sure the temple ran smoothly, knowing his actions affected his ability to retain access to his little pleasures in life. Instead, he wished he could lean into it without worrying about the consequences.

But his survival meant staying in control. All that mattered was keeping Xyl placated until … his mind stopped at that thought, mouth open and hand raised.

Until what?

He snapped his mouth closed, swallowed, and addressed the congregation. "As we have given our lamentation to Xyl of the loss of Percit, now we will give unto him the chorus of sounds that Percit cherished. The cries of pleasure driven by pain, of bodies being used to bring both, and the tears that we weep at her absence, tears created with the assistance of our partners."

"Forever shall we cry her name," they responded. Then they turned, and the orgy was on. Many had brought blankets or chairs, some still retained most of their clothes, while others exulted in the exhibitionism. For their part, the priests usually chose self-pleasure as they needed to make sure their sounds were harmonizing to some extent. The singers were encouraged to make the sounds of pleasure and pain via flogging, but that much Zayn had ensured was no worse than a light slap of leather. It sounded good, but even when he had it tested on him, there was little to no pain.

He watched as the people he thought he knew, thought he understood, reached for each other, and there was little of love or joy in their touches. Instead, anger, shame, fear, and sorrow drove their actions, and for those who performed their worship mostly clothed, he knew desperation drove them. Xyl was capable of, and had, punished those who avoided 'worshiping' correctly. On his desk sat reports of houses where the ground opened up, taking only the house, nothing else, or a bolt of lightning striking their best livestock. There were aspects of hope, of people finding gems in an area previously played out, or a sick relative recovering remarkably when they were seen to 'worship' with enough vigor.

As cantor, he was lucky and had no need to perform sex in public; instead, he stood there and sang. Something he much preferred to the idea of being naked in public while using a woman. The sky was blue with only white puffs of clouds, and the day unseasonably warm—a sign Xyl was pleased.

When the worship was over, no one stayed around and spoke anymore. They either fled or swaggered away, high on sex. Zayn headed back to his rooms, exhausted. He sank down on the chair awaiting him and poured a glass of fruist from the carafe. He dug out his supply of opi, noting how low it was. Maybe today he would be lucky and take enough that he would never wake up and this balancing act would be over. How much longer could Xyl's insanity last?

The answer was one he avoided. Because if he faced it, if he pulled the truth in and accepted it, it meant there was no hope. He had to resist the desire to give in to his darkest thoughts if he wanted to live.

Unless.

He shut his eyes and swirled the bit of black tar-like substance of the drug into his fruist. There had been no word from Lazul, and he had not spoken to the king since the day he delivered Xyl's commands. The question that he tried to avoid, the one drifting in the back of his mind, was had Lazul picked up on his clues, his attempt to give him information?

Unless.

At one point in his life, the power and ability to do anything he wanted would have delighted him. Even a mooncycle ago, it might have. But this was destroying everything. Creating a country that could not survive. Taking away the benefits of being the Cantor.

His hand shook as he took a hard swallow of the fruist, the bitterness of the opi coating his tongue and seeping into him. What else could he do? If he defied Xyl it would result only in his death. Nothing would change except maybe a person with fewer morals might become cantor.

A bark of laughter exploded out of his mouth. Fewer morals than him? Maybe that would make Xyl happy. And maybe it would leave a line of bodies at the altar of what their gods had become.

He had to stop thinking about it. The opi was pushing the thoughts back, and he needed something to distract himself, to sink into until he forgot how to think. Raging inside, Zayn pulled a call bell. The special one, the one that said he needed his treat.

When the boy arrived, Zayn had no tenderness left in him and lost himself in the pleasures of unwilling flesh, but all the while that little thought pulsed in the back of his mind.

Unless.

Unless they came.

Unless they could stop Xyl.

Unless there was an answer.

The tears that ran down his cheeks matched his victim's, even as Zayn sang in rage to Percit and Xyl trying to convince himself there was no other option. That Xyl approved of what he did. That thought soured the pleasure he would normally find.

When he was done, he sent the boy away, the act not providing power and pleasure as normal, instead he felt… unclean. Standing looking in the mirror, the handsome man he had always been was gone. The face was still the same, the same thick hair, unblemished skin, healthy body. One that now got even more attention from both genders.

But now he looked in the mirror and saw a man losing his power. A reflection of the insanity of the god he should worship. The loss of power and control. The glass of fruist flew from his hand and impacted the mirror, shattering the expensive luxury that had been shipped from Fivika. A moment later, a priest knocked at his door.

"Is something amiss, Cantor?"

"Clean this up," he ordered and stalked out. The 'worship' was still going on and he stood on the balcony watching it. The writhing bodies, the cries, the sobs

— it made him sick. And that was the only thing that kept him from diving from the second floor head first.

Maybe, just maybe, if this still horrified him, there was a chance.

If.

If they succeeded.

If Xyl was killed.

If… I can control the narrative.

Zayn turned and walked back to his quarters slowly, thinking. If Xyl was killed, he could take control again, guide the faith to a more suitable path. One where he was in command. But he still had no idea what the options would be or how he could select the optimal path.

Everything he had lost was too much. This time he reached for morphe, seeking the release of thought and caring. This was not why he had sought this role. He had wanted power, but this undermined the power of the church and minimized his ability to use the faith to his benefit. Using the singers was one thing, a private vice. Putting all perversions out in the open removed the joy in having them. If this continued, the poorest Char would have access to his slaves. That was unacceptable.

The thoughts chased each other like dogs chasing their tails until the rise of sweet oblivion swallowed it all.

CHAPTER NINETY

JADAYA

The smell and sounds of breakfast pulled her out of her sleep and Jadaya opened her eyes to see all the Leonaids in two-legged form, most without clothing. She sighed as she rose, stretching tall enough that her fingers could brush the bottom of the tent ceiling. Normally she felt tall, but Sher mimicking her actions and touching the highest point with ease made her feel tiny. It was an odd feeling.

"At least cloths to wrap around your waists?" Their time on the prison mountain had inured her to the majority of their nudity, but having their appendages waving about like that was distracting. And oddly discomfiting.

Shinala laughed. "We were just talking for a bit. These four will stay in saber form while the king and his not-queen come talk to us. But for now, I wanted to make sure they had no thoughts or concerns. All of them will fight with claws and teeth, and I will go in as a two-leg, so I have my chakram available. When it is time, we will go to warrior form, but until then, there is much damage they can do in their current shapes."

Jadaya moved over and grabbed some of the eggs that were cooked with cheese and other savory herbs. She settled down on the table near Shinala as she poured herself a telcha.

"That sounds good. Is there anything else you will need? For that matter, you have fought the… children before. What can you tell us?"

"Ah, that is true, but I think I will save that conversation for when the royals are here. It makes little sense to provide the same information and answer the same questions twice."

"As long as I get to extract my wife's price in blood, I care little what we do," Paka growled.

Jadaya knew the story and just nodded. "I am unable to make that promise, but if we do this, you will have your opportunity. Your claws can hurt him?"

Katel laughed. "Yes. We were all but made to hurt them. It will not be easy, but hurting him is well within our abilities."

Lev just grinned and winked at her.

They were sitting there sipping on telcha when a knock came at the door. After a glance at everyone, Mace went over and removed the bar as the other sabers took up positions in corners, giving them access to everyone that might be in the room.

The door opened and four people walked in, followed by servants with extra chairs. Jadaya remained seated, as did the others. These were not her rulers, and frankly, if she was going to die, they should bow to her, not the other way around.

Jadaya took the time to inspect each of them. One was the Captain from yesterday. In his hands was a roll of parchment that looked like a map. The other was Hauyne, looking fresher if still stressed. The servant was an older Char, if only from the silver in his short blond hair and his swollen joints.

That left the last man, the one wearing a crown. This one was a simple white metal circle with a large ruby in the center. It could not have weighed more than a ten tellaweight, but you would have thought it weighed closer to a thousand from the weariness in his steps. As with all Char, he had dark blond hair, though his had touches of red in it. His eyes were a darker blue that spoke of intelligence and determination. It was his face and body that caught her.

Char as a whole were a stocky people with curves, tending towards a generous body type, even the men had a nice layer of fat over them. Percit and Xyl had preferred their people to be comfortable to cuddle and exude warmth.

This man was nothing but whipcord and bone. His face had lost fat as had his body, if the way the clothes hung off of him was any indication. He moved as if every step shoved shards of obsidian into each joint in his body, but he never hesitated. Those sharp eyes trailed over each of them as he sat down, a soft sigh slipping out of his lips and his eyes closed for a moment in what only could be relief. But when they popped back open, Jadaya could see nothing soft about the man. That was not what she had heard about him in their travels. Something had changed.

"Sire, may I present our... guests," Hauyne said, stumbling for a second. "Guests, this is King Lazul Lapis, ruler of Charinsky. With him is Captain Diam Marcel and our chief of staff and steward, Actin." She finished her little speech and sat down, pulling out a small notebook from her chatelaine along with a graphine.

They all looked at each other, as the one thing they had forgotten to discuss was who would lead. Note shook his head and Jadaya agreed. Having him lead the conversation with the anger that still simmered would not be a good idea.

Rylix shrugged, and Jadaya sighed, speaking up. "King Lapis, it is good to meet you. What did you want to speak to us about? After all, we are here because of the efforts of your not-queen." She nodded at Hauyne at that point.

Lapis lifted an eyebrow and turned to look at Hauyne, a slight smile on his face. "My not-queen?"

She shrugged. "It is accurate, sire." Again, a level of teasing that warmed a part of Jadaya. There were layers to this.

"Ah. True." He shifted that piercing stare toward them. "Rumor is a funny thing and the rumor out there is you are coming to kill a god. Is that true?" His voice shook on the last part, losing his neutral tone. There was a touch of hope in there that made her swallow. To hide her reaction, she took a sip of telcha.

"That may be. But our original aim was different," she said slowly. They had the tools, the knowledge, but something made her want to address their original plan. What had started all this.

"And that was?" He had control of his voice again.

"To rescue the slaves. My people. To break them free of the chains you have them in," Note said, his voice harsh and tight. Jadaya cast him a sidelong look, and he clenched his hands around his mug of telcha and took a sip.

The king bowed his head for a second, then picked it up with effort, looking at them. "A worthy goal and one I regret would need to be done, but I admit to this failing of my people. And now what is your plan?"

"It seems now, given the changes that have occurred, the only option is to kill a mad god." The words fell from her lips with the weight of lead coins falling into a bowl of water. The reverberations of the sounds almost amplifying their impact. That was how much power they had.

His shoulders, all their visitors' shoulders, relaxed at that bit. Lapis bit his lip, then spoke. "And can you?"

Shinala grinned wide and fierce. "We can. But what happens when we do?"

That was something they had been arguing over. Until now, it had seemed so far away, something for a 'someday' discussion until suddenly that 'someday' was now.

"I have no idea, but I promise the singers … the slaves will be released and what possible reparations will be made. After that, I have no clue. There is no land without a god. What happens to us next is unknown." His voice was desperate, but honest.

"Will you or the populace hold us responsible?" That question had ridden in her mind, though she thought it should be a better question, but she had no idea how to ask it better.

Hauyne snorted at that, and after a quick nod from the king, she spoke. "They will hold you responsible and it will be hard to not proclaim you king, god, and hero at the same time. The damage being done to our people right now is more than has ever been done to our land. If it is not stopped soon, we will have no people worth saving."

That was from the heart, and Jadaya had seen what she meant as they traveled. She could understand wanting to prevent any more sliding down into that level of twisted depravity.

Jadaya set the telcha to the side and took a breath. "How can you help, and how do we do this?"

"You will fight him? You can kill him? How?" This came from the steward, Actin.

Jadaya opened her mouth, but Shinala lay a white hand over hers. "I promise you we can, but how we can do that may need to be the secret weapon. While none of the children can read minds, they are very good at registering certain words being said. I think explaining after his blood is on the street is a better option. But all of us have either the ability or the tools to spill the blood of a child of my creators."

Rylix smiled and spoke for the first time. "Besides, if we fail, you would have the ability to deny knowing who we were or what we intended."

The king shook his head. "I will guarantee you that the odds of me surviving this are nonexistent. But I agree with keeping information close. You never know what might be overheard and failing is not an option. My life is the least of my worries, but if something is not done, the country of Charinsky will no longer exist. And my people will be monsters wearing the skin of a Char."

His words rang off the stone walls and slipped through the tent roof with a level of truth that she could feel in her bones.

"Then how do we do this?" Jadaya said, looking at all of them.

"Oh, I can take care of that," two voices said at the same time.

CHAPTER NINETY-ONE

LAZUL

Lazul had been unsure of all of this, but walking in and seeing the sabers watching him with intelligent eyes, then the five waiting for him, a spark of hope ignited in his chest. One big man leaned against the back door either as a threat or charged with getting the door open if there was danger. Or both.

At the table were two women and two men. The men were normal almost. A Ged of young adult age and an Aoisan with hair that looked like he had rolled in ashes. But it was the women that entranced him.

He had met Zuyikans before. Even seen the two gods, Zula and Yika, once as a child when his parents took him to Zuyika on a rare trip. They had both had skin as black as the darkest mine. But this woman's skin was charcoal, black but with hints of light lacking on the other Zuyikans in the palace and as servants. Then there was the other woman. White skin, white hair, white eyes. Yet she was neither old nor young. While Charinsky changed little once they reached full adulthood, she looked ageless. The long white hair in twists that reached her waist and muscles corded to match the Zuyikan's. They were striking paired together, and he felt like he was looking at two sides of the same coin.

His worry they were the wrong people or worse, that all of this had been a false rumor, faded as he spoke to them and treacherous hope started to build deep in his heart. The same heart that clenched when both the white woman and a voice behind him spoke at the same time.

"Oh, I can take care of that."

He turned to see Cassix walking toward them. The god had a smile on his face, but rather than the loose robes similar to those the Ged wore, this time he had on tight leggings, a tabard with glimpses of chain mail under it, and a two-handed sword belted to his waist.

The sword threw him. A god with a sword. That somehow seemed more serious than the rest, and his world spun for a tiny moment.

"Now, now. No names. Not mine, and certainly not the white lady." He gave a bow that was both formal and teasing at the same time. Lazul was impressed with it. "While others might not remember your name, he will. I think the element of surprise is the best bet."

"My thoughts as well. You may simply call me Queen," the white lady responded with a smile. A smile with a few more teeth than seemed normal.

"Then if you know how to call him, my suggestions is this: let me change and we will all walk to the temple together. There is the best place to get his attention and a space where fighting might be possible, but also keep it contained. Be warned, though, he can summon animals, elements, and probably more. It is why I have no idea how to fight him, not to mention I saw him grab a blade from me with his bare hand and nothing happened. I tested the blade later and even pressing my finger against it had blood welling up." Lazul kept his attention on them as he spoke, gauging their reaction.

The white woman waved her hand dismissively. "Getting his attention is not an issue. The other aspect, though."

"Ah, but that is why I am here." Cassix gave a smile that had a hardness that Lazul recognized from the mirror. "I may be... enjoined to abstain from any fight against him, however I am not prevented from stopping his powers. I will prevent him from leveraging outside influences, but it will be up to you to defeat him. And remember, he is still a god."

"He is a child of a god. All of you are, and this time my attention, our attention will not be split." The words were said with an icy disdain that sent a twinge of fear down Lazul's spine. He turned to glance at Hauyne and she had both hands clamped over her mouth and her eyes wide.

She had been right. These are the Leonaids.

His eyes took in the woman, the four sabers, and the big man at the door. The man saw him looking at him and smiled, with too many teeth.

Lazul wanted to throw his head back and laugh. There now was a chance. They might be able to do this with the Leonaids. Maybe his land could be freed. They would deal with the aftermath when it happened. First, they had to free his people from a god that would drag them all down into his own insanity.

Instead, he pushed himself to his feet. "Then now? Is there any reason to wait?"

His four guests, his rescuers, the salvation of his nation, exchanged glances, then stood. "We need some time to dress and prepare. Say two fingers?"

He looked over at Captain Marcel, who nodded. "That is enough time. I called all the men in this morning."

"And what will they be doing?" asked the former Zuyikan, already working on re-twisting her hair into a tight cord down her back.

The captain ducked his head toward her. "My men would only get slaughtered if they interfered and if I thought it would make a difference, we would sacrifice ourselves, but instead we will ensure the populace stays out of your way and try to limit any noncombatants involved."

"The priests are just as guilty as your god is," the Aoisan said, his eyes dark and the amount of rage in those eyes made Lazul flinch back. He would need to figure out why the anger was so vibrant—after. Now the emotion could be used against Xyl.

The captain glanced back at Lazul, who just gave him a curt nod. There was something more here slipping past his understanding, but that also could wait until later. If there was a later.

"Understood," he said, as there was nothing more he could say.

"Then we will meet you at the outer door in two fingers," Lazul said, and everyone nodded. With that, he pushed himself to his feet and headed back to his chambers. He needed to change. And maybe pray to Aryix this made things better, not worse.

He was so focused on getting to his chambers and back that Hauyne's words caught him by surprise.

"Are you going to fight?"

He turned his head to look at her, warmed and surprised by the concern in her voice.

"Yes, and no. I will go in full kit, but I would manage a single swing before I collapsed. Already my body clamors for a surcease of the pain, but today it will have to endure. If we survive, it will not matter. If we die… well, then I suppose it matters little."

"And what happens if you die, but he does not?" Her question was soft, but there was trepidation in it, as if she suspected what the answer would be.

Lazul reached out and took her hand, squeezing it softly. "I left a succession plan. You will be announced as queen and will have full control of the country and what happens next. Besides, the councilors like you better than me, and none of them want to deal with Him."

He watched her pale, the flush on her nose becoming stark against her skin.

"I have no desire to have that level of responsibility," she protested, her voice cracking.

He squeezed her hand tighter as they walked. "I know and it hurts to know I am placing it on you. But the servants in the castle like and respect you. You have the lineage to deal with the council and nobles. Actin all but worships the ground you walk on. Both for dealing with me and your way of managing everything so effortlessly. Besides," he said with a grin that might have had a hint of actual humor in it. "Who else could I trust?"

Hauyne said nothing as they walked, reaching his chamber. With gritted teeth, Lazul pulled on his chain mail, leggings, and tabard. Exhaustion beat at him, but he refused to buckle as he belted his sword around his waist.

She broke the silence as he straightened, feeling more like a king than he had in a while. "Then you had better not die, because if you do, I will trade the place to the Snakes in Wysko," she said with thin lips and rough hands as she finished tucking in his outfit.

Lazul laughed. It was the first actual laugh he could remember in what seemed like mooncycles. "We both know you would never do that. I trust you. But I will pray to Aryix that you never have to take on this burden alone." He pressed a kiss to her forehead then turned to head back to meet the group.

"Is that who we are praying to now? Aryix?" She said with a sigh, coming up to walk with him.

Lazul shrugged. "Why not? It seems to work for the Ged and as he is still imprisoned, I am less worried about his reactions to us singing the wrong song."

She reached out to take his hand this time and squeezed. "Not my favorite, but anything, anyone, is better than our current option."

Lazul chuckled and pulled her closer. "Who knows? Maybe something will change. All we can do is try."

She nodded, and they walked in companionable silence through the castle, all too aware of the servants gathering as they walked, hope and fear mixed in their eyes. The cool morning air met them as they joined their hopeful saviors standing outside the back gate. In the past, this was so the Ged staying could easily get to their wagons and beasts. Now it formed a good mustering area.

Their visitors, he still did not know their names, were ready. Each of them held a weapon the likes of which he had never seen.

The tall, former Zuyikan with the brand on her cheek, stepped forward. "We are as ready as we can be. Where do we go?"

Lazul took a deep breath and forced a smile he willed to be real. "We head to the temple, and I guess you two will get him here?" He glanced at Cassix, who leaned against the wall, looking for all the world like a bored spectator.

"It will be my pleasure," said the god in question, flashing a smile that had the same hungry glee that Lazul felt swirling around in him.

Though his emotions also included stark fear and a fervent hope this was the right choice. Under all of that was the pain that he fought with every breath.

A little longer. Then it will be over one way or another.

The thought gave him little comfort. If he had his way, he would prefer to be alive to take Hauyne as his wife in fact, not just spirit.

"Stay here, with Actin. I feel you will know the outcome one way or the other." Lazul watched her for a moment and saw the instinctive refusal in her eyes. Then Hauyne snapped her mouth shut and nodded.

"I expect you to return. I will plan a lavish wedding," she replied instead, and the smile that spread across his face was the most real in his life.

"That sounds good to me." With a daring he had not had before, he leaned forward and kissed her gently in front of everyone. "I liked you when I met you at the dinner your brother held. I fell in love with you within tendays of you coming here. I plan on coming back and making you queen," he said when he pulled away.

Her eyes were suspiciously shining as she nodded. "If you get back here in one piece, then you can hear when I decided I loved you."

Another smile and he wanted to laugh. Here, when he was headed into a battle that would probably kill him, he felt more alive than he had in a mooncycle.

"Incentive indeed. Until I return." With strength gained from tendays of fighting the pain, he turned to the group watching him. Some with smirks on their faces, others just a soft smile. "This way," he said and faced the temple, his soldiers, the strangers, all falling in behind.

Lazul Lapis, king of Charinsky, turned and led the motley group toward the temple. His guards, a group of strangers, and a god. Either it would be enough, or they would all be dead and he would have the guilt of failure following him into the next existence.

CHAPTER NINETY-TWO

NOTE

Note had shed his hooded jacket and instead stood in his pants, shirt, and bracers. He felt oddly exposed after a tenday of wearing the shrouding outer gear. Trinity sat attached to his hip on his right, while Echo was in the bracer on his left arm. The bracer on his right held his normal knives. Soft leather boots with shark hide soles insured grip on the worn cobblestones. He kept his head on a swivel as they walked down the road, already gathering attention and for once, Note worried less about someone grabbing him than the ones watching them panicking.

No matter how jaded Note was, watching a king walk down the street—his sword secured at his waist, staggering every so often—was surreal. Five people armed to the teeth followed him, two of whom were so visually striking that Note fought to tear his eyes from the women warriors, one black, one white. It felt like the beginning of an epic story happening in real time. And he was part of it. Then there were the five sabers that paced after them as if the mortals were simply their entourage. All of it made the king's guard following behind them seem like an afterthought.

Turning around in a circle as they walked, Note smiled to himself. It was a parade indeed. And from the attention being garnered, there would be an audience to their battle. He let himself look at the city for the first time. When he had been enslaved here, he rarely saw anything outside the temple walls, and when he fled, it had been at night and everything had been looming buildings that held a chance of being caught. Now he finally looked and caught nuances that a tenset of suncycles ago he never would have.

There were signs of wind or other damage on most roofs, with clay tiles cracked or missing. The scent of wet bricks, new plaster, and fresh-cut wood was prevalent here. The buildings were rarely over two stories, but spread out. There were small buildings nestled together, with stores on the bottom and residences above.

It was from those residences that more and more blond heads stuck out watching them. A sea of virtual twins, unaging and ignorant to the depths their priests had gone to keep them alive.

He snarled and shoved down that momentary spurt of understanding. He refused, absolutely refused, to ever given them a smidgen of understanding for the torture, abuse, and enslavement of his people. And that the populace turned a blind eye to it made them just as complicit.

Yet, for all his anger, it was an attractive city. Where Pelisic had walls so white they were blinding, here everything was a soft gray. The gray mine dust they used to make their plasters, the gray of the stone they harvested to build with, the gray of the cobblestones under their feet. But touches of color, of joy, caught his eye at every turn. A window box of flowers here, gem castoffs made into light reflectors, laundry drying in colors of blue, green, and yellow.

The part that really made him uncomfortable was the lack of laughter. There was a heaviness he never sensed when he had been here before. He heard no children playing. The faces staring at him were worn with stress and worry, and even as more and more Chars started to follow them, they were silent. Like people observing an execution they knew they could not prevent. Even the dogs and cats sat silent as they watched them pass.

A shiver of foreboding washed down his spine, and he snapped his attention to the front where the king was leading them through the doors of the temple. Priests gaped at them in surprise and odd horror.

"Men, stay out here. Captain Marcel, keep everyone out," the king said as he walked in, all of them following.

Note fought down a wave of nausea as he crossed the threshold of the building he had fled all those suncycles ago. What he saw when he crossed into the open-air worship area caught him off guard. He had expected something, given the changes in the other temples he saw, but they had been smaller, with only a small section for the frieze depicting the love of Xyl for Percit. Here, there was much more space.

Gone was Xyl smiling up at his wife and Percit touching him with a love that Note had resented as he would never have that. The gifts of flowers and fruit laid at her feet, as she sat spinning. Always Xyl was there, never her alone, his obsession with her as prevalent when they depicted love as the images were now.

Here she screamed or laughed. If Xyl was using her, the depictions were of her screaming and crying, but for all that Note thought it was supposed to be in pleasure, he only saw pain and terror. In the ones where she was using implements on others, Xyl was watching and her eyes were always on him, not for his excitement, but he would have sworn she watched out of wariness.

He frowned. Before now, he had always resented Percit for dying and leaving Xyl behind to grieve. For a weird heartbeat of time, he felt sorry for her and thought death might have been her salvation.

Before he could chase down that thought, a man clad in robes of the cantor strode into the courtyard. "What is the meaning of this? This is not a place to practice your weapons, it is a place of worship."

That voice, that face, Note remembered him well and only the king speaking stopped him from his immediate reaction.

"Zayn, let us be. We need to stop him. That is what we are here for." The king turned to Shinala and Cassix. "The floor is yours." He stepped back toward the stairs the enslaved Aoisans would stand on and Note had a second to register that he sagged down, sitting on the first of the small risers, looking exhausted and gray.

The Cantor, his abuser, looked around and nodded at the priests gathering at the entrance, outrage and exhaustion mixed on their faces. "Stay back. I will deal with this," he ordered, and they moved back a bit, letting the king's guard create a block across the opening.

Trinity was in his hand, and Note ached to throw it. Three chances. Surely, he could kill the man in three throws. His aim was as close to perfect as he could get. The axe seemed to warm in his hand as he considered it. Rylix stood at his shoulder and he wondered if the man would stop him from murdering him. Somehow he thought the Ged might understand.

Shinala's voice pulled him away from his thoughts. "Xyl, I want to talk to you," she called out in a voice that carried through the air, struck the walls of the worship area and bounced back. Over and over her words rang, far past what the local acoustics could explain.

When the sounds faded, they still stood there, without a god. Or at least without another one. But the Cantor, his abuser, jailer, had gone even whiter. In the moments Note's attention had been on Shinala, the man had gone behind his pulpit and now held on to it as if it supported him.

"What are you doing? Do you think our god would just respond to your call, like a dog who seeks your love? Our god demands our worship, not begs like a child." His orator voice carried, but this time the walls swallowed the sound, leaving only an absence in their place. The cantor stood proudly, but his skin was gray as he stared down imperiously at them all.

Shinala turned to look at him with a sneer. "Oh, I know Xyl. He was a coward. He killed those who served him first. Just in case they might pledge their allegiance to someone else. Or should I repeat the rumors of him and Percit? That she asked the others to help her avoid the marriage? That she never loved him?"

"Loved him, loved him, loved him," the words bounced around the area, getting louder but fainter at the same time. A bolt of lightning slammed into the ground of the middle area, the grass bursting into flame, the marble shattering. A figure appeared even as thunder followed in a rolling crescendo that had more weight and power than any Note had ever heard.

He fought to blink away the aftermath of that burst of light across his eyes, the white line bisecting the figure that stood there. Taller even than Jadaya, with blond hair, blue eyes of the ripening sky, a body that sculptors would want to use as a model, and a face that embodied nobility. Then he screamed. There was nothing sane in that sound and Note found himself taking a step back in surprise.

Note watched Xyl turn to face Shinala, who stood there in her mortal form, a simple long shirt over her body. She had refused all armor, but agreed walking through the city naked might garner the wrong attention. The shirt would shred when she changed into her warrior form. Note fought his urge to kill the cantor as the Leonaid leader faced off with Xyl. His axes were as hungry as he was for blood, for vengeance, for a way to quiet the screaming in his mind. But for now, the god was the bigger threat. The cantor was mortal and would die soon enough.

"Who says my wife was less than perfect in her love for me? She worshiped me!" Xyl looked around wildly, dismissing the mortals. Then he focused on Shinala, taking in her form and that she was Leonaid. "You," Xyl snarled. "What are you doing off your prison island?" For a second, fear flickered across his face. "Are they free?"

Shinala shook her head. "No. I am here to deal with you."

All the power and arrogance flooded back into his face, and Xyl laughed. A dark sound that held nothing kind or gentle in it.

"I killed enough of yours back then. I have no problem adding the queen bitch to the pile of dead," he said with a sneer, lifting his hand. The snarl of an enraged saber pulled his attention to the side and Note saw Paka stalk forward, the scar present on his two-legged form clear across his saber form, dark and ropey as it traced from the outer corner of his left eye to his mouth.

"Xyl?" Cassix stepped forward and Note shook his head, realizing that he had not seen Cassix at all until this moment. A soft snarl to himself. Gods and their ability to not be seen was infuriating.

Xyl jerked back, looking at Cassix, his brows furrowed as he stared at the other god. "Cassix?"

"Yes, it is me. You can come with me. You have grieved long enough. She is gone. It is time to heal." He said with his hand out. "If you come with me, your siblings will help you. It is time to let her go."

Note wanted to scream, to protest, and from the shocked look on the others faces he figured they felt the same. But he could only stand there and watch, his voice and body refusing to respond to his urgent commands. He saw Rylix out of the corner of his eye, just as frozen as he was.

The confusion on Xyl's face drained away, and he brought up both hands to clutch at his hair. His fingers sunk into the golden blond waves and shook his head back and forth.

"No. She was going to leave me. She asked him to take her away. Percit was mine and I would never give her up. When she ran, I broke her legs so she could never run again. But he interfered. I tried to stop him, but he moved too fast. I went after him with my sword." A long silver weapon appeared in his hands. It was longer than Jadaya's arm and Note knew it would have taken even her two hands to manage it, but Xyl swung it around like it weighed nothing.

"What?" The word came from both Shinala and Cassix. Cassix's voice was shocked. While Shinala's held confusion.

"He was going to take her. I had to kill him. But she got in the way. Even with broken legs, she never listened to me. All she had to do was listen. She was mine. Why did she resist what would have been perfect? Percit, of all of them, was mine. She always had been. She made me kill her! Why could she not under-stand she was mine?" That last part was screamed out, but Note was unsure if it was rage or guilt. All he could hear was insanity and obsession.

"The rumors were true?" Shinala asked. "I had heard she asked the others to dissuade your suit, back when you were still young. Cassix, what did you say? Oh yes. 'Percit. He loves you. How could you not want him? Besides, there is no one else'." Shinala's words were mocking and directed at Cassix, who had gone pale under his tan skin. Even his hair seemed to have lost all color in his shock.

"I never, I thought she was…" he trailed off, jaw slack as he stared at the god. "Xyl? You killed her?"

"She was MINE," Xyl shrieked back, stepping up to Cassix, eyes raging and spittle landing on the ground, searing everything it touched, though Cassix had no reaction. "I threw the interloper onto his ship and set it to explode, but I failed. It broke her moon, our home, shattering it, and the ship came here. All of you noticed. I had to do something. It was all his fault. I told you the truth. He killed her. I would have never had to do it if he had stayed away. She made me because she wouldn't understand she was mine. She tried to leave me. Percit will always be mine!"

Cassix blinked. "Oh, Aryix," the words were meant to be a whisper, but they echoed around the room, amplifying over and over. Calling for an imprisoned god, begging forgiveness and more.

"Noooo!" Xyl screamed. "Never call him. He never approved, even my Leonaids knew. That was why I killed them all. No one could know she wanted away. She never understood she was mine. Now you all have to die as well. She was mine and will remain mine until the suns go dark," he snarled, swinging the sword toward Cassix.

Cassix jumped back as Shinala, moving like the wind, had her chakram up to block the sword. The sound of the clash between the two weapons rang through the courtyard, and one of the friezes cracked.

"May Aryix forgive me. I will stop his powers, but you must stop him," Cassix called as he jumped back. It was all Note had been waiting for.

Trinity separated and sat waiting in his hand. He threw each one as hard and fast as he could. They flew through the air, headed straight toward Xyl's back. This would be over in a moment.

Then Xyl ducked, spun, his sword intercepting the three axes in a triple stroke that Note could barely follow. Then the god was back swinging at Shinala as Jadaya launched her attack from the other side.

Note snarled, recalled Trinity and dove in. Throwing now would be too dangerous for his companions, so he joined the melee.

Three mortals, six Leonaids, and three witnesses, one of which was a god.

Time for the mad god to die.

CHAPTER NINETY-THREE

JADAYA

Jadaya was aware of the Leonaids shifting and vaguely heard the gasps from the king and the head clergyman, but all she cared about was Xyl's sword. She dove in with Immunity aimed toward him, but he pivoted, blocking her blade with his left forearm as he used his sword to block Shinala's dual pieced weapon.

"Mortals, you are so easy to kill. Your blood should have been spilled, not my beloved's," he said and flicked a finger at her.

Driven by feelings from the earring, she lifted her sword up in a high guard as a crack and the smell of burnt air hit her nose at the same time as her sword caught his lightning.

Immunity lived up to its name, and she grinned, turning the guard position into a slash toward his neck. Xyl ducked, slamming a sword toward the Leonaid, diving toward him. It caught Sher along the side, and the Leonaid screamed out in pain as it landed.

A flicker of white had her ducking as Shinala, in her warrior form, moved in a blur, flying toward Xyl with both curved blades intersecting to cut him. He pulled back just enough that they only grazed his stomach, leaving a delicate slice leaking blood behind.

"God weapons," he snarled as he kicked out, and his foot caught Katel in the chest as the saber charged him. It threw the Leonaid back into a frieze. "You still will lose."

"No," Jadaya said, "we will end your reign of terror." The words were shouted as she ducked and wove, working in concert with Shinala as if they had been fighting side by side for suns.

She ignored the flickers of silver gray as Note darted in and out, hitting with Trinity as one piece, leaving behind cuts and the occasional deeper wound.

But Xyl was so fast and his arms and legs could deflect swords, axes, even the whip. The Leonaids lashed out at him, but while their claws could cut, but they were the equivalent of scratches from a cat, not gashes from an ursoid.

"You will pay for Percit's death. She was one of the few I liked," Shinala snarled as well, her voice remarkably clear given the change in shape. Jadaya timed Shinala's strikes to move in between with stabs as Shinala created openings.

"Never. Instead, I will offer your hearts to my love on the altar I will build from your bones," Xyl said. He spun and blocked and lashed out like a whirl-wind. His sword cut as if edged in glass, leaving sliced skin behind. Jadaya and Shinala both collected small wounds from it, but if they stumbled even for a second, he would run them through.

"Why are my winds and animals not here?" he roared as he jumped, avoiding the claws of Paka trying to hamstring him.

"Every bit of power you bring, I counter. This is on you, to live or die as Xyl, without distracting those to whom you owe recompense," Cassix called out over the noise.

Jadaya's world had narrowed to blocking and attacking, letting her instincts and skills react, not her mind. With Shinala, Note, the Leonaids and the occasional crack of Rylix's whip to bite at the insane deity, she had to trust those instincts. More than once, the bracer Shinala created for her saved her life, but pain and bruises radiated out from under it, the force of Xyl's blows undeniable.

But even with all of them attacking, drawing blood, he still stood. Rylix stayed back, and only when one of them fell or there was a clear opening did the whip crack across the courtyard, the sound like the shattering of stone as it struck. Each strike hit home, but left only another tiny wound as Xyl fought. The whip itself was not enough to injure him, so Xyl ignored it the way Jadaya would ignore a biting insect.

The whirl of arms and swords and claws had only been going for a fraction of a finger, but already the attackers were injured worse than the god. Jadaya's breath and heartbeat pounded through her body as she pushed herself, raging against the heaviness growing in her arms.

Sher had leaped again, blood pouring down his side, arms spread wide to wrap his paws around Xyl. The mad god caught the huge Leonaid, his left arm wrapped around Sher's neck, and he twisted hard, snapping his neck in an instant and tossing the body of the dead Leonaid to the other side of the courtyard.

It happened so fast Jadaya barely had time to register the death, but she heard the roar from Shinala. A howl rose from the others still in saber form.

"Sher was mine, by oath and blood. You only know how to steal, not earn. Percit could never have loved you," Shinala spat, the silver arcs of her weapons weaving back and forth to the right of the god while Jadaya focused her attacks on the left.

"She worshiped me," Xyl screamed, then dropped into a crouch and the triple flash of axes flew across where his head had been, impacting the wall on the other side. One of them hit a carving of Percit and the frieze shattered. Xyl let loose another howl of rage and lunged at Jadaya.

Jadaya stumbled backward, falling, then rolling out of the way as he stomped down at her. Paka, still in saber form, dove in, seizing the moment as Xyl was off balance. He sank his teeth around the god's left knee as Mace, in warrior form, raked at his back with his right claw, leaning in as Xyl struggled to move.

"No," Xyl shouted and clouds crowded above them and the wind began to blow.

"I think not," Cassix said in a low voice that should have been overwhelmed by the other sound in the area, but carried clearly over the fight. The winds slowed back to the breeze they had been.

"Interloper," Xyl snarled, and reared back onto his right leg, lifting his left up, with the saber still attached, and slammed his sword through Paka's chest. The Leonaid roared in pain, his mouth opening as he cried out. Xyl grabbed him and threw him across the area, where he landed at Lazul's feet.

Jadaya, still scrambling back on all fours as Xyl attacked Paka, saw a flicker of motion as Lazul pulled back in shock, then dropped to his knees, pulling off his tabard to try to stop the wounded Leonaid's bleeding. The advisor beside him ripped off his robe and tied it around the Paka, working with Lazul to help.

Xyl raised his swords in the air, his face a mask of rage. "You will all die by my hand," he roared and something pulsed from him.

"Fight him. I think I can block that," Cassix said, but there was a hint of uncertainty under his words.

Jadaya caught herself and leaped to her feet. Sher and Paka were down, the other three Leonaids were striking when they could, and Xyl was covered with blood from fingersets of tiny cuts, but nothing dire enough to slow him down.

She raced toward his back and swung her sword, weaving a pattern that should give her multiple opportunities to strike, but he blocked or moved so they were only glancing blows. Already she felt herself slowing. Shinala was still going strong but even with all of them, with weapons that could cut through almost anything, they still were barely wounding him.

Jadaya realized it would take a direct hit for them to really damage him. That meant taking a chance. She kept attacking, but saw that Mace, Katel, and Lev worked in a pattern, the three of them almost seamless with lunges and slashes, avoiding the sword and usually Xyl's flicker-fast punches or stabs.

"Note," she called out, "when I say so, launch only Trinity, then Echo." With luck, Xyl would expect the three axes that Note had been attacking with, not a single strike. She had not yet seen Echo fly so hopefully the dagger would be yet one more surprise.

"Now!" she yelled, and Trinity came spinning over her head. Xyl dropped to let them go through, right into the path of the dagger. Echo slammed into his side between his hips and ribs. It sank all the way in, then Note recalled it as it disappeared.

Xyl turned in surprised pain, and she lunged forward. With Immunity gripped with both hands, she shoved the blade into his chest. Off-balance as she had hoped, and bleeding from the first serious wound, Immunity slid in through his ribs and into his heart.

Xyl hung there, surprised etched across his face. Shinala's attack to his right laid open two huge gashes as her blades sliced across him deeply this time, the god neither moving nor blocking the blows. At the same time, Trinity, this time in three, impacted into his back. Each of the axes thudded into him, sinking deep. This time, they stuck. The slashes that the Leonaids had left widened and blood rushed out of them, the wounds no longer being constrained by his power.

His knees buckled and Xyl sank downward, pulling Jadaya with him as he grabbed the sword and held on even as blood streamed from the blade.

"You hurt me," he said, looking at her in shock and bewilderment. "Mortals hurt me."

The others rushed over as he hit the ground and Jadaya pulled the sword out, looking at the god on the ground before her. She felt nothing but relief that it was over. She looked at Cassix with a sudden worry. Was it over?

Xyl clutched his chest, the heart wound obvious. He glared up at Jadaya, his eyes wild and crazy. "Then I die and Percit will be waiting for me. She is mine and always will be. No one else will touch her again. I made sure of that. Even in death, she will never escape me."

The words were slurred but burned into her brain and made her knees shake. What had he meant?

A wailing shriek of pain and rage slipped from his throat, body ravaged by fingersets of cuts inflicted by claws and blades, coating the area with blood, even her feet.

"She is mine! Even in death I will possess her." the scream cut short as Jadaya, driven by a fierce need to silence the keening, slashed Immunity across his throat. Blood sprayed out, soaking her, Shinala, Note, and Rylix, who had all come close to watch the dying god.

She dashed it from her eyes with a rub of her hand across her face. She looked at the god, slumped and bloody, at her feet.

"Is it done?" She asked, holding Immunity at the ready. If she needed, she would hack his body into pieces.

Cassix came over and crouched beside him. Of all of them, he was untouched. No blood marred his clothes or his skin, yet he looked tired and grey. He touched Xyl in the middle of the forehead, eyes closed. After a moment, he looked up at them.

"It is done. He is dead."

A sigh of relief escaped Jadaya, and she turned to check on the others. Mace walked over, carrying Paka in his arms. The Leonaid was dying. She had no idea how he was still alive.

"Show me," the mortally wounded warrior growled. Paka had shifted back to mortal form and Mace knelt, holding the Leonaid in his arms. Paka stared with hunger and sorrow at the body of Xyl.

"It is done. Your wife is avenged," Mace said quietly.

Paka let loose a long, slow breath. "Yes, now I can find her again." He closed his eyes, and the stress seemed to flow out of him like his lifeblood, leaving only peace. Then, he was gone.

Mace rose and walked over to lay Paka near Sher. The huge redhead had died with his neck broken by the god and lay against the wall like a discarded stuffed animal. Jadaya looked around and realized all of them had been injured in the fight, except for Rylix and Cassix. The fight had been too close for Rylix to help much, which was probably for the best. He was a trader, not a fighter. The distraction he provided with the whip had been enough.

Katel had a broken leg from one of Xyl's kicks. Mace and Lev had long, jagged cuts from the sword that bleed freely. Note had bruises on his face, and blood smears where she thought Xyl might have caught him with a backhand.

Shinala limped from a slash on her left thigh, bled from a slice on her right side, and favored a knee that was bruising and swelling already. She was in mortal form and you could see every bruise and bit of blood across her body.

"It is over?" Lazul asked, walking toward them, his tabard discarded and stained with Paka's blood. He looked different somehow.

Cassix nodded. "Xyl is dead. His magics should be stopping. Soon." As he spoke, the images around them changed back to what Note had told her about what they had looked like during his time in Char.

Following behind him was the cantor, looking both pale and relieved. "You did it. Is he really dead?"

"They did it Zayn. The torment is over," Lazul said quietly. He stood straighter and color was returning to his face. The lines of tension around his mouth and eyes had relaxed.

"Aryix bless," the man whispered. " Now it can get back to normal." He looked exhausted and elated at the same time.

Note snarled as he turned to face the man. " Normal? Normal! You want it back the way it was?"

The man turned to look at Note with a blank expression. " Of course. What Xyl wanted hurt Charinsky. But he was…… insane."

"Yes, and?" Note grated out as he stepped up into the man's space. The Charinsky was almost a hand taller than Note, but the sheer lethality radiating off the Aoisan made him look intimidating. "You still were the one who used the slaves you kept. The one who enjoyed the perks of rising through the ranks, no matter what damage you did to those you dragged to your bed." Each word had enough acid to sear through granite, and Jadaya felt her heart breaking for Note again.

The man paled and weaved a bit. "How?" he muttered weakly as Note bared his teeth.

"What? have you forgotten your favorite 'treat' so easily?" The mockery of the word "treat" had her swallowing, and Jadaya caught Shinala's wide eyes and Cassix's closed ones as Note faced down the priest.

The man's eyes went wide as his skin paled to the point the veins on his face stood out like roadmaps of indulgence. "Nok?" The word came out in a whisper.

"Nok died at your hands," Note snarled and his restraint snapped. Echo was in his hand, then he hurled the knife into the man's heart.

"What?" Lazul cried out as the man fell backward into his arms. The king sank to the ground, holding him as the robes grew darker as blood soaked into them.

Note stared down at the man, and Jadaya saw tears leaking from his eyes. "Now my vengeance is sated," he said, looking at the man dying not ten feet from him. With a gesture, Echo returned to his hand, leaving a hole and spreading patch of blood in the cantor's chest.

"What by Aryix is going on?" Lazul cried out, arms wrapped around Zayn, trying to stop the bleeding, but the throw had been perfect, and with each heartbeat blood geysered up, splashing the king and the ground with blood.

Jadaya watched the priest, held by a king who still sought answers that she had no right to provide, but his confusion drew words from her as Note turned away, his hands shaking.

"Your god not only hurt your country but turned a blind eye to the damage being done to those at the mercy of his priests. Damage to body and mind," she said, remembering the words Note had said in the belly of the *Starguide* a moon-cycle ago.

It took a moment, but realization flickered across the king's face and he stared down at the man. Lazul looked at the man who was supposed to protect his people from harm. Instead, he caused harm. "Zayn?"

CHAPTER NINETY-FOUR

LAZUL

Xyl appeared in the middle of them, and Lazul cringed. Part of him expected all of them to be struck down, killed for even daring to call on the god. But then Xyl started raving. The more the god said, the more the very foundation of Lazul's life shattered. Xyl had killed Percit. All this grief, this punishment, was misplaced guilt? Then who was the Usurper?

"Did he say *he* killed Percit? Then blamed someone else?"

Lazul jerked as he realized Zayn had sat down next to him. The man was as pale as Lazul had ever seen him. He had thrown on normal worship robes to run down here, but now they just leeched out what little color he had left.

"I think so, and she never loved him? He was abusive?" The idea of their god, gods, in an abusive relationship, shook him to the bones. What did that mean? Was there anything about their god that was true? Was anything worth saving or had everything the people of Charinsky had ever believed a lie?

Zayn gave a hollow laugh. "It makes sense. The more she slipped away, the more he held her tight. Then when he killed her, he cracked, blaming others. It explains so much."

"And does nothing but complicate things," Lazul murmured.

Then, like that, weapons were drawn and Lazul found his entire attention focused on the fight. He longed to get up and help, but he knew after a few heartbeats he would have been dead. Seeing the sabers shift into the legendary Leonaids and the speed of their attacks was breathtaking. He had never loved the art of war, though he made sure he knew how to use his sword. But this? He was barely a child compared to them, an infant maybe.

They *were* weapons. The black woman and the white Leonaid moved so fast with their attacks, counters, and avoidance that he could barely follow it. But what terrified him was that Xyl was faster.

The blocks, the strikes, the sound of flesh impacting stone, all created a music that his pulse matched. When the lightning came down and the woman caught it with the sword, Lazul was stunned, and hope crept into his heart. He watched, forgetting to breathe until his vision would go grey and a shudder would remind him to breathe again.

Then, like he missed an important part, there was a sword in Xyl's body and the god was sliding to the ground. Still raving about the goddess he had trapped and Lazul now knew abused. And her siblings had stood by and let it happen.

Then the pain that had hammered his mind and bones since the koxylitic sank its teeth into him started to fade. It took a few moments, but with every heartbeat, the pain lessened and his energy rose, pushing it back even more. A smile crossed his face as it faded to the point that he could ignore it.

"Is it over?" He said the words aloud, but part of them were to himself. Was it over? The pain, the exhaustion, the need for drugs?

Cassix rose back up. "Xyl is dead. His magics should be stopping. Soon."

Lazul saw flickering in the corner of his vision, but he kept his eyes on Xyl. Larger than a man, yes. But there, lying on the ground, he looked no different from any other dead body Lazul had ever seen. He pushed himself up and walked over to the god.

Zayn followed, his voice a shadow of its normal power. "You did it? Is he really dead?"

"They did it Zayn. The torment is over," Lazul said quietly. He straightened and felt his muscles unknot, unconscious resistance to the pain. He could breathe again, and a smile twitched at the sides of his mouth.

"Aryix bless," Zayn whispered. "Now it can get back to normal." He looked exhausted and elated at the same time. And Lazul wanted to reassure the man. Hauyne had caught the message Zayn tried to send. It all worked out.

The Aoisan whirled on Zayn snarling. "Normal? Normal! You want it back the way it was?"

Zayn moved as if in a trance, turning to look at the man. Lazul had never seen him so flustered. "Of course. What Xyl wanted hurt Charinsky. But he was… insane."

"Yes, and?" The Aoisan crowded up to Zayn, tilting his head to look up, but his rage made Lazul feel like Zayn was the small one. "You still were the one who used the slaves you kept. The one who savored the abuses made possible as you rose through the ranks. No matter what damage you did to those you dragged to your bed. Why would normal be what is desired?" The acid tone burned into every cell of Lazul's brain as he processed the words.

What? Zayn would never abuse his power.

The lie laughed in his mind even as tiny pieces clicked together. The empty rooms in the temple. The strange equipment in the healer's room. The way the singers, the slaves, avoided looking at the priests. They had been abusing them. Raping them. His stomach clenched in horror, and he found himself pulling back from the man.

Zayn's face was so white his veins popped out like bloody roads to failure. "How?"

That was Lazul's question. How had he missed this?

"What? have you forgotten your favorite 'treat' so easily?" The sneer on the Aoisan's face matched the rage making his body tremble.

"Nok?" Zayn's voice was but a whisper, but in Lazul's mind and heart it was a death knell that slammed the door on his guilt.

"Nok died at your hands."

Lazul could see the moment the man lost his control of his anger and the dagger appeared in his hand, then slammed into Zayn's chest.

"What?" Instinct drove him and he caught Zayn, going to the ground with him. "I am confused." It was a lie, he knew. He wanted to deny it, but he knew. He scrambled to stop the bleeding, but blood gushed out, a mortal wound as he held the cantor.

"Now my vengeance is taken," the man said coldly, his face a masterwork of pain and rage as he stared at Zayn bleeding out.

"What by Aryix is going on?" Lazul cried out, arms wrapped around Zayn, trying to stop the bleeding, but the throw had been perfect, and with each heart-beat blood geysered up, splashing him with blood.

"Your god not only hurt your country, but turned a blind eye to the damage being done to those at the mercy of his priests. Damage to body and mind." the Zuyikan's words were flat and Lazul watched the Aoisan walk away, his own blood, shed to protect his people, dripping on the ground.

The whispers that followed Zayn, the ones he'd never lowered himself to listen to sprang to his mind.

The rumors are true? He did more than wallow in his rank and power?

Lazul needed an explanation. "Zayn?"

"Sorry," Zayn gasped. "I wanted to keep my power. But Xyl was ruining that. So he needed to die."

The words made no sense and Lazul looked around for someone to help, but he saw only hard or curious faces. The Leonaids looked mildly confused, the three heroes hard, Cassix sad. No one seemed upset.

"Why?" Lazul managed to ask even as he could feel the heartbeat under his hands grow fainter.

The Aoisan stalked back over and crouched near Zayn looking down at him with a flat expression. "You made it all so much worse. You and your conductors." The words should have been said with a sneer, but there was only pain and sorrow in them.

The Aoisan with blood-spattered dark gray hair lifted silver eyes and caught Lazul's with them. "Taking it as a given, there is much you were unaware of in your church. At least you had better hope you were unknowing. Many of the priests use their child slaves for sexual pleasures. He was one of the worst, as no one would gainsay him. I was one of his 'treats', as he called us. I have dreamed of doing this for a tenset of suncycles. He has earned no pity, and I have only contempt. If you keep your country, king, do better."

The man stood back up and walked away, but Lazul could only look at Zayn, his hands covered with the cantor's lifeblood. And his heart and trust shattered in a way he thought might never heal.

"True. But I earned it. It was mine," Zayn rasped, and a smile twisted his pain-filled face. "I wanted it back."

Lazul just stared, bile collecting in his throat, but before he could say anything, Zayn's heart ceased beating and the man who had been a thorn in his side and sometimes he thought a friend was gone. Leaving behind questions and much more damage to repair.

Lazul sat there, everything he ever thought he knew in tatters at his feet.

"It is done, king. Now what?" The white Leonaid said as they stood there. She had shifted back into mortal form and her nakedness only increased the surrealism of the situation. Blood streaked her body, hers and Xyl's. The vivid red blood on her white skin acted as another stark and unpleasant reminder of everything.

Lazul closed his eyes. He wanted to run, to have time to comprehend these revelations, but in honesty, there was no time. He needed to get up and deal with it now.

With that thought, he stood, silently rejoicing at the power in his body. There was no pain. He took a heartbeat to revel in once again moving without agony, and then he opened his eyes.

"Obviously, there must be changes. But first, let us undo one of the biggest wrongs." He turned to see Captain Marcel approaching, his face pale and hand on his sword as his eyes were locked on the body of the god in the middle of the courtyard. "Diam, just who I need. Have the priests get the sing-" he broke off and cleared his throat, catching the glare from the Aoisan. "Get the captured Aoisans. Set them up in an inn here, everything paid for out of the crown's coffers. Then you detail five groups of men to go to every temple, spread the word that Xyl is dead and the church of Xyl and Percit is no more. At each temple, take the Aoisans and get them somewhere safe. Leave a man with each group to protect them. Those people have been hurt enough."

The captain nodded and turned on his heel, almost fleeing the courtyard and yelling orders as he headed deeper into the temple.

Lazul took a slow breath. The list of things that needed to be done quadrupled in his mind as he looked around.

"It will take time, but I will return them home with reparations," he said, looking at the small group. "And now I believe it would be safe for me to know your names? I feel off balance not knowing them." It was something small, and he hoped having names to call them would make this seem less like a fever dream.

It was the Ged that stepped forward. "I have contacts, and the Ged are willing to take them home. I can signal any in range to come here, if there are some supplies I can use."

"Of course, anything you need." Lazul rolled his shoulders slightly high from how little it hurt, but then the blood and the bodies caught his attention and the joy fled as if from a burst dam.

"I am Rylix, sire. The Aoisan is Note, the white Leonaid is Shinala, the former Zuyikan is Jadaya, and the others are Mace, Lev, and Katel. The fallen Leonaids are Sher and Paka."

Lazul nodded his head and turned to Shinala. Hauyne had been right. It was one of the Leonaids from the old stories. How could she be as old as the gods?

He cleared his throat. "Aryix bless for your assistance. I grieve for your losses, but honor the sacrifice they made."

Shinala tilted her head. "At least Paka is at peace, though I will miss Sher." Her voice was strangely contained, but he knew naught about her to have any idea what she might be feeling.

At a loss for anything else to say, he turned to Jadaya and Note, starting with the Aoisan. "There is no way to make amends for the suffering of you and your people, but I will try. Is there anything I can do now?"

Note opened his mouth, then closed it. He heaved a sigh and then looked at him with eyes that pierced through him. "You swear on your life that you will free them and do everything possible to get them home?"

"I swear," Lazul said without hesitation. That would be done if he had to beggar the crown.

"Then, once that is done, you will deal with Pel, Rian, and Ijo, the high priestess in Aois. They will decide what should be done for the untold suncycles of harm." The determination that had filled his face seemed to fade, and he stepped back, shaking his head. Rylix moved over and put a hand on his shoulder while Note stared at the ground.

Feeling like he watched a private moment, Lazul tore his eyes away and nodded at the tall young woman standing there, the sword in her hand still covered with Xyl's blood.

"You were amazing. Between you and Shinala, Xyl never stood a chance," he said, feeling out of place. He might be king, but these were people who would be legends. Stories would be created about them. But would he be a villain or a fool in the tales?

She smiled at him. "No. It took all of us. He moved so fast that alone we would have died. We owe much to Paka and Sher. I will miss Sher as well. Shinala was right about Paka being at peace now, but Sher was full of life and laughter."

Not sure what to say to that, Lazul looked at her. "Is there anything I can do for you?" He had seen the brand on her cheek declaring her Exile, but that he would let lay for a while until he had a better idea of how she would react. But if she wanted to become Charinsky and even if she wanted a role in the palace, he would give it to her without thinking.

"Now? I think we would like showers and food. A chance to realize what has happened and for some of us to grieve." Her eyes drifted to Shinala, who was standing near the other three Leonaids, all of them in mortal form and naked. Lazul found a priest standing there, looking lost, and told him to go get robes for their guests. The priest rushed away as if his robes were on fire.

Lazul turned back, looking at the people and wished for Actin or Hauyne. This required finesse, and at the moment, he was still reeling from the shock of the day. A long, low rumble shook the ground, and everyone froze. Groundquakes, while not common, were known, but this one went on and on. Leaving him wobbling when it finally finished.

Then a sound so loud he cried out came washing across the temple, the city, and further out. Terror grabbed his insides as he turned, hands over his ears, looking for the source.

CHAPTER NINETY-FIVE

SHINALA

First the ground rolled under her feet, then a sound she had never heard before assaulted her, so loud that she had to cover her ears in self-preservation. There was a strange silence as if the world held its breath, then an explosion so far in the distance it should have been impossible to hear or feel, but the force of the wave made the ground shake at her feet again and her body feel like a wave of air had slammed into it.

Weaker structures around the temple cracked and swayed. The groaning of timber and stone as the wave continued out away from them made talking impossible until it all abruptly ceased. The noise, the air, everything was quiet, as if the world held its breath. Confused, Shinala looked around and finally to the north she saw it. A vast cloud of smoke rising from what had been her home for so long, blotting out the sky with its darkness. She tilted her head, trying to figure out what she saw when it registered.

"Oh, Aryix. You escaped," she said in a whisper. Her mind and heart were numb. So much had happened, and now her creators had finally chosen to free themselves. Should she have tried to kill the children tensets of tensets of suncycles ago?

Jadaya spun to look at her, an expression of horror on her face. "What do you mean, escaped?" Her voice was a whisper, yet the world was so quiet that everyone heard it. Shinala found herself the center of attention as she dragged her eyes away from the cloud.

With forced nonchalance, she shrugged. "The gods have finally left their prison." Her males formed up behind her. Protecting her now, even from her gods. She purred softly, too low for mortals to hear, but her males responded with that same low vibration, giving her courage for what was about to come.

"What does that mean? They never had to stay? They are still there? Are they seeking vengeance for Xyl's death?"

The questions came at her from all sides from the king, her companions, but Shinala just stood quietly, her eyes still on the cloud that changed everything as competing thoughts battled in her brain.

My males. Are they safe?

My masters are free.

She stood frozen as she battled through both concepts, not knowing what to do or ask. As long as her males were safe, she would kneel gladly. But if they had been sacrificed? A lump formed in her throat as fear touched her for the first time in suncycles uncounted. Were her creators so cruel?

"They have?" Cassix stood in front of her, peering hard into her eyes. "Are you sure?" His face was pale and worry creased his brow.

Amusement at his fear rippled through her, and Shinala smiled. It had no mirth, only a sad resignation. "I feel them coming. Do you not?"

He stiffened, then his shoulders sagged. "This was not the change I was hoping for." He fell in next to her, waiting. Shinala stood watching the people around her react. The ruler of Charinsky and his people, priests, soldiers, and a few random citizens, moved back toward the raised steps where the singers had stood.

The three who had started all of this had formed up with their backs facing the wall with the images of Xyl and Percit. Jadaya in front, Immunity in her hand. Rylix and Note stood behind her and to the side, each with their own god-killing weapon in hand. Ready even now to face down gods.

That caused another whisper of thought. Would they kill her gods? The children were simple. But her gods had been in prison for so long. What if they were slow or limited in what they could do? Would she have to fight those she had come to regard as friends?

All the conflicting emotions and options battled inside her, leaving her trembling as she waited. Then her waiting was over. Between an inhale and an exhale, the courtyard was suddenly full of deities.

All of them wore only a loincloth or a chiton and were taller than Jadaya or Shinala, though Aryix was a good hand taller than Lyx, who was the smallest of them. They wore the same clothes they had been imprisoned in. Aryix with his hair of fire, skin of the rich dark earth, and eyes of clear blue water. Lyx standing next to him with hair darker than the night sky, skin the brown of tellanuts, eyes a blue that went to black when rage caught her. In between them stood Stari, a figure of neither male nor female, but both at the same time. Stari had hair the rich colors of a sunset at the beginning, the roots shifting into indigo blackness at the ends, and eyes of the purple dusk. The god smiled, and Shinala felt her heart unclench.

Quas stood apart, looking around and as his eyes of full-growth green, surrounded by skin the color of the moons, and hair that of starlight. When he caught her gaze, he also smiled.

That left Gela and Shinala broke ranks, walking over to her. Gela opened her arms, and Shinala went willingly into them. She had hair of a red the magma could have only wished for, her skin of freshly plowed soil, and eyes of emerald green. But the arms that wrapped around Shinala and held her tight were the most important part.

"MY CHILD. I MISSED YOU." The words rolled through the air as a physical force that rocked the mortals, but Shinala smiled into the hug. She had missed them, too.

"WE HAVE COME TO COLLECT OUR CHILD," Aryix said as Shinala pulled back from the hug. Multiple mortals had collapsed in prostration on the ground. She suspected it was a mix of fear and hearing the gods speak. Their children had always had softer voices. When these gods spoke, your very essence felt the words.

Shinala stepped away and pointed to the crumpled body. "He lays there. He said things at the end," she said slowly. As always, she never knew what they had heard or not hear.

"AH YES. THAT MUST BE ADDRESSED." Aryix looked at Quas and that god nodded. He lifted his hand and snapped his fingers. At that moment, the open doors that led from the antechamber to the worship area disappeared. In its place, there was a solid wall. The only mortals remaining in the worship court-yard were her three companions and the king, who sat stunned next to the body of the disgraced cantor. Then, as the snap faded, all the other gods were in the room.

The area filled with their power, their essence, and best of all, their fear. Shinala inhaled the sweet scent of fear from those upstart children who had hurt her gods. She opened and closed her hands, surprised to realize she had shifted back into warrior form, and she separated her chakram in two, ready to attack these cowards at the word of her gods.

Cries of outrage filled the air, but multiple gods sank to their knees, bowing their heads to their parents, who stood there, faces impassive.

"Shit," Cassix muttered and drifted over to stand near his siblings.

The children acted like they were about to be executed and Shinala was more than willing to be the executioner. From the rumbles behind her, she suspected her males agreed.

The fleeting thought of where her males were went through her mind again, and she glanced at Gela.

Gela caught the glanced, tilted her head, then there was a whisper in Shinala's mind. "YOUR MALES ARE FINE. WE DROPPED THEM ON THE DECK OF THE GED SHIP THAT DELIVERED YOU. WITH THE MESSAGE SHE WAS EXPECTED AT THIS HARBOR."

That removed the only question that had been on her mind. Her gods had protected hers, and as always, she was theirs to use. Her service once more being rewarded.

The children were protesting and blaming each other, but they fell silent as Lyx moved forward. The god knelt and picked up her son. Stari stood at her shoulder, assisting until she had a good hold on the limp form. Together, they moved back to stand with the other gods while the children watched in horror.

The mortals were all silent and trying very hard to be invisible, but Shinala knew her gods had made note of them.

Her eyes roved over the children and wanted to sneer as they wailed and clutched at each other. Even the mortals had more pride.

Pel and Rian held each other's hands, though they seemed relieved. Zula and Yika stood back to back, but occasionally they sneered at Jadaya, who kept her eyes on the true gods. Jovan and Sinka were pressed so close together they seemed to be joined, their hands in fists by their sides. Deox and Iryx, those who had the Wysko people, nestled into each other, as if what took one would take both.

Aegian and Sepha, sisters and friends, stood side by side, hands clasped in front of them and head down, refusing to look up at their parents. Sepha had been the one to make the takeover possible with her drugs. Shinala hoped her heart beat so fast with fear it hurt.

Linax and Shio. She had never figured out their relationship, just knelt on the ground, refusing to respond to anything. How had they ever been part of a rebellion?

Ord and Qian were the most relaxed. They stood waiting, their stances wide and ready for a blow. They reminded her of jacks getting ready to pull a load too heavy for them. Cassix stood next to them, a frown on his brow, but of them all, he simply struck her as a jelak player trying to deal with an unexpected move on the board.

The five gods scanned over their children, and Aryix heaved a sigh. "WE ARE LEAVING. IT IS TIME, JUST AS IT WAS TIME FOR YOU TO GO OUT ON YOUR OWN. FROM HERE OUT YOUR ACTIONS AND CHOICES ARE YOUR OWN. BUT THERE IS ONE ACTION I AM DEEPLY FRUSTRATED WITH." His words were a thud of fact against Shinala's heart, one she had missed.

Quas took up the thread, his voice a different impact that Aryix's. He had a sharpness to him, and she could see people reel back as he spoke. "PERCIT, YOUR SISTER, CAME TO YOU. TELLING YOU OF XYL'S OBSESSION. OF HER FEAR. YOU DISMISSED IT. YOU TOLD HER TO ENJOY IT. ENJOY ABUSE? FOR THAT I WILL NOT FORGIVE YOU. BUT WORSE, YOU BELIEVED HIM AND HIS STORIES, YOU NEVER ASKED. AND NOW THERE WILL BE CONSEQUENCES, BUT I WILL NOT DELIVER THEM."

Shinala felt like her heart was covered with paper cuts by the time he finished speaking. The crystals had blocked much of their power and she had forgotten the pain of his voice. But now she leaned into it, reveling in the sweet pain that she might never feel again.

"SHE WAS YOUR DAUGHTER TOO, AEGINA." Aryix's gaze snagged on the cowering Aegina, her head bowed and fingers white in their clench. "SHE CAME TO YOU FOR HELP AND YOU LAUGHED, SAYING XYL LOVED HER. HE KILLED HER." Aegina's head jerked up and the rest of the children stiffened.

Aryix continued. "HE KILLED HER AND THEN BLAMED THE VISITOR, THE ONE NONE OF YOU HAD SPOKEN TO. YOU BELIEVED HIM AND LOCKED THE VISITOR UP, NEVER HEARING ANYTHING BUT XYL'S WORDS. AVOIDING EVERYTHING. THEN YOU LET HIM BE, NOT WANTING TO INTERFERE." The amount of contempt in his voice could have left scars, and more than one of the children were crying.

Gela spoke, her words like the soft pounding of the surf in your mind. "AEGINA, I RAISED YOU BETTER THAN THIS. YOU CARED MORE ABOUT NOT CAUSING DISCORD THAN PROTECTING YOUR DAUGHTER. OF ALL OF YOU, THAT I WILL NEVER FORGIVE." Gela raised her hand and flicked her fingers at Aegina. "YOU WILL NEVER AGAIN KNOW THE FEEL OF A CHILD IN YOU. THAT IS A RIGHT YOU HAVE LOST."

A muffled sob escaped from Aegina, and Shinala just smiled. It seemed right, as they had ripped that ability from her just to waylay their own fears.

Quas spoke again, the words slashing in a different direction as wry humor filled his words. "YOUR CONSEQUENCES ARE COMING. THE VISITOR WAS MY OLDER BROTHER URELI. YOU HAVE IMPRISONED HIM IN HIS SHIP. HE IS BREAKING OUT. NOW YOU WILL NEED TO DEAL WITH HIS RAGE. IF YOU ARE LUCKY THERE WILL BE A WORLD LEFT WHEN HIS ANGER IS SLAKED."

Their gasps of horror were the best sounds Shinala ever heard, and she lost her battle to hold back the laughter. It rang through the court as everyone looked at her in shock.

Aryix smiled at her, but it was Stari who spoke, the voice a musical gift Xyl had always lusted after. "SHINALA, YOU WHO WERE ALWAYS FAITHFUL.

WE MUST LEAVE AND YOU WILL REMAIN BEHIND, BUT IT IS TIME. YOUR WISDOM WAY OUTSHINES YOUR SIBLINGS AND ALWAYS HAS. WE HOPED BY HAVING YOU LIVE CLOSER TO MORTALS THAN OUR CHILDREN DID, YOU MIGHT LEARN COMPASSION, LOVE, AND CHARITY. YOU PROVED YOUR LOYALTY, COURAGE, AND PASSION OVER AND OVER AS THE SUNCYCLES PASSED. THAT BEING SAID, WE GIVE YOU YOUR FULL BIRTHRIGHT AND UNDO WHAT YOUR SIBLINGS DID."

A wave of warmth flushed through her and Shinala staggered as something deep in her unlocked. A barrier she had never realized was there, vanished. The power in the courtyard sank into her and she purred as it flowed into her.

Lyx, still cradling the body of her dead son, smiled at her and spoke. Her voice was the rain beating down on you after a long day. "THE OTHERS TOOK AND CHOSE THEIR POWERS, THEIR SPHERES, WE GIVE THEM TO YOU."

Each of them whispered something that slammed into her, but from the confusion and jealousy on the faces of the others, she thought only she could hear it.

ARIA'S ANIMALS ARE YOURS TO CONTROL.

THE FERTILITY OF THE LEONAIDS AND HEALTHY CUBS.

FIRE OBEYS YOUR COMMAND.

DEATH IS A TOOL YOU CAN USE OR DENY TO ANY.

CHANGE AND CHAOS BOTH WANTED AND AVOIDED.

SEX AND ALL THE CONSENTING PLEASURE THAT CAN BRING.

WEATHER TO HELP THIS LAND HEAL.

TRUTH.

BASIC GIFTS, TRAVEL, HEARING YOUR NAME, AND MORE. MAYBE SOME OF THE CHILDREN WILL EXPLAIN OR YOU CAN EXPLORE YOUR ABILITIES.

BE HAPPY.

Aryix cleared his throat. "OUR TIME IS SHORT. OUR CHILDREN HAVE BEEN PUNISHED AND MUST DECIDE HOW TO DEAL WITH THAT IS COMING. BE WARNED. HE IS NOT AS PATIENT AS WE WERE."

Quas snapped his fingers, and the children disappeared, leaving only the Leonaids and the mortals.

Aryix turned his gaze to the king of Charinsky. "YOU DID WELL. YOU HAVE A NEW GOD. SHE IS BETTER THAN YOUR OLD ONE. YOU PERSISTED WHERE MOST WOULD HAVE BROKEN. I BLESS YOU." Aryix reached out and touched the king's forehead for a moment. A light washed through the king, then faded away and Aryix returned to his place.

Stari moved to look at Jadaya. "I REGRET MY CHILDREN ARE SO SELFISH AND SPOILED THAT THEY DID THIS. SO I GIVE YOU BACK YOURSELF."

The god touched her and a similar light washed through Jadaya. Her skin shifted to a richer, deeper black, and the brand on her face disappeared, but those were the only visible changes. Stari reached up and braided a five-strand plait into her red-orange hair. It then separated from her head, leaving her with a small braid about a hand long. "YOUR PATH HAS MANY OPTIONS AND WHAT YOU WILL NEED WILL BE DETERMINED BY THE CHOICES YOU MAKE. THESE ARE FIVE GIFTS. USE THEM WHEN YOU KNOW WHAT YOUR FUTURE HOLDS AND WHO YOU WISH TO BE. YOU CAN BE ANYTHING YOU IMAGINE. PEL AND RIAN STILL OWE YOU A DEBT. THINK ON WHAT YOU DESIRE, THEY DARE NOT DENY YOU."

Stari moved back and Lyx glanced at Gela, who nodded. Gela walked toward Note, who had been frozen watching all of this, Trinity in one hand, Echo in the other.

"YOU STOOD UP. YOU CHANGED THINGS. OUR CHILDREN FAILED THEIR PEOPLE. ALL WE CAN DO IS REWARD THE ONE WHO DID NOT FAIL HIS PEOPLE." Gela touched his head the way Lazul and Jadaya had been touched. The light went through him. He moaned, a sharp sound, and shifted unconsciously. His hair went to a black sable color, the same one he had tried to dye it to, but now it was from the roots.

"YOU ARE WHOLE AGAIN AND YOUR IDENTITY IS YOURS TO CHOOSE. I NOT ONLY MAKE YOU WHOLE, BUT GRANT YOU THE GIFT OF HEALING, MIND AND BODY. THE OCEANS THAT MY SON TOOK AS HIS TO COMMAND ARE ALSO YOURS, AS ARE ALL THE CREATURES OF ARIA IN IT. ALL THAT COME FROM THE SEAS MUST OBEY YOU. YOU MAY GIFT UNTO OTHERS THE ABILITY TO BREATHE WATER OR NOTHING AT ALL."

Shinala tilted her head at that. There was something about the way Gela had said that. A harder wave crashing against Note, instead of the soft pounding of the surf.

That left only Rylix, and he stood there, his face grey under his nut-brown skin.

Aryix laughed. The sound was a warm hug in a jiggling bosom, something you wanted to hold to you. "MY PEOPLE WHO NEVER GAVE UP THE OLD WAYS, BUT INSTEAD FORGED THEIR PATH. RATHER THAN BLESS YOU, I REMOVE THE CURSES MY CHILDREN PLACED ON OUR PEOPLE. NO LONGER WILL ROOF OR LAND PREVENT SLEEP. AS FOR YOU," Aryix paused to look at Rylix, who had wide eyes and looked about to faint. "SOME-THING SIMPLE. ALL THE LANGUAGES ARE YOURS. USE IT WELL KNOWING YOU CAN NOW UNDERSTAND ANYONE AND KNOW THEIR NEED OR DESIRE. YOU WILL ALWAYS KNOW WHERE YOU ARE IN RELA-TION TO ANYTHING ELSE. THE PATHS OF THE STARS AWAIT YOU."

Another single touch to Rylix's brow and he stepped back. Lyx leaned into him, still holding Xyl.

"IT IS TIME. WE MAY RETURN, BUT WE MAY NOT. SHINALA, BE ALL THAT OUR OTHER CHILDREN WERE NOT." Aryix looked at Quas, who nodded. A ribbon of silver surrounded them, moving faster and faster until they were no longer visible, only the whirl of silver was, then they were gone. At the same time, the door in the wall reappeared and a crowd of people stood there.

Chaos exploded around them and Shinala just stood there, the changes sinking in. She was a god? She was their *child*? She could have children of her own again?

Her knees buckled, and she might have fallen, but her males were there, looking at her. She blinked at them, worried for a moment that this would change something. Anything.

"Shinala, we are still yours. We always have been. But now maybe we can be a people in truth, instead of the remains of a dying race," Mace rumbled as he steadied her.

She looked around and smiled. "Yes. We have a lot of work to do."

EPILOGUE – RYLIX

Rylix had felt mostly useless during the entire battle. Then, when the rest of the revelations happened, he was more than glad to fade into the background, even if these were his gods, more than any others.

But when Aryix spoke to him and removed the charge from the Ged, he felt nothing but relief. The odds were most would not change their lives, but to be able to take shelter in solid buildings in bad weather or when injured or when his cousins were on land to not worry about a ship being nearby was priceless. And then there was the language. Rylix had always been good at languages. You had to be as a Ged, but there was something about how Aryix gave the gift that made him think there was more to it than that.

He shook his head. That was for later. The fight, the revelations, then the meeting of the gods had exhausted them and they had retreated to the Ged quarters, ate, and passed out. At least he had. Everyone else had needed baths prior to that, but now, fingers later, Shinala had disappeared with the king, leaving Katel here, his broken arm in a splint healing. The Leonaid was sound asleep; the rumbling snores almost like waves upon the shore.

Rylix sat at the table, a new notebook in front of him as he wrote and thought. But most of his thoughts just ended with the knowledge that the children were safe. That while he couldn't bring Kryx back, he no longer felt like the scales were unbalanced. No, he hadn't been the one to kill Xyl, but he had helped in the journey, and it was enough to erase his own guilt. Now he could think of her and no longer feel like he deserved to be punished.

He looked up as Jadaya and Note approached. They had similar expressions on their faces. Note looked different, he walked differently and Rylix had a suspicion, but asking it would be rude. Jadaya seemed more at ease, though her hand drifted up to check the unmarred skin on her cheek now, instead of the brand that had sat there since he met her.

"Do you feel better?" he asked, laying down his graphine.

"A bath helped. The blood of Xyl stung and left marks," Jadaya said, pointing to a few spots where her skin was still raw and healing, as if an ember had landed on her for a moment, burning her. "It just aches oddly. But it is fading. Shinala has the same and the marks look garish on her white skin."

With a wry grin, she settled down into one of the chairs at the table.

Note followed her example and Rylix glanced at his hair, now a silky black a Fivikan would have envied. The Aoisan must have seen his glance.

"I can change it now, if I want," he said with a wry smile. Rylix arched a brow as Jadaya leaned forward, curiosity on her face.

Note laughed, the sound having lost its bitter cynicism, instead now light and engaging. He thought for a moment and his hair rippled to a bright red. A color Rylix had never seen on an Aoisan before.

Jadaya blinked. "That is different," she said, looking at the hair. "Can you change the texture?"

"Texture?" Note asked, looking at her.

"Yes, make it curly like mine." She pulled out a strand of hair so he could feel it and see the spiral of curls that made up her hair.

"Let me try," he closed his eyes, one hand still feeling Jadaya's strand of hair. Then the red on his tightened and poofed up in an explosion of curls.

Rylix burst out in laughter, and Jadaya joined him. Giving both of them a look, Note got up to peer into one of the silver mirrors in the space. He started to laugh as well.

"The answer is yes. But I think this is not for me." He came back to the table and his hair resumed the straight charcoal black.

They all snickered for a moment before silence decided.

"It is over. We have become people there will be legends about," Rylix said softly. "Now what? I must say, I feel like the life of a trader might be a letdown after the last few mooncycles of excitement and adventure." He looked both of them in the eyes. "You have become my best friends and I have little desire to return to the orderly life that I thought I wanted. So, my amazing companions, do you have thoughts?"

He bit down on the fear that they might say they were done with him and focused on listening to their responses.

EPILOGUE – LAZUL

Lazul spent the next three fingers talking to Shinala, and he had to admit he had a hard time seeing her as a god, but then she seemed to have a hard time seeing herself as one.

"This is something that will take mooncycles to do and you have a kingdom to run," she finally said. "I know little about running a kingdom and less about being a god. I will come to visit in a few days. For now, you go deal with the populace and this temple will be my problem. Once the rest of my males get here, I will assist with updating the other temples to be..." she trailed off and shook her head. "Something else. When I know what I want, I will let you know."

With that, she shooed him out, and he gratefully headed toward the palace. Most of his citizens barely noticed him weaving through the crowd, and he was glad that he had never worried about threats to his life. Killing the king had little attraction when there was a mad god involved. And now?

Now he had no clue. But at the end of the day, a saber god had to be easier to deal with than one who had killed his wife.

Please let it be easier.

He repeated that thought as he headed into the palace, slipping in a door and heading right to his and Hauyne's sanctuary.

I still need a name for this room.

The thought flitted through his mind as he pushed open the door to find Hauyne and Actin sitting there. They had obviously been talking and both of them had notebooks with lists growing in them.

"He is dead. Xyl is dead." Both of them stared at him as the words seemed to boom throughout the chamber, though he had spoken them almost quietly.

"And you?" Hauyne said in a shaking voice as she stood, pressing against the chair as if it helped her stand.

Lazul felt the grin split his face as he took two swift steps to her side and pulled her into his arms, giving her the kiss he had wanted to for so long, but lacked the stamina and energy to do so. She froze for a moment, then responded with enthusiasm, her arms wrapping around him and holding him as tight as he held her. She was his anchor and as soon as all the aftermath was dealt with, he would marry her. The gods could go hang.

A clearing throat pulled them from their kiss, and he blinked to see Actin sitting there, the man's face an interesting shade of pink. "I would be more than happy to leave you to your pleasure, but you seem to be blocking my way out and if it is not too impertinent, what happened?" The last part of the sentence was said with an almost desperate growl.

Lazul laughed, and with great reluctance let Hauyne out of his arms. His familiar fruist and drugs sat there waiting for him and he pushed them away. He knew there might be a risk of craving the drugs, but when Aryix had touched him, he felt clean and present for the first time in a very long time. Maybe the god had been compassionate and removed the call of the drugs as well. That would be a boon, but if he could survive the pain, withdrawal had no chance against him.

He poured a glass of undrugged fruist, more to wet his throat than anything else. "There is much to tell," he said, then began to talk. The telling took a full four fingers, longer than the battle had taken, which had barely been moments. So much had happened in so short of a time.

When he was done, they stared at him, though halfway through the recitation Hauyne had grabbed her notebook and started making more lists.

"Let me see if I understand everything. The clergy of Xyl were abusing the sing- slaves both physically and sexually. Xyl actually killed Percit, and it was an abusive marriage, not a love match. The Usurper is the brother of Quas and Xyl blamed Percit's death on him and got the other gods to trap him. We have a new god who is the Leonaid Shinala of legends. And the old gods broke out of their prison, which they could have at any time, and have gone home?" Hauyne said all of this in a slow voice as she blinked at him.

Lazul tilted his head and nodded. "That sounds about accurate. But you forgot one important part."

She and Actin looked at him. "Oh?"

He rose with a smooth swiftness that he had lost for the mooncycles since Xyl showed up and knelt at her feet.

"You promised to marry me. Are you still willing with all of this facing us?" He looked up at her, his heart quivering as he waited for her answer.

Hauyne threw back her head and laughed, then lowered her so their foreheads touched. "Yes. Not even the gods can stop me from doing that."

This time Actin slipped by them before Lazul pulled Hauyne back into his arms.

EPILOGUE – NOTE

Note sat on the shore, his feet in the ocean's water, a finger's walk from Granite. There was too much noise in the city, especially as the citizens seemed torn between celebrating and being terrified about their new god.

The water soothed his mind as he listened to the steady thrum. He could sense the creatures that lived deep in the water and the small ones near the shore. He had played a bit, and they would come up to him, fearless and responsive. The power invigorated and terrified him. It also meant he would never go fishing for food again. The fish would just come up to him and that level of suicidal sacrifice made him uncomfortable.

The world had changed irrevocably. The gods were free. He was whole. And his people could return to their lives. So why was he hiding out here?

"Are you the Aoisan Note?" The voice came from behind him and he rose, turning, expecting to see a servant or something.

He froze as he took in the small crowd of Aoisans looking at him. Hauyne had let him know where they were being housed, but he had avoided seeing them. The idea that he had left them there made it too hard to face them.

Here was a mix of young and old, male and female, some that still had innocence in their eyes, others who had seen that which left scars on them. But he saw what he had feared the most. Familiar faces. Those of his people who had been enslaved with him.

But too many were missing. "Ali? Kan?" Ali had been an Aoisan in her late twenties when he came there. Already broken and cowed, she still protected and taught them the best she could. Kan had been the oldest Aoisan there. He had one leg broken and purposefully set wrong, so he walked with a limp. His baritone had been kept, so he was used a lot in the attempts to 'breed' them. From the rumors Note heard, his manhood worked poorly. Though in fact or for choice, he never asked.

"And me," another voice said, and a woman his age moved forward. The voice one that haunted his nightmares. The friendship forged on the ship across the sea when they had been ripped from their home. He and Sui had clung to each other. She was his best friend. And he had fled, leaving her there.

Guilt slammed into him, and he turned to stare out at the ocean, talking to it as he was unable to face his fellow slaves.

"You must hate me," he said, his voice thick with pain and guilt.

"Hate you, Nok?" It was Ali's voice, and he flinched as memories he had fought for so long to bury came flooding back, coaxed out by her voice and his once name. Images of her forcing a smile and being nice, even as he watched blood seep through her robes. Her quiet way of distracting the clergy from the children's misbehavior and then suffering for it. The food she snuck in when they were being punished for not knowing the songs perfectly. All of it slammed into him with the weight of a tidal wave.

He spun, shouting at them. "I left you. All you did for me, and I am the one that fled, leaving you behind. You suffered for me escaping."

All of them smiled at him and he flinched, the pain worse than before.

Sui walked up to him and took his hand. "We envied you your freedom. Nok, we were glad you made it out." Her hand was tight on his and he wanted her to hit him, scream, punish him for escaping and leaving them behind. And he needed them to stop using the name of the boy who had died so long ago.

"Note, that is the name you go by now, right?" Ali said, and he looked up to see all of them had drawn closer.

He nodded, his throat torn between screaming and begging, leaving him choking on his words and feelings.

"Nok died a long time ago," he managed staring at his feet.

"Note. I like it. Your escape was one of many. Some they brought back the bodies as proof. Always, anyone who escaped was presented to us as dead. When you escaped, the clergy informed us you had been eaten by the creatures of the deep as you tried to swim home. I feel a few must have made it back, but you… Note, you of all of them over the tenset of tensets of suncycles, you came back."

Kan laughed, a rich deep sound that reminded Note of thunder rolling across the long plains of Agrina. "Not only did you come back, you came back with weapons made by legends and killed a god for us."

Note tried to protest. "Jadaya actually killed him."

The three faces he recognized, others vaguely familiar and still others he had never seen, all smiled back at him. "You came back. You and your friends killed a god. All because you wanted to rescue us. You, a slave like us, did more for us than our gods. You are our savior."

"You should hate me," he said even as they got closer.

"Oh, Note," Ali whispered. "It is the opposite. We love you and you saved us all." With those last words, Note found himself in the middle of Aoisans all telling him he was loved, he was their savior, and blessing him in Aryix's name. There in the arms of people who knew what he had suffered, knew he had fled, knew he came back, Note found peace and the tears that he had walled off deep inside for so long broke free.

Together, he and the other Aoisan slaves cried, and their tears ran together into the ocean, a shimmering strand of pain, love, and hope. They healed scars in Note that a god could never touch, and his magic reached out to heal those who he had come back to save.

EPILOGUE – JADAYA

Jadaya had nothing to do. Recognizable everywhere in Granite, people constantly pushed things into her hands, items she had no idea what to do with. So she took the various gems, jewelry, and clothing to Shinala. At least she might have some use for it.

Shinala was turning out to be nothing like the former clergy and, in fact, had turned in several of them to the king for various crimes. The amount of luxuries she had stripped from the temple, all of which were being traded by the Ged as reparation for the Aoisans, was staggering.

The rooms formerly occupied by the clergy had been stripped and refurnished, and the Aoisans coming in from other temples were being kept there as more Ged ships showed up.

Jolyx had come a few days ago to bring all the Leonaids from the mount. She had left this morning with the first ship full of Aoisans, taking them home to Aois by way of Fivika and then down to the lower cities on the Aoisan archipelago.

No worship had been defined yet by Shinala, but Jadaya noticed a large amount of cats had migrated to the temple. She walked in to find some of the Leonaids in the courtyard lounging in saber form with children climbing all over them. Mace sat with an older Aoisan, looking at a ledger and rolls of building drawings. He glanced up as she walked in.

"Upstairs," he said, then went back to talking with the Aoisan, pointing at numbers and then at plans for something.

Curious but not wanting to impose, Jadaya went up the stairs to the second floor. Shinala had taken over the long galley that looked over the courtyard and was talking to Katel, whose arm was still in a brace.

"I brought more stuff for you. I have no idea what to do with it," Jadaya said, holding up the basket.

"Ah, a person I want to talk to," Shinala said with a smile. "Put it in the corner and it will be added to the other supplies."

Jadaya did so, then headed over as Shinala waved Katel away. "Tell Lazul as far as I care, he can just say he is married. If he wants a big ceremony, he can figure out what it should be. I care not. Just take the woman to bed and have younglings. It is not my business."

Katel shook his head and tugged on one of her braids with a laugh. "You just have younglings on the mind."

She smirked and gave him a side eye. "And?"

He just laughed and walked away.

Shinala smiled and waved at a chair. "Sit. And I swear if you start calling me a god, the workout you will get will leave you unable to walk for days."

Jadaya laughed and took a seat. She had wanted to talk to Shinala but now found the words not coming.

"Ah. You lack a purpose. I assume Zula and Yika have not come to talk to you?" Shinala sounded amused.

"Actually, they did. They apologized, asked me to come back as their palace major domo. It is the highest rank a Chosen can attain," she said quietly.

"And?"

"And I said no. They threw me away. Now that they perceive my value, they are willing to show me off? I think not. But what do I do? I am satisfied with who I am. The blessings I was given gave me back my sight and I can tweak alter my appearance, but I have zero desire to be anyone but me. Though I miss having a people. I am still a Zuyikan, but they are not my gods."

"Are you asking me to be your god?" There was more amusement in Shinala's voice.

"No, I think not," Jadaya said. It was hard to put into words what you felt when it was so nebulous.

"What about me?" The voice came from the far end of the chamber as the speaker moved toward them.

"Ah Cassix, I was wondering when you were going to show up," Shinala said, but there was a smile on her face.

"You be my god? But you have no people," Jadaya said with a touch of confusion.

"Not traditionally, but after the events of the last tenday, I have decided traditions can go hang," he said with a smile. Cassix waved his hand and a small stool appeared. He dropped onto it, joining their conversation. "I would have offered the same to Shinala, but my parents had different ideas and now I have a new sibling." He winked at her. "It is nice to have a sibling you actually like. Not one so full of themselves it is like talking to the wind."

Shinala snorted. "I think I might eat you before I became yours."

"Ah, but what a way to die," Cassix teased back. Then the smile fell from his face. "But no. I have tried to talk to the others. But they are fools," he said, spitting the words out. " Aegina is mourning what Gela took from her, and Sepha is almost as bad. Pel and Rian are too busy trying to make it up to their captured people coming home to even talk to me. Ord and Qian, as always, say it is not their problem and hide in their northern forts. The others are too busy celebrating that the threat of our parents is gone. None of them want to listen to me."

Shinala's humor had faded too, and Jadaya thought back to what Xyl and the old gods had said, and her stomach sank.

"The Usurper," she breathed.

"Yes. Quas said his name was Ureli. This happened a while ago, even the way we tell time. But I think he must have been in a deep sleep for a long while. Xyl lied to most of us, saying he wrapped him in gems. I now know it was a ship, and he is awake and angry."

"Would you not be?" Shinala asked dryly. "You come to see a sibling, are attacked, and locked away for longer than we have numbers? I would be more than annoyed."

Cassix nodded. "I agree. But if he comes out in a rage, he might destroy this world."

Jadaya blinked at that. This world. Were there others? She pushed it away for later contemplation. "And what are you seeking?"

Cassix smiled at her with a sly grin. "I was thinking there might be a group of heroes with weapons capable of hurting a god that might be interested in a quest to rescue a… god before he destroys everything."

Jadaya gave him a flat look, hiding the spurt of excitement his words brought. "Sounds dangerous."

"It is," he said.

"Sounds like there might be fighting," Shinala said, her claws sliding out from the tips of her fingers

"Probably," Cassix admitted.

"You might need help from multiple countries," Jadaya said. "So someone that can speak all languages might be a boon."

"That would, in fact, help." Cassix's smile was growing wider.

"And with the Usur- Ureli in the bottom of the sea, someone who could walk down there would be useful," Shinala commented while checking the sharpness of her claws.

"Most likely." His smile was a grin.

"Huh," Jadaya said. "I think I know some people like that who have mentioned a need to do something." Her smile was growing on her face as well.

"That is such a coincidence. Maybe I should talk to them," Cassix said in mock surprise. "You think they will help?"

"Never can tell. But it sounds like something they might write epic tales about," Jadaya said, rising. Already the idea of a new challenge and doing something no one else had ever done had eased the discontent that had been riding her.

"Indeed, it does. It also sounds much more interesting than being useless. If you can get them, I think I and some of mine will be interested," Shinala said, rising and letting her claws slip back into her hands. "An administrator is not the life for me."

Cassix rose as well. "Then it sounds like we have people to talk to. My lady Jadaya, if you would." He offered her his arm and laughing at the insanity of it all, Jadaya slipped her arm into the crook of the god's, one who was more like a mortal than she would have ever believed, and they headed out. Shinala trailed behind them, chuckling to herself.

Together, they left the former temple to see if Note and Rylix were ready for another adventure.

This novel was a rollercoaster to write and took so much longer than I expected, but Jadaya, Hauyne, Note, and Rylix got under my skin, and then there is Shinala. I hope you loved them as much as I did.

I did leave it open for another adventure, but that depends so much on you the reader. Leave reviews and talk about it.

For now, if you would like to read the Fall of the Gods, which tells the story of the children taking down their parents. You can find it via this QR Code.

If you haven't already, don't forget to sign up for my newsletter via this QR code.

I'll let you know about what is going on in my life and what stories are forth coming. If you enjoy this series and want a completed series to read that has more magic, familiars, and drama, check out the rest of my books on Amazon.

If you'd like to stay in touch, you can follow me on social media at the following places:

Website: https://badashpublishing.com/

Facebook: https://www.facebook.com/badashbooks/

Twitter: https://twitter.com/badashbooks

Instagram: https://www.instagram.com/badashbooks/

For those who are curious Two Moons is to the sung to tune of Scarborough Fair.

Mel Todd has three cats, none of which can turn into a form with opposable thumbs, which is good. If they could do that they wouldn't need her anymore. Writing and trying to start her empire, she decided creating her own worlds was less work than ruling this one.

ALSO BY MEL TODD

KAYLID CHRONICLES

- No Choice
- Commander
- Incoming
- Allies
- Family
- Kaylid Novellas

BLOOD WAR BY MEL TODD & DOUG BURBEY

- Rage
- Betray
- Fight/Power

STAND ALONE

- Puppet Master
- Vengeance

NOBLE'S LUCK

- Spark
- Lady
- Lord
- Bastard
- Bonfire

TWISTED LUCK SERIES

(ALSO AVAILABLE IN GERMAN & FRENCH)

- My Luck
- Hired Luck
- Educated Luck
- Drafted Luck
- Faded Luck
- Unbalanced Luck
- Balanced Luck

- Joined
- No Luck
- Shattered

WRITING AS RENEE LOVINS

- Fanfiction
- Ink Deep
- Glass Hearts
- Suddenly Single Collection
- Hitman, Inc Novellas

www.ingramcontent.com/pod-product-compliance
Lightning Source LLC
Chambersburg PA
CBHW070228200726
48293CB00005B/1524